MISTBORN

MISTBORN

THE FINAL EMPIRE

BRANDON SANDERSON

TOR

A TOM DOHERTY ASSOCIATES BOOK

NEW YORK

MISTBORN

Copyright © 2006 by Dragonsteel Entertainment, LLC

Brandon Sanderson® is a registered trademark of Dragonsteel Entertainment, LLC

All rights reserved.

Edited by Moshe Feder

Maps by Isaac Stewart

A Tor Teen Book
Published by Tom Doherty Associates
175 Fifth Avenue
New York, NY 10010

www.tor-forge.com

Tor® is a registered trademark of Macmillan Publishing Group, LLC.

Library of Congress Cataloging-in-Publication Data

Sanderson, Brandon.
    Mistborn : the final empire / Brandon Sanderson.—1st ed.
        p.   cm.
    "A Tom Doherty Associates book."
    ISBN 978-0-7653-1178-8 (hardcover)
    ISBN 978-1-4299-1456-7 (ebook)
    I. Title.
    PS3619.A533M57 2006
    813'.6—dc22

                                                    2005034496

Our books may be purchased in bulk for promotional, educational, or business use. Please contact your local bookseller or the Macmillan Corporate and Premium Sales Department at 1-800-221-7945, extension 5442, or by email at MacmillanSpecialMarkets@macmillan.com.

Printed in the United States of America

20   19   18   17

FOR BETH SANDERSON,

Who's been reading fantasy

For longer than I've been alive,

And fully deserves

To have a grandson as loony as she is.

ACKNOWLEDGMENTS

Once again, I find myself in need of thanking my wonderful agent, Joshua Bilmes, and equally amazing editor, Moshe Feder. They did a wonderful job with this book, and I'm proud to have the opportunity to work with them.

As always, my tireless writing groups have consistently provided feedback and encouragement: Alan Layton, Janette Layton, Kaylynne ZoBell, Nate Hatfield, Bryce Cundick, Kimball Larsen, and Emily Scorup. Alpha readers, who saw a version of this book in a much rougher form and helped me shape it into what you see now, included Krista Olson, Benjamin R. Olson, Micah Demoux, Eric Ehlers, Izzy Whiting, Stacy Whitman, Kristina Kugler, Megan Kauffman, Sarah Bylund, C. Lee Player, Ethan Skarstedt, Jillena O'Brien, Ryan Jurado, and the incalculable Peter Ahlstrom.

There are also a few people in particular whom I would like to thank. Isaac Stewart, who did the map work for this novel, was an invaluable resource both in the idea department and with visual cues. Heather Kirby had excellent advice to help me with the mysterious inner workings of a young woman's mind.

In addition, I'd like to acknowledge some of the very important people who work behind the scenes on the books that you buy. Irene Gallo, the art director at Tor, does a brilliant job—it's because of her that both this book and *Elantris* have the wonderful covers that they do. Also, David Moench, in the Tor publicity department, went far beyond the call of duty in helping make *Elantris* a success. Both have my thanks.

Finally, as always, I am thankful to my family for their continued support and enthusiasm.

In particular, I'd like to thank my brother, Jordan, for his enthusiasm, support, and loyalty. Check out his handiwork at my Web site: www.brandonsanderson.com.

THE FINAL EMPIRE

1. LUTHADEL

THE ASHMOUNTS

2. TYRIAN 3. ZERINAH
4. FALEAST 5. DORIEL
6. MORAG 7. KALLING 8. TORINOST

9. LAKE TYRIAN
10. LAKE LUTHADEL
11. THE BLACK LAKE
12. RIVER SEARAN

13. NORTH SEARAN
14. SOUTH SEARAN
15. THE RIVER CHANNEREL

TERRIS DOMINANCE

WESTERN DOMINANCE

FARMOST DOMINANCE

NORTHERN DOMINANCE

CENTRAL DOMINANCE

CRESCENT DOMINANCE

SOUTHERN DOMINANCE

SOUTHERN ISLANDS

EASTERN DOMINANCE

REMOTE DOMINANCE

2005

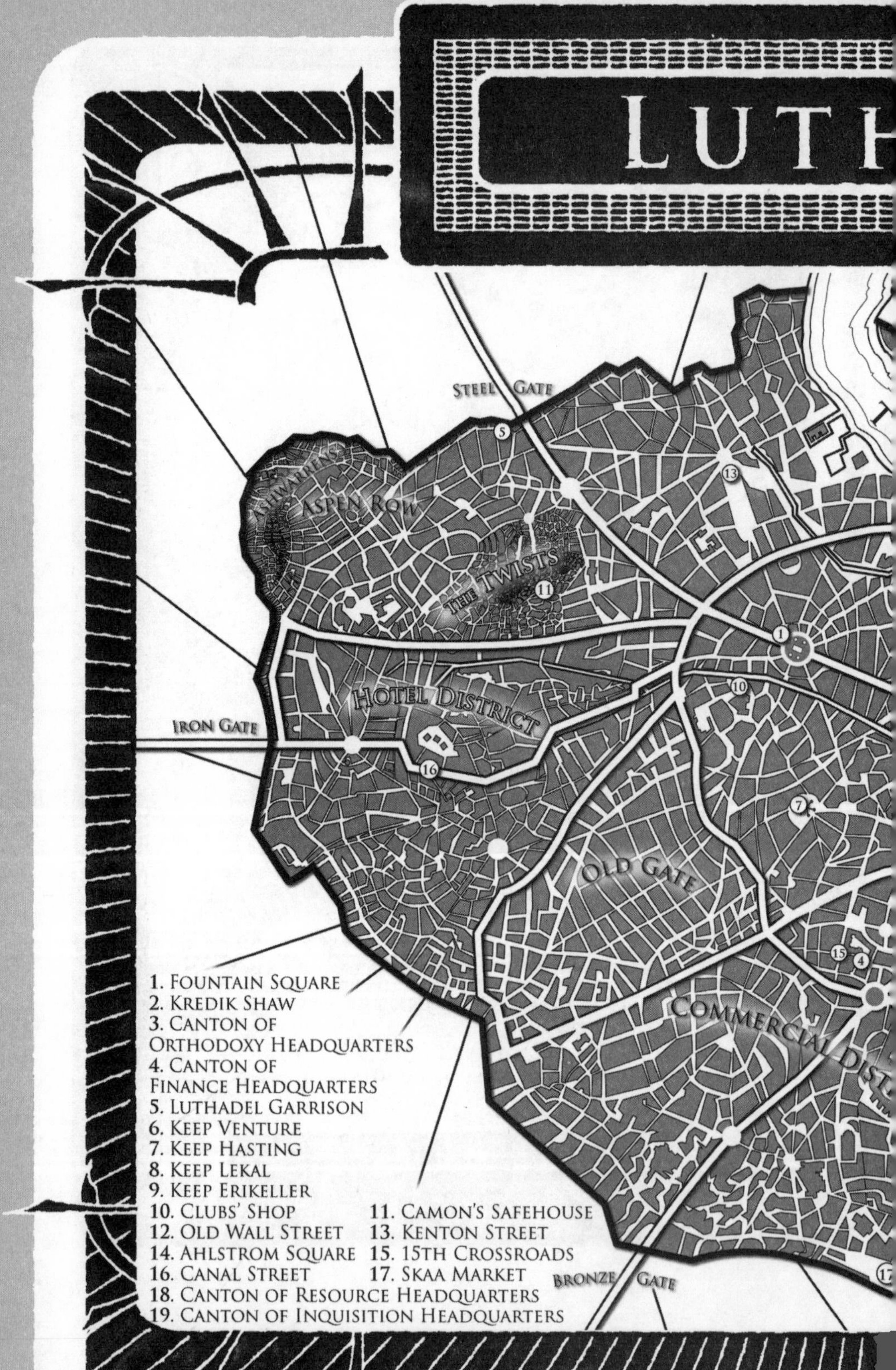

LUTH

STEEL GATE

5

13

ASHWARDENS
ASPEN ROW

THE TWISTS
11

IRON GATE

HOTEL DISTRICT
16

10

1

7

OLD GATE

15
4

COMMERCIAL DIST

BRONZE GATE

17

ADEL

TIN GATE

SOOTWARRENS

14

ALL BRIDGE

PEWTER GATE

6

12

8

BLOCKSTREET

3

2

ZINC GATE

19

18

INDUSTRIAL DISTRICT

TANNEREL

SOUTHBRIDGE

THE CRACKS

BRASSGATE

BRASS GATE

COPPER GATE

2005

MISTBORN

Sometimes, I worry that I'm not the hero everyone thinks I am.

The philosophers assure me that this is the time, that the signs have been met. But I still wonder if they have the wrong man. So many people depend on me. They say I will hold the future of the entire world on my arms.

What would they think if they knew that their champion—the Hero of Ages, their savior—doubted himself? Perhaps they wouldn't be shocked at all. In a way, this is what worries me most. Maybe, in their hearts, they wonder—just as I do.

When they see me, do they see a liar?

PROLOGUE

ASH FELL FROM THE SKY.

Lord Tresting frowned, glancing up at the ruddy midday sky as his servants scuttled forward, opening a parasol over Tresting and his distinguished guest. Ashfalls weren't that uncommon in the Final Empire, but Tresting had hoped to avoid getting soot stains on his fine new suit coat and red vest, which had just arrived via canal boat from Luthadel itself. Fortunately, there wasn't much wind; the parasol would likely be effective.

Tresting stood with his guest on a small hilltop patio that overlooked the fields. Hundreds of people in brown smocks worked in the falling ash, caring for the crops. There was a sluggishness to their efforts—but, of course, that was the way of the skaa. The peasants were an indolent, unproductive lot. They didn't complain, of course; they knew better than that. Instead, they simply worked with bowed heads, moving about their work with quiet apathy. The passing whip of a taskmaster would force them into dedicated motion for a few moments, but as soon as the taskmaster passed, they would return to their languor.

Tresting turned to the man standing beside him on the hill. "One would think," Tresting noted, "that a thousand years of working in fields would have bred them to be a little more effective at it."

The obligator turned, raising an eyebrow—the motion done as if to highlight his most distinctive feature, the intricate tattoos that laced the skin around his eyes. The tattoos were enormous, reaching all the way across his brow and up the sides of his nose. This was a full prelan—a very important obligator indeed. Tresting had his own, personal obligators back at the manor, but they were only minor functionaries, with barely a few marks around their eyes. This man had arrived from Luthadel with the same canal boat that had brought Tresting's new suit.

"You should see city skaa, Tresting," the obligator said, turning back to watch the skaa workers. "These are actually quite diligent, compared to those inside Luthadel. You have more . . . direct control over your skaa here. How many would you say you lose a month?"

"Oh, a half dozen or so," Tresting said. "Some to beatings, some to exhaustion."

"Runaways?"

"Never!" Tresting said. "When I first inherited this land from my father, I had a few runaways—but I executed their families. The rest quickly lost heart. I've never understood men who have trouble with their skaa—I find the creatures easy to control, if you show a properly firm hand."

The obligator nodded, standing quietly in his gray robes. He seemed pleased—which was a good thing. The skaa weren't actually Tresting's property. Like all skaa, they belonged to the Lord Ruler; Tresting only leased the workers from his God, much in the same way he paid for the services of His obligators.

The obligator looked down, checking his pocket watch, then glanced up at the sun. Despite the ashfall, the sun was bright this day, shining a brilliant crimson red behind the smoky blackness of the upper sky. Tresting removed a handkerchief and wiped his brow, thankful for the parasol's shade against the midday heat.

"Very well, Tresting," the obligator said. "I will carry your proposal to Lord Venture, as requested. He will have a favorable report from me on your operations here."

Tresting held in a sigh of relief. An obligator was required to witness any contract or business deal between noblemen. True, even a lowly obligator like the ones Tresting employed could serve as such a witness—but it meant so much more to impress Straff Venture's own obligator.

The obligator turned toward him. "I will leave back down the canal this afternoon."

"So soon?" Tresting asked. "Wouldn't you care to stay for supper?"

"No," the obligator replied. "Though there is another matter I wish to discuss with you. I came not only at the behest of Lord Venture, but to . . . look in on some matters for the Canton of Inquisition. Rumors say that you like to dally with your skaa women."

Tresting felt a chill.

The obligator smiled; he likely meant it to be disarming, but Tresting only found it eerie. "Don't worry yourself, Tresting," the obligator said. "If there had been any *real* worries about your actions, a Steel Inquisitor would have been sent here in my place."

Tresting nodded slowly. Inquisitor. He'd never seen one of the inhuman creatures, but he had heard . . . stories.

"I have been satisfied regarding your actions with the skaa women," the obligator said, looking back over the fields. "What I've seen and heard here indicate that you always clean up your messes. A man such as yourself—efficient, productive—could go far in Luthadel. A few more years of work, some inspired mercantile deals, and who knows?"

The obligator turned away, and Tresting found himself smiling. It wasn't a promise, or even an endorsement—for the most part, obligators were more bureaucrats and witnesses than they were priests—but to hear such praise from one of the Lord Ruler's own servants . . . Tresting knew that some nobility considered the obligators to be unsettling—some men even considered them a bother—but at that moment, Testing could have kissed his distinguished guest.

Tresting turned back toward the skaa, who worked quietly beneath the bloody sun and the lazy flakes of ash. Tresting had always been a country nobleman, living on his plantation, dreaming of perhaps moving into Luthadel itself. He had heard of the balls and the parties, the glamour and the intrigue, and it excited him to no end.

I'll have to celebrate tonight, he thought. There was that young girl in the fourteenth hovel that he'd been watching for some time. . . .

He smiled again. A few more years of work, the obligator had said. But could Tresting perhaps speed that up, if he worked a little harder? His skaa population had been growing lately. Perhaps if he pushed them a bit more, he could bring in an extra harvest this summer and fulfill his contract with Lord Venture in extra measure.

Tresting nodded as he watched the crowd of lazy skaa, some working with their hoes, others on hands and knees, pushing the ash away from the fledgling crops. They didn't complain. They didn't hope. They barely dared think. That was the way it should be, for they were skaa. They were—

Tresting froze as one of the skaa looked up. The man met Tresting's eyes, a spark—no, a fire—of defiance showing in his expression. Tresting had never seen anything like it, not in the face of a skaa. Tresting stepped backward reflexively, a chill running through him as the strange, straight-backed skaa held his eyes.

And smiled.

Tresting looked away. "Kurdon!" he snapped.

The burly taskmaster rushed up the incline. "Yes, my lord?"

Tresting turned, pointing at . . .

He frowned. Where had that skaa been standing? Working with their heads bowed, bodies stained by soot and sweat, they were so hard to tell apart. Tresting paused, searching. He thought he knew the place . . . an empty spot, where nobody now stood.

But, no. That couldn't be it. The man couldn't have disappeared from the group so quickly. Where would he have gone? He must be in there, somewhere, working with his head now properly bowed. Still, his moment of apparent defiance was inexcusable.

"My lord?" Kurdon asked again.

The obligator stood at the side, watching curiously. It would not be wise to let the man know that one of the skaa had acted so brazenly.

"Work the skaa in that southern section a little harder," Tresting ordered, pointing. "I see them being sluggish, even for skaa. Beat a few of them."

Kurdon shrugged, but nodded. It wasn't much of a reason for a beating—but, then, he didn't need much of a reason to give the workers a beating.

They were, after all, only skaa.

Kelsier had heard stories.

He had heard whispers of times when once, long ago, the sun had not been red. Times when the sky hadn't been clogged by smoke and ash, when plants hadn't struggled to grow, and when skaa hadn't been slaves. Times before the Lord Ruler. Those days, however, were nearly forgotten. Even the legends were growing vague.

Kelsier watched the sun, his eyes following the giant red disk as it crept toward the western horizon. He stood quietly for a long moment, alone in the empty fields. The day's work was done; the skaa had been herded back to their hovels. Soon the mists would come.

Eventually, Kelsier sighed, then turned to pick his way across the furrows and pathways, weaving between large heaps of ash. He avoided stepping on the plants—though he wasn't sure why he bothered. The crops hardly seemed worth the effort. Wan, with wilted brown leaves, the plants seemed as depressed as the people who tended them.

The skaa hovels loomed in the waning light. Already, Kelsier could see the mists beginning to form, clouding the air, and giving the moundlike buildings a surreal, intangible look. The hovels stood unguarded; there was no need for watchers, for no skaa would venture outside once night arrived. Their fear of the mists was far too strong.

I'll have to cure them of that someday, Kelsier thought as he approached one of the larger buildings. *But, all things in their own time.* He pulled open the door and slipped inside.

Conversation stopped immediately. Kelsier closed the door, then turned with a smile to confront the room of about thirty skaa. A firepit burned weakly at the center, and the large cauldron beside it was filled with vegetable-dappled water—the beginnings of an evening meal. The soup would be bland, of course. Still, the smell was enticing.

"Good evening, everyone," Kelsier said with a smile, resting his pack beside his feet and leaning against the door. "How was your day?"

His words broke the silence, and the women returned to their dinner preparations. A group of men sitting at a crude table, however, continued to regard Kelsier with dissatisfied expressions.

"Our day was filled with work, traveler," said Tepper, one of the skaa elders. "Something you managed to avoid."

"Fieldwork hasn't ever really suited me," Kelsier said. "It's far too hard on my delicate skin." He smiled, holding up hands and arms that were lined with layers and layers of thin scars. They covered his skin, running lengthwise, as if some beast had repeatedly raked its claws up and down his arms.

Tepper snorted. He was young to be an elder, probably barely into his forties—at most, he might be five years Kelsier's senior. However, the scrawny man held himself with the air of one who liked to be in charge.

"This is no time for levity," Tepper said sternly. "When we harbor a traveler, we expect him to behave himself and avoid suspicion. When you ducked away from the fields this morning, you could have earned a whipping for the men around you."

"True," Kelsier said. "But those men could also have been whipped for standing in the wrong place, for pausing too long, or for coughing when a taskmaster walked by. I once saw a man beaten because his master claimed that he had 'blinked inappropriately.'"

Tepper sat with narrow eyes and a stiff posture, his arm resting on the table. His expression was unyielding.

Kelsier sighed, rolling his eyes. "Fine. If you want me to go, I'll be off then." He slung his pack up on his shoulder and nonchalantly pulled open the door.

Thick mist immediately began to pour through the portal, drifting lazily across Kelsier's body, pooling on the floor and creeping across the dirt like a hesitant animal. Several people gasped in horror, though most of them were too stunned to make a sound. Kelsier stood for a moment, staring out into the dark mists, their shifting currents lit feebly by the cooking pit's coals.

"Close the door." Tepper's words were a plea, not a command.

Kelsier did as requested, pushing the door closed and stemming the flood of white mist. "The mist is not what you think. You fear it far too much."

"Men who venture into the mist lose their souls," a woman whispered. Her words raised a question. Had Kelsier walked in the mists? What, then, had happened to his soul?

If you only knew, Kelsier thought. "Well, I guess this means I'm staying." He waved for a boy to bring him a stool. "It's a good thing, too—it would have been a shame for me to leave before I shared my news."

More than one person perked up at the comment. This was the real reason they tolerated him—the reason even the timid peasants would harbor a man such as Kelsier, a skaa who defied the Lord Ruler's will by traveling from plantation to plantation. A renegade he might be—a danger to the entire community—but he brought news from the outside world.

"I come from the north," Kelsier said. "From lands where the Lord Ruler's touch is less noticeable." He spoke in a clear voice, and people leaned unconsciously toward him as they worked. On the next day, Kelsier's words would be repeated to the several hundred people who lived in other hovels. The skaa might be subservient, but they were incurable gossips.

"Local lords rule in the West," Kelsier said, "and they are far from the iron grip of the Lord Ruler and his obligators. Some of these distant noblemen are finding that happy skaa make better workers than mistreated skaa. One man, Lord Renoux, has even ordered his taskmasters to stop unauthorized beatings. There are whispers that he's considering paying wages to his plantation skaa, like city craftsmen might earn."

"Nonsense," Tepper said.

"My apologies," Kelsier said. "I didn't realize that Goodman Tepper had been to Lord Renoux's estates recently. When you dined with him last, did he tell you something that he did not tell me?"

Tepper blushed: Skaa did not travel, and they certainly didn't dine with lords. "You think me a fool, traveler," Tepper said, "but I know what you're doing. You're the one they call the Survivor; those scars on your arms give you away. You're a troublemaker—you travel the plantations, stirring up discontent. You eat our food, telling your grand stories and your lies, then you disappear and leave people like me to deal with the false hopes you give our children."

Kelsier raised an eyebrow. "Now, now, Goodman Tepper," he said. "Your worries are completely unfounded. Why, I have no intention of eating your food. I brought my own." With that, Kelsier reached over and tossed his pack onto the earth before Tepper's table. The loose bag slumped to the side, dumping an array of foods to the ground. Fine breads, fruits, and even a few thick, cured sausages bounced free.

A summerfruit rolled across the packed earthen floor and bumped lightly against Tepper's foot. The middle-aged skaa regarded the fruit with stunned eyes. "That's nobleman's food!"

Kelsier snorted. "Barely. You know, for a man of renowned prestige and rank, your Lord Tresting has remarkably poor taste. His pantry is an embarrassment to his noble station."

Tepper paled even further. "That's where you went this afternoon," he whispered. "You went to the manor. You . . . *stole from the master!*"

"Indeed," Kelsier said. "And, might I add that while your lord's taste in food is deplorable, his eye for soldiers is far more impressive. Sneaking into his manor during the day was quite a challenge."

Tepper was still staring at the bag of food. "If the taskmasters find this here . . ."

"Well, I suggest you make it disappear then," Kelsier said. "I'd be willing to bet that it tastes a fair bit better than watered-down farlet soup."

Two dozen sets of hungry eyes studied the food. If Tepper intended further arguments, he didn't make them quickly enough, for his silent pause was taken as agreement. Within a few minutes, the bag's contents had been inspected and distributed, and the pot of soup sat bubbling and ignored as the skaa feasted on a meal far more exotic.

Kelsier settled back, leaning against the hovel's wooden wall and watching the people devour their food. He had spoken correctly: The pantry's offerings had been depressingly mundane. However, this was a people who had been fed on nothing but soup and gruel since they were children. To them, breads and fruits were rare delicacies—usually eaten only as aging discards brought down by the house servants.

"Your storytelling was cut short, young man," an elderly skaa noted, hobbling over to sit on a stool beside Kelsier.

"Oh, I suspect there will be time for more later," Kelsier said. "Once all evidence of my thievery has been properly devoured. Don't you want any of it?"

"No need," the old man said. "The last time I tried lords' food, I had stomach pains for three days. New tastes are like new ideas, young man—the older you get, the more difficult they are for you to stomach."

Kelsier paused. The old man was hardly an imposing sight. His leathered skin and bald scalp made him look more frail than they did wise. Yet, he had to be stronger than he looked; few plantation skaa lived to such ages. Many lords didn't allow the elderly to remain home from daily work, and the frequent beatings that made up a skaa's life took a terrible toll on the elderly.

"What was your name again?" Kelsier asked.

"Mennis."

Kelsier glanced back at Tepper. "So, Goodman Mennis, tell me something. Why do you let him lead?"

Mennis shrugged. "When you get to be my age, you have to be very careful where you waste your energy. Some battles just aren't worth fighting." There was an implication in Mennis's eyes; he was referring to things greater than his own struggle with Tepper.

"You're satisfied with this, then?" Kelsier asked, nodding toward the hovel and its half-starved, overworked occupants. "You're content with a life full of beatings and endless drudgery?"

"At least it's a life," Mennis said. "I know what wages malcontent and rebellion bring. The eye of the Lord Ruler, and the ire of the Steel Ministry, can be far more terrible than a few whippings. Men like you preach change, but I wonder. Is this a battle we can really fight?"

"You're fighting it already, Goodman Mennis. You're just losing horribly."

Kelsier shrugged. "But, what do I know? I'm just a traveling miscreant, here to eat your food and impress your youths."

Mennis shook his head. "You jest, but Tepper might have been right. I fear your visit will bring us grief."

Kelsier smiled. "That's why I didn't contradict him—at least, not on the troublemaker point." He paused, then smiled more deeply. "In fact, I'd say calling me a troublemaker is probably the only accurate thing Tepper has said since I got here."

"How do you do that?" Mennis asked, frowning.

"What?"

"Smile so much."

"Oh, I'm just a happy person."

Mennis glanced down at Kelsier's hands. "You know, I've only seen scars like those on one other person—and he was dead. His body was returned to Lord Tresting as proof that his punishment had been carried out." Mennis looked up at Kelsier. "He'd been caught speaking of rebellion. Tresting sent him to the Pits of Hathsin, where he was worked until he died. The lad lasted less than a month."

Kelsier glanced down at his hands and forearms. They still burned sometimes, though he was certain the pain was only in his mind. He looked up at Mennis and smiled. "You ask why I smile, Goodman Mennis? Well, the Lord Ruler thinks he has claimed laughter and joy for himself. I'm disinclined to let him do so. This is one battle that doesn't take very much effort to fight."

Mennis stared at Kelsier, and for a moment Kelsier thought the old man might smile in return. However, Mennis eventually just shook his head. "I don't know. I just don't—"

The scream cut him off. It came from outside, perhaps to the north, though the mists distorted sounds. The people in the hovel fell silent, listening to the faint, high-pitched yells. Despite the distance and the mist, Kelsier could hear the pain contained in those screams.

Kelsier burned tin.

It was simple for him now, after years of practice. The tin sat with other Allomantic metals within his stomach, swallowed earlier, waiting for him to draw upon them. He reached inside with his mind and touched the tin, tapping powers he still barely understood. The tin flared to life within him, burning his stomach like the sensation of a hot drink swallowed too quickly.

Allomantic power surged through his body, enhancing his senses. The room around him became crisp, the dull firepit flaring to near blinding brightness. He could feel the grain in the wood of the stool beneath him. He could still taste the remnants of the loaf of bread he'd snacked on earlier. Most importantly, he could hear the screams with supernatural ears. Two separate people were yelling. One was an older woman, the other a younger woman—perhaps a child. The younger screams were getting farther and farther away.

"Poor Jess," a nearby woman said, her voice booming in Kelsier's enhanced ears. "That child of hers was a curse. It's better for skaa not to have pretty daughters."

Tepper nodded. "Lord Tresting was sure to send for the girl sooner or later. We all knew it. Jess knew it."

"Still a shame, though," another man said.

The screams continued in the distance. Burning tin, Kelsier was able to judge the direction accurately. Her voice was moving toward the lord's manor. The sounds set something off within him, and he felt his face flush with anger.

Kelsier turned. "Does Lord Tresting ever return the girls after he's finished with them?"

Old Mennis shook his head. "Lord Tresting is a law-abiding nobleman—he has the girls killed after a few weeks. He doesn't want to catch the eye of the Inquisitors."

That was the Lord Ruler's command. He couldn't afford to have half-breed children running around—children who might possess powers that skaa weren't even supposed to know existed. . . .

The screams waned, but Kelsier's anger only built. The yells reminded him of other screams. A woman's screams from the past. He stood abruptly, stool toppling to the ground behind him.

"Careful, lad," Mennis said apprehensively. "Remember what I said about wasting energy. You'll never raise that rebellion of yours if you get yourself killed tonight."

Kelsier glanced toward the old man. Then, through the screams and the pain, he forced himself to smile. "I'm not here to lead a rebellion among you, Goodman Mennis. I just want to stir up a little trouble."

"What good could that do?"

Kelsier's smile deepened. "New days are coming. Survive a little longer, and you just might see great happenings in the Final Empire. I bid you all thanks for your hospitality."

With that, he pulled open the door and strode out into the mist.

Mennis lay awake in the early hours of morning. It seemed that the older he became, the more difficult it was for him to sleep. This was particularly true when he was troubled about something, such as the traveler's failure to return to the hovel.

Mennis hoped that Kelsier had come to his senses and decided to move on. However, that prospect seemed unlikely; Mennis had seen the fire in Kelsier's eyes. It seemed such a shame that a man who had survived the Pits would instead find death here, on a random plantation, trying to protect a girl everyone else had given up for dead.

How would Lord Tresting react? He was said to be particularly harsh with anyone who interrupted his nighttime enjoyments. If Kelsier had managed to disturb the master's pleasures, Tresting might easily decide to punish the rest of his skaa by association.

Eventually, the other skaa began to awake. Mennis lay on the hard earth—bones aching, back complaining, muscles exhausted—trying to decide if it was worth rising. Each day, he nearly gave up. Each day, it was a little harder. One day, he would just stay in the hovel, waiting until the taskmasters came to kill those who were too sick or too elderly to work.

But not today. He could see too much fear in the eyes of the skaa—they knew that Kelsier's nighttime activities would bring trouble. They needed Mennis; they looked to him. He needed to get up.

And so, he did. Once he started moving, the pains of age decreased slightly, and he was able to shuffle out of the hovel toward the fields, leaning on a younger man for support.

It was then that he caught a scent in the air. "What's that?" he asked. "Do you smell smoke?"

Shum—the lad upon whom Mennis leaned—paused. The last remnants of the night's mist had burned away, and the red sun was rising behind the sky's usual haze of blackish clouds.

"I always smell smoke, lately," Shum said. "The Ashmounts are violent this year."

"No," Mennis said, feeling increasingly apprehensive. "This is different." He turned to the north, toward where a group of skaa were gathering. He let go of Shum, shuffling toward the group, feet kicking up dust and ash as he moved.

At the center of the group of people, he found Jess. Her daughter, the one they all assumed had been taken by Lord Tresting, stood beside her. The young girl's eyes were red from lack of sleep, but she appeared unharmed.

"She came back not long after they took her," the woman was explaining. "She came and pounded on the door, crying in the mist. Flen was sure it was just a mistwraith impersonating her, but I had to let her in! I don't care what he says, I'm not giving her up. I brought her out in the sunlight, and she didn't disappear. That proves she's not a mistwraith!"

Mennis stumbled back from the growing crowd. Did none of them see it? No taskmasters came to break up the group. No soldiers came to make the morning population counts. Something was very wrong. Mennis continued to the north, moving frantically toward the manor house.

By the time he arrived, others had noticed the twisting line of smoke that was just barely visible in the morning light. Mennis wasn't the first to arrive at the edge of the short hilltop plateau, but the group made way for him when he did.

The manor house was gone. Only a blackened, smoldering scar remained.

"By the Lord Ruler!" Mennis whispered. "What happened here?"

"He killed them all."

Mennis turned. The speaker was Jess's girl. She stood looking down at the fallen house, a satisfied expression on her youthful face.

"They were dead when he brought me out," she said. "All of them—the soldiers, the taskmasters, the lords . . . dead. Even Lord Tresting and his obligators. The master had left me, going to investigate when the noises began. On the way out, I saw him lying in his own blood, stab wounds in his chest. The man who saved me threw a torch in the building as we left."

"This man," Mennis said. "He had scars on his hands and arms, reaching past the elbows?"

The girl nodded silently.

"What kind of demon was that man?" one of the skaa muttered uncomfortably.

"Mistwraith," another whispered, apparently forgetting that Kelsier had gone out during the day.

But he did go out into the mist, Mennis thought. *And, how did he accomplish a feat like this . . . ? Lord Tresting kept over two dozen soldiers! Did Kelsier have a hidden band of rebels, perhaps?*

Kelsier's words from the night before sounded in his ears. *New days are coming. . . .*

"But, what of us?" Tepper asked, terrified. "What will happen when the Lord Ruler hears this? He'll think that we did it! He'll send us to the Pits, or maybe just send his koloss to slaughter us outright! Why would that troublemaker do something like this? Doesn't he understand the damage he's done?"

"He understands," Mennis said. "He warned us, Tepper. He came to stir up trouble."

"But, why?"

"Because he knew we'd never rebel on our own, so he gave us no choice."

Tepper paled.

Lord Ruler, Mennis thought. *I can't do this. I can barely get up in the mornings—I can't save this people.*

But what other choice was there?

Mennis turned. "Gather the people, Tepper. We must flee before word of this disaster reaches the Lord Ruler."

"Where will we go?"

"The caves to the east," Mennis said. "Travelers say there are rebel skaa hiding in them. Perhaps they'll take us in."

Tepper paled further. "But . . . we'd have to travel for days. Spend nights *in the mist.*"

"We can do that," Mennis said, "or we can stay here and die."

Tepper stood frozen for a moment, and Mennis thought the shock of it all might have overwhelmed him. Eventually, however, the younger man scurried off to gather the others, as commanded.

Mennis sighed, looking up toward the trailing line of smoke, cursing the man Kelsier quietly in his mind.

New days indeed.

PART ONE

THE SURVIVOR
OF HATHSIN

I consider myself to be a man of principle. But, what man does not? Even the cut-throat, I have noticed, considers his actions "moral" after a fashion.

Perhaps another person, reading of my life, would name me a religious tyrant. He could call me arrogant. What is to make that man's opinion any less valid than my own?

I guess it all comes down to one fact: In the end, I'm the one with the armies.

1

ASH FELL FROM THE SKY.

Vin watched the downy flakes drift through the air. Leisurely. Careless. Free. The puffs of soot fell like black snowflakes, descending upon the dark city of Luthadel. They drifted in corners, blowing in the breeze and curling in tiny whirlwinds over the cobblestones. They seemed so uncaring. What would that be like?

Vin sat quietly in one of the crew's watch-holes—a hidden alcove built into the bricks on the side of the safe house. From within it, a crewmember could watch the street for signs of danger. Vin wasn't on duty; the watch-hole was simply one of the few places where she could find solitude.

And Vin liked solitude. *When you're alone, no one can betray you.* Reen's words. Her brother had taught her so many things, then had reinforced them by doing what he'd always promised he would—by betraying her himself. *It's the only way you'll learn. Anyone will betray you, Vin. Anyone.*

The ash continued to fall. Sometimes, Vin imagined she was like the ash, or the wind, or the mist itself. A thing without thought, capable of simply *being*, not thinking, caring, or hurting. Then she could be . . . free.

She heard shuffling a short distance away, then the trapdoor at the back of the small chamber snapped open.

"Vin!" Ulef said, sticking his head into the room. "There you are! Camon's been searching for you for a half hour."

That's kind of why I hid in the first place.

"You should get going," Ulef said. "The job's almost ready to begin."

Ulef was a gangly boy. Nice, after his own fashion—naive, if one who had grown up in the underworld could ever really be called "naive." Of course, that didn't mean he wouldn't betray her. Betrayal had nothing to do with friendship; it was a simple fact of survival. Life was harsh on the streets, and if a skaa thief wanted to keep from being caught and executed, he had to be practical.

And ruthlessness was the very most practical of emotions. Another of Reen's sayings.

"Well?" Ulef asked. "You should go. Camon's mad."

When is he not? However, Vin nodded, scrambling out of the cramped—yet comforting—confines of the watch-hole. She brushed past Ulef and hopped out of the trapdoor, moving into a hallway, then a run-down pantry. The room was one of many at the back of the store that served as a front for the safe house. The crew's lair itself was hidden in a tunneled stone cavern beneath the building.

She left the building through a back door, Ulef trailing behind her. The job would happen a few blocks away, in a richer section of town. It was an intricate job—one of the most complex Vin had ever seen. Assuming Camon wasn't caught, the payoff would be great indeed. If he was caught . . . Well, scamming noblemen and obligators was a very dangerous profession—but it certainly beat working in the forges or the textile mills.

Vin exited the alleyway, moving out onto a dark, tenement-lined street in one of the city's many skaa slums. Skaa too sick to work lay huddled in corners and gutters, ash drifting around them. Vin kept her head down and pulled up her cloak's hood against the still falling flakes.

Free. No, I'll never be free. Reen made certain of that when he left.

"There you are!" Camon lifted a squat, fat finger and jabbed it toward her face. "Where were you?"

Vin didn't let hatred or rebellion show in her eyes. She simply looked down, giving Camon what he expected to see. There were other ways to be strong. That lesson she had learned on her own.

Camon growled slightly, then raised his hand and backhanded her across the face. The force of the blow threw Vin back against the wall, and her cheek blazed with pain. She slumped against the wood, but bore the punishment silently. Just another bruise. She was strong enough to deal with it. She'd done so before.

"Listen," Camon hissed. "This is an important job. It's worth thousands of boxings—worth more than you a hundred times over. I won't have you fouling it up. Understand?"

Vin nodded.

Camon studied her for a moment, his pudgy face red with anger. Finally, he looked away, muttering to himself.

He was annoyed about something—something more than just Vin. Perhaps he had heard about the skaa rebellion several days to the north. One of the provincial lords, Themos Tresting, had apparently been murdered, his manor burned to the ground. Such disturbances were bad for business; they made the aristocracy more alert, and less gullible. That, in turn, could cut seriously into Camon's profits.

He's looking for someone to punish, Vin though. *He always gets nervous before a job.* She looked up at Camon, tasting blood on her lip. She must have let some of her confidence show, because he glanced at her out of the corner of his eye, and his expression darkened. He raised his hand, as if to strike her again.

Vin used up a bit of her Luck.

She expended just a smidgen; she'd need the rest for the job. She directed the Luck at Camon, calming his nervousness. The crewleader paused—oblivious of Vin's touch, yet feeling its effects nonetheless. He stood for a moment; then he sighed, turning away and lowering his hand.

Vin wiped her lip as Camon waddled away. The thiefmaster looked very convincing in his nobleman's suit. It was as rich a costume as Vin had ever seen—it had a white shirt overlaid by a deep green vest with engraved gold buttons. The black suit coat was long, after the current fashion, and he wore a matching black hat. His fingers sparkled with rings, and he even carried a fine dueling cane. Indeed, Camon did an excellent job of imitating a nobleman; when it came to playing a role, there were few thieves more competent than Camon. Assuming he could keep his temper under control.

The room itself was less impressive. Vin pulled herself to her feet as Camon began to snap at some of the other crewmembers. They had rented one of the suites at the top of a local hotel. Not too lavish—but that was the idea. Camon was going to be playing the part of "Lord Jedue," a country nobleman who had hit upon hard financial times and come to Luthadel to get some final, desperate contracts.

The main room had been transformed into a sort of audience chamber, set with a large desk for Camon to sit behind, the walls decorated with cheap pieces of art. Two men stood beside the desk, dressed in formal stewards' clothing; they would play the part of Camon's manservants.

"What is this ruckus?" a man asked, entering the room. He was tall, dressed in a simple gray shirt and a pair of slacks, with a thin sword tied at his waist. Theron was the other crewleader—this particular scam was actually his. He'd brought in Camon as a partner; he'd needed someone to play Lord Jedue, and everyone knew that Camon was one of the best.

Camon looked up. "Hum? Ruckus? Oh, that was just a minor discipline problem. Don't bother yourself, Theron." Camon punctuated his remark with a dismissive wave of the hand—there was a reason he played such a good aristocrat. He was arrogant enough that he could have been from one of the Great Houses.

Theron's eyes narrowed. Vin knew what the man was probably thinking: He was deciding how risky it would be to put a knife in Camon's fat back once the scam was over. Eventually, the taller crewleader looked away from Camon, glancing at Vin. "Who's this?" he asked.

"Just a member of my crew," Camon said.

"I thought we didn't need anyone else."

"Well, we need her," Camon said. "Ignore her. My end of the operation is none of your concern."

Theron eyed Vin, obviously noting her bloodied lip. She glanced away. Theron's eyes lingered on her, however, running down the length of her body. She wore a simple white buttoned shirt and a pair of overalls. Indeed, she was hardly enticing; scrawny with a youthful face, she supposedly didn't even look her sixteen years. Some men preferred such women, however.

She considered using a bit of Luck on him, but eventually he turned away. "The obligator is nearly here," Theron said. "Are you ready?"

Camon rolled his eyes, settling his bulk down into the chair behind the desk. "Everything is perfect. Leave me be, Theron! Go back to your room and wait."

Theron frowned, then spun and walked from the room, muttering to himself.

Vin scanned the room, studying the decor, the servants, the atmosphere. Finally, she made her way to Camon's desk. The crewleader sat rifling through a stack of papers, apparently trying to decide which ones to put out on the desktop.

"Camon," Vin said quietly, "the servants are too fine."

Camon frowned, looking up. "What is that you're babbling?"

"The servants," Vin repeated, still speaking in a soft whisper. "Lord Jedue is supposed to be desperate. He'd have rich clothing left over from before, but he wouldn't be able to afford such rich servants. He'd use skaa."

Camon glared at her, but he paused. Physically, there was little difference between noblemen and skaa. The servants Camon had appointed, however, were dressed as minor noblemen—they were allowed to wear colorful vests, and they stood a little confidently.

"The obligator has to think that you're nearly impoverished," Vin said. "Pack the room with a lot of skaa servants instead."

"What do you know?" Camon said, scowling at her.

"Enough." She immediately regretted the word; it sounded too rebellious. Camon raised a bejeweled hand, and Vin braced herself for another slap. She couldn't afford to use up any more Luck. She had precious little remaining anyway.

However, Camon didn't hit her. Instead, he sighed and rested a pudgy hand on her shoulder. "Why do you insist on provoking me, Vin? You know the debts your brother left when he ran away. Do you realize that a less merciful man than myself would have sold you to the whoremasters long ago? How would you like that, serving in some nobleman's bed until he grew tired of you and had you executed?"

Vin looked down at her feet.

Camon's grip grew tight, his fingers pinching her skin where neck met shoulder, and she gasped in pain despite herself. He grinned at the reaction.

"Honestly, I don't know why I keep you, Vin," he said, increasing the pressure of his grip. "I should have gotten rid of you months ago, when your brother betrayed me. I suppose I just have too kindly a heart."

He finally released her, then pointed for her to stand over by the side of the room, next to a tall indoor plant. She did as ordered, orienting herself so she had a good view of the entire room. As soon as Camon looked away, she rubbed her shoulder. *Just another pain. I can deal with pain.*

Camon sat for a few moments. Then, as expected, he waved to the two "servants" at his side.

"You two!" he said. "You're dressed too richly. Go put on something that makes you look like skaa servants instead—and bring back six more men with you when you come."

Soon, the room was filled as Vin had suggested. The obligator arrived a short time later.

Vin watched Prelan Laird step haughtily into the room. Shaved bald like all obligators, he wore a set of dark gray robes. The Ministry tattoos around his eyes identified him as a prelan, a senior bureaucrat in the Ministry's Canton of Finance. A set of lesser obligators trailed behind him, their eye tattoos far less intricate.

Camon rose as the prelan entered, a sign of respect—something even the highest of Great House noblemen would show to an obligator of Laird's rank. Laird gave no bow or acknowledgment of his own, instead striding forward and taking the seat in front of Camon's desk. One of the crewmen impersonating a servant rushed forward, bringing chilled wine and fruit for the obligator.

Laird picked at the fruit, letting the servant stand obediently, holding the platter of food as if he were a piece of furniture. "Lord Jedue," Laird finally said. "I am glad we finally have the opportunity to meet."

"As am I, Your Grace," Camon said.

"Why is it, again, that you were unable to come to the Canton building, instead requiring that I visit you here?"

"My knees, Your Grace," Camon said. "My physicians recommend that I travel as little as possible."

And you were rightly apprehensive about being drawn into a Ministry stronghold, Vin thought.

"I see," Laird said. "Bad knees. An unfortunate attribute in a man who deals in transportation."

"I don't have to go on the trips, Your Grace," Camon said, bowing his head. "Just organize them."

Good, Vin thought. *Make sure you remain subservient, Camon. You need to seem desperate.*

Vin needed this scam to succeed. Camon threatened her and he beat her—but he considered her a good-luck charm. She wasn't sure if he knew why his plans went better when she was in the room, but he had apparently made the connection. That made her valuable—and Reen had always said that the surest way to stay alive in the underworld was to make yourself indispensable.

"I see," Laird said again. "Well, I fear that our meeting has come too late for your purposes. The Canton of Finance has already voted on your proposal."

"So soon?" Camon asked with genuine surprise.

"Yes," Laird replied, taking a sip of his wine, still not dismissing the servant. "We have decided not to accept your contract."

Camon sat for a moment, stunned. "I'm sorry to hear that, Your Grace."

Laird came to meet you, Vin thought. *That means he's still in a position to negotiate.*

"Indeed," Camon continued, seeing what Vin had. "That is especially unfortunate, as I was ready to make the Ministry an even better offer."

Laird raised a tattooed eyebrow. "I doubt it will matter. There is an element of the Council who feels that the Canton would receive better service if we found a more stable house to transport our people."

"That would be a grave mistake," Camon said smoothly. "Let us be frank, Your Grace. We both know that this contract is House Jedue's last chance. Now that we've lost the Farwan deal, we cannot afford to run our canal boats to Luthadel anymore. Without the Ministry's patronage, my house is financially doomed."

"This is doing very little to persuade me, Your Lordship," the obligator said.

"Isn't it?" Camon asked. "Ask yourself this, Your Grace—who will serve you better? Will it be the house that has dozens of contracts to divide its attention, or the house that views your contract as its last hope? The Canton of Finance will not find a more accommodating partner than a desperate one. Let my boats be the ones that bring your acolytes down from the north—let my soldiers escort them—and you will not be disappointed."

Good, Vin thought.

"I . . . see," the obligator said, now troubled.

"I would be willing to give you an extended contract, locked in at the price of fifty boxings a head per trip, Your Grace. Your acolytes would be able to travel our boats at their leisure, and would always have the escorts they need."

The obligator raised an eyebrow. "That's half the former fee."

"I told you," Camon said. "We're desperate. My house *needs* to keep its boats running. Fifty boxings will not make us a profit, but that doesn't matter. Once we have the Ministry contract to bring us stability, we can find other contracts to fill our coffers."

Laird looked thoughtful. It was a fabulous deal—one that might ordinarily have been suspicious. However, Camon's presentation created the image of a house on the brink of financial collapse. The other crewleader, Theron, had spent five years building, scamming, and finagling to create this moment. The Ministry would be remiss not to consider the opportunity.

Laird was realizing just that. The Steel Ministry was not just the force of bureaucracy and legal authority in the Final Empire—it was like a noble house unto itself. The more wealth it had, the better its own mercantile contracts, the more leverage the various Ministry Cantons had with each other—and with the noble houses.

Laird was still obviously hesitant, however. Vin could see the look in his eyes, the suspicion she knew well. He was not going to take the contract.

Now, Vin thought. *It's my turn.*

Vin used her Luck on Laird. She reached out tentatively—not even really sure what she was doing, or why she could even do it. Yet her touch was instinctive, trained through years of subtle practice. She'd been ten years old before she'd realized that other people couldn't do what she could.

She pressed against Laird's emotions, dampening them. He became less suspicious, less afraid. Docile. His worries melted away, and Vin could see a calm sense of control begin to assert itself in his eyes.

Yet, Laird still seemed slightly uncertain. Vin pushed harder. He cocked his head, looking thoughtful. He opened his mouth to speak, but she pushed against him again, desperately using up her last pinch of Luck.

He paused again. "Very well," he finally said. "I will take this new proposal to the Council. Perhaps an agreement can still be reached."

If men read these words, let them know that power is a heavy burden. Seek not to be bound by its chains. The Terris prophecies say that I will have the power to save the world.

They hint, however, that I will have the power to destroy it as well.

2

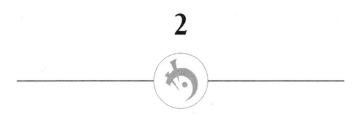

IN KELSIER'S OPINION, THE CITY OF Luthadel—seat of the Lord Ruler—was a gloomy sight. Most of the buildings had been built from stone blocks, with tile roofs for the wealthy, and simple, peaked wooden roofs for the rest. The structures were packed closely together, making them seem squat despite the fact that they were generally three stories high.

The tenements and shops were uniform in appearance; this was not a place to draw attention to oneself. Unless, of course, you were a member of the high nobility.

Interspersed throughout the city were a dozen or so monolithic keeps. Intricate, with rows of spearlike spires or deep archways, these were the homes of the high nobility. In fact, they were the *mark* of a high noble family: Any family who could afford to build a keep and maintain a high-profile presence in Luthadel was considered to be a Great House.

Most of the open ground in the city was around these keeps. The patches of space amid the tenements were like clearings in a forest, the keeps themselves like solitary mounts rising above the rest of the landscape. Black mountains. Like the rest of the city, the keeps were stained by countless years of ashfalls.

Every structure in Luthadel—virtually every structure Kelsier had ever seen—had been blackened to some degree. Even the city wall, upon which Kelsier now stood, was blackened by a patina of soot. Structures were generally darkest at the top, where the ash gathered, but rainwaters and evening condensations had carried the stains over ledges and down walls. Like paint running down a canvas, the darkness seemed to creep down the sides of buildings in an uneven gradient.

The streets, of course, were completely black. Kelsier stood waiting, scanning the city as a group of skaa workers worked in the street below, clearing away the latest mounds of ash. They'd take it to the River Channerel, which ran through the center of the city, sending the piles of ash to be washed away, lest it pile up and eventually bury the city. Sometimes, Kelsier wondered why the entire empire wasn't just one big mound of ash. He supposed the ash must break down into soil eventually. Yet, it took a ridiculous amount of effort to keep cities and fields clear enough to be used.

Fortunately, there were always enough skaa to do the work. The workers below him wore simple coats and trousers, ash-stained and worn. Like the plantation workers he had left behind several weeks before, they worked with beaten-down, despondent motions. Other groups of skaa passed the workers, responding to the bells in the distance, chiming the hour and calling them to their morning's work at the forges or mills. Luthadel's main export was metal; the city was home to hundreds of forges and refineries. However, the surgings of the river provided excellent locations for mills, both to grind grains and make textiles.

The skaa continued to work. Kelsier turned away from them, looking up into the distance, toward the city center, where the Lord Ruler's palace loomed like some kind of massive, multi-spined insect. Kredik Shaw, the Hill of a Thousand Spires. The palace was several times the size of any nobleman's keep, and was by far the largest building in the city.

Another ashfall began as Kelsier stood contemplating the city, the flakes falling lightly down upon the streets and buildings. *A lot of ashfalls, lately,* he thought, glad for the excuse to pull up the hood on his cloak. *The Ashmounts must be active.*

It was unlikely that anyone in Luthadel would recognize him—it had been three years since his capture. Still, the hood was reassuring. If all went well, there would come a time when Kelsier would want to be seen and recognized. For now, anonymity was probably better.

Eventually, a figure approached along the wall. The man, Dockson, was shorter than Kelsier, and he had a squarish face that seemed well suited to his moderately stocky build. A nondescript brown hooded cloak covered his black hair, and he wore the same short half beard that he'd sported since his face had first put forth whiskers some twenty years before.

He, like Kelsier, wore a nobleman's suit: colored vest, dark coat and trousers, and a thin cloak to keep off the ash. The clothing wasn't rich, but it was aristocratic—indicative of the Luthadel middle class. Most men of noble birth weren't wealthy enough to be considered part of a Great House—yet, in the Final Empire, nobility wasn't just about money. It was about lineage and history; the Lord Ruler was immortal, and he apparently still remembered the men who had supported him during the early years of his reign. The descendants of those men, no matter how poor they became, would always be favored.

The clothing would keep passing guard patrols from asking too many questions. In the cases of Kelsier and Dockson, of course, that clothing was a lie. Neither was actually noble—though, technically, Kelsier was a half-blood. In many ways, however, that was worse than being just a normal skaa.

Dockson strolled up next to Kelsier, then leaned against the battlement, resting a pair of stout arms on the stone. "You're a few days late, Kell."

"I decided to make a few extra stops in the plantations to the north."

"Ah," Dockson said. "So you *did* have something to do with Lord Tresting's death."

Kelsier smiled. "You could say that."

"His murder caused quite a stir among the local nobility."

"That was kind of the intention," Kelsier said. "Though, to be honest, I wasn't planning anything quite so dramatic. It was almost more of an accident than anything else."

Dockson raised an eyebrow. "How do you 'accidentally' kill a nobleman in his own mansion?"

"With a knife in the chest," Kelsier said lightly. "Or, rather, a pair of knives in the chest—it always pays to be careful."

Dockson rolled his eyes.

"His death isn't exactly a loss, Dox," Kelsier said. "Even among the nobility, Tresting had a reputation for cruelty."

"I don't care about Tresting," Dockson said. "I'm just considering the state of insanity that led me to plan another job with you. Attacking a provincial lord in his manor house, surrounded by guards . . . Honestly, Kell, I'd nearly forgotten how foolhardy you can be."

"Foolhardy?" Kelsier asked with a laugh. "That wasn't foolhardy—that was just a small diversion. You should see some of the things I'm *planning* to do!"

Dockson stood for a moment, then he laughed too. "By the Lord Ruler, it's good to have you back, Kell! I'm afraid I've grown rather boring during the last few years."

"We'll fix that," Kelsier promised. He took a deep breath, ash falling lightly around him. Skaa cleaning crews were already back at work on the streets below, brushing up the dark ash. Behind, a guard patrol passed, nodding to Kelsier and Dockson. They waited in silence for the men to pass.

"It's good to be back," Kelsier finally said. "There's something homey about Luthadel—even if it is a depressing, stark pit of a city. You have the meeting organized?"

Dockson nodded. "We can't start until this evening, though. How'd you get in, anyway? I had men watching the gates."

"Hmm? Oh, I snuck in last night."

"But how—" Dockson paused. "Oh, right. That's going to take some getting used to."

Kelsier shrugged. "I don't see why. You always work with Mistings."

"Yes, but this is different," Dockson said. He held up a hand to forestall further argument. "No need, Kell. I'm not hedging—I just said it would take some getting used to."

"Fine. Who's coming tonight?"

"Well, Breeze and Ham will be there, of course. They're very curious about this mystery job of ours—not to mention rather annoyed that I won't tell him what you've been up to these last few years."

"Good," Kelsier said with a smile. "Let them wonder. How about Trap?"

Dockson shook his head. "Trap's dead. The Ministry finally caught up with him a couple months ago. Didn't even bother sending him to the Pits—they beheaded him on the spot."

Kelsier closed his eyes, exhaling softly. It seemed that the Steel Ministry caught up with everyone eventually. Sometimes, Kelsier felt that a skaa Misting's life wasn't so much about surviving as it was about picking the right time to die.

"This leaves us without a Smoker," Kelsier finally said, opening his eyes. "You have any suggestions?"

"Ruddy," Dockson said.

Kelsier shook his head. "No. He's a good Smoker, but he's not a good enough man."

Dockson smiled. "Not a good enough man to be on a thieving crew . . . Kell, I *have* missed working with you. All right, who then?"

Kelsier thought for a moment. "Is Clubs still running that shop of his?"

"As far as I know," Dockson said slowly.

"He's supposed to be one of the best Smokers in the city."

"I suppose," Dockson said. "But . . . isn't he supposed to be kind of hard to work with?"

"He's not so bad," Kelsier said. "Not once you get used to him. Besides, I think he might be . . . amenable to this particular job."

"All right," Dockson said, shrugging. "I'll invite him. I think one of his relatives is a Tineye. Do you want me to invite him too?"

"Sounds good," Kelsier said.

"All right," Dockson said. "Well, beyond that, there's just Yeden. Assuming he's still interested . . ."

"He'll be there," Kelsier said.

"He'd better be," Dockson said. "He'll be the one paying us, after all."

Kelsier nodded, then frowned. "You didn't mention Marsh."

Dockson shrugged. "I warned you. Your brother never did approve of our methods, and now . . . well, you know Marsh. He won't even have anything to do with Yeden and the rebellion anymore, let alone with a bunch of criminals like us. I think we'll have to find someone else to infiltrate the obligators."

"No," Kelsier said. "He'll do it. I'll just have to stop by to persuade him."

"If you say so." Dockson fell silent then, and the two stood for a moment, leaning against the railing and looking out over the ash-stained city.

Dockson finally shook his head. "This is insane, eh?"

Kelsier smiled. "Feels good, doesn't it?"

Dockson nodded. "Fantastic."

"It will be a job like no other," Kelsier said, looking north—across the city and toward the twisted building at its center.

Dockson stepped away from the wall. "We have a few hours before the meeting. There's something I want to show you. I think there's still time—if we hurry."

Kelsier turned with curious eyes. "Well, I *was* going to go and chastise my prude of a brother. But . . ."

"This will be worth your time," Dockson promised.

Vin sat in the corner of the safe house's main lair. She kept to the shadows, as usual; the more she stayed out of sight, the more the others would ignore her. She couldn't afford to expend Luck keeping the men's hands off of her. She'd barely had time to regenerate what she'd used a few days before, during the meeting with the obligator.

The usual rabble lounged at tables in the room, playing at dice or discussing minor jobs. Smoke from a dozen different pipes pooled at the top of the chamber, and the walls were stained dark from countless years of similar treatment. The floor was darkened with patches of ash. Like most thieving crews, Camon's group wasn't known for its tidiness.

There was a door at the back of the room, and beyond it lay a twisting stone stairway that led up to a false rain grate in an alleyway. This room, like so many others hidden in the imperial capital of Luthadel, wasn't supposed to exist.

Rough laughter came from the front of the chamber, where Camon sat with a half-dozen cronies enjoying a typical afternoon of ale and crass jokes. Camon's table sat beside the bar, where the overpriced drinks were simply another way Camon exploited those who worked for him. The Luthadel criminal element had learned quite well from the lessons taught by the nobility.

Vin tried her best to remain invisible. Six months before, she wouldn't have believed that her life could actually get worse without Reen. Yet, despite her brother's abusive anger, he had kept the other crewmembers from having their way with Vin. There were relatively few women on thieving crews; generally, those women who got involved with the underworld ended up as whores. Reen had always told her that a girl needed to be tough—tougher, even, than a man—if she wanted to survive.

You think some crewleader is going to want a liability like you on his team? he had said. *I don't even want to have to work with you, and I'm your brother.*

Her back still throbbed; Camon had whipped her the day before. The blood would ruin her shirt, and she wouldn't be able to afford another one. Camon was already retaining her wages to pay the debts Reen had left behind.

But, I am strong, she thought.

That was the irony. The beatings almost didn't hurt anymore, for Reen's frequent abuses had left Vin resilient, while at the same time teaching her how to look pathetic and broken. In a way, the beatings were self-defeating. Bruises and welts mended, but each new lashing left Vin more hardened. Stronger.

Camon stood up. He reached into his vest pocket and pulled out his golden pocket watch. He nodded to one of his companions, then he scanned the room, searching for . . . her.

His eyes locked on Vin. "It's time."

Vin frowned. *Time for what?*

The Ministry's Canton of Finance was an imposing structure—but, then, *everything* about the Steel Ministry tended to be imposing.

Tall and blocky, the building had a massive rose window in the front, though the glass was dark from the outside. Two large banners hung down beside the window, the soot-stained red cloth proclaiming praises to the Lord Ruler.

Camon studied the building with a critical eye. Vin could sense his apprehension. The Canton of Finance was hardly the most threatening of Ministry offices—the Canton of Inquisition, or even the Canton of Orthodoxy, had a far more ominous reputation. However, voluntarily entering any Ministry office . . . putting yourself in the power of the obligators . . . well, it was a thing to do only after serious consideration.

Camon took a deep breath, then strode forward, his dueling cane tapping against the stones as he walked. He wore his rich nobleman's suit, and he was accompanied by a half-dozen crewmembers—including Vin—to act as his "servants."

Vin followed Camon up the steps, then waited as one of the crewmembers jumped forward to pull the door open for his "master." Of the six attendants, only Vin seemed to have been told nothing of Camon's plan. Suspiciously, Theron—Camon's supposed partner in the Ministry scam—was nowhere to be seen.

Vin entered the Canton building. Vibrant red light, sparkled with lines of blue, fell from the rose window. A single obligator, with midlevel tattoos around his eyes, sat behind a desk at the end of the extended entryway.

Camon approached, his cane thumping against the carpet as he walked. "I am Lord Jedue," he said.

What are you doing, Camon? Vin thought. *You insisted to Theron that you wouldn't meet with Prelan Laird in his Canton office. Yet, now you're here.*

The obligator nodded, making a notation in his ledger. He waved to the side.

"You may take one attendant with you into the waiting chamber. The rest must remain here."

Camon's huff of disdain indicated what he thought of that prohibition. The obligator, however, didn't look up from his ledger. Camon stood for a moment, and Vin couldn't tell if he was genuinely angry or just playing the part of an arrogant nobleman. Finally, he jabbed a finger at Vin.

"Come," he said, turning and waddling toward the indicated door.

The room beyond was lavish and plush, and several noblemen lounged in various postures of waiting. Camon chose a chair and settled into it, then pointed toward a table set with wine and red-frosted cakes. Vin obediently fetched him a glass of wine and a plate of food, ignoring her own hunger.

Camon began to pick hungrily at the cakes, smacking quietly as he ate.

He's nervous. More nervous, even, than before.

"Once we get in, you will say nothing," Camon grumbled between bites.

"You're betraying Theron," Vin whispered.

Camon nodded.

"But, how? Why?" Theron's plan was complex in execution, but simple in concept. Every year, the Ministry transferred its new acolyte obligators from a northern training facility south to Luthadel for final instruction. Theron had discovered, however, that those acolytes and their overseers brought down with them large amounts of Ministry funds—disguised as baggage—to be strongholded in Luthadel.

Banditry was very difficult in the Final Empire, what with the constant patrols along canal routes. However, if one were running the very canal boats that the acolytes were sailing upon, a robbery could become possible. Arranged at just the right time . . . the guards turning on their passengers . . . a man could make quite a profit, then blame it all on banditry.

"Theron's crew is weak," Camon said quietly. "He expended too many resources on this job."

"But, the return he'll make—" Vin said.

"Will never happen if I take what I can now, then run," Camon said, smiling. "I'll talk the obligators into a down payment to get my caravan boats afloat, then disappear and leave Theron to deal with the disaster when the Ministry realizes that it's been scammed."

Vin stood back, slightly shocked. Setting up a scam like this would have cost Theron thousands upon thousands of boxings—if the deal fell through now, he would be ruined. And, with the Ministry hunting him, he wouldn't even have time to seek revenge. Camon would make a quick profit, as well as rid himself of one of his more powerful rivals.

Theron was a fool to bring Camon into this, she thought. But, then, the amount Theron had promised to pay Camon was great; he probably assumed that Camon's greed would keep him honest until Theron himself could pull a double cross. Camon had simply worked faster than anyone, even Vin, had expected. How could Theron have known that Camon would undermine the job itself, rather than wait and try and steal the entire haul from the caravan boats?

Vin's stomach twisted. *It's just another betrayal*, she thought sickly. *Why does it still bother me so? Everyone betrays everyone else. That's the way life is. . . .*

She wanted to find a corner—someplace cramped and secluded—and hide. Alone.

Anyone will betray you. Anyone.

But there was no place to go. Eventually, a minor obligator entered and called for Lord Jedue. Vin followed Camon as they were ushered into an audience chamber.

The man who waited inside, sitting behind the audience desk, was not Prelan Laird.

Camon paused in the doorway. The room was austere, bearing only the desk and simple gray carpeting. The stone walls were unadorned, the only window barely a handspan wide. The obligator who waited for them had some of the most intricate tattoos around his eyes that Vin had ever seen. She wasn't even certain what rank they implied, but they extended all the way back to the obligator's ears and up over his forehead.

"Lord Jedue," the strange obligator said. Like Laird, he wore gray robes, but he was very different from the stern, bureaucratic men Camon had dealt with before. This man was lean in a muscular way, and his clean-shaven, triangular head gave him an almost predatory look.

"I was under the impression that I would be meeting with Prelan Laird," Camon said, still not moving into the room.

"Prelan Laird has been called away on other business. I am High Prelan Arriev—head of the board that was reviewing your proposal. You have a rare opportunity to address me directly. I normally don't hear cases in person, but Laird's absence has made it necessary for me to share in some of his work."

Vin's instincts made her tense. *We should go. Now.*

Camon stood for a long moment, and Vin could see him considering. Run now? Or, take a risk for the greater prize? Vin didn't care about prizes; she just wanted to live. Camon, however, had not become crewleader without the occasional gamble. He slowly moved into the room, eyes cautious as he took the seat opposite the obligator.

"Well, High Prelan Arriev," Camon said with a careful voice. "I assume that since I have been called back for another appointment, the board is considering my offer?"

"Indeed we are," the obligator said. "Though I must admit, there are some Council members who are apprehensive about dealing with a family that is so near to economic disaster. The Ministry generally prefers to be conservative in its financial operations."

"I see."

"But," Arriev said, "there are others on the board who are quite eager to take advantage of the savings you offered us."

"And with which group do you identify, Your Grace?"

"I, as of yet, have not made my decision." The obligator leaned forward. "Which is why I noted that you have a rare opportunity. Convince me, Lord Jedue, and you will have your contract."

"Surely Prelan Laird outlined the details of our offer," Camon said.

"Yes, but I would like to hear the arguments from you personally. Humor me."

Vin frowned. She remained near the back of the room, standing near the door, still half convinced she should run.

"Well?" Arriev asked.

"We need this contract, Your Grace," Camon said. "Without it we won't be able to continue our canal shipping operations. Your contract would give us a much needed period of stability—a chance to maintain our caravan boats for a time while we search for other contracts."

Arriev studied Camon for a moment. "Surely you can do better than that, Lord Jedue. Laird said that you were very persuasive—let me hear you *prove* that you deserve our patronage."

Vin prepared her Luck. She could make Arriev more inclined to believe . . . but something restrained her. The situation felt wrong.

"We are your best choice, Your Grace," Camon said. "You fear that my house will suffer economic failure? Well, if it does, what have you lost? At worst, my narrowboats would stop running, and you would have to find other merchants to deal with. Yet, if your patronage is enough to maintain my house, then you have found yourself an enviable long-term contract."

"I see," Arriev said lightly. "And why the Ministry? Why not make your deal with someone else? Surely there are other options for your boats—other groups who would jump at such rates."

Camon frowned. "This isn't about money, Your Grace, it is about the victory—the showing of confidence—that we would gain by having a Ministry contract. If you trust us, others will too. I *need* your support." Camon was sweating now. He was probably beginning to regret this gamble. Had he been betrayed? Was Theron behind the odd meeting?

The obligator waited quietly. He could destroy them, Vin knew. If he even suspected that they were scamming him, he could give them over to the Canton of Inquisition. More than one nobleman had entered a Canton building and never returned.

Gritting her teeth, Vin reached out and used her Luck on the obligator, making him less suspicious.

Arriev smiled. "Well, you have convinced me," he suddenly declared.

Camon sighed in relief.

Arriev continued, "Your most recent letter suggested that you need three thousand boxings as an advance to refurbish your equipment and resume shipping operations. See the scribe in the main hallway to finish the paperwork so that you may requisition the necessary funds."

The obligator pulled a sheet of thick bureaucratic paper from a stack, then stamped a seal at the bottom. He proffered it to Camon. "Your contract."

Camon smiled deeply. "I knew coming to the Ministry was the wise choice," he said, accepting the contract. He stood, nodding respectfully to the obligator, then motioned for Vin to open the door for him.

She did so. *Something is wrong. Something is very wrong.* She paused as Camon left, looking back at the obligator. He was still smiling.

A happy obligator was always a bad sign.

Yet, no one stopped them as they passed through the waiting room with its noble occupants. Camon sealed and delivered the contract to the appropriate scribe, and no soldiers appeared to arrest them. The scribe pulled out a small chest filled with coins, and then handed it to Camon with an indifferent hand.

Then, they simply left the Canton building, Camon gathering his other attendants with obvious relief. No cries of alarm. No tromping of soldiers. They were free. Camon had successfully scammed both the Ministry and another crewleader.

Apparently.

Kelsier stuffed another one of the little red-frosted cakes into his mouth, chewing with satisfaction. The fat thief and his scrawny attendant passed through the waiting room, entering the entryway beyond. The obligator who had interviewed the two thieves remained in his office, apparently awaiting his next appointment

"Well?" Dockson asked. "What do you think?"

Kelsier glanced at the cakes. "They're quite good," he said, taking another one. "The Ministry has always had excellent taste—it makes sense that they would provide superior snacks."

Dockson rolled his eyes. "About the girl, Kell."

Kelsier smiled as he piled four of the cakes in his hand, then nodded toward the doorway. The Canton waiting room was growing too busy for the discussion of delicate matters. On the way out, he paused and told the obligator secretary in the corner that they needed to reschedule.

Then the two crossed through the entry chamber—passing the overweight crewleader, who stood speaking with a scribe. Kelsier stepped out onto the street, pulled his hood up against the still falling ash, then led the way across the street. He paused beside an alleyway, standing where he and Dockson could watch the Canton building's doors.

Kelsier munched contentedly on his cakes. "How'd you find out about her?" he asked between bites.

"Your brother," Dockson replied. "Camon tried to swindle Marsh a few months ago, and he brought the girl with him then, too. Actually, Camon's little good-luck charm is becoming moderately famous in the right circles. I'm still not sure if he knows what she is or not. You know how superstitious thieves can get."

Kelsier nodded, dusting off his hands. "How'd you know she'd be here today?"

Dockson shrugged. "A few bribes in the right place. I've been keeping an eye on the girl ever since Marsh pointed her out to me. I wanted to give you an opportunity to see her work for yourself."

Across the street, the Canton building's door finally opened, and Camon made his way down the steps surrounded by a group of "servants." The small, short-haired girl was with him. The sight of her made Kelsier frown. She had a nervous anxiety to her step, and she jumped slightly whenever someone made a quick move. The right side of her face was still slightly discolored from a partially healed bruise.

Kelsier eyed the self-important Camon. *I'll have to come up with something particularly suitable to do to that man.*

"Poor thing," Dockson muttered.

Kelsier nodded. "She'll be free of him soon enough. It's a wonder no one discovered her before this."

"Your brother was right then?"

Kelsier nodded. "She's at least a Misting, and if Marsh says she's more, I'm inclined to believe him. I'm a bit surprised to see her using Allomancy on a member of the Ministry, especially inside a Canton building. I'd guess that she doesn't know that she's even using her abilities."

"Is that possible?" Dockson asked.

Kelsier nodded. "Trace minerals in the water can be burned, if just for a tiny bit of power. That's one of the reasons the Lord Ruler built his city here—lots of metals in the ground. I'd say that . . ."

Kelsier trailed off, frowning slightly. Something was wrong. He glanced toward Camon and his crew. They were still visible in the near distance, crossing the street and heading south.

A figure appeared in the Canton building's doorway. Lean with a confident air, he bore the tattoos of a high prelan of the Canton of Finance around his eyes. Probably the very man Camon had met with shortly before. The obligator stepped out of the building, and a second man exited behind him.

Beside Kelsier, Dockson suddenly grew stiff.

The second man was tall with a strong build. As he turned, Kelsier was able to see that a thick metal spike had been pounded tip-first through each of the man's eyes. With shafts as wide as an eye socket, the nail-like spikes were long enough that their sharp points jutted out about an inch from the back of the man's clean-shaven skull. The flat spike ends shone like two silvery disks, sticking out of the sockets in the front, where the eyes should have been.

A Steel Inquisitor.

"What's *that* doing here?" Dockson asked.

"Stay calm," Kelsier said, trying to force himself to do the same. The Inquisitor looked toward them, spiked eyes regarding Kelsier, before turning in the direction that Camon and the girl had gone. Like all Inquisitors, he wore intricate eye tattoos—mostly black, with one stark red line—that marked him as a high-ranking member of the Canton of Inquisition.

"He's not here for us," Kelsier said. "I'm not burning anything—he'll think that we're just ordinary noblemen."

"The girl," Dockson said.

Kelsier nodded. "You say Camon's been running this scam on the Ministry for a while. Well, the girl must have been detected by one of the obligators. They're trained to recognize when an Allomancer tampers with their emotions."

Dockson frowned thoughtfully. Across the street, the Inquisitor conferred with the other obligator, then the two of them turned to walk in the direction that Camon had gone. There was no urgency to their pace.

"They must have sent a tail to follow them," Dockson said.

"This is the Ministry," Kelsier said. "There'll be two tails, at least."

Dockson nodded. "Camon will lead them directly back to his safe house. Dozens of men will die. They're not all the most admirable people, but . . ."

"They fight the Final Empire, in their own way," Kelsier said. "Besides, I'm not about to let a possible Mistborn slip away from us—I want to talk to that girl. Can you deal with those tails?"

"I said I'd become boring, Kell," Dockson said. "Not sloppy. I can handle a couple of Ministry flunkies."

"Good," Kelsier said, reaching into his cloak pocket and pulling out a small vial. A collection of metal flakes floated in an alcohol solution within. Iron, steel, tin, pewter, copper, bronze, zinc, and brass—the eight basic Allomantic metals. Kelsier pulled off the stopper and downed the contents in a single swift gulp.

He pocketed the now empty vial, wiping his mouth. "I'll handle that Inquisitor."

Dockson looked apprehensive. "You're going to try and take him?"

Kelsier shook his head. "Too dangerous. I'll just divert him. Now, get going—we don't want those tails finding the safe house."

Dockson nodded. "Meet back at the fifteenth crossroad," he said before taking off down the alley and disappearing around a corner.

Kelsier gave his friend a count of ten before reaching within himself and burning his metals. His body came awash with strength, clarity, and power.

Kelsier smiled; then—burning zinc—he reached out and yanked firmly on the Inquisitor's emotions. The creature froze in place, then spun, looking back toward the Canton building.

Let's have a chase now, you and I, Kelsier thought.

We arrived in Terris earlier this week, and, I have to say, I find the countryside beautiful. The great mountains to the north—with their bald snowcaps and forested mantles—stand like watchful gods over this land of green fertility. My own lands to the south are mostly flat; I think that they might look less dreary if there were a few mountains to vary the terrain.

The people here are mostly herdsmen—though timber harvesters and farmers are not uncommon. It is a pastoral land, certainly. It seems odd that a place so remarkably agrarian could have produced the prophecies and theologies upon which the entire world now relies.

3

CAMON COUNTED HIS COINS, DROPPING THE golden boxings one by one into the small chest on his table. He still looked a bit stunned, as well he should have. Three thousand boxings was a fabulous amount of money—far more than Camon would earn in even a very good year. His closest cronies sat at the table with him, ale—and laughter—flowing freely.

Vin sat in her corner, trying to understand her feelings of dread. Three thousand boxings. The Ministry should never have let such a sum go so quickly. Prelan Arriev had seemed too cunning to be fooled with ease.

Camon dropped another coin into the chest. Vin couldn't decide if he was being foolish or clever by making such a display of wealth. Underworld crews worked under a strict agreement: Everyone received a cut of earnings in proportion to their status in the group. While it was sometimes tempting to kill the crewleader and take his money for yourself, a successful leader created more wealth for everyone. Kill him prematurely, and you would cut off future earnings—not to mention earn the wrath of the other crewmembers.

Still, three thousand boxings . . . that would be enough to tempt even the most logical thief. It was all wrong.

I have to get out of here, Vin decided. *Get away from Camon, and the lair, in case something happens.*

And yet . . . leave? By herself? She'd never been alone before; she'd always had Reen. He'd been the one to lead her from city to city, joining different thieving crews. She loved solitude. But the thought of being by herself, out in the city, horrified her. That was why she'd never run away from Reen; that was why she'd stayed with Camon.

She couldn't go. But she had to. She looked up from her corner, scanning the room. There weren't many people in the crew for whom she felt any sort of attachment. Yet, there were a couple that she would be sorry to see hurt, should the obligators actually move against the crew. A few men who hadn't tried to abuse her, or—in very rare cases—who had actually shown her some measure of kindness.

Ulef was at the top of that list. He wasn't a friend, but he was the closest thing she had now that Reen was gone. If he would go with her, then at least she wouldn't be alone. Cautiously, Vin stood and moved along the side of the room to where Ulef sat drinking with some of the other younger crewmembers.

She tugged on Ulef's sleeve. He turned toward her, only slightly drunk. "Vin?"

"Ulef," she whispered. "We need to go."

He frowned. "Go? Go where?"

"Away," Vin whispered. "Out of here."

"Now?"

Vin nodded urgently.

Ulef glanced back at his friends, who were chuckling among themselves, shooting suggestive looks at Vin and Ulef.

Ulef flushed. "You want to go somewhere, just you and I?"

"Not like that," Vin said. "Just . . . I need to leave the lair. And I don't want to be alone."

Ulef frowned. He leaned closer, a slight stink of ale on his breath. "What is this about, Vin?" he asked quietly.

Vin paused. "I . . . think something might happen, Ulef," she whispered. "Something with the obligators. I just don't want to be in the lair right now."

Ulef sat quietly for a moment. "All right," he finally said. "How long will this take?"

"I don't know," Vin said. "Until evening, at least. But we have to go. *Now.*"

He nodded slowly.

"Wait here for a moment," Vin whispered, turning. She shot a glance at Camon, who was laughing at one of his own jokes. Then she quietly moved through the ash-stained, smoky chamber into the lair's back room.

The crew's general sleeping quarters consisted of a simple, elongated corridor lined with bedrolls. It was crowded and uncomfortable, but it was far better than the cold alleyways she'd slept in during her years traveling with Reen.

Alleyways that I might have to get used to again, she thought. She had survived them before. She could do so again.

She moved to her pallet, the muffled sounds of men laughing and drinking sounding from the other room. Vin knelt down, regarding her few possessions. If something did happen to the crew, she wouldn't be able to come back to the lair. Ever. But, she couldn't take the bedroll with her now—it was far too obvious. That left only the small box that contained her personal effects: a pebble from each city she'd visited, the earring Reen said Vin's mother had given her, and a bit of obsidian the size of a large coin. It was chipped into an irregular pattern—Reen had carried it as some kind of good luck charm. It was the only thing he'd left behind when he'd snuck away from the crew half a year before. Abandoning her.

Just like he always said he would, Vin told herself sternly. *I never thought he'd actually go—and that's exactly why he had to leave.*

She gripped the bit of obsidian in her hand and pocketed the pebbles. The earring she put in her ear—it was a very simple thing. Little more than a stud, not even worth stealing, which was why she didn't fear leaving it in the back room. Still, Vin had rarely worn it, for fear that the ornamentation would make her look more feminine.

She had no money, but Reen had taught her how to scavenge and beg. Both were difficult in the Final Empire, especially in Luthadel, but she would find a way, if she had to.

Vin left her box and bedroll, slipping back out into the common room. Maybe she was overreacting; perhaps nothing would happen to the crew. But, if it did . . . well, if there was one thing Reen had taught her, it was how to protect her neck. Bringing Ulef was a good idea. He had contacts in Luthadel. If something happened to Camon's crew, Ulef could probably get her and him jobs on—

Vin froze just inside the main room. Ulef wasn't at the table where she had left him. Instead, he stood furtively near the front of the room. Near the bar. Near . . . Camon.

"What is this!" Camon stood, his face red as sunlight. He pushed his stool out of the way, then lurched toward her, half drunk. "Running away? Off to betray me to the Ministry, are you!"

Vin dashed toward the stairwell door, desperately scrambling around tables and past crewmembers.

Camon's hurled wooden stool hit her square in the back, throwing her to the ground. Pain flared between her shoulders; several crewmembers cried out as the stool bounced off of her and thumped against the floorboards nearby.

Vin lay in a daze. Then . . . something within her—something she knew of but didn't understand—gave her strength. Her head stopped swimming, her pain becoming a focus. She climbed awkwardly to her feet.

Camon was there. He backhanded her even as she stood. Her head snapped to the side from the blow, twisting her neck so painfully that she barely felt herself hit the floor again.

Camon bent over, grabbing her by the front of her shirt and pulling her up, raising his fist. Vin didn't pause to think or to speak; there was only one thing to do. She used up all of her Luck in a single furious effort, pushing against Camon, calming his fury.

Camon teetered. For a moment, his eyes softened. He lowered her slightly.

Then the anger returned to his eyes. Hard. Terrifying.

"Damn wench," Camon muttered, grabbing her by the shoulders and shaking her. "That backstabbing brother of yours never respected me, and you're the same. I was too easy on you both. Should have . . ."

Vin tried to twist free, but Camon's grip was firm. She searched desperately for aid from the other crewmembers—however, she knew what she would find. Indifference. They turned away, their faces embarrassed but not concerned. Ulef still stood near Camon's table, looking down guiltily.

In her mind, she thought she heard a voice whispering to her. Reen's voice. *Fool! Ruthlessness—it's the most logical of emotions. You don't have any friends in the underworld. You'll never have any friends in the underworld!*

She renewed her struggles, but Camon hit her again, knocking her to the ground. The blow stunned her, and she gasped, breath knocked from her lungs.

Just endure, she thought, mind muddled. *He won't kill me. He needs me.*

Yet, as she turned weakly, she saw Camon looming above her in the caliginous room, drunken fury showing in his face. She knew this time would be different; it would be no simple beating. He thought that she intended to betray him to the Ministry. He wasn't in control.

There was murder in his eyes.

Please! Vin thought with desperation, reaching for her Luck, trying to make it work. There was no response. Luck, such as it was, had failed her.

Camon bent down, muttering to himself as he grabbed her by the shoulder. He raised an arm—his meaty hand forming another fist, his muscles tensing, an angry bead of sweat slipping off his chin and hitting her on the cheek.

A few feet away, the stairwell door shook, then burst open. Camon paused, arm upraised as he glared toward the door and whatever unfortunate crewmember had chosen such an inopportune moment to return to the lair.

Vin seized the distraction. Ignoring the newcomer, she tried to shake herself free from Camon's grip, but she was too weak. Her face blazed from where he'd hit her, and she tasted blood on her lip. Her shoulder had been twisted awkwardly, and her side ached from where she'd fallen. She clawed at Camon's hand, but she suddenly felt weak, her inner strength failing her just as her Luck had. Her pains suddenly seemed greater, more daunting, more . . . demanding.

She turned toward the door desperately. She was close—painfully close. She had nearly escaped. Just a little farther . . .

Then she saw the man standing quietly in the stairwell doorway. He was unfamiliar to her. Tall and hawk-faced, he had light blond hair and wore a relaxed nobleman's suit, his cloak hanging free. He was, perhaps, in his mid-thirties. He wore no hat, nor did he carry a dueling cane.

And he looked very, very angry.

"What is this?" Camon demanded. "Who are you?"

How did he get by the scouts . . . ? Vin thought, struggling to get her wits back. Pain. She could deal with pain. *The obligators . . . did they send him?*

The newcomer looked down at Vin, and his expression softened slightly. Then he looked up at Camon and his eyes grew dark.

Camon's angry demands were cut off as he was thrown backward as if had been punched by a powerful force. His arm was ripped free from Vin's shoulder, and he toppled to the ground, causing the floorboards to shake.

The room fell quiet.

Have to get away, Vin thought, forcing herself up to her knees. Camon groaned in pain from a few feet away, and Vin crawled away from him, slipping beneath an unoccupied table. The lair had a hidden exit, a trapdoor beside the far back wall. If she could crawl to it—

Suddenly, Vin felt an overwhelming peace. The emotion slammed into her like a sudden weight, her emotions squished silent, as if crushed by a forceful hand. Her fear puffed out like an extinguished candle, and even her pain seemed unimportant.

She slowed, wondering why she had been so worried. She stood up, pausing as she faced the trapdoor. She breathed heavily, still a little dazed.

Camon just tried to kill me! the logical part of her mind warned. *And someone else is attacking the lair. I have to get away!* However, her emotions didn't match the logic. She felt . . . serene. Unworried. And more than a little bit curious.

Someone had just used Luck on her.

She recognized it somehow, even though she'd never felt it upon her before. She paused beside the table, one hand on the wood, then slowly turned around. The newcomer still stood in the stairwell doorway. He studied her with a critical eye, then smiled in a disarming sort of way.

What is going on?

The newcomer finally stepped into the room. The rest of Camon's crew remained sitting at their tables. They looked surprised, but oddly unworried.

He's using Luck on them all. But . . . how can he do it to so many at once? Vin had never been able to store up enough Luck to do more than give the occasional, brief push.

As the newcomer entered the room, Vin could finally see that a second person stood in the stairwell behind him. This second man was less imposing. He was shorter, with a dark half beard and close-cropped straight hair. He also wore a nobleman's suit, though his was less sharply tailored.

On the other side of the room, Camon groaned and sat up, holding his head. He glanced at the newcomers. "Master Dockson! Why, uh, well, this is a surprise!"

"Indeed," said the shorter man—Dockson. Vin frowned, realizing she sensed a slight familiarity to these men. She recognized them from somewhere.

The Canton of Finance. They were sitting in the waiting room when Camon and I left.

Camon climbed to his feet, studying the blond newcomer. Camon looked down at the man's hands, both of which were lined with strange, overlapping scars. "By the Lord Ruler . . ." Camon whispered. "The Survivor of Hathsin!"

Vin frowned. The title was unfamiliar to her. Should she know this man? Her wounds still throbbed despite the peace she felt, and her head was dizzy. She leaned on the table for support, but did not sit.

Whoever this newcomer was, Camon obviously thought him important. "Why, Master Kelsier!" Camon sputtered. "This is a rare honor!"

The newcomer—Kelsier—shook his head. "You know, I'm not really interested in listening to you."

Camon let out an "urk" of pain as he was thrown backward again. Kelsier made no obvious gesture to perform the feat. Yet, Camon collapsed to the ground, as if shoved by some unseen force.

Camon fell quiet, and Kelsier scanned the room. "The rest of you know who I am?"

Many of the crewmembers nodded.

"Good. I've come to your lair because you, my friends, owe me a great debt."

The room was silent save for Camon's groans. Finally, one of the crewmen spoke. "We . . . do, Master Kelsier?"

"Indeed you do. You see, Master Dockson and I just saved your lives. Your rather incompetent crewleader left the Ministry's Canton of Finance about an hour ago, returning directly to this safe house. He was followed by two Ministry scouts, one high-ranking prelan . . . and a single Steel Inquisitor."

No one spoke.

Oh, Lord . . . Vin thought. She'd been right—she just hadn't been fast enough. If there was an Inquisitor—

"I dealt with the Inquisitor," Kelsier said. He paused, letting the implication hang in the air. What kind of person could so lightly claim to have "dealt" with an Inquisitor? Rumors said the creatures were immortal, that they could see a man's soul, and that they were unmatched warriors.

"I require payment for services rendered," Kelsier said.

Camon didn't get up this time; he had fallen hard, and he was obviously disoriented. The room remained still. Finally, Milev—the dark-skinned man who was Camon's second—scooped up the coffer of Ministry boxings and dashed forward with it. He proffered it to Kelsier.

"The money Camon got from the Ministry," Milev explained. "Three thousand boxings."

Milev is so eager to please him, Vin thought. *This is more than just Luck—either that, or it's some sort of Luck I've never been able to use.*

Kelsier paused, then accepted the coin chest. "And you are?"

"Milev, Master Kelsier."

"Well, Crewleader Milev, I will consider this payment satisfactory—assuming you do one other thing for me."

Milev paused. "What would that be?"

Kelsier nodded toward the near-unconscious Camon. "Deal with him."

"Of course," Milev said.

"I want him to live, Milev," Kelsier said, holding up a finger. "But I don't want him to enjoy it."

Milev nodded. "We'll make him a beggar. The Lord Ruler disapproves of the profession—Camon won't have an easy time of it here in Luthadel."

And Milev will dispose of him anyway as soon as he thinks this Kelsier isn't paying attention.

"Good," Kelsier said. Then he opened the coin chest and began counting out some golden boxings. "You're a resourceful man, Milev. Quick on your feet, and not as easily intimidated as the others."

"I've had dealings with Mistings before, Master Kelsier," Milev said.

Kelsier nodded. "Dox," he said, addressing his companion, "where were we going to have our meeting tonight?"

"I was thinking that we should use Clubs's shop," said the second man.

"Hardly a neutral location," Kelsier said. "Especially if he decides not to join us."

"True."

Kelsier looked to Milev. "I'm planning a job in this area. It would be useful to have the support of some locals." He held out a pile of what looked like a hundred boxings. "We'll require use of your safe house for the evening. This can be arranged?"

"Of course," Milev said, taking the coins eagerly.

"Good," Kelsier said. "Now, get out."

"Out?" Milev asked hesitantly.

"Yes," Kelsier said. "Take your men—including your former leader—and leave. I want to have a private conversation with Mistress Vin."

The room grew silent again, and Vin knew she wasn't the only one wondering how Kelsier knew her name.

"Well, you heard him!" Milev snapped. He waved for a group of thugs to go grab Camon, then he shooed the rest of the crewmembers up the stairs.

Vin watched them go, growing apprehensive. This Kelsier was a powerful man, and instinct told her that powerful men were dangerous. Did he know of her Luck? Obviously; what other reason would he have for singling her out?

How is this Kelsier going to try and use me? she thought, rubbing her arm where she'd hit the floor.

"By the way, Milev," Kelsier said idly. "When I say 'private,' I mean that I don't want to be spied on by the four men watching us through peek-holes behind the far wall. Kindly take them up into the alley with you."

Milev paled. "Of course, Master Kelsier."

"Good. And, in the alleyway you'll find the two dead Ministry spies. Kindly dispose of the corpses for us."

Milev nodded, turning.

"And Milev," Kelsier added.

Milev turned back again.

"See that none of your men betray us," Kelsier said quietly. And Vin felt it again—a renewed pressure on her emotions. "This crew already has the eye of the Steel Ministry—do not make an enemy of me as well."

Milev nodded sharply, then disappeared into the stairwell, pulling the door closed behind him. A few moments later, Vin heard footsteps from the peek room; then all was still. She was alone with a man who was—for some reason—so singularly impressive that he could intimidate an entire room full of cutthroats and thieves.

She eyed the bolt door. Kelsier was watching her. What would he do if she ran?

He claims to have killed an Inquisitor, Vin thought. *And . . . he used Luck. I have to stay, if just long enough to find out what he knows.*

Kelsier's smile deepened, then finally he laughed. "That was *far* too much fun, Dox."

The other man, the one Camon had called Dockson, snorted and walked toward the front of the room. Vin tensed, but he didn't move toward her, instead strolling to the bar.

"You were insufferable enough before, Kell," Dockson said. "I don't know how I'm going to handle this new reputation of yours. At least, I'm not sure how I'm going to handle it and maintain a straight face."

"You're jealous."

"Yes, that's it," Dockson said. "I'm terribly jealous of your ability to intimidate petty criminals. If it's of any note to you, I think you were too harsh on Camon."

Kelsier walked over and took a seat at one of the room's tables. His mirth darkened slightly as he spoke. "You saw what he was doing to the girl."

"Actually, I didn't," Dockson said dryly, rummaging through the bar's stores. "Someone was blocking the doorway."

Kelsier shrugged. "Look at her, Dox. The poor thing's been beaten nearly senseless. I don't feel any sympathy for the man."

Vin remained where she was, keeping watch on both men. As the tension of the moment grew weaker, her wounds began to throb again. The blow between her shoulder blades—that would be a large bruise—and the slap to her face burned as well. She was still a little dizzy.

Kelsier was watching her. Vin clinched her teeth. Pain. She could deal with pain.

"You need anything, child?" Dockson asked. "A wet handkerchief for that face, perhaps?"

She didn't respond, instead remaining focused on Kelsier. *Come on. Tell me what you want with me. Make your play.*

Dockson finally shrugged, then ducked beneath the bar for a moment. He eventually came up with a couple of bottles.

"Anything good?" Kelsier asked, turning.

"What do you think?" Dockson asked. "Even among thieves, Camon isn't exactly known for his refinement. I have socks worth more than this wine."

Kelsier sighed. "Give me a cup anyway." Then he glanced back at Vin. "You want anything?"

Vin didn't respond.

Kelsier smiled. "Don't worry—we're far less frightening than your friends think."

"I don't think they were her friends, Kell," Dockson said from behind the bar.

"Good point," Kelsier said. "Regardless, child, you don't have anything to fear from us. Other than Dox's breath."

Dockson rolled his eyes. "Or Kell's jokes."

Vin stood quietly. She could act weak, the way she had with Camon, but instincts told her that these men wouldn't respond well to that tactic. So, she remained where she was, assessing the situation.

The calmness fell upon her again. It encouraged her to be at ease, to be trusting, to simply do as the men were suggesting. . . .

No! She stayed where she was.

Kelsier raised an eyebrow. "That's unexpected."

"What?" Dockson asked as he poured a cup of wine.

"Nothing," Kelsier said, studying Vin.

"You want a drink or not, lass?" Dockson asked.

Vin said nothing. All her life, as long as she could remember, she'd had her Luck. It made her strong, and it gave her an edge over other thieves. It was probably why she was still alive. Yet, all that time, she'd never really known what it was or why she could use it. Logic and instinct now told her the same thing—that she needed to find out what this man knew.

However he intended to use her, whatever his plans, she needed to endure them. She had to find out how he'd grown so powerful.

"Ale," she finally said.

"Ale?" Kelsier asked. "That's it?"

Vin nodded, watching him carefully. "I like it."

Kelsier rubbed his chin. "We'll have to work on that," he said. "Anyway, have a seat."

Hesitant, Vin walked over and sat down opposite Kelsier at the small table. Her wounds throbbed, but she couldn't afford to show weakness. Weakness killed. She had to pretend to ignore the pain. At least, sitting as she was, her head cleared.

Dockson joined them a moment later, giving Kelsier a glass of wine and Vin her mug of ale. She didn't take a drink.

"Who are you?" she asked in a quiet voice.

Kelsier raised an eyebrow. "You're a blunt one, eh?"

Vin didn't reply.

Kelsier sighed. "So much for my intriguing air of mystery."

Dockson snorted quietly.

Kelsier smiled. "My name is Kelsier. I'm what you might call a crewleader—but I run a crew that isn't like any you've probably known. Men like Camon, along with his crew, like to think of themselves as predators, feeding off of the nobility and the various organizations of the Ministry."

Vin shook her head. "Not predators. Scavengers." One would have thought, perhaps, that so close to the Lord Ruler, such things as thieving crews would not be able to exist. Yet, Reen had shown her that the opposite was true: Powerful, rich nobility congregated around the Lord Ruler. And, where power and riches existed, so did corruption—especially since the Lord Ruler tended to police his nobility far less than he did the skaa. It had to do, apparently, with his fondness for their ancestors.

Either way, thieving crews like Camon's were the rats who fed on the city's corruption. And, like rats, they were impossible to entirely exterminate—especially in a city with the population of Luthadel.

"Scavengers," Kelsier said, smiling; apparently he did that a lot. "That's an appropriate description, Vin. Well, Dox and I, we're scavengers too . . . we're just a higher quality of scavenger. We're more well-bred, you might say—or perhaps just more ambitious."

She frowned. "You're noblemen?"

"Lord, no," Dockson said.

"Or, at least," Kelsier said, "not full-blooded ones."

"Half-breeds aren't supposed to exist," Vin said carefully. "The Ministry hunts them."

Kelsier raised an eyebrow. "Half-breeds like you?"

Vin felt a shock. *How . . . ?*

"Even the Steel Ministry isn't infallible, Vin," Kelsier said. "If they can miss you, then they can miss others."

Vin paused thoughtfully. "Milev. He called you Mistings. Those are some kind of Allomancer, right?"

Dockson glanced at Kelsier. "She's observant," the shorter man said with an appreciative nod.

"Indeed," Kelsier agreed. "The man did call us Mistings, Vin—though the appellation was a bit hasty, since neither Dox nor I are technically Mistings. We do, however, associate with them quite a bit."

Vin sat quietly for a moment, sitting beneath the scrutiny of the two men. Allomancy. The mystical power held by the nobility, granted to them by the Lord Ruler some thousand years before as a reward for their loyalty. It was basic Ministry doctrine; even a skaa like Vin knew that much. The nobility had Allomancy and privilege because of their ancestors; the skaa were punished for the same reason.

The truth was, however, that she didn't really know what Allomancy was. It had something to do with fighting, she'd always assumed. One "Misting," as they were called, was said to be dangerous enough to kill an entire thieving team. Yet, the skaa she knew spoke of the power in whispered, uncertain tones. Before this moment, she'd never even paused to consider the possibility that it might simply be the same thing as her Luck.

"Tell me, Vin," Kelsier said, leaning forward with interest. "Do you realize what you did to that obligator in the Canton of Finance?"

"I used my Luck," Vin said quietly. "I use it to make people less angry."

"Or less suspicious," Kelsier said. "Easier to scam."

Vin nodded.

Kelsier held up a finger. "There are a lot of things you're going to have to learn. Techniques, rules, and exercises. One lesson, however, cannot wait. *Never* use emotional Allomancy on an obligator. They're all trained to recognize when their passions are being manipulated. Even the high nobility are forbidden from Pulling or Pushing the emotions of a obligator. You are what caused that obligator to send for an Inquisitor."

"Pray the creature never catches your trail again, lass," Dockson said quietly, sipping his wine.

Vin paled. "You didn't kill the Inquisitor?"

Kelsier shook his head. "I just distracted him for a bit—which was quite dangerous enough, I might add. Don't worry, many of the rumors about them aren't true. Now that he's lost your trail, he won't be able to find you again."

"Most likely," Dockson said.

Vin glanced at the shorter man apprehensively.

"Most likely," Kelsier agreed. "There are a lot of things we don't know about the Inquisitors—they don't seem to follow the normal rules. Those spikes through their eyes, for instance, should kill them. Nothing I've learned about Allomancy has ever provided an explanation for how those creatures keep living. If it were only a regular Misting Seeker on your trail, we wouldn't need to worry. An Inquistor . . . well, you'll want to keep your eyes open. Of course, you already seem pretty good at that."

Vin sat uncomfortably for a moment. Eventually, Kelsier nodded to her mug of ale. "You aren't drinking."

"You might have slipped something in it," Vin said.

"Oh, there was no need for me to sneak something into your drink," Kelsier said with a smile, pulling an object out of his suit coat pocket. "After all, you're going to drink this vial of mysterious liquid quite willingly."

He set a small glass vial on the tabletop. Vin frowned, regarding the liquid within. There was a dark residue at its bottom. "What is it?" she asked.

"If I told you, it wouldn't be mysterious," Kelsier said with a smile.

Dockson rolled his eyes. "The vial is filled with an alcohol solution and some flakes of metal, Vin."

"Metal?" she asked with a frown.

"Two of the eight basic Allomantic metals," Kelsier said. "We need to do some tests."

Vin eyed the vial.

Kelsier shrugged. "You'll have to drink it if you want to know any more about this Luck of yours."

"You drink half first," Vin said.

Kelsier raised an eyebrow. "A bit on the paranoid side, I see."

Vin didn't respond.

Finally, he sighed, picking up the vial and pulling off the plug.

"Shake it up first," Vin said. "So you get some of the sediment."

Kelsier rolled his eyes, but did as requested, shaking the vial, then downing half of its contents. He set it back on the table with a click.

Vin frowned. Then she eyed Kelsier, who smiled. He knew that he had her. He had shown off his power, had tempted her with it. *The only reason to be subservient to those with power is so that you can learn to someday take what they have.* Reen's words.

Vin reached out and took the vial, then she downed its contents. She sat, waiting for some magical transformation or surge of power—or even signs of poison. She felt nothing.

How . . . anticlimactic. She frowned, leaning back in her chair. Out of curiosity, she felt at her Luck.

And felt her eyes widen in shock.

It was there, like a massive golden hoard. A storage of power so incredible that it stretched her understanding. Always before, she had needed to be a scrimp with her Luck, holding it in reserve, using up morsels sparingly. Now she felt like a starving woman invited to a high nobleman's feast. She sat, stunned, regarding the enormous wealth within her.

"So," Kelsier said with a prodding voice. "Try it. Soothe me."

Vin reached out, tentatively touching her newfound mass of Luck. She took a bit, and directed it at Kelsier.

"Good." Kelsier leaned forward eagerly. "But we already knew you could do that. Now the real test, Vin. Can you go the other way? You can dampen my emotions, but can you enflame them too?"

Vin frowned. She'd never used her Luck in such a way; she hadn't even realized that she could. Why was he so eager?

Suspicious, Vin reached for her source of Luck. As she did so, she noticed something interesting. What she had first interpreted as one massive source of power was actually two different sources of power. There were different types of Luck.

Eight. He'd said there were eight of them. But . . . what do the others do?

Kelsier was still waiting. Vin reached to the second, unfamiliar source of Luck, doing as she'd done before and directing it at him.

Kelsier's smile deepened, and he sat back, glancing at Dockson. "That's it then. She did it."

Dockson shook his head. "To be honest, Kell, I'm not sure what to think. Having one of you around was unsettling enough. Two, though . . ."

Vin regarded them with narrowed, dubious eyes. "Two what?"

"Even among the nobility, Vin, Allomancy is modestly rare," Kelsier said. "True, it's a hereditary skill, with most of its powerful lines among the high nobility. However, breeding alone doesn't guarantee Allomantic strength.

"Many high noblemen only have access to a single Allomantic skill. People like that—those who can only perform Allomancy in one of its eight basic aspects—are called Mistings. Sometimes these abilities appear in skaa—but only if that skaa has noble blood in his or her near ancestry. You can usually find one Misting in . . . oh, about ten thousand mixed-breed skaa. The better, and closer, the noble ancestry, the more likely the skaa is to be a Misting."

"Who were your parents, Vin?" Dockson asked. "Do you remember them?"

"I was raised by my half brother, Reen," Vin said quietly, uncomfortable. These were not things she discussed with others.

"Did he speak of your mother and father?" Dockson asked.

"Occasionally," she admitted. "Reen said that our mother was a whore. Not out of choice, but the underworld . . ." She trailed off. Her mother had tried to kill her, once, when she was very young. She vaguely remembered the event. Reen had saved her.

"What about your father, Vin?" Dockson asked.

Vin looked up. "He is a high prelan in the Steel Ministry."

Kelsier whistled softly. "Now, *that's* a slightly ironic breach of duty."

Vin looked down at the table. Finally, she reached over and took a healthy pull on her mug of ale.

Kelsier smiled. "Most ranking obligators in the Ministry are high noblemen. Your father gave you a rare gift in that blood of yours."

"So . . . I'm one of these Mistings you mentioned?"

Kelsier shook his head. "Actually, no. You see, this is what made you so interesting to us, Vin. Mistings only have access to one Allomantic skill. You just proved you have two. And, if you have access to at least two of the eight, then you have access to the rest as well. That's the way it works—if you're an Allomancer, you either get one skill or you get them all."

Kelsier leaned forward. "You, Vin, are what is generally called a Mistborn. Even amongst the nobility, they're incredibly rare. Amongst skaa . . . well, let's just say I've only met one other skaa Mistborn in my entire life."

Somehow, the room seemed to grow more quiet. More still. Vin stared at her mug with distracted, uncomfortable eyes. *Mistborn.* She'd heard the stories, of course. The legends.

Kelsier and Dockson sat quietly, letting her think. Eventually, she spoke. "So . . . what does this all mean?"

Kelsier smiled. "It means that you, Vin, are a very special person. You have a power that most high noblemen envy. It is a power that, had you been born an aristocrat, would have made you one of the most deadly and influential people in all of the Final Empire."

Kelsier leaned forward again. "But, you weren't born an aristocrat. You're not noble, Vin. You don't have to play by their rules—and that makes you even *more* powerful."

Apparently, the next stage of my quest will take us up into the highlands of Terris. This is said to be a cold, unforgiving place—a land where the mountains themselves are made of ice.

Our normal attendants will not do for such a trip. We should probably hire some Terris packmen to carry our gear.

4

"YOU HEARD WHAT HE SAID! He's planning a job." Ulef's eyes shone with excitement. "I wonder which of the Great Houses he's going to strike."

"It'll be one of the most powerful ones," said Disten, one of Camon's head pointmen. He was missing a hand, but his eyes and ears were among the keenest in the crew. "Kelsier never bothers himself with small-time jobs."

Vin sat quietly, her mug of ale—the same one Kelsier had given her—still sitting mostly full on the tabletop. Her table was crowded with people; Kelsier had let the thieves return to their home for a bit before his meeting began. Vin, however, would have preferred to remain by herself. Life with Reen had accustomed her to loneliness—if you let someone get too close, it would just give them better opportunities to betray you.

Even after Reen's disappearance, Vin had kept to herself. She hadn't been willing to leave; however, she also hadn't felt the need to become familiar with the other crewmembers. They had, in turn, been perfectly willing to let her alone. Vin's position had been precarious, and associating with her could have tainted them by association. Only Ulef had made any moves to befriend her.

If you let someone get close to you, it will only hurt more when they betray you, Reen seemed to whisper in her mind.

Had Ulef even really been her friend? He'd certainly sold her out quickly enough. In addition, the crewmembers had taken Vin's beating and sudden rescue in stride, never mentioning their betrayal or refusal to help her. They'd only done what was expected.

"The Survivor hasn't bothered himself with *any* jobs lately," said Harmon, an older, scraggly-bearded burglar. "He's barely been seen in Luthadel a handful of times during the last few years. In fact, he hasn't pulled any jobs since . . ."

"This is the first one?" Ulef asked eagerly. "The first since he escaped the Pits? Then it's bound to be something spectacular!"

"Did he say anything about it, Vin?" Disten asked. "Vin?" He waved a stumpy arm in her direction, catching her attention.

"What?" she asked, looking up. She had cleaned herself slightly since her beating at Camon's hand, finally accepting a handkerchief from Dockson to wipe the blood from her face. There was little she could do about the bruises, however. Those still throbbed. Hopefully, nothing was broken.

"Kelsier," Disten repeated. "Did he say anything about the job he's planning?"

Vin shook her head. She glanced down at the bloodied handkerchief. Kelsier and Dockson had left a short time ago, promising to return after she'd had some time to think about the things they had told her. There was an implication in their words, however—an offer. Whatever job they were planning, she was invited to participate.

"Why'd he pick you to be his twixt, anyway, Vin?" Ulef asked. "Did he say anything about that?"

That's what the crew assumed—that Kelsier had chosen her to be his contact with Camon's . . . Milev's . . . crew.

There were two sides to the Luthadel underground. There were the regular crews, like Camon's. Then there were . . . the *special* ones. Groups composed of the extremely skillful, the extremely foolhardy, or the extremely talented. Allomancers.

The two sides of the underworld didn't mix; regular thieves left their betters alone. However, occasionally one of these Misting crews hired a regular team to do some of its more mundane work, and they would choose a twixt—a go-between—to work with both crews. Hence Ulef's assumption about Vin.

Milev's crewmembers noticed her unresponsiveness, and turned to another topic: Mistings. They spoke of Allomancy with uncertain, whispered tones, and she listened, uncomfortable. How could she be associated with something they held in such awe? Her Luck . . . her Allomancy . . . was something small, something she used to survive, but something really quite unimportant.

But, such power . . . she thought, looking in at her Luck reserve.

"What's Kelsier been doing these last few years, I wonder?" Ulef asked. He had seemed a bit uncomfortable around her at the beginning of the conversation, but that had passed quickly. He'd betrayed her, but this was the underworld. No friends.

It didn't seem that way between Kelsier and Dockson. They appeared to trust each other. A front? Or were they simply one of those rare teams that actually didn't worry about each other's betrayal?

The most unsettling thing about Kelsier and Dockson had been their openness with her. They seemed willing to trust, even accept, Vin after a relatively short time. It couldn't be genuine—no one could survive in the underworld following such tactics. Still, their friendliness was disconcerting.

"Two years . . ." said Hrud, a flat-faced, quiet thug. "He must have spent the entire time planning for this job."

"It must be some job indeed. . . ." Ulef said.

"Tell me about him," Vin said quietly.

"Kelsier?" Disten asked.

Vin nodded.

"They didn't talk about Kelsier down south?"

Vin shook her head.

"He was the best crewleader in Luthadel," Ulef explained. "A legend, even among the Mistings. He robbed some of the wealthiest Great Houses in the city."

"And?" Vin asked.

"Someone betrayed him," Harmon said in a quiet voice.

Of course, Vin thought.

"The Lord Ruler himself caught Kelsier," Ulef said. "Sent Kelsier and his wife to the Pits of Hathsin. But *he escaped.* He escaped from the Pits, Vin! He's the only one who ever has."

"And the wife?" Vin asked.

Ulef glanced at Harmon, who shook his head. "She didn't make it."

So, he's lost someone too. How can he laugh so much? So honestly?

"That's where he got those scars, you know," Disten said. "The ones on his arms. He got them at the Pits, from the rocks on a sheer wall he had to climb to escape."

Harmon snorted. "That's not how he got them. He killed an Inquisitor while escaping—that's where he got the scars."

"I heard he got them fighting one of the monsters that guard the Pits," Ulef said. "He reached into its mouth and strangled it *from the inside.* The teeth scraped his arms."

Disten frowned. "How do you strangle someone from the inside?"

Ulef shrugged. "That's just what I heard."

"The man isn't natural," Hrud muttered. "Something happened to him in the Pits, something bad. He wasn't an Allomancer before then, you know. He entered the Pits a regular skaa, and now . . . Well, he's a Misting for sure—if he's even human anymore. Been out in the mists a lot, that one has. Some say that the real Kelsier is dead, that the thing wearing his face is . . . something else."

Harmon shook his head. "Now, that's just plantation-skaa foolishness. We've all gone out in the mists."

"Not in the mists outside the city," Hrud insisted. "The mistwraiths are out there. They'll grab a man and take his face, sure as the Lord Ruler."

Harmon rolled his eyes.

"Hrud's right about one thing," Disten said. "That man isn't human. He might not be a mistwraith, but he's not skaa either. I've heard of him doing things, things like only *they* can do. The ones that come out at night. You saw what he did to Camon."

"Mistborn," Harmon muttered.

Mistborn. Vin had heard the term before Kelsier had mentioned it to her, of course. Who hadn't? Yet, the rumors about Mistborn made stories of Inquisitors and Mistings seem rational. It was said that Mistborn were heralds of the mists themselves, endowed with great powers by the Lord Ruler. Only high noblemen could be Mistborn; they were said to be a secret sect of assassins who served him, only going out at night. Reen had always taught her that they were a myth, and Vin had assumed he was right.

And Kelsier says I—like he himself—am one of them. How could she be what he said? Child of a prostitute, she was nobody. She was nothing.

Never trust a man who tells you good news, Reen had always said. *It's the oldest, but easiest, way to con someone.*

Yet, she did have her Luck. Her Allomancy. She could still sense the reserves Kelsier's vial had given her, and had tested her powers on the crewmembers. No longer limited to just a bit of Luck a day, she found she could produce far more striking effects.

Vin was coming to realize that her old goal in life—simply staying alive—was uninspired. There was so much more she could be doing. She had been a slave to Reen; she had been a slave to Camon. She would be a slave to this Kelsier too, if it would lead her to eventual freedom.

At his table, Milev looked at his pocket watch, then stood. "All right, everyone out."

The room began to clear in preparation for Kelsier's meeting. Vin remained where she was; Kelsier had made it quite clear to the others that she was invited. She sat quietly for a bit, the room feeling far more comfortable to her now that it was empty. Kelsier's friends began to arrive a short time later.

The first man down the steps had the build of a soldier. He wore a loose, sleeveless shirt that exposed a pair of well-sculpted arms. He was impressively muscular, but not massive, and had close-cropped hair that stuck up slightly on his head.

The soldier's companion was a sharply dressed man in a nobleman's suit—plum vest, gold buttons, black overcoat—complete with short-brimmed hat and dueling cane. He was older than the soldier, and was a bit portly. He removed his hat upon entering the room, revealing a head of well-styled black hair. The two men were chatting amiably as they walked, but they paused when they saw the empty room.

"Ah, this must be our twixt," said the man in the suit. "Has Kelsier arrived yet, my dear?" He spoke with a simple familiarity, as if they were longtime friends. Suddenly, despite herself, Vin found herself liking this well-dressed, articulate man.

"No," she said quietly. Though overalls and a work shirt had always suited her, she suddenly wished that she owned something nicer. This man's very bearing seemed to demand a more formal atmosphere.

"Should have known that Kell would be late to his own meeting," the soldier said, sitting down at one of the tables near the center of the room.

"Indeed," said the suited man. "I suppose his tardiness leaves us with a chance for some refreshment. I could so use something to drink. . . ."

"Let me get you something," Vin said quickly, jumping to her feet.

"How gracious of you," the suited man said, choosing a chair next to the solider. He sat with one leg crossed over the other, his dueling cane held to the side, tip against the floor, one hand resting on the top.

Vin walked to the bar and began rummaging for drinks.

"Breeze . . ." the soldier said with a warning tone as Vin selected a bottle of Camon's most expensive wine and began pouring a cup.

"Hum . . . ?" the suited man said, raising an eyebrow.

The soldier nodded toward Vin.

"Oh, very well," the suited man said with a sigh.

Vin paused, wine half poured, and frowned slightly. *What am I doing?*

"I swear, Ham," the suited man said, "you are dreadfully stiff sometimes."

"Just because you can Push someone around doesn't mean you should, Breeze."

Vin stood, dumbfounded. *He . . . used Luck on me.* When Kelsier had tried to manipulate her, she'd felt his touch and had been able to resist. This time, however, she hadn't even realized what she was doing.

She looked up at the man, thinning her eyes. "Mistborn."

The suited man, Breeze, chuckled. "Hardly. Kelsier's the only skaa Mistborn you're likely to ever meet, my dear—and pray you never are in a situation where you meet a noble one. No, I am just an ordinary, humble Misting."

"Humble?" Ham asked.

Breeze shrugged.

Vin looked down at the half-full cup of wine. "You Pulled on my emotions. With . . . Allomancy, I mean."

"I Pushed on them, actually," Breeze said. "Pulling makes a person less trusting and more determined. Pushing on emotions—Soothing them—makes a person more trusting."

"Regardless, you controlled me," Vin said. "You made me fetch you a drink."

"Oh, I wouldn't say that I *made* you do it," Breeze said. "I just altered your emotions slightly, putting you in a frame of mind where you'd be more likely to do as I wished."

Ham rubbed his chin. "I don't know, Breeze. It's an interesting question. By influencing her emotions, did you take away her ability to choose? If, for instance, she were to kill or steal while under your control, would the crime be hers or yours?"

Breeze rolled his eyes. "There's really no question to it at all. You shouldn't think about such things, Hammond—you'll hurt your brain. I offered her encouragement, I simply did it through an irregular means."

"But—"

"I'm not going to argue it with you, Ham."

The beefy man sighed, looking a little bit forlorn.

"Are you going to bring me the drink . . . ?" Breeze asked hopefully, looking at Vin. "I mean, you're already up, and you're going to have to come back this direction to reach your seat anyway. . . ."

Vin examined her emotions. Did she feel irregularly drawn to do as the man asked? Was he manipulating her again? Finally, she simply walked away from the bar, leaving the drink where it was.

Breeze sighed. He didn't stand to go get the drink himself, however.

Vin walked tentatively toward the two men's table. She was accustomed to shadows and corners—close enough to eavesdrop, but far enough away to escape. Yet, she couldn't hide from these men—not while the room was so empty. So, she chose a chair at the table beside the one that the two men were using, then sat cautiously. She needed information—as long as she was ignorant, she was going to be at a severe disadvantage in this new world of Misting crews.

Breeze chuckled. "Nervous little thing, aren't you?"

Vin ignored the comment. "You," Vin said, nodding to Ham. "You're a . . . a Misting too?"

Ham nodded. "I'm a Thug."

Vin frowned in confusion.

"I burn pewter," Ham said.

Again, Vin looked at him questioningly.

"He can make himself stronger, my dear," Breeze said. "He hits things—particularly other people—who try to interfere with what the rest of us are doing."

"There's much more to it than that," Ham said. "I run general security for jobs, providing my crewleader with manpower and warriors, assuming such are necessary."

"And he'll try and bore you with random philosophy when it isn't," Breeze added.

Ham sighed. "Breeze, honestly, sometimes I don't know why I . . ." Ham trailed off as the door opened again, admitting another man.

The newcomer wore a dull tan overcoat, a pair of brown trousers, and a simple white shirt. However, his face was far more distinctive than his clothing. It was knotted and gnarled, like a twisted piece of wood, and his eyes shone with the level of disapproving dissatisfaction only the elderly can display. Vin couldn't quite place his age—he was young enough that he wasn't stooped over, yet he was old enough that he made even the middle-aged Breeze look youthful.

The newcomer looked over Vin and the others, huffed disdainfully, then walked to a table on the other side of the room and sat down. His steps were marked by a distinct limp.

Breeze sighed. "I'm going to miss Trap."

"We all will," Ham said quietly. "Clubs is very good, though. I've worked with him before."

Breeze studied the newcomer. "I wonder if I could get *him* to bring my drink over. . . ."

Ham chuckled. "I'd pay money to see you try it."

"I'm sure you would," Breeze said.

Vin eyed the newcomer, who seemed perfectly content to ignore her and the other two men. "What's he?"

"Clubs?" Breeze asked. "He, my dear, is a Smoker. He is what will keep the rest of us from being discovered by an Inquisitor."

Vin chewed on her lip, digesting the new information as she studied Clubs. The man shot her a glare, and she looked away. As she turned, she noticed that Ham was looking at her.

"I like you, kid," he said. "The other twixts I've worked with have either been too intimidated to talk to us, or they've been jealous of us for moving into their territory."

"Indeed," Breeze said. "You're not like most crumbs. Of course, I'd like you a great deal more if you'd go fetch me that glass of wine. . . ."

Vin ignored him, glancing at Ham. "Crumb?"

"That's what some of the more self-important members of our society call lesser thieves," Ham said. "They call you crumbs, since you tend to be involved with . . . less inspired projects."

"No offense intended, of course," Breeze said.

"Oh, I wouldn't ever take offense at—" Vin paused, feeling an irregular desire to please the well-dressed man. She glared at Breeze. "Stop that!"

"See, there," Breeze said, glancing at Ham. "She still retains her ability to choose."

"You're hopeless."

They assume I'm a twixt, Vin thought. *So Kelsier hasn't told them what I am. Why?* Time constraints? Or, was the secret too valuable to share? How trustworthy were these men? And, if they thought her a simple "crumb," why were they being so nice to her?

"Who else are we waiting upon?" Breeze asked, glancing at the doorway. "Besides Kell and Dox, I mean."

"Yeden," Ham said.

Breeze frowned with a sour expression. "Ah, yes."

"I agree," Ham said. "But, I'd be willing to bet that he feels the same way about us."

"I don't even see why he was invited," Breeze said.

Ham shrugged. "Something to do with Kell's plan, obviously."

"Ah, the infamous 'plan,'" Breeze said musingly. "What job could it be, what indeed . . . ?"

Ham shook his head. "Kell and his cursed sense of drama."

"Indeed."

The door opened a few moments later, and the one they had spoken of, Yeden, entered. He turned out to be an unassuming man, and Vin had trouble understanding why the other two were so displeased about his attendance. Short with curly brown hair, Yeden was dressed in simple gray skaa clothing and a patched, soot-stained brown worker's coat. He regarded the surroundings with a look of disapproval, but he was nowhere near as openly hostile as Clubs, who still sat on the other side of the room scowling at anyone who looked in his direction.

Not a very big crew, Vin thought. *With Kelsier and Dockson, that makes six of them.* Of course, Ham had said that he led a group of "Thugs." Were the men at this meeting simply representatives? The leaders of smaller, more specialized groups? Some crews worked that way.

Breeze checked his pocket watch three more times before Kelsier finally arrived. The Mistborn crewleader burst through the door with his cheery enthusiasm, Dockson sauntering along behind. Ham stood immediately, smiling broadly and clasping hands with Kelsier. Breeze stood as well, and while his greeting was a bit more reserved, Vin had to admit that she had never seen any crewleader welcomed so happily by his men.

"Ah," Kelsier said, looking toward the other side of the room. "Clubs and Yeden too. So, everyone's here. Good—I absolutely loathe being made to wait."

Breeze raised an eyebrow as he and Ham settled back into their chairs, Dockson taking a seat at the same table. "Are we to receive any explanation for your tardiness?"

"Dockson and I were visiting my brother," Kelsier explained, walking toward the front of the lair. He turned and leaned back against the bar, scanning the room. When Kelsier's eyes fell on Vin, he winked.

"Your brother?" Ham said. "Is Marsh coming to the meeting?"

Kelsier and Dockson shared a look. "Not tonight," Kelsier said. "But he'll join the crew eventually."

Vin studied the others. They were skeptical. *Tension between Kelsier and his brother, perhaps?*

Breeze raised his dueling cane, pointing the tip at Kelsier. "All right, Kelsier, you've kept this 'job' secret from us for eight months now. We know it's big, we know you're excited, and we're all properly annoyed at you for being so secretive. So, why don't you just go ahead and tell us what it is?"

Kelsier smiled. Then he stood up straight, waving a hand toward the dirty, plain-looking Yeden. "Gentlemen, meet your new employer."

This was, apparently, quite a shocking statement.

"*Him?*" Ham asked.

"Him," Kelsier said with a nod.

"What?" Yeden asked, speaking for the first time. "You have trouble working with someone who actually has morals?"

"It's not that, my dear man," Breeze said, setting his dueling cane across his lap. "It's just that, well, I was under the strange impression that you didn't *like* our types very much."

"I don't," Yeden said flatly. "You're selfish, undisciplined, and you've turned your backs on the rest of the skaa. You dress nicely, but on the inside you're dirty as ash."

Ham snorted. "I can already see that this job is going to be *great* for crew morale."

Vin watched quietly, chewing on her lip. Yeden was obviously a skaa worker, probably a member of a forge or textile mill. What connection did he have with the underground? And . . . how would he be able to afford the services of a thieving crew, especially one as apparently specialized as Kelsier's team?

Perhaps Kelsier noticed her confusion, for she found him looking at her as the others continued to speak.

"I'm still a little confused," Ham said. "Yeden, we're all aware of how you regard thieves. So . . . why hire us?"

Yeden squirmed a bit. "Because," he finally said, "everyone knows how effective you are."

Breeze chuckled. "Disapproving of our morals doesn't make you unwilling to make use of our skills, I see. So, what is the job, then? What does the skaa rebellion wish of us?"

Skaa rebellion? Vin thought, a piece of the conversation falling into place. There were two sides to the underworld. The far larger portion was made up of the thieves, crews, whores, and beggars who tried to survive outside of mainstream skaa culture.

And then there were the rebels. The people who worked against the Final Empire. Reen had always called them fools—a sentiment shared by most of the people, both underworlders and regular skaa, that Vin had met.

All eyes slowly turned to Kelsier, who leaned back against the bar again. "The skaa rebellion, courtesy of its leader, Yeden, has hired us for something very specific."

"What?" Ham asked. "Robbery? Assassination?"

"A little of both," Kelsier said, "and, at the same time, neither one. Gentlemen, this isn't going to be a regular job. It's going to be different from anything any crew has ever tried to pull. We're going to help Yeden overthrow the Final Empire."

Silence.

"Excuse me?" Ham asked.

"You heard me right, Ham," Kelsier said. "That's the job I've been planning—the destruction of the Final Empire. Or, at least, its center of government. Yeden has hired us to supply him with an army, then provide him with a favorable opportunity to seize control of this city."

Ham sat back, then shared a glance with Breeze. Both men turned toward Dockson, who nodded solemnly. The room remained quiet for a moment longer; then the silence was broken as Yeden began to laugh ruefully to himself.

"I should never have agreed to this," Yeden said, shaking his head. "Now that you say it, I realize how ridiculous it all sounds."

"Trust me, Yeden," Kelsier said. "These men have made a habit of pulling off plans that seem ridiculous at first glance."

"That may be true, Kell," Breeze said. "But, in this case, I find myself agreeing with our disapproving friend. Overthrow the Final Empire . . . that is something that skaa rebels have been working toward for a thousand years! What makes you think that we can achieve anything where those men have failed?"

Kelsier smiled. "We'll succeed because we have vision, Breeze. That's something the rebellion has always lacked."

"Excuse me?" Yeden said indignantly.

"It's true, unfortunately," Kelsier said. "The rebellion condemns people like us because of our greed, but for all their high morals—which, by the way, I respect—they never get anything done. Yeden, your men hide in woods and in hills, plotting how they'll someday rise up and lead a glorious war against the Final Empire. But your kind has no idea how to develop and execute a proper plan."

Yeden's expression grew dark. "And *you* have no idea what you are talking about."

"Oh?" Kelsier said lightly. "Tell me, what has your rebellion accomplished during its thousand-year struggle? Where are your successes and your victories? The Massacre of Tougier three centuries ago, where seven thousand skaa rebels were slaughtered? The occasional raid of a traveling canal boat or the kidnapping of a minor noble official?"

Yeden flushed. "That's the best we can manage with the people we have! Don't blame my men for their failures—blame the rest of the skaa. We can't ever get them to help. They've been beaten down for a millennium; they haven't got any spirit left. It's difficult enough to get one in a thousand to listen to us, let alone rebel!"

"Peace, Yeden," Kelsier said, holding up a hand. "I'm not trying to insult your courage. We're on the same side, remember? You came to me specifically because you were having trouble recruiting people for your army."

"I'm regretting that decision more and more, thief," Yeden said.

"Well, you've already paid us," Kelsier said. "So it's a little late to back out now. But, we'll get you that army, Yeden. The men in this room are the most capable, most clever, and most skilled Allomancers in the city. You'll see."

The room grew quiet again. Vin sat at her table, watching the interaction with a frown. *What is your game, Kelsier?* His words about overthrowing the Final Empire were obviously a front. It seemed most likely to her that he intended to scam the skaa rebellion. But . . . if he'd already been paid, then why continue the charade?

Kelsier turned from Yeden to Breeze and Ham. "All right, gentlemen. What do you think?"

The two men shared a look. Finally Breeze spoke. "Lord Ruler knows, I've never been one to turn down a challenge. But, Kell, I do question your reasoning. Are you sure we can do this?"

"I'm positive," Kelsier said. "Previous attempts to overthrow the Lord Ruler have failed because they lacked proper organization and planning. We're thieves, gentlemen—and we're extraordinarily good ones. We can rob the unrobbable and fool the unfoolable. We know how to take an incredibly large task and break it down to manageable pieces, then deal with each of those pieces. We know how to get what we want. These things make us perfect for this particular task."

Breeze frowned. "And . . . how much are we getting paid for achieving the impossible?"

"Thirty thousand boxings," Yeden said. "Half now, half when you deliver the army."

"Thirty thousand?" Ham said. "For an operation this big? That will barely cover expenses. We'll need a spy among the nobility to watch for rumors, we'll need a couple of safe houses, not to mention someplace big enough to hide and train an entire army. . . ."

"No use haggling now, thief," Yeden snapped. "Thirty thousand may not sound like much to *your* type, but it's the result of decades of saving on our part. We can't pay you more because we don't have anything more."

"It's good work, gentlemen," Dockson noted, joining the conversation for the first time.

"Yes, well, that's all great," Breeze said. "I consider myself a nice enough fellow. But . . . this just seems a bit too altruistic. Not to mention stupid."

"Well . . ." Kelsier said, "there might be a little bit more in it for us. . . ."

Vin perked up, and Breeze smiled.

"The Lord Ruler's treasury," Kelsier said. "The plan, as it stands now, is to provide Yeden with an army and an opportunity to seize the city. Once he takes the palace, he'll capture the treasury and use its funds to secure power. And, central to that treasury . . ."

"Is the Lord Ruler's atium," Breeze said.

Kelsier nodded. "Our agreement with Yeden promises us half of the atium reserves we find in the palace, no matter how vast they may be."

Atium. Vin had heard of the metal, but she had never actually seen any. It was incredibly rare, supposedly used only by noblemen.

Ham was smiling. "Well, now," he said slowly, "that's almost a big enough prize to be tempting."

"That atium stockpile is supposed to be enormous," Kelsier said. "The Lord Ruler sells the metal only in small bits, charging outrageous sums to the nobility. He *has* to keep a huge reserve of it to make certain he controls the market, and to make certain he has enough wealth for emergencies."

"True . . ." Breeze said. "But, are you sure you want to try something like this so soon after . . . what happened the last time we tried getting into the palace?"

"We're going to do things differently this time," Kelsier said. "Gentlemen, I'll be frank with you. This isn't going to be an easy job, but it *can* work. The plan is simple. We're going to find a way to neutralize the Luthadel Garrison—leaving the area without a policing force. Then, we're going to throw the city into chaos."

"We've got a couple of options on how to do that," Dockson said. "But we can talk about that later."

Kelsier nodded. "Then, in that chaos, Yeden will march his army into Luthadel and seize the palace, taking the Lord Ruler prisoner. While Yeden secures the city, we'll pilfer the atium. We'll give half to him, then disappear with the other half. After that, it's his job to hang on to what he's grabbed."

"Sounds a little dangerous for you, Yeden," Ham noted, glancing at the rebel leader.

He shrugged. "Perhaps. But, if we do, by some miracle, end up in control of the palace, then we'll have at least done something no skaa rebellion has ever achieved before. For my men, this isn't just about riches—it isn't even about surviving. It's about doing something grand, something wonderful, to give the skaa hope. But, I don't expect you people to understand things like that."

Kelsier shot a quieting glance at Yeden, and the man sniffed and sat back. *Did he use Allomancy?* Vin wondered. She'd seen employer-crew relationships before, and it seemed that Yeden was much more in Kelsier's pocket than the other way around.

Kelsier turned back to Ham and Breeze. "There's more to all this than simply a show of daring. If we do manage to steal that atium, it will be a sound blow to the Lord Ruler's financial foundation. He depends on the money that atium provides—without it, he could very well be left without the means to pay his armies.

"Even if he escapes our trap—or, if we decide to take the city when he's gone to minimize having to deal with him—he'll be financially ruined. He won't be able to march soldiers in to take the city away from Yeden. If this works right, we'll have the city in chaos anyway, and the nobility will be too weak to react against the rebel forces. The Lord Ruler will be left confused, and unable to mount a sizable army."

"And the koloss?" Ham asked quietly.

Kelsier paused. "If he marches those creatures on his own capital city, the destruction it would cause could be even more dangerous than financial instability. In the chaos, the provincial noblemen will rebel and set themselves up as kings, and the Lord Ruler won't have the troops to bring them into line. Yeden's rebels will be able to hold Luthadel, and we, my friends, will be very, very rich. Everyone gets what they want."

"You're forgetting the Steel Ministry," Clubs snapped, sitting almost forgotten at the side of the room. "Those Inquisitors won't just let us throw their pretty theocracy into chaos."

Kelsier paused, turning toward the gnarled man. "We will have to find a way to deal with the Ministry—I've got a few plans for that. Either way, problems like that are the things that we—as a crew—will have to work out. We have to get rid of the Luthadel Garrison—there's no way we'll be able to get anything done with them policing the streets. We'll have to come up with an appropriate way to throw the city into chaos, and we'll have to find a way to keep the obligators off our trail.

"But, if we play this right, we might be able to force the Lord Ruler to send the palace guard—maybe even the Inquisitors—into the city to restore order. That will leave the palace itself exposed, giving Yeden a perfect opportunity to strike. After that, it won't matter what happens with the Ministry or the Garrison—the Lord Ruler won't have the money to maintain control of his empire."

"I don't know, Kell," Breeze said, shaking his head. His flippancy was subdued; he seemed to be honestly considering the plan. "The Lord Ruler got that atium somewhere. What if he just goes and mines some more?"

Ham nodded. "No one even knows where the atium mine is."

"I wouldn't say *no one*," Kelsier said with a smile.

Breeze and Ham shared a look.

"You know?" Ham asked.

"Of course," Kelsier said. "I spent a year of my life working there."

"The Pits?" Ham asked with surprise.

Kelsier nodded. "That's why the Lord Ruler makes certain nobody survives working there—he can't afford to let his secret out. It's not just a penal colony, not just a hellhole where skaa are sent to die. It's a mine."

"Of course . . ." Breeze said.

Kelsier stood up straight, stepping away from the bar and walking toward Ham and Breeze's table. "We have a chance here, gentlemen. A chance to do something great—something no other thieving crew has ever done. We'll rob from the Lord Ruler himself!

"But, there's more. The Pits nearly killed me, and I've seen things . . . differently since I escaped. I see the skaa, working without hope. I see the thieving crews, trying to survive on aristocratic leavings, often getting themselves—and other skaa—killed in the process. I see the skaa rebellion trying so hard to resist the Lord Ruler, and never making any progress.

"The rebellion fails because it's too unwieldy and spread out. Anytime one of its many pieces gains momentum, the Steel Ministry crushes it. That's not the way to defeat the Final Empire, gentlemen. But, a small team—specialized and highly skilled—has a hope. We can work without great risk of exposure. We know how to avoid the Steel Ministry's tendrils. We understand how the high nobility thinks, and how to exploit its members. We can do this!"

He paused beside Breeze and Ham's table.

"I don't know, Kell," Ham said. "It's not that I'm disagreeing with your motives. It's just that . . . well, this seems a bit foolhardy."

Kelsier smiled. "I know it does. But you're going to go along with it anyway, aren't you?"

Ham paused, then nodded. "You know I'll join your crew no matter what the job. This sounds crazy, but so do most of your plans. Just . . . just tell me. Are you serious about overthrowing the Lord Ruler?"

Kelsier nodded. For some reason, Vin was almost tempted to believe him.

Ham nodded firmly. "All right, then. I'm in."

"Breeze?" Kelsier asked.

The well-dressed man shook his head. "I'm not sure, Kell. This is a bit extreme, even for you."

"We need you, Breeze," Kell said. "No one can Soothe a crowd like you can. If we're going to raise an army, we'll need your Allomancers—and your powers."

"Well, that much is true," Breeze said. "But, even still . . ."

Kelsier smiled, then he set something on the table—the cup of wine Vin had poured for Breeze. She hadn't even noticed that Kelsier had grabbed it off of the bar.

"Think of the challenge, Breeze," Kelsier said.

Breeze glanced at the cup, then looked up at Kelsier. Finally, he laughed, reaching for the wine. "Fine. I'm in."

"It's impossible," a gruff voice said from the back of the room. Clubs sat with folded arms, regarding Kelsier with a scowl. "What are you really planning, Kelsier?"

"I'm being honest," Kelsier replied. "I plan to take the Lord Ruler's atium and overthrow his empire."

"You can't," the man said. "It's idiocy. The Inquisitors will hang us all by hooks through our throats."

"Perhaps," Kelsier said. "But think of the reward if we succeed. Wealth, power, and a land where the skaa can live like men, rather than slaves."

Clubs snorted loudly. Then he stood, his chair toppling backward onto the floor behind him. "No reward would be enough. The Lord Ruler tried to have you killed once—I see that you won't be satisfied until he gets it right." With that, the older man turned and stalked in a limping gait from the room, slamming the door behind him.

The lair grew quiet.

"Well, guess we'll need a different Smoker," Dockson said.

"You're just going to let him go?" Yeden demanded. "He knows everything!"

Breeze chuckled. "Aren't you supposed to be the moral one in this little group?"

"Morals doesn't have anything to do with it," Yeden said. "Letting someone go like that is foolish! He could bring the obligators down on us in minutes."

Vin nodded in agreement, but Kelsier just shook his head. "I don't work that way, Yeden. I invited Clubs to a meeting where I outlined a dangerous plan— one some people might even call stupid. I'm not going to have him assassinated because he decided it was too dangerous. If you do things like that, pretty soon nobody will come listen to your plans in the first place."

"Besides," Dockson said. "We wouldn't invite someone to one of these meetings unless we trusted him not to betray us."

Impossible, Vin thought, frowning. He had to be bluffing to keep up crew morale; nobody was that trusting. After all, hadn't the others said that Kelsier's failure a few years before—the event that had sent him to the Pits of Hathsin— had come because of a betrayal? He probably had assassins following Clubs at that very moment, watching to make certain he didn't go to the authorities.

"All right, Yeden," Kelsier said, getting back to business. "They accepted. The plan is on. Are you still in?"

"Will you give the rebellion's money back if I say no?" Yeden asked.

The only response to that was a quiet chuckle from Ham. Yeden's expression darkened, but he just shook his head. "If I had any other option . . ."

"Oh, stop complaining," Kelsier said. "You're officially part of a thieving crew now, so you might as well come over here and sit with us."

Yeden paused for a moment, then sighed and walked over to sit at Breeze, Ham, and Dockson's table, beside which Kelsier was still standing. Vin still sat at the next table over.

Kelsier turned, looking over toward Vin. "What about you, Vin?"

She paused. *Why is he asking me? He already knows he has a hold over me. The job doesn't matter, as long as I learn what he knows.*

Kelsier waited expectantly.

"I'm in," Vin said, assuming that was what he wanted to hear.

She must have guessed correctly, for Kelsier smiled, then nodded to the last chair at the table.

Vin sighed, but did as he indicated, standing and walking over to take the last seat.

"Who is the child?" Yeden asked.

"Twixt," Breeze said.

Kelsier cocked an eyebrow. "Actually, Vin is something of a new recruit. My brother caught her Soothing his emotions a few months back."

"Soother, eh?" Ham asked. "Guess we can always use another of those."

"Actually," Kelsier noted, "it seems she can Riot people's emotions as well." Breeze started.

"Really?" Ham asked.

Kelsier nodded. "Dox and I tested her just a few hours ago."

Breeze chuckled. "And here I was telling her that she'd probably never meet another Mistborn besides yourself."

"A second Mistborn on the team . . ." Ham said appreciatively. "Well, that increases our chances somewhat."

"What are you saying?" Yeden sputtered. "Skaa can't be Mistborn. I'm not even sure if Mistborn exist! *I've* certainly never met one."

Breeze raised an eyebrow, then laid a hand on Yeden's shoulder. "You should try not to talk so much, friend," he suggested. "You'll sound far less stupid that way."

Yeden shook off Breeze's hand, and Ham laughed. Vin, however, sat quietly, considering the implications of what Kelsier had said. The part about stealing the atium reserves was tempting, but seizing the city to do it? Were these men really that reckless?

Kelsier pulled a chair over to the table for himself and sat down on it the wrong way, resting his arms on the seatback. "All right," he said. "We have a crew. We'll plan specifics at the next meeting, but I want you all to be thinking about the job. I have some plans, but I want fresh minds to consider our task. We'll need to discuss ways to get the Luthadel Garrison out of the city, and ways that we can throw this place into so much chaos that the Great Houses can't mobilize their forces to stop Yeden's army when it attacks."

The members of the group, save Yeden, nodded.

"Before we end for the evening, however," Kelsier continued, "there is one more part of the plan I want to warn you about."

"More?" Breeze asked with a chuckle. "Stealing the Lord Ruler's fortune and overthrowing his empire aren't enough?"

"No," Kelsier said. "If I can, I'm going to kill him too."

Silence.

"Kelsier," Ham said slowly. "The Lord Ruler is the Sliver of Infinity. He's a piece of God Himself. You can't kill him. Even *capturing* him will probably prove impossible."

Kelsier didn't reply. His eyes, however, were determined.

That's it, Vin thought. *He has to be insane.*

"The Lord Ruler and I," Kelsier said quietly, "we have an unsettled debt. He took Mare from me, and he nearly took my own sanity as well. I'll admit to you all that part of my reason for this plan is to get revenge on him. We're going to take his government, his home, and his fortune from him.

"However, for that to work, we'll have to get rid of him. Perhaps imprison him in his own dungeons—at the very least, we'll have to get him out of the city. However, I can think of something far better than either option. Down those pits where he sent me, I Snapped and came to an awakening of my Allomantic powers. Now I intend to use them to kill him."

Kelsier reached into his suit pocket and pulled something out. He set it on the table.

"In the north, they have a legend," Kelsier said. "It teaches that the Lord Ruler isn't immortal—not completely. They say he can be killed with the right metal. The Eleventh Metal. That metal."

Eyes turned toward the object on the table. It was a thin bar of metal, perhaps as long and wide as Vin's small finger, with straight sides. It was silvery white in color.

"The Eleventh Metal?" Breeze asked uncertainly. "I've heard of no such legend."

"The Lord Ruler has suppressed it," Kelsier said. "But it can still be found, if you know where to look. Allomantic theory teaches of ten metals: the eight basic metals, and the two high metals. There is another one, however, unknown to most. One far more powerful, even, than the other ten."

Breeze frowned skeptically.

Yeden, however, appeared intrigued. "And, this metal can somehow kill the Lord Ruler?"

Kelsier nodded. "It's his weakness. The Steel Ministry wants you to believe that he's immortal, but even he can be killed—by an Allomancer burning this."

Ham reached out, picking up the thin bar of metal. "Where did you get it?"

"In the north," Kelsier said. "In a land near the Far Peninsula, a land where people still remember what their old kingdom was called in the days before the Ascension."

"How does it work?" Breeze asked.

"I'm not sure," Kelsier said frankly. "But I intend to find out."

Ham regarded the porcelain-colored metal, turning it over in his fingers.

Kill the Lord Ruler? Vin thought. The Lord Ruler was a force, like the winds or the mists. One did not kill such things. They didn't live, really. They simply *were.*

"Regardless," Kelsier said, accepting the metal back from Ham, "you don't need to worry about this. Killing the Lord Ruler is my task. If it proves impossible, we'll settle for tricking him outside of the city, then robbing him silly. I just thought that you should know what I'm planning."

I've bound myself to a madman, Vin thought with resignation. But that didn't really matter—not as long as he taught her Allomancy.

I don't even understand what I'm supposed to do. The Terris philosophers claim that I'll know my duty when the time comes, but that's a small comfort.

The Deepness must be destroyed, and apparently I'm the only one who can do so. It ravages the world even now. If I don't stop it soon, there will be nothing left of this land but bones and dust.

5

"AHA!" KELSIER'S TRIUMPHANT FIGURE POPPED UP from behind Camon's bar, a look of satisfaction on his face. He brought his arm up and thunked a dusty wine bottle down on the countertop.

Dockson looked over with amusement. "Where'd you find it?"

"One of the secret drawers," Kelsier said, dusting off the bottle.

"I thought I'd found all of those," Dockson said.

"You did. One of them had a false back."

Dockson chuckled. "Clever."

Kelsier nodded, unstoppering the bottle and pouring out three cups. "The trick is to never stop looking. There's *always* another secret." He gathered up the three cups and walked over to join Vin and Dockson at the table.

Vin accepted her cup with a tentative hand. The meeting had ended a short time earlier, Breeze, Ham, and Yeden leaving to ponder the things Kelsier had told them. Vin felt that she should have left as well, but she had nowhere to go. Dockson and Kelsier seemed to take it for granted that she would remain with them.

Kelsier took a long sip of the rubicund wine, then smiled. "Ah, that's *much* better."

Dockson nodded in agreement, but Vin didn't taste her own drink.

"We're going to need another Smoker," Dockson noted.

Kelsier nodded. "The others seemed to take it well, though."

"Breeze is still uncertain," Dockson said.

"He won't back out. Breeze likes a challenge, and he'll never find a challenge greater than this one." Kelsier smiled. "Besides, it'd drive him insane to know that we were pulling a job that he wasn't in on."

"Still, he's right to be apprehensive," Dockson said. "I'm a little worried myself."

Kelsier nodded his agreement, and Vin frowned. *So, are they serious about the plan? Or is this still a show for my sake?* The two men seemed so competent. Yet, overthrowing the Final Empire? They'd sooner stop the mists from flowing or the sun from rising.

"When do your other friends get here?" Dockson asked.

"A couple days," Kelsier said. "We'll need to have another Smoker by then. I'm also going to need some more atium."

Dockson frowned. "Already?"

Kelsier nodded. "I spent most of it buying OreSeur's Contract, then used my last bit at Tresting's plantation."

Tresting. The nobleman who had been killed in his manor the week before. *How was Kelsier involved? And, what was it Kelsier said before about atium?* He'd claimed that the Lord Ruler kept control of the high nobility by maintaining a monopoly on the metal.

Dockson rubbed his bearded chin. "Atium's not easy to come by, Kell. It took nearly eight months of planning to steal you that last bit."

"That's because you had to be delicate," Kelsier said with a devious smile.

Dockson eyed Kelsier with a look of slight apprehension. Kelsier just smiled more broadly, and finally Dockson rolled his eyes, sighing. Then he glanced at Vin. "You haven't touched your drink."

Vin shook her head.

Dockson waited for an explanation, and eventually Vin was forced to respond. "I don't like to drink anything I didn't prepare myself."

Kelsier chuckled. "She reminds me of Vent."

"Vent?" Dockson said with a snort. "The lass is a bit paranoid, but she's not *that* bad. I swear, that man was so jumpy that his own heartbeat could startle him."

The two men shared a laugh. Vin, however, was only made more uncomfortable by the friendly air. *What do they expect from me? Am I to be an apprentice of some sort?*

"Well, then," Dockson said, "are you going to tell me how you plan on getting yourself some atium?"

Kelsier opened his mouth to respond, but the stairs clattered with the sound of someone coming down. Kelsier and Dockson turned; Vin, of course, had seated herself so she could see both entrances to the room without having to move.

Vin expected the newcomer to be one of Camon's crewmembers, sent to see if Kelsier was done with the lair yet. Therefore, she was completely surprised when the door swung open to reveal the surly, gnarled face of the man called Clubs.

Kelsier smiled, eyes twinkling.

He's not surprised. Pleased, perhaps, but not surprised.

"Clubs," Kelsier said.

Clubs stood in the doorway, giving the three of them an impressively disapproving stare. Finally, he hobbled into the room. A thin, awkward-looking teenage boy followed him.

The boy fetched Clubs a chair and put it by Kelsier's table. Clubs settled down, grumbling slightly to himself. Finally, he eyed Kelsier with a squinting, wrinkle-nosed expression. "The Soother is gone?"

"Breeze?" Kelsier asked. "Yes, he left."

Clubs grunted. Then he eyed the bottle of wine.

"Help yourself," Kelsier said.

Clubs waved for the boy to go fetch him a cup from the bar, then turned back to Kelsier. "I had to be sure," he said. "Never can trust yourself when a Soother is around—especially one like him."

"You're a Smoker, Clubs," Kelsier said. "He couldn't do much to you, not if you didn't want him to."

Clubs shrugged. "I don't like Soothers. It's not just Allomancy—men like that . . . well, you can't trust that you aren't being manipulated when they are around. Copper or no copper."

"I wouldn't rely on something like that to get your loyalty," Kelsier said.

"So I've heard," Clubs said as the boy poured him a cup of wine. "Had to be sure, though. Had to think about things without that Breeze around." He scowled, though Vin had trouble determining why, then took the cup and downed half of it in one gulp.

"Good wine," he said with a grunt. Then he looked over at Kelsier. "So, the Pits really did drive you insane, eh?"

"Completely," Kelsier said with a straight face.

Clubs smiled, though on his face the expression had a decidedly twisted look. "You mean to go through with this, then? This so-called job of yours?"

Kelsier nodded solemnly.

Clubs downed the rest of his wine. "You've got yourself a Smoker then. Not for the money, though. If you're really serious about toppling this government, then I'm in."

Kelsier smiled.

"And don't smile at me," Clubs snapped. "I hate that."

"I wouldn't dare."

"Well," Dockson said, pouring himself another drink, "that solves the Smoker problem."

"Won't matter much," Clubs said. "You're going to fail. I've spent my life trying to hide Mistings from the Lord Ruler and his obligators. He gets them all eventually anyway."

"Why bother helping us, then?" Dockson asked.

"Because," Clubs said, standing. "The Lord's going to get me sooner or later. At least this way, I'll be able to spit in his face as I go. Overthrowing the Final Empire . . ." He smiled. "It's got style. Let's go, kid. We've got to get the shop ready for visitors."

Vin watched them go, Clubs limping out the door, the boy pulling it closed behind them. Then she glanced at Kelsier. "You knew he'd come back."

He shrugged, standing and stretching. "I hoped. People are attracted to vision. The job I'm proposing . . . well, it just isn't the sort of thing you walk away from—at least, not if you're a bored old man who's generally annoyed at life. Now, Vin, I assume that your crew owns this entire building?"

Vin nodded. "The shop upstairs is a front."

"Good," Kelsier said, checking his pocket watch, then handing it to Dockson. "Tell your friends that they can have their lair back—the mists are probably already coming out."

"And us?" Dockson asked.

Kelsier smiled. "We're going to the roof. Like I told you, I have to fetch some atium."

By day Luthadel was a blackened city, scorched by soot and red sunlight. It was hard, distinct, and oppressive.

At night, however, the mists came to blur and obscure. High noble keeps became ghostly, looming silhouettes. Streets seemed to grow more narrow in the fog, every thoroughfare becoming a lonely, dangerous alleyway. Even noblemen and thieves were apprehensive about going out at night—it took a strong heart to brave the foreboding, misty silence. The dark city at night was a place for the desperate and the foolhardy; it was a land of swirling mystery and strange creatures.

Strange creatures like me, Kelsier thought. He stood upon the ledge that ran around the lip of the flat-roofed lair. Shadowed buildings loomed in the night around him, and the mists made everything seem to shift and move in the darkness. Weak lights peeked from the occasional window, but the tiny beads of illumination were huddled, frightened things.

A cool breeze slipped across the rooftop, shifting the haze, brushing against Kelsier's mist-wetted cheek like an exhaled breath. In days past—back before everything had gone wrong—he had always sought out a rooftop on the evening before a job, wishing to overlook the city. He didn't realize he was observing his old custom this night until he glanced to the side, expecting Mare to be there next to him, as she always had been.

Instead, he found only the empty air. Lonely. Silent. The mists had replaced her. Poorly.

He sighed and turned. Vin and Dockson stood behind him on the rooftop. Both looked apprehensive to be out in the mists, but they dealt with their fear. One did not get far in the underworld without learning to stomach the mists.

Kelsier had learned to do far more than "stomach" them. He had gone among them so often during the last few years that he was beginning to feel more comfortable at night, within the mists' obscuring embrace, than he did at day.

"Kell," Dockson said, "do you *have* to stand on the ledge like that? Our plans may be a bit crazy, but I'd rather not have them end with you splattered across the cobblestones down there."

Kelsier smiled. *He still doesn't think of me as a Mistborn*, he thought. *It will take some getting used to for all of them.*

Years before, he had become the most infamous crewleader in Luthadel, and he had done it without even being an Allomancer. Mare had been a Tineye, but he and Dockson . . . they had just been regular men. One a half-breed with no powers, the other a runaway plantation skaa. Together, they had brought Great Houses to their knees, stealing brashly from the most powerful men in the Final Empire.

Now Kelsier was more, so much more. Once he had dreamed of Allomancy, wishing for a power like Mare's. She had been dead before he'd Snapped, coming to his powers. She would never see what he would do with them.

Before, the high nobility had feared him. It had taken a trap set by the Lord Ruler himself to capture Kelsier. Now . . . the Final Empire itself would shake before he was finished with it.

He scanned the city once more, breathing in the mists, then hopped down off the ledge and strolled over to join Dockson and Vin. They carried no lights; ambient starlight diffused by the mists was enough to see by in most cases.

Kelsier took off his jacket and vest, handing them to Dockson, then he untucked his shirt, letting the long garment hang loose. The fabric was dark enough that it wouldn't give him away in the night.

"All right," Kelsier said. "Who should I try?"

Dockson frowned. "You're sure you want to do this?"

Kelsier smiled.

Dockson sighed. "Houses Urbain and Teniert have been hit recently, though not for their atium."

"Which house is the strongest right now?" Kelsier asked, squatting down and undoing the ties on his pack, which rested by Dockson's feet. "Who would no one consider hitting?"

Dockson paused. "Venture," he finally said. "They've been on top for the last few years. They keep a standing force of several hundred men, and the local house nobility includes a good two dozen Mistings."

Kelsier nodded. "Well, that's where I'll go, then. They're certain to have some atium." He pulled open the pack, then whipped out a dark gray cloak. Large and enveloping, the cloak wasn't constructed from a single piece of cloth—rather, it was made up of hundreds of long, ribbonlike strips. They were sewn together at the shoulders and across the chest, but mostly they hung separate from one another, like overlapping streamers.

Kelsier threw on the garment, its strips of cloth twisting and curling, almost like the mists themselves.

Dockson exhaled softly. "I've never been so close to someone wearing one of those."

"What is it?" Vin asked, her quiet voice almost haunting in the night mists.

"A Mistborn cloak," Dockson said. "They all wear the things—it's kind of like a . . . sign of membership in their club."

"It's colored and constructed to hide you in the mist," Kelsier said. "And it warns city guards and other Mistborn not to bother you." He spun, letting the cloak flare dramatically. "I think it suits me."

Dockson rolled his eyes.

"All right," Kelsier said, bending down and pulling a cloth belt from his pack. "House Venture. Is there anything I need to know?"

"Lord Venture supposedly has a safe in his study," Dockson said. "That's where he'd probably keep his atium stash. You'll find the study on the third floor, three rooms in from the upper southern balcony. Be careful, House Venture keeps about a dozen hazekillers in addition to its regular troops and Mistings."

Kelsier nodded, tying on the belt—it had no buckle, but it did contain two small sheaths. He pulled a pair of glass daggers from the bag, checked them for nicks, and slid them into the sheaths. He kicked off his shoes and stripped off his stockings, leaving himself barefoot on the chill stones. With the shoes also went the last bit of metal on his person save for his coin pouch and the three vials of metals in his belt. He selected the largest one, downed its contents, then handed the empty vial to Dockson.

"That it?" Kelsier asked.

Dockson nodded. "Good luck."

Beside him, the girl Vin was watching Kelsier's preparations with intense curiosity. She was a quiet, small thing, but she hid an intensity that he found impressive. She was paranoid, true, but not timid.

You'll get your chance, kid, he thought. *Just not tonight.*

"Well," he said, pulling a coin from his pouch and tossing it off the side of the building. "Guess I'll be going. I'll meet you back at Clubs's shop in a bit."

Dockson nodded.

Kelsier turned and walked back up onto the roof's ledge. Then he jumped off the building.

Mist curled in the air around him. He burned steel, second of the basic Allomantic metals. Translucent blue lines sprang into existence around him, visible only to his eyes. Each one led from the center of his chest out to a nearby source of metal. The lines were all relatively faint—a sign that they pointed to metal sources that were small: door hinges, nails, and other bits. The type of source metal didn't matter. Burning iron or steel would point blue lines at all kinds of metal, assuming they were close enough and large enough to be noticeable.

Kelsier chose the line that pointed directly beneath him, toward his coin. Burning steel, he Pushed against the coin.

His descent immediately stopped, and he was thrown back up into the air in the opposite direction along the blue line. He reached out to the side, selected a passing window clasp, and Pushed against it, angling himself to the side. The careful nudge sent him up and over the lip of the building directly across the street from Vin's lair.

Kelsier landed with a lithe step, falling into a crouch and running across the building's peaked roof. He paused in the darkness at the other side, peering through the swirling air. He burned tin, and felt it flare to life in his chest, enhancing his senses. Suddenly the mists seemed less deep. It wasn't that the night around him grew any lighter; his ability to perceive simply increased. In the distance to the north, he could just barely make out a large structure. Keep Venture.

Kelsier left his tin on—it burned slowly, and he probably didn't need to worry about running out. As he stood, the mists curled slightly around his body. They twisted and spun, running in a slight, barely noticeable current beside him. The mists knew him; they claimed him. They could sense Allomancy.

He jumped, Pushing against a metal chimney behind him, sending himself in a wide horizontal leap. He tossed a coin even as he jumped, the tiny bit of metal flickering through the darkness and fog. He Pushed against the coin before it hit the ground, the force of his weight driving it downward in a sharp motion. As soon as it hit the cobblestones, Kelsier's Pushing forced him upward, turning the second half of his leap into a graceful arc.

Kelsier landed on another peaked wooden rooftop. Steelpushing and Ironpulling were the first things that Gemmel had taught him. *When you Push on something, it's like you're throwing your weight against it,* the old lunatic had said. *And you can't change how much you weigh—you're an Allomancer, not some northern mystic. Don't Pull on something that weighs less than you unless you want it to come flying at you, and don't Push on something heavier than you unless you want to get tossed in the other direction.*

Kelsier scratched his scars, then pulled his mistcloak tight as he crouched on the roof, the wooden grain biting his unshod toes. He often wished that burning tin didn't enhance all of the senses—or, at least, not all of them at once. He needed the improved eyesight to see in the darkness, and he made good use of the improved hearing as well. However, burning tin made the night seem even more chilly to his overly sensitive skin, and his feet registered every pebble and wooden ripple they touched.

Keep Venture rose before him. Compared with the murky city, the keep seemed to blaze with light. High nobles kept different schedules from regular people; the ability to afford, even squander, lamp oil and candles meant that the wealthy didn't have to bow before the whims of season or sun.

The keep was majestic—that much was visible simply from the architecture. While it maintained a defensive wall around the grounds, the keep itself was more an artistic construction than a fortification. Sturdy buttressings arched out from the sides, allowing for intricate windows and delicate spires. Brilliant stained-glass windows stretched high along the sides of the rectangular building, and they shone with light from within, giving the surrounding mists a variegated glow.

Kelsier burned iron, flaring it strong and searching the night for large sources of metal. He was too far away from the keep to use small items like coins or hinges. He'd need a larger anchor to cover this distance.

Most of the blue lines were faint. Kelsier marked a couple of them moving in a slow pattern up ahead—probably a pair of guards standing on the rooftop. Kelsier would be sensing their breastplates and weapons. Despite Allomantic considerations, most noblemen still armed their soldiers with metal. Mistings who could Push or Pull metals were uncommon, and full Mistborn were even more so. Many lords thought it impractical to leave one's soldiers and guards relatively defenseless in order to counter such a small segment of the population.

No, most high noblemen relied on other means to deal with Allomancers. Kelsier smiled. Dockson had said that Lord Venture kept a squad of hazekillers; if that was true, Kelsier would probably meet them before the night was through. He ignored the soldiers for the moment, instead focusing on a solid line of blue pointing toward the keep's lofty top. It likely had bronze or copper sheeting on the roof. Kelsier flared his iron, took a deep breath, and Pulled on the line.

With a sudden jerk, he was yanked into the air.

Kelsier continued to burn iron, pulling himself toward the keep at a tremendous speed. Some rumors claimed that Mistborn could fly, but that was a wistful exaggeration. Pulling and Pushing against metals usually felt less like flying than it did like falling—only in the wrong direction. An Allomancer had to Pull hard in order to get the proper momentum, and this sent him hurtling toward his anchor at daunting speeds.

Kelsier shot toward the keep, mists curling around him. He easily cleared the protective wall surrounding the keep's grounds, but his body dropped slightly toward the ground as he moved. It was his pesky weight again; it tugged him down. Even the swiftest of arrows angled slightly toward the ground as it flew.

The drag of his weight meant that instead of shooting right up to the roof, he swung in an arc. He approached the keep wall several dozen feet below the rooftop, still traveling at a terrible speed.

Taking a deep breath, Kelsier burned pewter, using it to enhance his physical strength much in the same way that tin enhanced his senses. He turned himself in the air, hitting the stone wall feet-first. Even his strengthened muscles protested at the treatment, but he stopped without breaking any bones. He immediately released his hold on the roof, dropping a coin and Pushing against it even as he began to fall. He reached out, selecting a source of metal above him—one of the wire housings of a stained-glass window—and Pulled on it.

The coin hit the ground below and was suddenly able to support his weight. Kelsier launched himself upward, Pushing on the coin and Pulling on the window at the same time. Then, extinguishing both metals, he let momentum carry him the last few feet up through the dark mists. Cloak flapping quietly, he crested the lip of the keep's upper service walkway, flipped himself up over the stone railing, and landed quietly on the ledge.

A startled guard stood not three paces away. Kelsier was upon the man in a second, jumping into the air, Pulling slightly on the guard's steel breastplate and throwing the man off balance. Kelsier whipped out one of his glass daggers, allowing the strength of his Ironpull to bring him toward the guard. He landed with both feet against the man's chest, then crouched and sliced with a pewter-enhanced swing.

The guard collapsed with a slit throat. Kelsier landed lithely beside him, ears straining in the night, listening for sounds of alarm. There were none.

Kelsier left the guard to his gurgling demise. The man was likely a lesser nobleman. The enemy. If he were, instead, a skaa soldier—enticed into betraying his people in exchange for a few coins . . . Well, then, Kelsier was even happier to send such men into their eternity.

He Pushed off the dying man's breastplate, hopping up off the stone service walkway and onto the rooftop itself. The bronze roof was chill and slick beneath his feet. He scurried along it, heading toward the southern side of the building, looking for the balcony Dockson had mentioned. He wasn't too worried about being spotted; one purpose of this evening was to steal some atium, the tenth and most powerful of the generally known Allomantic metals. His other purpose, however, was to cause a commotion.

He found the balcony with ease. Wide and broad, it was probably a sitting balcony, used to entertain small groups. It was quiet at the moment, however—empty save for two guards. Kelsier crouched silently in the night mists above the balcony, furled gray cloak obscuring him, toes curling out over the side of the roof's metallic lip. The two guards chatted unwittingly below.

Time to make a bit of noise.

Kelsier dropped to the ledge directly between the guards. Burning pewter to strengthen his body, he reached out and fiercely Steelpushed against both men at the same time. Braced as he was at the center, his Push threw the guards away in opposite directions. The men cried out in surprise as the sudden force threw them backward, hurling them over the balcony railing into the darkness beyond.

The guards screamed as they fell. Kelsier threw open the balcony doors, letting a wall of mist fall inward around him, its tendrils creeping forward to claim the darkened room beyond.

Third room in, Kelsier thought, moving forward in a crouching run. The second room was a quiet, greenhouse-like conservatory. Low beds containing cultivated bushes and small trees ran through the room, and one wall was made up of enormous floor-to-ceiling windows to provide sunlight for the plants. Though it was dark, Kelsier knew that the plants would all be of slightly different colors than the typical brown—some would be white, others ruddy, and perhaps even a few light yellow. Plants that weren't brown were a rarity cultivated and kept by the nobility.

Kelsier moved quickly through the conservatory. He paused at the next doorway, noting its lighted outline. He extinguished his tin lest his enhanced eyes be blinded when he entered the lit room, and threw open the door.

He ducked inside, blinking against the light, a glass dagger in each hand. The room, however, was empty. It was obviously a study; a lantern burned on each wall beside bookcases, and it had a desk in the corner.

Kelsier replaced his knives, burning steel and searching for sources of metal. There was a large safe in the corner of the room, but it was too obvious. Sure enough, another strong source of metal shone from inside the eastern wall. Kelsier approached, running his fingers along the plaster. Like many walls in noble keeps, this one was painted with a soft mural. Foreign creatures lounged beneath a red sun. The false section of wall was under two feet square, and it had been placed so that its cracks were obscured by the mural.

There's always another secret, Kelsier thought. He didn't bother trying to figure out how to open the contraption. He simply burned steel, reaching in and tugging against the weak source of metal that he assumed was the trapdoor's locking mechanism. It resisted at first, pulling him against the wall, but he burned pewter and yanked harder. The lock snapped, and the panel swung open, revealing a small safe embedded in the wall.

Kelsier smiled. It looked small enough for a pewter-enhanced man to carry, assuming he could get it out of the wall.

He jumped up, Ironpulling against the safe, and landed with his feet against the wall, one foot on either side of the open panel. He continued to Pull, holding himself in place, and flared his pewter. Strength flooded his legs, and he flared his steel as well, Pulling against the safe.

He strained, grunting slightly at the exertion. It was a test to see which would give out first—the safe, or his legs.

The safe shifted in its mountings. Kelsier Pulled harder, muscles protesting. For an extended moment, nothing happened. Then the safe shook and ripped free of the wall. Kelsier fell backward, burning steel and Pushing against the safe to get out of the way. He landed maladroitly, sweat dripping from his brow as the safe crashed to the wooden floor, throwing up splinters.

A pair of startled guards burst into the room.

"About time," Kelsier noted, raising a hand and Pulling on one of the soldier's swords. It whipped out of the sheath, spinning in the air and streaking toward Kelsier point-first. He extinguished his iron, stepping to the side and catching the sword by its hilt as momentum carried it past.

"Mistborn!" the guard screamed.

Kelsier smiled and jumped forward.

The guard pulled out a dagger. Kelsier Pushed it, tearing the weapon out of the man's hand, then swung, shearing the guard's head from his body. The second guard cursed, tugging free the release tie on his breastplate.

Kelsier Pushed on his own sword even as he completed his swing. The sword ripped from his fingers and hissed directly toward the second guard. The man's armor dropped free—preventing Kelsier from Pushing against it—just as the first guard's corpse fell to the ground. A moment later, Kelsier's sword planted itself in the second guard's now unarmored chest. The man stumbled quietly, then collapsed.

Kelsier turned from the bodies, cloak rustling. His anger was quiet, not as fierce as it had been the night he'd killed Lord Tresting. But he felt it still, felt it in the itching of his scars and in the remembered screams of the woman he loved. As far as Kelsier was concerned, any man who upheld the Final Empire also forfeited his right to live.

He flared his pewter, strengthening his body, then squatted down and lifted the safe. He teetered for a second beneath its weight, then got his balance and began to shuffle back toward the balcony. Perhaps the safe held atium; perhaps it didn't. However, he didn't have time to search out other options.

He was halfway through the conservatory when he heard footsteps from behind. He turned to see the study flooding with figures. There were eight of them, each one wearing a loose gray robe and carrying a dueling cane and a shield instead of a sword. Hazekillers.

Kelsier let the safe drop to the ground. Hazekillers weren't Allomancers, but they were trained to fight Mistings and Mistborn. There wouldn't be a single bit of metal on their bodies, and they would be ready for his tricks.

Kelsier stepped back, stretching and smiling. The eight men fanned into the study, moving with quiet precision.

This should be interesting.

The hazekillers attacked, dashing by twos into the conservatory. Kelsier pulled out his daggers, ducking beneath the first attack and slicing at a man's chest. The hazekiller jumped back, however, and forced Kelsier away with a swing of his cane.

Kelsier flared his pewter, letting strengthened legs carry him back in a powerful jump. With one hand, he whipped out a handful of coins and Pushed them against his opponents. The metal disks shot forward, zipping through the air, but his enemies were ready for this: They raised their shields, and the coins bounced off the wood, throwing up splinters but leaving the men unharmed.

Kelsier eyed the other hazekillers as they filled the room, advancing on him. They couldn't hope to fight him in an extended battle—their tactic would be to rush him at once, hoping for quick end to the fight, or to at least to stall him until Allomancers could be awakened and brought to fight. He glanced at the safe as he landed.

He couldn't leave without it. He needed to end the fight quickly as well. Flaring pewter, he jumped forward, trying an experimental dagger swipe, but he couldn't get inside his opponent's defenses. Kelsier barely ducked away in time to avoid getting cracked on the head by the end of a cane.

Three of the hazekillers dashed behind him, cutting off his retreat into the balcony room. *Great*, Kelsier thought, trying to keep an eye on all eight men at once. They advanced on him with careful precision, working as a team.

Gritting his teeth, Kelsier flared his pewter again; it was running low, he noticed. Pewter was the fastest-burning of the basic eight metals.

No time to worry about that now. The men behind him attacked, and Kelsier jumped out of the way—Pulling on the safe to tug himself toward the center of the room. He Pushed as soon as he hit the ground near the safe, launching himself into the air at an angle. He tucked, flipping over the heads of two attackers, and landed on the ground beside a well-cultivated tree bed. He spun, flaring his pewter and raising his arm in defense against the swing he knew would come.

The dueling cane connected with his arm. A burst of pain ran down his forearm, but his pewter-enhanced bone held. Kelsier kept moving, driving his other hand forward and slamming a dagger into his opponent's chest.

The man stumbled back in surprise, the motion ripping away Kelsier's dagger. A second hazekiller attacked, but Kelsier ducked, then reached down with his free hand, ripping his coin pouch off of his belt. The hazekiller prepared to block Kelsier's remaining dagger, but Kelsier raised his other hand instead, slamming the coin pouch into the man's shield.

Then he Pushed on the coins inside.

The hazekiller cried out, the force of the intense Steelpush throwing him backward. Kelsier flared his steel, Pushing so hard that he tossed himself backward as well—away from the pair of men who tried to attack him. Kelsier and his enemy flew away from each other, hurled in opposite directions. Kelsier collided with the far wall, but kept Pushing, smashing his opponent—pouch, shield, and all—against one of the massive conservatory windows.

Glass shattered, sparkles of lanternlight from the study playing across its shards. The hazekiller's desperate face disappeared into the darkness beyond, and mist—quiet, yet ominous—began to creep in through the shattered window.

The other six men advanced relentlessly, and Kelsier was forced to ignore the pain in his arm as he ducked two swings. He spun out of the way, brushing past a small tree, but a third hazekiller attacked, smashing his cane into Kelsier's side.

The attack threw Kelsier into the tree bed. He tripped, then collapsed near the entrance to the lit study, dropping his dagger. He gasped in pain, rolling to his knees and holding his side. The blow would have broken another man's ribs. Even Kelsier would have a massive bruise.

The six men moved forward, spreading to surround him again. Kelsier stumbled to his feet, vision growing dizzy from pain and exertion. He gritted his teeth, reaching down and pulling out one of his remaining vials of metal. He downed its contents in a single gulp, replenishing his pewter, then burned tin. The light nearly blinded him, and the pain in his arm and side suddenly seemed more acute, but the burst of enhanced senses cleared his head.

The six hazekillers advanced in a sudden, coordinated attack.

Kelsier whipped his hand to the side, burning iron and searching for metal. The closest source was a thick silvery paperweight on a desk just inside the study. Kelsier flipped it into his hand, then turned, arm held toward the advancing men, falling into an offensive stance.

"All right," he growled.

Kelsier burned steel with a flash of strength. The rectangular ingot ripped from his hand, streaking through the air. The foremost hazekiller raised his shield, but he moved too slowly. The ingot hit the man's shoulder with a crunch, and he dropped, crying out.

Kelsier spun to the side, ducking a staff swing and putting a hazekiller between himself and the fallen man. He burned iron, Pulling the ingot back toward him. It whipped through the air, cracking the second hazekiller in the side of the head. The man collapsed as the ingot flipped into the air.

One of the remaining men cursed, rushing forward to attack. Kelsier Pushed the still airborne ingot, flipping it away from him—and away from the attacking hazekiller, who had his shield raised. Kelsier heard the ingot hit the ground behind him, and he reached up—burning pewter—and caught the hazekiller's cane mid-swing.

The hazekiller grunted, struggling against Kelsier's enhanced strength. Kelsier didn't bother trying to pull the weapon free; instead he Pulled sharply on the ingot behind him, bringing it toward his own back at a deadly speed. He twisted at the last moment, using his momentum to spin the hazekiller around—right into the ingot's path.

The man dropped.

Kelsier flared pewter, steadying himself against attacks. Sure enough, a cane smashed against his shoulders. He stumbled to his knees as the wood cracked, but flared tin kept him conscious. Pain and lucidity flashed through his mind. He Pulled on the ingot—ripping it out of the dying man's back—and stepped to the side, letting the impromptu weapon shoot past him.

The two hazekillers nearest him crouched warily. The ingot snapped into one of the men's shields, but Kelsier didn't continue Pushing, lest he throw himself off balance. Instead, he burned iron, wrenching the ingot back toward himself. He ducked, extinguishing iron and feeling the ingot whoosh through the air above him. There was a crack as it collided with the man who had been sneaking up on him.

Kelsier spun, burning iron then steel to send the ingot soaring toward the final two men. They stepped out of the way, but Kelsier tugged on the ingot, dropping it to the ground directly in front of them. The men regarded it warily, distracted as Kelsier ran and jumped, Steelpushing himself against the ingot and flipping over the men's heads. The hazekillers cursed, spinning. As Kelsier landed, he Pulled the ingot again, bringing it up to smash into a man's skull from behind.

The hazekiller fell silently. The ingot flipped a few times in the darkness, and Kelsier snatched it from the air, its cool surface slick with blood. Mist from the shattered window flowed by his feet, curling up around his legs. He brought his hand down, pointing it directly at the last remaining hazekiller.

Somewhere in the room, a fallen man groaned.

The remaining hazekiller stepped back, then dropped his weapon and dashed away. Kelsier smiled, lowering his hand.

Suddenly, the ingot was Pushed from his fingers. It shot across the room, smashing through another window. Kelsier cursed, spinning to see another, larger group of men pouring into the study. They wore the clothing of noblemen. Allomancers.

Several of them raised hands, and a flurry of coins shot toward Kelsier. He flared steel, Pushing the coins out of the way. Windows shattered and wood splintered as the room was sprayed with coins. Kelsier felt a tug on his belt as his final vial of metal was ripped away, Pulled toward the other room. Several burly men ran forward in a crouch, staying beneath the shooting coins. Thugs—Mistings who, like Ham, could burn pewter.

Time to go, Kelsier thought, deflecting another wave of coins, gritting his teeth against the pain in his side and arm. He glanced behind him; he had a few moments, but he was never going to make it back to the balcony. As more Mistings advanced, Kelsier took a deep breath and dashed toward one of the broken, floor-to-ceiling windows. He leapt out into the mists, turning in the air as he fell, and reached out to Pull firmly on the fallen safe.

He jerked in midair, swinging down toward the side of the building as if tied to the safe by a tether. He felt the safe slide forward, grinding against the floor of the conservatory as Kelsier's weight pulled against it. He slammed against the side of the building, but continued to Pull, catching himself on the upper side of a windowsill. He strained, standing upside down in the window well, Pulling on the safe.

The safe appeared over the lip of the floor above. It teetered, then fell out the window and began to plummet directly toward Kelsier. He smiled, extinguishing his iron and pushing away from the building with his legs, throwing himself out into the mists like some insane diver. He fell backward through the darkness, barely catching sight of an angry face poking out of the broken window above.

Kelsier Pulled carefully against the safe, moving himself in the air. Mists curled around him, obscuring his vision, making him feel as if he weren't falling at all—but hanging in the middle of nothingness.

He reached the safe, then twisted in the air and Pushed against it, throwing himself upward.

The safe crashed into the cobblestones just below. Kelsier Pushed against the safe slightly, slowing himself until he eventually jerked to a halt in the air just a few feet above the ground. He hung in the mists for a moment, ribbons from his cloak curling and flapping in the wind, then let himself drop to the ground beside the safe.

The strongbox had been shattered by the fall. Kelsier pried open its mangled front, tin-enhanced ears listening to calls of alarm from the building above. Inside the safe, he found a small pouch of gemstones and a couple of tenthousand boxing letters of credit, all of which he pocketed. He felt around inside, suddenly worried that the night's work had been for naught. Then his fingers found it—a small pouch at the very back.

He pulled it open, revealing a grouping of dark, beadlike bits of metal. Atium. His scars flared, memories of his time in the Pits returning to him.

He pulled the pouch tight and stood. With amusement, he noticed a twisted form lying on the cobblestones a short distance away—the mangled remains of the hazekiller he'd thrown out the window. Kelsier walked over, and retrieved his coin pouch with a tug of Ironpulling.

No, this night was not a waste. Even if he hadn't found the atium, any night that ended with a group of dead noblemen was a successful one, in Kelsier's opinion.

He gripped his pouch in one hand and the bag of atium in the other. He kept his pewter burning—without the strength it lent his body, he'd probably collapse from the pain of his wounds—and dashed off into the night, heading toward Clubs's shop.

I never wanted this, true. But somebody has to stop the Deepness. And, apparently, Terris is the only place this can be done.

On this fact, however, I don't have to take the word of the philosophers. I can feel our goal now, can sense it, though the others cannot. It . . . pulses, in my mind, far off in the mountains.

6

VIN AWOKE TO A QUIET ROOM, red morning sunlight peeking through cracks in the shutters. She lay in bed for a moment, unsettled. Something felt wrong. It wasn't that she was waking up in an unfamiliar place—traveling with Reen had accustomed her to a nomadic lifestyle. It took her a moment to realize the source of her discomfort.

The room was empty.

Not only was it empty, it was open. Uncrowded. And it was . . . comfortable. She lay on an actual mattress, raised on posts, with sheets and a plush quilt. The room was decorated with a sturdy wooden armoire, and even had a circular rug. Perhaps another might have found the room cramped and spartan, but to Vin it seemed lavish.

She sat up, frowning. It felt wrong to have a room all to herself. She had always been crammed into tight bunkrooms filled with crewmembers. Even while traveling, she had slept in beggars' alleys or rebel caves, and Reen had been there with her. She had always been forced to fight to find privacy. Being given it so easily seemed to devalue the years she had spent relishing her brief moments of solitude.

She slipped out of bed, not bothering to open the shutters. The sunlight was faint, which meant it was still early morning, but she could already hear people moving in the hallway. She crept to the door, creaking it open and peeking out.

After leaving Kelsier the night before, Dockson had led Vin to Clubs's shop. Because of the late hour, Clubs had immediately led them to their separate rooms. Vin, however, had not gone to bed immediately. She had waited until everyone was asleep, then had snuck out to inspect her surroundings.

The residence was almost more of an inn than it was a shop. Though it had a showroom below and a large workshop in the back, the building's second floor was dominated by several long hallways lined with guestrooms. There was a third floor, and the doors were more widely spaced there, implying larger rooms. She hadn't tapped for trapdoors or false walls—the noise might have awakened someone—but experience told her that it wouldn't be a proper lair if it didn't have at least a secret basement and some bolt-holes.

Overall, she was impressed. The carpentry equipment and half-finished projects below indicated a reputable, working front. The lair was secure, well stocked, and well maintained. Watching through the crack in her door, Vin made out a group of about six groggy young men coming out of the hallway opposite her own. They wore simple clothing, and made their way down the stairs toward the workroom.

Apprentice carpenters, Vin thought. *That's Clubs's front—he's a skaa craftsman.* Most skaa lived lives of drudgery on the plantations; even those who lived in a city were generally forced to do menial labor. However, some talented few were allowed a trade. They were still skaa; they were paid poorly and were always subject to the whims of the nobility. However, they had a measure of freedom that most skaa would envy.

Clubs was probably a master carpenter. What would entice such a man—one who had, by skaa standards, an amazing life—to risk joining the underground?

He is a Misting, Vin thought. *Kelsier and Dockson called him a "Smoker."* She would probably have to figure out what that meant on her own; experience told her that a powerful man like Kelsier would withhold knowledge from her as long as he could, stringing her along with occasional tidbits. His knowledge was what bound her to him—it would be unwise to give away too much too quickly.

Footsteps sounded outside, and Vin continued to peek through the crack.

"You'll want to get ready, Vin," Dockson said as he passed her door. He wore a nobleman's dress shirt and slacks, and he already looked awake and trim. He paused, continuing. "There's a fresh bath for you in the room at the end of the hallway, and I had Clubs scrounge you up a few changes of clothing. They should fit well enough until we can get you something more appropriate. Take your time in the bath—Kell's planned a meeting for this afternoon, but we can't start until Breeze and Ham arrive."

Dockson smiled, eyeing her through the cracked door, then continued on down the hallway. Vin flushed at being caught. *These are observant men. I'm going to have to remember that.*

The hallway grew quiet. She slipped out her door and crept down to the indicated room, and was half surprised to find that there was indeed a warm bath waiting for her. She frowned, studying the tiled chamber and metal tub. The water smelled scented, after the fashion of noble ladies.

These men are more like noblemen than skaa, Vin thought. She wasn't certain what she thought of that. However, they obviously expected her to do as they did, so she closed and bolted the door, then disrobed and crawled into the tub.

She smelled funny.

Even though the scent was faint, Vin still caught whiffs of herself occasionally. It was the smell of a passing noblewoman, the scent of a perfumed drawer opened by her brother's burgling fingers. The smell grew less noticeable as the morning progressed, but it still worried her. It would distinguish her from other skaa. If this crew expected her to take those baths regularly, she would have to request that the perfumes be removed.

The morning meal was more up to her expectations. Several skaa women of various ages worked the shop's kitchen, preparing baywraps—rolls of thin, flat bread stuffed with boiled barley and vegetables. Vin stood by the kitchen doorway, watching the women work. None of them smelled like she did, though they were far more cleanly and well groomed than average skaa.

In fact, there was an odd sense of cleanliness to the entire building. She hadn't noticed it the night before, because of the darkness, but the floor was scrubbed clean. All of the workers—kitchen women or apprentices—had clean faces and hands. It felt odd to Vin. She was accustomed to her own fingers being black with ashstains; with Reen, if she'd ever washed her face, she had quickly rubbed it with ash again. A clean face stood out on the streets.

No ash in the corners, she thought, eyeing the floor. *The room is kept swept.* She'd never lived in such a place before. It was almost like living in some nobleman's house.

She glanced back at the kitchen women. They wore simple dresses of white and gray, with scarves around the tops of their heads and long tails of hair hanging out the back. Vin fingered her own hair. She kept it short, like a boy's—her current, ragged cut had been given by one of the other crewmembers. She wasn't like these women—she never had been. By Reen's command, Vin had lived so that other crewmembers would think of her as a thief first and a girl second.

But, what am I now? Perfumed by her bath, yet wearing the tan trousers and buttoning shirt of an apprentice craftsman, she felt distinctly out of place. And that was bad—if she felt awkward, then she undoubtedly looked awkward too. Something else to make her stand out.

Vin turned, eyeing the workroom. The apprentices were already about their morning labors, working on various bits of furniture. They stayed in the back while Clubs worked in the main showroom, putting detailed finishing touches on the pieces.

The back kitchen door suddenly slammed open. Vin slipped reflexively to the side, putting her back to a wall and peeking around into the kitchen.

Ham stood in the kitchen doorway, framed by red sunlight. He wore a loose shirt and vest, both sleeveless, and carried several large packs. He wasn't dirtied by soot—none of the crew had ever been, the few times Vin had seen them.

Ham walked through the kitchen and into the workroom. "So," he said, dropping his packs, "anyone know which room is mine?"

"I'll ask Master Cladent," one of the apprentices said, moving into the front room.

Ham smiled, stretching, then turned toward Vin. "Morning, Vin. You know, you don't have to hide from me. We're on the same team."

Vin relaxed but remained where she was, standing beside a line of mostly finished chairs. "You're going to live here too?"

"It always pays to stay near the Smoker," Ham said, turning and disappearing back into the kitchen. He returned a moment later with a stack of four large baywraps. "Anyone know where Kell is?"

"Sleeping," Vin said. "He came in late last night, and hasn't gotten up yet."

Ham grunted, taking a bite of a baywrap. "Dox?"

"In his room on the third floor," Vin said. "He got up early, came down to get something to eat, and went back upstairs." She didn't add that she knew, from peeking through the keyhole, that he was sitting at his desk scribbling on some papers.

Ham raised an eyebrow. "You always keep track of where everyone is like that?"

"Yes."

Ham paused, then chuckled. "You're an odd kid, Vin." He gathered up his packs as the apprentice returned, and the two moved up the stairs. Vin stood, listening to their footsteps. They stopped about halfway down the first hallway, perhaps a few doors from her room.

The scent of steamed barley enticed her. Vin eyed the kitchen. Ham had gone in and taken food. Was she allowed to do the same?

Trying to look confident, Vin strode into the kitchen. A pile of baywraps sat on a platter, probably to be delivered to the apprentices as they worked. Vin picked up two of them. None of the women objected; in fact, a few of them even nodded respectfully toward her.

I'm an important person now, she thought with a measure of discomfort. Did they know that she was . . . Mistborn? Or was she simply treated with respect because she was a guest?

Eventually, Vin took a third baywrap and fled to her room. It was more food than she could possibly eat; however, she intended to scrape out the barley and save the flatbread, which would keep well should she need it later.

A knock came at her door. Vin answered it, pulling the door open with a careful motion. A young man stood outside—the boy who had been with Clubs back at Camon's lair the night before.

Thin, tall, and awkward-looking, he was dressed in gray clothing. He was perhaps fourteen, though his height might have made him look older than he was. He seemed nervous for some reason.

"Yes?" Vin asked.

"Um . . ."

Vin frowned. "What?"

"You're wanted," he said in a thick Eastern accent. "Ups in the where above with the doing. With Master Jumps to the third floor. Uh, I've gotta go." The boy blushed, then turned and hurried away, scrambling up the stairs.

Vin stood in the doorway of her room, dumbfounded. *Was that supposed to make any sense?* she wondered.

She peeked into the hallway. The boy had seemed like he expected her to follow him. Finally, she decided to do so, carefully making her way up the steps.

Voices were coming from an open door at the end of the hallway. Vin approached and peeked around the corner to find a well-decorated room, set with a fine rug and comfortable-looking chairs. A hearth burned at the side of the room, and the chairs were arranged to point toward a large charcoal writing board set atop an easel.

Kelsier stood, leaning one elbow resting against the brick hearth, a cup of wine in his hand. Angling herself slightly, Vin could see that he was talking to Breeze. The Soother had arrived well into midday, and had appropriated half of Clubs's apprentices to unload his possessions. Vin had watched from her window as the apprentices had carried the luggage—disguised as boxes of lumber scraps—up to Breeze's room. Breeze himself hadn't bothered to help.

Ham was there, as was Dockson, and Clubs was settling himself into the large, overstuffed chair farthest from Breeze. The boy who had fetched Vin sat on a stool beside Clubs, and he was obviously making a point of trying not to look at her. The final occupied chair held the man Yeden, dressed—as before—in common skaa worker's clothing. He sat in his chair without resting against its back, as if he disapproved of its plushness. His face was darkened with soot, as Vin expected of a skaa worker.

There were two empty chairs. Kelsier noticed Vin standing by the doorway, and gave her one of his inviting smiles. "Well, there she is. Come in."

Vin scanned the room. There was a window, though its shutters were closed against approaching gloom. The only chairs were the ones in Kelsier's half circle. Resigned, she moved forward and took the empty chair beside

Dockson. It was too big for her, and she settled into it with her knees folded beneath her.

"That's all of us," Kelsier said.

"Who's the last chair for?" Ham asked.

Kelsier smiled, winked, but ignored the question. "All right, let's talk. We've got something of a task ahead of ourselves, and the sooner we begin outlining a plan, the better."

"I thought you had a plan," Yeden said uncomfortably.

"I have a framework," Kelsier said. "I know what needs to happen, and I have a few ideas on how to do it. But, you don't gather a group like this and just tell them what to do. We need to work this out together, beginning with a list of problems we need to deal with if we want the plan to work."

"Well," Ham said, "let me get the framework straight first. The plan is to gather Yeden an army, cause chaos in Luthadel, secure the palace, steal the Lord Ruler's atium, then leave the government to collapse?"

"Essentially," Kelsier said.

"Then," Ham said, "our main problem is the Garrison. If we want chaos in Luthadel, then we can't have twenty thousand troops here to keep the peace. Not to mention the fact that Yeden's troops will never take the city while there is any sort of armed resistance on the walls."

Kelsier nodded. Picking up a piece of chalk, he wrote *Luthadel Garrison* up on the board. "What else?"

"We'll need a way to make said chaos in Luthadel," Breeze said, gesturing with a cup of wine. "Your instincts are right, my dear man. This city is where the Ministry makes its headquarters and the Great Houses run their mercantile empires. We'll need to bring Luthadel down if we want to break the Lord Ruler's ability to govern."

"Mentioning the nobility brings up another point," Dockson added. "The Great Houses all have guard forces in the city, not to mention their Allomancers. If we're going to deliver the city to Yeden, we'll have to deal with those noblemen."

Kelsier nodded, writing *Chaos* and *Great Houses* beside *Luthadel Garrison* on his board.

"The Ministry," Clubs said, leaning back in his plush chair so much that Vin almost couldn't see his grumpy face. "There'll be no change in government as long as the Steel Inquisitors have anything to say about it."

Kelsier added *Ministry* to the board. "What else?"

"Atium," Ham said. "You might as well write it up there—we'll need to secure the palace quickly, once general mayhem starts, and make certain nobody else takes the opportunity to slip into the treasury."

Kelsier nodded, writing *Atium: Secure Treasury* on the board.

"We will need to find a way to gather Yeden's troops," Breeze added. "We'll have to be quiet, but quick, and train them somewhere that the Lord Ruler won't find them."

"We also might want to make certain that the skaa rebellion is ready to take control of Luthadel," Dockson added. "Seizing the palace and digging in will make for a spectacular story, but it would be nice if Yeden and his people were actually ready to govern, once this is all over."

Troops and *Skaa Rebellion* were added to the board. "And," Kelsier said, "I'm going to add 'Lord Ruler.' We'll at least want a plan to get him out of the city, should other options fail." After writing *Lord Ruler* on the list, he turned back toward the group. "Did I forget anything?"

"Well," Yeden said dryly, "if you're listing problems we'll have to overcome, you should write up there that we're all bloody insane—though I doubt we can fix that fact."

The group chuckled, and Kelsier wrote *Yeden's Bad Attitude* on the board. Then he stepped back, looking over the list. "When you break it down like that, it doesn't sound so bad, does it?"

Vin frowned, trying to decide if Kelsier was attempting a joke or not. The list wasn't just daunting—it was disturbing. Twenty thousand imperial soldiers? The collected forces and power of the high nobility? The Ministry? One Steel Inquisitor was said to be more powerful than a thousand troops.

More discomforting, however, was how matter-of-factly they regarded the issues. How could they even think of resisting the Lord Ruler? He was . . . well, he was the *Lord*. He ruled all of the world. He was the creator, protector, and punisher of mankind. He had saved them from the Deepness, then had brought the ash and the mists as a punishment for the people's lack of faith. Vin wasn't particularly religious—intelligent thieves knew to avoid the Steel Ministry— but even she knew the legends.

And yet, the group regarded their list of "problems" with determination. There was a grim mirth about them—as if they understood that they had a better chance of making the sun rise at night than they did of overthrowing the Final Empire. Yet, they were still going to try.

"By the Lord Ruler," Vin whispered. "You're *serious*. You really mean to do this."

"Don't use his name as an oath, Vin," Kelsier said. "Even blasphemy honors him—when you curse by that creature's name, you acknowledge him as your god."

Vin fell silent, sitting back in her chair, a bit numb.

"Anyway," Kelsier said, smiling lightly. "Anyone have any ideas on how to overcome these problems? Besides Yeden's attitude, of course—we all know he's hopeless."

The room was quiet and thoughtful.

"Thoughts?" Kelsier asked. "Angles? Impressions?"

Breeze shook his head. "Now that it's all up there, I can't help wondering if the child has a point. This is a daunting task."

"But it *can* be done," Kelsier said. "Let's start by talking about how to break the city. What can we do that would be so threatening that it would throw the nobility into chaos, maybe even get the palace guard out into the city, exposing them to our troops? Something that would distract the Ministry, and the Lord Ruler himself, while we move our troops in to attack?"

"Well, a general revolution among the populace comes to mind," Ham said.

"Won't work," Yeden said firmly.

"Why not?" Ham asked. "You know how the people are treated. They live in slums, work in mills and smithies the entire day, and half of them *still* starve."

Yeden shook his head. "Don't you understand? The rebellion has been trying for a *thousand years* to get the skaa in this city to rise up. It never works. They're too beaten down—they don't have the will or the hope to resist. That's why I had to come to you to get an army."

The room fell still. Vin, however, slowly nodded her head. She'd seen it— she'd *felt* it. One didn't fight the Lord Ruler. Even living as a thief, crouching at the edge of society, she knew that. There would be no rebellion.

"He's right, I'm afraid," Kelsier said. "The skaa won't rise up, not in their current state. If we're going to overthrow this government, we'll need to do it without the help of the masses. We can probably recruit our soldiers from among them, but we can't count on the general populace."

"Could we cause a disaster of some sort?" Ham asked. "A fire maybe?"

Kelsier shook his head. "It might disrupt trade for a while, but I doubt it would have the effect we want. Besides, the cost in skaa lives would be too high. The slums would burn, not stone nobleman keeps."

Breeze sighed. "What, then, would you have us do?"

Kelsier smiled, eyes twinkling. "What if we turned the Great Houses against each other?"

Breeze paused. "A house war . . ." he said, taking a speculative sip of his wine. "It's been a while since the city had one of those."

"Which means that tensions have had plenty of time to brew," Kelsier said. "The high nobility are growing increasingly powerful—the Lord Ruler barely has control over them anymore, which is why we have a chance of shattering his grip. Luthadel's Great Houses are the key—they control imperial trade, not to mention enslave the greatest majority of the skaa."

Kelsier pointed at the board, moving his finger between the line that said *Chaos* and the line that said *Great Houses*.

"If we can turn the houses inside Luthadel against each other, we can bring down the city. Mistborn will start assassinating house leaders. Fortunes will collapse. It won't take long before there is open warfare in the streets. Part of our contract with Yeden states that we'll give him an opening to seize the city for himself. Can you think of a better one than that?"

Breeze nodded with a smile. "It has flair—and I do like the idea of having the noblemen kill each other."

"You *always* like it better when someone else does the work, Breeze," Ham noted.

"My dear friend," Breeze replied, "the entire point of life is to find ways to get others to do your work for you. Don't you know anything about basic economics?"

Ham raised an eyebrow. "Actually, I—"

"It was a rhetorical question, Ham," Breeze interrupted, rolling his eyes.

"Those are the best kind!" Ham replied.

"Philosophy later, Ham," Kelsier said. "Stay on task. What do you think of my suggestion?"

"It could work," Ham said, settling back. "But I can't see the Lord Ruler letting things go that far."

"It's our job to see that he doesn't have a choice," Kelsier said. "He's known to let his nobility squabble, probably to keep them off-balance. We fan those tensions, then we somehow force the Garrison to pull out. When the houses start fighting in earnest, the Lord Ruler won't be able to do anything to stop them—except, perhaps, send his palace guard into the streets, which is exactly what we want him to do."

"He could also send for a koloss army," Ham noted.

"True," Kelsier said. "But they're stationed a moderate distance away. That's a flaw we need to exploit. Koloss troops make wonderful grunts, but they have to be kept away from civilized cities. The very center of the Final Empire is exposed, yet the Lord Ruler is confident in his strength—and why shouldn't he be? He hasn't faced a serious threat in centuries. Most cities only need small policing forces."

"Twenty thousand men is hardly a 'small' number," Breeze said.

"It is on a national scale," Kelsier said, holding up a finger. "The Lord Ruler keeps most of his troops on the edges of his empire, where the threat of rebellion is strongest. That's why we're going to strike him here, in Luthadel itself— and that's why we're going to succeed."

"Assuming we can deal with that Garrison," Dockson noted.

Kelsier nodded, turning to write *House War* underneath *Great Houses* and *Chaos*. "All right, then. Let's talk about the Garrison. What are we going to do about it?"

"Well," Ham said speculatively, "historically, the best way to deal with a large force of soldiers is to have your own large force of soldiers. We're going to raise Yeden an army—why not let them attack the Garrison? Isn't that kind of the point of raising the army in the first place?"

"That won't work, Hammond," Breeze said. He regarded his empty cup of wine, then held it up toward the boy sitting beside Clubs, who immediately scurried over to refill it.

"If we wanted to defeat the Garrison," Breeze continued, "we'd need our own force of *at least* its same size. We'd probably want one much larger, since our men will be newly trained. We might be able to raise Yeden an army—we might even be able to get him one large enough to hold the city for a while. But, getting him one large enough to take on the Garrison inside its fortifications? We might as well give up now, if that's our plan."

The group fell silent. Vin squirmed in her chair, looking over each man in turn. Breeze's words had a profound effect. Ham opened his mouth to speak, then closed it again, sitting back to reconsider.

"All right," Kelsier finally said. "We'll get back to the Garrison in a moment. Let's look at our own army. How can we raise one of substantial size and hide it from the Lord Ruler?"

"Again, that will be difficult," Breeze said. "There is a very good reason why the Lord Ruler feels safe in the Central Dominance. There are constant patrols on the roadways and canals, and you can hardly spend a day traveling without running into a village or plantation. This isn't the sort of place where you can raise an army without attracting notice."

"The rebellion has those caves up to the north," Dockson said. "We might be able to hide some men there."

Yeden paled. "You *know* about the Arguois caverns?"

Kelsier rolled his eyes. "Even the Lord Ruler knows about them, Yeden. The rebels there just aren't dangerous enough to bother him yet."

"How many people do you have, Yeden?" Ham asked. "In Luthadel and around it, caves included? What do we have to start with?"

Yeden shrugged. "Maybe three hundred—including women and children."

"And how many do you think those caves could hide?" Ham asked.

Yeden shrugged again.

"The caves could support a larger group, for certain," Kelsier said. "Perhaps ten thousand. I've been there—the rebellion has been hiding people in them for years, and the Lord Ruler has never bothered to destroy them."

"I can imagine why," Ham said. "Cave fighting is nasty business, especially for the aggressor. The Lord Ruler likes to keep defeats to a minimum—he's nothing if not vain. Anyway, ten thousand. That's a decent number. It could hold the palace with ease—might even be able to hold the city, if it had the walls."

Dockson turned to Yeden. "When you asked for an army, what size were you thinking?"

"Ten thousand sounds like a good number, I suppose," Yeden said. "Actually . . . it's a bit larger than I was thinking."

Breeze tipped his cup slightly, swirling the wine. "I hate to sound contrary again—that's usually Hammond's job—but I do have to return to our earlier problem. Ten thousand men. That won't even *frighten* the Garrison. We're talking about twenty thousand well-armed, well-trained troops."

"He has a point, Kell," Dockson said. He had found a small book somewhere, and had begun taking notes on the meeting.

Kelsier frowned.

Ham nodded. "Any way you look at it, Kell, that Garrison is going to be a tough stone to break. Perhaps we should just focus on the nobility. Maybe we can cause enough chaos that even the Garrison won't be able to suppress it."

Kelsier shook his head. "Doubtful. The Garrison's primary duty is to maintain order in the city. If we can't deal with those troops, we'll never pull this off." He paused, then eyed Vin. "What do you think, Vin? Any suggestions?"

She froze. Camon had never asked her opinion. What did Kelsier want from her? She pulled back into her chair slightly as she realized that the other members of the crew had turned, looking at her.

"I . . ." Vin said slowly.

"Oh, don't intimidate the poor thing, Kelsier," Breeze said with a wave of his hand.

Vin nodded, but Kelsier didn't turn away from her. "No, really. Tell me what you're thinking, Vin. You've got a much larger enemy threatening you. What do you do?"

"Well," she said slowly. "You don't fight him, that's for certain. Even if you won somehow, you'd be so hurt and broken that you couldn't fight off anyone else."

"Makes sense," Dockson said. "But we might not have a choice. We have to get rid of that army somehow."

"And if it just left the city?" she asked. "That would work too? If I had to deal with someone big, I'd try and distract him first, get him to leave me alone."

Ham chuckled. "Good luck getting the Garrison to leave Luthadel. The Lord Ruler sends squads out on patrol sometimes, but the only time I know of the entire Garrison leaving was when that skaa rebellion broke out down in Courteline a half century ago."

Dockson shook his head. "Vin's idea is too good to dismiss that easily, I think. Really, we can't fight the Garrison—at least, not while they're entrenched. So, we need to get them to leave the city somehow."

"Yes," Breeze said, "but it would take a particular crisis to require involving the Garrison. If the problem weren't threatening enough, the Lord Ruler wouldn't send the entire Garrison. If it were too dangerous, he'd hunker down and send for his koloss."

"A rebellion in one of the nearby cities?" Ham suggested.

"That leaves us with the same problem as before," Kelsier said, shaking his head. "If we can't get the skaa here to rebel, we'll never get ones outside the city to do so."

"What about a feint of some sort, then?" Ham asked. "We're assuming that we'll be able to raise a sizable group of soldiers. If they pretend to attack someplace nearby, perhaps the Lord Ruler would send the Garrison out to help."

"I doubt he'd send them away to protect another city," Breeze said. "Not if it left him exposed in Luthadel."

The group fell silent, thinking again. Vin glanced around, then found Kelsier's eyes on her.

"What?" he asked.

She squirmed a bit, glancing down. "How far away are the Pits of Hathsin?" she finally asked.

The crew paused.

Finally, Breeze laughed. "Oh, now *that's* devious. The nobility don't know that the Pits produce atium, so the Lord Ruler couldn't make much of a fuss— not without revealing that there's something very special about those Pits. That means no koloss."

"They wouldn't arrive in time anyway," Ham said. "The Pits are only a couple of days away. If they were threatened, the Lord Ruler would have to respond quickly. The Garrison would be the only force in striking distance."

Kelsier smiled, eyes alight. "And it wouldn't take much of an army to threaten the Pits, either. A thousand men could do it. We send them to attack, then when the Garrison leaves, we march our second, larger force in and seize Luthadel itself. By the time the Garrison realized that they'd been duped, they wouldn't be able to get back in time to stop us from taking the city walls."

"Could we keep them, though?" Yeden asked apprehensively.

Ham nodded eagerly. "With ten thousand skaa, I could hold this city against the Garrison. The Lord Ruler would have to send for his koloss."

"By then, we'd have the atium," Kelsier said. "And the Great Houses won't be in any position to stop us—they'll be weakened and frail because of their internal fighting."

Dockson was scribbling furiously on his pad. "We'll need to use Yeden's caves, then. They're within striking distance of both our targets, and they're closer to Luthadel than the Pits are. If our army left from there, it could get here before the Garrison could return from the Pits."

Kelsier nodded.

Dockson continued to scribble. "I'll have to start stockpiling supplies in those caves, maybe make a trip out to check conditions there."

"And, how are we going to get the soldiers there?" Yeden asked. "That's a week outside the city—and skaa aren't allowed to travel on their own."

"I've already got someone who can help us there," Kelsier said, writing *Attack Pits of Hathsin* beneath *Luthadel Garrison* on his board. "I have a friend that can give us a front to run canal boats to the north."

"Assuming," Yeden said, "you can even make good on your first and primary promise. I paid you to gather me an army. Ten thousand men is a great number, but I've still to see an adequate explanation of how you're going to raise them. I've already told you the kinds of problems we've had trying to recruit in Luthadel."

"We won't need the general population to support us," Kelsier said. "Just a small percentage of them—there are nearly a million workers in and around Luthadel. This should actually be the easiest part of the plan, since we happen to be in the presence of one of the world's greatest Soothers. Breeze, I'm counting on you and your Allomancers to force us up a nice selection of recruits."

Breeze sipped his wine. "Kelsier, my good man. I wish you wouldn't use words like 'force' in reference to my talents. I simply encourage people."

"Well, can you encourage us up an army?" Dockson asked.

"How much time do I have?" Breeze asked.

"A year," Kelsier said. "We'll plan this to go off next fall. Assuming the Lord Ruler does gather his forces to attack Yeden once we take the city, we might as well make him do it in the winter."

"Ten thousand men," Breeze said with a smile, "gathered from a resistant population in less than a year. It would certainly be a challenge."

Kelsier chuckled. "From you, that's as good as a yes. Start in Luthadel, then move to the surrounding cities. We need people who are close enough to gather at the caves."

Breeze nodded.

"We'll also need weapons and supplies," Ham said. "And we'll need to train the men."

"I've already got a plan to get weapons," Kelsier said. "Can you find some men to do the training?"

Ham paused thoughtfully. "Probably. I know some skaa soldiers who fought in one of the Lord Ruler's Suppression Campaigns."

Yeden paled. "Traitors!"

Ham shrugged. "Most of them aren't proud of what they did," he said. "But most of them also like to eat. It's a hard world, Yeden."

"My people will never work with such men," Yeden said.

"They'll have to," Kelsier said sternly. "A large number of skaa rebellions fail because their men are poorly trained. We're going to give you an army of well-equipped, well-fed men—and I'll be damned if I'm going to let you get them slaughtered because they were never taught which end of the sword to hold."

Kelsier paused, then eyed Ham. "However, I do suggest that you find men who are bitter against the Final Empire for what it forced them to do. I don't trust men whose loyalty only goes as far as the boxings in their pockets."

Ham nodded, and Yeden quieted. Kelsier turned, writing *Ham: Training* and *Breeze: Recruitment* beneath *Troops* on the board.

"I'm interested in your plan to get weapons," Breeze said. "How, exactly, do you intend to arm ten thousand men without making the Lord Ruler suspicious? He keeps a *very* careful eye on the armament flows."

"We could make the weapons," Clubs said. "I have enough extra wood that we could churn out a war staff or two every day. Could probably get you some arrows too."

"I appreciate the offer, Clubs," Kelsier said. "And I think that's a good idea. However, we're going to need more than staves. We'll need swords, shields, and armor—and we need them quickly enough to begin training."

"How, then, are you going to do it?" Breeze asked.

"The Great Houses can get weapons," Kelsier said. "They don't have any problems arming their personal retinues."

"You want us to steal from them?"

Kelsier shook his head. "No, for once we're going to do things somewhat legally—we're going to buy our weapons. Or, rather, we're going to have a sympathetic nobleman buy them for us."

Clubs laughed bluntly. "A nobleman sympathetic to the skaa? It will never happen."

"Well, 'never' happened a short time ago, then," Kelsier said lightly. "Because I've already found someone to help us."

The room fell silent save for the crackling of the fireplace. Vin squirmed slightly in her chair, glancing at the others. They seemed shocked.

"Who?" Ham asked.

"His name is Lord Renoux," Kelsier said. "He arrived in the area a few days back. He's staying in Fellise—he doesn't quite have enough influence to establish himself in Luthadel. Besides, I think it's prudent to keep Renoux's activities a bit removed from the Lord Ruler."

Vin cocked her head. Fellise was a small, suburb-style city an hour outside of Luthadel; she and Reen had worked there before moving into the capital city. How had Kelsier recruited this Lord Renoux? Had he bribed the man, or was it some sort of scam?

"I know of Renoux," Breeze said slowly. "He's a Western lord; he has a great deal of power in the Farmost Dominance."

Kelsier nodded. "Lord Renoux recently decided to try and elevate his family to high noble status. His official story is that he came south in order to expand his mercantile efforts. He hopes that by shipping fine Southern weaponry to the North, he can earn enough money—and make enough connections—to build himself a keep in Luthadel by the end of the decade."

The room was quiet.

"But," Ham said slowly, "those weapons will be coming to us instead."

Kelsier nodded. "We'll have to fake the shipping records, just in case."

"That's . . . quite an ambitious front, Kell," Ham said. "A lord's family working on our side."

"But," Breeze said, looking confused. "Kelsier, you *hate* noblemen."

"This one's different," Kelsier said with a sly smile.

The crew studied Kelsier. They didn't like working with a nobleman; Vin could tell that much easily. It probably didn't help that Renoux was so powerful.

Suddenly, Breeze laughed. He leaned back in his chair, downing the last of his wine. "You blessed madman! You killed him, didn't you? Renoux—you killed him and replaced him with an impostor."

Kelsier's smile broadened.

Yeden cursed, but Ham simply smiled. "Ah. Now *that* makes sense. Or, at least, it makes sense if you're Kelsier the Foolhardy."

"Renoux is going to take up permanent residence in Fellise," Kelsier said. "He'll be our front if we need to do anything official. I'll use him to purchase armaments and supplies, for instance."

Breeze nodded thoughtfully. "Efficient."

"Efficient?" Yeden asked. "You've killed a nobleman! A very important one."

"You're planning to overthrow the entire empire, Yeden," Kelsier noted. "Renoux isn't going to be the last aristocratic casualty in this little endeavor."

"Yes, but impersonating him?" Yeden asked. "That sounds a little risky to me."

"You hired us because you wanted extraordinary results, my dear man," Breeze said, sipping his wine. "In our line of work, extraordinary results usually require extraordinary risks."

"We minimize them as best we can, Yeden," Kelsier said. "My actor is *very* good. However, these are the sorts of things we're going to be doing in this job."

"And if I order you to stop a few of them?" Yeden asked.

"You can shut down the job at any time," Dockson said, not looking up from his ledgers. "But as long as it is in motion, Kelsier has final say on plans, objectives, and procedures. That is how we work; you knew that when you hired us."

Yeden shook his head ruefully.

"Well?" Kelsier asked. "Do we continue or not? The call is yours, Yeden."

"Feel free to call an end to it, friend," Breeze said with a helpful voice. "Don't be afraid of offending us. I, for one, look favorably upon free money."

Vin saw Yeden pale slightly. In Vin's estimation, he was fortunate that Kelsier hadn't simply taken his money and stabbed him in the chest. But, she was becoming increasingly convinced that wasn't the way things worked around here.

"This is insane," Yeden said.

"Trying to overthrow the Lord Ruler?" Breeze asked. "Why, yes, as a matter of fact, it is."

"All right," Yeden said, sighing. "We continue."

"Good," Kelsier said, writing *Kelsier: Equipment* under *Troops*. "The Renoux front will also give us an 'in' with Luthadel high society. This will be a very important advantage—we'll need to keep careful track of Great House politics if we're going to start a war."

"This house war might not be as easy to pull off as you think, Kelsier," Breeze warned. "The current lot of high noblemen is a careful, discriminating group."

Kelsier smiled. "Then it's good that you're here to help, Breeze. You're an expert at making people do what you want—together, you and I will plan how to make the high nobility turn on each other. Major house wars seem to happen every couple of centuries or so. The current group's competence will only make them more dangerous, so getting them riled up shouldn't be *that* hard. In fact, I've already started the process. . . ."

Breeze raised an eyebrow, then glanced at Ham. The Thug grumbled a bit, pulling out a golden ten-boxing coin and flipping it across the room to the self-satisfied Breeze.

"What was that about?" Dockson asked.

"We had a bet," Breeze said, "regarding whether or not Kelsier was involved in last night's disturbance."

"Disturbance?" Yeden asked. "What disturbance?"

"Someone attacked House Venture," Ham said. "The rumors claim that three full Mistborn were sent to assassinate Straff Venture himself."

Kelsier snorted. "Three? Straff certainly has an elevated opinion of himself. I didn't go anywhere near His Lordship. I was there for the atium—and to make certain that I was seen."

"Venture isn't sure who to blame," Breeze said. "But because Mistborn were involved, everyone assumes that it was one of the Great Houses."

"That was the idea," Kelsier said happily. "The high nobility take Mistborn attacks very seriously—they have an unspoken agreement that they won't use Mistborn to assassinate each other. A few more strikes like this, and I'll have them snapping at each other like frightened animals."

He turned, adding *Breeze: Planning* and *Kelsier: General Mayhem* beneath *Great Houses* on the board.

"Anyway," Kelsier continued, "we'll need to keep an eye on local politics to find out which Houses are making alliances. That means sending a spy to some of their functions."

"Is that really necessary?" Yeden asked uncomfortably.

Ham nodded. "It's standard procedure for *any* Luthadel job, actually. If there is information to be had, it will pass through the lips of the court's powerful. It always pays to keep an open set of ears moving through their circles."

"Well, that should be easy," Breeze said. "We just bring up your impostor and send him into the parties."

Kelsier shook his head. "Unfortunately, Lord Renoux himself won't be able to come to Luthadel."

Yeden frowned. "Why not? Won't your impostor hold up to close scrutiny?"

"Oh, he looks just like Lord Renoux," Kelsier said. "*Exactly* like Lord Renoux, actually. We just can't let him get near an Inquisitor. . . ."

"Ah," Breeze said, exchanging a glance with Ham. "One of *those*. Well, then."

"What?" Yeden asked. "What does he mean?"

"You don't want to know," Breeze said.

"I don't?"

Breeze shook his head. "You know how unsettled you just were when Kelsier said he'd replaced Lord Renoux with an impostor? Well, this is about a dozen times worse. Trust me—the less you know, the more comfortable you'll be."

Yeden looked toward Kelsier, who was smiling broadly. Yeden paled, then leaned back in his chair. "I think you're probably right."

Vin frowned, eying the others in the room. They seemed to know what Kelsier was talking about. She'd have to study this Lord Renoux sometime.

"Anyway," Kelsier said, "we have to send someone to the social functions. Dox, therefore, will be playing Renoux's nephew and heir, a scion of the family who has recently gained favor with Lord Renoux."

"Wait a moment, Kell," Dockson said. "You didn't tell me about this."

Kelsier shrugged. "We're going to need someone to be our dupe with the nobility. I assumed that you'd fit the role."

"Can't be me," Dockson said. "I got marked during the Eiser job just a couple months back."

Kelsier frowned.

"What?" Yeden asked. "Do I want to know what they're talking about this time?"

"He means that the Ministry is watching for him," Breeze said. "He pretended to be a nobleman, and they found out."

Dockson nodded. "The Lord Ruler himself saw me on one occasion, and he's got a flawless memory. Even if I managed to avoid him, someone's bound to recognize me eventually."

"So . . ." Yeden said.

"So," Kelsier said, "we'll need someone else to play Lord Renoux's heir."

"Don't look at me," Yeden said apprehensively.

"Trust me," Kelsier said flatly, "nobody was. Clubs is out too—he's far too prominent a local skaa craftsman."

"I'm out as well," Breeze said. "I already have several aliases among the nobility. I suppose I could use one of them, but I couldn't go to any major balls or parties—it would be rather embarrassing if I met someone who knew me by a different alias."

Kelsier frowned thoughtfully.

"I could do it," Ham said. "But you know I'm no good at acting."

"What about my nephew?" Clubs said, nodding to the young man at his side.

Kelsier studied the boy. "What's your name, son?"

"Lestibournes."

Kelsier raised an eyebrow. "That's a mouthful. You don't have a nickname?"

"Not of the yetting yet."

"We'll have to work on that," Kelsier said. "Do you always speak in that Eastern street slang?"

The boy shrugged, obviously nervous at being such a center of attention. "Wasing the place when I was young."

Kelsier glanced at Dockson, who shook his head. "I don't think it's a good idea, Kell."

"Agreed." Kelsier turned to Vin, then smiled. "I guess that leaves you. How good are you at imitating a noblewoman?"

Vin paled slightly. "My brother gave me a few lessons. But, I've never actually tried to. . . ."

"You'll do fine," Kelsier said, writing *Vin: Infiltration* underneath *Great Houses*. "All right. Yeden, you should probably begin planning how you're to keep control of the empire once this is all through."

Yeden nodded. Vin felt a little sorry for the man, seeing how much the planning—the sheer outrageousness of it all—seemed to be overwhelming him. Still, it was hard to feel sympathy for him, considering what Kelsier had just said regarding *her* part in all this.

Playing a noblewoman? she thought. *Surely there's someone else who could do a better job. . . .*

Breeze's attention was still on Yeden and his obvious discomfort. "Don't look so solemn, my dear fellow," Breeze said. "Why, you'll probably never actually have to *rule* the city. Chances are, we'll all get caught and executed long before that happens."

Yeden smiled wanly. "And if we don't? What's to keep you all from just knifing me and taking the empire for yourselves?"

Breeze rolled his eyes. "We're thieves, my dear man, not politicians. A nation is far too unwieldy a commodity to be worth our time. Once we have our atium, we'll be happy."

"Not to mention rich," Ham added.

"The two words are synonyms, Hammond," Breeze said.

"Besides," Kelsier said to Yeden. "We won't be giving you the entire empire—hopefully, it will shatter once Luthadel destabilizes. You'll have this city, and probably a good piece of the Central Dominance—assuming you can bribe the local armies into supporting you."

"And . . . the Lord Ruler?" Yeden asked.

Kelsier smiled. "I'm still planning to deal with him personally—I just have to figure out how to make the Eleventh Metal work."

"And if you don't?"

"Well," Kelsier said, writing *Yeden: Preparation and Rule* beneath *Skaa Rebellion* on the board, "we'll try and find a way to trick him out of the city. Perhaps we can get him to go with his army to the Pits and secure things there."

"Then what?" Yeden asked.

"You find some way to deal with him," Kelsier said. "You didn't hire us to kill the Lord Ruler, Yeden—that's just a possible perk I intend to throw in if I can."

"I wouldn't worry *too* much, Yeden," Ham added. "He won't be able to do much without funds or armies. He's a powerful Allomancer, but by no means omnipotent."

Breeze smiled. "Though, if you think about it, hostile, dethroned pseudo-deities probably make disagreeable neighbors. You'll have to figure out something to do with him."

Yeden didn't appear to like that idea much, but he didn't continue the argument.

Kelsier turned. "That should be it, then."

"Uh," Ham said, "what about the Ministry? Shouldn't we at least find a way to keep an eye on those Inquisitors?"

Kelsier smiled. "We'll let my brother deal with them."

"Like hell you will," a new voice said from the back of the room.

Vin jumped to her feet, spinning and glancing toward the room's shadowed doorway. A man stood there. Tall and broad-shouldered, he had a statuesque rigidity. He wore modest clothing—a simple shirt and trousers with a loose skaa jacket. His arms were folded in dissatisfaction, and he had a hard, square face that looked a bit familiar.

Vin glanced back at Kelsier. The similarity was obvious.

"Marsh?" Yeden said, standing. "Marsh, it *is* you! He promised you'd be joining the job, but I . . . well . . . welcome back!"

Marsh's face remained impassive. "I'm not certain if I'm 'back' or not, Yeden. If you all don't mind, I'd like to speak privately with my little brother."

Kelsier didn't seem intimidated by Marsh's harsh tone. He nodded to the group. "We're done for the evening, folks."

The others rose slowly, giving Marsh a wide berth as they left. Vin followed them, pulling the door shut and walking down the stairs to give the appearance of retiring to her room.

Less than three minutes later she was back at the door, listening carefully to the conversation going on inside.

Rashek is a tall man—of course, most of these Terrismen are tall. He is young to receive so much respect from the other packmen. He has charisma, and the women of court would probably describe him as handsome, in a rugged sort of way.

Yet, it amazes me that anyone would give heed to a man who speaks such hatred. He has never seen Khlennium, yet he curses the city. He does not know me, yet I can already see the anger and hostility in his eyes.

7

THREE YEARS HADN'T CHANGED MARSH'S appearance much. He was still the stern, commanding person Kelsier had known since childhood. There was still that glint of disappointment in his eyes, and he spoke with the same air of disapproval.

Yet, if Dockson were to be believed, Marsh's attitudes had changed much since that day three years before. Kelsier still found it hard to believe that his brother had given up leadership of the skaa rebellion. He had always been so passionate about his work.

Apparently, that passion had dimmed. Marsh walked forward, regarding the charcoal writing board with a critical eye. His clothing was stained slightly by dark ash, though his face was relatively clean, for a skaa. He stood for a moment, looking over Kelsier's notes. Finally, Marsh turned and tossed a sheet of paper onto the chair beside Kelsier.

"What is this?" Kelsier asked, picking it up.

"The names of the eleven men you slaughtered last night," Marsh said. "I thought you might at least want to know."

Kelsier tossed the paper into the crackling hearth. "They served the Final Empire."

"They were *men*, Kelsier," Marsh snapped. "They had lives, families. Several of them were skaa."

"Traitors."

"People," Marsh said. "People who were just trying to do the best with what life gave them."

"Well, I'm just doing the same thing," Kelsier said. "And, fortunately, life gave *me* the ability to push men like them off the tops of buildings. If they want to stand against me like noblemen, then they can die like noblemen."

Marsh's expression darkened. "How can you be so flippant about something like this?"

"Because, Marsh," Kelsier said, "humor is the only thing I've got left. Humor and determination."

Marsh snorted quietly.

"You should be happy," Kelsier said. "After decades of listening to your lectures, I've finally decided to do something worthwhile with my talents. Now that you're here to help, I'm sure—"

"I'm not here to help," Marsh interrupted.

"Then why did you come?"

"To ask you a question." Marsh stepped forward, stopping right in front of Kelsier. They were about the same height, but Marsh's stern personality always made him seem to loom taller.

"How dare you do this?" Marsh asked quietly. "I dedicated my life to overthrowing the Final Empire. While you and your thieving friends partied, I hid runaways. While you planned petty burglaries, I organized raids. While you lived in luxury, I watched brave people die of starvation."

Marsh reached up, stabbing a finger at Kelsier's chest. "*How dare you?* How dare you try and hijack the rebellion for one of your little 'jobs'? How dare you use this dream as a way of enriching yourself?"

Kelsier pushed Marsh's finger away. "That's not what this is about."

"Oh?" Marsh asked, tapping the word *atium* on the board. "Why the games, Kelsier? Why lead Yeden along, pretending to accept him as your 'employer'? Why act like you care about the skaa? We both know what you're really after."

Kelsier clenched his jaw, a bit of his humor melting away. *He always could do that to me.* "You don't know me anymore, Marsh," Kelsier said quietly. "This isn't about money—I once had more wealth than any man could spend. This job is about something different."

Marsh stood close, studying Kelsier's eyes, as if searching for truth in them. "You always were a good liar," he finally said.

Kelsier rolled his eyes. "Fine, think what you want. But don't preach to me. Overthrowing the empire might have been your dream once—but now you've become a good little skaa, staying in your shop and fawning over noblemen when they visit."

"I've faced reality," Marsh said. "Something you've never been good at. Even if you're serious about this plan, you'll fail. Everything the rebellion has done—the raids, the thefts, the deaths—has accomplished nothing. Our best efforts were never even a mild annoyance for the Lord Ruler."

"Ah," Kelsier said, "but being an annoyance is something that *I* am very good at. In fact, I'm far more than just a 'mild' annoyance—people tell me I can be downright frustrating. Might as well use this talent for the cause of good, eh?"

Marsh sighed, turning away. "This isn't about a 'cause,' Kelsier. It's about revenge. It's about you, just like everything always is. I'll believe that you aren't after the money—I'll even believe that you intend to deliver Yeden this army he's apparently paying you for. But I won't believe that you care."

"That's where you are wrong, Marsh," Kelsier said quietly. "That's where you've always been wrong about me."

Marsh frowned. "Perhaps. How did this start, anyway? Did Yeden come to you, or did you go to him?"

"Does it matter?" Kelsier asked. "Look, Marsh. I need someone to infiltrate the Ministry. This plan won't go anywhere if we don't discover a way to keep an eye on those Inquisitors."

Marsh turned. "You actually expect me to help you?"

Kelsier nodded. "That's why you came here, no matter what you say. You once told me that you thought I could do great things if I ever applied myself to a worthy goal. Well, that's what I'm doing now—and you're going to help."

"It's not that easy anymore, Kell," Marsh said with a shake of his head. "Some people are different now. Others are . . . gone."

Kelsier let the room grow quiet. Even the hearth's fire was starting to die out. "I miss her too."

"I'm sure that you do—but I have to be honest with you, Kell. Despite what she did . . . sometimes I wish that you hadn't been the one to survive the Pits."

"I wish the same thing every day."

Marsh turned, studying Kelsier with his cold, discerning eyes. The eyes of a Seeker. Whatever he saw reflected inside of Kelsier must have finally met with his approval.

"I'm leaving," Marsh said. "But, for some reason you actually seem sincere this time. I'll come back and listen to whatever insane plan you've concocted. Then . . . well, we'll see."

Kelsier smiled. Beneath it all, Marsh was a good man—a better one than Kelsier had ever been. As Marsh turned toward the door, Kelsier caught a flicker of shadowed movement from beneath the doorway. He immediately burned iron, and the translucent blue lines shot out from his body, connecting him to nearby sources of metal. Marsh, of course, had none on his person—not even any coins. Traveling through skaa sectors of town could be very dangerous for a man who looked even marginally prosperous.

Someone else, however, hadn't yet learned not to carry metal on her person. The blue lines were thin and weak—they didn't do well penetrating wood—but they were just strong enough to let Kelsier locate the belt latch of a person out in the hallway, moving quickly away from the door on silent feet.

Kelsier smiled to himself. The girl was remarkably skilled. Her time on the streets, however, had also left her with remarkable scars. Hopefully, he would be able to encourage the skills while helping heal the scars.

"I'll return tomorrow," Marsh said as he reached the door.

"Just don't come by too early," Kelsier said with a wink. "I've got some things to do tonight."

Vin waited quietly in her darkened room, listening to footsteps clomp down the stairs to the ground floor. She crouched beside her door, trying to determine if both sets had continued down the steps or not. The hallway fell silent, and eventually she breathed a quiet sigh of relief.

A knock sounded on the door just inches from her head.

Her start of surprise nearly knocked her to the ground. *He's good!* she thought.

She quickly ruffled her hair and rubbed her eyes, trying to make it appear as if she had been sleeping. She untucked her shirt, and waited until the knock came again before pulling open the door.

Kelsier lounged against the doorframe, backlit by the hallway's single lantern. The tall man raised an eyebrow at her disheveled state.

"Yes?" Vin asked, trying to sound drowsy.

"So, what do you think of Marsh?"

"I don't know," Vin said, "I didn't see much of him before he kicked us out."

Kelsier smiled. "You're not going to admit that I caught you, are you?"

Vin almost smiled back. Reen's training came to her rescue. *The man who wants you to trust him is the one you must fear the most.* Her brother's voice almost seemed to whisper in her head. It had grown stronger since she'd met Kelsier, as if her instincts were on edge.

Kelsier studied her for a moment, then stepped back from the doorframe. "Tuck in that shirt and follow me."

Vin frowned. "Where are we going?"

"To begin your training."

"Now?" Vin asked, glancing at the dark shutters to her room.

"Of course," Kelsier said. "It's a perfect night for a stroll."

Vin straightened her clothing, joining him in the hallway. If he actually planned to begin teaching her, then she wasn't going to complain, no matter what the hour. They walked down the steps to the first floor. The workroom was dark, furniture projects lying half finished in the shadows. The kitchen, however, was bright with light.

"Just a minute," Kelsier said, walking toward the kitchen.

Vin paused just inside the shadows of the workroom, letting Kelsier enter the kitchen without her. She could just barely see inside. Dockson, Breeze, and Ham sat with Clubs and his apprentices around a wide table. Wine and ale were present, though in small amounts, and the men were munching on a simple evening snack of puffed barley cakes and battered vegetables.

Laughter trickled out into the workroom. Not raucous laughter, such as had often sounded from Camon's table. This was something softer—something indicative of genuine mirth, of good-natured enjoyment.

Vin wasn't certain what kept her out of the room. She hesitated—as if the light and the humor were a barrier—and she instead remained in the quiet, solemn workroom. She watched from the darkness, however, and wasn't completely able to suppress her longing.

Kelsier returned a moment later, carrying his pack and a small cloth bundle. Vin regarded the bundle with curiosity, and he handed it to her with a smile. "A present."

The cloth was slick and soft in Vin's fingers, and she quickly realized what it was. She let the gray material unroll in her fingers, revealing a Mistborn cloak. Like the garment Kelsier had worn the night before, it was tailored completely from separate, ribbonlike strips of cloth.

"You look surprised," Kelsier noted.

"I . . . assumed that I'd have to earn this somehow."

"What's there to earn?" Kelsier said, pulling out his own cloak. "This is who you are, Vin."

She paused, then threw the cloak over her shoulders and tied it on. It felt . . . different. Thick and heavy on her shoulders, but light and unconstraining around her arms and legs. The ribbons were sewn together at the top, allowing her to pull it tight by the mantle if she wished. She felt . . . enveloped. Protected.

"How does it feel?" Kelsier asked.

"Good," Vin said simply.

Kelsier nodded, pulling out several glass vials. He handed two to her. "Drink one; keep the other in case you need it. I'll show you how to mix new vials later."

Vin nodded, downing the first vial and tucking the second into her belt.

"I'm having some new clothing tailored for you," Kelsier said. "You'll want to get into the habit of wearing things that don't have any metal on them: belts with no buckles, shoes that slip on and off, trousers without clasps. Perhaps later, if you're feeling daring, we'll get you some women's clothing."

Vin flushed slightly.

Kelsier laughed. "I'm just teasing you. However, you're entering a new world now—you may find that there are situations where it will be to your advantage to look less like a crew thief and more like a young lady."

Vin nodded, following Kelsier as he walked to the shop's front door. He pushed the portal open, revealing a wall of darkly shifting mists. He stepped out into them. Taking a deep breath, Vin followed.

Kelsier shut the door behind them. The cobbled street felt muffled to Vin, the shifting mists making everything just a bit damp. She couldn't see far in either direction, and the street ends seemed to fade into nothingness, paths into eternity. Above, there was no sky, just swirling currents of gray upon gray.

"All right, let's begin," Kelsier said. His voice felt loud in the quiet, empty street. There was a confidence to his tone, something that—confronted with the mists all around—Vin certainly didn't feel.

"Your first lesson," Kelsier said, strolling down the street, Vin trailing along beside him, "isn't about Allomancy, but attitude." He swept his hand forward. "This, Vin. This is *ours*. The night, the mists—they belong to us. Skaa avoid the mists as if they were death. Thieves and soldiers go out at night, but they fear it nonetheless. Noblemen feign nonchalance, but the mist makes them uncomfortable."

He turned, regarding her. "The mists are your friend, Vin. They hide you, they protect you . . . and they give you power. Ministry doctrine—something rarely shared with skaa—claims that the Mistborn are descendants of the only men who remained true to the Lord Ruler during the days before his Ascension. Other legends whisper that we are something beyond even the Lord Ruler's power, something that was born on that day when the mists first came upon the land."

Vin nodded slightly. It seemed odd to hear Kelsier speak so openly. Buildings filled with sleeping skaa loomed on either side of the street. And yet, the dark shutters and quiet air made Vin feel as if she and Kelsier were alone. Alone in the most densely populated, overcrowded city in all of the Final Empire.

Kelsier continued to walk, the spring in his step incongruent with the dark gloom.

"Shouldn't we be worried about soldiers?" Vin asked quietly. Her crews always had to be careful of nighttime Garrison patrols.

Kelsier shook his head. "Even if we were careless enough to be spotted, no imperial patrol would dare bother Mistborn. They'd see our cloaks and pretend not to see us. Remember, nearly all Mistborn are members of the Great Houses—and the rest are from lesser Luthadel houses. Either way, they're very important individuals."

Vin frowned. "So, the guards just ignore the Mistborn?"

Kelsier shrugged. "It's bad etiquette to acknowledge that the skulking rooftop figure you see is actually a very distinguished and proper high lord—or even high lady. Mistborn are so rare that houses can't afford to apply gender prejudices to them.

"Anyway, most Mistborn live two lives—the life of the courtgoing aristocrat, and the life of the sneaking, spying Allomancer. Mistborn identities are closely guarded house secrets—rumors regarding who is Mistborn are always a focus of high noble gossip."

Kelsier turned down another street, Vin following, still a bit nervous. She wasn't certain where he was taking her; it was easy to get lost in the night. Perhaps he didn't even have a destination, and was just accustoming her to the mists.

"All right," Kelsier said, "let's get you used to the basic metals. Can you feel your metal reserves?"

Vin paused. If she focused, she could distinguish eight sources of power within her—each one far larger, even, than her two had been on the day when Kelsier had tested her. She had been reticent to use her Luck much since then. She was coming to realize that she had been using a weapon she'd never really understood—a weapon that had accidentally drawn the attention of a Steel Inquisitor.

"Begin burning them, one at a time," Kelsier said.

"Burning?"

"That's what we call it when you activate an Allomantic ability," Kelsier said. "You 'burn' the metal associated with that power. You'll see what I mean. Start with the metals you don't know about yet—we'll work on Soothing and Raging emotions some other time."

Vin nodded, pausing in the middle of the street. Tentatively, she reached out to one of the new sources of power. One of them was slightly familiar to her. Had she used it before without realizing it? What would it do?

Only one way to find out . . . Uncertain what, exactly, she was supposed to do, Vin gripped the source of power and tried to use it.

Immediately, she felt a flare of heat from within her chest. It wasn't discomforting, but it was obvious and distinct. Along with the warmth came something else—a feeling of rejuvenation, and of power. She felt . . . more *solid*, somehow.

"What happened?" Kelsier asked.

"I feel different," Vin said. She held up her hand, and it seemed as if the limb reacted just a bit too quickly. The muscles were eager. "My body is strange. I don't feel tired anymore, and I feel alert."

"Ah," Kelsier said. "That's pewter. It enhances your physical abilities, making you stronger, more able to resist fatigue and pain. You'll react more quickly when you're burning it, and your body will be tougher."

Vin flexed experimentally. Her muscles didn't seem any bigger, yet she could feel their strength. It wasn't just in her muscles, however—it was everything about her. Her bones, her flesh, her skin. She reached out to her reserve, and could feel it shrinking.

"I'm running out," she said.

Kelsier nodded. "Pewter burns relatively quickly. The vial I gave you was measured to contain about ten minutes' worth of continuous burning—though it will go faster if you flare often and slower if you are careful about when you use it."

"Flare?"

"You can burn your metals a little more powerfully if you try," Kelsier said. "It makes them run out much faster, and it's difficult to maintain, but it can give you an extra boost."

Vin frowned, trying to do as he said. With a push of effort, she was able to stoke the flames within her chest, flaring the pewter.

It was like the inhaled breath before a daring leap. A sudden rush of strength and power. Her body grew tense with anticipation, and for just a moment she felt invincible. Then it passed, her body relaxing slowly.

Interesting, she thought, noting how quickly her pewter had burned during that brief moment.

"Now, there's something you need to know about Allomantic metals," Kelsier said as they strolled forward in the mists. "The more pure they are, the more effective they are. The vials we prepare contain absolutely pure metals, prepared and sold specifically for Allomancers.

"Alloys—like pewter—are even trickier, since the metal percentages have to be mixed just right, if you want maximum power. In fact, if you aren't careful when you buy your metals, you could end up with the wrong alloy entirely."

Vin frowned. "You mean, someone might scam me?"

"Not intentionally," Kelsier said. "The thing is, most of the terms that people use—words like 'brass,' 'pewter,' and 'bronze'—are really quite vague, when you get down to it. Pewter, for instance, is generally accepted as an alloy of tin mixed with lead, with perhaps some copper or silver, depending on the use and the circumstances. *Allomancer's pewter*, however, is an alloy of ninety-one percent tin, nine percent lead. If you want maximum strength from your metal, you have to use those percentages."

"And . . . if you burn the wrong percentage?" Vin asked.

"If the mixture is only off by a bit, you'll still get some power out of it," Kelsier said. "However, if it's too far off, burning it will make you sick."

Vin nodded slowly. "I . . . think I've burned this metal before. Once in a while, in very small amounts."

"Trace metals," Kelsier said. "From drinking water contaminated by metals, or by eating with pewter utensils."

Vin nodded. Some of the mugs in Camon's lair had been pewter.

"All right," Kelsier said. "Extinguish the pewter and let's move on to another metal."

Vin did as asked. The withdrawal of power left her feeling weak, tired, and exposed.

"Now," Kelsier said, "you should be able to notice a kind of pairing between your reserves of metal."

"Like the two emotion metals," Vin said.

"Exactly. Find the metal linked to pewter."

"I see it," Vin said.

"There are two metals for every power," Kelsier said. "One Pushes, one Pulls—the second is usually an alloy of the first. For emotions—the external mental powers—you Pull with zinc and Push with brass. You just used pewter to Push your body. That's one of the internal physical powers."

"Like Ham," Vin said. "He burns pewter."

Kelsier nodded. "Mistings who can burn pewter are called Thugs. A crude term, I suppose—but they tend to be rather crude people. Our dear Hammond is something of an exception to that rule."

"So, what does the other internal physical metal do?"

"Try it and see."

Vin did so eagerly, and the world suddenly became brighter around her. Or . . . well, that wasn't quite right. She could see better, and she could see farther, but the mists were still there. They were just . . . more translucent. The ambient light around her seemed brighter, somehow.

There were other changes. She could feel her clothing. She realized that she had always been able to feel it, but she usually ignored it. Now, however, it felt closer. She could sense the textures, and was acutely aware of the places where the cloth was tight on her.

She was hungry. That, too, she had been ignoring—yet now her hunger seemed far more pressing. Her skin felt wetter, and she could smell the crisp air mixed with scents of dirt, soot, and refuse.

"Tin enhances your senses," Kelsier said, his voice suddenly seeming quite loud. "And it's one of the slowest-burning metals—the tin in that vial is enough to keep you going for hours. Most Mistborn leave their tin on whenever they're out in the mists—I've had mine on since we left the shop."

Vin nodded. The wealth of sensations was nearly overwhelming. She could hear creaks and scuffles in the darkness, and they made her want to jump in alarm, certain that someone was sneaking up behind her.

This is going to take some getting used to.

"Leave it burning," Kelsier said, waving for her to walk beside him as he continued down the street. "You'll want to accustom yourself to the enhanced senses. Just don't flare it all the time. Not only would you run out of it very quickly, but perpetually flaring metals does . . . strange things to people."

"Strange?" Vin asked.

"Metals—especially tin and pewter—stretch your body. Flaring the metals only pushes this stretching further. Stretch it too far for too long, and things start to break."

Vin nodded uncomfortably. Kelsier fell quiet, and they continued to walk, letting Vin explore her new sensations and the detailed world that tin revealed. Before, her vision had been restricted to a tiny pocket within the night. Now, however, she saw an entire city enveloped by a blanket of shifting, swirling mist. She could make out keeps like small, dark mountains in the distance, and could see specks of light from windows, like pin-pricked holes in the night. And above . . . she saw lights in the sky.

She stopped, gazing up with wonder. They were faint, blurred to even her tin-enhanced eyes, but she could just barely make them out. Hundreds of them. Thousands of them. So small, like the dying embers of candles recently extinguished.

"Stars," Kelsier said, strolling up beside her. "You can't see them very often, even with tin. It must be a particularly clear night. People used to be able to look up and see them every night—that was before the mists came, before the Ashmounts erupted ash and smoke into the sky."

Vin glanced at him. "How do you know?"

Kelsier smiled. "The Lord Ruler has tried very hard to crush memories of those days, but still some remain." He turned, not really having answered her question, and continued to walk. Vin joined him. Suddenly, with tin, the mists around her didn't seem so ominous. She was beginning to see how Kelsier could walk about at night with such confidence.

"All right," Kelsier eventually said. "Let's try another metal."

Vin nodded, leaving her tin on but picking another metal to burn as well. When she did so, a very strange thing happened—a multitude of faint blue lines sprung from her chest, streaking out into the spinning mists. She froze, gasping slightly and looking down at her chest. Most of the lines were thin, like translucent pieces of twine, though a couple were as thick as yarn.

Kelsier chuckled. "Leave that metal and its partner alone for the moment. They're a bit more complicated than the others."

"What . . . ?" Vin asked, tracing the lines of blue light with her eyes. They pointed at random objects. Doors, windows—a couple even pointed at Kelsier.

"We'll get to it," he promised. "Extinguish that one and try one of the last two."

Vin extinguished the strange metal and ignored its companion, picking one of the last metals. Immediately, she felt a strange vibration. Vin paused. The pulses didn't make a sound that she could hear, yet she could feel them washing across her. They seemed to be coming from Kelsier. She looked at him, frowning.

"That's probably bronze," Kelsier said. "The internal mental Pulling metal. It lets you sense when someone is using Allomancy nearby. Seekers, like my brother, use it. Generally it's not that useful—unless you happen to be a Steel Inquisitor searching for skaa Mistings."

Vin paled. "Inquisitors can use Allomancy?"

Kelsier nodded. "They're all Seekers—I'm not sure if that's because Seekers are chosen to become Inquisitors, or if the process of becoming an Inquisitor grants the power. Either way, since their main duties are to find half-breed children and noblemen who use Allomancy improperly, it's a useful skill for them to have. Unfortunately, 'useful' for them means 'rather annoying' for us."

Vin began to nod, then froze. The pulsing had stopped.

"What happened?" she asked.

"I started burning copper," Kelsier said, "the companion to bronze. When you burn copper, it hides your use of powers from other Allomancers. You can try burning it now, if you want, though you won't sense much."

Vin did so. The only change was a feeling of slight vibration within her.

"Copper is a vital metal to learn," Kelsier said. "It will hide you from Inquisitors. We probably don't have anything to worry about tonight—the Inquisitors would assume us to be regular noble Mistborn, out for training. However, if you're ever in a skaa guise and need to burn metals, make sure you turn on your copper first."

Vin nodded appreciatively.

"In fact," Kelsier said, "many Mistborn keep their copper on all the time. It burns slowly, and it makes you invisible to other Allomancers. It hides you from bronze, and it also prevents others from manipulating your emotions."

Vin perked up.

"I thought that might interest you," Kelsier said. "Anyone burning copper is immune to emotional Allomancy. In addition, copper's influence occurs in a bubble around you. This cloud—called a coppercloud—hides anyone inside of it from the senses of a Seeker, though it won't make them immune to emotional Allomancy, like it will you."

"Clubs," Vin said. "That's what a Smoker does."

Kelsier nodded. "If one of our people is noticed by a Seeker, they can run back to the lair and disappear. They can also practice their abilities without fear of being discovered. Allomantic pulses coming from a shop in a skaa sector of town would be a quick giveaway to a passing Inquisitor."

"But, you can burn copper," Vin said. "Why were you so worried about finding a Smoker for the crew?"

"I can burn copper, true," Kelsier said. "And so can you. We can use all of the powers, but we can't be everywhere. A successful crewleader needs to know how to divide labor, especially on a job as big as this one. Standard practice has a coppercloud going at all times in the lair. Clubs doesn't do it all himself—several of those apprentices are Smokers too. When you hire a man like Clubs, it's understood that he'll provide you with a base of operations and a team of Smokers competent enough to keep you hidden at all times."

Vin nodded. However, she was more interested in copper's ability to protect her emotions. She would need to locate enough of it to keep it burning all the time.

They started walking again, and Kelsier gave her more time to get used to burning tin. Vin's mind, however, began to wander. Something didn't feel . . . right to her. Why was Kelsier telling her all of these things? It seemed like he was giving away his secrets too easily.

Except one, she thought suspiciously. *The metal with the blue lines. He hasn't gone back to it yet.* Perhaps that was the thing he was going to keep from her, the power he would hold in reserve to maintain control over her.

It must be strong. The most powerful of the eight.

As they walked through the quiet streets, Vin reached tentatively inside. She eyed Kelsier, then carefully burned that unknown metal. Again, the lines sprang up around her, pointing in seemingly random directions.

The lines moved with her. One end of each thread stayed stuck to her chest, while the other end remained attached to a given place along the street. New lines appeared as she walked, and old ones faded, disappearing behind. The lines came in various widths, and some of them were brighter than others.

Curious, Vin tested the lines with her mind, trying to discover their secret. She focused on a particularly small and innocent-looking one, and found that she could feel it individually if she concentrated. She almost felt like she could touch it. She reached out with her mind and gave it a slight tug.

The line shook, and something immediately flew out of the darkness toward her. Vin yelped, trying to jump away, but the object—a rusty nail—shot directly toward her.

Suddenly, something grabbed the nail, ripping it away and throwing it back out into the darkness.

Vin came up from her roll in a tense crouch, mistcloak fluttering around her. She scanned the darkness, then glanced at Kelsier, who was chuckling softly.

"I should have known you'd try that," he said.

Vin flushed in embarrassment.

"Come on," he said, waving her over. "No harm done."

"The nail attacked me!" *Did that metal bring objects to life? That would be an incredible power indeed.*

"Actually, you kind of attacked yourself," Kelsier said.

Vin stood carefully, then joined him as he began to walk down the street again.

"I'll explain what you did in a moment," he promised. "First, there's something you have to understand about Allomancy."

"Another rule?"

"More a philosophy," Kelsier said. "It has to do with consequences."

Vin frowned. "What do you mean?"

"Every action we take has consequences, Vin," Kelsier said. "I've found that in both Allomancy and life, the person who can best judge the consequences of their actions will be the most successful. Take burning pewter, for instance. What are its consequences?"

Vin shrugged. "You get stronger."

"What happens if you're carrying something heavy when your pewter runs out?"

Vin paused. "I suppose you'd drop it."

"And, if it's too heavy, you could hurt yourself seriously. Many a Misting Thug has shrugged off a dire wound while fighting, only to die from that same wound once their pewter ran out."

"I see," Vin said quietly.

"Ha!"

Vin jumped in shock, throwing her hands up over her enhanced ears. "Ow!" she complained, glaring at Kelsier.

He smiled. "Burning tin has consequences too. If someone produces a sudden light or sound, you can be blinded or stunned."

"But, what does that have to do with those last two metals?"

"Iron and steel give you the ability to manipulate other metals around you," Kelsier explained. "With iron, you can Pull a metal source toward yourself. With steel, you can Push one away. Ah, here we are."

Kelsier stopped, looking up ahead.

Through the mist, Vin could see the massive city wall looming above them. "What are we doing here?"

"We're going to practice Ironpulling and Steelpushing," Kelsier said. "But first, some basics." He pulled something out of his belt—a clip, the smallest denomination of coin. He held it up before her, standing to the side. "Burn steel, the opposite of the metal you burned a few moments ago."

Vin nodded. Again, the blue lines sprang up around her. One of them pointed directly at the coin in Kelsier's hand.

"All right," Kelsier said. "Push on it."

Vin reached toward the proper thread and Pushed slightly. The coin flipped out of Kelsier's fingers, traveling directly away from Vin. She continued to focus on it, Pushing the coin through the air until it snapped against the wall of a nearby house.

Vin was thrown violently backward in a sudden, jerking motion. Kelsier caught her and kept her from falling to the ground.

Vin stumbled and righted herself. Across the street, the coin—now released from her control—plinked to the ground.

"What happened?" Kelsier asked her.

She shook her head. "I don't know. I Pushed on the coin, and it flew away. But when it hit the wall, I was pushed away."

"Why?"

Vin frowned thoughtfully. "I guess . . . I guess the coin couldn't go anywhere, so I had to be the one that moved."

Kelsier nodded approvingly. "Consequences, Vin. You use your own weight when you Steelpush. If you're a lot heavier than your anchor, it will fly away from you like that coin did. However, if the object is heavier than you are—or if it runs into something that is—you'll be Pushed away. Ironpulling is similar—either you'll be Pulled toward the object or it will be Pulled toward you. If your weights are similar, then you'll both move.

"This is the great art of Allomancy, Vin. Knowing how much, or how little, you will move when you burn steel or iron will give you a major advantage over your opponents. You'll find that these two are the most versatile and useful of your abilities."

Vin nodded.

"Now, remember," he continued. "In both cases, the force of your Push or Pull is *directly* away from or toward you. You can't flip things around with your mind, controlling them to go wherever you want. That's not the way that Allomancy works, because that's not the way the physical world works. When you push against something—whether with Allomancy or with your hands—it goes directly in the opposite direction. Force, reactions, consequences. Understand?"

Vin nodded again.

"Good," Kelsier said happily. "Now, let's go jump over that wall."

"*What?*"

He left her standing dumbfounded in the street. She watched him approach the base of the wall, then scurried over to him.

"You're insane!" she said quietly.

Kelsier smiled. "I think that's the second time today you've said that to me. You need to pay better attention—if you'd been listening to everyone else, you'd know that my sanity departed long ago."

"Kelsier," she said, looking up at the wall. "I can't. . . . I mean, I've never really even used Allomancy before this evening!"

"Yes, but you're such a quick learner," Kelsier said, pulling something out from beneath his cloak. It appeared to be a belt. "Here, put this on. It's got metal weights strapped to it. If something goes wrong, I'll probably be able to catch you."

"Probably?" Vin asked nervously, strapping on the belt.

Kelsier smiled, then dropped a large metal ingot at his feet. "Put the ingot directly below you, and remember to Steelpush, not Ironpull. Don't stop Pushing until you reach the top of the wall."

Then he bent down and jumped.

Kelsier shot into the air, his dark form vanishing into the curling mists. Vin waited for a moment, but he didn't plummet back down to his doom.

All was still, even to her enhanced ears. The mists whirled playfully around her. Taunting her. Daring her.

She glanced down at the ingot, burning steel. The blue line glowed with a faint, ghostly light. She stepped over to the ingot, standing with one foot on either side of it. She glanced up at the mists, then down one last time.

Finally, she took a deep breath and Pushed against the ingot with all of her strength.

"He shall defend their ways, yet shall violate them. He will be their savior, yet they shall call him heretic. His name shall be Discord, yet they shall love him for it."

8

VIN SHOT INTO THE AIR. She suppressed a scream, remembering to continue Pushing despite her fear. The stone wall was a blur of motion just a few feet away from her. The ground disappeared below, and the line of blue pointing toward the ingot grew fainter and fainter.

What happens if it disappears?

She began to slow. The fainter the line grew, the more her speed decreased. After just a few moments of flight, she crept to a halt—and was left hanging in the air above a nearly invisible blue line.

"I've always liked the view from up here."

Vin glanced to the side. Kelsier stood a short distance away; she had been so focused that she hadn't noticed that she was hovering just a few feet from the top of the wall.

"Help!" she said, continuing to Push desperately, lest she fall. The mists below her shifted and spun, like some dark ocean of damned souls.

"You don't have to worry too much," Kelsier said. "It's easier to balance in the air if you have a tripod of anchors, but you can do fine with a single anchor. Your body is used to balancing itself. Part of what you've been doing since you learned to walk transfers to Allomancy. As long as you stay still, hanging at the very edge of your Pushing ability, you'll be pretty stable—your mind and body will correct any slight deviations from the base center of your anchor below, keeping you from falling to the sides.

"If you were to Push on something else, or move too much to one side, though . . . well, you'd lose your anchor below, and wouldn't be pushing directly up anymore. Then you'd have problems—you'd tip over like a lead weight on the top of a very tall pole."

"Kelsier . . ." Vin said.

"I hope you aren't afraid of heights, Vin," Kelsier said. "That's quite a disadvantage for a Mistborn."

"I'm . . . not . . . afraid . . . of . . . heights," Vin said through gritted teeth. *"But I'm also not accustomed to hanging in the air a hundred feet above the bloody street!"*

Kelsier chuckled, but Vin felt a force tug against her belt, pulling her through the air toward him. He grabbed her and pulled her up over the stone railing, then set her down beside him. He reached an arm over the side of the wall. A second later, the ingot shot up through the air, scraping along the side of the wall, until it flipped into his waiting hand.

"Good job," he said. "Now we go back down." He tossed the ingot over his shoulder, casting it into the dark mists on the other side of the wall.

"We're really going outside?" Vin asked. "Outside the city walls? *At night?*"

Kelsier smiled in that infuriating way of his. He walked over and climbed onto the battlements. "Varying the strength with which you Push or Pull is difficult, but possible. It's better to just fall a bit, then Push to slow yourself. Let go and fall some more, then Push again. If you get the rhythm right, you'll reach the ground just fine."

"Kelsier," Vin said, approaching the wall. "I don't . . ."

"You're at the top of the city wall now, Vin," he said, stepping out into the air. He hung, hovering, balanced as he'd explained to her before. "There are only two ways down. Either you jump off, or you try and explain to that guard patrol why a Mistborn needs to use their stairwell."

Vin turned with concern, noting an approaching bob of lanternlight in the dark mists.

She turned back to Kelsier, but he was gone. She cursed, bending over the side of the wall and looking down into the mists. She could hear the guards behind her, speaking softly to one another as they walked along the wall.

Kelsier was right: She didn't have many options. Angry, she climbed up onto the battlement. She wasn't afraid of heights in particular, but who wouldn't be apprehensive, standing atop the wall, looking down at her doom? Vin's heart fluttered, her stomach twisting.

I hope Kelsier's out of the way, she thought, checking the blue line to make certain she was above the ingot. Then, she stepped off.

She immediately began to plummet toward the ground. She Pushed reflexively with her steel, but her trajectory was off; she had fallen to the side of the ingot, not directly toward it. Consequently, her Push nudged her to the side even farther, and she began to tumble through the air.

Alarmed, she Pushed again—harder this time, flaring her steel. The sudden effort launched her back upward. She arced sideways through the air, popping up into the air alongside the walltop. The passing guards spun with surprise, but their faces soon became indistinct as Vin fell back down toward the ground.

Mind muddled by terror, she reflexively reached out and Pulled against the ingot, trying to yank herself toward it. And, of course, it obediently shot up toward her.

I'm dead.

Then her body lurched, pulled upward by the belt. Her descent slowed until she was drifting quietly through the air. Kelsier appeared in the mists, standing on the ground beneath her; he was—of course—smiling.

He let her drop the last few feet, catching her, then setting her upright on the soft earth. She stood quivering for a moment, breathing in terse, anxious breaths.

"Well, that was fun," Kelsier said lightly.

Vin didn't respond.

Kelsier sat down on a nearby rock, obviously giving her time to gather her wits. Eventually, she burned pewter, using the sensation of solidness it provided to steady her nerves.

"You did well," Kelsier said.

"I nearly died."

"Everybody does, their first time," Kelsier said. "Ironpulling and Steelpushing are dangerous skills. You can impale yourself with a bit of metal that you Pull into your own body, you can jump and leave your anchor too far behind, or you can make a dozen other mistakes.

"My experience—limited though it is—has been that it's better to get into those extreme circumstances early, when someone can watch over you. Anyway, I assume you can understand why it's important for an Allomancer to carry as little metal on their body as possible."

Vin nodded, then paused, reaching up to her ear. "My earring," she said. "I'll have to stop wearing it."

"Does it have a clip on the back?" Kelsier asked.

Vin shook her head. "It's just a small stud, and the pin on the back bends down."

"Then you'll be all right," Kelsier said. "Metal in your body—even if only a bit of it is in your body—can't be Pushed or Pulled. Otherwise another Allomancer could rip the metals out of your stomach while you were burning them."

Good to know, Vin thought.

"It's also why those Inquisitors can walk around so confidently with a pair of steel spikes sticking out of their heads. The metal pierces their bodies, so it can't be affected by another Allomancer. Keep the earring—it's small, so you won't be able to do much with it, but you could use it as a weapon in an emergency."

"All right."

"Now, you ready to go?"

She looked up at the wall, preparing to jump again, then nodded.

"We're not going back up," Kelsier said. "Come on."

Vin frowned as Kelsier began to walk out into the mists. *So, does he have a destination after all—or has he just decided to wander some more?* Oddly, his affable nonchalance made him very difficult to read.

Vin hurried to keep up, not wanting to be left alone in the mists. The landscape around Luthadel was barren save for scrub and weeds. Prickles and dried leaves—both dusted with ash from an earlier ashfall—rubbed against her legs as they walked. The underbrush crunched as they walked, quiet and a bit sodden with mist dew.

Occasionally, they passed heaps of ash that had been carted out of the city. Most of the time, however, ash was thrown into the River Channerel, which passed through the city. Water broke it down eventually—or, at least, that was what Vin assumed. Otherwise the entire continent would have been buried long ago.

Vin stayed close to Kelsier as they walked. Though she had traveled outside cities before, she had always moved as part of a group of boatmen—the skaa workers who ran narrowboats and barges up and down the many canal routes in the Final Empire. It had been hard work—most noblemen used skaa instead of horses to pull the boats along the towpath—but there had been a certain freedom to knowing that she was traveling at all, for most skaa, even skaa thieves, never left their plantation or town.

The constant movement from city to city had been Reen's choice; he had been obsessive about never getting locked down. He usually got them places on canal boats run by underground crews, never staying in one place for more than a year. He had kept moving, always going. As if running from something.

They continued to walk. At night, even the barren hills and scrub-covered plains took on a forbidding air. Vin didn't speak, though she tried to make as little noise as possible. She had heard tales of what went abroad in the land at night, and the cover of the mists—even pierced by tin as it now was—made her feel as if she were being watched.

The sensation grew more unnerving as they traveled. Soon, she began to hear noises in the darkness. They were muffled and faint—crackles of weeds, shuffles in the echoing mist.

You're just being paranoid! she told herself as she jumped at some half-imagined sound. Eventually, however, she could stand it no more.

"Kelsier!" she said with an urgent whisper—one that sounded betrayingly loud to her enhanced ears. "I think there's something out there."

"Hum?" Kelsier asked. He looked lost in his thoughts.

"I think something is following us!"

"Oh," Kelsier said. "Yes, you're right. It's a mistwraith."

Vin stopped dead in her tracks. Kelsier, however, kept going.

"Kelsier!" she said, causing him to pause. "You mean *they're real?*"

"Of course they are," Kelsier said. "Where do you think all the stories came from?"

Vin stood in dumbfounded shock.

"You want to go look at it?" Kelsier asked.

"Look at the mistwraith?" Vin asked. "Are you—" She stopped.

Kelsier chuckled, strolling back to her. "Mistwraiths might be a bit disturbing to look at, but they're relatively harmless. They're scavengers, mostly. Come on."

He began to retrace their footsteps, waving her to follow. Reluctant—but morbidly curious—Vin followed. Kelsier walked at a brisk pace, leading her to the top of a relatively scrub-free hill. He crouched down, motioning for Vin to do likewise.

"Their hearing isn't very good," he said as she knelt in the rough, ashen dirt beside him. "But their sense of smell—or, rather, taste—is quite acute. It's probably following our trail, hoping that we'll discard something edible."

Vin squinted in the darkness. "I can't see it," she said, searching the mists for a shadowed figure.

"There," Kelsier said, pointing toward a squat hill.

Vin frowned, imagining a creature crouching atop the hill, watching her as she looked for it.

Then the hill moved.

Vin jumped slightly. The dark mound—perhaps ten feet tall and twice as long—lurched forward in a strange, shuffling gait, and Vin leaned forward, trying to get a better look.

"Flare your tin," Kelsier suggested.

Vin nodded, calling upon a burst of extra Allomantic power. Everything immediately became lighter, the mists becoming even less of an obstruction.

What she saw caused her to shiver—fascinated, revolted, and more than a little disturbed. The creature had smoky, translucent skin, and Vin could see its bones. It had dozens upon dozens of limbs, and each one looked as if it had come from a different animal. There were human hands, bovine hooves, canine haunches, and others she couldn't identify.

The mismatched limbs let the creature walk—though it was more of a shamble. It crawled along slowly, moving like an awkward centipede. Many of the limbs, in fact, didn't even look functional—they jutted from the creature's flesh in a twisted, unnatural fashion.

Its body was bulbous and elongated. It wasn't just a blob, though . . . there was a strange logic to its form. It had a distinct skeletal structure, and—squinting through tin-enhanced eyes—she thought she could make out translucent muscles and sinew wrapping the bones. The creature flexed odd jumbles of muscles as it moved, and appeared to have a dozen different ribcages. Along the main body, arms and legs hung at unnerving angles.

And heads—she counted six. Despite the translucent skin, she could make out a horse head sitting beside that of a deer. Another head turned toward her, and she could see its human skull. The head sat atop a long spinal cord attached to some kind of animal torso, which was in turn attached to a jumble of strange bones.

Vin nearly retched. "What . . . ? How . . . ?"

"Mistwraiths have malleable bodies," Kelsier said. "They can shape their skin around any skeletal structure, and can even re-create muscles and organs if they have a model to mimic."

"You mean . . . ?"

Kelsier nodded. "When they find a corpse, they envelop it and slowly digest the muscles and organs. Then, they use what they've eaten as a pattern, creating an exact duplicate of the dead creature. They rearrange the parts a little bit—excreting the bones they don't want, while adding the ones they do want to their body—forming a jumble like what you see out there."

Vin watched the creature shamble across the field, following her tracks. A flap of slimy skin drooped from its underbelly, trailing along the ground. *Tasting for scents*, Vin thought. *Following the smell of our passing.* She let her tin return to normal, and the mistwraith once again became a shadowed mound. The silhouette, however, only seemed to heighten its abnormality.

"Are they intelligent, then?" Vin asked. "If they can split up a . . . body and put the pieces where they want?"

"Intelligent?" Kelsier asked. "No, not one this young. More instinctual than intelligent."

Vin shivered again. "Do people know about these things? I mean, other than the legends?"

"What do you mean by 'people'?" Kelsier asked. "A lot of Allomancers know about them, and I'm sure the Ministry does. Regular people . . . well, they just don't go out at night. Most skaa fear and curse mistwraiths, but go their entire lives without actually seeing one."

"Lucky for them," Vin muttered. "Why doesn't someone do something about these things?"

Kelsier shrugged. "They're not that dangerous."

"That one has a human head!"

"It probably found a corpse," Kelsier said. "I've never heard of a mistwraith attacking a full-grown, healthy adult. That's probably why everyone leaves them alone. And, of course, the high nobility have devised their own uses for the creatures."

Vin looked at him questioningly, but he said no more, rising and walking down the hillside. She shot one more glance at the unnatural creature, then took off, following Kelsier.

"Is that what you brought me out here to see?" Vin asked.

Kelsier chuckled. "Mistwraiths might look eerie, but they're hardly worth such a long trip. No, we're heading over there."

She followed his gesture, and was able to make out a change in the landscape ahead. "The imperial highroad? We've circled around to the front of the city."

Kelsier nodded. After a short walk—during which Vin glanced backward no less than three times to make certain the mistwraith hadn't gained on them—they left the scrub and stepped onto the flat, packed earth of the imperial highroad. Kelsier paused, scanning the road in either direction. Vin frowned, wondering what he was doing.

Then she saw the carriage. It was parked by the side of the highroad, and Vin could see that there was a man waiting beside it.

"Ho, Sazed," Kelsier said, walking forward.

The man bowed. "Master Kelsier," he said, his smooth voice carrying well in the night air. It had a higher pitch to it, and he spoke with an almost melodic accent. "I almost thought that you had decided not to come."

"You know me, Saze," Kelsier said, jovially slapping the man on the shoulder. "I'm the soul of punctuality." He turned and waved a hand toward Vin. "This apprehensive little creature is Vin."

"Ah, yes," Sazed said, speaking in a slow, well-enunciated way. There was something strange about his accent. Vin approached cautiously, studying the man. Sazed had a long, flat face and a willowy body. He was even taller than Kelsier—tall enough to be a bit abnormal—and his arms were unusually long.

"You're a Terrisman," Vin said. His earlobes had been stretched out, and the ears themselves contained studs that ran around their perimeter. He wore the lavish, colorful robes of a Terris steward—the garments were made of embroidered, overlapping V shapes, alternating among the three colors of his master's house.

"Yes, child," Sazed said, bowing. "Have you known many of my people?"

"None," Vin said. "But I know that the high nobility prefer Terrismen stewards and attendants."

"Indeed they do, child," Sazed said. He turned to Kelsier. "We should go, Master Kelsier. It is late, and we are still an hour away from Fellise."

Fellise, Vin thought. *So, we're going to see the impostor Lord Renoux.*

Sazed opened the carriage door for them, then closed it after they climbed in. Vin settled on one of the plush seats as she heard Sazed climb atop the vehicle and set the horses in motion.

Kelsier sat quietly in the carriage. The window shades were closed against the mist, and a small lantern, half shielded, hung in the corner. Vin rode on the seat directly across from him—her legs tucked up underneath her, her enveloping mistcloak pulled close, hiding her arms and legs.

She always does that, Kelsier thought. *Wherever she is, she tries to be as small and unnoticeable as possible. So tense.* Vin didn't sit, she crouched. She didn't walk, she prowled. Even when she was sitting in the open, she seemed to be trying to hide.

She's a brave one, though. During his own training, Kelsier hadn't been quite so willing to throw himself off of a city wall—old Gemmel had been forced to push him.

Vin watched him with those quiet, dark eyes of hers. When she noticed his attention, she glanced away, huddling down a little more within her cloak. Unexpectedly, however, she spoke.

"Your brother," she said in her soft near-whisper of a voice. "You two don't get along very well."

Kelsier raised an eyebrow. "No. We never have, really. It's a shame. We should, but we just . . . don't."

"He's older than you?"

Kelsier nodded.

"Did he beat you often?" Vin asked.

Kelsier frowned. "Beat me? No, he didn't beat me at all."

"You stopped him, then?" Vin said. "Maybe that's why he doesn't like you. How did you escape? Did you run, or were you just stronger than him?"

"Vin, Marsh never *tried* to beat me. We argued, true—but we never really wanted to hurt one another."

Vin didn't contradict him, but he could see in her eyes that she didn't believe him.

What a life . . . Kelsier thought, falling silent. There were so many children like Vin in the underground. Of course, most died before reaching her age. Kelsier had been one of the lucky ones: His mother had been a resourceful mistress of a high nobleman, a clever woman who had managed to hide the fact that she was skaa from her lord. Kelsier and Marsh had grown up privileged—considered illegitimate, but still noble—until their father had finally discovered the truth.

"Why did you teach me those things?" Vin asked, interrupting his thoughts. "About Allomancy, I mean."

Kelsier frowned. "I promised you that I would."

"Now that I know your secrets, what is to keep me from running away from you?"

"Nothing," Kelsier said.

Once again, her distrusting glare told him that she didn't believe his answer. "There are metals you didn't tell me about. Back in our meeting on the first day, you said there were ten."

Kelsier nodded, leaning forward. "There are. But I didn't leave the last two out because I wanted to keep things from you. They're just . . . difficult to get used to. It will be easier if you practice with the basic metals first. However, if you want to know about the last two, I can teach you once we arrive in Fellise."

Vin's eyes narrowed.

Kelsier rolled his eyes. "I'm not trying to trick you, Vin. People serve on my crews because they want to, and I'm effective because they can rely on one another. No distrust, no betrayals."

"Except one," Vin whispered. "The betrayal that sent you to the Pits."

Kelsier froze. "Where did you hear that?"

Vin shrugged.

Kelsier sighed, rubbing his forehead with one hand. That wasn't what he wanted to do—he wanted to scratch his scars, the ones that ran all along his fingers and hands, twisting up his arms toward his shoulders. He resisted.

"That isn't something worth talking about," he said.

"But there was a traitor," Vin said.

"We don't know for certain." That sounded weak, even to him. "Regardless, my crews rely on trust. That means no coercions. If you want out, we can go back to Luthadel right now. I'll show you the last two metals, then you can be on your way."

"I don't have enough money to survive on my own," Vin said.

Kelsier reached inside of his cloak and pulled out a bag of coins, then tossed it onto the seat beside her. "Three thousand boxings. The money I took from Camon."

Vin glanced at the bag distrustfully.

"Take it," Kelsier said. "You're the one who earned it—from what I've been able to gather, your Allomancy was behind most of Camon's recent successes, and you were the one who risked Pushing the emotions of a obligator."

Vin didn't move.

Fine, Kelsier thought, reaching up and knocking on the underside of the coachman's chair. The carriage stopped, and Sazed soon appeared at his window.

"Turn the carriage around please, Saze," Kelsier said. "Take us back to Luthadel."

"Yes, Master Kelsier."

Within moments, the carriage was rolling back in the direction it had come. Vin watched in silence, but she seemed a little less certain of herself. She eyed the bag of coins.

"I'm serious, Vin," Kelsier said. "I can't have someone on my team who doesn't want to work with me. Turning you away isn't a punishment; it's just the way things must be."

Vin didn't respond. Letting her go would be a gamble—but forcing her to stay would be a bigger one. Kelsier sat, trying to read her, trying to understand her. Would she betray them to the Final Empire if she left? He thought not. She wasn't a bad person.

She just thought that everybody else was.

"I think your plan is crazy," she said quietly.

"So do half the people on the crew."

"You can't defeat the Final Empire."

"We don't have to," Kelsier said. "We just have to get Yeden an army, then seize the palace."

"The Lord Ruler will stop you," Vin said. "You can't beat him—he's immortal."

"We have the Eleventh Metal," Kelsier said. "We'll find a way to kill him."

"The Ministry is too powerful. They'll find your army and destroy it."

Kelsier leaned forward, looking Vin in the eye. "You trusted me enough to jump off the top of the wall, and I caught you. You're going to have to trust me this time too."

She obviously didn't like the word "trust" very much. She studied him in the weak lanternlight, remaining quiet long enough that the silence grew uncomfortable.

Finally, she snatched the bag of coins, quickly hiding it beneath her cloak. "I'll stay," she said. "But not because I trust you."

Kelsier raised an eyebrow. "Why, then?"

Vin shrugged, and she sounded perfectly honest when she spoke. "Because I want to see what happens."

Having a keep in Luthadel qualified a house for high noble status. However, having a keep didn't mean that one had to live in it, especially not all of the time. Many families also maintained a residence in one of Luthadel's outskirt cities.

Less crowded, cleaner, and less strict in its observance of imperial laws, Fellise was a rich town. Rather than containing imposing, buttressed keeps, it was filled with lavish manors and villas. Trees even lined some of the streets; most of them were aspens, whose bone-white bark was somehow resistant to the discoloring of the ash.

Vin watched the mist-cloaked city through her window, the carriage lantern extinguished at her request. Burning tin, she was able to study the neatly organized and well-groomed streets. This was a section of Fellise she had rarely seen; despite the town's opulence, its slums were remarkably similar to the ones in every other city.

Kelsier watched the city through his own window, frowning.

"You disapprove of the waste," Vin guessed, her voice a whisper. The sound would carry to Kelsier's enhanced ears. "You see the riches of this city and think of the skaa who worked to create it."

"That's part of it," Kelsier said, his own voice barely a whisper. "There's more, though. Considering the amount of money spent on it, this city should be beautiful."

Vin cocked her head. "It is."

Kelsier shook his head. "The homes are still stained black. The soil is still arid and lifeless. The trees still grow leaves of brown."

"Of course they're brown. What else would they be?"

"Green," Kelsier said. "Everything should be green."

Green? Vin thought. *What a strange thought.* She tried to imagine trees with green leaves, but the image seemed silly. Kelsier certainly had his quirks—though, anyone who had spent so long at the Pits of Hathsin was bound to be left a bit strange.

He turned back toward her. "Before I forget, there are a couple more things you should know about Allomancy."

Vin nodded.

"First," Kelsier said, "remember to burn away any unused metals you have inside of you at the end of the night. Some of the metals we use can be poisonous if digested; it's best not to sleep with them in your stomach."

"All right," Vin said.

"Also," Kelsier said, "never try to burn a metal that isn't one of the ten. I warned you that impure metals and alloys can make you sick. Well, if you try to burn a metal that isn't Allomantically sound at all, it could be deadly."

Vin nodded solemnly. *Good to know,* she thought.

"Ah," Kelsier said, turning back toward the window. "Here we are: the newly purchased Manor Renoux. You should probably take off your cloak—the people here are loyal to us, but it always pays to be careful."

Vin agreed completely. She pulled off the cloak, letting Kelsier tuck it in his pack. Then she peeked out the carriage window, peering through the mists at the approaching manor. The grounds had a low stone wall and an iron gate; a pair of guards opened the way as Sazed identified himself.

The roadway inside was lined with aspens, and atop the hill ahead Vin could see a large manor house, phantom light spilling from its windows.

Sazed pulled the carriage up before the manor, then handed the reins to a servant and climbed down. "Welcome to Manor Renoux, Mistress Vin," he said, opening the door and gesturing to help her down.

Vin eyed his hand, but didn't take it, instead scrambling down on her own. The Terrisman didn't seem offended by her refusal.

The steps to the manor house were lit by a double line of lantern poles. As Kelsier hopped from the carriage, Vin could see a group of men gathering at the top of the white marble stairs. Kelsier climbed the steps with a springy stride; Vin followed behind, noticing how clean the steps were. They would have to be scrubbed regularly to keep the ash from staining them. Did the skaa who maintained the building know that their master was an imposter? How was Kelsier's "benevolent" plan to overthrow the Final Empire helping the common people who cleaned these steps?

Thin and aging, "Lord Renoux" wore a rich suit and a pair of aristocratic spectacles. A sparse, gray mustache colored his lip, and—despite his age—he didn't carry a cane for support. He nodded respectfully to Kelsier, but maintained a dignified air. Immediately, Vin was struck by one obvious fact: *This man knows what he is doing.*

Camon had been skilled at impersonating noblemen, but his self-importance had always struck Vin as a bit juvenile. While there were noblemen like Camon, the more impressive ones were like this Lord Renoux: calm, and self-confident. Men whose nobility was in their bearing rather than their ability to speak scornfully to those around them. Vin had to resist cringing when the impostor's eyes fell on her—he seemed far too much a nobleman, and she had been trained to reflexively avoid their attention.

"The manor is looking much better," Kelsier said, shaking hands with Renoux.

"Yes, I'm impressed with its progress," Renoux said. "My cleaning crews are quite proficient—give us a bit more time, and the manor will be so grand that I wouldn't hesitate to host the Lord Ruler himself."

Kelsier chuckled. "Wouldn't *that* be an odd dinner party." He stepped back, gesturing toward Vin. "This is the young lady I spoke of."

Renoux studied her, and Vin glanced away. She didn't like it when people looked at her that way—it made her wonder how they were going to try and use her.

"We will need to speak further of this, Kelsier," Renoux said, nodding toward the mansion's entrance. "The hour is late, but . . ."

Kelsier stepped into the building. "Late? Why, it's barely midnight. Have your people prepare some food—Lady Vin and I missed dinner."

A missed meal was nothing new to Vin. However, Renoux immediately waved to some servants, and they leapt into motion. Renoux walked into the building, and Vin followed. She paused in the entryway, however, Sazed waiting patiently behind her.

Kelsier paused, turning when he noticed that she wasn't following. "Vin?"

"It's so . . . clean," Vin said, unable to think of any other description. On jobs, she'd occasionally seen the homes of noblemen. However, those times had happened at night, in dark gloom. She was unprepared for the well-lit sight before her.

The white marble floors of Manor Renoux seemed to glow, reflecting the light of a dozen lanterns. Everything was . . . pristine. The walls were white except where they had been wash-painted with traditional animal murals. A brilliant chandelier sparkled above a double staircase, and the room's other decorations—crystal sculptures, vases set with bundles of aspen branches—glistened, unmarred by soot, smudge, or fingerprint.

Kelsier chuckled. "Well, her reaction speaks highly of your efforts," he said to Lord Renoux.

Vin allowed herself to be led into the building. The group turned right, entering a room whose whites were muted slightly by the addition of maroon furnishings and drapes.

Renoux paused. "Perhaps the lady could enjoy some refreshment here for a moment," he said to Kelsier. "There are some matters of a . . . delicate nature that I would discuss with you."

Kelsier shrugged. "Fine with me," he said, following Renoux toward another doorway. "Saze, why don't you keep Vin company while Lord Renoux and I talk?"

"Of course, Master Kelsier."

Kelsier smiled, eyeing Vin, and somehow she knew that he was leaving Sazed behind to keep her from eavesdropping.

She shot the departing men an annoyed look. *What was that you said about "trust," Kelsier?* However, she was even more annoyed at herself for getting unsettled. Why should she care if Kelsier excluded her? She had spent her entire life being ignored and dismissed. It had never bothered her before when other crewleaders left her out of their planning sessions.

Vin took a seat in one of the stiffly upholstered maroon chairs, tucking her feet up beneath her. She knew what the problem was. Kelsier had been showing her too much respect, making her feel too important. She was beginning to think that she *deserved* to be part of his secret confidences. Reen's laughter in the back of her mind discredited those thoughts, and she sat, annoyed at both herself and Kelsier, feeling ashamed, but not exactly certain why.

Renoux's servants brought her a platter of fruits and breads. They set up a small stand beside her chair, and even gave her a crystalline cup filled with a glistening red liquid. She couldn't tell if it was wine or juice, and she didn't intend to find out. She did, however, pick at the food—her instincts wouldn't let her pass up a free meal, even if it was prepared by unfamiliar hands.

Sazed walked over and took a position standing just behind her chair to the right. He waited with a stiff posture, hands clasped in front of him, eyes forward. The stance was obviously intended to be respectful, but his looming posture didn't help her mood any.

Vin tried to focus on her surroundings, but this only reminded her of how rich the furnishings were. She was uncomfortable amid such finery; she felt as if she stood out like a black spot on a clean rug. She didn't eat the breads for fear that she would drop crumbs on the floor, and she worried at her feet and legs—which had been stained with ash while walking through the countryside—marring the furnishings.

All of this cleanliness came at some skaa's expense, Vin thought. *Why should I worry about disturbing it?* However, she had trouble feeling outraged, for she knew this was only a front. "Lord Renoux" had to maintain a certain level of finery. It would be suspicious to do otherwise.

In addition, something else kept her from resenting the waste. The servants were happy. They went about their duties with a businesslike professionalism, no sense of drudgery about their efforts. She heard laughter in the outer hall-way. These were not mistreated skaa; whether they had been included in Kelsier's plans or not was irrelevant.

So, Vin sat and forced herself to eat fruit, yawning occasionally. It was turning out to be a long night indeed. The servants eventually left her alone, though Sazed continued to loom just behind her.

I can't eat like this, she finally thought with frustration. "Could you not stand over my shoulder like that?"

Sazed nodded. He took two steps forward so that he stood next to her chair, rather than behind it. He adopted the same stiff posture, looming above her just as he had before.

Vin frowned in annoyance, then noticed the smile on Sazed's lips. He glanced down at her, eyes twinkling at his joke, then walked over and seated himself in the chair beside hers.

"I've never known a Terrisman with a sense of humor before," Vin said dryly.

Sazed raised an eyebrow. "I was under the impression that you hadn't known any Terrismen at all, Mistress Vin."

Vin paused. "Well, I've never *heard* of one with a sense of humor. You're supposed to be completely rigid and formal."

"We're just subtle, Mistress," Sazed said. Though he sat with a stiff posture, there was still something . . . relaxed about him. It was as if he were as comfortable when sitting properly as other people were when lounging.

That's how they're supposed to be. The perfect serving men, completely loyal to the Final Empire.

"Is something troubling you, Mistress Vin?" Sazed asked as she studied him.

How much does he know? Perhaps he doesn't even realize that Renoux is an imposter. "I was just wondering how you . . . came here," she finally said.

"You mean, how did a Terrisman steward end up as part of a rebellion intending to overthrow the Final Empire?" Sazed asked in his soft voice.

Vin flushed. Apparently he was well versed indeed.

"That is an intriguing question, Mistress," Sazed said. "Certainly, my situation is not common. I would say that I arrived at it because of belief."

"Belief?"

"Yes," Sazed said. "Tell me, Mistress. What is it that you believe?"

Vin frowned. "What kind of question is that?"

"The most important kind, I think."

Vin sat for a moment, but he obviously expected a reply, so she finally shrugged. "I don't know."

"People often say that," Sazed said, "but I find that it is rarely true. Do you believe in the Final Empire?"

"I believe that it is strong," Vin said.

"Immortal?"

Vin shrugged. "It has been so far."

"And the Lord Ruler? Is he the Ascended Avatar of God? Do you believe that he, as the Ministry teaches, is a Sliver of Infinity?"

"I . . . I've never thought about it before."

"Perhaps you should," Sazed said. "If, upon examination, you find that the Ministry's teachings do not suit you, then I would be pleased to offer you an alternative."

"What alternative?"

Sazed smiled. "That depends. The right belief is like a good cloak, I think. If it fits you well, it keeps you warm and safe. The wrong fit, however, can suffocate."

Vin paused, frowning slightly, but Sazed just smiled. Eventually, she turned her attention back to her meal. After a short wait, the side door opened, and Kelsier and Renoux returned.

"Now," Renoux said as he and Kelsier seated themselves, a group of servants bringing another plate of food for Kelsier, "let us discuss this child. The man you were going to have play my heir will not do, you say?"

"Unfortunately," Kelsier said, making quick work of his food.

"That complicates things greatly," Renoux said.

Kelsier shrugged. "We'll just have Vin be your heir."

Renoux shook his head. "A girl her age *could* inherit, but it would be suspicious for me to pick her. There are any number of legitimate male cousins in the Renoux line who would be far more suitable choices. It was going to be difficult enough to get a middle-aged man past courtly scrutiny. A young girl . . . no, too many people would investigate her background. Our forged family lines will survive passing scrutiny, but if someone were to actually send messengers to search out her holdings . . ."

Kelsier frowned.

"Besides," Renoux added. "There is another issue. If I were to name a young, unmarried girl as my heir, hers would instantly become one of the most sought-after hands in Luthadel. It would be very difficult for her to spy if she were to receive that much attention."

Vin flushed at the thought. Surprisingly, she found her heart sinking as the old imposter spoke. *This was the only part Kelsier gave me in the plan. If I can't do it, what good am I to the crew?*

"So, what do you suggest?" Kelsier asked.

"Well, she doesn't *have* to be my heir," Renoux said. "What if, instead, she were simply a young scion I brought with me to Luthadel? Perhaps I promised her parents—distant but favored cousins—that I would introduce their daughter to the court? Everyone would assume that my ulterior motive is to marry her off to a high noble family, thereby gaining myself another connection to those in power. However, she wouldn't draw much attention—she would be of low status, not to mention somewhat rural."

"Which would explain why she's a bit less refined than other court members," Kelsier said. "No offense, Vin."

Vin looked up from hiding a piece of napkin-wrapped bread in her shirt pocket. "Why would I be offended?"

Kelsier smiled. "Never mind."

Renoux nodded to himself. "Yes, this will work much better. Everyone assumes that House Renoux will eventually join the high nobility, so they'll accept Vin into their ranks out of courtesy. However, she herself will be unimportant enough that most people will ignore her. That is the ideal situation for what we will want her to do."

"I like it," Kelsier said. "Few people expect a man of your age and mercantile concerns to bother himself with balls and parties, but having a young socialite to send instead of a rejection note will serve as an advantage to your reputation."

"Indeed," Renoux said. "She'll need some refinement, however—and not just in appearance."

Vin squirmed a bit beneath their scrutiny. It looked as if her part in the plan would go forward, and she suddenly realized what that meant. Being around Renoux made her uncomfortable—and he was a *fake* nobleman. How would she react to an entire room full of real ones?

"I'm afraid I'll have to borrow Sazed from you for a while," Kelsier said.

"Quite all right," Renoux said. "He's really not my steward, but yours."

"Actually," Kelsier said, "I don't think he's *anybody's* steward anymore, eh Saze?"

Sazed cocked his head. "A Terrisman without a master is like a soldier with no weapon, Master Kelsier. I have enjoyed my time attending to Lord Renoux, as I am certain that I shall enjoy returning to your service."

"Oh, you won't be returning to my service," Kelsier said.

Sazed raised an eyebrow.

Kelsier nodded toward Vin. "Renoux is right, Saze. Vin needs some coaching, and I know plenty of high noblemen who are less refined than yourself. Do you think you could help the girl prepare?"

"I am certain that I could offer the young lady some aid," Sazed said.

"Good," Kelsier said, popping one last cake in his mouth, then rising. "I'm glad that's settled, because I'm starting to feel tired—and poor Vin looks like she's about to nod off in the middle of her fruit plate."

"I'm fine," Vin said immediately, the assertion weakened slightly by a stifled yawn.

"Sazed," Renoux said, "would you show them to the appropriate guest chambers?"

"Of course, Master Renoux," Sazed said, rising from his seat in a smooth motion.

Vin and Kelsier trailed the tall Terrisman from the room as a group of servants took away the remnants of the meal. *I left food behind,* Vin noticed, feeling a bit drowsy. She wasn't certain what to think of the occurrence.

As they crested the stairs and turned into a side hallway, Kelsier fell into place beside Vin. "I'm sorry for excluding you back there, Vin."

She shrugged. "There's no reason for me to know all of your plans."

"Nonsense," Kelsier said. "Your decision tonight makes you as much a part of this team as anyone else. Renoux's words in private, however, were of a personal nature. He is a marvelous actor, but he feels very uncomfortable with people knowing the specifics of how he took Lord Renoux's place. I promise you, nothing we discussed has any bearing on your part in the plan."

Vin continued walking. "I . . . believe you."

"Good," Kelsier said with a smile, clapping her on the shoulder. "Saze, I know my way to the men's guest quarters—I was, after all, the one who bought this place. I can make my way from here."

"Very well, Master Kelsier," Sazed said with a respectful nod. Kelsier shot Vin a smile, then turned down a hallway, walking with his characteristically lively step.

Vin watched him go, then followed Sazed down a different side passage, pondering the Allomancy training, her discussion with Kelsier in the carriage, and finally Kelsier's promise just a few moments before. The three thousand boxings—a fortune in coins—was a strange weight tied to her belt.

Eventually, Sazed opened a particular door for her, walking in to light the lanterns. "The linens are fresh, and I will send maids to prepare you a bath in the morning." He turned, handing her his candle. "Will you require anything else?"

Vin shook her head. Sazed smiled, bid her good evening, then walked back out in the hallway. Vin stood quietly for a short moment, studying the room. Then she turned, glancing once again in the direction Kelsier had gone.

"Sazed?" she said, peeking back out into the hallway.

The steward paused, turning back. "Yes, Mistress Vin?"

"Kelsier," Vin said quietly. "He's a good man, isn't he?"

Sazed smiled. "A very good man, Mistress. One of the best I've known."

Vin nodded slightly. "A good man . . ." she said softly. "I don't think I've ever known one of those before."

Sazed smiled, then bowed his head respectfully and turned to leave.

Vin let the door swing shut.

THE END OF PART ONE

PART TWO

REBELS BENEATH
A SKY OF ASH

In the end, I worry that my arrogance shall destroy us all.

9

VIN PUSHED AGAINST THE COIN AND threw herself up into the mist. She flew away from earth and stone, soaring through the dark currents of the sky, wind fluttering her cloak.

This is freedom, she thought, breathing deeply of the cool, damp air. She closed her eyes, feeling the passing wind. *This was what I was always missing, yet never knew it.*

She opened her eyes as she began to descend. She waited until the last moment, then flicked a coin. It hit the cobblestones, and she Pushed against it lightly, slowing her descent. She burned pewter with a flash and hit the ground running, dashing along Fellise's quiet streets. The late-autumn air was cool, but winters were generally mild in the Central Dominance. Some years passed without even a flake of snow.

She tossed a coin backward, then used it to Push herself slightly up and to the right. She landed on a low stone wall, barely breaking stride as she ran spryly along the wall's top. Burning pewter enhanced more than muscles—it increased all the body's physical abilities. Keeping pewter at a low burn gave her a sense of balance that any night burglar would have envied.

The wall turned north, and Vin paused at the corner. She fell into a crouch, bare feet and sensitive fingers gripping the chill stone. Her copper on to hide her Allomancy, she flared tin to strain her senses.

Stillness. Aspens made insubstantial ranks in the mist, like emaciated skaa standing in their work lines. Estates rolled in the distance—each one walled, manicured, and well guarded. There were far fewer dots of light in the city than there were in Luthadel. Many of the homes were only part-time residences, their masters away visiting some other sliver of the Final Empire.

Blue lines suddenly appeared before her—one end of each pointing at her chest, the other disappearing into the mists. Vin immediately jumped to the side, dodging as a pair of coins shot past in the night air, leaving trails in the mist. She flared pewter, landing on the cobbled street beside the wall. Her tin-enhanced ears picked out a scraping sound; then a dark form shot into the sky, a few blue lines pointing to his coin pouch.

Vin dropped a coin and threw herself into the air after her opponent. They soared for a moment, flying over the grounds of some unsuspecting nobleman. Vin's opponent suddenly changed course in the air, jerking toward the mansion itself. Vin followed, letting go of the coin below her, instead burning iron and Pulling on one of the mansion's window latches.

Her opponent hit first, and she heard a thud as he ran into the side of the building. He was off a second later.

A light brightened, and a confused head poked out of a window as Vin spun in the air, landing feet-first against the mansion. She immediately kicked off of the vertical surface, angling herself slightly and Pushing against the same window latch. Glass cracked, and she shot away into the night before gravity could reclaim her.

Vin flew through the mists, eyes straining to keep track of her quarry. He shot a couple of coins back at her, but she Pushed them away with a dismissive thought. A hazy blue line fell downward—a dropped coin—and her opponent moved to the side again.

Vin dropped her own coin and Pushed. However, her coin suddenly jerked backward along the ground—the result of a Push from her opponent. The sudden move changed the trajectory of Vin's jump, throwing her sideways. She cursed, flicking another coin to the side, using it to Push herself back on track. By then, she'd lost her quarry.

All right . . . she thought, hitting the soft ground just inside the wall. She emptied a few coins into her hand, then tossed the mostly full pouch into the air, giving it a strong Push in the direction she had seen her quarry disappear. The pouch disappeared into the mists, trailing a faint blue Allomantic line.

A scattering of coins suddenly shot from the bushes ahead, streaking toward her bag. Vin smiled. Her opponent had assumed that the flying pouch was Vin herself. He was too far away to see the coins in her hand, just as he had been too far away for her to see the coins he carried.

A dark figure jumped out of the bushes, hopping up onto the stone wall. Vin waited quietly as the figure ran along the wall and slipped down onto the other side.

Vin launched herself straight up into the air, then threw her handful of coins at the figure passing below. He immediately Pushed, sending the coins streaking away—but they were only a distraction. Vin landed on the ground before him, twin glass knives whipping from her sheathes. She lunged, slashing, but her opponent jumped backward.

Something's wrong. Vin ducked and threw herself to the side as a handful of glittering coins—her coins, the ones her opponent had Pushed away—shot back down from the sky into her opponent's hand. He turned and sprayed them in her direction.

Vin dropped her daggers with a quiet yelp, thrusting her hands forward and Pushing on the coins. Immediately, she was thrown backward as her Push was matched by her opponent.

One of the coins lurched in the air, hanging directly between the two of them. The rest of the coins disappeared into the mists, pushed sideways by conflicting forces.

Vin flared her steel as she flew, and heard her opponent grunt as he was Pushed backward as well. Her opponent hit the wall. Vin slammed into a tree, but she flared pewter and ignored the pain. She used the wood to brace herself, continuing to Push.

The coin quivered in the air, trapped between the amplified strength of two Allomancers. The pressure increased. Vin gritted her teeth, feeling the small aspen bend behind her.

Her opponent's Pushing was relentless.

Will . . . not . . . be beaten! Vin thought, flaring both steel and pewter, grunting slightly as she threw the entire force of her strength at the coin.

There was a moment of silence. Then Vin lurched backward, the tree cracking with a loud snap in the night air.

Vin hit the ground in a tumble, splinters of wood scattering around her. Even tin and pewter weren't enough to keep her mind clear as she rolled across the cobblestones, eventually coming to a dizzy rest. A dark figure approached, mistcloak ribbons billowing around him. Vin lurched to her feet, grasping for knives she'd forgotten that she'd dropped.

Kelsier put down his hood and held her knives toward her. One was broken. "I know it's instinctual, Vin, but you don't have to put your hands forward when you Push—nor do you have to drop what you're holding."

Vin grimaced in the darkness, rubbing her shoulder and nodding as she accepted the daggers.

"Nice job with the pouch," Kelsier said. "You had me for a moment."

"For all the good it did," Vin grumbled.

"You've only been doing this for a few months, Vin," he said lightly. "All things considered, your progress is fantastic. I would, however, recommend that you avoid Push-matches with people who weigh more than you." He paused, eyeing Vin's short figure and thin frame. "Which probably means avoiding them with pretty much everybody."

Vin sighed, stretching slightly. She'd have more bruises. *At least they won't be visible.* Now that the bruises Camon had given her face were finally gone, Sazed had warned her to be careful. Makeup could only cover so much, and she would have to look like a "proper" young noblewoman if she were going to infiltrate the court.

"Here," Kelsier said, handing her something. "A souvenir."

Vin held up the object—the coin they had Pushed between them. It was bent and flattened from the pressure.

"I'll see you back at the mansion," Kelsier said.

Vin nodded, and Kelsier disappeared into the night. *He's right,* she thought. *I'm smaller, I weigh less, and I have a shorter reach than anyone I'm likely to fight. If I attack someone head on, I'll lose.*

The alternative had always been her method anyway—to struggle quietly, to stay unseen. She had to learn to use Allomancy the same way. Kelsier kept saying that she was developing amazingly fast as an Allomancer. He seemed to think it was his teaching, but Vin felt it was something else. The mists . . . the night prowling . . . it all felt *right* to her. She was not worried about mastering Allomancy in time to help Kelsier against other Mistborn.

It was her other part in the plan that worried her.

Sighing, Vin hopped over the wall to search for her coin pouch. Up at the mansion—not Renoux's home, but one owned by some other nobleman—lights were on and people milled about. None of them ventured deeply into the night. The skaa would fear mistwraiths; the nobility would have guessed that Mistborn had caused the disturbance. Neither one was something a sane person would want to confront.

Vin eventually traced her pouch by steel-line to the upper branches of a tree. She Pulled it slightly, tugging it down into her hand, then made her way back out to the street. Kelsier probably would have left the pouch behind— the two dozen or so clips it contained wouldn't have been worth his time. However, for most of her life Vin had scrounged and starved. She just couldn't force herself to be wasteful. Even tossing coins to jump with made her uncomfortable.

So, she used her coins sparingly as she traveled back toward Renoux's mansion, instead Pushing and Pulling off of buildings and discarded bits of metal. The half-jumping, half-running gait of a Mistborn came naturally to her now, and she didn't have to think much about her movements.

How would she fare, trying to pretend to be a noblewoman? She couldn't hide her apprehensions, not from herself. Camon had been good at imitating noblemen because of his self-confidence, and that was one attribute Vin knew she didn't have. Her success with Allomancy only proved that her place was in corners and shadows, not striding around in pretty dresses at courtly balls.

Kelsier, however, refused to let her back out. Vin landed in a crouch just outside Mansion Renoux, puffing slightly from exertion. She regarded the lights with a slight feeling of apprehension.

You've got to learn to do this, Vin, Kelsier kept telling her. *You're a talented Al-*

lomancer, but you'll need more than Steelpushes to succeed against the nobility. Until you can move in their society as easily as you do in the mists, you'll be at a disadvantage.

Letting out a quiet sigh, Vin rose from her crouch, then took off her mist-cloak and stuffed it away for later retrieval. Then she walked up the steps and into the building. When she asked after Sazed, the mansion servants directed her to the kitchens, so she made her way into the closed-off, hidden section of the mansion that was the servants' quarters.

Even these parts of the building were kept immaculately clean. Vin was beginning to understand why Renoux made such a convincing impostor: He didn't allow for imperfection. If he maintained his impersonation half as well as he maintained order in his mansion, then Vin doubted anyone would ever discover the ruse.

But, she thought, *he must have some flaw. Back in the meeting two months ago, Kelsier said that Renoux wouldn't be able to withstand scrutiny by an Inquisitor. Perhaps they'd be able to sense something about his emotions, something that gives him away?*

It was a small item, but Vin had not forgotten it. Despite Kelsier's words about honesty and trust, he still had his secrets. Everyone did.

Sazed was, indeed, to be found in the kitchens. He stood with a middle-aged servant. She was tall for a skaa woman—though standing next to Sazed made her look diminutive. Vin recognized her as a member of the mansion staff; Cosahn was her name. Vin had made an effort to memorize all of the names of the local staff, if only to keep tabs on them.

Sazed looked over as Vin entered. "Ah, Mistress Vin. Your return is quite timely." He gestured to his companion. "This is Cosahn."

Cosahn studied Vin with a businesslike air. Vin longed to return to the mists, where people couldn't look at her like that.

"It is long enough now, I think," Sazed said.

"Probably," Cosahn said. "But I cannot perform miracles, Master Vaht."

Sazed nodded. "Vaht" was, apparently, the proper title for a Terrisman steward. Not quite skaa, but definitely not noblemen, the Terrismen held a very strange place in imperial society.

Vin studied the two of them suspiciously.

"Your hair, Mistress," Sazed said with a calm tone. "Cosahn is going to cut it for you."

"Oh," Vin said, reaching up. Her hair was getting a bit long for her taste—though somehow she doubted that Sazed was going to let her have it cropped boyishly short.

Cosahn waved to a chair, and Vin reluctantly seated herself. She found it unnerving to sit docilely while someone worked with shears so close to her head, but there was no getting around it.

After a few moments of running her hands through Vin's hair, "tisk"ing quietly, Cosahn began to snip. "Such beautiful hair," she said, almost as if to herself, "thick, with a nice deep black color. It's a shame to see it cared for so poorly, Master Vaht. Many courtly women would die for hair like this—it has just enough body to lie full, but is straight enough to work with easily."

Sazed smiled. "We'll have to see that it receives better care in the future," he said.

Cosahn continued her work, nodding to herself. Eventually, Sazed walked over and took a seat just a few feet in front of Vin.

"Kelsier hasn't returned yet, I assume?" Vin asked.

Sazed shook his head, and Vin sighed. Kelsier didn't think she was practiced enough go with him on his nightly raids, many of which he went on directly following his training sessions with Vin. During the last two months, Kelsier had put in appearances on the properties of a dozen different noble houses, both in Luthadel and in Fellise. He varied his disguises and apparent motives, trying to create an air of confusion among the Great Houses.

"What?" Vin asked, eyeing Sazed, who was regarding her with a curious look.

The Terrisman nodded his head slightly with respect. "I was wondering if you might be willing to listen to another proposal."

Vin sighed, rolling her eyes. "Fine." *It isn't like I can do anything else but sit here.*

"I think I have the perfect religion for you," Sazed said, his normally stoic face revealing a glimmer of eagerness. "It is called 'Trelagism,' after the god Trell. Trell was worshipped by a group known as the Nelazan, a people who lived far to the north. In their land, the day and night cycle was very odd. During some months of the year, it was dark for most of the day. During the summer, however, it only grew dark for a few hours at a time.

"The Nelazan believed that there was beauty in darkness, and that the daylight was more profane. They saw the stars as the Thousand Eyes of Trell watching them. The sun was the single, jealous eye of Trell's brother, Nalt. Since Nalt only had one eye, he made it blaze brightly to outshine his brother. The Nelazan, however, were not impressed, and preferred to worship the quiet Trell, who watched over them even when Nalt obscured the sky."

Sazed fell silent. Vin wasn't sure how to respond, so she didn't say anything.

"It really is a good religion, Mistress Vin," Sazed said. "Very gentle, yet very powerful. The Nelazan were not an advanced people, but they were quite determined. They mapped the entire night sky, counting and placing every major star. Their ways suit you—especially their preference of the night. I can tell you more, if you wish."

Vin shook her head. "That's all right, Sazed."

"Not a good fit, then?" Sazed said, frowning slightly. "Ah, well. I shall have to consider it some more. Thank you, Mistress—you are very patient with me, I think."

"Consider it some more?" Vin asked. "That's the fifth religion you've tried to convert me to, Saze. How many more can there be?"

"Five hundred and sixty two," Sazed said. "Or, at least, that is the number of belief systems I know. There are, likely and unfortunately, others that have passed from this world without leaving traces for my people to collect."

Vin paused. "And you have all of these religions *memorized?*"

"As much as is possible," Sazed said. "Their prayers, their beliefs, their mythologies. Many are very similar—break-offs or sects of one another."

"Even still, how can you remember all of that?"

"I have . . . methods," Sazed said.

"But, what's the point?"

Sazed frowned. "The answer should be obvious, I think. People are valuable, Mistress Vin, and so—therefore—are their beliefs. Since the Ascension a thousand years ago, so many beliefs have disappeared. The Steel Ministry forbids the worship of anyone but the Lord Ruler, and the Inquisitors have quite diligently destroyed hundreds of religions. If *someone* doesn't remember them, then they will simply disappear."

"You mean," Vin said incredulously, "you're trying to get me to believe in religions that have been dead for a thousand years?"

Sazed nodded.

Is everyone involved with Kelsier insane?

"The Final Empire cannot last forever," Sazed said quietly. "I do not know if Master Kelsier will be the one who finally brings its end, but that end *will* come. And when it does—when the Steel Ministry no longer holds sway— men will wish to return to the beliefs of their fathers. On that day they will look to the Keepers, and on that day we shall return to mankind his forgotten truths."

"Keepers?" Vin asked as Cosahn moved around to begin snipping at her bangs. "There are more like you?"

"Not many," Sazed said. "But some. Enough to pass the truths on to the next generation."

Vin sat thoughtfully, resisting the urge to squirm beneath Cosahn's ministrations. The woman certainly was taking her time—when Reen had cut Vin's hair, he had been finished after just a few quick hacks.

"Shall we go over your lessons while we wait, Mistress Vin?" Sazed asked.

Vin eyed the Terrisman, and he smiled just slightly. He knew that he had her captive; she couldn't hide, or even sit at the window, staring out into the mists. All she could do was sit and listen. "Fine."

"Can you name all ten Great Houses of Luthadel in order of power?"

"Venture, Hasting, Elariel, Tekiel, Lekal, Erikeller, Erikell, Haught, Urbain, and Buvidas."

"Good," Sazed said. "And you are?"

"I am the Lady Valette Renoux, fourth cousin to Lord Teven Renoux, who owns this mansion. My parents—Lord Hadren and Lady Fellette Renoux—live in Chakath, a city in the Western Dominance. Major export, wool. My family works in trading dyes, specifically blushdip red, from the snails that are common there, and callowfield yellow, made from tree bark. As part of a trade agreement with their distant cousin, my parents sent me down here to Luthadel, so I can spend some time at court."

Sazed nodded. "And how do you feel about this opportunity?"

"I am amazed and a little overwhelmed," Vin said. "People will pay attention to me because they wish to curry favor with Lord Renoux. Since I'm not familiar with the ways of court, I will be flattered by their attention. I will ingratiate myself to the court community, but I will stay quiet and out of trouble."

"Your memorization skills are admirable, Mistress," Sazed said. "This humble attendant wonders how much more successful might you be if you dedicated yourself to learning, rather than dedicating yourself to avoiding our lessons."

Vin eyed him. "Do all Terrisman 'humble attendants' give their masters as much lip as you do?"

"Only the successful ones."

Vin eyed him for a moment, then sighed. "I'm sorry, Saze. I don't mean to avoid your lessons. I just . . . the mists . . . I get distracted sometimes."

"Well, fortunately and honestly, you are very quick to learn. However, the people of the court have had their entire lives to study etiquette. Even as a rural noblewoman, there are certain things you would know."

"I know," Vin said. "I don't want to stand out."

"Oh, you can't avoid that, Mistress. A newcomer, from a distant part of the empire? Yes, they will notice you. We just don't want to make them suspicious. You must be considered, then dismissed. If you act too much like a fool, that will be suspect in and of itself."

Great.

Sazed paused, cocking his head slightly. A few seconds later, Vin heard footsteps in the hallway outside. Kelsier sauntered into the room, bearing a self-satisfied smile. He pulled off his mistcloak, then paused as he saw Vin.

"What?" she asked, sinking a little further into the chair.

"The haircut looks good," Kelsier said. "Nice job, Cosahn."

"It was nothing, Master Kelsier." Vin could hear the blush in her voice. "I just work with what I have."

"Mirror," Vin said, holding out her hand.

Cosahn handed her one. Vin held it up, and what she saw gave her pause. She looked . . . like a girl.

Cosahn had done a remarkable job of evening out the hair, and she had managed to get rid of the snags. Vin had always found that if her hair got too long, it had a tendency to stand up. Cosahn had done something about this too. Vin's hair still wasn't very long—it barely hung down over her ears—but at least it lay flat.

You don't want them to think of you as a girl, Reen's voice warned. Yet, for once, she found herself wanting to ignore that voice.

"We might actually turn you into a lady, Vin!" Kelsier said with a laugh, earning him a glare from Vin.

"First we'll have to persuade her not to scowl so often, Master Kelsier," Sazed noted.

"That's going to be hard," Kelsier said. "She's quite fond of making faces. Anyway, well done, Cosahn."

"I've still got a little bit of trimming to do, Master Kelsier," the woman said.

"By all means, continue," Kelsier said. "But I'm going to filch Sazed for a moment."

Kelsier winked at Vin, smiled at Cosahn, then he and Sazed retreated from the room—once again leaving Vin where she couldn't eavesdrop.

Kelsier peeked into the kitchen, watching Vin sit sullenly in her chair. The haircut really was good. However, his compliments had an ulterior motive—he suspected that Vin had spent far too much of her life being told that she was worthless. Perhaps if she had a bit more self-confidence, she wouldn't try to hide so much.

He let the door slide shut, turning to Sazed. The Terrisman waited, as always, with restful patience.

"How is the training going?" Kelsier asked.

"Very well, Master Kelsier," Sazed said. "She already knew some things from training she received at her brother's hands. Above that, however, she is an extremely intelligent girl—perceptive and quick to memorize. I didn't expect such skill from one who grew up in her circumstances."

"A lot of the street children are clever," Kelsier said. "The ones who aren't dead."

Sazed nodded solemnly. "She is extremely reserved, and I sense that she doesn't see the full value in my lessons. She is very obedient, but is quick to exploit mistakes or misunderstandings. If I don't tell her exactly when and where to meet, I often have to search the entire mansion for her."

Kelsier nodded. "I think it's her way of maintaining a bit of control in her life. Anyway, what I really wanted to know is whether she's ready or not."

"I'm not sure, Master Kelsier," Sazed replied. "Pure knowledge is not the equivalent of skill. I'm not certain if she has the . . . poise to imitate a noblewoman, even a young and inexperienced one. We've done practice dinners, gone over conversational etiquette, and memorized gossip. She seems skilled at it all, in a controlled situation. She's even done well sitting in on tea meetings when Renoux entertains noble guests. However, we won't really be able to tell if she can do this until we put her alone in a party full of aristocrats."

"I wish she could practice some more," Kelsier said with a shake of his head. "But every week we spend preparing increases the chances that the Ministry will discover our budding army in the caves."

"It is a test of balance, then," Sazed said. "We must wait long enough to gather the men we need, yet move soon enough to avoid discovery."

Kelsier nodded. "We can't pause for one crewmember—we'll have to find someone else to be our mole if Vin does badly. Poor girl—I wish I had time to train her better in Allomancy. We've barely covered the first four metals. I just don't have enough *time!*"

"If I might make a suggestion . . ."

"Of course, Saze."

"Send the child with some of the Misting crewmembers," Sazed said. "I hear that the man Breeze is a very accomplished Soother, and surely the others are equally skilled. Let them show Mistress Vin how to use her abilities."

Kelsier paused thoughtfully. "That's a good idea, Saze."

"But?"

Kelsier glanced back toward the door, beyond which Vin was still petulantly getting her haircut. "I'm not sure. Today, when we were training, we got into a Steelpush shoving match. The kid has to weigh less than half what I do, but she gave me a decent pummeling anyway."

"Different people have different strengths in Allomancy," Sazed said.

"Yes, but the variance isn't usually this great," Kelsier said. "Plus, it took me months and months to learn how to manipulate my Pushes and Pulls. It's not as easy as it sounds—even something as simple as Pushing yourself up onto a rooftop requires an understanding of weight, balance, and trajectory.

"But Vin . . . she seems to know all these things instinctively. True, she can only use the first four metals with any skill, but the progress she's made is amazing."

"She is a special girl."

Kelsier nodded. "She deserves more time to learn about her powers. I feel a little guilty about pulling her into our plans. She'll probably end up at a Ministry execution ceremony with the rest of us."

"But that guilt won't stop you from using her to spy on the aristocracy."

Kelsier shook his head. "No," he said quietly. "It won't. We'll need every advantage we can get. Just . . . watch over her, Saze. From now on, you'll act as Vin's steward and guardian at the functions she attends—it won't be odd for her to bring a Terrisman servant with her."

"Not at all," Sazed agreed. "In fact, it would be strange to send a girl her age to courtly functions without an escort."

Kelsier nodded. "Protect her, Saze. She might be a powerful Allomancer, but she's inexperienced. I'll feel a lot less guilty about sending her into those aristo-cratic dens if I know you're with her."

"I will protect her with my life, Master Kelsier. I promise you this."

Kelsier smiled, resting a thankful hand on Sazed's shoulder. "I feel pity for the man who gets in your way."

Sazed bowed his head humbly. He looked innocuous, but Kelsier knew the strength that Sazed hid. Few men, Allomancers or not, would fare well in a fight with a Keeper whose anger had been roused. That was probably why the Ministry had hunted the sect virtually to extinction.

"All right," Kelsier said. "Get back to your teaching. Lord Venture is throw-ing a ball at the end of the week, and—ready or not—Vin is going to be there."

It amazes me how many nations have united behind our purpose. There are still dissenters, of course—and some kingdoms, regrettably, have fallen to wars that I could not stop.

Still, this general unity is glorious, even humbling, to contemplate. I wish that the nations of mankind hadn't required such a dire threat to make them see the value of peace and cooperation.

10

VIN WALKED ALONG A STREET in the Cracks—one of Luthadel's many skaa slums—with her hood up. For some reason, she found the muffled heat of a hood preferable to the oppressive red sunlight.

She walked with a slouch, eyes down, sticking near to the side of the street. The skaa she passed had similar airs of dejection. No one looked up; no one walked with a straight back or an optimistic smile. In the slums, those things would make one look suspicious.

She'd almost forgotten how oppressive Luthadel could be. Her weeks in Fellise had accustomed her to trees and washed stone. Here, there was nothing white—no creeping aspens, no whitewashed granite. All was black.

Buildings were stained by countless, repetitive ashfalls. Air curled with smoke from the infamous Luthadel smithies and a thousand separate noble kitchens. Cobblestones, doorways, and corners were clogged with soot—the slums were rarely swept clean.

It's like . . . things are actually brighter at night than they are during the day, Vin thought, pulling her patched skaa cloak close, turning a corner. She passed beggars, huddled on corners, hands outstretched and hoping for an offering, their pleadings falling vainly on the ears of people who were themselves starving. She passed workers, walking with heads and shoulders bowed, caps or hoods pulled down to keep ash out of their eyes. Occasionally, she passed squads of Garrison town guards, walking with full armor—breastplate, cap, and black cloak—trying to look as intimidating as possible.

This last group moved through the slums, acting as the Lord Ruler's hands in an area most obligators found too distasteful to visit. The Garrisoners kicked at beggars to make certain they were truly invalids, stopped wandering workers to harass them about being on the streets instead of working, and made a general nuisance of themselves. Vin ducked down as a group passed, pulling her hood close. She was old enough that she should have been either bearing children or working in a mill, but her size often made her look younger in profile.

Either the ruse worked, or this particular squad wasn't interested in looking for ditchers, for they let her pass with barely a glance. She ducked around a corner, walking down an ash-drifted alley, and approached the soup kitchen at the end of the small street.

Like most of its kind, the kitchen was dingy and poorly maintained. In an economy where workers were rarely, if ever, given direct pay, kitchens had to be supported by the nobility. Some local lords—probably the owners of the mills and forges in the area—paid the kitchen owner to provide food for the local skaa. The workers would be given meal tokens for their time, and would be allowed a short break at midday to go eat. The central kitchen would allow the smaller businesses to avoid the costs of providing on-site meals.

Of course, since the kitchen owner was paid directly, he could pocket whatever he could save on ingredients. In Vin's experience, kitchen food was about as tasty as ashwater.

Fortunately, she hadn't come to eat. She joined the line at the door, waiting quietly as workers presented their meal chips. When her turn came, she pulled out a small wooden disk and passed it to the skaa man at the door. He accepted the chip with a smooth motion, nodding almost imperceptibly to his right.

Vin walked in the indicated direction, passing through a filthy dining room, floor scattered with tracked-in ash. As she approached far wall, she could see a splintery wooden door set in the room's corner. A man seated by the door caught her eyes, nodded slightly, and pushed the door open. Vin passed quickly into the small room beyond.

"Vin, my dear!" Breeze said, lounging at a table near the center of the room. "Welcome! How was Fellise?"

Vin shrugged, taking a seat at the table.

"Ah," Breeze said. "I'd almost forgotten what a fascinating conversationalist you are. Wine?"

Vin shook her head.

"Well, I would certainly like some." Breeze wore one of his extravagant suits, dueling cane resting across his lap. The chamber was only lit by a single lantern, but it was far cleaner than the room outside. Of the four other men in the room, Vin recognized only one—an apprentice from Clubs's shop. The two by the door were obviously guards. The last man appeared to be a regular skaa worker—complete with blackened jacket and ashen face. His self-confident air, however, proved that he was a member of the underground. Probably one of Yeden's rebels.

Breeze held up his cup, tapping its side with his fingernail. The rebel regarded it darkly.

"Right now," Breeze said, "you're wondering if I'm using Allomancy on you. Perhaps I am, perhaps I am not. Does it matter? I'm here by your leader's invitation, and he ordered you to see that I was made comfortable. And, I assure you, a cup of wine in my hand is *absolutely* necessary for my comfort."

The skaa man waited for a moment, then snatched the cup and stalked away, grumbling under his breath about foolish costs and wasted resources.

Breeze raised an eyebrow, turning to Vin. He seemed quite pleased with himself.

"So, did you Push him?" she asked.

Breeze shook his head. "Waste of brass. Did Kelsier tell you why he asked you to come here today?"

"He told me to watch you," Vin said, a bit annoyed at being handed off to Breeze. "He said he didn't have time to train me in all the metals."

"Well," Breeze said, "let us begin, then. First, you must understand that Soothing is about more than just Allomancy. It's about the delicate and noble art of manipulation."

"Noble indeed," Vin said.

"Ah, you sound like one of *them*," Breeze said.

"Them who?"

"Them everyone else," Breeze said. "You saw how that skaa gentleman treated me? People don't like us, my dear. The idea of someone who can play with their emotions, who can 'mystically' get them to do certain things, makes them uncomfortable. What they do not realize—and what you *must* realize—is that manipulating others is something that all people do. In fact, manipulation is at the core of our social interaction."

He settled back, raising his dueling cane and gesturing with it slightly as he spoke. "Think about it. What is a man doing when he seeks the affection of a young lady? Why, he is trying to manipulate her to regard him favorably. What happens when old two friends sit down for a drink? They tell stories, trying to impress each other. Life as a human being is about posturing and influence. This isn't a bad thing—in fact, we depend upon it. These interactions teach us how to respond to others."

He paused, pointing at Vin with the cane. "The difference between Soothers and regular people is that we are aware of what we're doing. We also have a slight . . . advantage. But, is it really that much more 'powerful' than having a charismatic personality or a fine set of teeth? I think not."

Vin paused.

"Besides," Breeze added, "as I mentioned, a good Soother must be skilled far beyond his ability to use Allomancy. Allomancy can't let you read minds or even emotions—in a way, you're as blind as anyone else. You fire off pulses of emotions, targeted at a single person or in an area, and your subjects will have their emotions altered—hopefully producing the effect that you wished. However, great Soothers are those who can successfully use their eyes and instincts to know how a person is feeling *before* they get Soothed."

"What does it matter how they're feeling?" Vin said, trying to cover her annoyance. "You're just going to Soothe them anyway, right? So, when you're done, they'll feel how you want them to."

Breeze sighed, shaking his head. "What would you say if you knew I'd Soothed you on three separate occasions during our conversation?"

Vin paused. "When?" she demanded.

"Does it matter?" Breeze asked. "This is the lesson you must learn, my dear. If you can't read how someone is feeling, then you'll never have a subtle touch with emotional Allomancy. Push someone too hard, and even the most blind of skaa will realize that they're being manipulated somehow. Touch too softly, and you won't produce a noticeable effect—other, more powerful emotions will still rule your subject."

Breeze shook his head. "It's all about understanding people," he continued. "You have to read how someone is feeling, change that feeling by nudging it in the proper direction, then channel their newfound emotional state to your advantage. That, my dear, is the challenge in what we do! It is difficult, but for those who can do it well . . ."

The door opened, and the sullen skaa man returned, bearing an entire bottle of wine. He put it and a cup on the table before Breeze, then went over to stand on the other side of the room, beside peepholes looking into the dining room.

"There are vast rewards," Breeze said with a quiet smile. He winked at her, then poured some wine.

Vin wasn't certain what to think. Breeze's opinion seemed cruel. Yet, Reen had trained her well. If she didn't have power over this thing, others would gain power over her through it. She started burning copper—as Kelsier had taught her—to shield herself from further manipulations on Breeze's part.

The door opened again, and a familiar vest-wearing form tromped in. "Hey, Vin," Ham said with a friendly wave. He walked over to the table, eyeing the wine. "Breeze, you know that the rebellion doesn't have the money for that kind of thing."

"Kelsier will reimburse them," Breeze said with a dismissive wave. "I simply cannot work with a dry throat. How is the area?"

"Secure," Ham said. "But I've got Tineyes on the corners just in case. Your bolt-exit is behind that hatch in the corner."

Breeze nodded, and Ham turned, looking at Clubs's apprentice. "You Smoking back there, Cobble?"

The boy nodded.

"Good lad," Ham said. "That's everything, then. Now we just have to wait for Kell's speech."

Breeze checked his pocket watch. "He's not scheduled for another few minutes. Shall I have someone fetch you a cup?"

"I'll pass," Ham said.

Breeze shrugged, sipping his wine.

There was a moment of silence. Finally, Ham spoke. "So . . ."

"No," Breeze interrupted.

"But—"

"Whatever it is, we don't want to hear about it."

Ham gave the Soother a flat stare. "You can't Push me into complacence, Breeze."

Breeze rolled his eyes, taking a drink.

"What?" Vin asked. "What were you going to say?"

"Don't encourage him, my dear," Breeze said.

Vin frowned. She glanced at Ham, who smiled.

Breeze sighed. "Just leave me out of it. I'm not in the mood for one of Ham's inane debates."

"Ignore him," Ham said eagerly, pulling his chair a little bit closer to Vin. "So, I've been wondering. By overthrowing the Final Empire are we doing something good, or are we doing something bad?"

Vin paused. "Does it matter?"

Ham looked taken aback, but Breeze chuckled. "Well answered," the Soother said.

Ham glared at Breeze, then turned back to Vin. "Of course it matters."

"Well," Vin said, "I guess we're doing something good. The Final Empire has oppressed the skaa for centuries."

"Right," Ham said. "But, there's a problem. The Lord Ruler is God, right?"

Vin shrugged. "Does it matter?"

Ham glared at her.

She rolled her eyes. "All right. The Ministry claims that he is God."

"Actually," Breeze noted, "the Lord Ruler is only a *piece* of God. He is the Sliver of Infinity—not omniscient or omnipresent, but an independent section of a consciousness that *is*."

Ham sighed. "I thought you didn't want to be involved."

"Just making certain everyone has their facts correct," Breeze said lightly.

"Anyway," Ham said. "God is the creator of all things, right? He is the force that dictates the laws of the universe, and is therefore the ultimate source of ethics. He is absolute morality."

Vin blinked.

"You see the dilemma?" Ham asked.

"I see an idiot," Breeze mumbled.

"I'm confused," Vin said. "What's the problem?"

"We claim to be doing good," Ham said. "But, the Lord Ruler—as God— *defines* what is good. So, by opposing him we're actually evil. But, since he's doing the wrong thing, does evil actually count as good in this case?"

Vin frowned.

"Well?" Ham asked.

"I think you gave me a headache," Vin said.

"I warned you," Breeze noted.

Ham sighed. "But, don't you think it's worth thinking about?"

"I'm not sure."

"I am," Breeze said.

Ham shook his head. "No one around here likes to have decent, intelligent discussions."

The skaa rebel in the corner suddenly perked up. "Kelsier's here!"

Ham raised an eyebrow, then stood. "I should go watch the perimeter. Think about that question, Vin."

"All right . . ." Vin said as Ham left.

"Over here, Vin," Breeze said, rising. "There are peepholes on the wall for us. Be a dear and bring my chair over, would you?"

Breeze didn't look back to see if she did as requested. She paused, uncertain. With her copper on, he couldn't Soothe her, but . . . Eventually, she sighed and carried both chairs over to the side of the room. Breeze slid back a long, thin slat in the wall, revealing a view of the dining room.

A group of dirtied skaa men sat around tables, wearing brown work coats or ragged cloaks. They were a dark group, with ash-stained skin and slumped postures. However, their presence at the meeting meant that they were willing to listen. Yeden sat at a table near the front of the room, wearing his usual patched worker's coat, his curly hair cut short during Vin's absence.

Vin had expected some kind of grand entrance from Kelsier. Instead, however, he simply walked quietly out of the kitchen. He paused by Yeden's table, smiling and speaking quietly with the man for a moment, then he stepped up before the seated workers.

Vin had never seen him in such mundane clothing before. He wore a brown skaa coat and tan trousers, like many of the audience. Kelsier's outfit, however, was clean. No soot stained the cloth, and while it was of the same rough material that skaa commonly used, it bore no patches or tears. The difference was stark enough, Vin decided—if he'd come in a suit, it would have been too much.

He put his arms behind his back, and slowly the crowd of workers quieted. Vin frowned, watching through the peep slit, wondering at Kelsier's ability to quiet a room of hungry men by simply standing before them. Was he using Allomancy, perhaps? Yet, even with her copper on, she felt a . . . presence from him.

Once the room fell quiet, Kelsier began to speak. "You've probably all heard of me, by now," he said. "And, you wouldn't be here if you weren't at least a little bit sympathetic to my cause."

Beside Vin, Breeze sipped his drink. "Soothing and Rioting aren't like other kinds of Allomancy," he said quietly. "With most metals, Pushing and Pulling have opposite effects. With emotions, however, you can often produce the same result regardless of whether you Soothe or Riot.

"This doesn't hold for extreme emotional states—complete emotionlessness or utter passion. However, in most cases, it doesn't matter which power you use. People are not like solid bricks of metal—at any given time, they will have a dozen different emotions churning within them. An experienced Soother can dampen everything but the emotion he wants to remain dominant."

Breeze turned slightly. "Rudd, send in the blue server, please."

One of the guards nodded, cracking the door and whispering something to the man outside. A moment later, Vin saw a serving girl wearing a faded blue dress move through the crowd, filling drinks.

"My Soothers are mixed with the crowd," Breeze said, his voice growing distracted. "The serving girls are a sign, telling my men which emotions to Soothe away. They will work, just as I do. . . ." He trailed off, concentrating as he looked into the crowd.

"Fatigue . . ." he whispered. "That's not a necessary emotion right now. Hunger . . . distracting. Suspicion . . . definitely not helpful. Yes, and as the Soothers work, the Rioters enflame the emotions we want the crowd to be feeling. Curiosity . . . that's what they need now. Yes, listen to Kelsier. You've heard legends and stories. See the man for yourself, and be impressed."

"I know why you came today," Kelsier said quietly. He spoke without much of the flamboyance Vin associated with the man, his tone quiet, but direct. "Twelve-hour days in a mill, mine, or forge. Beatings, lack of pay, poor food. And, for what? So that you can return to your tenements at the day's end to find another tragedy? A friend, slain by an uncaring taskmaster. A daughter, taken to be some nobleman's plaything. A brother, dead at the hand of a passing lord who was having an unpleasant day."

"Yes," Breeze whispered. "Good. Red, Rudd. Send in the girl in light red."

Another serving girl entered the room.

"Passion and anger," Breeze said, his voice almost a mumble. "But just a bit. Just a nudge—a reminder."

Curious, Vin extinguished her copper for a moment, burning bronze instead, trying to sense Breeze's use of Allomancy. No pulses came from him.

Of course, she thought. *I forgot about Clubs's apprentice—he'd keep me from sensing any Allomantic pulses.* She turned her copper back on.

Kelsier continued to speak. "My friends, you're not alone in your tragedy. There are millions, just like you. And they need you. I've not come to beg— we've had enough of that in our lives. I simply ask you to think. Where would you rather your energy be spent? On forging the Lord Ruler's weapons? Or, on something more valuable?"

He's not mentioning our troops, Vin thought. *Or even what those who join with him are going to do. He doesn't want the workers to know details. Probably a good idea—those he recruits can be sent to the army, and the rest won't be able to give away specific information.*

"You know why I am here," Kelsier said. "You know my friend, Yeden, and what he represents. Every skaa in the city knows about the rebellion. Perhaps you've considered joining it. Most of you will not—most of you will go back to your soot-stained mills, to your burning forges, to your dying homes. You'll go because this terrible life is familiar. But some of you . . . some of you will come with me. And those are the men who will be remembered in the years to come. Remembered for having done something grand."

Many of the workers shared glances, though some just stared at their half-empty soup bowls. Finally, someone near the back of the room spoke. "You're a fool," the man said. "The Lord Ruler will kill you. You don't rebel against God in his *own city*."

The room fell silent. Tense. Vin sat up as Breeze whispered to himself.

In the room, Kelsier stood quietly for a moment. Finally, he reached up and pulled back the sleeves on his jacket, revealing the crisscrossed scars on his arms. "The Lord Ruler is not our god," he said quietly. "And he cannot kill me. He tried, but he failed. For I am the thing that he can never kill."

With that, Kelsier turned, walking from the room the way he had come.

"Hum," Breeze said, "well, that was a little dramatic. Rudd, bring back the red and send out the brown."

A serving woman in brown walked into the crowd.

"Amazement," Breeze said. "And, yes, pride. Soothe the anger, for now. . . ."

The crowd sat quietly for a moment, the dining room eerily motionless. Finally, Yeden stood up to speak and give some further encouragement, as well as an explanation of what the men should do, should they wish to hear more. As he talked, the men returned to their meals.

"Green, Rudd," Breeze said. "Hum, yes. Let's make you all thoughtful, and give you a nudge of loyalty. We wouldn't want anyone to run to the obligators, would we? Kell's covered his tracks quite well, but the less the authorities hear, the better, eh? Oh, and what about you, Yeden? You're a bit too nervous. Let's Soothe that, take away your worries. Leave only that passion of yours—hopefully, it will be enough to cover up that stupid tone in your voice."

Vin continued to watch. Now that Kelsier had gone, she found it easier to focus on the crowd's reactions, and on Breeze's work. As Yeden spoke, the workers outside seemed to react exactly according to Breeze's mumbled instructions. Yeden, too, showed effects of the Soothing: He grew more comfortable, his voice more confident, as he spoke.

Curious, Vin let her copper drop again. She concentrated, seeing if she could sense Breeze's touch on her emotions; she would be included in his general Allomantic projections. He didn't have time to pick and choose individuals, except maybe Yeden. It was very, very difficult to sense. Yet, as Breeze sat mumbling to himself, she began to feel the exact emotions he described.

Vin couldn't help but be impressed. The few times that Kelsier had used Allomancy on her emotions, his touch has been like a sudden, blunt punch to the face. He had strength, but very little subtlety.

Breeze's touch was incredibly delicate. He Soothed certain emotions, dampening them while leaving others unaffected. Vin thought she could sense his men Rioting on her emotions, too, but these touches weren't nearly as subtle as Breeze's. She left her copper off, watching for touches on her emotions as Yeden continued his speech. He explained that the men who joined with them would have to leave family and friends for a time—as long as a year—but would be fed well during that time.

Vin felt her respect for Breeze continue to rise. Suddenly, she didn't feel so annoyed with Kelsier for handing her off. Breeze could only do one thing, but he obviously had a great deal of practice at it. Kelsier, as a Mistborn, had to learn all of the Allomantic skills; it made sense that he wouldn't be as focused in any one power.

I need to make certain he sends me to learn from the others, Vin thought. *They'll be masters at their own powers.*

Vin turned her attention back to the dining room as Yeden wrapped up. "You heard Kelsier, the Survivor of Hathsin," he said. "The rumors about him are true—he's given up his thieving ways, and turned his considerable attention toward working for the skaa rebellion! Men, we are preparing for something grand. Something that may, indeed, end up being our last struggle against the Final Empire. Join with us. Join with your brothers. Join with the Survivor himself!"

The dining room fell silent.

"Bright red," Breeze said. "I want those men to leave feeling passionate about what they've heard."

"The emotions will fade, won't they?" Vin said as a red-clothed serving girl entered the crowd.

"Yes," Breeze said, sitting back and sliding the panel closed. "But memories stay. If people associate strong emotion with an event, they'll remember it better."

A few moments later, Ham entered through the back door. "That went well. The men are leaving invigorated, and a number of them are staying behind. We'll have a good set of volunteers to send off to the caves."

Breeze shook his head. "It's not enough. Dox takes a few days to organize each of these meetings, and we only get about twenty men from each one. At this rate, we'll never hit ten thousand in time."

"You think we need more meetings?" Ham asked. "That's going to be tough—we have to be very careful with these things, so only those who can be reasonably trusted are invited."

Breeze sat for a moment. Finally, he downed the rest of his wine. "I don't know—but we'll have to think of something. For now, let's return to the shop. I believe Kelsier wishes to hold a progress meeting this evening."

Kelsier looked to the west. The afternoon sun was a poisonous red, shining angrily through a sky of smoke. Just below it, Kelsier could see the silhouetted tip of a dark peak. Tyrian, closest of the Ashmounts.

He stood atop Clubs's flat-roofed shop, listening to workers returning home on the streets below. A flat roof meant having to shovel off ash occasionally, which was why most skaa buildings were peaked, but in Kelsier's opinion the view was often worth a bit of trouble.

Below him, the skaa workers trudged in despondent ranks, their passing kicking up a small cloud of ash. Kelsier turned away from them, looking toward the northern horizon . . . toward the Pits of Hathsin.

Where does it go? he thought. *The atium reaches the city, but then disappears. It isn't the Ministry—we've watched them—and no skaa hands touch the metal. We assume it goes into the treasury. We hope it does, at least.*

While burning atium, a Mistborn was virtually unstoppable, which was part of why it was so valuable. But, his plan was about more than just wealth. He knew how much atium was harvested at the pits, and Dockson had researched the amounts that the Lord Ruler doled out—at exorbitant prices—to the nobility. Barely a tenth of what was mined eventually found its way into noble hands.

Ninety percent of the atium produced in the world had been stockpiled, year after year, for a thousand years. With that much of the metal, Kelsier's team could intimidate even the most powerful of the noble houses. Yeden's plan to hold the palace probably seemed futile to many—indeed, on its own, it was doomed to fail. However, Kelsier's other plans . . .

Kelsier glanced down at the small, whitish bar in his hand. The Eleventh Metal. He knew the rumors about it—he'd started them. Now, he just had to make good on them.

He sighed, turning eyes east, toward Kredik Shaw, the Lord Ruler's palace. The name was Terris; it meant "The Hill of a Thousand Spires." Appropriate, since the imperial palace resembled a patch of enormous black spears thrust into the ground. Some of the spires twisted, others were straight. Some were thick towers, other were thin and needlelike. They varied in height, but each one was tall. And each one ended in a point.

Kredik Shaw. That's where it had ended three years before. And he needed to go back.

The trap door opened, and a figure climbed onto the roof. Kelsier turned with a raised eyebrow as Sazed brushed off his robe, then approached in his characteristically respectful posture. Even a rebellious Terrisman maintained the form of his training.

"Master Kelsier," Sazed said with a bow.

Kelsier nodded, and Sazed stepped up beside him, looking toward the imperial palace. "Ah," he said to himself, as if understanding Kelsier's thoughts.

Kelsier smiled. Sazed had been a valuable find indeed. Keepers were necessarily secretive, for the Lord Ruler had hunted them practically since the Day of Ascension itself. Some legends claimed that the Ruler's complete subjugation of the Terris people—including the breeding and stewardship programs—was simply an outgrowth of his hatred for Keepers.

"I wonder what he would think if he knew a Keeper was in Luthadel," Kelsier said, "barely a short walk from the palace itself."

"Let us hope we never find out, Master Kelsier," Sazed said.

"I appreciate your willingness to come here to the city, Saze. I know it's a risk."

"This is a good work," Sazed said. "And this plan is dangerous for all involved. Indeed, simply living is dangerous for me, I think. It is not healthy to belong to a sect that the Lord Ruler himself fears."

"Fears?" Kelsier asked, turning to look up at Sazed. Despite Kelsier's above-average height, the Terrisman was still a good head taller. "I'm not sure if he fears anything, Saze."

"He fears the Keepers," Sazed said. "Definitely and inexplicably. Perhaps it is because of our powers. We are not Allomancers, but . . . something else. Something unknown to him."

Kelsier nodded, turning back toward the city. He had so many plans, so much work to do—and at the core of it all were the skaa. The poor, humble, defeated skaa.

"Tell me about another one, Saze," Kelsier said. "One with power."

"Power?" Sazed asked. "That is a relative term when applied to religion, I think. Perhaps you would like to hear of Jaism. Its followers were quite faithful and devout."

"Tell me about them."

"Jaism was founded by a single man," Sazed said. "His true name is lost, though his followers simply called him 'the Ja.' He was murdered by a local king for preaching discord—something he was apparently very good at—but that only made his following larger.

"The Jaists thought that they earned happiness proportional to their overt devotion, and were known for frequent and fervent professions of faith. Apparently, speaking with a Jaist could be frustrating, since they tended to end nearly every sentence with 'Praise the Ja.'"

"That's nice, Saze," Kelsier said. "But power is more than just words."

"Oh, quite indeed," Sazed agreed. "The Jaists were strong in their faith. Legends say that the Ministry had to wipe them out completely, since not one Jaist would accept the Lord Ruler as God. They didn't last long past the Ascension, but only because they were so blatant that they were easy to hunt down and kill."

Kelsier nodded, then he smiled, eyeing Sazed. "You didn't ask me if I wanted to convert."

"My apologies, Master Kelsier," Sazed said, "but the religion does not suit you, I think. It has a level of brashness that you might find appealing, but you would find the theology simplistic."

"You're getting to know me too well," Kelsier said, still regarding the city. "In the end, after kingdoms and armies had fallen, the religions were still fighting, weren't they?"

"Indeed," Sazed said. "Some of the more resilient religions lasted all the way until the fifth century."

"What made them so strong?" Kelsier said. "How did they do it, Saze? What gave these theologies such power over people?"

"It wasn't any one thing, I think," Sazed said. "Some were strong through honest faith, others because of the hope they promised. Others were coercive."

"But they all had passion," Kelsier said.

"Yes, Master Kelsier," Sazed said with a nod. "That is a quite true statement."

"That's what we've lost," Kelsier said, looking over the city with its hundreds of thousands, barely a handful of whom would dare fight. "They don't have faith in the Lord Ruler, they simply fear him. They don't have anything left to believe in."

"What do *you* believe in, if I may ask, Master Kelsier?"

Kelsier raised an eyebrow. "I'm not exactly sure yet," he admitted. "But overthrowing the Final Empire seems like a good start. Are there any religions on your list that include the slaughter of noblemen as a holy duty?"

Sazed frowned disapprovingly. "I do not believe so, Master Kelsier."

"Maybe I should found one," Kelsier said with an idle smile. "Anyway, have Breeze and Vin returned yet?"

"They arrived just before I came up here."

"Good," Kelsier said with a nod. "Tell them I'll be down in a moment."

Vin sat in her overstuffed chair in the conference room, legs tucked beneath her, trying to study Marsh out of the corner of her eye.

He looked so much like Kelsier. He was just . . . stern. He wasn't angry, nor was he grumpy like Clubs. He just wasn't happy. He sat in his chair, a neutral expression on his face.

The others had all arrived except for Kelsier, and they were chatting quietly amongst themselves. Vin caught Lestibournes's eye and waved him over. The teenage boy approached and crouched beside her chair.

"Marsh," Vin whispered beneath the general hum of the room. "Is that a nickname?"

"Notting without the call of his parents."

Vin paused, trying to decipher the boy's eastern dialect. "Not a nickname, then?"

Lestibournes shook his head. "He wasing one though."

"What was it?"

"Ironeyes. Others stopped using it. Too calling close to an iron in the real eyes, eh? Inquisitor."

Vin glanced at Marsh again. His expression was hard, his eyes unwavering, almost like they *were* made of iron. She could see why people would stop using the nickname; even referring to a Steel Inquisitor made her shiver.

"Thanks."

Lestibournes smiled. He was an earnest boy. Strange, intense, and jumpy— but earnest. He retreated to his stool as Kelsier finally arrived.

"All right, crew," he said. "What've we got?"

"Besides the bad news?" Breeze asked.

"Let's hear it."

"It's been twelve weeks, and we've gathered under two thousand men," Ham said. "Even with the numbers the rebellion already has, we're going to fall short."

"Dox?" Kelsier asked. "Can we get more meetings?"

"Probably," Dockson said from his seat beside a table stacked with ledgers.

"Are you sure you want to take that risk, Kelsier?" Yeden asked. His attitude had improved during the last few weeks—especially once Kelsier's recruits had begun to file in. As Reen had always said, results made quick friends.

"We're already in danger," Yeden continued. "Rumors are all over the under-ground. If we make any more of a stir, the Ministry is going to realize that something major is happening."

"He's probably right, Kell," Dockson said. "Besides, there are only so many skaa willing to listen. Luthadel is big, true, but our movement here is limited."

"All right," Kelsier said. "So, we'll start working the other towns in the area. Breeze, can you split your crew into two effective groups?"

"I suppose," Breeze said hesitantly.

"We can have one team work in Luthadel and the other work in surrounding towns. I can probably make it to all of the meetings, assuming we organize them so they don't happen at the same time."

"That many meetings will expose us even more," Yeden said.

"And that, by the way, brings up another problem," Ham said. "Weren't we supposed to be working on infiltrating the Ministry's ranks?"

"Well?" Kelsier asked, turning to Marsh.

Marsh shook his head. "The Ministry is tight—I need more time."

"It's not going to happen," Clubs grumbled. "Rebellion's already tried it."

Yeden nodded. "We've tried to get spies into the Inner Ministries a dozen times. It's impossible."

The room fell silent.

"I have an idea," Vin said quietly.

Kelsier raised an eyebrow.

"Camon," she said. "He was working on a job before you recruited me. Actually, it was the job that got us spotted by the obligators. The core of that plan was organized by another thief, a crewleader named Theron. He was setting up a fake canal convoy to carry Ministry funds to Luthadel."

"And?" Breeze asked.

"Those same canal boats would have brought new Ministry acolytes to Luthadel for the final part of their training. Theron has a contact along the route, a lesser obligator who was open to bribes. Maybe we could get him to add an 'acolyte' to the group from his local chapter."

Kelsier nodded thoughtfully. "It's worth looking into."

Dockson scribbled something on a sheet with his fountain pen. "I'll contact Theron and see if his informant is still viable."

"How are our resources coming?" Kelsier asked.

Dockson shrugged. "Ham found us two ex-soldier instructors. The weapons, however . . . well, Renoux and I are making contacts and initiating deals, but we can't move very quickly. Fortunately, when the weapons come, they should come in bulk."

Kelsier nodded. "That's everything, right?"

Breeze cleared his throat. "I've . . . been hearing a lot of rumors on the streets, Kelsier," he said. "The people are talking about this Eleventh Metal of yours."

"Good," Kelsier said.

"Aren't you worried that the Lord Ruler will hear? If he has forewarning of what you're going to do, it will be much more difficult to . . . resist him."

He didn't say "kill," Vin thought. *They don't think that Kelsier can do it.*

Kelsier just smiled. "Don't worry about the Lord Ruler—I've got things under control. In fact, I intend to pay the Lord Ruler a personal visit sometime during the next few days."

"*Visit?*" Yeden asked uncomfortably. "You're going to visit the Lord Ruler? Are you insa . . ." Yeden trailed off, then glanced at the rest of the room. "Right. I forgot."

"He's catching on," Dockson noted.

Heavy footsteps sounded in the hallway, and one of Ham's guards entered a moment later. He made his way to Ham's chair and whispered a brief message.

Ham frowned.

"What?" Kelsier asked.

"An incident," Ham said.

"Incident?" Dockson asked. "What kind of incident?"

"You know that lair we met in a few weeks back?" Ham said. "The one where Kell first introduced his plan?"

Camon's lair, Vin thought, growing apprehensive.

"Well," Ham said, "apparently the Ministry found it."

It seems Rashek represents a growing faction in Terris culture. A large number of the youths think that their unusual powers should be used for more than just field-work, husbandry, and stonecarving. They are rowdy, even violent—far different from the quiet, discerning Terris philosophers and holy men that I have known.

They will have to be watched carefully, these Terrismen. They could be very dangerous, if given the opportunity and the motivation.

11

KELSIER PAUSED IN THE DOORWAY, BLOCKING Vin's view. She stooped down, trying to peek past him into the lair, but too many people were in the way. She could only tell that the door hung at an angle, splintered, the upper hinge torn free.

Kelsier stood for a long moment. Finally, he turned, looking past Dockson toward her. "Ham is right, Vin. You may not want to see this."

Vin stood where she was, looking at him resolutely. Finally, Kelsier sighed, stepping into the room. Dockson followed, and Vin could finally see what they had been blocking.

The floor was scattered with corpses, their twisted limbs shadowed and haunting in the light of Dockson's solitary lantern. They weren't rotting yet—the attack had happened only that morning—but there was still a smell of death about the room. The scent of blood drying slowly, the scent of misery and of terror.

Vin remained in the doorway. She'd seen death before—seen it often, on the streets. Knifings in alleys. Beatings in lairs. Children dead of starvation. She had once seen an old woman's neck snapped by the backhand of an annoyed lord. The body had lain in the street for three days before a skaa corpse crew had finally come for it.

Yet, none of those incidents had the same air of intentional butchery that she saw in Camon's lair. These men hadn't simply been killed, they had been torn apart. Limbs lay separated from torsos. Broken chairs and tables impaled chests. There were only a few patches of floor that were not covered in sticky, dark blood.

Kelsier glanced at her, obviously expecting some sort of reaction. She stood, looking over the death, feeling . . . numb. What should her reaction be? These were the men who had mistreated her, stolen from her, beaten her. And yet, these were the men who had sheltered her, included her, and fed her when others might have simply given her to the whoremasters.

Reen probably would have berated her for the traitorous sadness she felt at the sight. Of course, he had always been angry when—as a child—she'd cried as they left one town for another, not wanting to leave the people she'd grown to know, no matter how cruel or indifferent they were. Apparently, she hadn't quite gotten over that weakness. She stepped into the room, not shedding any tears for these men, yet at the same time wishing that they had not come to such an end.

In addition, the gore itself was disturbing. She tried to force herself to maintain a stiff face in front of the others, but she found herself cringing occasionally, glancing away from mangled corpses. The ones who had performed the attack had been quite . . . thorough.

This seems extreme, even for the Ministry, she thought. *What kind of person would do something like this?*

"Inquisitor," Dockson said quietly, kneeling by a corpse.

Kelsier nodded. Behind Vin, Sazed stepped into the room, careful to keep his robes clear of the blood. Vin turned toward the Terrisman, letting his actions distract her from a particularly grisly corpse. Kelsier was a Mistborn, and Dockson was supposedly a capable warrior. Ham and his men were securing the area. However, others—Breeze, Yeden, and Clubs—had stayed behind. The area was too dangerous. Kelsier had even resisted Vin's desire to come.

Yet, he had brought Sazed without apparent hesitation. The move, subtle though it was, made Vin regard the steward with a new curiosity. Why would it be too dangerous for Mistings, yet safe enough for a Terrisman Steward? Was Sazed a warrior? How would he have learned to fight? Terrismen were supposedly raised from birth by very careful trainers.

Sazed's smooth step and calm face gave her few clues. He didn't appear shocked by the carnage, however.

Interesting, Vin thought, picking her way through shattered furniture, stepping clear of blood pools, making her way to Kelsier's side. He crouched beside a pair of corpses. One, Vin noticed in a moment of shock, had been Ulef. The boy's face was contorted and pained, the front of his chest a mass of broken bones and ripped flesh—as if someone had forcibly torn the rib cage apart with his hands. Vin shivered, looking away.

"This isn't good," Kelsier said quietly. "Steel Inquisitors don't generally bother with simple thieving crews. Usually, the obligators would just come down with their troops and take everyone captive, then use them to make a good show on an execution day. An Inquisitor would only get involved if it had a special interest in the crew."

"You think . . ." Vin said. "You think it might be the same one as before?"

Kelsier nodded. "There are only about twenty Steel Inquisitors in the whole of the Final Empire, and half of them are out of Luthadel at any given time. I find it too much of a coincidence that you would catch one's interest, escape, and then have your old lair get hit."

Vin stood quietly, forcing herself to look down at Ulef's body and confront her sorrow. He had betrayed her in the end, but for a time he had almost been a friend.

"So," she said quietly, "the Inquisitor still has my scent?"

Kelsier nodded, standing.

"Then this is my fault," Vin said. "Ulef and the others . . ."

"It was Camon's fault," Kelsier said firmly. "He's the one who tried to scam an obligator." He paused, then looked over at her. "You going to be all right?"

Vin looked up from Ulef's mangled corpse, trying to remain strong. She shrugged. "None of them were my friends."

"That's kind of coldhearted, Vin."

"I know," she said with a quiet nod.

Kelsier regarded her for a moment, then crossed the room to speak with Dockson.

Vin looked back at Ulef's wounds. They looked like the work of some crazed animal, not a single man.

The Inquisitor must have had help, Vin told herself. *There is no way one person, even an Inquisitor, could have done all this.* There was a pileup of bodies near the bolt exit, but a quick count told her that most—if not all—of the crew was accounted for. One man couldn't have gotten to all of them quickly enough . . . could he have?

There are a lot of things we don't know about the Inquisitors, Kelsier had told her. *They don't quite follow the normal rules.*

Vin shivered again.

Footsteps sounded on the stairs, and Vin grew tense, crouching and preparing to run.

Ham's familiar figure appeared in the stairwell. "Area's secure," he said, holding up a second lantern. "No sign of obligators or Garrisoners."

"That's their style," Kelsier said. "They want the massacre to be discovered—they left the dead as a sign."

The room fell silent save for a low mumbling from Sazed, who stood at the far left side of the room. Vin picked her way over to him, listening to the rhythmic cadence of his voice. Eventually, he stopped speaking, then bowed his head and closed his eyes.

"What was that?" Vin asked as he looked up again.

"A prayer," Sazed said. "A death chant of the Cazzi. It is meant to awaken the spirits of the dead and entice them free from their flesh so that they may return to the mountain of souls." He glanced at her. "I can teach you of the religion, if you wish, Mistress. The Cazzi were an interesting people—very familiar with death."

Vin shook her head. "Not right now. You said their prayer—is this the religion you believe in, then?"

"I believe in them all."

Vin frowned. "None of them contradict each other?"

Sazed smiled. "Oh, often and frequently they do. But, I respect the truths behind them all—and I believe in the need for each one to be remembered."

"Then, how did you decide which religion's prayer to use?" Vin asked.

"It just seemed . . . appropriate," Sazed said quietly, regarding the scene of shadowed death.

"Kell," Dockson called from the back of the room. "Come look at this."

Kelsier moved to join him, as did Vin. Dockson stood by the long corridor-like chamber that had been her crew's sleeping quarters. Vin poked her head inside, expecting to find a scene similar to the one in the common room. Instead, there was only a single corpse tied to a chair. In the weak light she could barely make out that his eyes had been gouged out.

Kelsier stood quietly for a moment. "That's the man I put in charge."

"Milev," Vin said with a nod. "What about him?"

"He was killed slowly," Kelsier said. "Look at the amount of blood on the floor, the way his limbs are twisted. He had time to scream and struggle."

"Torture," Dockson said, nodding.

Vin felt a chill. She glanced up at Kelsier.

"Shall we move our base?" Ham asked.

Kelsier slowly shook his head. "When Clubs came to this lair, he would have worn a disguise to and from the meeting, hiding his limp. It's his job as a Smoker to make certain that you can't find him just by asking around on the street. None of the people in this crew could have betrayed us—we should still be safe."

No one spoke the obvious. *The Inquisitor shouldn't have been able to find this lair either.*

Kelsier stepped back into the main room, pulling Dockson aside and speaking to him in a quiet voice. Vin edged closer, trying to hear what they were saying, but Sazed placed a restraining hand on her shoulder.

"Mistress Vin," he said disapprovingly, "if Master Kelsier wanted us to hear what he was saying, would he not speak in a louder voice?"

Vin shot the Terrisman an angry glance. Then she reached inside and burned tin.

The sudden stench of blood almost staggered her. She could hear Sazed's breathing. The room was no longer dark—in fact, the brilliant light of two lanterns made her eyes water. She became aware of the stuffy, unventilated air.

And she could hear, quite distinctly, Dockson's voice.

". . . went to check on him a couple times, like you asked. You'll find him three streets west of the Fourwell Crossroads."

Kelsier nodded. "Ham," he said in a loud voice, causing Vin to jump.

Sazed looked down at her with disapproving eyes.

He knows something of Allomancy, Vin thought, reading the man's expression. *He guessed what I was doing.*

"Yes, Kell?" Ham said, peeking out of the back room.

"Take the others back to the shop," Kelsier said. "And be careful."

"Of course," Ham promised.

Vin eyed Kelsier, then resentfully allowed herself to be ushered from the lair with Sazed and Dockson.

I should have taken the carriage, Kelsier thought, frustrated by his slow pace. *The others could have walked back from Camon's lair.*

He itched to burn steel and begin jumping toward his destination. Unfortunately, it was very difficult to remain inconspicuous when flying through the city during the full light of day.

Kelsier adjusted his hat and continued walking. A nobleman pedestrian was not an irregular sight, especially in the commercial district, where more fortunate skaa and less fortunate noblemen mixed on the streets—though each group did its best to ignore the other.

Patience. Speed doesn't matter. If they know about him, he's already dead.

Kelsier entered a large crossroad square. Four wells sat in its corners, and a massive copper fountain—its green skin caked and blackened by soot—dominated the square's center. The statue depicted the Lord Ruler, standing dramatically in cloak and armor, a formless representation of the Deepness dead in the water at his feet.

Kelsier passed the fountain, its waters flaked from a recent ashfall. Skaa beggars called out from the streetsides, their pitiful voices walking a fine line between audibility and annoyance. The Lord Ruler barely suffered them; only skaa with severe disfigurements were allowed to beg. Their pitiful life, however, was not something even plantation skaa would envy.

Kelsier tossed them a few clips, not caring that doing so made him stand out, and continued to walk. Three streets over, he found a much smaller crossroads. It was also rimmed by beggars, but no fine fountain splashed the center of this intersection, nor did the corners contain wells to draw traffic.

The beggars here were even more pathetic—these were the sorry individuals who were too wretched to fight themselves a spot in a major square. Malnourished children and age-withered adults called out with apprehensive voices; men missing two or more limbs huddled in corners, their soot-stained forms almost invisible in the shadows.

Kelsier reached reflexively for his coin purse. *Stay on track,* he told himself. *You can't save them all, not with coins. There will be time for these once the Final Empire is gone.*

Ignoring the piteous cries—which became louder once the beggars realized he was watching them—Kelsier studied each face in turn. He had only seen Camon briefly, but he thought that he'd recognize the man. However, none of the faces looked right, and none of the beggars had Camon's girth, which should have still been noticeable despite weeks of starvation.

He's not here, Kelsier thought with dissatisfaction. Kelsier's order—given to Milev, the new crewleader—that Camon be made a beggar had been carried out. Dockson had checked on Camon to make certain.

Camon's absence in the square could simply mean that he'd gained a better spot. It could also mean that the Ministry had found him. Kelsier stood quietly for a moment, listening to the beggars' haunted moanings. A few flakes of ash began to float down from the sky.

Something was wrong. There weren't any beggars near the north corner of the intersection. Kelsier burned tin, and smelled blood on the air.

He kicked off his shoes, then pulled his belt free. His cloak clasp went next, the fine garment dropping to the cobblestones. That done, the only metal remaining on his body was in his coin pouch. He dumped a few coins into his hand, then carefully made his way forward, leaving his discarded garments for the beggars.

The smell of death grew stronger, but he didn't hear anything except scrambling beggars behind him. He edged onto the northern street, immediately noticing a thin alleyway to his left. Taking a breath, he flared pewter and ducked inside.

The thin, dark alley was clogged with refuse and ash. No one waited for him—at least, no one living.

Camon, crewleader turned beggar, hung quietly from a rope tied far above. His corpse spun leisurely in the breeze, ash falling lightly around it. He hadn't been hanged in the conventional fashion—the rope had been tied to a hook, then rammed down his throat. The bloodied end of the hook jutted from his skin below the chin, and he swung with head tipped back, rope running out of his mouth. His hands were tied, his still plump body showing signs of torture.

This isn't good.

A foot scraped the cobblestones behind, and Kelsier spun, flaring steel and spraying forth a handful of coins.

With a girlish yelp, a small figure ducked to the ground, coins deflected as she burned steel.

"Vin?" Kelsier said. He cursed, reaching out and yanking her into the alleyway. He glanced around the corner, watching the beggars perk up as they heard coins hit the cobblestones.

"What are you doing here?" he demanded, turning back. Vin wore the same brown overalls and gray shirt she had before, though she at least had the sense to wear a nondescript cloak with the hood up.

"I wanted to see what you were doing," she said, cringing slightly before his anger.

"This could have been dangerous!" Kelsier said. "What were you thinking?"

Vin cowered further.

Kelsier calmed himself. *You can't blame her for being curious,* he thought as a few brave beggars scuttled in the street after the coins. *She's just—*

Kelsier froze. It was so subtle he almost missed it. Vin was Soothing his emotions.

He glanced down. The girl was obviously trying to make herself invisible against the corner of the wall. She seemed so timid, yet he caught a hidden glimmer of determination in her eyes. This child had made an art of making herself seem harmless.

So subtle! Kelsier thought. *How did she get so good so quickly?*

"You don't have to use Allomancy, Vin," Kelsier said softly. "I'm not going to hurt you. You know that."

She flushed. "I didn't mean it . . . it's just habit. Even still."

"It's all right," Kelsier said, laying a hand on her shoulder. "Just remember— no matter what Breeze says, it's bad manners to touch the emotions of your friends. Plus, the noblemen consider it an insult to use Allomancy in formal settings. Those reflexes will get you into trouble if you don't learn to control them."

She nodded, rising to study Camon. Kelsier expected her to turn away in disgust, but she just stood quietly, a look of grim satisfaction on her face.

No, this one isn't weak, Kelsier thought. *No matter what she'd have you believe.*

"They tortured him here?" she asked. "Out in the open?"

Kelsier nodded, imagining the screams reverberating out to the uncomfortable beggars. The Ministry liked to be very visible with its punishments.

"Why the hook?" Vin asked.

"It's a ritual killing reserved for the most reprehensible of sinners: people who misuse Allomancy."

Vin frowned. "Camon was an Allomancer?"

Kelsier shook his head. "He must have admitted to something heinous during his torture." Kelsier glanced at Vin. "He must have known what you were, Vin. He used you intentionally."

She paled slightly. "Then . . . the Ministry knows that I'm a Mistborn?"

"Perhaps. It depends on whether Camon knew or not. He could have assumed you were just a Misting."

She stood quietly for a moment. "What does this mean for my part in the job, then?"

"We'll continue as planned," Kelsier said. "Only a couple of obligators saw you at the Canton building, and it takes a very rare man to connect the skaa servant and the well-dressed noblewoman as the same person."

"And the Inquisitor?" Vin asked softly.

Kelsier didn't have an answer to that one. "Come on," he finally said. "We've already attracted too much attention."

What would it be like if every nation—from the isles in the South to the Terris hills in the North—were united under a single government? What wonders could be achieved, what progress could be made, if mankind were to permanently set aside its squabblings and join together?

It is too much, I suppose, to even hope for. A single, unified empire of man? It could never happen.

12

VIN RESISTED THE URGE TO PICK at her noblewoman's dress. Even after a half week of being forced to wear one—Sazed's suggestion—she found the bulky garment uncomfortable. It pulled tightly at her waist and chest, then fell to the floor with several layers of ruffled fabric, making it difficult to walk. She kept feeling as if she were going to trip—and, despite the gown's bulk, she felt as if she were somehow exposed by how tight it was through the chest, not to mention the neckline's low curve. Though she had exposed nearly as much skin when wearing normal, buttoning shirts, this seemed different somehow.

Still, she had to admit that the gown made quite a difference. The girl who stood in the mirror before her was a strange, foreign creature. The light blue dress, with its white ruffles and lace, matched the sapphire barrettes in her hair. Sazed claimed he wouldn't be happy until her hair was at least shoulder-length, but he had still suggested that she purchase the broochlike barrettes and put them just above each ear.

"Often, aristocrats don't hide their deficiencies," he had explained. "Instead, they highlight them. Draw attention to your short hair, and instead of thinking you're unfashionable, they might be impressed by the statement you are making."

She also wore a sapphire necklace—modest by noble standards, but still worth more than two hundred boxings. It was complemented by a single ruby bracelet for accentuation. Apparently, the current fashion dictated a single splash of a different color to provide contrast.

And it was all hers, paid for by crew funds. If she ran, taking the jewelry and her three thousand boxings, she could live for decades. It was more tempting than she wanted to admit. Images of Camon's men, their corpses twisted and dead in the quiet lair, kept returning to her. That was probably what waited for her if she remained.

Why, then, didn't she go?

She turned from the mirror, putting on a light blue silken shawl, the female aristocrat's version of a cloak. Why didn't she leave? Perhaps it was her promise to Kelsier. He had given her the gift of Allomancy, and he depended on her. Perhaps it was her duty to the others. In order to survive, crews needed each person to do their separate job.

Reen's training told her that these men were fools, but she was tempted, enticed, by the possibility that Kelsier and the others offered. In the end, it wasn't the wealth or the job's thrill that made her stay. It was the shadowed prospect—unlikely and unreasonable, but still seductive—of a group whose members actually trusted one another. She had to stay. She *had* to know if it lasted, or if it was—as Reen's growing whispers promised—all a lie.

She turned and left her room, walking toward the front of Mansion Renoux, where Sazed waited with a carriage. She had decided to stay, and that meant she had to do her part.

It was time to make her first appearance as a noblewoman.

The carriage shook suddenly, and Vin jumped in surprise. The vehicle continued normally, however, and Sazed didn't move from his place in the driver's seat.

A sound came from above. Vin flared her metals, tensing, as a figure dropped down off the top of the carriage and landed on the footman's rest just outside her door. Kelsier smiled as he peeked his head in the window.

Vin let out a relieved breath, settling back into her seat. "You could have just asked us to pick you up."

"No need," Kelsier said, pulling open the carriage door and swinging inside. It was already dark outside, and he wore his mistcloak. "I warned Sazed I'd be dropping by sometime during the trip."

"And you didn't tell me?"

Kelsier winked, pulling the door shut. "I figured I still owed you for surprising me in that alleyway last week."

"How very adult of you," Vin said flatly.

"I've always been very confident in my immaturity. So, are you ready for this evening?"

Vin shrugged, trying to hide her nervousness. She glanced down. "How . . . uh, do I look?"

"Splendid," Kelsier said. "Just like a noble young lady. Don't be nervous, Vin—the disguise is perfect."

For some reason, that didn't feel like the answer she'd wanted to hear. "Kelsier?"

"Yes?"

"I've been meaning to ask this for a while," she said, glancing out the window, though all she could see is mist. "I understand that you think this is important—having a spy among the nobility. But . . . well, do we really have to do it this way? Couldn't we get street informants to tell us what we need to know about house politics?"

"Perhaps," Kelsier said. "But those men are called 'informants' for a reason, Vin. Every question you ask them gives a clue about your true motives—even meeting with them reveals a bit of information that they could sell to someone else. It's better to rely on them as little as possible."

Vin sighed.

"I don't send you into danger heedlessly, Vin," Kelsier said, leaning forward. "We do need a spy among the nobility. Informants generally get their information from servants, but most aristocrats are not fools. Important meetings go on where no servant can overhear them."

"And you expect me to be able to get into such meetings?"

"Perhaps," Kelsier said. "Perhaps not. Either way, I've learned that it's always useful to have someone infiltrate the nobility. You and Sazed will overhear vital items that street informants wouldn't think important. In fact, just by being at these parties—even if you don't overhear anything—you will get us information."

"How so?" Vin asked, frowning.

"Make note of the people who seem interested in you," Kelsier said. "Those will be of the houses we want to watch. If they pay attention to you, they're probably paying attention to Lord Renoux—and there's one good reason why they would be doing that."

"Weapons," Vin said.

Kelsier nodded. "Renoux's position as a weapons merchant will make him valuable to those who are planning military action. These are the houses on which I'll need to focus my attention. There should already be a sense of tension among the nobility—hopefully, they're starting to wonder which houses are turning against the others. There hasn't been an all-out war among the Great Houses for over a century, but the last one was devastating. We need to replicate it."

"That could mean the deaths of a lot of noblemen," Vin said.

Kelsier smiled. "I can live with that. How about you?"

Vin smiled despite her tension.

"There's another reason for you to do this," Kelsier said. "Sometime during this fiasco of a plan of mine, we might need to face the Lord Ruler. I have a feeling that the fewer people we need to sneak into his presence, the better.

Having a skaa Mistborn hiding among the nobility . . . well, it could be a powerful advantage."

Vin felt a slight chill. "The Lord Ruler . . . will he be there tonight?"

"No. There will be obligators in attendance, but probably no Inquisitors—and certainly not the Lord Ruler himself. A party like this is far beneath his attention."

Vin nodded. She'd never seen the Lord Ruler before—she'd never wanted to.

"Don't worry so much," Kelsier said. "Even if you were to meet him, you'd be safe. He can't read minds."

"Are you sure?"

Kelsier paused. "Well, no. But, if he *can* read minds, he doesn't do it to everyone he meets. I've known several skaa who pretended to be noblemen in his presence—I did it several times myself, before . . ." He trailed off, glancing down toward his scar-covered hands.

"He caught you eventually," Vin said quietly.

"And he'll probably do so again," Kelsier said with a wink. "But, don't worry about him for now—our goal this evening is to establish Lady Valette Renoux. You won't need to do anything dangerous or unusual. Just make an appearance, then leave when Sazed tells you. We'll worry about building confidences later."

Vin nodded.

"Good girl," Kelsier said, reaching out and pushing open the door. "I'll be hiding near the keep, watching and listening."

Vin nodded gratefully, and Kelsier jumped out of the carriage door, disappearing into the dark mists.

Vin was unprepared for how bright Keep Venture would be in the darkness. The massive building was enveloped in an aura of misty light. As the carriage approached, Vin could see that eight enormous lights blazed along the outside of the rectangular building. They were as bright as bonfires, yet far more steady, and they had mirrors arranged behind them to make them shine directly on the keep. Vin had trouble determining their purpose. The ball would happen indoors—why light the outside of the building?

"Head inside, please, Mistress Vin," Sazed said from his position above. "Proper young ladies do not gawk."

Vin shot him a glare he couldn't see, but ducked her head back inside, waiting with impatient nervousness as the carriage pulled up to the massive keep. It eventually rolled to a stop, and a Venture footman immediately opened her door. A second footman approached and held out a hand to help her down.

Vin accepted his hand, trying with as much grace as possible to pull the frilled, bulky bottom of her dress out of the carriage. As she carefully descended—trying not to trip—she was grateful for the footman's steadying hand, and she finally realized why men were expected to help a lady out of her carriage. It wasn't a silly custom after all—the clothing was the silly part.

Sazed surrendered the carriage and took his place a few steps behind her. He wore robes even more fine than his standard fare; though they still maintained the same V-like pattern, they had a belted waist and wide, enveloping sleeves.

"Forward, Mistress," Sazed coached quietly from behind. "Up the carpet, so that your dress doesn't rub on the cobbles, and in through the main doors."

Vin nodded, trying to swallow her discomfort. She walked forward, passing noblemen and ladies in various suits and gowns. Though they weren't looking at her, she felt exposed. Her steps were nowhere near as graceful as those of the other ladies, who looked beautiful and comfortable in their gowns. Her hands began to sweat inside her silky, blue-white gloves.

She forced herself to continue. Sazed introduced her at the door, presenting her invitation to the attendants. The two men, dressed in black and red servant's suits, bowed and waved her in. A crowd of aristocrats was pooling slightly in the foyer, waiting to enter the main hall.

What am I doing? she thought frantically. She could challenge mist and Allomancy, thieves and burglaries, mistwraiths and beatings. Yet, facing these noblemen and their ladies . . . going amongst them in the light, visible, unable to hide . . . this terrified her.

"Forward, Mistress," Sazed said in a soothing voice. "Remember your lessons."

Hide! Find a corner! Shadows, mists, anything!

Vin kept her hands clasped rigidly before her, walking forward. Sazed walked beside her. Out of the corner of her eyes, she could see concern on his normally calm face.

And well he should worry! Everything he had taught her seemed fleeting—vaporous, like the mists themselves. She couldn't remember names, customs, anything.

She stopped just inside the foyer, and an imperious-looking nobleman in a black suit turned to regard her. Vin froze.

The man looked her over with a dismissive glance, then turned away. She distinctly heard the word "Renoux" whispered, and she glanced apprehensively to the side. Several women were looking at her.

And yet, it didn't feel like they were seeing her at all. They were studying the gown, the hair, and the jewelry. Vin glanced to the other side, where a group of younger men were watching her. They saw the neckline, the pretty dress and the makeup, but they didn't see *her.*

None of them could see Vin, they could only see the face she had put on—the face she wanted them to see. They saw Lady Valette. It was as if Vin weren't there.

As if . . . she were hiding, hiding right in front of their eyes.

And suddenly, her tension began to retreat. She let out a long, calming breath, anxiety flowing away. Sazed's training returned, and she adopted the look of a girl amazed by her first formal ball. She stepped to the side, handing her shawl to an attendant, and Sazed relaxed beside her. Vin shot him a smile, then swept forward into the main hall.

She could *do* this. She was still nervous, but the moment of panic was over. She didn't need shadows or corners—she just needed a mask of sapphires, makeup, and blue fabric.

The Venture main hall was a grand and imposing sight. Four or five daunting stories high, the hall was several times as long as it was wide. Enormous, rectangular stained-glass windows ran in rows along the hall, and the strange, powerful lights outside shone on them directly, throwing a cascade of colors across the room. Massive, ornate stone pillars were set into the walls, running between the windows. Just before the pillars met the floor, the wall fell away, indenting and creating a single-story gallery beneath the windows themselves. Dozens of white-clothed tables sat in this area, shadowed behind the pillars and beneath the overhang. In the distance, at the far end of the hallway, Vin could make out a low balcony set into the wall, and this held a smaller group of tables.

"The dining table of Lord Straff Venture," Sazed whispered, gesturing toward the far balcony.

Vin nodded. "And those lights outside?"

"Limelights, Mistress," Sazed explained. "I'm not certain the process used—somehow, the quicklime stones can be heated to brilliance without melting them."

A string orchestra played on a platform to her left, providing music for the couples who danced in the very center of the hall. To her right, serving tables held platter upon platter of foods being attended by scurrying serving men in white.

Sazed approached an attendant and presented Vin's invitation. The man nodded, then whispered something in a younger servant's ear. The young man bowed to Vin, then led the way into the room.

"I asked for a small, solitary table," Sazed said. "You won't need to mingle during this visit, I think. Just be seen."

Vin nodded gratefully.

"The solitary table will mark you as single," Sazed warned. "Eat slowly—once your meal is through, men will come to ask you to dance."

"You didn't teach me to dance!" Vin said in an urgent whisper.

"There wasn't time, Mistress," Sazed said. "Worry not—respectfully and rightly, you can refuse these men. They will assume that you are simply flustered by your first ball, and no harm will be done."

Vin nodded, and the serving man led them to a small table near the center of the hallway. Vin seated herself in the only chair while Sazed ordered her meal. He then stepped up to stand behind her chair.

Vin sat primly, waiting. Most of the tables lay just beneath the overhang of the gallery—up close to the dancing—and that left a corridorlike walkway behind them, near the wall. Couples and groups passed along this, speaking quietly. Occasionally someone gestured or nodded toward Vin.

Well, that part of Kelsier's plan is working. She was getting noticed. She had to force herself not to cringe or sink down in her chair, however, as a high prelan strolled along the pathway behind her. He wasn't the one she had met, fortunately, though he had the same gray robes and dark tattoos around his eyes.

Actually, there were a fair number of obligators at the party. They strolled about, mingling with the partygoers. And yet, there was an . . . aloofness to them. A division. They hovered about, almost like chaperones.

The Garrison watches the skaa, Vin thought. *Apparently, the obligators perform a similar function for the nobility.* It was an odd sight—she'd always thought of the noblemen as being free. And, truthfully, they were far more confident than the skaa. Many seemed to be enjoying themselves, and the obligators didn't seem to be acting really as police, or even specifically as spies. And yet, they were there. Hovering about, joining in conversations. A constant reminder of the Lord Ruler and his empire.

Vin turned her attention away from the obligators—their presence still made her a bit uncomfortable—and instead focused on something else: the beautiful windows. Sitting where she was, she could see some of the ones directly across and up from where she sat.

They were religious, like many scenes preferred by the aristocracy. Perhaps it was to show devotion, or perhaps it was required. Vin didn't know enough— but, likely, that was something Valette wouldn't know either, so it was all right.

She did, fortunately, recognize some of the scenes—mostly because of Sazed's teachings. He seemed to know as much about the Lord Ruler's mythology as he did about other religions, though it seemed odd to her that he would study the very religion he found so oppressive.

Central to many of the windows was the Deepness. Dark black—or, in window terms, violet—it was formless, with vengeful, tentaclelike masses creeping across several windows. Vin looked up at it, along with the brilliantly colored depictions of the Lord Ruler, and found herself a little bit transfixed by the backlit scenes.

What was it? she wondered. *The Deepness? Why depict it so formlessly—why not show what it really was?*

She'd never really wondered about the Deepness before, but Sazed's lessons left her wondering. Her instincts whispered scam. The Lord Ruler had invented some terrible menace that he'd been able to destroy in the past, therefore "earning" his place as emperor. And yet, staring up at the horrible, twisting thing, Vin could almost believe.

What if something like that *had* existed? And, if it had, how had the Lord Ruler managed to defeat it?

She sighed, shaking her head at the thoughts. Already, she was beginning to think too much like a noblewoman. She was admiring the beauty of the decorations—thinking about what they meant—without giving more than a passing thought to the wealth that had created them. It was just that everything here was so wondrous and ornate.

The pillars in the hall weren't just normal columns, they were carved masterpieces. Wide banners hung from the ceiling just above the windows, and the arching, lofty ceiling was crisscrossed by structural buttressings and dotted with capstones. Somehow she knew each of those capstones was intricately carved, despite the fact that they were too far away to be seen from below.

And the dancers matched, perhaps even outshone, the exquisite setting. Couples moved gracefully, stepping to the soft music with seemingly effortless motions. Many were even chatting with one another while they danced. The ladies moved freely in their dresses—many of which, Vin noticed, made her own frilly garment look plain by comparison. Sazed was right: Long hair was certainly the fashion, though an equal number kept their hair up as left it down.

Surrounded by the majestic hall, the sharp-suited noblemen looked different, somehow. Distinguished. Were these the same creatures that beat her friends and enslaved the skaa? They seemed too . . . perfect, too well-mannered, for such horrible acts.

I wonder if they even notice the outside world, she thought, crossing her arms on the table as she watched the dancing. *Perhaps they can't see beyond their keeps and their balls—just like they can't see past my dress and makeup.*

Sazed tapped her shoulder, and Vin sighed, adopting a more ladylike posture. The meal arrived a few moments later—a feast of such strange flavors that she would have been daunted, had she not eaten similar fare often during the last few months. Sazed's lessons might have omitted dancing, but they had been quite extensive regarding dining etiquette, for which Vin was grateful. As Kelsier had said, her main purpose of the evening was to make an appearance—and so it was important that she make a proper one.

She ate delicately, as instructed, and that allowed her to be slow and meticulous. She didn't relish the idea of being asked to dance; she was half afraid she'd panic again if anyone actually spoke to her. However, a meal could only be extended so long—especially one with a lady's small portions. She soon finished, and set her fork across the plate, indicating that she was done.

The first suitor approached not two minutes later. "Lady Valette Renoux?" the young man asked, bowing just slightly. He wore a green vest beneath his long, dark suit coat. "I am Lord Rian Strobe. Would you care to dance?"

"My lord," Vin said, glancing down demurely. "You are kind, but this is my first ball, and everything here is so grand! I fear that I'll stumble from nervousness on the dance floor. Perhaps, next time . . . ?"

"Of course, my lady," he said with a courteous nod, then withdrew.

"Very well done, Mistress," Sazed said quietly. "Your accent was masterful. You will, of course, have to dance with him at the next ball. We shall surely have you trained by then, I think."

Vin flushed slightly. "Maybe he won't attend."

"Perhaps," Sazed said. "But not likely. The young nobility are quite fond of their nightly diversions."

"They do this every night?"

"Nearly," Sazed said. "The balls are, after all, a prime reason people come to Luthadel. If one is in town and there is a ball—and there almost always is—one generally attends, especially if one is young and unmarried. You won't be expected to attend quite so frequently, but we should probably get you up to attending two or three a week."

"Two or three . . ." Vin said. "I'm going to need more gowns!"

Sazed smiled. "Ah, thinking like a noblewoman already. Now, Mistress, if you will excuse me . . ."

"Excuse you?" Vin asked, turning.

"To the steward's dinner," Sazed said. "A servant of my rank is generally dismissed once my master's meal is finished. I hesitate to go and leave you, but that room will be filled with the self-important servants of the high nobility. There will be conversations there that Master Kelsier wishes me to overhear."

"You're leaving me by myself?"

"You've done well so far, Mistress," Sazed said. "No major mistakes—or, at least, none that wouldn't be expected of a lady new to court."

"Like what?" Vin asked apprehensively.

"We shall discuss them later. Just remain at your table, sipping your wine— try not to get it refilled too often—and wait for my return. If other young men approach, turn them away as delicately as you did the first."

Vin nodded hesitantly.

"I shall return in about an hour," Sazed promised. He remained, however, as if waiting for something.

"Um, you are dismissed," Vin said.

"Thank you, Mistress," he said, bowing and withdrawing. Leaving her alone.

Not alone, she thought. *Kelsier's out there somewhere, watching in the night.* The thought comforted her, though she wished she didn't feel the empty space beside her chair quite so keenly.

Three more young men approached her for dances, but each one accepted her polite rejection. No others came after them; word had probably gotten around that she wasn't interested in dancing. She memorized the names of the four men who had approached her—Kelsier would want to know them—and began to wait.

Oddly, she soon found herself growing bored. The room was well ventilated, but she still felt hot beneath the layers of fabric. Her legs were especially bad, since they had to deal with her ankle-long undergarments. The long sleeves didn't help either, though the silky material was soft against her skin. The dancing continued, and she watched with interest for a time. However, her attention soon turned to the obligators.

Interestingly, they did seem to serve some sort of function at the party. Though they often stood apart from the groups of chatting nobility, occasionally they would join in. And, every so often, a group would pause and seek out an obligator, waving one over with a respectful gesture.

Vin frowned, trying to decide what she was missing. Eventually, a group at a nearby table waved to a passing obligator. The table was too far away to hear unaided, but with tin . . .

She reached inside to burn the metal, but then paused. *Copper first,* she thought, turning the metal on. She would have to grow accustomed to leaving it on almost all the time, so that she wouldn't expose herself.

Her Allomancy hidden, she burned tin. Immediately, the light in the room became blinding, and she had to close her eyes. The band's music became louder, and a dozen conversations around her turned from buzzes to audible voices. She had to try hard to focus on the one she was interested in, but the table was the one closest to her, so she eventually singled out the appropriate voices.

". . . swear that I'll share news of my engagement with him before anyone else," one of the people said. Vin opened her eyes a slit—it was one of the noblemen at the table.

"Very well," said the obligator. "I witness and record this."

The nobleman reached out a hand, and coins clinked. Vin extinguished her tin, opening her eyes all the way in time to see the obligator wandering away from the table, slipping something—likely the coins—into a pocket of his robes.

Interesting, Vin thought.

Unfortunately, the people at that table soon rose and went their separate ways, leaving Vin without anyone close enough to eavesdrop upon. Her boredom returned as she watched the obligator stroll across the room toward one of his companions. She began to tap on the table, idly watching the two obligators until she realized something.

She recognized one of them. Not the one who had taken the money earlier, but his companion, an older man. Short and firm-featured, he stood with an imperious air. Even the other obligator seemed deferential to him.

At first, Vin thought her familiarity came from her visit to the Canton of Finance with Camon, and she felt a stab of panic. Then, however, she realized that this wasn't the same man. She'd seen him before, but not there. He was . . .

My father, she realized with stupefaction.

Reen had pointed him out once, when they had first come to Luthadel, a year ago; he had been inspecting the workers at a local forge. Reen had taken Vin, sneaking her in, insisting that she at least see her father once—though she still didn't understand why. She had memorized the face anyway.

She resisted the urge to shrink down in her chair. There was no way the man would be able to recognize her—he didn't even know she existed. She forcibly turned her attention away from him, looking up at the windows instead. She couldn't get that good a look at them, however, because the pillars and overhang restricted her view.

As she sat, she noticed something she hadn't seen before—a lofty, inset balcony that ran just above the entire far wall. It was like a counterpart to the alcove beneath the windows, except it ran at the top of the wall, between the stained-glass windows and the ceiling. She could see movement upon it, couples and singles strolling along, looking down upon the party below.

Her instincts drew her toward the balcony, from where she could watch the party without being seen herself. It would also give her a wonderful view of the banners and the windows directly above her table, not to mention let her study the stonework without seeming to gawk.

Sazed had told her to stay, but the more she sat, the more she found her eyes drawn toward the hidden balcony. She itched to stand up and move, to stretch her legs and perhaps air them out a bit. The presence of her father—oblivious of her or not—served only as another motivation for her to leave the main floor.

It isn't like anyone else is asking me to dance, she thought. *And I've done what Kelsier wanted, I've been seen by the nobility.*

She paused, then waved for a serving boy.

He approached with alacrity. "Yes, Lady Renoux?"

"How do I get up there?" Vin asked, pointing toward the balcony.

"There are stairs just to the side of the orchestra, my lady," the boy said. "Climb them to the top landing."

Vin nodded her thanks. Then, determined, she stood and made her way to the front of the room. No one gave her passing more than a glance, and she walked with more confidence as she crossed the hallway to the stairwell.

The stone corridor twisted upward, curling upon itself, its steps short but steep. Little stained glass windows, no wider than her hand, ran up the outside wall—though they were dark in color, lacking backlight. Vin climbed eagerly, working away her restless energy, but she soon began to puff from the weight of the dress and the difficulty of holding it up so that she didn't trip. A spark of burned pewter, however, made the climb effortless enough that she didn't sweat and ruin her makeup.

The climb proved to be worth the effort. The upper balcony was dark—lit only by several small blue-glassed lanterns on the walls—and it gave an amazing view of the stained-glass windows. The area was quiet, and Vin felt practically alone as she approached the iron railing between two pillars, looking down. The stone tiles of the floor below formed a pattern she hadn't noticed, a kind of freeform curving of gray upon white.

Mists? she wondered idly, leaning against the railing. It, like the lantern bracket behind her, was intricate and detailed—both had been wrought in the form of thick, curving vines. To her sides, the tops of the pillars were carved into stone animals that appeared frozen in the motion of jumping off of the balcony.

"Now, see, here's the problem with going to refill your cup of wine."

The sudden voice made Vin jump, and she spun. A young man stood behind her. His suit wasn't the finest she had seen, nor was his vest as bright as most. Both coat and shirt seemed to fit too loosely, and his hair was just a bit disheveled. He carried a cup of wine, and the outer pocket of his suit coat bulged with the shape of a book that was just a bit too big for its confines.

"The problem is," the young man said, "you return to find that your favorite spot has been stolen by a pretty girl. Now, a gentleman would move on to another place, leaving the lady to her contemplations. However, this *is* the best spot on the balcony—it's the only place close enough to a lantern to have good reading light."

Vin flushed. "I'm sorry, my lord."

"Ah, see, now I feel guilty. All for a cup of wine. Look, there's plenty of room for two people here—just scoot over a bit."

Vin paused. Could she politely refuse? He obviously wanted her to stay near him—did he know who she was? Should she try to find out his name, so she could tell Kelsier?

She stepped a bit to the side, and the man took a place next to her. He leaned back against the side pillar, and, surprisingly, took out his book and began to read. He was right: The lantern shined directly on the pages. Vin stood for a moment, watching him, but he seemed completely absorbed. He didn't even pause to look up at her.

Isn't he going to pay me any attention at all? Vin thought, puzzled at her own annoyance. *Maybe I should have worn a fancier dress.*

The man sipped at his wine, focused on the book.

"Do you always read at balls?" she asked.

The young man looked up. "Whenever I can get away with it."

"Doesn't that kind of defeat the purpose of coming?" Vin asked. "Why attend if you're just going to avoid socializing?"

"You're up here too," he pointed out.

Vin flushed. "I just wanted to get a brief view of the hall."

"Oh? And why did you refuse all three men who asked you to dance?"

Vin paused. The man smiled, then turned back to his book.

"There were four," Vin said with a huff. "And I refused them because I don't know how to dance very well."

The man lowered his book slightly, eyeing her. "You know, you're a lot less timid than you look."

"Timid?" Vin asked. "I'm not the one staring at his book when there's a young lady standing by him, never having properly introduced himself."

The man raised a speculative eyebrow. "Now, see, you sound like my father. Far better looking, but just as grumpy."

Vin glared at him. Finally, he rolled his eyes. "Very well, let me be a gentleman, then." He bowed to her with a refined, formal step. "I am Lord Elend. Lady Valette Renoux, might I have the pleasure of sharing this balcony with you whilst I read?"

Vin folded her arms. *Elend? Family name or given name? Should I even care? He just wanted his spot back. But . . . how did he know that I'd refused dancing partners?* Somehow, she had a suspicion that Kelsier would want to hear about this particular conversation.

Oddly, she didn't feel a desire to shrug this man away as she had the others. Instead, she felt another stab of annoyance as he again raised his book.

"You still haven't told me why you would rather read than participate," she said.

The man sighed, lowering the book again. "Well, see, I'm not exactly the best dancer either."

"Ah," Vin said.

"But," he said, raising a finger, "that's only part of it. You may not realize this yet, but it's not that hard to get overpartied. Once you attend five or six hundred of these balls, they start to feel a bit repetitive."

Vin shrugged. "You'd probably learn to dance better if you practiced."

Elend raised an eyebrow. "You're not going to let me get back to my book, are you?"

"I wasn't intending to."

He sighed, tucking the book back into his jacket pocket—which was beginning to show signs of book-shaped wear. "Well, then. Do you want to go dance instead?"

Vin froze. Elend smiled nonchalantly.

Lord! He's either incredibly smooth or socially incompetent. It was disturbing that she couldn't determine which.

"That's a no, I assume?" Elend said. "Good—I thought I should offer, since we've established that I'm a gentleman. However, I doubt the couples below would appreciate us trampling their toes."

"Agreed. What were you reading?"

"Dilisteni," Elend said. "*Trials of Monument.* Heard of it?"

Vin shook her head.

"Ah, well. Not many have." He leaned over the railing, looking below. "So, what do you think of your first experience at court?"

"It's very . . . overwhelming."

Elend chuckled. "Say what you will about House Venture—they know how to throw a party."

Vin nodded. "You don't like House Venture, then?" she said. Perhaps this was one of the rivalries Kelsier was watching for.

"Not particularly, no," Elend said. "They're an ostentatious lot, even for high nobility. They can't just have a party, they have to throw the *best* party. Never mind that they run their servants ragged setting it up, then beat the poor things in retribution when the hall isn't perfectly clean the very next morning."

Vin cocked her head. *Not words I'd expect to hear from a nobleman.*

Elend paused, looking a little embarrassed. "But, well, never mind that. I think your Terrisman is looking for you."

Vin started, glancing over the side of the balcony. Sure enough, Sazed's tall form stood by her now-empty table, speaking to a serving boy.

Vin yelped quietly. "I've got to go," she said, turning toward the stairwell.

"Ah, well then," Elend said, "back to reading it is." He gave her a half wave of farewell, but he had his book open before she passed the first step.

Vin reached the bottom out of breath. Sazed saw her immediately.

"I'm sorry," she said, chagrined as she approached.

"Do not apologize to me, Mistress," Sazed said quietly. "Is it both unseemly and unnecessary. Moving about a bit was a good idea, I think. I would have suggested it, had you not seemed so nervous."

Vin nodded. "Is it time for us to go, then?"

"It is a proper time to withdraw, if you wish," he said, glancing up at the balcony. "May I ask what you were doing up there, Mistress?"

"I wanted to get a better look at the windows," Vin said. "But I ended up talking to someone. He seemed interested in me at first, but now I don't think he ever intended to pay me much attention. It doesn't matter—he didn't seem important enough to bother Kelsier with his name."

Sazed paused. "Who was it you were speaking to?"

"The man in the corner there, on the balcony," Vin said.

"One of Lord Venture's friends?"

Vin froze. "Is one of them named Elend?"

Sazed paled visibly. "You were chatting with Lord *Elend Venture?*"

"Um . . . yes?"

"Did he ask you to dance?"

Vin nodded. "But I don't think he meant it."

"Oh, dear," Sazed said. "So much for controlled anonymity."

"Venture?" Vin asked, frowning. "Like, Keep Venture?"

"Heir to the house title," Sazed said.

"Hum," Vin said, realizing that she should probably be a bit more intimidated than she felt. "He was a bit annoying—in a pleasant sort of way."

"We shouldn't be discussing this here," Sazed said. "You're far, far below his station. Come, let us retire. I shouldn't have gone away to the dinner. . . ."

He trailed off, mumbling to himself as he led Vin to the entryway. She got one more glimpse into the main chamber as she retrieved her shawl, and she burned tin, squinting against the light and seeking the balcony above.

He held the book, closed, in one hand—and she could have sworn that he was looking down in her direction. She smiled, and let Sazed usher her to their carriage.

I know that I shouldn't let a simple packman perturb me. However, he is from Terris, where the prophecies originated. If anyone could spot a fraud, would it not be he?

Nevertheless, I continue my trek, going where the scribbled auguries proclaim that I will meet my destiny—walking, feeling Rashek's eyes on my back. Jealous. Mocking. Hating.

13

VIN SAT WITH HER LEGS CROSSED beneath her on one of Lord Renoux's fine easy chairs. It felt good to be rid of the bulky dress, instead getting back to a more familiar shirt and trousers.

However, Sazed's calm displeasure made her want to squirm. He stood on the other side of the room, and Vin got the distinct impression that she was in trouble. Sazed had questioned her in depth, seeking out every detail of her conversation with Lord Elend. Sazed's inquiries had been respectful, of course, but they had also been forceful.

The Terrisman seemed, in Vin's opinion, unduly worried about her exchange with the young nobleman. They hadn't really talked about anything important, and Elend himself was decidedly unspectacular for a Great House lord.

But, there *had* been something odd about him—something Vin hadn't admitted to Sazed. She'd felt . . . comfortable with Elend. Looking back on the experience, she realized that for those few moments, she hadn't really been Lady Valette. Nor had she been Vin, for that part of her—the timid crewmember—was almost as fake as Valette was.

No, she'd simply been . . . whoever she was. It was a strange experience. She had occasionally felt the same way during her time with Kelsier and the others, but in a more limited manner. How had Elend been able to evoke her true self so quickly and so thoroughly?

Maybe he used Allomancy on me! she thought with a start. Elend was a high nobleman; perhaps he was a Soother. Maybe there was more to the conversation than she had thought.

Vin sat back in her chair, frowning to herself. She'd had copper on, and that meant he *couldn't* have used emotional Allomancy on her. Somehow, he had simply gotten her to let her guard down. Vin thought back to the experience, thinking about how oddly comfortable she'd felt. In retrospect, it was clear that she hadn't been careful enough.

I'll be more cautious next time. She assumed that they would meet again. They'd better.

A servant entered and whispered quietly to Sazed. A quick burn of tin let Vin hear the conversation—Kelsier had finally returned.

"Please send word to Lord Renoux," Sazed said. The white-clothed servant nodded, leaving the room with a quick step.

"The rest of you may leave," Sazed said calmly, and the room's attendants scampered away. Sazed's quiet vigil had forced them to stand, waiting in the tense room, not speaking or moving.

Kelsier and Lord Renoux arrived together, chatting quietly. As always, Renoux wore a rich suit cut in the unfamiliar Western style. The aging man kept his gray mustache trimmed thin and neat, and he walked with a confident air. Even after spending an entire evening among the nobility, Vin was again struck by his aristocratic bearing.

Kelsier still wore his mistcloak. "Saze?" he said as he entered. "You have news?"

"I am afraid so, Master Kelsier," Sazed said. "It appears that Mistress Vin caught the attention of Lord Elend Venture at the ball tonight."

"Elend?" Kelsier asked, folding his arms. "Isn't he the heir?"

"He is indeed," Renoux said. "I met the lad perhaps four years ago, when his father visited the West. He struck me as a bit undignified for one of his station."

Four years? Vin thought. *There's no way he's been imitating Lord Renoux for that long. Kelsier only escaped the Pits two years ago!* She eyed the impostor, but—as always—was unable to detect a flaw in his bearing.

"How attentive was the boy?" Kelsier asked.

"He asked her to dance," Sazed said. "But Mistress Vin was wise enough to decline. Apparently, their meeting was a matter of idle happenstance—but I fear she may have caught his eye."

Kelsier chuckled. "You taught her too well, Saze. In the future, Vin, perhaps you should try to be a little less charming."

"Why?" Vin asked, trying to mask her annoyance. "I thought we *wanted* me to be well liked."

"Not by a man as important as Elend Venture, child," Lord Renoux said. "We sent you to court so you could make alliances—not scandals."

Kelsier nodded. "Venture is young, eligible, and heir to a powerful house. Your having a relationship with him could make serious problems for us. The women of the court would be jealous of you, and the older men would disapprove of the rank difference. You'd alienate yourself from large sections of the court. To get the information we need, we need the aristocracy to see you as uncertain, unimportant, and—most importantly—unthreatening."

"Besides, child," Lord Renoux said. "It is unlikely that Elend Venture has any real interest in you. He is known to be a court eccentric—he is probably just trying to heighten his reputation by doing the unexpected."

Vin felt her face flush. *He's probably right,* she told herself sternly. Still, she couldn't help feeling annoyed at the three of them—especially Kelsier, with his flippant, unconcerned attitude.

"Yes," Kelsier said, "it's probably best that you avoid Venture completely. Try to offend him or something. Give him a couple of those glares you do."

Vin regarded Kelsier with a flat look.

"That's the one!" Kelsier said with a laugh.

Vin clinched her teeth, then forced herself to relax. "I saw my father at the ball tonight," she said, hoping to distract Kelsier and the others away from Lord Venture.

"Really?" Kelsier asked with interest.

Vin nodded. "I recognized him from a time my brother pointed him out to me."

"What is this?" Renoux asked.

"Vin's father is an obligator," Kelsier said. "And, apparently an important one if he has enough pull to go to a ball like this. Do you know what his name is?"

Vin shook her head.

"Description?" Kelsier asked.

"Uh . . . bald, eye tattoos . . ."

Kelsier chuckled. "Just point him out to me sometime, all right?"

Vin nodded, and Kelsier turned to Sazed. "Now, did you bring me the names of which noblemen asked Vin to dance?"

Sazed nodded. "She gave me a list, Master Kelsier. I also have several interesting tidbits to share from the stewards' meal."

"Good," Kelsier said, glancing at the grandfather clock in the corner. "You'll have to save them for tomorrow morning, though. I've got to be going."

"Going?" Vin asked, perking up. "But you just got in!"

"That's the funny thing about arriving somewhere, Vin," he said with a wink. "Once you're there, the only thing you can really do is leave again. Get some sleep—you're looking a bit ragged."

Kelsier waved a farewell to the group, then ducked out of the room, whistling amiably to himself.

Too nonchalant, Vin thought. *And too secretive. He usually tells us which families he plans to hit.*

"I think I *will* retire," Vin said, yawning.

Sazed eyed her suspiciously, but let her go as Renoux began speaking quietly to him. Vin scrambled up the stairs to her room, threw on her mistcloak, and pushed open her balcony doors.

Mist poured into the room. She flared iron, and was rewarded with the sight of a fading blue metal line, pointing into the distance.

Let's see where you're going, Master Kelsier.

Vin burned steel, Pushing herself into the cold, humid autumn night. Tin enhanced her eyes, making the wet air tickle her throat as she breathed. She Pushed hard behind her, then Pulled slightly on the gates below. The maneuver swung her in a soaring arc over the steel gates, which she then Pushed against to throw herself farther into the air.

She kept an eye on the trail of blue that pointed toward Kelsier, following him at enough of a distance to remain unseen. She wasn't carrying any metal— not even coins—and she kept her copper burning to hide her use of Allomancy. Theoretically, only sound could alert Kelsier of her presence, and so she moved as quietly as possible.

Surprisingly, Kelsier didn't head into town. After passing the mansion's gates, he turned north out of the city. Vin followed, landing and running quietly on the rough ground.

Where is he going? she thought with confusion. *Is he circling Fellise? Heading for one of the peripheral mansions?*

Kelsier continued northward for a short time, then his metal line suddenly began to grow dim. Vin paused, stopping beside a group of stumpy trees. The line faded at a rapid rate: Kelsier had suddenly sped up. She cursed to herself, breaking into a dash.

Ahead, Kelsier's line vanished into the night. Vin sighed, slowing. She flared her iron, but it was barely enough to catch a glimpse of him disappearing again in the distance. She'd never keep up.

Her flared iron, however, showed her something else. She frowned, continuing forward until she reached a stationary source of metal—two small bronze bars stuck into the ground a couple feet from each other. She flipped one up into her hand, then looked into the swirling mists to the north.

He's jumping, she thought. *But why?* Jumping *was* faster than walking, but there didn't seem much point to it in the empty wilderness.

Unless . . .

She walked forward, and she soon found two more bronze bars embedded in the earth. Vin glanced backward. It was hard to tell in the night, but it seemed that the four bars made a line that pointed directly toward Luthadel.

So that's how he does it, she thought. Kelsier had an uncanny ability to move between Luthadel and Fellise with remarkable speed. She'd assumed that he was using horses, but it appeared that there was a better way. He—or perhaps someone before him—had laid down an Allomantic road between the two cities.

She gripped the first bar in her palm—she'd need it to soften her landing if she was wrong—then stepped up in front of the second pair of bars and launched herself into the air.

She Pushed hard, flaring her steel, throwing herself as far up into the sky as she could. As she flew, she flared her iron, searching for other sources of metal. They soon appeared—two directly north, and two more in the distance to either side of her.

The ones on the sides are for course corrections, she realized. She'd have to keep moving directly north if she wanted to stay on the bronze highway. She nudged herself slightly to the left—moving so that she passed directly between the two adjacent bars of the main path—then hurled herself forward again in an arcing leap.

She got the hang of it quickly, hopping from point to point, never dropping even close to the ground. In just a few minutes, she had the rhythm down so well that she barely had to do any corrections from the sides.

Her progress across the scraggly landscape was incredibly swift. The mists blew by, her mistcloak whipping and flapping behind her. Still, she forced herself to speed up. She'd spent too long studying the bronze bars. She had to catch up to Kelsier; otherwise she'd arrive in Luthadel, but not know where to go from there.

She began to throw herself from point to point at an almost reckless speed, watching desperately for some sign of Allomantic motion. After about ten minutes of leaping, a line of blue finally appeared ahead of her—one pointing up, rather than down toward bars in the ground. She breathed in relief.

Then a second line appeared, and a third.

Vin frowned, letting herself drop to the ground with a muted thump. She flared tin, and a massive shadow appeared in the night before her, its top sparkling with balls of light.

The city wall, she thought with amazement. *So soon? I made the trip twice as fast as a man on horseback!*

However, that meant she'd lost Kelsier. Frowning to herself, she used the bar she'd been carrying to throw herself up onto the battlements. Once she landed on the damp stone, she reached behind and Pulled the bar up into her hand. Then she approached the other side of the wall, hopping up and crouching on the stone railing as she scanned the city.

What now? she thought with annoyance. *Head back to Fellise? Stop by Clubs's shop and see if he went there?*

She sat uncertainly for a moment, then threw herself off the wall and began making her way across the rooftops. She wandered randomly, pushing off of window clasps and bits of metal, using the bronze bar—then pulling it back into her hand—when long jumps were necessary. It wasn't until she arrived that she realized she'd unconsciously gone to a specific destination.

Keep Venture rose before her in the night. The limelights had been extinguished, and only a few phantom torches burned near guard posts.

Vin crouched on the lip on a rooftop, trying to decide what had led her back to the massive keep. The cool wind ruffled her hair and cloak, and she thought she felt a few tiny raindrops on her cheek. She sat for a long moment, her toes growing cold.

Then she noticed motion to her right. She crouched immediately, flaring her tin.

Kelsier sat on a rooftop not three houses away, just barely lit by ambient light. He didn't seem to have noticed her. He was watching the keep, his face too distant for her to read his expression.

Vin watched him with suspicious eyes. He'd dismissed her meeting with Elend, but perhaps it worried him more than he'd admitted. A sudden spike of fear made her tense.

Could he be here to kill Elend? The assassination of a high noble heir would certainly create tension amongst the nobility.

Vin waited apprehensively. Eventually, however, Kelsier stood and walked away, Pushing himself off the rooftop and into the air.

Vin dropped her bronze bar—it would give her away—and dashed after him. Her iron showed blue lines moving in the distance, and she hurriedly jumped out over the street and Pushed herself off a sewer grate below, determined not to lose him again.

He moved toward the center of the city. Vin frowned, trying to guess his destination. Keep Erikeller was in that direction, and it was a major supplier of armaments. Perhaps Kelsier planned to do something to interrupt its supplies, making House Renoux more vital to the local nobility.

Vin landed on a rooftop and paused, watching Kelsier shoot off into the night. *He's moving fast again. I—*

A hand fell on her shoulder.

Vin yelped, jumping back, flaring pewter.

Kelsier regarded her with a cocked eyebrow. "You're supposed to be in bed, young lady."

Vin glanced to the side, toward the line of metal. "But—"

"My coin pouch," Kelsier said, smiling. "A good thief can steal clever tricks as easily as he steals boxings. I've started being more careful since you tailed me last week—at first, I assumed you were a Venture Mistborn."

"They have some?"

"I'm sure they do," Kelsier said. "Most of the Great Houses do—but your friend Elend isn't one of them. He's not even a Misting."

"How do you know? He could be hiding it."

Kelsier shook his head. "He nearly died in a raid a couple of years ago—if there were ever a time to show your powers, it would have been then."

Vin nodded, still looking down, not meeting Kelsier's eyes.

He sighed, sitting down on the slanted rooftop, one leg hanging over the side. "Have a seat."

Vin settled herself on the tile roof across from him. Above, the cool mists continued to churn, and it had begun to drizzle slightly—but that wasn't much different from the regular nightly humidity.

"I can't have you tailing me like this, Vin," Kelsier said. "Do you remember our discussion about trust?"

"If you trusted me, you'd tell me where you were going."

"Not necessarily," Kelsier said. "Maybe I just don't want you and the others to worry about me."

"Everything you do is dangerous," Vin said. "Why would we worry any more if you told us specifics?"

"Some tasks are even more dangerous than others," Kelsier said quietly.

Vin paused, then glanced to the side, in the direction Kelsier had been going. Toward the center of the city.

Toward Kredik Shaw, the Hill of a Thousand Spires. The Lord Ruler's palace.

"You're going to confront the Lord Ruler!" Vin said quietly. "You said last week that you were going to pay him a visit."

"'Visit' is, perhaps, too strong a word," Kelsier said. "I *am* going to the palace, but I sincerely hope I don't run into the Lord Ruler himself. I'm not ready for him yet. Regardless, *you* are going straight to Clubs's shop."

Vin nodded.

Kelsier frowned. "You're just going to try and follow me again, aren't you?"

Vin paused, then she nodded again.

"Why?"

"Because I want to help," Vin said quietly. "So far, my part in this all has essentially boiled down to going to a party. But, I'm Mistborn—you've trained me yourself. I'm not going to sit back and let everyone else do dangerous work while I sit, eat dinner, and watch people dance."

"What you're doing at those balls is important," Kelsier said.

Vin nodded, glancing down. She'd just let him go, then she'd follow him. Part of her reasoning was what she'd said before: She was beginning to feel a camaraderie for this crew, and it was like nothing she had ever known. She wanted to be part of what it was doing; she wanted to help.

However, another part of her whispered that Kelsier wasn't telling her everything. He might trust her; he might not. However, he certainly had secrets. The Eleventh Metal, and therefore the Lord Ruler, were involved in those secrets.

Kelsier caught her eyes, and he must have seen her intention to follow in them. He sighed, leaning back. "I'm serious, Vin! You can't go with me."

"Why not?" she asked, abandoning pretense. "If what you're doing is so dangerous, wouldn't it be safer if you had another Mistborn watching your back?"

"You still don't know all of the metals," Kelsier said.

"Only because you haven't taught me."

"You need more practice."

"The best practice is doing," Vin said. "My brother trained me to steal by taking me on burglaries."

Kelsier shook his head. "It's too dangerous."

"Kelsier," she said in a serious tone. "We're planning to *overthrow the Final Empire*. I don't really expect to live until the end of the year anyway.

"You keep telling the others what an advantage it is to have two Mistborn on the team. Well, it's not going to be much of an advantage unless you actually let me *be* a Mistborn. How long are you going to wait? Until I'm 'ready'? I don't think that will ever happen."

Kelsier eyed her for a moment, then he smiled. "When we first met, half the time I couldn't get you to say a word. Now you're lecturing me."

Vin blushed. Finally, Kelsier sighed, reaching beneath his cloak to pull something out. "I can't believe I'm considering this," he muttered, handing her the bit of metal.

Vin studied the tiny, silvery ball of metal. It was so reflective and bright that it almost seemed to be a drop of liquid, yet it was solid to the touch.

"Atium," Kelsier said. "Tenth, and most powerful, of the known Allomantic metals. That bead is worth more than the entire bag of boxings I gave you before."

"This little bit?" she asked with surprise.

Kelsier nodded. "Atium only comes from one place—the Pits of Hathsin—where the Lord Ruler controls its production and distribution. The Great Houses get to buy a monthly stipend of atium, which is one of the main ways the Lord Ruler controls them. Go ahead and swallow it."

Vin eyed the bit of metal, uncertain she wanted to waste something so valuable.

"You can't sell it," Kelsier said. "Thieving crews try, but they get tracked down and executed. The Lord Ruler is very protective of his atium supply."

Vin nodded, then swallowed the metal. Immediately, she felt a new well of power appear within her, waiting to be burned.

"All right," Kelsier said, standing. "Burn it as soon as I start walking."

Vin nodded. As he began to walk forward, she drew upon her new well of strength and burned atium.

Kelsier seemed to fuzz slightly to her eyes; then a translucent, wraithlike image shot out into the mists in front of him. The image looked just like Kelsier, and it walked just a few steps in front of him. A very faint, trailing after-image extended from the duplicate back to Kelsier himself.

It was like . . . a reverse shadow. The duplicate did everything Kelsier did—except, the image moved *first*. It turned, and then Kelsier followed its same path.

The image's mouth began moving. A second later, Kelsier spoke. "Atium lets you see just a bit into the future. Or, at least, it lets you see what people are going to do a little bit in the future. In addition, it enhances your mind, allowing you to deal with the new information, allowing you to react more quickly and collectedly."

The shadow stopped, then Kelsier walked up to it, stopping as well. Suddenly, the shadow reached out and slapped her, and Vin moved reflexively, putting her hand up just as Kelsier's real hand began to move. She caught his arm midswing.

"While you're burning atium," he said, "nothing can surprise you. You can swing a dagger, knowing confidently that your enemies will run right into it. You can dodge attacks with ease because you'll be able to see where every blow will fall. Atium makes you quite nearly invincible. It enhances your mind, making you able to make use of all the new information."

Suddenly, dozens of other images shot from Kelsier's body. Each one sprang in a different direction, some striding across the roof, others jumping into the air. Vin released his arm, rising and backing away in confusion.

"I just burned atium too," Kelsier said. "I can see what you're going to do, and that changes what I'm going to do—which in turn changes what you're going to do. The images reflect each of the possible actions we might take."

"It's confusing," Vin said, watching the insane jumble of images, old ones constantly fading, new ones constantly appearing.

Kelsier nodded. "The only way to defeat someone who is burning atium is to burn it yourself—that way, neither of you has an advantage."

The images vanished.

"What did you do?" Vin asked with a start.

"Nothing," Kelsier said. "Your atium probably ran out."

Vin realized with surprise that he was right—the atium was gone. "It burns so quickly!"

Kelsier nodded, sitting down again. "That's probably the fastest fortune you've ever blown, eh?"

Vin nodded, stunned. "It seems like such a waste."

Kelsier shrugged. "Atium is only valuable because of Allomancy. So, if we didn't burn it, it wouldn't be worth the fortune that it is. Of course, if we do burn it, we make it even more rare. It's kind of an interesting relationship—ask Ham about it sometimes. He loves talking about atium economics.

"Anyway, any Mistborn you face will probably have atium. However, they'll be reluctant to use it. In addition, they won't have swallowed it yet—atium is fragile, and your digestive juices will ruin it in a matter of hours. So, you have to walk a line between conservation and effectiveness. If it looks like your opponent is using atium, then you'd better use yours too—however, make sure he doesn't lure you into using up your reserve before he does."

Vin nodded. "Does this mean you're taking me tonight?"

"I'll probably regret it," Kelsier said, sighing. "But I don't see any way to make you stay behind—short of tying you up, perhaps. But, I warn you Vin. This could be dangerous. *Very* dangerous. I don't intend to meet the Lord Ruler, but I do intend to sneak into his stronghold. I think I know where we might find a clue on how to defeat him."

Vin smiled, stepping forward as Kelsier waved her toward him. He reached into his pouch and pulled out a vial, which he handed to her. It was like regular Allomantic vials, except the liquid inside held only a single drop of metal. The atium bead was several times larger than the one he had given her to practice on.

"Don't use it unless you have to," Kelsier warned. "You need any other metals?"

Vin nodded. "I burned up most of my steel getting here."

Kelsier handed her another vial. "First, let's go retrieve my coin pouch."

Sometimes I wonder if I'm going mad.

Perhaps it is due to the pressure of knowing that I must somehow bear the burden of an entire world. Perhaps it is caused by the death I have seen, the friends I have lost. The friends I have been forced to kill.

Either way, I sometimes see shadows following me. Dark creatures that I don't understand, nor wish to understand. Are they, perhaps, some figment of my overtaxed mind?

14

IT STARTED RAINING just after they located the coin pouch. It wasn't a hard rain, but it seemed to clear the mist slightly. Vin shivered, pulling up her hood, crouching beside Kelsier on a rooftop. He didn't pay the weather much heed, so neither did she. A little dampness wouldn't hurt—in fact, it would probably help, as the rainfall would cover the sounds of their approach.

Kredik Shaw lay before them. The peaked spires and sheer towers rose like dark talons in the night. They varied greatly in thickness—some were wide enough to house stairwells and large rooms, but others were simply thin rods of steel jutting up into the sky. The variety gave the mass a twisted, off-center symmetry—an almost-balance.

The spikes and towers had a foreboding cast in the damp, misty night—like the ash-blackened bones of a long-weathered carcass. Looking at them, Vin thought she felt something . . . a *depression*, as if simply being close to the building was enough to suck away her hope.

"Our target is a tunnel complex at the base of one of the far right spires," Kelsier said, his voice barely carrying over the quiet hush of the falling rain. "We're heading for a room at the very center of that complex."

"What's inside?"

"I don't know," Kelsier said. "That's what we're going to find out. Once every three days—and today isn't one of them—the Lord Ruler visits this chamber. He stays for three hours, then leaves. I tried to get in once before. Three years ago."

"The job," Vin whispered. "The one that . . ."

"Got me captured," Kelsier said with a nod. "Yes. At the time, we thought that the Lord Ruler stored riches in the room. I don't think that's true, now, but I'm still curious. The way he visits is so regular, so . . . odd. Something's in that room, Vin. Something important. Maybe it holds the secret to his power and immortality."

"Why do we need to worry about that?" Vin asked. "You have the Eleventh Metal to defeat him, right?"

Kelsier frowned slightly. Vin waited for an answer, but he didn't ever give one. "I failed to get in last time, Vin," he said instead. "We got close, but we got there too easily. When we arrived, there were Inquisitors outside the room. Waiting for us."

"Someone told them you were coming?"

Kelsier nodded. "We planned that job for months. We were overconfident, but we had reason to be. Mare and I were the best—the job should have gone flawlessly." Kelsier paused, then he turned to Vin. "Tonight, I didn't plan at all. We're just going in—we'll quiet anyone who tries to stop us, then break into that room."

Vin sat quietly, feeling the chill rainwater on her wet hands and damp arms. Then she nodded.

Kelsier smiled slightly. "No objections?"

Vin shook her head. "I made you take me with you. It's not my place to object now."

Kelsier chuckled. "Guess I've been hanging out with Breeze too long. I just don't feel right unless someone tells me I'm crazy."

Vin shrugged. However, as she moved on the rooftop, she felt it again—the sense of depression coming from Kredik Shaw.

"There is something, Kelsier," she said. "The palace feels . . . wrong, somehow."

"That's the Lord Ruler," Kelsier said. "He radiates like an incredibly powerful Soother, smothering the emotions of everyone who gets close to him. Turn on your copper; that will make you immune."

Vin nodded, burning copper. Immediately, the sensation went away.

"Good?" Kelsier asked.

She nodded again.

"All right, then," he said, giving her a handful of coins. "Stay close to me, and keep your atium handy—just in case."

With that, he threw himself off the roof. Vin followed, her cloak tassels spraying rainwater. She burned pewter as she fell, and hit the ground with Allomantically strengthened legs.

Kelsier took off at a dash, and she followed. Her speed on the wet cobblestones would have been reckless, but her pewter-fueled muscles reacted with precision, strength, and balance. She ran in the wet, misty night, burning tin and copper—one to let her see, the other to let her hide.

Kelsier rounded the palace complex. Oddly, the grounds had no outer wall. *Of course they don't. Who would dare attack the Lord Ruler?*

Flat space, covered in cobblestones, was all that surrounded the Hill of a Thousand Spires. No tree, foliage, or structure stood to distract one's eye from the disturbing, asymmetric collection of wings, towers, and spires that was Kredik Shaw.

"Here we go," Kelsier whispered, his voice carrying to her tin-enhanced ears. He turned, dashing directly toward a squat, bunkerlike section of the palace. As they approached, Vin saw a pair of guards standing by an ornate, gatelike door.

Kelsier was on the men in a flash, cutting one down with slashing knives. The second man tried to cry out, but Kelsier jumped, slamming both feet into the man's chest. Thrown to the side by the inhumanly strong kick, the guard crashed into the wall, then slumped to the ground. Kelsier was on his feet a second later, slamming his weight against the door and pushing it open.

Weak lanternlight spilled out of a stone corridor within. Kelsier ducked through the door. Vin dimmed her tin, then followed in a crouching dash, her heart pounding. Never, in all her time as a thief, had she done something like this. Hers had been a life of sneaky burgling and scamming, not raids or muggings. As she followed Kelsier down the corridor—their feet and cloaks leaving a wet trail on the smooth stonework—she nervously pulled out a glass dagger, gripping the leather-wrapped handle in a sweaty palm.

A man stepped into the hallway just ahead, exiting what appeared to be some sort of guard chamber. Kelsier jumped forward and elbowed the soldier in the stomach, then slammed him against the wall. Even as the guard collapsed, Kelsier ducked into the room.

Vin followed, stepping into chaos. Kelsier Pulled a metal candelabrum from the corner up into his hands, then began to spin with it, striking down soldier after soldier. Guards cried out, scrambling and grabbing staves from the side of the room. A table covered in half-eaten meals was thrown to the side as men tried to make room.

A soldier turned toward Vin, and she reacted without thinking. She burned steel and threw out a handful of coins. She Pushed, and the missiles shot forward, tearing through the guard's flesh and dropping him.

She burned iron, Pulling the coins back to her hand. She turned with a bloodied fist, spraying the room with metal, dropping three soldiers. Kelsier felled the last with his impromptu staff.

I just killed four men, Vin thought, stunned. Before, Reen had always done the killing.

There was rustling behind. Vin spun to see another squadron of soldiers enter through a door opposite her. To the side, Kelsier dropped his candelabrum and stepped forward. The room's four lanterns suddenly ripped from their mountings, slamming directly toward him. He ducked to the side, letting the lanterns crash together.

The room fell dark. Vin burned tin, her eyes adapting to light from the corridor outside. The guards, however, stumbled to a halt.

Kelsier was amidst them a second later. Daggers flashing in the darkness. Men screaming. Then all was silent.

Vin stood surrounded by death, bloodied coins dribbling from her stunned fingers. She kept a tight grip on her dagger, however—if only to steady her quivering arm.

Kelsier lay a hand on her shoulder, and she jumped.

"These were evil men, Vin," he said. "Every skaa knows in his heart that it is the greatest of crimes to take up arms in defense of the Final Empire."

Vin nodded numbly. She felt . . . wrong. Maybe it was the death, but now that she was actually within the building, she swore that she could still feel the Lord Ruler's power. Something seemed to Push her emotions, making her more depressed despite her copper.

"Come. Time is short." Kelsier took off again, hopping lithely over corpses, and Vin felt herself following.

I made him bring me, she thought. *I wanted to fight, like him. I'm going to have to get used to this.*

They dashed into a second corridor, and Kelsier jumped into the air. He lurched, then shot forward. Vin did the same, leaping and seeking an anchor far down the corridor, then using it to Pull herself through the air.

Side corridors whipped past, the air a rushing howl in her tin-enhanced ears. Ahead, two soldiers stepped into the corridor. Kelsier slammed feet-first into one, then flipped up and rammed a dagger into the other's neck. Both men fell.

No metal, Vin thought, dropping to the ground. *None of the guards in this place wear metal.* Hazekillers, they were called. Men trained to fight Allomancers.

Kelsier ducked down a side corridor, and Vin had to sprint to keep up with him. She flared pewter, willing her legs to move faster. Ahead, Kelsier paused, and Vin lurched to a stop beside him. To their right was an open, arching doorway, and it shone with a light far brighter than that of the small corridor lanterns. Vin extinguished her tin, following Kelsier through the archway and into the room.

Six braziers burned with open flames at the corners of the large, dome-roofed chamber. In contrast to the simple corridors, this room was covered with silver-inlayed murals. Each obviously represented the Lord Ruler; they were like the windows she had seen earlier, except less abstract. She saw a mountain. A large cavern. A pool of light.

And something very dark.

Kelsier strode forward, and Vin turned. The center of the room was dominated by a small structure—a building within the building. Ornate, with carved stone and flowing patterns, the single-story building stood reverently before them. All in all, the quiet, empty chamber gave Vin a strange feeling of solemnity.

Kelsier walked forward, bare feet falling on smooth black marble. Vin followed in a nervous crouch; the room seemed empty, but there had to be other guards. Kelsier walked up to a large oaken door set into the inner building, its surface carved with letterings Vin didn't recognize. He reached out and pulled open the door.

A Steel Inquisitor stood inside. The creature smiled, lips curling in an eerie expression beneath the two massive spikes that had been pounded point-first through its eyes.

Kelsier paused for just a moment. Then he yelled, *"Vin, run!"* as the Inquisitor's hand snapped forward, grabbing him by the throat.

Vin froze. To the sides, she saw two other black-robed Inquisitors stride through open archways. Tall, lean, and bald, they were also marked by their spikes and intricate Ministry eye tattoos.

The closest Inquisitor lifted Kelsier up into the air by his neck. "Kelsier, the Survivor of Hathsin," the creature said in a grinding voice. Then he turned toward Vin. "And . . . you. I've been looking for you. I'll let this one die quickly if you'll tell me which nobleman spawned you, half-breed."

Kelsier coughed, struggling for breath as he pried at the creature's grip. The Inquisitor turned, regarding Kelsier with spike-end eyes. Kelsier coughed again, as if trying to say something, and the Inquisitor curiously pulled Kelsier a bit closer.

Kelsier's hand whipped out, ramming a dagger into the creature's neck. As the Inquisitor stumbled, Kelsier slammed his fist into the creature's forearm, shattering the bone with a snap. The Inquisitor dropped him, and Kelsier fell to the reflective marble floor, coughing.

Gasping for breath, Kelsier looked up at Vin with intense eyes. "I said *run!*" he croaked, tossing something to her.

Vin paused, reaching out to catch the coin pouch. However, it lurched suddenly in the air, shooting forward. Abruptly, she realized Kelsier wasn't throwing it to her, but *at* her.

The bag hit her in the chest. Pushed by Kelsier's Allomancy, it hurled her across the room—past the two surprised Inquisitors—until she finally dropped awkwardly to the floor, skidding on the marble.

Vin looked up, slightly dazed. In the distance, Kelsier regained his feet. The main Inquisitor, however, didn't seem very concerned about the dagger in his neck. The other two Inquisitors stood between her and Kelsier. One turned toward her, and Vin felt chilled by its horrifying, unnatural gaze.

"RUN!" The word echoed in the domed chamber. And this time, finally, it struck home.

Vin scrambled to her feet—fear shocking her, screaming at her, making her move. She dashed toward the nearest archway, uncertain if it was the one she had come in through. She clutched Kelsier's coin pouch and burned iron, frantically seeking an anchor down the corridor.

Must get away!

She grabbed the first bit of metal she saw and yanked, tearing herself off the ground. She shot down the corridor at an uncontrolled speed, terror flaring her iron.

She lurched suddenly, and everything spun. She hit the ground at an awkward angle—her head slamming against the rough stone—then lay dizzily, wondering what had happened. The coin pouch . . . someone had Pulled on it, using its metal to yank her backward.

Vin rolled over and saw a dark form shooting down the corridor. The Inquisitor's robes fluttered as he dropped lightly to his feet a short distance from Vin. He strode forward, his face impassive.

Vin flared tin and pewter, clearing her mind and pushing away the pain. She whipped out a few coins, Pushing them at the Inquisitor.

He raised a hand, and both coins froze in the air. Vin's own Push suddenly threw her backward, and she tumbled across the stones, skidding and sliding.

She heard the coins pling against the floor as she came to a rest. She shook her head, a dozen new bruises flaring angrily across her body. The Inquisitor stepped over the discarded coins, walking toward her with a smooth gait.

I have to get away! Even Kelsier had been afraid to face an Inquisitor. If he couldn't fight one, what chance did she have?

None. She dropped the pouch and jumped to her feet, then she ran, ducking through the first doorway she saw. The room beyond was empty of people, but a golden altar stood at its center. Between the altar, the four candelabra at the corners, and the cluttering of other religious paraphernalia, the space was cramped.

Vin turned, Pulling a candelabrum into her hands, remembering Kelsier's trick from before. The Inquisitor stepped into the room, then raised an almost amused hand, ripping the candelabra from her hands in an easy Allomantic Pull.

He's so strong! Vin thought with horror. He was probably steadying himself by Pulling against the lantern brackets behind. However, the force of his Iron-pulls was far more powerful than Kelsier's had ever been.

Vin jumped, Pulling herself slightly up and over the altar. At the doorway, the Inquisitor reached over to a bowl that sat atop a short pillar, pulling out what appeared to be a handful of small metal triangles. They were sharp on all sides, and they cut the creature's hand in a dozen different places. He ignored the wounds, raising a bloody hand toward her.

Vin yelped, ducking behind the altar as pieces of metal sprayed against the back wall.

"You are trapped," the Inquisitor said in a scratchy voice. "Come with me."

Vin glanced to the side. There weren't any other doors in the room. She peeked up, glancing at the Inquisitor, and a piece of metal shot at her face. She Pushed against it, but the Inquisitor was too strong. She had to duck and let the metal go, lest his power pin her back against the wall.

I'll need something to block with. Something that isn't made of metal.

As she heard the Inquisitor step into the room, she found what she needed—a large, leather-bound book sitting beside the altar. She grabbed it, then paused. There was no use in being rich if she died. She pulled out Kelsier's vial and downed the atium, then burned it.

The Inquisitor's shadow stepped around the side of the altar, then the actual Inquisitor followed a second later. The atium-shadow opened its hand, and a spray of tiny, translucent daggers shot at her.

Vin raised her book as the real daggers followed. She swung the book through the shadow trails just as the real daggers shot toward her. She caught every one, their sharp, jagged edges digging deeply into the book's leather cover.

The Inquisitor paused, and she was rewarded by what seemed to be a look of confusion on its twisted face. Then a hundred shadow images shot from his body.

Lord Ruler! Vin thought. He had atium too.

Not pausing to worry about what that meant, Vin hopped over the altar, carrying the book with her as protection against further missiles. The Inquisitor spun, spike-eyes following her as she ducked back into the hallway.

A squad of soldiers stood waiting for her. However, each one bore a future-shadow. Vin ducked between them, barely watching where their weapons would fall, somehow avoiding the attacks of twelve different men. And, for a moment, she almost forgot the pain and fear—and they were replaced by an incredible sense of power. She dodged effortlessly, staves swinging above and beside her, each one missing by just inches. She was invincible.

She spun through the ranks of the men, not bothering to kill or hurt them—she only wanted to escape. As she passed the last one, she turned around a corner.

And a second Inquisitor, his body springing with shadow images, stepped up and slammed something sharp into her lower side.

Vin gasped in pain. There was a sickening sound as the creature pulled his weapon free of her body; it was a length of wood affixed with sharp obsidian blades. Vin grasped her side, stumbling backward, feeling a terrifying amount of warm blood seeping from the wound.

The Inquisitor looked familiar. *The first one, from the other room,* she thought through the pain. *Does . . . that mean that Kelsier is dead?*

"Who is your father?" the Inquisitor asked.

Vin kept her hand at her side, trying to stop the blood. It was a large wound. A bad wound. She had seen such wounds before. They always killed.

Yet, she still stood. *Pewter,* her confused mind thought. *Flare pewter!*

She did so, the metal giving her body strength, letting her stay on her feet. The soldiers stepped back to let the second Inquisitor approach her from the side. Vin looked in horror from one Inquisitor to the other, both descending upon her, blood pouring between her fingers and down her side. The lead Inquisitor still carried the axelike weapon, its edge coated with blood. Her blood.

I'm going to die, she thought with terror.

And then she heard it. Rain. It was faint, but her tin-ears picked it out behind her. She spun, lurching through a door, and was rewarded by the sight of a large archway on the other side of the room. Mist pooled at the room's floor, and rain slapped the stones outside.

Must have been where the guards came from, she thought. She kept her pewter flared, amazed at how well her body still worked, and stumbled out into the rain, reflexively clutching the leather book to her chest.

"You think to escape?" the lead Inquisitor asked from behind, his voice amused.

Numbly, Vin reached into the sky and Pulled against one of the palace's many spires. She heard the Inquisitor curse as she pitched into the air, hurling up into the dark night.

The thousand spires rose around her. She Pulled against one, then switched to another. The rain was strong now, and it made the night black. There was no mist to reflect ambient light, and the stars were hidden by clouds above. Vin couldn't see where she was going; she had to use Allomancy to sense the metallic tips of the spires, and hope there was nothing in between.

She hit a spire, catching hold of it in the night and pulling to a stop. *Have to bandage the wound . . .* she thought weakly. She was beginning to grow numb, her head cloudy despite her pewter and tin.

Something slammed against the spire above her, and she heard a low growl. Vin Pushed off even as she felt the Inquisitor slash the air beside her.

She had one chance. Midjump, she Pulled herself sideways, toward a different spire. At the same time, she Pushed against the book in her hands—it still had bits of metal embedded into its cover. The book continued in the direction she had been going, metal lines glowing weakly in the night. It was the only metal she had on her.

Vin caught the next spire lightly, trying to make as little sound as possible. She strained in the night, burning tin, the rainfall becoming a thunder in her ears. Over it, she thought she heard the distinct sound of something hitting a spire in the direction she had Pushed the book.

The Inquisitor had fallen for her ruse. Vin sighed, hanging from the spire, rain splattering her body. She made sure her copper was still burning, Pulled lightly against the spire to hold herself in place, and ripped off a piece of her shirt to bandage the wound. Despite her numb mind, she couldn't help noticing how big the gash was.

Oh, Lord, she thought. Without pewter, she would have fallen unconscious long ago. She should be dead.

Something sounded in the darkness. Vin felt a chill, looking up. All was black around her.

It can't be. He can't—

Something slammed into her spire. Vin cried out, jumping away. She Pulled herself toward another spire, caught it weakly, then immediately Pushed off again. The Inquisitor followed, thuds sounding as he jumped from spire to spire behind her.

He found me. He couldn't see me, hear me, or sense me. But he found me.

Vin hit a spire, holding it by one hand, limply hanging in the night. Her strength was nearly gone. *I . . . have to get away . . . hide. . . .*

Her hands were numb, and her mind felt nearly the same. Her fingers slipped from the cold, wet metal of the spire, and she felt herself drop free into the darkness.

She fell with the rain.

However, she went only a short distance before thudding against something hard—the roof of a particularly tall bit of the palace. Dazed, she climbed to her knees, crawling away from the spire, seeking a corner.

Hide . . . hide . . . hide . . .

She crawled weakly to the nook formed by another tower. She huddled against the dark corner, lying in a deep puddle of ashy rainwater, arms wrapped around herself. Her body was wet with rain and blood.

She thought, for just a moment, that she might have escaped.

A dark form thumped to the rooftop. The rain was letting up, and her tin revealed a head set with two spikes, a body cloaked in a dark robe.

She was too weak to move, too weak to do more than shiver in the puddle of water, clothing plastered to her skin. The Inquisitor turned toward her.

"Such a small, troubling thing you are," he said. He stepped forward, but Vin could barely hear his words.

It was growing dark again . . . no, it was just her mind. Her vision grew dark, her eyes closing. Her wound didn't hurt anymore. She couldn't . . . even . . . think. . . .

A sound, like shattering branches.

Then arms gripped her. Warm arms, not the arms of death. She forced her eyes open.

"Kelsier?" she whispered.

But it wasn't Kelsier's face that looked back at her, streaked with concern. It was a different, kinder face. She sighed in relief, drifting away as the strong arms pulled her close, making her feel oddly safe in the terrible storms of night.

I don't know why Kwaan betrayed me. Even still, this event haunts my thoughts. He was the one who discovered me; he was the Terris philosopher who first called me the Hero of Ages. It seems ironically surreal that now—after his long struggle to convince his colleagues—he is the only major Terris holy man to preach against my reign.

15

"YOU TOOK HER WITH YOU?" Dockson demanded, bursting into the room. "You took Vin into Kredik Shaw? Are you *bloody insane?"*

"Yes," Kelsier snapped. "You've been right all along. I'm a madman. A lunatic. Perhaps I should have just died in the Pits and never come back to bother any of you!"

Dockson paused, taken aback by the force in Kelsier's words. Kelsier pounded the table in frustration, and the wood splintered from the force of the blow. He still burned pewter, the metal helping him resist his several wounds. His mistcloak lay in tatters, his body sliced by a half-dozen different small cuts. His entire right side burned with pain. He'd have a massive bruise there, and he'd be lucky if none of his ribs were cracked.

Kelsier flared the pewter. The fire within felt good—it gave him a focus for his anger and self-loathing. One of the apprentices worked quickly, tying a bandage around Kelsier's largest gash. Clubs sat with Ham at the side of the kitchen; Breeze was away visiting a suburb.

"By the Lord Ruler, Kelsier," Dockson said quietly.

Even Dockson, Kelsier though. *Even my oldest friend swears by the Lord Ruler's name. What are we doing? How can we face this?*

"There were three Inquisitors waiting for us, Dox," Kelsier said.

Dockson paled. "And you *left* her there?"

"She got out before I did. I tried to distract the Inquisitors as long as I could, but . . ."

"But?"

"One of the three followed her. I couldn't get to it—maybe the other two Inquisitors were simply trying to keep me busy so that their companion could find her."

"Three Inquisitors," Dockson said, accepting a small cup of brandy from one of the apprentices. He downed it.

"We must have made too much noise going in," Kelsier said. "Either that, or they were already there for some reason. And we *still* don't know what's in that room!"

The kitchen fell silent. The rain outside picked up again, assaulting the building with a reproachful fury.

"So . . ." Ham said, "what of Vin?"

Kelsier glanced at Dockson, and saw pessimism in his eyes. Kelsier had barely escaped, and he had years of training. If Vin was still in Kredik Shaw . . .

Kelsier felt a sharp, twisting pain in his chest. *You let her die too. First Mare, then Vin. How many more will you lead to slaughter before this is through?*

"She might be hiding somewhere in the city," Kelsier said. "Afraid to come to the shop because the Inquisitors are looking for her. Or . . . perhaps for some reason she went back to Fellise."

Maybe she's out there somewhere, dying alone in the rain.

"Ham," Kelsier said, "you and I are heading back to the palace. Dox, take Lestibournes and visit other thieving crews. Maybe one of their scouts saw something. Clubs, send an apprentice to Renoux's mansion to see if she went there."

The solemn group started to move, but Kelsier didn't need to state the obvious. He and Ham wouldn't be able to get close to Kredik Shaw without running afoul of guard patrols. Even if Vin was hiding in the city somewhere, the Inquisitors would probably find her first. They would have—

Kelsier froze, his sudden jerk causing the others to pause. He'd heard something.

Hurried footsteps sounded as Lestibournes rushed down the stairs and into the room, his lanky form wet with rain. "Someone's coming! Out the night with the calling!"

"Vin?" Ham asked hopefully.

Lestibournes shook his head. "Big man. Robe."

This is it, then. I've brought death to the crew—I've led the Inquisitors right to them.

Ham stood, picking up a wooden stave. Dockson pulled out a pair of daggers, and Clubs's six apprentices moved to the back of the room, eyes wide with fright.

Kelsier flared his metals.

The back door to the kitchen slammed open. A tall, dark form in wet robes stood in the rain. And he carried a cloth-wrapped figure in his arms.

"Sazed!" Kelsier said.

"She is badly wounded," Sazed said, stepping quickly into the room, his fine robes streaming with rainwater. "Master Hammond, I require some pewter. Her supply is exhausted, I think."

Ham rushed forward as Sazed set Vin on the kitchen table. Her skin was clammy and pale, her thin frame soaked and wet.

She's so small, Kelsier thought. *Barely more than a child. How could I have thought to take her with me?*

She bore a massive, bloody wound in her side. Sazed set something aside—a large book he'd been carrying in his arms beneath Vin—and accepted a vial from Hammond, then bent down and poured the liquid down the unconscious girl's throat. The room fell silent, the sound of pounding rain coming through the still open door.

Vin's face flushed slightly with color, and her breathing seemed to steady. To Kelsier's Allomantic bronze senses, she began to pulse softly with a rhythm not unlike a second heartbeat.

"Ah, good," Sazed said, undoing Vin's makeshift bandage. "I feared that her body was too unfamiliar with Allomancy to burn metals unconsciously. There is hope for her, I think. Master Cladent, I shall require a pot of boiled water, some bandages, and the medical bag from my rooms. Quickly, now!"

Clubs nodded, waving for his apprentices to do as instructed. Kelsier cringed as he watched Sazed's work. The wound was bad—worse than any he himself had survived. The cut went deeply into her gut; it was the type of wound that killed slowly, but consistently.

Vin, however, was no ordinary person—pewter would keep an Allomancer alive long after their body should have given out. In addition, Sazed was no ordinary healer. Religious rites were not the only things that Keepers stored in their uncanny memories; their metalminds contained vast wealths of information on culture, philosophy, and science.

Clubs ushered his apprentices from the room as the surgery began. The procedure took an alarming amount of time, Ham applying pressure to the wound as Sazed slowly stitched Vin's insides back together. Finally, Sazed closed the outer wound and applied a clean bandage, then asked Ham to carefully carry the girl up to her bed.

Kelsier stood, watching Ham carry Vin's weak, limp form out of the kitchen. Then, he turned to Sazed questioningly. Dockson sat in the corner, the only other one still in the room.

Sazed shook his head gravely. "I do not know, Master Kelsier. She could survive. We will need to keep her supplied with pewter—it will help her body make new blood. Even still, I have seen many strong men die from wounds smaller than this one."

Kelsier nodded.

"I arrived too late, I think," Sazed said. "When I found her gone from Renoux's mansion, I came to Luthadel as quickly as I could. I used up an entire metalmind to make the trip with haste. I was still too late. . . ."

"No, my friend," Kelsier said. "You've done well this night. Far better than I."

Sazed sighed, then reached over and fingered the large book he'd set aside before beginning the surgery. The tome was wet with rainwater and blood. Kelsier regarded it, frowning. "What is that, anyway?"

"I don't know," Sazed said. "I found at the palace, while I was searching for the child. It is written in Khlenni."

Khlenni, the language of Khlennium—the ancient, pre-Ascension homeland of the Lord Ruler. Kelsier perked up a bit. "Can you translate it?"

"Perhaps," Sazed said, suddenly sounding very tired. "But . . . not for a time, I think. After this evening, I shall need to rest."

Kelsier nodded, calling for one of the apprentices to prepare Sazed a room. The Terrisman nodded thankfully, then walked wearily up the stairs.

"He saved more than Vin's life tonight," Dockson said, approaching quietly from behind. "What you did was stupid, even for you."

"I had to know, Dox," he said. "I had to go back. What if the atium really is in there?"

"You said that it isn't."

"I said that," Kelsier said with a nod, "and I'm mostly sure. But what if I'm wrong?"

"That's no excuse," Dockson said angrily. "Now Vin is dying and the Lord Ruler is alerted to us. Wasn't it enough that you got Mare killed trying to get into that room?"

Kelsier paused, but he was too drained to feel any anger. He sighed, sitting down. "There's more, Dox."

Dockson frowned.

"I've avoided talking about the Lord Ruler to the others," Kelsier said, "but . . . I'm worried. The plan is good, but I have this terrible, haunting feeling that we'll never succeed as long as he's alive. We can take his money, we can take his armies, we can trick him out of the city . . . but I still worry that we won't be able to stop him."

Dockson frowned. "You're serious about this Eleventh Metal business, then?"

Kelsier nodded. "I searched for two years to find a way to kill him. Men have tried everything—he ignores normal wounds, and decapitation only annoys him. A group of soldiers burned down his inn during one of the early wars. The Lord Ruler walked out as barely more than a skeleton, then healed in a matter of seconds.

"Only the stories of the Eleventh Metal offered any hope. But I can't make it work! That's why I had to go back to the palace. The Lord Ruler's hiding *some-*

thing in that room—I can feel it. I can't help thinking that if we knew what it was, we'd be able to stop him."

"You didn't have to take Vin with you."

"She followed me," Kelsier said. "I worried that she'd try to get in on her own if I left her. The girl has a headstrong streak, Dox—she hides it well, but she's blasted stubborn when she wants to be."

Dockson sighed, then nodded quietly. "And we *still* don't know what's in that room."

Kelsier eyed the book Sazed had set on the table. The rainwater had marked it, but the tome was obviously designed to endure. It was strapped tightly to prevent water from seeping in, and the cover was of well-cured leather.

"No," Kelsier finally said. "We don't." *But we do have that, whatever it is.*

"Was it worth it, Kell?" Dockson asked. "Was this insane stunt really worth nearly getting yourself—and the child—killed?"

"I don't know," Kelsier said honestly. He turned to Dockson, meeting his friend's eyes. "Ask me once we know whether or not Vin will live."

THE END OF PART TWO

PART THREE

CHILDREN OF
A BLEEDING SUN

Many think that my journey started in Khlennium, that great city of wonder. They forget that I was no king when my quest began. Far from it.

I think it would do men well to remember that this task was not begun by emperors, priests, prophets, or generals. It didn't start in Khlennium or Kordel, nor did it come from the great nations to the east or the fiery empire of the West.

It began in a small, unimportant town whose name would mean nothing to you. It began with a youth, the son of a blacksmith, who was unremarkable in every way—except, perhaps, in his ability to get into trouble.

It began with me.

16

WHEN VIN AWOKE, THE PAIN TOLD her that Reen had beaten her again. What had she done? Had she been too friendly to one of the other crewmembers? Had she made a foolish comment, drawing the crewleader's ire? She was to remain quiet, always quiet, staying away from the others, never calling attention to herself. Otherwise he would beat her. She had to learn, he said. She had to learn. . . .

But, her pain seemed too strong for that. It had been a long time since she could remember hurting this much.

She coughed slightly, opening her eyes. She lay in a bed that was far too comfortable, and a lanky teenage boy sat in a chair beside her bed.

Lestibournes, she thought. *That's his name. I'm in Clubs's shop.*

Lestibournes jumped to his feet. "You're awaking!"

She tried to speak, but just coughed again, and the boy hurriedly gave her a cup of water. Vin sipped it thankfully, grimacing at the pain in her side. In fact, her entire body felt like it had been pummeled soundly.

"Lestibournes," she finally croaked.

"Notting as the now," he said. "Kelsier wasing the hit with my name; changed it to Spook."

"Spook?" Vin asked. "It fits. How long have I been asleep?"

"Two weeks," the boy said. "Wait here." He scrambled away, and she could hear him calling out in the distance.

Two weeks? She sipped at the cup, trying to organize her muddled memories. Reddish afternoon sunlight shone through the window, lighting the room. She set the cup aside, checking her side, where she found a large white bandage.

That's where the Inquisitor hit me, she thought. *I should be dead.*

Her side was bruised and discolored from where she'd hit the roof after falling, and her body bore a dozen other nicks, bruises, and scrapes. All in all, she felt absolutely terrible.

"Vin!" Dockson said, stepping into the room. "You're awake!"

"Barely," Vin said with a groan, lying back against her pillow.

Dockson chuckled, walking over and sitting on Lestibournes's stool. "How much do you remember?"

"Most everything, I think," she said. "We fought our way into the palace, but there were Inquisitors. They chased us, and Kelsier fought—" She stopped, looking at Dockson. "Kelsier? Is he—"

"Kell's fine," Breeze said. "He came out of the incident in far better shape than you did. He knows the palace fairly well, from the plans we made three years ago, and he . . ."

Vin frowned as Dockson trailed off. "What?"

"He said the Inquisitors didn't seem very focused on killing him. They left one to chase him, and sent two after you."

Why? Vin thought. *Did they simply want to concentrate their energy on the weakest enemy first? Or, is there another reason?* She sat back thoughtfully, working through the events of that night.

"Sazed," Vin she finally said. "He saved me. The Inquisitor was about to kill me, but . . . Dox, what *is* he?"

"Sazed?" Dockson asked. "That's probably a question I should let him answer."

"Is he here?"

Dockson shook his head. "He had to return to Fellise. Breeze and Kell are out recruiting, and Ham left last week to inspect our army. He won't be back for another month at least."

Vin nodded, feeling drowsy.

"Drink the rest of your water," Dockson suggested. "There's something in it to help with the pain."

Vin downed the rest of the drink, then rolled over and let sleep take her again.

Kelsier was there when she awoke. He sat on the stool by her bed, hands clasped with his elbows on his knees, watching her by the faint light of a lantern. He smiled when she opened her eyes. "Welcome back."

She immediately reached for the cup of water on the bedstand. "How's the job going?"

He shrugged. "The army is growing, and Renoux has begun to purchase weapons and supplies. Your suggestion regarding the Ministry turned out to be a good one—we found Theron's contact, and we've nearly negotiated a deal that will let us place someone as a Ministry acolyte."

"Marsh?" Vin asked. "Will he do it himself?"

Kelsier nodded. "He's always had a . . . certain fascination with the Ministry. If any skaa can pull off imitating an obligator, it will be Marsh."

Vin nodded, sipping her drink. There was something different about Kelsier. It was subtle—a slight alteration in his air and attitude. Things had changed during her sickness.

"Vin," Kelsier said hesitantly. "I owe you an apology. I nearly got you killed."

Vin snorted quietly. "It's not your fault. I made you take me."

"You shouldn't have been able to make me," Kelsier said. "My original decision to send you away was the right one. Please accept the apology."

Vin nodded quietly. "What do you need me to do now? The job has to go forward, right?"

Kelsier smiled. "Indeed it does. As soon as you're up to it, I'd like you to move back to Fellise. We created a cover story saying that Lady Valette has taken sick, but rumors are starting to appear. The sooner you can be seen in the flesh by visitors, the better."

"I can go tomorrow," Vin said.

Kelsier chuckled. "I doubt it, but you can go soon. For now, just rest." He stood, moving to leave.

"Kelsier?" Vin asked, causing him to pause. He turned, looking at her.

Vin struggled to formulate what she wanted to say. "The palace . . . the Inquisitors . . . We're not invincible, are we?" She flushed; it sounded stupid when she said it that way.

Kelsier, however, just smiled. He seemed to understand what she meant. "No, Vin," he said quietly. "We're far from it."

Vin watched the landscape pass outside her carriage window. The vehicle, sent from Mansion Renoux, had supposedly taken Lady Valette for a ride through Luthadel. In reality, it hadn't picked up Vin until it had stopped briefly by

Clubs's street. Now, however, her window shades were open, showing her again to the world—assuming anyone cared.

The carriage made its way back toward Fellise. Kelsier had been right: She'd had to rest three more days in Clubs's shop before feeling strong enough to make the trip. In part, she'd waited simply because she had dreaded struggling into a noblewoman's dresses with her bruised arms and wounded side.

Still, it felt good to be up again. There had been something . . . wrong about simply recovering in bed. Such a lengthy period of rest wouldn't have been given to a regular thief; thieves either got back to work quickly or were abandoned for dead. Those who couldn't bring in money for food couldn't be allowed to take up space in the lair.

But, that isn't the only way people live, Vin thought. She was still uncomfortable with that knowledge. It hadn't mattered to Kelsier and the others that she drained their resources—they hadn't exploited her weakened state, but had cared for her, each one spending time at her bedside. Most notable among the vigilists had been the young Lestibournes. Vin didn't even feel that she knew him very well, yet Kelsier said that the boy had spent hours watching over her during her coma.

What did one make of a world where a crewleader agonized over his people? In the underground, each person bore responsibility for what happened to them—the weaker segment of a crew had to be allowed to die, lest they keep everyone else from earning enough to survive. If a person got captured by the Ministry, you left them to their fate and hoped that they didn't betray too much. You didn't worry about your own guilt at putting them in danger.

They're fools, Reen's voice whispered. *This entire plan will end in disaster— and your death will be your own fault for not leaving when you could.*

Reen had left when he could. Perhaps he'd known that the Inquisitors would eventually hunt her down for the powers she unwittingly possessed. He always had known when to leave—it was no accident, she thought, that he hadn't ended up slaughtered with the rest of Camon's crew.

And yet, she ignored Reen's promptings in her head, instead letting the carriage pull her toward Fellise. It wasn't that she felt completely secure in her place with Kelsier's crew—indeed, in a way, her place with these people was making her even more apprehensive. What if they stopped needing her? What if she became useless to them?

She had to prove to them that she could do what they needed her to. There were functions to attend, a society to infiltrate. She had so much work to do; she couldn't afford to spend any more of it sleeping.

In addition, she needed to return to her Allomantic practice sessions. It had only taken a few short months for her to grow dependent upon her powers, and she longed for the freedom of leaping through the mists, of Pulling and Pushing her way through the skies. Kredik Shaw had taught her that she wasn't invincible—but Kelsier's survival with barely a scratch proved that it was possible to be much better than she was. Vin needed to practice, to grow in strength, until she too could escape Inquisitors like Kelsier had.

The carriage turned a bend and rolled into Fellise. The familiar, pastoral suburb made Vin smile to herself, and she leaned against the open carriage window, feeling the breeze. With luck, some streetgoers would gossip that Lady Valette had been seen riding through the city. She arrived at Mansion Renoux a few short turns later. A footman opened the door, and Vin was surprised to see Lord Renoux himself waiting outside the carriage to help her down.

"My lord?" she said, giving him her hand. "Surely you have more important things to attend to."

"Nonsense," he said. "A lord must be allowed time to dote upon his favored niece. How was your ride?"

Does he ever break character? He didn't ask after the others in Luthadel, or give any indication that he knew of her wound.

"It was refreshing, Uncle," she said as they walked up the steps to the mansion doors. Vin was thankful for the pewter burning lightly in her stomach to give strength to her still weak legs. Kelsier had warned against using it too much, lest she grow dependent upon its power, but she saw little alternative until she was healed.

"That is wonderful," Renoux said. "Perhaps, once you are feeling better, we should take lunch together on the garden balcony. It has been warm lately, despite the coming winter."

"That would be very pleasant," Vin said. Before, she'd found the impostor's noble bearing intimidating. Yet, as she slipped into the persona of Lady Valette, she experienced the same calmness as before. Vin the thief was nothing to a man such as Renoux, but Valette the socialite was another matter.

"Very good," Renoux said, pausing inside the entryway. "However, let us attend to that on another day—for now, you would likely prefer to rest from your journey."

"Actually, my lord, I'd like to visit Sazed. I have some matters I must discuss with the steward."

"Ah," Renoux said. "You will find him in the library, working on one of my projects."

"Thank you," Vin said.

Renoux nodded, then walked away, his dueling cane clicking against the white marble floor. Vin frowned, trying to decide if he was completely sane. Could someone really adopt a persona that wholly?

You do it, Vin reminded herself. *When you become Lady Valette, you show a completely different side of yourself.*

She turned, flaring pewter to help her climb the northern set of stairs. She let her flare lapse as she reached the top, returning to a normal burn. As Kelsier said, it was dangerous to flare metals for too extended a period; an Allomancer could quickly make their body dependent.

She took a few breaths—climbing the stairs had been difficult, even with pewter—then walked down the corridor to the library. Sazed sat at a desk beside a small coal stove on the far side of the small room, writing on a pad of paper. He wore his standard steward's robes, and a pair of thin spectacles sat at the end of his nose.

Vin paused in the doorway, regarding the man who had saved her life. *Why is he wearing spectacles? I've seen him read before without them.* He seemed completely absorbed by his work, periodically studying a large tome on the desk, then turning to scribble notes on his pad.

"You're an Allomancer," Vin said quietly.

Sazed paused, then set down his pen and turned. "What makes you say that, Mistress Vin?"

"You got to Luthadel too quickly."

"Lord Renoux keeps several swift messenger horses in his stables. I could have taken one of those."

"You found me at the palace," Vin said.

"Kelsier told me of his plans, and I correctly assumed that you had followed him. Locating you was a stroke of luck, one that nearly took me too long to achieve."

Vin frowned. "You killed the Inquisitor."

"Killed?" Sazed asked. "No, Mistress. It takes far more power than I posses to kill one of those monstrosities. I simply . . . distracted him."

Vin stood in the doorway for a moment longer, trying to figure out why Sazed was being so ambiguous. "So, are you an Allomancer or not?"

He smiled, then he pulled a stool out from beside the desk. "Please, sit down."

Vin did as requested, crossing the room and sitting on the stool, her back to a massive bookshelf.

"What would you think if I told you that I wasn't an Allomancer?" Sazed asked.

"I'd think that you were lying," Vin said.

"Have you known me to lie before?"

"The best liars are those who tell the truth most of the time."

Sazed smiled, regarding her through bespectacled eyes. "That is true, I think. Still, what proof have you that I am an Allomancer?"

"You did things that couldn't have been done without Allomancy."

"Oh? A Mistborn for two months, and already you know all that is possible in the world?"

Vin paused. Up until just recently, she hadn't even known much about Allomancy. Perhaps there was more to the world than she had assumed.

There's always another secret. Kelsier's words.

"So," she said slowly, "what exactly *is* a 'Keeper'?"

Sazed smiled. "Now, *that* is a far more clever question, Mistress. Keepers are . . . storehouses. We remember things, so that they can be used in the future."

"Like religions," Vin said.

Sazed nodded. "Religious truths are my particular specialty."

"But, you remember other things too?"

Sazed nodded.

"Like what?"

"Well," Sazed said, closing the tome he had been studying. "Languages, for instance."

Vin immediately recognized the glyph-covered cover. "The book I found in the palace! How did you get it?"

"I happened across it while searching for you," the Terrisman said. "It is written in a very old language, one that hasn't been spoken regularly in nearly a millennium."

"But you speak it?" Vin asked.

Sazed nodded. "Enough to translate this, I think."

"And . . . how many languages do you know?"

"A hundred and seventy-two," Sazed said. "Most of them, such as Khlenni, are no longer spoken. The Lord Ruler's unity movement of the fifth century made certain of that. The language people now speak is actually a distant dialect of Terris, the language of my homeland."

A *hundred and seventy-two,* Vin thought with amazement. "That . . . sounds impossible. One man couldn't remember that much."

"Not one man," Sazed said. "One Keeper. What I do is similar to Allomancy, but not the same. You draw power from metals. I . . . use them to create memories."

"How?" Vin asked.

Sazed shook his head. "Perhaps another time, Mistress. My kind . . . we prefer to maintain our secrets. The Lord Ruler hunts us with a remarkable, confusing passion. We are far less threatening than Mistborn—yet, he ignores Allomancers and seeks to destroy us, hating the Terris people because of us."

"Hating?" Vin asked. "You're treated better than regular skaa. You're given positions of respect."

"That is true, Mistress," Sazed said. "But, in a way, the skaa are more free. Most Terrismen are raised from birth to be stewards. There are very few of us left, and the Lord Ruler's breeders control our reproduction. No Terrisman steward is allowed to have a family, or even to bear children."

Vin snorted. "That seems like it would be hard to enforce."

Sazed paused, hand laying on the cover of the large book. "Why, not at all," he said with a frown. "All Terrisman stewards are eunuchs, child. I assumed you knew that."

Vin froze, then she blushed furiously. "I . . . I'm . . . sorry. . . ."

"Truly and surely, no apology is required. I was castrated soon after my birth, as is standard for those who will be stewards. Often, I think I would have easily traded my life for that of a common skaa. My people are less than slaves . . . they're fabricated automatons, created by breeding programs, trained from birth to fulfill the Lord Ruler's wishes."

Vin continued to blush, cursing her lack of tact. Why hadn't anyone told her? Sazed, however, didn't seem offended—he never seemed to get angry about anything.

Probably a function of his . . . condition, Vin thought. *That's what the breeders must want. Docile, even-tempered stewards.*

"But," Vin said, frowning, "you're a rebel, Sazed. You're fighting the Lord Ruler."

"I am something of a deviant," Sazed said. "And, my people are not as completely subjugated as the Lord Ruler would believe, I think. We hide Keepers beneath his very eyes, and some of us even gather the courage to break our training."

He paused, then shook his head. "It is not an easy thing, however. We are a weak people, Mistress. We are eager to do as we are told, quick to seek subjugation. Even I, whom you dub a rebel, immediately sought out a position of stewardship and subservience. We are not so brave as we would wish, I think."

"You were brave enough to save me," Vin said.

Sazed smiled. "Ah, but there was an element of obedience in that too. I promised Master Kelsier that I would see to your safety."

Ah, she thought. She had wondered if he'd had a reason for his actions. After all, who would risk their life simply to save Vin? She sat for a moment in thought, and Sazed turned back to his book. Finally, she spoke again, drawing the Terrisman's attention. "Sazed?"

"Yes, Mistress?"

"Who betrayed Kelsier three years ago?"

Sazed paused, then set down his fountain pen. "The facts are unclear, Mistress. Most of the crew assumes it was Mare, I think."

"Mare?" Vin asked. "Kelsier's wife?"

Sazed nodded. "Apparently, she was one of the only people who could have done it. In addition, the Lord Ruler himself implicated her."

"But, wasn't she was sent to the Pits too?"

"She died there," Sazed said. "Master Kelsier is reticent about the Pits, but I sense that the scars he bears from that horrid place go much deeper than the ones you see on his arms. I don't think he ever knew if she was the traitor or not."

"My brother said that anyone would betray you, if they had the right chance and a good enough motive."

Sazed frowned. "Even if such a thing were true, I would not want to live believing it."

It seems better than what happened to Kelsier: being turned over to the Lord Ruler by one you thought you loved.

"Kelsier is different lately," Vin said. "He seems more reserved. Is that because he feels guilty for what happened to me?"

"I suspect that is part of it," Sazed said. "However, he is also coming to realize that there is a large difference between heading a small crew of thieves and organizing a large rebellion. He can't take the risks he once did. The process is changing him for the better, I think."

Vin wasn't so certain. However, she remained silent, realizing with frustration how tired she was. Even sitting on a stool seemed strenuous to her now.

"Go and sleep, Mistress," Sazed said, picking up his pen and relocating his place in the tome with his finger. "You survived something that probably should have killed you. Give your body the thanks it deserves; let it rest."

Vin nodded tiredly, then climbed to her feet and left him scribbling quietly in the afternoon light.

Sometimes I wonder what would have happened if I'd remained there, in that lazy village of my birth. I'd have become a smith, like my father. Perhaps I'd have a family, sons of my own.

Perhaps someone else would have come to carry this terrible burden. Someone who could bear it far better than I. Someone who deserved to be a hero.

17

BEFORE COMING TO MANSION RENOUX, VIN had never seen a cultivated garden. On burglaries or scouting missions, she had occasionally seen ornamental plants, but she'd never given them much heed—they, like many noble interests, had seemed frivolous to her.

She hadn't realized how beautiful the plants could be when arranged carefully. Mansion Renoux's garden balcony was a thin, oval structure that overlooked the grounds below. The gardens weren't large—they required too much water and attention to form more than a thin perimeter around the back of the building.

Still, they were marvelous. Instead of mundane browns and whites, the cultivated plants were of deeper, more vibrant colors—shades of red, orange, and yellow, with the colors concentrated in their leaves. The groundskeepers had planted them to make intricate, beautiful patterns. Closer to the balcony, exotic trees with colorful yellow leaves gave shade and protected from ashfalls. It was a very mild winter, and most of the trees still held their leaves. The air felt cool, and the rustling of branches in the wind was soothing.

Almost soothing enough, in fact, to make Vin forget how annoyed she was.

"Would you like more tea, child?" Lord Renoux asked. He didn't wait for an answer; he simply waved for a servant to rush forward and refill her cup.

Vin sat on a plush cushion, her wicker chair designed for comfort. During the last four weeks, her every whim and desire had been met. Servants cleaned up after her, primped her, fed her, and even helped bathe her. Renoux saw that anything she asked for was given her, and she certainly wasn't expected to do anything strenuous, dangerous, or even slightly inconvenient.

In other words, her life was maddeningly boring. Before, her time at Mansion Renoux had been monopolized by Sazed's lessons and Kelsier's training. She'd slept during the days, having only minimal contact with the mansion staff.

Now, however, Allomancy—at least, the nighttime jumping kind—was forbidden her. Her wound was only partially healed, and too much motion re-opened it. Sazed still gave her occasional lessons, but his time was dominated by translating the book. He spent long hours in the library, poring over its pages with an uncharacteristically excited air.

He's found a new bit of lore, Vin thought. *To a Keeper, that's probably as intoxicating as streetspice.*

She sipped at her tea with repressed petulance, eyeing the nearby servants. They seemed like scavenger birds, roosting and waiting for any opportunity to make Vin as comfortable—and as frustrated—as possible.

Renoux wasn't much help either. His idea of "taking lunch" with Vin was to sit and attend to his own duties—making notes on ledgers or dictating letters—while eating. Her attendance seemed important to him, but he rarely paid much attention to her other than to ask how her day had been.

Yet, she forced herself to act the part of a prim noblewoman. Lord Renoux had hired some new servants that didn't know about the job—not house staff, but gardeners and workmen. Kelsier and Renoux had worried that the other houses would grow suspicious if they couldn't get at least a few servant-spies onto the Renoux grounds. Kelsier didn't see it as a danger to the job, but it did mean that Vin had to maintain her persona whenever possible.

I can't believe that people live like this, Vin thought as some servants began clearing away the meal. *How can noblewomen fill their days with so much nothing? No wonder everyone's eager to attend those balls!*

"Is your respite pleasant, dear?" Renoux asked, pouring over another ledger.

"Yes, Uncle," Vin said through tight lips. "Quite."

"You should be up to a shopping trip soon," Renoux said, looking up at her. "Perhaps you would like to visit Kenton Street? Get some new earrings to replace that pedestrian stud you wear?"

Vin reached a hand to her ear, where her mother's earring still sat. "No," she said. "I'll keep this."

Renoux frowned, but said no more, for a servant approached and drew his attention. "My lord," the servant said to Renoux. "A carriage just arrived from Luthadel."

Vin perked up. That was the servants' way of saying that a member of the crew had arrived.

"Ah, very good," Renoux said. "Show them up, Tawnson."

"Yes, my lord."

A few minutes later, Kelsier, Breeze, Yeden, and Dockson walked out onto the balcony. Renoux discreetly waved to the servants, who closed the glass balcony doors and left the crew in privacy. Several men took up position just inside, watching to make certain that the wrong people didn't have an opportunity to eavesdrop.

"Are we interrupting your meal?" Dockson asked.

"No!" Vin said quickly, cutting off Lord Renoux's reply. "Sit, please."

Kelsier strolled over to the balcony's ledge, looking out over the garden and grounds. "Nice view you have here."

"Kelsier, is that wise?" Renoux asked. "Some of the gardeners are men for whom I cannot vouch."

Kelsier chuckled. "If they can recognize me from this distance, they deserve more than the Great Houses are paying them." However, he did leave the balcony edge, walking over to the table and spinning a chair, then sitting down on it the wrong way. Over the last few weeks, he had mostly returned to his old, familiar self. Yet, there were still changes. He held meetings more often, discussed more of his plans with the crew. He also still seemed different, more . . . thoughtful.

Sazed was right, Vin thought. *Our attack on the palace might have been near-deadly for me, but it has changed Kelsier for the better.*

"We thought we'd have our meeting here this week," Dockson said, "since you two rarely get to participate."

"That was most thoughtful of you, Master Dockson," Lord Renoux said. "But your concern is unnecessary. We are doing just fine—"

"No," Vin interrupted. "No, *we* aren't. Some of us need information. What's happening with the crew? How is the recruitment going?"

Renoux eyed her with dissatisfaction. Vin, however, ignored him. *He's not really a lord,* she told herself. *He's just another crewmember. My opinion counts as much as his! Now that the servants are gone, I can speak how I want.*

Kelsier chuckled. "Well, captivity's made her a bit more outspoken, if nothing else."

"I don't have anything to *do*," Vin said. "It's driving me insane."

Breeze set his cup of wine on the table. "Some would find your state quite enviable, Vin."

"Then they must *already* be insane."

"Oh, they're mostly noblemen," Kelsier said. "So, yes, they're quite mad."

"The job," Vin reminded. "What's happening?"

"Recruitment is still too slow," Dockson said. "But we're improving."

"We may have to sacrifice further security for numbers, Kelsier," Yeden said.

That's a change too, she thought, impressed as she noted Yeden's civility. He had taken to wearing nicer clothing—not quite a full gentlemen's suit like

Dockson or Breeze, but at least a well-cut jacket and trousers, with a buttoning shirt beneath, all kept clean of soot.

"That can't be helped, Yeden," Kelsier said. "Fortunately, Ham's doing well with the troops. I had a message from him just a few days ago. He's impressed with their progress."

Breeze snorted. "Be warned—Hammond does tend to be a bit optimistic about these kinds of things. If the army were made up of one-legged mutes, he would praise their balance and their listening skills."

"I should like to see the army," Yeden said eagerly.

"Soon," Kelsier promised.

"We should be able to get Marsh into the Ministry within the month," Dockson said, nodding to Sazed as the Terrisman passed their sentries and entered the balcony. "Hopefully, Marsh will be able to give some insight as to how to deal with the Steel Inquisitors."

Vin shivered.

"They are a concern," Breeze agreed. "Considering what a couple of them did to you two, I don't envy capturing the palace with them in there. They are as dangerous as Mistborn."

"More," Vin said quietly.

"Can the army really fight them?" Yeden asked uncomfortably. "I mean, they're supposed to be immortal, aren't they?"

"Marsh will find the answer," Kelsier promised.

Yeden paused, then nodded, accepting Kelsier's word.

Yes, changed indeed, Vin thought. It appeared that not even Yeden could resist Kelsier's charisma for an extended period of time.

"In the meantime," Kelsier said, "I'm hoping to hear what Sazed has learned about the Lord Ruler."

Sazed sat, laying his tome on the tabletop. "I will tell you what I can, though this is not the book that I first assumed it to be. I thought that Mistress Vin had recovered some ancient religious text—but it is of a far more mundane nature."

"Mundane?" Dockson asked. "How?"

"It is a journal, Master Dockson," Sazed said. "A record that appears to have been penned by the Lord Ruler himself—or, rather, the man who became the Lord Ruler. Even Ministry teachings agree that before the Ascension, he was a mortal man.

"This book tells of his life just prior to his final battle at the Well of Ascension a thousand years ago. Mostly, it is a record of his travels—a narration of the people he met, the places he visited, and the trials he faced during his quest."

"Interesting," Breeze said, "but how does it help us?"

"I am not certain, Master Ladrian," Sazed said. "However, understanding the real history behind the Ascension will be of use, I think. At the very least, it will give us some insight to the Lord Ruler's mind."

Kelsier shrugged. "The Ministry thinks it's important—Vin said she found it in some kind of shrine in the central palace complex."

"Which, of course," Breeze noted, "doesn't at *all* raise any questions regarding its authenticity."

"I do not believe it to be a fabrication, Master Ladrian," Sazed said. "It contains a remarkable level of detail, especially regarding unimportant issues—like packmen and supplies. In addition, the Lord Ruler it depicts is very conflicted. If the Ministry were going to devise a book for worship, they would present their god with more . . . divinity, I think."

"I'll want to read it when you are done, Saze," Dockson said.

"And I," Breeze said.

"Some of Clubs's apprentices occasionally work as scribes," Kelsier said. "We'll have them make a copy for each of you."

"Handy lot, those," Dockson noted.

Kelsier nodded. "So, where does that leave us?"

The group paused, then Dockson nodded to Vin. "With the nobility."

Kelsier frowned slightly.

"I can go back to work," Vin said quickly. "I'm mostly healed, now."

Kelsier shot a look at Sazed, who raised an eyebrow. He checked on her wound periodically. Apparently, he didn't like what he saw.

"Kell," Vin said. "I'm going *insane*. I grew up as a thief, scrambling for food and space—I can't just sit around and let these servants pamper me." *Besides, I have to prove that I can still be useful to this crew.*

"Well," Kelsier said. "You're one of the reasons we came here today. There's a ball this weekend that—"

"I'll go," Vin said.

Kelsier held up a finger. "Hear me out, Vin. You've been through a lot lately, and this infiltration could get dangerous."

"Kelsier," Vin said flatly. "My whole *life* has been dangerous. I'm going."

Kelsier didn't look convinced.

"She has to do it, Kell," Dockson said. "For one thing, the nobility is going to get suspicious if she doesn't start going to parties again. For another, we need to know what she sees. Having servant spies on the staff isn't the same as having a spy listening to local plots. You know that."

"All right, then," Kelsier finally said. "But you have to promise not to use physical Allomancy until Sazed says otherwise."

Later that evening, Vin still couldn't believe how eager she was to go the ball. She stood in her room, looking over the different gown ensembles that Dockson had found for her. Since she had been forced to wear noblewoman's attire for a good month straight, she was beginning to find dresses just a shade more comfortable than she once had.

Not that they aren't frivolous, of course, she thought, inspecting the four gowns. *All of that lace, the layers of material . . . a simple shirt and trousers are so much more practical.*

Yet, there *was* something special about the gowns—something in their beauty, like the gardens outside. When regarded as static items, like a solitary plant, the dresses were only mildly impressive. However, when she considered attending the ball, the gowns took on a new meaning. They were beautiful, and they would make her beautiful. They were the face she would show to the court, and she wanted to choose the right one.

I wonder if Elend Venture will be there. . . . Didn't Sazed say that most of the younger aristocrats attended every ball?

She lay a hand on one dress, black with silver embroiderings. It would match her hair, but was it too dark? Most of the other women wore colorful dresses; muted colors seemed reserved for men's suits. She eyed a yellow gown, but it just seemed a little too . . . perky. And the white one was too ornate.

That left the red. The neckline was lower—not that she had a lot to show—but it was beautiful. A bit gossamer, with full sleeves that were made of translucent mesh in places, it enticed her. But it seemed so . . . blatant. She picked it up, feeling the soft material in her fingers, imagining herself wearing it.

How did I get to this? Vin thought. *This thing would be impossible to hide in! These frilly creations, these aren't me.*

And yet . . . part of her longed to be back at the ball again. The daily life of a noblewoman frustrated her, but her memories of that one night were alluring. The beautiful couples dancing, the perfect atmosphere and music, the marvelous crystalline windows . . .

I don't even realize when I'm wearing perfume anymore, she realized with shock. She found it preferable to bathe in scented water each day, and the servants even perfumed her clothing. It was all subtle, of course, but it would be enough to give her away while sneaking.

Her hair had grown longer, and had been carefully cut by Renoux's stylist so that it fell around her ears, curling just slightly. She no longer looked quite so scrawny in the mirror, despite her lengthy sickness; regular meals had filled her out.

I'm becoming . . . Vin paused. She didn't know what she was becoming. Certainly not a noblewoman. Noblewomen didn't get annoyed when they couldn't to go out stalking at night. Yet, she wasn't really Vin the urchin anymore. She was . . .

Mistborn.

Vin carefully laid the beautiful red dress back on her bed, then crossed the room to look out the window. The sun was close to setting; soon, the mists would come—though, as usual, Sazed would have guards posted to make certain that she didn't go on any unauthorized Allomantic romps. She hadn't complained at the precautions. He was right: Unwatched, she probably would have broken her promise long ago.

She caught a glimpse of motion to her right, and could just barely make out a figure standing out on the garden balcony. Kelsier. Vin stood for a moment, then left her rooms.

Kelsier turned as she walked onto the balcony. She paused, not wanting to interrupt, but he gave her one of his characteristic smiles. She walked forward, joining him at the carved stone balcony railing.

He turned and looked westward—not at the grounds, but beyond them. Toward the wilderness, lit by a setting sun, outside of town. "Does it ever look wrong to you, Vin?"

"Wrong?" she asked.

Kelsier nodded. "The dry plants, the angry sun, the smoky-black sky."

Vin shrugged. "How can those things be right or wrong? That's just the way things are."

"I suppose," Kelsier said. "But, I think your mind-set is part of the wrongness. The world shouldn't look like this."

Vin frowned. "How do you know that?"

Kelsier reached into his vest pocket and pulled out a piece of paper. He unfolded it with a gentle touch, then handed it to Vin.

She accepted the sheet, holding it carefully; it was so old and worn that it seemed close to breaking at the creases. It didn't contain any words, just an old, faded picture. It depicted a strange shape—something like a plant, though not one Vin had ever seen. It was too . . . flimsy. It didn't have a thick stalk, and its leaves were far too delicate. At its top, it had a strange collection of leaves that were a different color from the rest.

"It's called a flower," Kelsier said. "They used to grow on plants, before the Ascension. Descriptions of them appear in the old poems and stories—things that only Keepers and rebel sages know about anymore. Apparently, these plants were beautiful, and they had a pleasant smell."

"Plants that smell?" Vin asked. "Like fruit?"

"Something like that, I think. Some of the reports even claim that these flowers *grew into* fruit, in the days before the Ascension."

Vin stood quietly, frowning, trying to imagine such a thing.

"That picture belonged to my wife, Mare," Kelsier said quietly. "Dockson found it in her things after we were taken. He kept it, hoping that we would return. He gave it to me after I escaped."

Vin looked down at the picture again.

"Mare was fascinated by pre-Ascension times," Kelsier said, still staring out over the gardens. In the distance, the sun touched the horizon, and grew an even deeper red. "She collected things like that paper: pictures and descriptions of the old times. I think that fascination—along with the fact that she was a Tineye—is part of what led her to the underground, and to me. She's the one who first introduced me to Sazed, though I didn't use him in my crew at the time. He wasn't interested in thieving."

Vin folded up the paper. "And you keep this picture still? After . . . what she did to you?"

Kelsier fell silent for a moment. Then he eyed her. "Been listening at doors again, have we? Oh, don't worry. I suppose it's common enough knowledge." In the distance, the setting sun became a blaze, its ruddy light illuminating clouds and smoke alike.

"Yes, I keep the flower," Kelsier said. "I'm not really sure why. But . . . do you stop loving someone just because they betray you? I don't think so. That's what makes the betrayal hurt so much—pain, frustration, anger . . . and I still loved her. I still do."

"How?" Vin asked. "How can you? And, how can you possibly trust people? Didn't you learn from what she did to you?"

Kelsier shrugged. "I think . . . I think given the choice between loving Mare—betrayal included—and never knowing her, I'd choose love. I risked, and I lost, but the risk was still worth it. It's the same with my friends. Suspicion is healthy in our profession—but only to an extent. I'd rather trust my men than worry about what will happen if they turn on me."

"That sounds foolish," Vin said.

"Is happiness foolish?" Kelsier asked, turning toward her. "Where have you been happier, Vin? On my crew, or back with Camon?"

Vin paused.

"I don't know for sure if Mare betrayed me," Kelsier said, looking back at the sunset. "She always claimed that she didn't."

"And she was sent to the Pits, right?" Vin said. "That doesn't make sense, if she sided with the Lord Ruler."

Kelsier shook his head, still staring into the distance. "She showed up at the Pits a few weeks after I was sent there—we were separated, after we were caught. I don't know what happened during that time, or why she was eventually sent to Hathsin. The fact that she *was* sent to die hints that maybe she really didn't betray me, but . . ."

He turned toward Vin. "You didn't hear him when he caught us, Vin. The Lord Ruler . . . he thanked her. Thanked her for betraying me. His words—spoken with such an eerie sense of honesty—mixed with the way that the plan was set up . . . well, it was hard to believe Mare. That didn't change my love, though—not deep down. I nearly died when she did a year later, beaten before the slavemasters at the Pits. That night, after her corpse was taken away, I Snapped."

"You went mad?" Vin asked.

"No," Kelsier said. "Snapping is an Allomantic term. Our powers are latent at first—they only come out after some traumatic event. Something intense—

something almost deadly. The philosophers say that a man can't command the metals until he has seen death and rejected it."

"So . . . when did it happen to me?" Vin asked.

Kelsier shrugged. "It's hard to tell. Growing up as you did, there were probably ample opportunities for you to Snap."

He nodded as if to himself. "For me," he said, "it was that night. Alone in the Pits, my arms bleeding from the day's work. Mare was dead, and I feared that I was responsible—that my lack of faith took away her strength and will. She died knowing that I questioned her loyalty. Maybe, if I'd really loved her, I wouldn't have ever questioned. I don't know."

"But, you didn't die," Vin said.

Kelsier shook his head. "I decided that I'd see her dream fulfilled. I'd make a world where flowers returned, a world with green plants, a world where no soot fell from the sky. . . ." He trailed off, then sighed. "I know. I'm insane."

"Actually," Vin said quietly, "it kind of makes sense. Finally."

Kelsier smiled. The sun sank beneath the horizon, and while its light was still a flare in the west, the mists began to appear. They didn't come from one specific place, they just sort of . . . grew. They extended like translucent, twisting vines in the sky—curling back and forth, lengthening, dancing, melding.

"Mare wanted children," Kelsier said suddenly. "Back when we were first married, a decade and a half ago. I . . . didn't agree with her. I wanted to become the most famous skaa thief of all time, and didn't have time for things that would slow me down.

"It's probably a good thing that we didn't have children. The Lord Ruler might have found and killed them. But, he might not have—Dox and the others survived. Now, sometimes, I wish that I had a piece of her with me. A child. A daughter, perhaps, with Mare's same dark hair and resilient stubbornness."

He paused, then looked down at Vin. "I don't want to be responsible for something happening to you, Vin. Not again."

Vin frowned. "I'm not spending any more time locked in this mansion."

"No, I don't suppose you will. If we try and keep you in much longer, you'll probably just show up at Clubs's shop one night having done something very foolish. We're a bit too much alike that way, you and I. Just . . . be careful."

Vin nodded. "I will."

They stood for a few more minutes, watching the mists gather. Finally, Kelsier stood up straight, stretching. "Well, for what it's worth, I'm glad you decided to join us, Vin."

Vin shrugged. "To tell you the truth, I'd kind of like to see one of those flowers for myself."

You could say that circumstances forced me to leave my home behind—certainly, if I had stayed, I would now be dead. During those days—running without knowing why, carrying a burden I didn't understand—I assumed that I would lose myself in Khlennium and seek a life of indistinction.

I am slowly coming to understand that anonymity, like so many other things, has already been lost to me forever.

18

SHE DECIDED TO WEAR THE RED dress. It was definitely the boldest choice, but that felt right. After all, she hid her true self behind an aristocratic appearance; the more visible that appearance was, the easier it should be for her to hide.

A footman opened the carriage door. Vin took a deep breath—chest a little confined by the special corset she was wearing to hide her bandages—then accepted the footman's hand and climbed down. She straightened her dress, nodded to Sazed, then joined the other aristocrats making their way up the steps to Keep Elariel. It was a bit smaller than the keep of House Venture. However, Keep Elariel apparently had a separate party ballroom, while House Venture had its gatherings in the enormous main hall.

Vin eyed the other noblewomen, and felt a bit of her confidence vanish. Her dress was beautiful, but the other women had so much more than just gowns. Their long, flowing hair and self-assured airs matched their bejeweled figures. They filled out the upper portions of their dresses with voluptuous curves, and moved elegantly in the frilled splendor of the lower folds. Vin occasionally caught glimpses of the women's feet, and they didn't wear simple slippers like her own, but rather high-heeled shoes.

"Why don't I have shoes like that?" she asked quietly as they climbed the carpet-covered stairs.

"Heels take practice to walk in, Mistress," Sazed replied. "Since you've only just learned to dance, it might be best if you wore regular shoes for a time."

Vin frowned, but accepted the explanation. Sazed's mention of dancing, however, increased her discomfort. She remembered the flowing poise of the dancers at her last ball. She certainly wouldn't be able to imitate that—she barely even knew the basic steps.

That won't matter, she thought. *They won't see me—they'll see Lady Valette. She's supposed to be new and uncertain, and everyone thinks she's been ill lately. It will make sense for her to be a poor dancer.*

That thought in mind, Vin reached the top of the stairs feeling a bit more secure.

"I must say, Mistress," Sazed said. "You seem far less nervous this time—in fact, you even seem excited. This is the proper attitude for Valette to display, I think."

"Thank you," she said, smiling. He was right: She *was* excited. Excited to be part of the job again—excited, even, to be back among the nobility, with their splendor and grace.

They stepped up to the squat ballroom building—one of several low wings extending from the main keep—and a servant took her shawl. Vin paused a moment just inside the doorway, waiting as Sazed arranged her table and meal.

The Elariel ballroom was very different from the majestic Venture grand hall. The dim room was only a single story high, and while it had a lot of stained-glass windows, they were all in the ceiling. Circular rose-window skylights shone from above, lit by small limelights on the roof. Each table was set with candles, and despite the light from above, there was a reserved darkness about the room. It seemed . . . private, despite the numerous people in attendance.

This room had obviously been designed to accommodate parties. A sunken dancing floor lay at its center, and this was better lit than the rest of the room. There were two tiers of tables circling the dancing floor: The first tier was only a few feet above, the other was farther back and about twice as high.

A servant led her to a table at the rim of the room. She sat, Sazed taking his customary place beside her, and began to wait for her meal to arrive.

"How exactly am I supposed to get the information Kelsier wants?" she asked quietly, scanning the dark room. The deep, crystalline colors from above projected patterns across tables and people, creating an impressive atmosphere, yet making it difficult to distinguish faces. Was Elend here somewhere amidst the ball-goers?

"Tonight, some men should ask you to dance," Sazed said. "Accept their invitations—this will give you an excuse to seek them out later and mingle in their groups. You don't need to participate in conversations—you just have to listen. At future balls, perhaps some of the young men will begin to ask you to accompany them. Then you'll be able to sit at their table and listen to all of their discussions."

"You mean, sit with one man the entire time?"

Sazed nodded. "It's not uncommon. You would dance only with him that night as well."

Vin frowned. However, she let the matter drop, turning to inspect the room again. *He's probably not even here—he said he avoided balls when possible. Even if he were here, he'd be off on his own. You won't even—*

A muted thump sounded as someone dropped a stack of books onto her table. Vin jumped in startlement, turning as Elend Venture pulled over a chair, then sat down with a relaxed posture. He leaned back in the chair, angling toward a candelabrum beside her table, and opened a book to begin reading.

Sazed frowned. Vin hid a smile, eyeing Elend. He still didn't look as if he had bothered to brush his hair, and again wore his suit without the buttons done up. The garment wasn't shabby, but nor was it as rich as others at the party. It seemed to have been tailored to be loose and relaxed, defying the traditional sharp, well-cut fashion.

Elend flipped through his book. Vin waited patiently for him to acknowledge her, but he just continued to read. Finally, Vin raised an eyebrow. "I don't remember giving you permission to sit at my table, Lord Venture," she said.

"Don't mind me," Elend said, not looking up. "You've got a big table—there's plenty of room for both of us."

"Both of us, perhaps," Vin said. "But I'm not sure about those books. Where are the servers going to put my meal?"

"There's a bit of space to your left," Elend said offhandedly.

Sazed's frown deepened. He stepped forward, gathering up the books and setting them on the floor beside Elend's chair.

Elend continued to read. He did, however, raise a hand to gesture. "See, now, that's why I don't ever use Terrismen servants. They're an insufferably efficient lot, I must say."

"Sazed is hardly insufferable," Vin said coolly. "He is a good friend, and is probably a better man than you will ever be, Lord Venture."

Elend finally looked up. "I'm . . . sorry," he said in a frank tone. "I apologize."

Vin nodded. Elend, however, opened his book and began reading again.

Why sit with me if he's just going to read? "What did you do at these parties before you had me to pester?" she asked in an annoyed tone.

"See, now, how can I be pestering you?" he asked. "I mean, really, Valette. I'm just sitting here, reading quietly to myself."

"At *my* table. I'm certain you could get your own—you're the Venture heir. Not that you were forthcoming about that fact during our last meeting."

"True," Elend said. "I *do*, however, recall telling you that the Ventures were an annoying lot. I'm just trying to live up to the description."

"You're the one that made up the description!"

"Convenient, that," Elend said, smiling slightly as he read.

Vin sighed in frustration, scowling.

Elend peeked up over his book. "That's a stunning dress. It's almost as beautiful as you are."

Vin froze, jaw hanging open slightly. Elend smiled mischievously, then turned back to his book, eyes sparkling as if to indicate that he'd made the comment simply because he knew the reaction he'd get.

Sazed loomed over the table, not bothering to mask his disapproval. Yet, he said nothing. Elend was obviously too important to be chastised by a simple steward.

Vin finally found her tongue. "How is it, Lord Venture, that an eligible man like yourself comes to these balls alone?"

"Oh, I don't," Elend said. "My family usually has one girl or another lined up to accompany me. Tonight's fare is the Lady Stase Blanches—she's the one in the green dress sitting on the lower tier across from us."

Vin glanced across the room. Lady Blanches was a gorgeous blond woman. She kept glancing up at Vin's table, covering a scowl.

Vin flushed, turning away. "Um, shouldn't you be down there with her?"

"Probably," Elend said. "But, see, I'll tell you a secret. The truth is, I'm not really much of a gentleman. Besides, *I* didn't invite her—it wasn't until I got into the carriage that I was informed regarding my accompaniment."

"I see," Vin said with a frown.

"My behavior is, nonetheless, deplorable. Unfortunately, I'm quite prone to such bouts of deplorability—take, for instance, my fondness for reading books at the dinner table. Excuse me for a moment; I'm going to go get something to drink."

He stood, tucking the book into his pocket, and walked toward one of the room's bar tables. Vin watched him go, both annoyed and bemused.

"This is not good, Mistress," Sazed said in a low tone.

"He's not *that* bad."

"He's using you, Mistress," Sazed said. "Lord Venture is infamous for his unconventional, disobedient attitude. Many people dislike him—precisely because he does things like this."

"Like this?"

"He is sitting with you because he knows that it will annoy his family," Sazed said. "Oh, child—I do not wish to bring you pain, but you must understand the ways of the court. This young man is not romantically interested in you. He is a young, arrogant lord who chafes at his father's restrictions—so he rebels, acting rude and offensive. He knows that his father will relent if he acts spoiled enough for long enough."

Vin felt her stomach twist. *Sazed's probably right, of course. Why else would*

Elend seek me out? I'm exactly what he needs—someone lowborn enough to annoy his father, but inexperienced enough not to see the truth.

Her meal arrived, but Vin didn't have much of an appetite anymore. She began to pick at the food as Elend returned, settling down with a large goblet filled with some mixed drink. He sipped as he read.

Let's see how he reacts if I don't interrupt his reading, Vin thought in annoyance, remembering her lessons, and eating her food with a lady's grace. It wasn't a large meal—mostly some rich, buttered vegetables—and the sooner she finished, the sooner she could get to dancing. At least then she wouldn't have to sit with Elend Venture.

The young lord paused several times as she ate, peeking at her over the top of his book. He obviously expected her to say something, but she never did. As she ate, however, her anger faded. She glanced at Elend, studying his slightly disheveled appearance, watching the earnestness with which he read his book. Could this man really hide the twisted sense of manipulation Sazed implied? Was he really just using her?

Anyone will betray you, Reen whispered. *Everyone will betray you.*

Elend just seemed so . . . genuine. He felt like a real person, not a front or a face. And it did seem like he wanted her to talk to him. It felt like a personal victory to Vin when he finally sat the book down and looked at her.

"Why are you here, Valette?" he asked.

"Here at the party?"

"No, here in Luthadel."

"Because it's the center of everything," Vin said.

Elend frowned. "I suppose it is. But, the empire is a big place to have such a small center. I don't think we really understand how large it is. How long did it take you to get here?"

Vin felt a moment of panic, but Sazed's lessons snapped quickly into her mind. "Almost two months by canal, with some stops."

"Such a long time," Elend said. "They say it can take half a year to travel from one end of the empire to the other, yet most of us ignore everything but this little bit at the center."

"I . . ." Vin trailed off. With Reen, she'd been all across the Central Dominance. It was the smallest of the dominances, however, and she'd never visited the more exotic places in the empire. This central area was good for thieves; oddly, the place closest to the Lord Ruler was also the one with the most corruption, not to mention the most riches.

"What do you think of the city, then?" Elend asked.

Vin paused. "It's . . . dirty," she said honestly. In the dim light, a servant arrived to remove her empty plate. "It's dirty, and it's full. The skaa are treated terribly, but I guess that's true everywhere."

Elend cocked his head, giving her a strange look.

I shouldn't have mentioned the skaa. That wasn't very noble-like.

He leaned forward. "You think the skaa here are treated worse than the ones on your plantation? I always thought they would be better off in the city."

"Um . . . I'm not sure. I didn't go to the fields very often."

"So, you didn't interact with them very much?"

Vin shrugged. "Why does it matter? They're just skaa."

"See, now, that's what we always say," Elend said. "But I don't know. Maybe I'm too curious, but they interest me. Did you ever hear them talk to one another? Did they sound like regular people?"

"What?" Vin asked. "Of course they did. What else would they sound like?"

"Well, you know what the Ministry teaches."

She didn't. However, if it was regarding the skaa, it probably wasn't flattering. "I make it a rule to never completely believe anything the Ministry says."

Elend paused again, cocking his head. "You're . . . not what I expected, Lady Valette."

"People rarely are."

"So, tell me about the plantation skaa. What are they like?"

Vin shrugged. "Like skaa everywhere else."

"Are they intelligent?"

"Some are."

"But, not like you and me, right?" Elend asked.

Vin paused. *How would a noblewoman respond?* "No, of course not. They're just skaa. Why are you so interested in them?"

Elend seemed . . . disappointed. "No reason," he said, sitting back in his chair and opening his book. "I think some of those men over there want to ask you to dance."

Vin turned, noticing that there was indeed a group of young men standing a short distance from her table. They looked away as soon as she turned. After a few moments, one of the men pointed at another table; then he walked over and asked a young lady to dance.

"Several people have noticed you, my lady," Sazed said. "However, they never approach. Lord Venture's presence intimidates them, I think."

Elend snorted. "They should know that I am anything but intimidating."

Vin frowned, but Elend just continued to read. *Fine!* she thought, turning back toward the young men. She caught one man's eye, smiling slightly.

A few moments later, the young man approached. He spoke to her in a stiff, formal tone. "Lady Renoux, I am Lord Melend Liese. Would you care to dance?"

Vin shot a glance at Elend, but he didn't look up from his book.

"I would love to, Lord Liese," Vin said, taking the young man's hand and rising.

He led her down to the dance floor, and as they approached, Vin's nervousness returned. Suddenly, one week of practice didn't seem like enough. The music stopped, allowing for couples to leave or enter the floor, and Lord Liese led her forward.

Vin fought down her paranoia, reminding herself that everyone saw the dress and the rank, not Vin herself. She looked up into Lord Liese's eyes and saw, surprisingly, apprehension.

The music began, as did the dancing. Lord Liese's face took on a look of consternation. She could feel his palm sweating in her hands. *Why, he's just as nervous as I am! Perhaps even more.*

Liese was younger than Elend, closer to her own age. He probably wasn't very experienced with balls—he certainly didn't look like he'd danced much. He focused so much on the steps that his motions felt rigid.

It makes sense, Vin realized, relaxing and letting her body move in the motions Sazed had taught. *The experienced ones wouldn't ask me to dance, not when I'm so new. I'm beneath their notice.*

But, why is Elend paying attention to me? Is it simply what Sazed said—a ploy to annoy his father? Why, then, does he seem interested in what I have to say?

"Lord Liese," Vin said. "Do you know much of Elend Venture?"

Liese looked up. "Um, I . . ."

"Don't focus so much on the dancing," Vin said. "My instructor says that it will flow more naturally if you don't try too hard."

He blushed.

Lord Ruler! Vin thought. *How fresh is this boy?*

"Um, Lord Venture . . ." Liese said. "I don't know. He's a very important person. Far more important than I am."

"Don't let his lineage intimidate you," Vin said. "From what I've seen, he's pretty harmless."

"I don't know, my lady," Liese said. "Venture is a very influential house."

"Yes, well, Elend doesn't live up to that reputation. He seems very fond of ignoring those in his company—does he do that to everyone?"

Liese shrugged, dancing more naturally now that they were talking. "I don't know. You . . . seem to know him better than I, my lady."

"I . . ." Vin trailed off. She *felt* as if she knew him well—far better than she should know a man after two brief encounters. She couldn't very well explain that to Liese, however.

But, maybe . . . Didn't Renoux say that he'd met Elend once?

"Oh, Elend is a friend of the family," Vin said as they spun beneath a crystalline skylight.

"He is?"

"Yes," Vin said. "It was very kind of my uncle to ask Elend to watch over me at these parties, and so far he's been quite a dear. I do wish that he'd pay less attention to those books of his and more attention to introducing me, though."

Liese perked up, and he seemed to grow a little less insecure. "Oh. Why, that makes sense."

"Yes," Vin said, "Elend has been like an older brother to me during my time here in Luthadel."

Liese smiled.

"I ask you about him because he doesn't speak much of himself," Vin said.

"The Ventures have all been quiet lately," Liese said. "Ever since the attack on their keep several months back."

Vin nodded. "You know much about that?"

Liese shook his head. "No one tells me anything." He glanced down, watching their feet. "You're very good at dancing, Lady Renoux. You must have attended many balls back in your home city."

"You flatter me, my lord," Vin said.

"No, really. You're so . . . graceful."

Vin smiled, feeling a slight surge of confidence.

"Yes," Liese said, almost to himself. "You're not at all like Lady Shan said—" He stopped, jerking slightly, as if realizing what he was saying.

"What?" Vin said.

"Nothing," Liese said, his blush rising. "I'm sorry. It was nothing."

Lady Shan, Vin thought. *Remember that name.*

She prodded Liese further as the dance progressed, but he was obviously too inexperienced to know much. He did feel that there was a tension rising between the houses; though the balls continued, there were more and more absences as people didn't attend parties thrown by their political rivals.

When the dance ended, Vin felt good about her efforts. She probably hadn't discovered much of value to Kelsier—however, Liese was only the beginning. She'd work up to more important people.

Which means, Vin thought as Liese led her back to her table, *I'm going to have to attend a lot more of these balls.* It wasn't that the balls themselves were unpleasant—especially now that she was more confident in her dancing. However, more balls meant fewer chances to be out in the mists.

Not that Sazed would let me go anyway, she thought with an inward sigh, smiling politely as Liese bowed and retreated.

Elend had spread his books across the table, and her alcove was lit by several more candelabra—apparently filched from other tables.

Well, Vin thought, *we've at least got thieving in common.*

Elend hunched over the table, making notations in a small, pocket-sized book. He didn't look up as she sat. Sazed, she noticed, was nowhere to be seen.

"I sent the Terrisman to dinner," Elend said distractedly as he scribbled. "No need for him to go hungry while you twirled down below."

Vin raised an eyebrow, regarding the books that dominated her tabletop. Even as she watched, Elend pushed one tome aside—leaving it open to a specific page—and pulled over another. "So, how was the aforementioned twirling, anyway?" he said.

"It was actually kind of fun."

"I thought you weren't very good at it."

"I wasn't," Vin said. "I practiced. You may find this information surprising, but sitting in the back of a room reading books in the dark doesn't exactly help one become a better dancer."

"Is that a proposition?" Elend asked, pushing aside his book and selecting another. "It's unladylike to ask a man to dance, you know."

"Oh, I wouldn't want to take you away from your reading," Vin said, turning a book toward her. She grimaced—the text was written in a small, cramped hand. "Besides, dancing with you would undermine all of the work I just did."

Elend paused. Then he finally looked up. "Work?"

"Yes," Vin said. "Sazed was right—Lord Liese finds you intimidating, and he found me intimidating by association. It could be quite disastrous to a young lady's social life if all of the young men assumed her unavailable simply because an annoying lord decided to study at her table."

"So . . ." Elend said.

"So I told him that you were simply showing me the ways of court. Kind of like an . . . older brother."

"Older brother?" Elend asked, frowning.

"*Much* older," Vin said, smiling. "I mean, you've got to be at least twice my age."

"Twice your . . . Valette, I'm *twenty-one*. Unless you're a *very* mature ten-year-old, I'm nowhere near 'twice your age.'"

"I've never been good with math," Vin said offhandedly.

Elend sighed, rolling his eyes. Nearby, Lord Liese was speaking quietly with his group of friends, gesturing toward Vin and Elend. Hopefully, one would come ask her to dance soon.

"Do you know a Lady Shan?" Vin asked idly as she waited.

Surprisingly, Elend looked up. "Shan Elariel?"

"I assume so," Vin said. "Who is she?"

Elend turned back to his book. "Nobody important."

Vin raised an eyebrow. "Elend, I've only been doing this for a few months, but even *I* know not to trust a comment like that."

"Well . . ." Elend said. "I might be engaged to her."

"You have a fiancée?" Vin asked with exasperation.

"I'm not exactly sure. We haven't really done anything about the situation for a year or so. Everyone's likely forgotten the matter by now."

Great, Vin thought.

A moment later, one of Liese's friends approached. Glad to be rid of the frustrating Venture heir, Vin stood, accepting the young lord's hand. As she walked to the dance floor, she glanced at Elend, and caught him peeking over the book at her. He immediately turned back to his research with an overtly indifferent air.

Vin sat down at her table, feeling a remarkable level of exhaustion. She resisted the urge to pull off her shoes and massage her feet; she suspected that wouldn't be very ladylike. She quietly turned on her copper, then burned pewter, strengthening her body and washing away a bit of her fatigue.

She let her pewter, then her copper, lapse. Kelsier had assured her that with copper on, she couldn't be spotted as an Allomancer. Vin wasn't so certain. With pewter burning, her reactions were too fast, her body too strong. It seemed to her that an observant person would be able to notice such inconsistencies, whether or not they themselves were an Allomancer.

With the pewter off, her fatigue returned. She'd been trying to wean herself off constant pewter lately. Her wound was to the point that it only hurt badly if she twisted the wrong way, and she wanted to recover her strength on her own, if she could.

In a way, her fatigue this evening was a good thing—it was a result of an extended period of dancing. Now that the young men regarded Elend as a guardian, rather than a romantic interest, they had no qualms about asking Vin to dance. And, worried that she would make an unintended political statement by refusing, Vin had agreed to each request. A few months ago, she would have laughed at the idea of exhaustion from dancing. However, her sore feet, aching side, and tired legs were only part of it. The effort of memorizing names and houses—not to mention putting up with her dancing partners' fluffy conversation—left her mentally drained.

It's a good thing Sazed had me wear slippers instead of heels, Vin thought with a sigh, sipping her chilled juice. The Terrisman hadn't returned from his dinner yet. Notably, Elend wasn't at the table either—though his books still lay scattered across its top.

Vin eyed the tomes. Perhaps if she appeared to be reading, the young men would leave her alone for a bit. She reached over, rifling through the books for a likely candidate. The one she was most interested in—Elend's small, leather-bound notebook—was missing.

Instead, she picked a large, blue tome and hefted it over to her side of the table. She had picked it for its large lettering—was paper really so expensive that scribes needed to cram as many lines to a page as possible? Vin sighed, leafing through the volume.

I can't believe people read books this big, she thought. Despite the large lettering, each page was filled with words. It would take days and days to read the entire thing. Reen had taught her reading so that she would be able to decipher contracts, write notes, and perhaps play a noblewoman. However, her training hadn't extended to texts this massive.

Historical Practices in Imperial Political Rule, the first page read. The chapters had titles like "The Fifth Century Governorship Program" and "The Rise of Skaa Plantations." She flipped through to the end of the book, figuring it would probably be the most interesting. The final chapter was titled "Current Political Structure."

So far, she read, *the plantation system has produced a far more stable government than previous methodologies. The structure of Dominances with each provincial lord taking command of—and responsibility for—his skaa has fostered a competitive environment where discipline is harshly enforced.*

The Lord Ruler apparently finds this system troubling because of the freedom it allows the aristocracy. However, the relative lack of organized rebellion is undoubtedly enticing; during the two hundred years that the system has been in place, there hasn't been a major uprising in the Five Inner Dominances.

Of course, this political system is only an extension of the greater theocratic rulership. The aristocracy's independence has been tempered by a renewed vigor in obligator enforcement. No lord, no matter how lofty, would be advised to think himself above their law. The call from an Inquisitor can come to anyone.

Vin frowned. While the text itself was dry, she was surprised that the Lord Ruler allowed such analytical discussions of his empire. She settled back in her chair, holding up the book, but she didn't read any more. She was too exhausted from the hours she had spent covertly trying to wiggle information out of her dancing partners.

Unfortunately, politics didn't pay heed to Vin's state of exhaustion. Though she did her best to appear absorbed in Elend's book, a figure soon approached her table.

Vin sighed, preparing herself for another dance. She soon realized, however, that the newcomer wasn't a nobleman, but a Terrisman steward. Like Sazed, he wore robes with overlapping **V** designs, and was very fond of jewelry.

"Lady Valette Renoux?" the tall man asked in a faintly accented voice.

"Yes," Vin said hesitantly.

"My mistress, Lady Shan Elariel, requires your presence at her table."

Requires? Vin thought. She already didn't like that tone, and she had little desire to meet with Elend's former betrothed. Unfortunately, House Elariel was one of the more powerful Great Houses—probably not someone to dismiss offhandedly.

The Terrisman waited expectantly.

"Very well," Vin said, rising with as much grace as she could muster.

The Terrisman led Vin toward a table a short distance from her own. The table was well attended, with five women seated around it, and Vin picked out

Shan immediately. Lady Elariel was obviously the statuesque woman with long dark hair. She wasn't participating in the conversation, but seemed to dominate it nonetheless. Her arms sparkled with lavender bracelets that matched her dress, and she turned dismissive eyes toward Vin as she approached.

Those dark eyes, however, were keen. Vin felt exposed before them— stripped of her fine dress, reduced to a dirty urchin once again.

"Excuse us, ladies," Shan said. The women immediately did as ordered, departing the table in a stately flurry.

Shan picked up a fork and began to meticulously dissect and devour a small piece of dessert cake. Vin stood uncertainly, the Terrisman steward taking up a position behind Shan's chair.

"You may sit," Shan said.

I feel like a skaa again, Vin thought, sitting. *Noblemen treat each other this way too?*

"You are in an enviable position, child," Shan said.

"How is that?" Vin asked.

"Address me as 'Lady Shan,'" Shan said, her tone unchanged. "Or, perhaps, 'Your Ladyship.'"

Shan waited expectantly, taking petite bites of the cake. Finally, Vin said, "Why is that, Your Ladyship?"

"Because young Lord Venture has decided to use you in his games. That means you have the opportunity to be used by me as well."

Vin frowned. *Remember to stay in character. You're the easily intimidated Valette.*

"Wouldn't it would be better to not be used at all, Your Ladyship?" Vin said carefully.

"Nonsense," Shan replied. "Even an uncultured simpleton like yourself must see the importance of being useful to your betters." Shan said the words, even the insult, without vehemence; she simply seemed to take it for granted that Vin would agree.

Vin sat, dumbfounded. None of the other nobility had treated her in such a manner. Of course, the only member of a Great House she'd met so far was Elend.

"I trust from your vapid look that you accept your place," Shan said. "Do well, child, and perhaps I will let you join my retinue. You could learn much from the ladies here in Luthadel."

"Such as?" Vin asked, trying to keep the snappishness out of her voice.

"Look at yourself sometime, child. Hair like you've undergone some terrible disease, so scrawny that your dress hangs like a bag. Being a noblewoman in Luthadel requires . . . perfection. Not *that*." She said the last word while waving her hand dismissively toward Vin.

Vin flushed. There was a strange power to this woman's demeaning attitude. With a start, Vin realized that Shan reminded her of some crewleaders she had known, Camon the latest of them—men who would hit a person, fully expecting no resistance. Everyone knew that resisting such men only made the beating worse.

"What do you want from me?" Vin asked.

Shan raised an eyebrow as she set aside her fork, the cake only half-eaten. The Terrisman took the plate and walked off with it. "You really are a dull-minded thing, aren't you?" Shan asked.

Vin paused. "What does *Her Ladyship* want from me?"

"I'll tell you eventually—assuming Lord Venture decides to keep playing with you." Vin caught just the barest flash of hatred in her eyes when she said Elend's name.

"For now," Shan continued, "tell me of your conversation with him this evening."

Vin opened her mouth to respond. But . . . something felt wrong. She only caught the barest flicker of it—she wouldn't have even noticed that much without Breeze's training.

A Soother? Interesting.

Shan was trying to make Vin complacent. So that she would talk, perhaps? Vin began to relate her conversation with Elend, staying away from anything interesting. However, something still felt odd to her—something about the way that Shan was playing with her emotions. From the corner of her eye, Vin saw Shan's Terrisman return from the kitchens. However, he didn't walk back toward Shan's table—he headed in the other direction.

Toward Vin's own table. He paused beside it, and began to poke through Elend's books.

Whatever he wants, I can't let him find it.

Vin stood suddenly, finally provoking an overt reaction in Shan as the woman looked up with surprise.

"I just remembered that I told my Terrisman to find me at my table!" Vin said. "He'll be worried if I'm not sitting there!"

"Oh, for the Lord Ruler's sake," Shan muttered under her breath. "Child, there is no need—"

"I'm sorry, Your Ladyship," Vin said. "I've got to go."

It was a bit obvious, but it was the best she could manage. Vin curtsied and withdrew from Shan's table, leaving the displeased woman behind. The Terrisman was good—by the time Vin was a few steps away from Shan's table, he had noticed Vin and continued on his way, his motions impressively smooth.

Vin arrived back at her table, wondering if she'd made a blunder by leaving Shan so rudely. However, she was growing too tired to care. As she noticed another group of young men eyeing her, she hurriedly sat, plopping open one of Elend's books.

Fortunately, the ploy worked better this time. The young men eventually trailed away, leaving Vin in peace, and she sat back, relaxing slightly with the book open before her. The evening was growing late, and the ballroom was slowly beginning to empty.

The books, she thought with a frown, picking up her cup of juice to take a sip. *What did the Terrisman want with them?*

She scanned the table, trying to notice if anything had been disturbed, but Elend had left the books in such a state of disarray that it was hard to tell. However, a small book sitting beneath another tome caught her eye. Most of the other texts lay open to a specific page, and she had seen Elend perusing them. This particular book, however, was closed—and she couldn't remember him ever opening it. It had been there before—she recognized it because it was so much thinner than the others—so the Terrisman hadn't left it behind.

Curious, Vin reached over and slid the book out from underneath the larger book. It had had a black leather cover, and the spine read *Weather Patterns of the Northern Dominance.* Vin frowned, turning the book over in her hands. There was no title page, nor was an author listed. It launched directly into text.

When regarding the Final Empire in its entirety, one certain fact is unmistakable. For a nation ruled by a self-proclaimed divinity, the empire has experienced a frightening number of colossal leadership errors. Most of these have been successfully covered up, and can only be found in the metalminds of Feruchemists or on the pages of banned texts. However, one only need look to the near past to note such blunders as the Massacre at Devanex, the revision of the Deepness Doctrine, and the relocation of the Renates peoples.

The Lord Ruler does not age. That much, at least, is undeniable. This text, however, purports to prove that he is by no means infallible. During the days before the Ascension, mankind suffered chaos and uncertainty caused by an endless cycle of kings, emperors, and other monarchs. One would think that now, with a single, immortal governor, society would finally have an opportunity to find stability and enlightenment. It is the remarkable lack of either attribute in the Final Empire that is the Lord Ruler's most grievous oversight.

Vin stared at the page. Some of the words were beyond her skill, but she was able to grasp the author's meaning. He was saying . . .

She snapped the book closed and hurriedly put it back in its place. What would happen if the obligators discovered that Elend owned such a text? She glanced to the sides. They were there, of course, mingling with the crowds like at the other ball, marked by their gray robes and tattooed faces. Many sat at tables with noblemen. Friends? Or spies for the Lord Ruler? Nobody seemed quite as comfortable when an obligator was nearby.

What is Elend doing with a book like that? A powerful nobleman like himself? Why would he read texts that malign the Lord Ruler?

A hand fell on her shoulder, and Vin spun reflexively, pewter and copper flaring in her stomach.

"Whoa," Elend said, stepping back and raising his hand. "Has anyone ever told you how jumpy you are, Valette?"

Vin relaxed, sitting back in her chair and extinguishing her metals. Elend sauntered over to his place and sat down. "Enjoying Heberen?"

Vin frowned, and Elend nodded to the larger, thick book that still sat before her.

"No," Vin said. "It's boring. I was just pretending to read so that the men would leave me alone for a bit."

Elend chuckled. "Now, see, your cleverness is coming back to snap at you."

Vin raised an eyebrow as Elend began to gather up his books, stacking them on the table. He didn't appear to notice that she'd moved the "weather" book, but he did carefully slide it into the middle of the stack.

Vin turned her eyes from the book. *I probably shouldn't tell him about Shan—not until I talk to Sazed.* "I think my cleverness did its job well," she said instead. "After all, I came to the ball to dance."

"I find dancing overrated."

"You can't remain aloof from the court forever, Lord Venture—you're the heir of a very important house."

He sighed, stretching and leaning back in his chair. "I suppose you're right," he said with surprising frankness. "But the longer I hold out, the more annoyed my father will become. That, in itself, is a worthy goal."

"He's not the only one you hurt," Vin said. "What of the girls that never get asked to dance because you're too busy rummaging through your books?"

"As I recall," Elend said, setting the last book on the top of his pile, "someone was just pretending to read in order to *avoid* dancing. I don't think the ladies have any trouble finding more amicable partners than myself."

Vin raised an eyebrow. "I didn't have trouble because I'm new and I'm low-ranked. I suspect that the ladies closer to your station have trouble finding partners, amicable or not. As I understand it, noblemen are uncomfortable dancing with women above their station."

Elend paused, obviously searching for a comeback.

Vin leaned forward. "What is it, Elend Venture? Why are you so intent on avoiding your duty?"

"Duty?" Elend asked, leaning toward her, his posture earnest. "Valette, this isn't duty. This ball . . . this is fluff and distraction. A waste of time."

"And women?" Vin asked. "Are they a waste too?"

"Women?" Elend asked. "Women are like . . . thunderstorms. They're beautiful to look at, and sometimes they're nice to listen to—but most of the time they're just plain inconvenient."

Vin felt her jaw drop slightly. Then she noticed the twinkle in his eye, the smile at the edges of his lips, and she found herself smiling as well. "You say these things just to provoke me!"

His smile deepened. "I'm charming that way." He stood, looking at her fondly. "Ah, Valette. Don't let them trick you into taking yourself too seriously. It's not worth the effort. But, I must bid you a good evening. Try not to let months pass between balls you attend in the future."

Vin smiled. "I'll think about it."

"Please do," Elend said, bending down and scooting the tall stack of books off the table and into his arms. He teetered for a moment, then steadied himself and peeked to the side. "Who knows—maybe one of these days you'll actually get me to dance."

Vin smiled, nodding as the nobleman turned and walked off, circling the perimeter of the ballroom's second tier. He was soon met by two other young men. Vin watched curiously as one of the men clapped Elend on the shoulder in a friendly way, then took half of the books. The three began to walk together, chatting.

Vin didn't recognize the newcomers. She sat thoughtfully as Sazed finally appeared out of a side hallway, and Vin eagerly waved him forward. He approached with a hurried step.

"Who are those men with Lord Venture?" Vin asked, pointing toward Elend.

Sazed squinted behind his spectacles. "Why . . . one of them is Lord Jastes Lekal. The other is a Hasting, though I don't know his given name."

"You sound surprised."

"Houses Lekal and Hasting are both political rivals of House Venture, Mistress. Noblemen often visit with each other in smaller, after-ball parties, making alliances. . . ." The Terrisman paused, turning back to her. "Master Kelsier will wish to hear of this, I think. It is time we retire."

"I agree," Vin said, rising. "And so do my feet. Let's go."

Sazed nodded, and the two of them made their way to the front doors. "What took you so long?" Vin asked as they waited for an attendant to fetch her shawl.

"I came back several times, Mistress," Sazed said. "But you were always dancing. I decided I would be of far more use speaking with the servants than I would be standing beside your table."

Vin nodded, accepting her shawl, then walked out the front steps and down the carpeted stairs, Sazed just behind her. Her step was quick—she wanted to get back and tell Kelsier the names she'd memorized before she forgot the whole list. She paused at the landing, waiting for a servant to fetch her carriage. As she did, she noticed something odd. A small disturbance was going on a short distance away in the mists. She stepped forward, but Sazed put a hand on her shoulder, holding her back. A lady wouldn't wander off into the mists.

She reached to burn copper and tin, but waited—the disturbance was getting closer. It resolved as a guard appeared from the mists, pulling a small, struggling form: a skaa boy in dirty clothing, face soot-stained. The soldier gave Vin a wide berth, nodding apologetically to her as he approached one of the guard captains. Vin burned tin to hear what was said.

"Kitchen boy," the soldier said quietly. "Tried to beg from one of the noblemen inside a carriage when they stopped for the gates to open."

The captain simply nodded. The soldier pulled his captive back out into the mists, walking toward the far courtyard. The boy struggled, and the soldier grunted with annoyance, keeping a tight grip. Vin watched him go, Sazed's hand on her shoulder, as if to hold her back. Of course she couldn't help the boy. He shouldn't have—

In the mists, beyond the eyesight of regular people, the soldier drew out a dagger and slit the boy's throat. Vin jumped, shocked, as the sounds of the boy's struggling tapered off. The guard dropped the body, then grabbed it by a leg and began to drag it away.

Vin stood, stunned, as her carriage pulled up.

"Mistress," Sazed prompted, but she simply stood there.

They killed him, she thought. *Right here, just a few paces away from where noblemen wait for their carriages. As if . . . the death were nothing out of the ordinary. Just another skaa, slaughtered. Like an animal.*

Or less than an animal. Nobody would slaughter pigs in a keep courtyard. The guard's posture as he'd performed the murder indicated that he'd simply been too annoyed with the struggling boy to wait for a more appropriate location. If any of the other nobility around Vin had noticed the event, they paid it no heed, continuing their chatting as they waited. Actually, they seemed a little more chatty, now that the screams had stopped.

"Mistress," Sazed said again, pushing her forward.

She allowed herself to be led into the carriage, her mind still distracted. It seemed such an impossible contrast to her. The pleasant nobility, dancing, just inside a room sparkling with light and dresses. Death in the courtyard. Didn't they care? Didn't they know?

This is the Final Empire, Vin, she told herself as the carriage rolled away. *Don't forget the ash because you see a little silk. If those people in there knew you were skaa, they'd have you slaughtered just as easily as they did that poor boy.*

It was a sobering thought—one that absorbed her during the entire trip back to Fellise.

Kwaan and I met by happenstance—though, I suppose, he would use the word "providence."

I have met many other Terris philosophers since that day. They are, every one, men of great wisdom and ponderous sagaciousness. Men with an almost palpable importance.

Not so Kwaan. In a way, he is as unlikely a prophet as I am a hero. He never had an air of ceremonious wisdom—nor was he even a religious scholar. When we first met, he was studying one of his ridiculous interests in the great Khlenni library—I believe he was trying to determine whether or not trees could think.

That he should be the one who finally discovered the great Hero of Terris prophecy is a matter that would cause me to laugh, had events turned out just a little differently.

19

KELSIER COULD FEEL ANOTHER ALLOMANCER PULSING in the mists. The vibrations washed over him like rhythmic waves brushing up against a tranquil shore. They were faint, but unmistakable.

He crouched atop a low garden wall, listening to the vibrations. The curling white mist continued its normal, placid wafting—indifferent, save for the bit closest to his body, which curled in the normal Allomantic current around his limbs.

Kelsier squinted in the night, flaring tin and seeking out the other Allomancer. He thought he saw a figure crouching atop a wall in the distance, but he couldn't be certain. He recognized the Allomantic vibrations, however. Each metal, when burned, gave off a distinct signal, recognizable to one who was well practiced with bronze. The man in the distance burned tin, as did the four others Kelsier had sensed hiding around Keep Tekiel. The five Tineyes formed a perimeter, watching the night, searching for intruders.

Kelsier smiled. The Great Houses were growing nervous. Keeping five Tineyes on watch wouldn't be that hard for a house like Tekiel, but the noblemen Allomancers would resent being forced into simple guard duty. And if there were five Tineyes on watch, chances were good that a number of Thugs, Coinshots, and Lurchers were on call as well. Luthadel was quietly in a state of alert.

The Great Houses were growing so wary, in fact, that Kelsier had trouble finding cracks in their defenses. He was only one man, and even Mistborn had limits. His success so far had been achieved through surprise. However, with five Tineyes on watch, Kelsier wouldn't be able to get very close to the keep without serious risk of being spotted.

Fortunately, Kelsier didn't need to test Tekiel's defenses this night. Instead, he crept along the wall toward the outer grounds. He paused near the garden well, and—burning bronze to make certain no Allomancers were near—reached into a stand of bushes to retrieve a large sack. It was heavy enough that he had to burn pewter to pull it free and throw it over his shoulder. He paused in the night for a moment, straining for sounds in the mist, then hauled the sack back toward the keep.

He stopped near a large, whitewashed garden veranda that sat beside a small reflecting pool. Then, he heaved the sack off his shoulder and dumped its contents—a freshly killed corpse—onto the ground.

The body—which had belonged to one Lord Charrs Entrone—rolled to a stop with its face in the dirt, twin dagger wounds glistening in its back. Kelsier had ambushed the half-drunken man on a street just outside of a skaa slum, ridding the world of another nobleman. Lord Entrone, in particular, would not be missed—he was infamous for his twisted sense of pleasure. Skaa bloodfights, for instance, were a particular enjoyment of his. That was where he had spent this evening.

Entrone had, not coincidentally, been a major political ally of House Tekiel. Kelsier left the corpse sitting in its own blood. The gardeners would locate it first—and once the servants knew about the death, no amount of noble obstinacy would keep it quiet. The murder would cause an outcry, and immediate blame would probably be placed upon House Izenry, House Tekiel's rival. However, Entrone's suspiciously unexpected death might make House Tekiel wary. If they began poking around, they would find that Entrone's gambling opponent at the night's bloodfight had been Crews Geffenry—a man whose house had been petitioning the Tekiels for a stronger alliance. Crews was a known Mistborn, and a very competent knife-fighter.

And so, the intrigue would begin. Had House Izenry done the murder? Or, perhaps, had the death been an attempt by House Geffenry to push Tekiel into a higher state of alarm—thereby encouraging them to seek allies among the lesser nobility? Or, was there a third answer—a house that wanted to strengthen the rivalry between Tekiel and Izenry?

Kelsier hopped off the garden wall, scratching at the fake beard he wore. It didn't really matter whom House Tekiel decided to blame; Kelsier's real purpose was to make them question and worry, to make them mistrust and misunderstand. Chaos was his strongest ally in fostering a house war. When that war finally came, each noblemen killed would be one less person that the skaa would have to face in their rebellion.

As soon as Kelsier got a short distance from Keep Tekiel, he flipped a coin and went to the rooftops. Occasionally, he wondered what the people in the houses beneath him thought, hearing footsteps from above. Did they know that Mistborn found their homes a convenient highway, a place where they could move without being bothered by guards or thieves? Or, did the people attribute the knockings to the ever-blamable mistwraiths?

They probably don't even notice. Sane people are asleep when the mists come out. He landed on a peaked roof, retrieved his pocket watch from a nook to check the time, then stowed it—and the dangerous metal from which it was made—away again. Many nobility blatantly wore metal, a foolish form of bravado. The habit had been inherited directly from the Lord Ruler. Kelsier, however, didn't like carrying any metal—watch, ring, or bracelet—on him that he didn't have to.

He launched himself into the air again, making his way toward the Sootwarrens, a skaa slum on the far northern side of town. Luthadel was an enormous, sprawling city; every few decades or so, new sections were added, the city wall expanded through the sweat and effort of skaa labor. With the advent of the modern canal era, stone was growing relatively cheap and easy to move.

I wonder why he even bothers with the wall, Kelsier thought, moving along rooftops parallel to the massive structure. *Who would attack? The Lord Ruler controls everything. Not even the western isles resist anymore.*

There hadn't been a true war in the Final Empire for centuries. The occasional "rebellion" consisted of nothing more than a few thousand men hiding in hills or caves, coming out for periodic raids. Even Yeden's rebellion wouldn't rely much on force—they were counting on the chaos of a house war, mixed with the strategic misdirection of the Luthadel Garrison, to give them an opening. If it came down to an extended campaign, Kelsier would lose. The Lord Ruler and the Steel Ministry could marshal literally millions of troops if the need arose.

Of course, there was his other plan. Kelsier didn't speak of it, he barely even dared consider it. He probably wouldn't even have an opportunity to implement it. But, if the opportunity did arrive . . .

He dropped to the ground just outside of the Sootwarrens, then pulled his mistcloak tight and walked along the street with a confident step. His contact sat in the doorway of a closed shop, puffing quietly on a pipe. Kelsier raised an eyebrow; tobacco was an expensive luxury. Hoid was either very wasteful, or he was just as successful as Dockson implied.

Hoid calmly put away the pipe, then climbed to his feet—though that didn't make him much taller. The scrawny bald man bowed deeply in the misty night. "Greetings, my lord."

Kelsier paused in front of the man, arms tucked carefully inside his mistcloak. It wouldn't do for a street informant to realize that the unidentified "nobleman" he was meeting with had the scars of Hathsin on his arms.

"You come highly recommended," Kelsier said, mimicking the haughty accent of a nobleman.

"I am one of the best, my lord."

Anyone who can survive as long as you have must be good, Kelsier thought. Lords didn't like the idea of other men knowing their secrets. Informants generally didn't live very long.

"I need to know something, informant," Kelsier said. "But first you must vow never to speak of this meeting to anyone."

"Of course, my lord," Hoid said. He'd likely break the promise before the night was out—another reason informants didn't tend to live very long. "There is, however, the matter of payment. . . ."

"You'll have your money, skaa," Kelsier snapped.

"Of course, my lord," Hoid said with a quick bob of the head. "You requested information regarding House Renoux, I believe. . . ."

"Yes. What is known about it? Which houses is it aligned with? I must know these things."

"There isn't really much to know, my lord," Hoid said. "Lord Renoux is very new to the area, and he is a careful man. He's making neither allies nor enemies at the moment—he's buying a large number of weapons and armor, but is probably just purchasing from a wide variety of houses and merchants, thereby ingratiating himself to them all. A wise tactic. He will, perhaps, have an excess of merchandise, but he will also have an excess of friends, yes?"

Kelsier snorted. "I don't see why I should pay you for that."

"He'll have too much merchandise, my lord," Hoid said quickly. "You could make a clever profit, knowing that Renoux is shipping at a loss."

"I'm no merchant, skaa," Kelsier said. "I don't care about profits and shipping!" *Let him chew on that. Now he thinks I'm of a Great House—of course, if he hadn't suspected that because of the mistcloak, then he doesn't deserve his reputation.*

"Of course, my lord," Hoid said quickly. "There is more, of course. . . ."

Ah, and here we see it. Does the street know that House Renoux is connected to the rumblings of rebellion? If anyone had discovered that secret, then Kelsier's crew was in serious jeopardy.

Hoid coughed quietly, holding out his hand.

"Insufferable man!" Kelsier snapped, tossing a pouch at Hoid's feet.

"Yes, my lord," Hoid said, falling to his knees and searching about with his hand. "I apologize, my lord. My eyesight is weak, you know. I can barely see my own fingers held in front of my face."

Clever, Kelsier thought as Hoid found the pouch and tucked it away. The comment about eyesight was, of course, a lie—no man would get far in the underground with such an impediment. However, a nobleman who thought his informant to be half blind would be far less paranoid about being identified. Not that Kelsier himself was worried—he wore one of Dockson's best disguises. Beside the beard, he had a fake, but realistic, nose, along with platforms in the shoes and makeup to lighten his skin.

"You said there was more?" Kelsier said. "I swear, skaa, if it isn't good . . ."

"It is," Hoid said quickly. "Lord Renoux is considering a union between his niece, the Lady Valette, and Lord Elend Venture."

Kelsier paused. *Wasn't expecting that . . .* "That's silly. Venture is *far* above Renoux."

"The two youths were seen speaking—at length—at the Venture ball a month ago."

Kelsier laughed derisively. "Everyone knows about that. It meant nothing."

"Did it?" Hoid asked. "Does everyone know that Lord Elend Venture spoke very highly of the girl to his friends, the group of nobleling philosophers that lounge at the Broken Quill?"

"Young men speak of girls," Kelsier said. "It means nothing. You will be returning those coins."

"Wait!" Hoid said, sounding apprehensive for the first time. "There is more. Lord Renoux and Lord Venture have had secret dealings."

What?

"It is true," Hoid continued. "This is fresh news—I heard it barely an hour ago myself. There is a connection between Renoux and Venture. And, for some reason, Lord Renoux was able to demand that Elend Venture be assigned to watch over Lady Valette at balls." He lowered his voice. "It is even whispered that Lord Renoux has some kind of . . . leverage over House Venture."

What happened at that ball tonight? Kelsier thought. Out loud, however, he said, "This all sounds very weak, skaa. You have nothing more than idle speculations?"

"Not about House Renoux, my lord," Hoid said. "I tried, but your worry over this house is meaningless! You should pick a house more central to politics. Like, say, House Elariel . . ."

Kelsier frowned. By mentioning Elariel, Hoid was implying that he had some important tidbit that would be worth Kelsier's payment. It seemed that House Renoux's secrets were safe. It was time to move the discussion along to other houses, so that Hoid wouldn't get suspicious of Kelsier's interest in Renoux.

"Very well," Kelsier said. "But if this isn't worth my time . . ."

"It is, my lord. Lady Shan Elariel is a Soother."

"Proof?"

"I felt her touch on my emotions, my lord," Hoid said. "During a fire at Keep Elariel a week ago, she was there calming the emotions of the servants."

Kelsier had started that fire. Unfortunately, it hadn't spread beyond the guardhouses. "What else?"

"House Elariel has recently given her leave to use her powers more at court functions," Hoid said. "They fear a house war, and wish her to make whatever allegiances possible. She always carries a thin envelope of shaved brass in her right glove. Get a Seeker close to her at a ball, and you shall see. My lord, I do not lie! My life as an informant depends solely upon my reputation. Shan Elariel *is* a Soother."

Kelsier paused, as if musing. The information was useless to him, but his true purpose—finding out about House Renoux—had already been fulfilled. Hoid had earned his coins, whether he realized it or not.

Kelsier smiled. *Now to sow a little more chaos.*

"What of Shan's covert relationship with Salmen Tekiel?" Kelsier said, picking the name of a likely young nobleman. "Do you think that she used her powers to gain his favor?"

"Oh, most certainly, my lord," Hoid said quickly. Kelsier could see the glimmer of excitement in his eyes; he assumed that Kelsier had given him a luscious bit of political gossip free of charge.

"Perhaps she was the one who secured Elariel the deal with House Hasting last week," Kelsier said musingly. There had been no such deal.

"Most likely, my lord."

"Very well, skaa," Kelsier said. "You have earned your coins. Perhaps I shall call upon you another time."

"Thank you, my lord," Hoid said, bowing very low.

Kelsier dropped a coin and launched himself into the air. As he landed on a rooftop, he caught a glimpse of Hoid scuttling over to pluck the coin off the ground. Hoid didn't have any trouble locating it, despite his "weak eyesight." Kelsier smiled, then kept moving. Hoid hadn't mentioned Kelsier's tardiness, but Kelsier's next appointment would not be so forgiving.

He made his way eastward, toward Ahlstrom Square. He pulled off his mistcloak as he moved, then ripped off his vest, revealing the tattered shirt hidden beneath. He dropped to an alleyway, discarding cloak and vest, then grabbed a double handful of ash from the corner. He rubbed the crusty, dark flakes on his arms, masking his scars, then ground them onto his face and false beard.

The man who stumbled out of the alleyway seconds later was very different from the nobleman who had met with Hoid. The beard, once neat, now jutted out in an unkempt frazzle. A few, select bits had been removed, making it look patchy and sickly. Kelsier stumbled, pretending to have a lame leg, and called out to a shadowed figure standing near the square's quiet fountain.

"My lord?" Kelsier asked in a raspy voice. "My lord, is that you?"

Lord Straff Venture, leader of House Venture, was a domineering man, even for a nobleman. Kelsier could make out a pair of guards standing at his side; the lord himself didn't seem the least bit bothered by the mists—it was openly known that he was a Tineye. Venture stepped forward firmly, dueling cane tapping the ground beside him.

"You are late, skaa!" he snapped.

"My lord, I . . . I . . . I was waiting in the alley, my lord, like we agreed!"

"We agreed to no such thing!"

"I'm sorry, my lord," Kelsier said again, bowing—then stumbling because of his "lame" leg. "I'm sorry, I'm sorry. I was just in the alley. I didn't mean to make you wait."

"Couldn't you see us, man?"

"I'm sorry, my lord," Kelsier said. "My eyesight . . . it isn't very good, you know. I can barely see my own hands in front of my face." *Thanks for the tip, Hoid.*

Venture snorted, handing his dueling cane to a guard, then slapped Kelsier smartly across the face.

Kelsier stumbled to the ground, holding his cheek. "I'm sorry, my lord," he mumbled again.

"Next time you make me wait, it will be the cane," Venture said curtly.

Well, I know where to go next time I need a corpse to dump on someone's lawn, Kelsier thought, stumbling to his feet.

"Now," Venture said. "Let us get down to business. What is this important news you promised to deliver?"

"It's about House Erikell, my lord," Kelsier said. "I know Your Lordship has had dealings with them in the past."

"And?"

"Well, my lord, they are cheating you dearly. They have been selling their swords and canes to House Tekiel for half the price you've been paying!"

"Proof?"

"You need only look to Tekiel's new armaments, my lord," Kelsier said. "My word is true. I have nothing but my reputation! If I have not that, I have not my life."

And he wasn't lying. Or, at least, not completely. It would be useless of Kelsier to spread information that Venture could corroborate or dismiss with ease. Some of what he said was true—Tekiel was giving a slight advantage to Erikell. Kelsier was overstating it, of course. If he played the game well, he could start a rift between Erikell and Venture, while at the same time making Venture jealous of Tekiel. And, if Venture came to Renoux for weapons instead of Erikell . . . well, that would just be a side benefit.

Straff Venture snorted. His house was powerful—incredibly powerful—and relied on no specific industry or enterprise to fuel its wealth. That was a very difficult position to achieve in the Final Empire, considering the Lord Ruler's taxes and atium costs. It also made Venture a powerful tool to Kelsier. If he could give this man the right mixture of truth and fiction . . .

"This is of little use to me," Venture said suddenly. "Let's see how much you *really* know, informant. Tell me about the Survivor of Hathsin."

Kelsier froze. "Excuse me, my lord?"

"You want to get paid?" Venture asked. "Well, tell me about the Survivor. Rumors say he's returned to Luthadel."

"Rumors only, my lord," Kelsier said quickly. "I have never met this Survivor, but I doubt he is in Luthadel—if, indeed, he even lives."

"I've heard that he's gathering a skaa rebellion."

"There are always fools whispering rebellion to the skaa, my lord," Kelsier said. "And there are always those who try to use the name of the Survivor, but I do not believe that any man could have lived through the Pits. I could seek more information on this, if you wish, but I worry you will be disappointed in what I find. The Survivor is dead—the Lord Ruler . . . he does not allow such oversights."

"True," Venture said contemplatively. "But the skaa seem convinced about this rumor of an 'Eleventh Metal.' Have you heard of it, informant?"

"Ah, yes," Kelsier said, covering his shock. "A legend, my lord."

"One I've never heard of," Venture said. "And I pay *very* close attention to such things. This is no 'legend.' Someone very clever is manipulating the skaa."

"An . . . interesting conclusion, my lord," Kelsier said.

"Indeed," Venture said. "And, assuming the Survivor *did* die in the Pits, and if someone had gotten ahold of his corpse . . . his bones . . . there are ways to imitate a man's appearance. You know of what I speak?"

"Yes, my lord," Kelsier said.

"Watch for this," Venture said. "I don't care about your gossip—bring me something about this man, or whatever he is, that leads the skaa. *Then* you'll get some coin of me."

Venture spun in the darkness, waving to his men and leaving a thoughtful Kelsier behind.

Kelsier arrived at Mansion Renoux a short time later; the spikeway between Fellise and Luthadel made for quick travel between the cities. He hadn't placed the spikes himself; he didn't know who had. He often wondered what he would do if, while traveling the spikeway, he met another Mistborn traveling in the opposite direction.

We'd probably just ignore each other, Kelsier thought as he landed in Mansion Renoux's courtyard. *We're pretty good at doing that.*

He peered through the mists at the lantern-lit mansion, his recovered mistcloak flapping slightly in the calm wind. The empty carriage indicated that Vin and Sazed had returned from House Elariel. Kelsier found them inside, waiting in the sitting room and speaking quietly with Lord Renoux.

"That's a new look for you," Vin noted as Kelsier walked into the room. She still wore her dress—a beautiful red gown—though she sat in an unladylike position, legs tucked beneath her.

Kelsier smiled to himself. *A few weeks ago she would have changed out of that gown as soon as she got back. We'll turn her into a lady yet.* He found a seat, picking at the fake, soot-stained beard. "You mean this? I hear beards are going to make a return soon. I'm just trying to stay on the edge of fashionability."

Vin snorted. "The edge of beggar fashion, maybe."

"How did the evening go, Kelsier?" Lord Renoux asked.

Kelsier shrugged. "Like most others. Fortunately, it appears that House Renoux remains free of suspicion—though I myself am something of a concern to some of the nobility."

"You?" Renoux asked.

Kelsier nodded as a servant brought him a warm, damp cloth to clean his face and arms—though Kelsier wasn't certain if the servants were worried about his comfort or the ash he might get on the furniture. He wiped off his arms, exposing the pale white scratch scars, then began to pick off the beard.

"It seems that the general skaa have gotten wind of the Eleventh Metal," he continued. "Some of the nobility have heard the building rumors, and the more intelligent ones are growing worried."

"How does this affect us?" Renoux asked.

Kelsier shrugged. "We'll spread opposite rumors to make the nobility focus more on each other and less on me. Though, amusingly, Lord Venture encouraged me to search out information about myself. A man could get very confused from this kind of playacting—I don't know how you do it, Renoux."

"It is who I am," the kandra said simply.

Kelsier shrugged again, turning to Vin and Sazed. "So, how did your evening go?"

"Frustratingly," Vin said with a surly tone.

"Mistress Vin is a tad annoyed," Sazed said. "On the way back from Luthadel, she told me the secrets she'd gathered while dancing."

Kelsier chuckled. "Not much of interest?"

"Sazed already knew it all!" Vin snapped. "I spent hours twirling and twittering for those men, and it was all worthless!"

"Hardly worthless, Vin," Kelsier said, pulling off the last bit of false beard. "You made some contacts, you were seen, and you practiced your twittering. As for information—well, nobody's going to tell you anything important yet. Give it some time."

"How much time?"

"Now that you're feeling better, we can have you start attending the balls regularly. After a few months, you should have gathered enough contacts to begin finding the kind of information we need."

Vin nodded, sighing. She didn't seem quite as opposed to the idea of regularly attending balls as she once had, however.

Sazed cleared his throat. "Master Kelsier, I feel that I must mention something. Our table was attended by Lord Elend Venture for most of the evening, though Mistress Vin did find a way to make his attentions less threatening to the court."

"Yes," Kelsier said, "so I understand. What did you tell those people, Vin? That Renoux and Venture are friends?"

Vin paled slightly. "How do you know?"

"I'm mysteriously powerful," Kelsier said with a wave of his hand. "Anyway, everyone thinks that House Renoux and House Venture have had secret business dealings. They probably assume that Venture has been stockpiling weapons."

Vin frowned. "I didn't mean it to go that far. . . ."

Kelsier nodded, rubbing the glue from his chin. "That's the way court is, Vin. Things can get out of hand quickly. However, this isn't much of a problem— though it does mean that you're going to have to be very careful when dealing with House Venture, Lord Renoux. We'll want to see what kind of reaction they have to Vin's comments."

Lord Renoux nodded. "Agreed."

Kelsier yawned. "Now, if there isn't anything else, playing both nobleman and beggar in one evening has made me dreadfully tired. . . ."

"There is one other thing, Master Kelsier," Sazed said. "At the end of the evening, Mistress Vin saw Lord Elend Venture leaving the ball with young lords of Houses Lekal and Hasting."

Kelsier paused, frowning. "That's an odd combination."

"So I thought," Sazed said.

"He's probably just trying to annoy his father," Kelsier said musingly. "Fraternizing with the enemy in public . . ."

"Perhaps," Sazed said. "But the three did seem to be good friends."

Kelsier nodded, standing. "Investigate this further, Saze. There's a chance that Lord Venture and his son are playing us all for fools."

"Yes, Master Kelsier," Sazed said.

Kelsier left the room, stretching and handing his mistcloak to a servant. As he walked up the eastern stairway, he heard quick footsteps. He turned to find Vin scooting up behind him, shimmering red dress held up as she climbed the steps.

"Kelsier," she said quietly. "There was something else. Something I'd like to talk about."

Kelsier raised an eyebrow. *Something she doesn't even want Sazed to hear?* "My room," he said, and she followed him up the stairs and into the chamber.

"What is this about?" he asked as she shut the door behind her.

"Lord Elend," Vin said, looking down, seeming a bit embarrassed. "Sazed already doesn't like him, so I didn't want to mention this in front of the others. But, I found something strange tonight."

"What?" Kelsier asked curiously, leaning back against his bureau.

"Elend had a stack of books with him," Vin said.

First name, Kelsier thought with disapproval. *She is falling for the boy.*

"He's known to read a lot," Vin continued, "but some of these books . . . well, when he was gone, I picked through them."

Good girl. The streets gave you at least a few good instincts.

"One of them drew my attention," she said. "The title said something about the weather, but the words inside spoke about the Final Empire and its flaws."

Kelsier raised an eyebrow. "What exactly did it say?"

Vin shrugged. "Something about how since the Lord Ruler is immortal, his empire should be more advanced and peaceful."

Kelsier smiled. "*Book of the False Dawn*—any Keeper can quote the entire thing to you. I didn't think there were any physical copies left. Its author— Deluse Couvre—went on to write some books that were even more damning. Though he didn't blaspheme against Allomancy, the obligators made an exception in his case and strung him up on a hook anyway."

"Well," Vin said, "Elend has a copy. I think one of the other noblewomen was trying to find the book. I saw one of her servants rifling through them."

"Which noblewoman?"

"Shan Elariel."

Kelsier nodded. "Former fiancée. She's probably searching for something to blackmail the Venture boy with."

"I think she's an Allomancer, Kelsier."

Kelsier nodded distractedly, thinking about the information. "She's a Soother. She probably had the right idea with those books—if the Venture heir is reading a book like *False Dawn*, not to mention foolish enough to carry it around with him . . ."

"Is it that dangerous?" Vin asked.

Kelsier shrugged. "Moderately. It's an older book, and it didn't actually encourage rebellion, so it might slide."

Vin frowned. "The book sounded pretty critical of the Lord Ruler. He allows the nobility to read things like that?"

"He doesn't really 'allow' them to do such things," Kelsier said. "More, he sometimes ignores it when they do. Banning books is tricky business, Vin—the more stink the Ministry makes about a text, the more attention it will draw, and the more people will be tempted to read it. *False Dawn* is a stuffy volume, and by *not* forbidding it, the Ministry doomed it to obscurity."

Vin nodded slowly.

"Besides," Kelsier said, "the Lord Ruler is far more lenient with the nobility than he is with skaa. He sees them as the children of his long-dead friends and allies, the men who supposedly helped him defeat the Deepness. He occasionally lets them get away with things like reading edgy texts or assassinating family members."

"So . . . the book is nothing to worry about?" Vin asked.

Kelsier shrugged. "I wouldn't say that either. If young Elend has *False Dawn*, he might also have other books that *are* explicitly forbidden. If obligators had proof of that, they'd hand young Elend over to the Inquisitors—nobleman or not. The question is, how do we make certain that happens? If the Venture heir were to be executed, it would certainly add to Luthadel's political turmoil."

Vin paled visibly.

Yes, Kelsier thought with an internal sigh. *She's definitely falling for him. I should have foreseen this. Sending a young, pretty girl into noble society? One vulture or another was bound to latch on to her.*

"I didn't tell you this so we could get him killed, Kelsier!" she said. "I thought, maybe . . . well, he's reading forbidden books, and he seems like a good man. Maybe we can use him as an ally or something."

Oh, child, Kelsier thought. *I hope he doesn't hurt you too much when he discards you. You should know better than this.*

"Don't count on it," he said out loud. "Lord Elend might be reading a forbidden book, but that doesn't make him our friend. There have always been noblemen like him—young philosophers and dreamers who think that their ideas are new. They like to drink with their friends and grumble about the Lord Ruler; but, in their hearts, they're still noblemen. They'll never overthrow the establishment."

"But—"

"No, Vin," Kelsier said. "You have to trust me. Elend Venture doesn't care about us or the skaa. He's a gentleman anarchist because it's fashionable and exciting."

"He talked to me about the skaa," Vin said. "He wanted to know if they were intelligent, and if they acted like real people."

"And was his interest compassionate or intellectual?"

She paused.

"See," Kelsier said. "Vin, that man is *not* our ally—in fact, I distinctly recall telling you to stay away from him. When you spend time with Elend Venture, you put the operation—and your fellow crewmembers—in jeopardy. Understand?"

Vin looked down, nodding.

Kelsier sighed. *Why do I suspect that staying away from him is the last thing she intends to do? Bloody hell—I don't have time to deal with this right now.*

"Go get some sleep," Kelsier said. "We can talk more about this later."

It isn't a shadow.

This dark thing that follows me, the thing that only I can see—It isn't really a shadow. It's blackish and translucent, but it doesn't have a shadowlike solid outline. It's insubstantial—wispy and formless. Like it's made out of a dark fog.

Or mist, perhaps.

20

VIN WAS GROWING very tired of the scenery between Luthadel and Fellise. She'd made the same trip at least a dozen times during the last few weeks—watching the same brown hills, scraggly trees, and rug of weedy underbrush. She was beginning to feel as if she could individually identify each and every bump in the road.

She attended numerous balls—but they were only the beginning. Luncheons, sitting parties, and other forms of daily entertainment were just as popular. Often, Vin traveled between the cites two or even three times a day. Apparently, young noblewomen didn't have anything better to do than sit in carriages for six hours a day.

Vin sighed. In the near distance, a group of skaa trudged along the towpath beside a canal, pulling a barge toward Luthadel. Her life could be much worse.

Still, she felt frustration. It was still midday, but there weren't any important events happening until the evening, so she had nowhere to go but back to Fellise. She kept thinking about how much faster she could make the trip if she used the spikeway. She longed to leap through the mists again, but Kelsier had been reluctant to continue her training. He allowed her out for a short time each night to maintain her skills, but she wasn't allowed any extreme, exciting leaps. Just some basic moves—mostly Pushing and Pulling small objects while standing on the ground.

She was beginning to grow frustrated with her continued weakness. It had been over three months since her encounter with the Inquisitor; the worst of winter had passed without even a flake of snow. How long was it going to take her to recover?

At least I can still go to balls, she thought. Despite her annoyance at the constant traveling, Vin was coming to enjoy her duties. Pretending to be a noblewoman was actually far less tense than regular thieving work. True, her life would be forfeit if her secret were ever discovered, but for now the nobility seemed willing to accept her—to dance with her, dine with her, and chat with her. It was a good life—a bit unexciting, but her eventual return to Allomancy would fix that.

That left her with two frustrations. The first was her inability to gather useful information; she was getting increasingly annoyed at having her questions avoided. She was growing experienced enough to tell that there was a great deal of intrigue going on, yet she was still too new to be allowed a part in it.

Still, while her outsider status was annoying, Kelsier was confident that it would eventually change. Vin's second major annoyance wasn't so easily dealt with. Lord Elend Venture had been notably absent from several balls during the last few weeks, and he had yet to repeat his act of spending the entire evening with her. While she rarely had to sit alone anymore, she was quickly coming to realize that none of the other noblemen had the same . . . depth as Elend. None of them had his droll wit, or his honest, earnest eyes. The others didn't feel *real*. Not like he did.

He didn't seem to be avoiding her. However, he also didn't seem to be making much of an effort to spend time with her.

Did I misread him? she wondered as the carriage reached Fellise. Elend was so hard to understand sometimes. Unfortunately, his apparent indecision hadn't changed his former fiancée's temperament. Vin was beginning to realize why Kelsier had warned her to avoid catching the attention of anyone too important. She didn't run into Shan Elariel often, thankfully—but when they did meet, Shan took every occasion to deride, insult, and demean Vin. She did it with a calm, aristocratic manner, even her bearing reminding Vin just how inferior she was.

Perhaps I'm just becoming too attached to my Valette persona, Vin thought. Valette was just a front; she was supposed to be all the things Shan said. However, the insults still stung.

Vin shook her head, putting both Shan and Elend out of her mind. Ash had fallen during her trip to the city, and though it was done now, its aftermath was visible in small drifts and flurries of black blowing across the town's streets. Skaa workers moved about, sweeping the soot into bins and carrying it out of the city. They occasionally had to hurry to get out of the way of a passing noble carriage, none of which bothered to slow for the workers.

Poor things, Vin thought, passing a group of ragged children who were shaking aspen trees to get the ash out so that it could be swept up—it wouldn't do for a passing nobleman to get an unexpected dump of tree-borne ash on his head. The children shook, two to a tree, bringing furious black showers down on their heads. Careful, cane-wielding taskmasters walked up and down the street, making certain the work continued.

Elend and the others, she thought. *They must not understand how bad life is for the skaa. They live in their pretty keeps, dancing, never really understanding the extent of the Lord Ruler's oppression.*

She could see beauty in the nobility—she wasn't like Kelsier, hating them outright. Some of them seemed quite kind, in their own way, and she was beginning to think some of the stories skaa told about their cruelty must be exaggerated. And yet, when she saw events like that poor boy's execution or the skaa children, she had to wonder. How could the nobility not see? How could they not understand?

She sighed, looking away from the skaa as the carriage finally rolled up to Mansion Renoux. She immediately noticed a large gathering in the inner courtyard, and she grabbed a fresh vial of metals, worrying that the Lord Ruler had sent soldiers to arrest Lord Renoux. However, she quickly realized that the crowd wasn't made up of soldiers, but of skaa in simple worker's clothing.

The carriage rolled through the gates, and Vin's confusion deepened. Boxes and sacks lay in heaps among the skaa—many of them dusted with soot from the recent ashfall. The workers themselves bustled with activity, loading a series of carts. Vin's carriage pulled to a stop in front of the mansion, and she didn't wait for Sazed to open the door. She hopped out on her own, holding up her dress and stalking over to Kelsier and Renoux, who stood surveying the operation.

"You're running goods to the caves out of *here*?" Vin asked under her breath as she reached the two men.

"Curtsey to me, child," Lord Renoux said. "Maintain appearances while we can be seen."

Vin did as ordered, containing her annoyance.

"Of course we are, Vin," Kelsier said. "Renoux has to do *something* with all of the weapons and supplies he's been gathering. People would start getting suspicious if they didn't see him sending them away."

Renoux nodded. "Ostensibly, we're sending this all via canal barges to my plantation in the west. However, the barges will stop to drop off supplies—and many of the canalmen—at the rebellion caverns. The barges and a few men will continue on to keep up appearances."

"Our soldiers don't even know that Renoux is in on the plan," Kelsier said, smiling. "They think he's a nobleman that I'm scamming. Besides, this will be a great opportunity for us to go and inspect the army. After a week or so at the caves, we can return to Luthadel on one of Renoux's barges coming east."

Vin paused. "'We'?" she asked, suddenly imagining weeks spent on the barge, watching the same, dull scenery day, after day, after day as they traveled.

That would be even worse than traveling back and forth between Luthadel and Fellise.

Kelsier raised an eyebrow. "You sound worried. Apparently, someone's coming to enjoy her balls and parties."

Vin flushed. "I just thought that I should be here. I mean, after all the time I missed by being sick, I—"

Kelsier held up his hand, chuckling. "You're staying; Yeden and I are the ones going. I need to inspect the troops, and Yeden is going to take a turn watching over the army so that Ham can come back to Luthadel. We'll also take my brother with us, then drop him at his insertion point with the Ministry acolytes up in Vennias. It's a good thing you're back—I want you to spent a little time with him before we leave."

Vin frowned. "With Marsh?"

Kelsier nodded. "He's a Misting Seeker. Bronze is one of the less useful metals, especially for a full Mistborn, but Marsh claims he can show you a few tricks. This will probably be your last chance to train with him."

Vin glanced toward the gathering caravan. "Where is he?"

Kelsier frowned. "He's late."

Runs in the family, I guess.

"He should be here soon, child," Lord Renoux said. "Perhaps you'd like to go take some refreshment inside?"

I've had plenty of refreshment lately, she thought, controlling her annoyance. Instead of going into the mansion, she wandered across the courtyard, studying the goods and workers, who were packing the supplies onto carts for transport to the local canal docks. The grounds were kept well maintained, and though the ash hadn't been cleaned up yet, the low-cut grass meant that she didn't have to hold her dress up much to keep it from dragging.

Beyond that, ash was surprisingly easy to get out of clothing. With proper washing, and some expensive soaps, even a white garment could be rendered clean of ash. That was why the nobility could always have new-looking clothing. It was such an easy, simple thing to divide the skaa and the aristocracy.

Kelsier's right, Vin thought. *I am coming to enjoy being a noblewoman.* And she was concerned about the changes her new lifestyle was encouraging inside of her. Once, her problems had been things like starvation and beatings—now they were things like extended carriage rides and companions who arrived late for appointments. What did a transformation like that do to a person?

She sighed to herself, walking amidst the supplies. Some of the boxes would be filled with weapons—swords, war staves, bows—but the bulk of the material was sacked foodstuffs. Kelsier said that forming an army required far more grain than it did steel.

She trailed her fingers along one stack of boxes, careful not to brush the ash that was on top of them. She'd known that they'd be sending out a barge this day, but she hadn't expected Kelsier to go with it. Of course, he probably hadn't made the decision to go until a short time before—even the new, more responsible Kelsier was an impulsive man. Perhaps that was a good attribute in a leader. He wasn't afraid to incorporate new ideas, no matter when they occurred to him.

Maybe I should ask to go with him, Vin thought idly. *I've been playing the noblewoman far too much lately.* The other day, she'd caught herself sitting straight-backed in her carriage with a prim posture, despite the fact that she was alone. She feared that she was losing her instincts—being Valette was almost more natural to her now than being Vin was.

But of course she couldn't leave. She had a lunch appointment with Lady Flavine to attend, not to mention the Hasting ball—it was going to be the social event of the month. If Valette was absent, it would take weeks to repair the damage. Besides, there was always Elend. He'd probably forget about her if she disappeared again.

He's already forgotten you, she told herself. *He's barely spoken to you during the last three parties. Keep your head on, Vin. This is all just another scam—a game, like the ones you pulled before. You're building your reputation to gain information, not so that you can flirt and play.*

She nodded to herself, resolute. To her side, a few skaa men loaded one of the carts. Vin paused, standing beside a large stack of boxes and watching the men work. According to Dockson, the army's recruitment was picking up.

We're gaining momentum, Vin thought. *I guess word is spreading.* That was good—assuming it didn't spread *too* far.

She watched the packmen for a moment, sensing something . . . odd. They seemed unfocused. After a few moments, she was able to determine the source of their distraction. They kept shooting looks at Kelsier, whispering as they worked. Vin inched closer—keeping to the side of the boxes—and burned tin.

". . . no, that's him for certain," one of the men whispered. "I saw the scars."

"He's tall," another said.

"Of course he is. What did you expect?"

"He spoke at the meeting where I was recruited," another said. "The Survivor of Hathsin." There was awe in his tone.

The men moved on, walking over to gather more boxes. Vin cocked her head, then began to move among the workers, listening. Not all of them were discussing Kelsier, but a surprising number were. She also heard a number of references to the "Eleventh Metal."

So that's why, Vin thought. *The rebellion's momentum isn't gathering—Kelsier's is.* The men spoke of him in quiet, almost reverent, tones. For some reason, that made Vin uncomfortable. She would never have been able to stand hearing similar things said about her. Yet, Kelsier took them in stride; his charismatic ego probably just fueled the rumors even more.

I wonder if he'll be able to let it go when this is all through. The other crewmembers obviously had no interest in leadership, but Kelsier seemed to thrive on it. Would he really let the skaa rebellion take over? Would any man be able to relinquish that kind of power?

Vin frowned. Kelsier was a good man; he'd probably make a good ruler. However, if he did try to take control, it would smell of betrayal—a reneging on the promises that he had made to Yeden. She didn't want to see that from Kelsier.

"Valette," Kelsier called.

Vin jumped slightly, feeling a bit guilty. Kelsier pointed toward a carriage that was pulling onto the mansion grounds. Marsh had arrived. She walked back as the carriage pulled up, and she reached Kelsier about the same time that Marsh did.

Kelsier smiled, nodding toward Vin. "We won't be ready to leave for a while yet," he said to Marsh. "If you have time, could you show the kid a few things?"

Marsh turned toward her. He shared Kelsier's lanky build and blond hair, but he wasn't as handsome. Maybe it was the lack of a smile.

He pointed up, toward the mansion's fore-balcony. "Wait for me up there."

Vin opened her mouth to reply, but something about Marsh's expression made her shut it again. He reminded her of the old times, several months ago, when she had not questioned her superiors. She turned, leaving the three, and made her way into the mansion.

It was a short trip up the stairs to the fore-balcony. When she arrived, she pulled over a chair and seated herself beside the whitewashed wooden railing. The balcony had, of course, already been scrubbed clean of ash. Below, Marsh was still speaking with Kelsier and Renoux. Beyond them, beyond even the sprawling caravan, Vin could see the barren hills outside of the city, lit by red sunlight.

Only a few months playing noblewoman, and I already find anything that isn't cultivated to be inferior. She'd never thought of the landscape as "barren" during the years she'd traveled with Reen. *And Kelsier says the entire land used to be even more fertile than a nobleman's garden.*

Did he think to reclaim such things? Keepers could, perhaps, memorize languages and religions, but they couldn't create seeds for plants that had long been extinct. They couldn't make the ash stop falling or the mists go away. Would the world really change that much if the Final Empire were gone?

Besides, didn't the Lord Ruler have *some* right to his place? He'd defeated the Deepness, or so he claimed. He'd saved the world, which—in a twisted sort of way—made it his. What right did they have to try and take it from him?

She wondered about such things often, though she didn't express her worries to the others. They all seemed committed to Kelsier's plan; some even seemed to share his vision. But Vin was more hesitant. She had learned, as Reen had taught, to be skeptical of optimism.

And if there were ever a plan to be hesitant about, this was the one.

However, she was getting past the point where she questioned herself. She knew the reason she stayed in the crew. It wasn't the plan; it was the people. She liked Kelsier. She liked Dockson, Breeze, and Ham. She even liked the strange little Spook and his crotchety uncle. This was a crew unlike any other she'd worked with.

Is that a good enough reason to let them get you killed? Reen's voice asked.

Vin paused. She had been hearing his whispers in her mind less frequently lately, but they were still there. Reen's teachings, drilled into her over sixteen years of life, could not be idly discarded.

Marsh arrived on the balcony a few moments later. He glanced at her with those hard eyes of his, then spoke. "Kelsier apparently expects me to spend the evening training you in Allomancy. Let us get started."

Vin nodded.

Marsh eyed her, obviously expecting more of a response. Vin sat quietly. *You're not the only one who can be terse, friend.*

"Very well," Marsh said, sitting beside her, resting one arm on the balcony railing. His voice sounded a little less annoyed when he continued. "Kelsier says that you have spent very little time training with the internal mental abilities. Correct?"

Vin nodded again.

"I suspect that many full Mistborn neglect these powers," Marsh said. "And that is a mistake. Bronze and copper may not be as flashy as other metals, but they can be very powerful in the hands of someone properly trained. The Inquisitors work though their manipulation of bronze, and the Misting underground survives because of its reliance upon copper.

"Of the two powers, bronze is by far the more subtle. I can teach you how to use it properly—if you practice what I show you, then you will have an advantage that many Mistborn dismiss."

"But, don't other Mistborn know to burn copper?" Vin asked. "What is the use of learning bronze if everyone you fight is immune to its powers?"

"I see that you already think like one of them," Marsh said. "Not everyone is Mistborn, girl—in fact, very, very few people are. And, despite what your kind likes to think, normal Mistings can kill people too. Knowing that the man attacking you is a Thug rather than a Coinshot could very easily save your life."

"All right," Vin said.

"Bronze will also help you identify Mistborn," Marsh said. "If you see someone using Allomancy when there is no Smoker nearby, and yet don't sense them giving off Allomantic pulses, then you know that they are Mistborn—either that, or they're an Inquisitor. In either case, you should run."

Vin nodded silently, the wound in her side throbbing slightly.

"There are great advantages to burning bronze, rather than just running around with your copper on. True, you Smoke yourself by using copper—but in a way you also blind yourself. Copper makes you immune to having your emotions Pushed or Pulled."

"But that's a good thing."

Marsh cocked his head slightly. "Oh? And what would be the greater advantage? Being immune to—but ignorant of—some Soother's attentions? Or instead knowing—from your bronze—exactly which emotions he is trying to suppress?"

Vin paused. "You can see something that specific?"

Marsh nodded. "With care and practice, you can recognize very minute changes in your opponents' Allomantic burnings. You can identify precisely which parts of a person's emotions a Soother or Rioter intends to influence. You'll also be able to tell when someone is flaring their metal. If you grow very skilled, you might even be able to tell when they're running low on metals."

Vin paused in thought.

"You begin to see the advantage," Marsh said. "Good. Now burn bronze."

Vin did so. Immediately, she felt two rhythmic thumpings in the air. The soundless pulses washed over her, like the beating of drums or the washings of ocean waves. They were mixed and muddled.

"What do you sense?" Marsh asked.

"I . . . think there are two different metals being burned. One's coming from Kelsier down below; the other is coming from you."

"Good," Marsh said appreciatively. "You've practiced."

"Not much," Vin admitted.

He cocked an eyebrow. "Not much? You can already determine pulse origins. That takes practice."

Vin shrugged. "It seems natural to me."

Marsh was still for a moment. "Very well," he eventually said. "Are the two pulses different?"

Vin concentrated, frowning.

"Close your eyes," Marsh said. "Remove other distractions. Focus only on the Allomantic pulses."

Vin did so. It wasn't like hearing—not really. She had to concentrate to distinguish anything specific about the pulses. One felt . . . like it was beating against her. The other, in a strange sensation, felt like it was actually pulling her toward it with each beat.

"One's a Pulling metal, isn't it?" Vin asked, opening her eyes. "That one's Kelsier. You're Pushing."

"Very good," Marsh said. "He is burning iron, as I asked him to so that you could practice. I—of course—am burning bronze."

"Do they all do that?" Vin asked. "Feel distinct, I mean?"

Marsh nodded. "You can tell a Pulling metal from a Pushing metal by the Allomantic signature. Actually, that's how some of the metals were originally divided into their categories. It isn't intuitive, for instance, that tin Pulls while pewter Pushes. I didn't tell you to open your eyes."

Vin shut them.

"Focus on the pulses," Marsh said. "Try and distinguish their lengths. Can you tell the difference between them?"

Vin frowned. She focused as hard as she could, but her sense of the metals seemed . . . muddled. Fuzzy. After a few minutes, the lengths of the separate pulses still seemed the same to her.

"I can't sense anything," she said, dejected.

"Good," Marsh said flatly. "It took me six months of practice to distinguish pulse lengths—if you'd done it on the first try, I'd have felt incompetent."

Vin opened her eyes. "Why ask me to do it, then?"

"Because you need to practice. If you can tell Pulling metals from Pushing metals already . . . well, you apparently have talent. Perhaps as much talent as Kelsier has been bragging about."

"What was I supposed to see, then?" Vin asked.

"Eventually, you'll be able to sense two different pulse lengths. Internal metals, like bronze and copper, give off longer pulses than external metals, like iron and steel. Practice will also let you sense the three patterns within the pulses: one for the physical metals, one for the mental metals, and one for the two greater metals.

"Pulse length, metal group, and Push-Pull variance—once you know these three things, you will be able to tell exactly which metals your opponent is burning. A long pulse that beats against you and has a quick pattern will be pewter—the internal Pushing physical metal."

"Why the names?" Vin asked. "External and internal?"

"Metals come in groups of four—or, at least, the lower eight do. Two external metals, two internal metals—one each that Pushes, one each that Pulls. With iron, you Pull on something outside of yourself, with steel you Push on something outside of yourself. With tin you Pull on something inside of yourself, with pewter you Push on something inside of yourself."

"But, bronze and copper," Vin said. "Kelsier called them internal metals, but it seems like they affect external things. Copper keeps people from sensing when you use Allomancy."

Marsh shook his head. "Copper doesn't change your opponents, it changes something within yourself that has an effect on your opponents. That's why it is an internal metal. Brass, however, alters another person's emotions directly— and is an external metal."

Vin nodded thoughtfully. Then she turned, glancing toward Kelsier. "You know a lot about all the metals, but you're just a Misting, right?"

Marsh nodded. He didn't look like he intended to respond, though.

Let's try something, then, Vin thought, extinguishing her bronze. She lightly began burning copper to mask her Allomancy. Marsh didn't react, instead continuing to look down at Kelsier and the caravan.

I should be invisible to his senses, she thought, carefully burning both zinc and brass. She reached, just as Breeze had been training her to do, and subtly touched Marsh's emotions. She suppressed his suspicions and inhibitions, while at the same time bringing out his sense of wistfulness. Theoretically, that would make him more likely to talk.

"You must have learned somewhere?" Vin asked carefully. *He'll see what I did for sure. He's going to get angry and—*

"I Snapped when I was very young," Marsh said. "I've had a long time to practice."

"So have a lot of people," Vin said.

"I . . . had reasons. They're hard to explain."

"They always are," Vin said, slightly increasing her Allomantic pressure.

"You know how Kelsier feels about the nobility?" Marsh asked, turning toward her, his eyes like ice.

Ironeyes, she thought. *Like they said.* She nodded to his question.

"Well, I feel the same way about the obligators," he said, turning away. "I'll do anything to hurt them. They took our mother—that's when I Snapped, and that's when I vowed to destroy them. So, I joined the rebellion and started learning all I could about Allomancy. Inquisitors use it, so I had to understand it—understand everything I could, be as *good* as I could, and are you Soothing me?"

Vin started, abruptly extinguishing her metals. Marsh turned back toward her again, his expression cold.

Run! Vin thought. She almost did. It was nice to know that the old instincts were still there, if buried just a bit.

"Yes," she said meekly.

"You *are* good," Marsh said. "I'd have never known if I hadn't started rambling. Stop it."

"I already have."

"Good," Marsh said. "That's the second time you've altered my emotions. Never do it again."

Vin nodded. "Second time?"

"The first was in my shop, eight months ago."

That's right. Why don't I remember him? "I'm sorry."

Marsh shook his head, finally turning away. "You're Mistborn—that's what you do. He does the same thing." He was looking down at Kelsier.

They sat quietly for a few moments.

"Marsh?" Vin asked. "How did you know I was Mistborn? I only knew how to Soothe back then."

Marsh shook his head. "You knew the other metals instinctively. You were burning pewter and tin that day—just a tiny bit, barely noticeable. You probably got the metals from water and dining utensils. Did you ever wonder why you survived when so many others died?"

Vin paused. *I did live through a lot of beatings. A lot of days with no food, nights spent in alleys during rain or ashfalls . . .*

Marsh nodded. "Very few people, even Mistborn, are so attuned to Allomancy that they burn metals instinctively. That's what interested me in you—that's why I kept track of you and told Dockson where to find you. And, are you Pushing my emotions again?"

Vin shook her head. "I promise."

Marsh frowned, studying her with one of his stony gazes.

"So stern," Vin said quietly. "Like my brother."

"Were you close?"

"I hated him," Vin whispered.

Marsh paused, then turned away. "I see."

"Do you hate Kelsier?"

Marsh shook his head. "No, I don't hate him. He's frivolous and self-important, but he's my brother."

"And that's enough?" Vin asked.

Marsh nodded.

"I . . . have trouble understanding that," Vin said honestly, looking out over the field of skaa, boxes, and sacks.

"Your brother didn't treat you well, I presume?"

Vin shook her head.

"What about your parents?" Marsh said. "One was a nobleman. The other?"

"Mad," Vin said. "She heard voices. It got so bad that my brother was afraid to leave us alone with her. But, of course, he didn't have a choice. . . ."

Marsh sat quietly, not speaking. *How did this get turned back to me?* Vin thought. *He's no Soother, yet he's getting as much out of me as I'm getting out of him.*

Still, it was good to speak it finally. She reached up, idly fingering her earring. "I don't remember it," she said, "but Reen said that he came home one day and found my mother covered in blood. She'd killed my baby sister. Messily. Me, however, she hadn't touched—except to give me an earring. Reen said . . . He said she was holding me on her lap, babbling and proclaiming me a queen, my sister's corpse at our feet. He took me from my mother, and she fled. He saved my life, probably. That's part of why I stayed with him, I guess. Even when it was bad."

She shook her head, glancing at Marsh. "Still, you don't know how lucky you are, having Kelsier as a brother."

"I suppose," Marsh said. "I just . . . wish he wouldn't treat people like playthings. I've been known to kill obligators, but murdering men just because they're noble . . ." Marsh shook his head. "It's not just that, either. He likes people to fawn over him."

He had a point. However, Vin also detected something in his voice. Jealousy? *You're the older brother, Marsh. You were the responsible one—you joined the rebellion instead of working with thieves. It must have hurt that Kelsier was the one everybody liked.*

"Still," Marsh said, "he's getting better. The Pits changed him. Her . . . death changed him."

What's this? Vin thought, perking up slightly. There was definitely something here, too. Hurt. Deep hurt, more than a man should feel for a sister-in-law.

So that's it. It wasn't just "everyone" who liked Kelsier more, it was one person in particular. Someone you loved.

"Anyway," Marsh said, his voice growing more firm. "The arrogance of the past is behind him. This plan of his is insane, and I'm sure he's partially doing it just so he can enrich himself, but . . . well, he didn't have to go to the rebellion. He's trying to do something good—though it will probably get him killed."

"Why go along if you're so sure he'll fail?"

"Because he's going to get me into the Ministry," Marsh said. "The information I gather there will help the rebellion for centuries after Kelsier and I are dead."

Vin nodded, glancing down at the courtyard. She spoke hesitantly. "Marsh, I don't think it's *all* behind him. The way he's setting himself up with the skaa . . . the way they're starting to look at him . . ."

"I know," Marsh said. "It started with that 'Eleventh Metal' scheme of his. I don't know that we have to worry—this is just Kell playing his usual games."

"It makes me wonder why he's leaving on this trip," Vin said. "He'll be away from the action for a good month."

Marsh shook his head. "He'll have an entire army full of men to perform for. Besides, he needs to get out of the city. His reputation is growing too unwieldy, and the nobility is becoming too interested in the Survivor. If rumors got out that a man with scars on his arms is staying with Lord Renoux . . ."

Vin nodded, understanding.

"Right now," Marsh said, "he's playing the part of one of Renoux's distant relatives. That man has to leave before someone connects him to the Survivor. When Kell gets back, he'll have to keep a low profile—sneaking into the mansion instead of walking up the steps, keeping his hood up when he's in Luthadel."

Marsh trailed off, then stood. "Anyway, I've given you the basics. Now you just need to practice. Whenever you're with Mistings, have them burn for you and focus on their Allomantic pulses. If we meet again, I'll show you more, but there's nothing else I can do until you've practiced."

Vin nodded, and Marsh walked out the door without any other farewell. A few moments later, she saw him approach Kelsier and Renoux again.

They really don't hate each other, Vin thought, resting with both arms crossed atop the railing. *What would that be like?* After some thought, she decided that the concept of loving siblings was a little like the Allomantic pulse lengths she was supposed to be looking for—they were just too unfamiliar for her to understand at the moment.

"The Hero of Ages shall be not a man, but a force. No nation may claim him, no woman shall keep him, and no king may slay him. He shall belong to none, not even himself."

21

KELSIER SAT QUIETLY, READING AS HIS boat moved slowly along the canal to the north. *Sometimes, I worry that I'm not the hero everyone thinks I am,* the text said.

What proof do we have? The words of men long dead, only now deemed divinatory? Even if we accept the prophecies, only tenuous interpretation links them to me. Is my defense of the Summer Hill really the "Burden by which the Hero shall be dubbed"? My several marriages could give me a "Bloodless bond to the world's kings," if you look at it the right way. There are dozens of similar phrases that could refer to events in my life. But, then again, they could all just be coincidences.

The philosophers assure me that this is the time, that the signs have been met. But I still wonder if they have the wrong man. So many people depend on me. They say I will hold the future of the entire world on my arms. What would they think if they knew that their champion—the Hero of Ages, their savior—doubted himself?

Perhaps they wouldn't be shocked at all. In a way, this is what worries me most. Maybe, in their hearts, they wonder—just like I do. When they see me, do they see a liar?

Rashek seems to think so. I know that I shouldn't let a simple packman perturb me. However, he is from Terris, where the prophecies originated. If anyone could spot a fraud, would it not be he?

Nevertheless, I continue my trek, going where the scribbled auguries proclaim that I will meet my destiny—walking, feeling Rashek's eyes on my back. Jealous. Mocking. Hating.

In the end, I worry that my arrogance shall destroy us all.

Kelsier lowered the booklet, his cabin shaking slightly from the efforts of the pullers outside. He was glad that Sazed had provided him with a copy of the translated portions of the Lord Ruler's logbook before the caravan boats' departure. There was blessed little else to do during the trip.

Fortunately, the logbook was fascinating. Fascinating, and eerie. It was disturbing to read words that had originally been written by the Lord Ruler himself. To Kelsier the Lord Ruler was less a man, and more a . . . creature. An evil force that needed to be destroyed.

Yet, the person presented in the logbook seemed all too mortal. He questioned and pondered—he seemed a man of depth, and even of character.

Though, it would be best not to trust his narrative too closely, Kelsier thought, running his fingers across the page. *Men rarely see their own actions as unjustified.*

Still, the Lord Ruler's story reminded Kelsier of the legends he had heard—stories whispered by skaa, discussed by noblemen, and memorized by Keepers. They claimed that once, before the Ascension, the Lord Ruler had been the greatest of men. A beloved leader, a man entrusted with the fate of all mankind.

Unfortunately, Kelsier knew how the story ended. The Final Empire itself was the logbook's legacy. The Lord Ruler hadn't saved mankind; he had enslaved it instead. Reading a firsthand account, seeing the Lord Ruler's self-doubt and internal struggles, only made the story that much more tragic.

Kelsier raised the booklet to continue; however, his boat began to slow. He glanced out the window of his cabin, looking up the canal. Dozens of men trudged along the towpath—a small road alongside the canal—pulling the four barges and two narrowboats that made up their convoy. It was an efficient, if labor-intensive, way to travel; men pulling a barge across a canal could move hundreds more pounds of weight than they could if forced to carry packs.

The men had pulled to a stop, however. Ahead, Kelsier could make out a lock mechanism, beyond which the canal split into two sections. A kind of crossroads of waterways. *Finally,* Kelsier thought. His weeks of travel were over.

Kelsier didn't wait for a messenger. He simply stepped out onto the deck of his narrowboat and slipped a few coins from his pouch into his hand. *Time to be a bit ostentatious,* he thought, dropping a coin to the wood. He burned steel and Pushed himself into the air.

He lurched upward at an angle, quickly gaining a height where he could see the entire line of men—half pulling the boats, half walking and waiting for their shifts. Kelsier flew in an arc, dropping another coin as he passed over one of the supply-laden barges, then Pushing against it when he began to descend. Would-be soldiers looked up, pointing in awe as Kelsier soared above the canal.

Kelsier burned pewter, strengthening his body as he thumped to the deck of the narrowboat leading the caravan.

Yeden stepped out of his cabin, surprised. "Lord Kelsier! We've, uh, arrived at the crossroads."

"I can see that," Kelsier said, glancing back along the line of boats. The men on the towpath spoke excitedly, pointing. It felt strange to use Allomancy so obviously in the daylight, and before so many people.

There's no help for it, he thought. *This visit is the last chance the men will have to see me for months. I need to make an impression, give them something they can hold on to, if this is all going to work. . . .*

"Shall we go see if the group from the caves has arrived to meet us?" Kelsier asked, turning back to Yeden.

"Of course," Yeden said, waving for a servant to pull his narrowboat up to the side of the canal and throw out the plank. Yeden looked excited; he really was an earnest man, and that much Kelsier could respect, even if he was a bit lacking in presence.

Most of my life, I've had the opposite problem, Kelsier thought with amusement, walking with Yeden off of the boat. *Too much presence, not enough earnestness.*

The two of them walked up the line of canal workers. Near the front of the men, one of Ham's Thugs—playing the part of Kelsier's guard captain—saluted. "We've reached the crossroads, Lord Kelsier."

"I can see that," Kelsier repeated. A dense stand of birch trees grew ahead, running up a slope into the hills. The canals ran away from the woods—there were better sources of wood in other parts of the Final Empire. The forest stood alone and ignored by most.

Kelsier burned tin, wincing slightly at the suddenly blinding sunlight. His eyes adjusted, however, and he was able to pick out detail—and a slight bit of motion—in the forest.

"There," he said, flipping a coin into the air, then Pushing it. The coin zipped forward and thocked against a tree. The prearranged sign given, a small group of camouflaged men left the tree line, crossing the ash-stained earth toward the canal.

"Lord Kelsier," the foremost man said, saluting. "My name is Captain Demoux. Please, gather the recruits and come with me—General Hammond is eager to meet with you."

"Captain" Demoux was a young man to be so disciplined. Barely into his twenties, he led his small squad of men with a level of solemnity that might have seemed self-important had he been any less competent.

Younger men than he have led soldiers into battle, Kelsier thought. *Just because I was a fop when I was that age doesn't mean that everyone is. Look at poor Vin—only sixteen, already a match for Marsh in seriousness.*

They took a roundabout passage through the forest—by Ham's order, each troop took a different path to avoid wearing a trail. Kelsier glanced back at the two hundred or so men behind, frowning slightly. Their trail would probably still be visible, but there was little he could do about that—the movements of so many men would be nearly impossible to mask.

Demoux slowed, waving, and several members of his squad scrambled forward; they didn't have half their leader's sense of military decorum. Still, Kelsier was impressed. The last time he'd visited, the men had been typically ragtag and uncoordinated, like most skaa outcasts. Ham and his officers had done their work well.

The soldiers pulled away some false underbrush, revealing a crack in the ground. It was dark within, the sides jutting with crystalline granite. It wasn't a regular hillside cavern, but instead a simple rend in the ground leading directly down.

Kelsier stood quietly, looking down at the black, stone-laced rift. He shivered slightly.

"Kelsier?" Yeden asked, frowning. "What is it?"

"It reminds me of the Pits. They looked like this—cracks in the ground."

Yeden paled slightly. "Oh. I, uh . . ."

Kelsier waved dismissively. "I knew this was coming. I climbed down inside those caves every day for a year, and I always came back out. I beat them. They have no power over me."

To prove his words, he stepped forward and climbed down into the thin crack. It was just wide enough for a large man to slip through. As Kelsier descended, he saw the soldiers—both Demoux's squad and the new recruits—watching quietly. He had intentionally spoken loud enough for them to hear.

Let them see my weakness, and let them see me overcome it.

They were brave thoughts. However, once he passed beneath the surface, it was as if he were back again. Smashed between two walls of stone, questing downward with shaking fingers. Cold, damp, dark. Slaves had to be the ones who recovered the atium. Allomancers might have been more effective, but using Allomancy near atium crystals shattered them. So, the Lord Ruler used condemned men. Forcing them into the pits. Forcing them to crawl downward, ever downward . . .

Kelsier forced himself onward. This wasn't Hathsin. The crack wouldn't go down for hours, and there would be no crystal-lined holes to reach through with torn, bleeding arms—stretching, seeking the atium geode hidden within. One geode; that bought one more week of life. Life beneath the taskmasters' lashes. Life beneath the rule of a sadistic god. Life beneath the sun gone red.

I will change things for the others, Kelsier thought. *I will make it better!*

The climb was difficult for him, more difficult than he ever would have admitted. Fortunately, the crack soon opened up to a larger cavern beneath, and Kelsier caught a glimpse of light from below. He let himself drop the rest of the way, landing on the uneven stone floor, and smiled at the man who stood waiting.

"Hell of an entryway you've got there, Ham," Kelsier said, dusting off his hands.

Ham smiled. "You should see the bathroom."

Kelsier laughed, moving to make way for the others. Several natural tunnels led off of the chamber, and a small rope ladder hung from the bottom of the rift to facilitate going back up. Yeden and Demoux soon climbed down the ladder into the cavern, their clothing scraped and dirtied from the descent. It wasn't an easy entrance to get through. That, however, was the idea.

"It's good to see you, Kell," Ham said. It was odd to see him in clothing that wasn't missing the sleeves. In fact, his militaristic outfit looked rather formal, with square-cut lines and buttons down the front. "How many have you brought me?"

"Just over two hundred and forty."

Ham raised his eyebrows. "Recruitment has picked up, then?"

"Finally," Kelsier said with a nod. Soldiers began to drop into the cavern, and several of Ham's aides moved forward, helping the newcomers and directing them down a side tunnel.

Yeden moved over to join Kelsier and Ham. "This cavern is amazing, Lord Kelsier! I've never actually been to the caves myself. No wonder the Lord Ruler hasn't found the men down here!"

"The complex is completely secure," Ham said proudly. "There are only three entrances, all of them cracks like this one. With proper supplies, we could hold this place indefinitely against an invading force."

"Plus," Kelsier said, "this isn't the only cave complex beneath these hills. Even if the Lord Ruler were determined to destroy us, his army could spend weeks searching and still not find us."

"Amazing," Yeden said. He turned, eyeing Kelsier. "I was wrong about you, Lord Kelsier. This operation . . . this army . . . well, you've done something impressive here."

Kelsier smiled. "Actually, you were right about me. You believed in me when this started—we're only here because of you."

"I . . . guess I did, didn't I?" Yeden said, smiling.

"Either way," Kelsier said, "I appreciate the vote of confidence. It's probably going to take some time to get all these men down the crack—would you mind directing things here? I'd like to talk to Hammond for a bit."

"Of course, Lord Kelsier." There was respect—even a growing bit of adulation—in his voice.

Kelsier nodded to the side. Ham frowned slightly, picking up a lantern, then followed Kelsier from the first chamber. They entered a side tunnel, and once they were out of earshot, Ham paused, glancing backward.

Kelsier stopped, raising an eyebrow.

Ham nodded back toward the entry chamber. "Yeden certainly has changed."

"I have that effect on people."

"Must be your awe-inspiring humility," Ham said. "I'm serious, Kell. How do you do it? That man practically hated you; now he looks at you like a kid idolizing his big brother."

Kelsier shrugged. "Yeden's never been part of an effective team before—I think he's started to realize that we might actually have a chance. In little over half a year, we've gathered a rebellion larger than he's ever seen. Those kind of results can convert even the stubborn."

Ham didn't look convinced. Finally, he just shrugged, beginning to walk again. "What was it you wanted to talk about?"

"Actually, I'd like to visit the other two entrances, if we could," Kelsier said.

Ham nodded, pointing to a side tunnel and leading the way. The tunnel, like most of the others, hadn't been hollowed by human hands; it was a natural growth of the cave complex. There were hundreds of similar cave systems in the Central Dominance, though most weren't as extensive. And only one—the Pits of Hathsin—grew atium geodes.

"Anyway, Yeden's right," Ham said, twisting his way through a narrow place in the tunnel. "You picked a great place to hide these people."

Kelsier nodded. "Various rebel groups have been using the cavern complexes in these hills for centuries. They're frighteningly close to Luthadel, but the Lord Ruler has never led a successful raid against anyone here. He just ignores the place now—one too many failures, probably."

"I don't doubt it," Ham said. "With all the nooks and bottlenecks down here, this would be a nasty place to have a battle." He stepped out of the passageway, entering another small cavern. This one also had a rift in the ceiling, and faint sunlight trickled down. A squad of ten soldiers stood guard in the room, and they snapped to attention as soon as Ham entered.

Kelsier nodded approvingly. "Ten men at all times?"

"At each of the three entrances," Ham said.

"Good," Kelsier said. He walked forward, inspecting the soldiers. He wore his sleeves up, his scars showing, and he could see the men eyeing them. He didn't really know what to inspect, but he tried to look discriminating. He examined their weapons—staves for eight of the men, swords for two—and dusted off a few shoulders, though none of the men wore uniforms.

Finally, he turned to a soldier who bore an insignia on his shoulder. "Who do you let out of the caverns, soldier?"

"Only men bearing a letter sealed by General Hammond himself, sir!"

"No exceptions?" Kelsier asked.

"No, sir!"

"And if I wanted to leave right now?"

The man paused. "Uh . . ."

"You'd stop me!" Kelsier said. "No one is exempt, soldier. Not me, not your bunkmate, not an officer—no one. If they don't have that seal, they don't leave!"

"Yes, sir!" the soldier said.

"Good man," Kelsier said. "If all of your soldiers are this fine, General, then the Lord Ruler has good reason to be afraid."

The soldiers puffed up slightly at the words.

"Carry on, men," Kelsier said, waving for Ham to follow as he left the room.

"That was kind of you," Ham said softly. "They've been anticipating your visit for weeks."

Kelsier shrugged. "I just wanted to see that they were guarding the crack properly. Now that you have more men, I want you to post guards at any tunnels leading to these exit caverns."

Ham nodded. "Seems a bit extreme, though."

"Humor me," Kelsier said. "A single runaway or malcontent could betray us all to the Lord Ruler. It's nice that you feel that you could defend this place, but if there's an army camped outside trapping you in, this army will effectively become useless to us."

"All right," Ham said. "You want to see the third entrance?"

"Please," Kelsier said.

Ham nodded, leading him down another tunnel.

"Oh, one other thing," Kelsier said after a bit of walking. "Get together groups of a hundred men—all ones you trust—to go tromp around up in the forest. If someone comes looking for us, we won't be able to hide the fact that lots of people have passed through the area. However, we might be able to muddle the tracks so much that the trails all lead nowhere."

"Good idea."

"I'm full of 'em," Kelsier said as they stepped into another cave chamber, this one far larger than the previous two. It wasn't an entrance rift, but instead a practice room. Groups of men stood with swords or staves, sparring beneath the eye of uniformed instructors. Uniforms for the officers had been Dockson's idea. They couldn't afford to outfit all the men—it would be too expensive, and obtaining that many uniforms would look suspicious. However, maybe seeing their leaders in uniform would help give the men a sense of cohesion.

Ham paused at the edge of the room rather than continuing onward. He eyed the soldiers, speaking softly. "We need to talk about this sometime, Kell. The men are starting to feel like soldiers, but . . . Well, they're skaa. They've spent their lives working in mills or fields. I don't know how well they'll do when we actually get them onto a battlefield."

"If we do everything right, they won't have to do much fighting," Kelsier said.

"The Pits are only guarded by a couple hundred soldiers—the Lord Ruler can't have too many men there, lest he hint at the location's importance. Our thousand men can take the Pits with ease, then retreat as soon as the Garrison arrives. The other nine thousand might have to face a few Great House guard squads and the palace soldiers, but our men should have the upper hand in numbers."

Ham nodded, though his eyes still seemed uncertain.

"What?" Kelsier asked, leaning against the smooth, crystalline mouth of the cavern juncture.

"And when we're done with them, Kell?" Ham asked. "Once we have our atium, we give the city—and the army—over to Yeden. Then what?"

"That's up to Yeden," Kelsier said.

"They'll be slaughtered," Ham said very softly. "Ten thousand men can't hold Luthadel against the entire Final Empire."

"I intend to give them a better chance than you think, Ham," Kelsier said. "If we can turn the nobility against each other and destabilize the government . . ."

"Maybe," Ham said, still not convinced.

"You agreed to the plan, Ham," Kelsier said. "This was what we were intending all along. Raise an army, deliver it to Yeden."

"I know," Ham said, sighing and leaning back against the cavern wall. "I guess . . . Well, it's different, now that I've been leading them. Maybe I'm just not meant to be in charge like this. I'm a bodyguard, not a general."

I know how you feel, my friend, Kelsier thought. *I'm a thief, not a prophet. Sometimes, we just have to be what the job requires.*

Kelsier laid a hand on Ham's shoulder. "You did a fine job here."

Ham paused. "'Did' fine?"

"I brought Yeden to replace you. Dox and I decided it would be better to rotate him in as the army's commander—that way, the troops get used to him as their leader. Besides, we need you back in Luthadel. Someone has to visit the Garrison and gather intelligence, and you're the only one with any military contacts."

"So, I'm going back with you?" Ham asked.

Kelsier nodded.

Ham looked crestfallen for just a moment, then he relaxed, smiling. "I'll finally be able get out of this uniform! But, do you think Yeden can handle it?"

"You said yourself, he's changed a lot during the last few months. And, he really is an excellent administrator—he's done a fine job with the rebellion since my brother left."

"I suppose. . . ."

Kelsier shook his head ruefully. "We're spread thin, Ham. You and Breeze are two of the only men I know I can trust, and I need you back in Luthadel. Yeden's not perfect for the job here, but the army is going to be his, eventually. Might as well let him lead it for a time. Besides, it will give him something to do; he's growing a bit touchy about his place in the crew." Kelsier paused, then smiled in amusement. "I think he's jealous of the attention I pay the others."

Ham smiled. "That *is* a change."

They began to walk again, leaving the practice chamber behind. They entered another twisting stone tunnel, this one leading slightly downward, Ham's lantern providing their only light.

"You know," Ham said after a few minutes of walking, "there's something else nice about this place. You've probably noticed this before, but it certainly is beautiful down here sometimes."

Kelsier hadn't noticed. He glanced to the side as they walked. One edge of the chamber had been formed of dripping minerals from the ceiling, thin stalactites and stalagmites—like dirty icicles—melding together to form a kind of banister. Minerals twinkled in Ham's light, and the path in front of them seemed to be frozen in the form of a tumbling molten river.

No, Kelsier thought. *No, I don't see its beauty, Ham.* Other men might see art in the layers of color and melted rock. Kelsier only saw the Pits. Endless caves, most of them going straight down. He'd been forced to wiggle through cracks, plunging downward in the darkness, not even given a light to brighten his way.

Often, he'd considered not climbing back up. But, then he would find a corpse in the caves—the body of another prisoner, a man who had gotten lost, or who had perhaps just given up. Kelsier would feel their bones and promise himself more. Each week, he'd found an atium geode. Each week he'd avoided execution by brutal beating.

Except that last time. He didn't deserve to be alive—he should have been killed. But, Mare had given him an atium geode, promising him that she'd found two that week. It wasn't until after he'd turned it in that he'd discovered her lie. She'd been beaten to death the next day. Beaten to death right in front of him.

That night, Kelsier had Snapped, coming into his powers as a Mistborn. The next night, men had died.

Many men.

Survivor of Hathsin. A man who shouldn't live. Even after watching her die, I couldn't decide if she'd betrayed me or not. Did she give me that geode out of love? Or did she do it out of guilt?

No, he couldn't see beauty in the caverns. Other men had been driven mad by the Pits, becoming terrified of small, enclosed spaces. That hadn't happened to Kelsier. However, he knew that no matter what wonders the labyrinths held—no mater how amazing the views or delicate the beauties—he would never acknowledge them. Not with Mare dead.

I can't think about this anymore, Kelsier decided, the cavern seeming to grow darker around him. He glanced to the side. "All right, Ham. Go ahead. Tell me what you're thinking about."

"Really?" Ham said eagerly.

"Yes," Kelsier said with a sense of resignation.

"All right," Ham said. "So, here's what I've been worried about lately: Are skaa different from noblemen?"

"Of course they are," Kelsier said. "The aristocracy has the money and the land; the skaa don't have anything."

"I don't mean economics—I'm talking about physical differences. You know what the obligators say, right?"

Kelsier nodded.

"Well, is it true? I mean, skaa really do have a lot of children, and I've heard that aristocrats have trouble reproducing."

The Balance, it was called. It was supposedly the way that the Lord Ruler ensured that there weren't too many noblemen for the skaa to support, and the way he made certain that—despite beatings and random killings—there were always enough skaa to grow food and work in mills.

"I've always just assumed it to be Ministry rhetoric," Kelsier said honestly.

"I've known skaa women to have as many as a dozen children," Ham said. "But I can't name a single major noble family with more than three."

"It's just cultural."

"And the height difference? They say you used to be able to tell skaa and noblemen apart by sight alone. That's changed, probably through interbreeding, but most skaa are still kind of short."

"That's nutritional. Skaa don't get enough to eat."

"What about Allomancy?"

Kelsier frowned.

"You have to admit that there's a physical difference there," Ham said. "Skaa never become Mistings unless they have aristocratic blood somewhere in their last five generations."

That much, at least, was true.

"Skaa think differently from noblemen, Kell," Ham said. "Even these soldiers are kind of timid, and they're the brave ones! Yeden's right about the general skaa population—it will never rebel. What if . . . what if there really is something physically different about us? What if the noblemen are *right* to rule over us?"

Kelsier froze in the hallway. "You don't really mean that."

Ham stopped as well. "I guess . . . no, I don't. But I do wonder sometimes. The noblemen have Allomancy, right? Maybe they're meant to be in charge."

"Meant by who? The Lord Ruler?"

Ham shrugged.

"No, Ham," Kelsier said. "It isn't right. *This* isn't right. I know it's hard to see—things have been this way for so long—but something very serious is wrong with the way skaa live. You *have* to believe that."

Ham paused, then nodded.

"Let's go," Kelsier said. "I want to visit that other entrance."

The week passed slowly. Kelsier inspected the troops, the training, the food, the weapons, the supplies, the scouts, the guards, and just about everything else he could think of. More important, he visited the men. He complimented and encouraged them—and he made certain to use Allomancy frequently in front of them.

While many skaa had heard of "Allomancy," very few knew specifically what it could do. Nobleman Mistings rarely used their powers in front of other people, and half-breeds had to be even more careful. Ordinary skaa, even city skaa, didn't know of things like Steelpushing or Pewter-burning. When they saw Kelsier flying through the air or sparring with supernatural strength, they would just attribute it to formless "Allomancy Magics." Kelsier didn't mind the misunderstanding at all.

Despite all of the week's activities, however, he never forgot his conversation with Ham.

How could he even wonder if skaa are inferior? Kelsier thought, poking at his meal as he sat at the high table in the central meeting cavern. The massive "room" was large enough to hold the entire army of seven thousand men, though many sat in side chambers or halfway out into tunnels. The high table sat on a raised rock formation at the far end of the chamber.

I'm probably worrying too much. Ham was prone to think about things that no sane man would consider; this was just another of his philosophical dilemmas. In fact, he already seemed to have forgotten his earlier concerns. He laughed with Yeden, enjoying his meal.

As for Yeden, the gangly rebel leader looked quite satisfied with his general's uniform, and had spent the week taking very serious notes from Ham regarding the army's operation. He seemed to be falling quite naturally into his duties.

In fact, Kelsier seemed to be the only one who wasn't enjoying the feast. The evening's foods—brought on the barges especially for the occasion—were humble by aristocratic standards, but were much finer than what the soldiers were used to. The men relished the meal with a joyful boisterousness, drinking their small allotment of ale and celebrating the moment.

And still, Kelsier worried. What did these men think they were fighting for? They seemed enthusiastic about their training, but that might have just been due to the regular meals. Did they actually believe that they deserved to overthrow the Final Empire? Did they think that skaa were inferior to noblemen?

Kelsier could sense their reservations. Many of the men realized the impending danger, and only the strict exit rules kept them from fleeing. While they were eager to speak of their training, they avoided talking about their final task—that of seizing the palace and city walls, then holding off the Luthadel Garrison.

They don't think they can succeed, Kelsier guessed. *They need confidence. The rumors about me are a start, but . . .*

He nudged Ham, getting the man's attention.

"Are there any men who have given you discipline problems?" Kelsier asked quietly.

Ham frowned at the odd question. "There are a couple, of course. I'd think there are always dissidents in a group this large."

"Anyone in particular?" Kelsier asked. "Men who have wanted to leave? I need someone outspoken in their opposition to what we're doing."

"There are a couple in the brig right now," Ham said.

"Anyone here?" Kelsier asked. "Preferably someone sitting at a table we can see?"

Ham thought for a moment, scanning the crowd. "The man sitting at the second table with the red cloak. He was caught trying to escape a couple weeks ago."

The man in question was scrawny and twitchy; he sat at his table with a hunched, solitary posture.

Kelsier shook his head. "I need someone a bit more charismatic."

Ham rubbed his chin in thought. Then he paused, and nodded toward another table. "Bilg. The big guy sitting at the fourth table over on the right."

"I see him," Kelsier said. Bilg was a brawny man wearing a vest and a full beard.

"He's too clever to be insubordinate," Ham said, "but he's been making trouble quietly. He doesn't think we have a chance against the Final Empire. I'd lock him up, but I can't really punish a man for expressing fear—or, at least, if I did, I'd have to do the same for half the army. Besides, he's too good a warrior to discard idly."

"He's perfect," Kelsier said. He burned zinc, then looked toward Bilg. While zinc wouldn't let him read the man's emotions, it was possible—when burning the metal—to isolate just a single individual for Soothing or Rioting, much as one was able to isolate a single bit of metal from hundreds to Pull on.

Even still, it was difficult to single Bilg out from such a large crowd, so Kelsier just focused on the entire tableful of men, keeping their emotions "in hand" for later use. Then he stood. Slowly, the cavern quieted.

"Men, before I leave, I wish to express one last time how much I was impressed by this visit." His words rang through the room, amplified by the cavern's natural acoustics.

"You are becoming a fine army," Kelsier said. "I apologize for stealing General Hammond, but I leave a very competent man in his place. Many of you know General Yeden—you know of his many years serving as rebellion leader. I have confidence in his ability to train you even further in the ways of soldiers."

He began to Riot Bilg and his companions, enflaming their emotions, counting on the fact that they'd be feeling disagreeable.

"It is a great task I ask of you," Kelsier said, not looking at Bilg. "Those skaa outside of Luthadel—indeed, most skaa everywhere—have no idea what you are about to do for them. They aren't aware of the training you endure or the battles you prepare to fight. However, they will reap the rewards. Someday, they will call you heroes."

He Rioted Bilg's emotions even harder.

"The Garrison of Luthadel is strong," Kelsier said, "but we can defeat it—especially if we take the city walls quickly. Do not forget why you came here. This isn't simply about learning to swing a sword or wear a helm. This is about a revolution such as the world has never seen—it is about taking the government for ourselves, about ousting the Lord Ruler. Do not lose sight of your goal."

Kelsier paused. From the corner of his eye, he could see dark expressions from the men at Bilg's table. Finally, in the silence, Kelsier heard a muttered comment from the table—carried by cavern acoustics to many ears.

Kelsier frowned, turning toward Bilg. The entire cavern seemed to grow even more still. "Did you say something?" Kelsier asked. *Now, the moment of decision. Will he resist, or will he be cowed?*

Bilg looked back. Kelsier hit the man with a flared Riot. His reward came as Bilg stood from his table, face red.

"Yes, *sir*," the brawny man snapped. "I did say something. I said that some of us haven't lost sight of our 'goal.' We think about it every day."

"And why is that?" Kelsier asked. Rumbling whispers began to sound at the back of the cavern as soldiers passed the news to those too far away to hear.

Bilg took a deep breath. "Because, *sir*, we think that this is suicide you're sending us to. The Final Empire's armies are bigger than just one garrison. It won't matter if we take the walls—we'll get slaughtered eventually anyway. You don't overthrow an empire with a couple thousand soldiers."

Perfect, Kelsier thought. *I'm sorry, Bilg. But someone needed to say it, and it certainly couldn't be me.*

"I see we have a disagreement," Kelsier said loudly. "*I* believe in these men, and in their purpose."

"I believe that you are a deluded fool," Bilg bellowed. "And I was a bigger fool for coming to these bloody caves. If you're so certain about our chances, then why can't anyone leave? We're trapped here until you send us to die!"

"You insult me," Kelsier snapped. "You know very well why men aren't allowed to leave. Why do you want to go, soldier? Are you that eager to sell out your companions to the Lord Ruler? A few quick boxings in exchange for four thousand lives?"

Bilg's face grew redder. "I would never do such a thing, but I'm certainly not going to let you send me to my death, either! This army is a waste."

"You speak treason," Kelsier said. He turned, scanning the crowd. "It is not fitting for a general to fight a man beneath his command. Is there a soldier here who is willing to defend the honor of this rebellion?"

Immediately, a couple dozen men stood up. Kelsier noticed one in particular. He was smaller than the rest, but he had the simple earnestness that Kelsier had noticed earlier. "Captain Demoux."

Immediately, the young captain jumped forward.

Kelsier reached over, grabbing his own sword and tossing it down to the man. "You can use a sword, lad?"

"Yes, sir!"

"Someone fetch a weapon for Bilg and a pair of studded vests." Kelsier turned toward Bilg. "Noblemen have a tradition. When two men have a dispute, they settle it with a duel. Defeat my champion, and you are free to leave."

"And if he defeats me?" Bilg asked.

"Then you'll be dead," Kelsier said.

"I'm dead if I stay," Bilg said, accepting a sword from a nearby soldier. "I accept the terms."

Kelsier nodded, waving for some men to pull aside tables and make an open space before the high table. Men began to stand, crowding around to watch the contest.

"Kell, what are you doing!" Ham hissed at his side.

"Something that needs to be done."

"Needs to be . . . Kelsier, that boy is no match for Bilg! I trust Demoux—that's why I promoted him—but he's not that great a warrior. Bilg's one of the finest swordsmen in the army!"

"The men know this?" Kelsier asked.

"Of course," Ham said. "Call this off. Demoux is nearly half Bilg's size—he's at a disadvantage in reach, strength, and skill. He'll get slaughtered!"

Kelsier ignored the request. He sat quietly as Bilg and Demoux hefted their weapons, a pair of soldiers tying on their leather cuirasses. When they were done, Kelsier waved a hand, motioning for the battle to begin.

Ham groaned.

It would be a short fight. Both men had longswords and little armor. Bilg stepped forward with confidence, making a few testing swings toward Demoux. The boy was at least competent—he blocked the blows, but he revealed a great deal about his abilities as he did so.

Taking a deep breath, Kelsier burned steel and iron.

Bilg swung, and Kelsier nudged the blade to the side, giving Demoux room to escape. The boy tried a thrust, but Bilg easily knocked it away. The larger warrior then attacked with a barrage, sending Demoux stumbling backward. Demoux tried to jump out of the way of the last swing, but he was too slow. The blade fell with awful inevitability.

Kelsier flared iron—stabilizing himself by Pulling against a lantern bracket behind—then grabbed the iron studs on Demoux's vest. Kelsier Pulled as Demoux jumped, yanking the boy backward in a small arc away from Bilg.

Demoux landed with a maladroit stumble as Bilg's sword smashed into the stone ground. Bilg looked up with surprise, and a low rumble of amazement moved through the crowd.

Bilg growled, running forward with weapon held high. Demoux blocked the powerful swing, but Bilg knocked the boy's weapon aside with a careless sweep. Bilg struck again, and Demoux raised a hand in reflexive defense.

Kelsier Pushed, freezing Bilg's sword in midswing. Demoux stood, hand forward, as if he had stopped the attacking weapon with a thought. The two stood like that for a moment, Bilg trying to force the sword forward, Demoux staring in awe at his hand. Standing up a bit straighter, Demoux tentatively forced his hand forward.

Kelsier Pushed, throwing Bilg backward. The large warrior tumbled to the ground with a cry of surprise. When he rose a moment later, Kelsier didn't have to Riot his emotions to make him angry. He bellowed in rage, grabbing his sword in two hands and rushing toward Demoux.

Some men don't know when to quit, Kelsier thought as Bilg swung.

Demoux began to dodge. Kelsier shoved the boy to the side, getting him out of the way. Then Demoux turned, gripping his own weapon in two hands and swinging at Bilg. Kelsier grabbed Demoux's weapon in mid-arc and Pulled against it forcefully, ripping the steel forward with a mighty flare of iron.

The swords smashed together, and Demoux's Kelsier-enhanced blow knocked Bilg's weapon out of his hands. There was a loud snap, and the large miscreant fell to the floor—thrown completely off balance by the force of Demoux's blow. Bilg's weapon bounced to the stone floor a distance away.

Demoux stepped forward, raising his weapon over the stunned Bilg. And then, he stopped. Kelsier burned iron, reaching out to grab the weapon and Pull it down, to force the killing blow, but Demoux resisted.

Kelsier paused. *This man should die,* he thought angrily. On the ground, Bilg groaned quietly. Kelsier could just barely see his twisted arm, its bone shattered by the powerful strike. It was bleeding.

No, Kelsier thought. *This is enough.*

He released Demoux's weapon. Demoux lowered his sword, staring down at Bilg. Then, Demoux raised his hands, regarding them with wonder, his arms quivering slightly.

Kelsier stood, and the crowd fell to a hush once again.

"Do you think I would send you against the Lord Ruler unprepared?" Kelsier demanded in a loud voice. "Do you think I would just send you off to die? You fight for what is just, men! You fight for *me.* I will not leave you unaided when you go against the soldiers of the Final Empire."

Kelsier thrust his hand into the air, holding aloft a tiny bar of metal. "You've heard of this, haven't you? You know the rumors of the Eleventh Metal? Well, I have it—and I will use it. The Lord Ruler will die!"

The men began to cheer.

"This is not our only tool!" Kelsier bellowed. "You soldiers have power untold inside of you! You have heard of the arcane magics that the Lord Ruler uses? Well, we have some of our own! Feast, my soldiers, and don't fear the battle to come. Look forward to it!"

The room erupted in a riot of cheers, and Kelsier waved for more ale to be delivered. A couple of servants rushed forward to help Bilg from the room.

When Kelsier sat, Ham was frowning deeply. "I don't like this, Kell," he said.

"I know," Kelsier said quietly.

Ham was about to speak further, but Yeden leaned across him. "That was amazing! I . . . Kelsier, I didn't know! You should have told me you could pass your powers to others. Why, with these abilities, how can we possibly lose?"

Ham laid a hand on Yeden's shoulder, pushing the man back into his seat. "Eat," he ordered. Then, he turned to Kelsier, pulling his chair closer and speaking in a low voice. "You just lied to my entire army, Kell."

"No, Ham," Kelsier said quietly. "I lied to *my* army."

Ham paused. Then his face darkened.

Kelsier sighed. "It was only a partial lie. They don't need to be warriors, they just have to look threatening long enough for us to grab the atium. With it, we can bribe the Garrison, and our men won't even have to fight. That's virtually the same thing as what I promised them."

Ham didn't respond.

"Before we leave," Kelsier said, "I want you to select a few dozen of our most trustworthy and devoted soldiers. We'll send them back to Luthadel—with vows that they can't reveal where the army is—so that word of this evening can spread amongst the skaa."

"So this is about your ego?" Ham snapped.

Kelsier shook his head. "Sometimes we need to do things that we find distasteful, Ham. My ego may be considerable, but this is about something else entirely."

Ham sat for a moment, then turned back to his meal. He didn't eat, however—he just sat staring at the blood on the ground before the high table.

Ah, Ham, Kelsier thought. *I wish I could explain everything to you.*

Plots behind plots, plans beyond plans.

There was always another secret.

At first, there were those who didn't think the Deepness was a serious danger, at least not to them. However, it brought with it a blight that I have seen infect nearly every part of the land. Armies are useless before it. Great cities are laid low by its power. Crops fail, and the land dies.

This is the thing I fight. This is the monster I must defeat. I fear that I have taken too long. Already, so much destruction has occurred that I fear for mankind's survival.

Is this truly the end of the world, as many of the philosophers predict?

22

We arrived in Terris earlier this week, *Vin read*, and, I have to say, I find the countryside beautiful. The great mountains to the north—with their bald snowcaps and forested mantles—stand like watchful gods over this land of green fertility. My own lands to the south are mostly flat; I think that they might look less dreary if there were a few mountains to vary the terrain.

The people here are mostly herdsmen—though timber harvesters and farmers are not uncommon. It is a pastoral land, certainly. It seems odd that a place so remarkably agrarian could have produced the prophecies and theologies upon which the entire world now relies.

We picked up a group of Terris packmen to guide us through the difficult mountain passages. Yet, these are no ordinary men. The stories are apparently true—some Terrismen have a remarkable ability that is most intriguing.

Somehow, they can store up their strength for use on the next day. Before they sleep at night, they spend an hour lying in their bedrolls, during which time they suddenly grow very frail in appearance—almost as if they had aged by half a century. Yet, when they wake the next morning, they become quite muscular. Apparently, their powers have something to do with the metal bracelets and earrings that they always wear.

The leader of the packmen is named Rashek, and he is rather taciturn. Nevertheless, Braches—inquisitive, as always—has promised to interrogate him in the hopes of discovering exactly how this wondrous strength-storing is achieved.

Tomorrow, we begin the final stage of our pilgrimage—the Far Mountains of Terris. There, hopefully, I will find peace—both for myself, and for our poor land.

AS SHE READ her copy of the logbook, Vin was quickly coming to several decisions. First was the firm belief that she did *not* like reading. Sazed didn't listen to her complaints; he just claimed that she hadn't practiced enough. Couldn't he see that reading was hardly as practical a skill as being able to handle a dagger or use Allomancy?

Still, she continued to read as per his orders—if only to stubbornly prove that she could. Many of the logbook's words were difficult to her, and she had to read in a secluded part of Renoux's mansion where she could sound out the words to herself, trying to decipher the Lord Ruler's odd style of writing.

The continued reading led to her second conclusion: The Lord Ruler was far more whiny than any god had a right to be. When pages of the logbook weren't filled with boring notes about the Lord Ruler's travels, they were instead packed with internal contemplations and lengthy moralistic ramblings. Vin was beginning to wish that she'd never found the book in the first place.

She sighed, settling back into her wicker chair. A cool early-spring breeze blew through the lower gardens, passing over the petite fountain brook to her left. The air was comfortably moist, and the trees overhead shaded her from the afternoon sun. Being nobility—even fake nobility—certainly did have its perks.

A quiet footfall sounded behind her. It was distant, but Vin had grown into the habit of burning a little bit of tin at all times. She turned, shooting a covert glance over her shoulder.

"Spook?" she said with surprise as young Lestibournes walked down the garden path. "What are you doing here?"

Spook froze, blushing. "Wasing with the Dox to come and be without the stay."

"Dockson?" Vin said. "He's here too?" *Maybe he has news of Kelsier!*

Spook nodded, approaching. "Weapons for the getting, giving for the time to be."

Vin paused. "You lost me on that one."

"We needed the drop off some more weapons," Spook said, struggling to speak without his dialect. "Storing them here for a while."

"Ah," Vin said, rising and brushing off her dress. "I should go see him."

Spook looked suddenly apprehensive, flushing again, and Vin cocked her head. "Was there something else?"

With a sudden movement, Spook reached into his vest and pulled something out. Vin flared pewter in response, but the item was simply a pink-and-white handkerchief. Spook thrust it toward her.

Vin took it hesitantly. "What's this for?"

Spook flushed again, then turned and dashed away.

Vin watched him go, dumbfounded. She looked down at the handkerchief. It was made of soft lace, but there didn't seem to be anything unusual about it.

That is one strange boy, she thought, tucking the handkerchief inside her sleeve. She picked up her copy of the logbook, then began to work her way up the garden path. She was growing so accustomed to wearing a dress that she barely had to pay attention to keep the gown's lower layers from brushing against underbrush or stones.

I guess that in itself is a valuable skill, Vin thought as she reached the mansion's garden entrance without having snagged her dress on a single branch. She pushed open the many-paned glass door and stopped the first servant she saw.

"Master Delton has arrived?" she asked, using Dockson's fake name. He played the part of one of Renoux's merchant contacts inside Luthadel.

"Yes, my lady," the servant said. "He's in conference with Lord Renoux."

Vin let the servant go. She could probably force her way into the conference, but it would look bad. Lady Valette had no reason to attend a mercantile meeting between Renoux and Delton.

Vin chewed her lower lip in thought. Sazed was always telling her she had to keep up appearances. *Fine,* she thought. *I'll wait. Maybe Sazed can tell me what that crazy boy expects me to do with this handkerchief.*

She sought out the upper library, maintaining a pleasant ladylike smile, inwardly trying to guess what Renoux and Dockson were talking about. Dropping off the weapons was an excuse; Dockson wouldn't have come personally to do something so mundane. Perhaps Kelsier had been delayed. Or, maybe Dockson had finally gotten a communication from Marsh—Kelsier's brother, along with the other new obligator initiates, should be arriving back in Luthadel soon.

Dockson and Renoux could have sent for me, she thought with annoyance. Valette often entertained guests with her uncle.

She shook her head. Even though Kelsier had named her a full member of the crew, the others obviously still regarded her as something of a child. They were friendly and accepting, but they didn't think to include her. It was probably unintentional, but that didn't make it any less frustrating.

Light shone from the library ahead. Sure enough, Sazed sat inside, translating the last group of pages from the logbook. He looked up as Vin entered, smiling and nodding respectfully.

No spectacles this time either, Vin noted. *Why did he wear them for that short time before?*

"Mistress Vin," he said, rising and fetching her a chair. "How are your studies of the logbook going?"

Vin looked down at the loosely bound pages in her hand. "All right, I suppose. I don't see why I have to bother reading them—you gave copies to Kell and Breeze too, didn't you?"

"Of course," Sazed said, setting the chair down beside his desk. "However, Master Kelsier asked every member of the crew to read the pages. He is correct to do so, I think. The more eyes that read those words, the more likely we will be to discover the secrets hidden within them."

Vin sighed slightly, smoothing her dress and seating herself. The white and blue dress was beautiful—though intended for daily use, it was only slightly less luxurious than one of her ball gowns.

"You must admit, Mistress," Sazed said as he sat, "the text is amazing. This work is a Keeper's dream. Why, I'm discovering things about my culture that even I did not know!"

Vin nodded. "I just got to the part where they reach Terris." *Hopefully, the next part will contain fewer supply lists. Honestly, for an evil god of darkness, he certainly can be dull.*

"Yes, yes," Sazed said, speaking with uncharacteristic enthusiasm. "Did you see what he said, how he described Terris as a place of 'green fertility'? Keeper legends speak of this. Terris is now a tundra of frozen dirt—why, almost no plants can survive there. But, once it was green and beautiful, like the text says."

Green and beautiful, Vin thought. *Why would green be beautiful? That would be like having blue or purple plants—it would just be weird.*

However, there was something about the logbook that made her curious—something that both Sazed and Kelsier had been strangely closemouthed about. "I just read the part where the Lord Ruler gets some Terris packmen," Vin said carefully. "He talked about how they grow stronger during the day because they let themselves be weak at night."

Sazed suddenly grew more subdued. "Yes, indeed."

"You know something about this? Does it have to do with being a Keeper?"

"It does," Sazed said. "But, this should remain a secret, I think. Not that you aren't worthy of trust, Mistress Vin. However, if fewer people know about Keepers, then fewer rumors will be told of us. It would be best if the Lord Ruler began to believe that he had destroyed us completely, as has been his goal for the last thousand years."

Vin shrugged. "Fine. Hopefully, none of the secrets Kelsier wants us to discover in this text are related to the Terrisman powers—if they are, I'll miss them completely."

Sazed paused.

"Ah, well," Vin said nonchalantly, flipping through the pages she hadn't read. "Looks like he spends a lot of time talking about the Terrismen. Guess I won't be able to give much input when Kelsier gets back."

"You make a good point," Sazed said slowly. "Even if you make it a bit melodramatically."

Vin smiled pertly.

"Very well," Sazed said with a sigh. "We should not have let you spend so much time with Master Breeze, I think."

"The men in the logbook," Vin said. "They're Keepers?"

Sazed nodded. "What we now call Keepers were far more common back then—perhaps even more common than Mistings are among modern nobility. Our art is called 'Feruchemy,' and it grants the ability to store certain physical attributes inside bits of metal."

Vin frowned. "You burn metals too?"

"No, Mistress," Sazed said with a shake of his head. "Feruchemists aren't like Allomancers—we don't 'burn' away our metals. We use them as storage. Each piece of metal, dependent upon size and alloy, can store a certain physical quality. The Feruchemist saves up an attribute, then draws upon that reserve at a later time."

"Attribute?" Vin asked. "Like strength?"

Sazed nodded. "In the text, the Terris packmen make themselves weaker during the evening, storing up strength in their bracelets for use on the next day."

Vin studied Sazed's face. "That's why you wear so many earrings!"

"Yes, Mistress," he said, reaching over to pull up his sleeves. Underneath his robe, he wore thick iron bracers around his upper arms. "I keep some of my reserves hidden—but wearing many rings, earrings, and other items of jewelry has always been a part of Terris culture. The Lord Ruler once tried to enforce a ban upon Terrismen touching or owning any metal—in fact, he tried to make wearing metal a noble privilege, rather than a skaa one."

Vin frowned. "That's odd," she said. "One would think that the nobility *wouldn't* want to wear metal, because that would make them vulnerable to Allomancy."

"Indeed," Sazed said. "However, it has long been imperial fashion to accent one's wardrobe with metal. It began, I suspect, with the Lord Ruler's desire to deny the Terrismen the right to touch metal. He himself began wearing metal rings and bracelets, and the nobility always follows him in fashion. Nowadays, the most wealthy often wear metal as a symbol of power and pride."

"Sounds foolish," Vin said.

"Fashion often is, Mistress," Sazed said. "Regardless, the ploy failed—many of the nobility only wear wood painted to look like metal, and the Terris managed to weather the Lord Ruler's discontent in this area. It was simply too impractical to never let stewards handle metal. That hasn't stopped the Lord Ruler from trying to exterminate the Keepers, however."

"He fears you."

"And hates us. Not just Feruchemists, but all Terrismen." Sazed laid a hand on the still untranslated portion of the text. "I hope to find that secret in here as well. No one remembers why the Lord Ruler persecutes the Terris people, but I suspect that it has something to do with those packmen—their leader, Rashek, appears to be a very contrary man. The Lord Ruler often speaks of him in the narrative."

"He mentioned religion," Vin said. "The Terris religion. Something about prophecies?"

Sazed shook his head. "I cannot answer that question, Mistress, for I don't know any more of the Terris religion than you do."

"But, you collect religions," Vin said. "You don't know about your own?"

"I do not," Sazed said solemnly. "You see, Mistress, this was why the Keepers were formed. Centuries ago, my people hid away the last few Terris Feruchemists. The Lord Ruler's purges of the Terris people were growing quite violent—this was before he began the breeding program. Back then, we weren't stewards or servants—we weren't even skaa. We were something to be destroyed.

"Yet, something kept the Lord Ruler from wiping us out completely. I don't know why—perhaps he thought genocide too kind a punishment. Anyway, he successfully destroyed our religion during the first two centuries of his rule. The organization of Keepers was formed during the next century, its members intent upon discovering that which had been lost, then remembering for the future."

"With Feruchemy?"

Sazed nodded, rubbing his fingers across the bracer on his right arm. "This one is made of copper; it allows for the storage of memories and thoughts. Each Keeper carries several bracers like this, filled with knowledge—songs, stories, prayers, histories, and languages. Many Keepers have a particular area of interest—mine is religion—but we all remember the entire collection. If just one of us survives until the death of the Lord Ruler, then the world's people will be able to recover all that they have lost."

He paused, then pulled down his sleeve. "Well, not *all* that was lost. There are still things we are missing."

"Your own religion," Vin said quietly. "You never found it, did you?"

Sazed shook his head. "The Lord Ruler implies in this logbook that it was our prophets that led him to the Well of Ascension, but even this is new information for us. What did we believe? What, or whom, did we worship? Where did these Terris prophets come from, and how did they predict the future?"

"I'm . . . sorry."

"We continue to look, Mistress. We will find our answers eventually, I think. Even if we do not, we will still have provided an invaluable service for mankind. Other people call us docile and servile, but we have fought him, in our own way."

Vin nodded. "So, what other things can you store? Strength and memories. Anything else?"

Sazed eyed her. "I have said too much already, I think. You understand the mechanics of what we do—if the Lord Ruler mentions these things in his text, you will not be confused."

"Sight," Vin said, perking up. "That's why you wore glasses for a few weeks after you rescued me. You needed to be able to see better that night when you saved me, so you used up your storage. Then you spent a few weeks with weak vision so that you could refill it."

Sazed didn't respond to the comment. He picked up his pen, obviously intending to turn back to his translation. "Was there anything else, Mistress?"

"Yes, as a matter of fact," Vin said, pulling the handkerchief from her sleeve. "Do you have any idea what this is?"

"It appears to be a handkerchief, Mistress."

Vin raised a droll eyebrow. "Very funny. You've spent far too long around Kelsier, Sazed."

"I know," he said with a quiet sigh. "He has corrupted me, I think. Regardless, I do not understand your question. What is distinctive about that particular handkerchief?"

"That's what *I* want to know," Vin said. "Spook gave it to me just a little bit ago."

"Ah. That makes sense, then."

"What?" Vin demanded.

"In noble society, Mistress, a handkerchief is the traditional gift a young man gives a lady that he wishes to seriously court."

Vin paused, regarding the handkerchief with shock. "*What?* Is that boy crazy?"

"Most young men his age are somewhat crazy, I think," Sazed said with a smile. "However, this is hardly unexpected. Haven't you noticed how he stares at you when you enter the room?"

"I just thought he was creepy. What is he thinking? He's so much younger than me."

"The boy is fifteen, Mistress. That only makes him one year your junior."

"Two," Vin said. "I turned seventeen last week."

"Still, he isn't really that much younger than you."

Vin rolled her eyes. "I don't have time for his attentions."

"One would think, Mistress, that you would appreciate the opportunities you have. Not everyone is so fortunate."

Vin paused. *He's a eunuch, you fool.* "Sazed, I'm sorry. I . . ."

Sazed waved a hand. "It is something I have never known enough of to miss, Mistress. Perhaps I am fortunate—a life in the underground does not make it easy to raise a family. Why, poor Master Hammond has been away from his wife for months."

"Ham's *married?*"

"Of course," Sazed said. "So is Master Yeden, I believe. They protect their families by separating them from underground activities, but this necessitates spending large periods of time apart."

"Who else?" Vin asked. "Breeze? Dockson?"

"Master Breeze is a bit too . . . self-motivated for a family, I think. Master Dockson hasn't spoken of his romantic life, but I suspect that there is something painful in his past. That is not uncommon for plantation skaa, as you might expect."

"Dockson is from a plantation?" Vin asked with surprise.

"Of course. Don't you ever spend time talking with your friends, Mistress?"

Friends. I have friends. It was an odd realization.

"Anyway," Sazed said, "I should continue my work. I am sorry to be so dismissive, but I am nearly finished with the translation. . . ."

"Of course," Vin said, standing and smoothing her dress. "Thank you."

She found Dockson sitting in the guest study, writing quietly on a piece of paper, a pile of documents organized neatly on the desktop. He wore a standard nobleman's suit, and always looked more comfortable in the clothing than the others did. Kelsier was dashing, Breeze immaculate and lavish, but Dockson . . . he simply looked natural in the outfit.

He looked up as she entered. "Vin? I'm sorry—I should have sent for you. For some reason I assumed you were out."

"I often am, these days," she said, closing the door behind her. "I stayed home today; listening to noblewomen prattle over their lunches can get a bit annoying."

"I can imagine," Dockson said, smiling. "Have a seat."

Vin nodded, strolling into the room. It was a quiet place, decorated in warm colors and deep woods. It was still somewhat light outside, but Dockson already had the evening drapes drawn and was working by candlelight.

"Any news from Kelsier?" Vin asked as she sat.

"No," Dockson said, setting aside his document. "But that's not unexpected. He wasn't going to stay at the caves for long, so sending a messenger back would have been a bit silly—as an Allomancer, he might even be able to get back before a man on horseback. Either way, I suspect he'll be a few days late. This is Kell we're talking about, after all."

Vin nodded, then sat quietly for a moment. She hadn't spent as much time with Dockson as she had with Kelsier and Sazed—or even Ham and Breeze. He seemed like a kind man, however. Very stable, and very clever. While most of the others contributed some kind of Allomantic power to the crew, Dockson was valuable because of his simple ability to organize.

When something needed to be purchased—such as Vin's dresses—Dockson saw that it got done. When a building needed to be rented, supplies procured, or a permit secured, Dockson made it happen. He wasn't out front, scamming noblemen, fighting in the mists, or recruiting soldiers. Without him, however, Vin suspected that the entire crew would fall apart.

He's a nice man, she told herself. *He won't mind if I ask him.* "Dox, what was it like living on a plantation?"

"Hmm? The plantation?"

Vin nodded. "You grew up on one, right? You're a plantation skaa?"

"Yes," Dockson said. "Or, at least, I was. What was it like? I'm not sure how to answer, Vin. It was a hard life, but most skaa live hard lives. I wasn't allowed to leave the plantation—or even go outside of the hovel community—without permission. We ate more regularly than a lot of the street skaa, but we were worked as hard as any millworker. Perhaps more.

"The plantations are different from the cities. Out there, every lord is his own master. Technically, the Lord Ruler owns the skaa, but the noblemen rent them, and are allowed to kill as many as they want. Each lord just has to make certain that his crops come in."

"You seem so . . . unemotional about it," Vin said.

Dockson shrugged. "It's been a while since I lived there, Vin. I don't know that the plantation was overly traumatic. It was just life—we didn't know anything better. In fact, I now know that amongst plantation lords, mine was actually rather lenient."

"Why did you leave, then?"

Dockson paused. "An event," he said his voice growing almost wistful. "You know that the law says that a lord can bed any skaa woman that he wishes?"

Vin nodded. "He just has to kill her when he's done."

"Or soon thereafter," Dockson said. "Quickly enough that she can't birth any half-breed children."

"The lord took a woman you loved, then?"

Dockson nodded. "I don't talk about it much. Not because I can't, but because I think it would be pointless. I'm not the only skaa to lose a loved one to a lord's passion, or even to a lord's indifference. In fact, I'll bet you'd have trouble finding a skaa who *hasn't* had someone they love murdered by the aristocracy. That's just . . . the way it is."

"Who was she?" Vin asked.

"A girl from the plantation. Like I said, my story isn't that original. I remember . . . sneaking between the hovels at night to spend time with her. The entire community played along, hiding us from the taskmasters—I wasn't supposed to be out after dark, you see. I braved the mists for the first time for her, and while many thought me foolish to go out at night, others got over their superstition and encouraged me. I think the romance inspired them; Kareien and I reminded everyone that there was something to live for.

"When Kareien was taken by Lord Devinshae—her corpse returned the next morning for burial—something just . . . died in the skaa hovels. I left that next evening. I didn't know there was a better life, but I just couldn't stay, not with Kareien's family there, not with Lord Devinshae watching us work. . . ."

Dockson sighed, shaking his head. Vin could finally see some emotion in his face. "You know," he said, "it amazes me sometimes that we even try. With everything they've done to us—the deaths, the tortures, the agonies—you'd think that we would just give up on things like hope and love. But we don't. Skaa still fall in love. They still try to have families, and they still struggle. I mean, here we are . . . fighting Kell's insane little war, resisting a god we know is just going to slaughter us all."

Vin sat quietly, trying to comprehend the horror of what he described. "I . . . thought you said that your lord was a kind one."

"Oh, he was," Dockson said. "Lord Devinshae rarely beat his skaa to death, and he only purged the elderly when the population got completely out of control. He has an impeccable reputation among the nobility. You've probably seen him at some of the balls—he's been in Luthadel lately, over the winter, between planting seasons."

Vin felt cold. "Dockson, that's horrible! How could they let a monster like that among them?"

Dockson frowned, then he leaned forward slightly, resting his arms on the desktop. "Vin, they're *all* like that."

"I know that's what some of the skaa say, Dox," Vin said. "But, the people at the balls, they aren't like that. I've met them, danced with them. Dox, a lot of them are good people. I don't think they realize how terrible things are for the skaa."

Dockson looked at her with a strange expression. "Am I really hearing this from you, Vin? Why do you think we're fighting against them? Don't you realize the things those people—all of those people—are capable of?"

"Cruelty, perhaps," Vin said. "And indifference. But they aren't monsters, not all of them—not like your former plantation lord."

Dockson shook his head. "You just aren't seeing well enough, Vin. A nobleman can rape and murder a skaa woman one night, then be praised for his morality and virtue the next day. Skaa just aren't people to them. Noblewomen don't even consider it cheating when their lord sleeps with a skaa woman."

"I . . ." Vin trailed off, growing uncertain. This was the one area of noble culture she hadn't wanted to confront. Beatings, she could perhaps forgive, but this . . .

Dockson shook his head. "You're letting them dupe you, Vin. Things like this are less visible in the cities because of whorehouses, but the murders still happen. Some brothels use women of very poor—but noble—birth. Most, however, just kill off their skaa whores periodically to keep the Inquisitors placated."

Vin felt a little weak. "I . . . know about the brothels, Dox. My brother always threatened to sell me to one. But, just because brothels exist doesn't mean that all the men go to them. There are lots of workers who don't visit the skaa whorehouses."

"Noblemen are different, Vin," Dockson said sternly. "They're horrible creatures. Why do you think I don't complain when Kelsier kills them? Why do you think I'm working with him to overthrow their government? You should ask some of those pretty boys you dance with how often they've slept with a skaa woman they knew would be killed a short time later. They've all done it, at one point or another."

Vin looked down.

"They can't be redeemed, Vin," Dockson said. He didn't seem as passionate about the topic as Kelsier, he just seemed . . . resigned. "I don't think that Kell will be happy until they're all dead. I doubt we have to go that far—or even that we can—but I, for one, would be more than happy to see their society collapse."

Vin sat quietly. *They can't* all *be like that,* she thought. *They're so beautiful, so distinguished. Elend has never taken and murdered a skaa woman . . . has he?*

I sleep but a few hours each night. We must press forward, traveling as much as we can each day—but when I finally lie down, I find sleep elusive. The same thoughts that trouble me during the day are only compounded by the stillness of night.

And, above it all, I hear the thumping sounds from above, the pulsings from the mountains. Drawing me closer with each beat.

23

"THEY SAY THAT the deaths of the Geffenry brothers were a retaliation for the murder of Lord Entrone," Lady Kliss said quietly. Behind Vin's group, the musicians played upon their stage, but the evening was growing late, and few people danced.

Lady Kliss's circle of partygoers frowned at the news. There were about six of them, including Vin and her companion—one Milen Davenpleu, a young heir to a minor house title.

"Kliss, really," Milen said. "Houses Geffenry and Tekiel are allies. Why would Tekiel assassinate two Geffenry noblemen?"

"Why indeed?" Kliss said, leaning forward conspiratorially, her massive blond bun wobbling slightly. Kliss had never displayed much fashion sense. She was an excellent source of gossip, however.

"You remember when Lord Entrone was found dead in the Tekiel gardens?" Kliss asked. "Well, it *seemed* obvious that one of House Tekiel's enemies had killed him. But, House Geffenry has been petitioning Tekiel for an alliance—apparently, a faction within the house thought that if something happened to enflame the Tekiels, they would be more willing to seek allies."

"You're saying that Geffenry *purposely* killed a Tekiel ally?" asked Rene, Kliss's date. He scrunched up his ample brow in thought.

Kliss patted Rene's arm. "Don't worry about it too much, dear," she advised, then turned eagerly back to the conversation. "Don't you see? By secretly killing Lord Entrone, Geffenry hoped to get the allegiance it needs. *That* would give it access to those Tekiel canal routes through the eastern plains."

"But it backfired," Milen said thoughtfully. "Tekiel discovered the ruse, and killed Ardous and Callins."

"I danced with Ardous a couple of times at the last ball," Vin said. *Now he's dead, his corpse left on the streets outside a skaa slum.*

"Oh?" Milen asked. "Was he any good?"

Vin shrugged. "Not very." *That's all you can ask, Milen? A man is dead, and you just want to know if I liked him more than you?*

"Well, now he's dancing with the worms," said Tyden, the final man in the group.

Milen gave the quip a pity laugh, which was more than it deserved. Tyden's attempts at humor generally left something to be desired. He seemed like the type who would have been more at home with the ruffians of Camon's crew than the noblemen of the dance hall.

Of course, Dox says they're all like that, underneath.

Vin's conversation with Dockson still dominated her thoughts. When she'd started coming to the noblemen's balls back on that first night—the night she'd nearly been killed—she'd thought about how fake everything seemed. How had she forgotten that original impression? How had she let herself get taken in, to begin admiring their poise and their splendor?

Now, every nobleman's arm around her waist made her cringe—as if she could feel the rot within their hearts. How many skaa had Milen killed? What about Tyden? He seemed like the type who would enjoy a night with the whores.

But, still she played along. She had finally worn her black gown this evening, somehow feeling the need to set herself apart from the other women with their bright colors and often brighter smiles. However, she couldn't avoid the others' company; Vin had finally begun to gain the confidences her crew needed. Kelsier would be delighted to know that his plan for House Tekiel was working, and that wasn't the only thing she had been able to discover. She had dozens of little tidbits that would be of vital use to the crew's efforts.

One such tidbit was about House Venture. The family was bunkering up for what it expected to be an extended house war; one evidence of this was the fact that Elend attended far fewer balls than he once had. Not that Vin minded. When he did come, he generally avoided her, and she didn't really want to talk to him anyway. Memories of what Dockson had said made her think that she might have trouble remaining civil toward Elend.

"Milen?" Lord Rene asked. "Are you still planning on joining us for a game of shelldry tomorrow?"

"Of course, Rene," Milen said.

"Didn't you promise that last time?" Tyden asked.

"I'll be there," Milen said. "Something came up last time."

"And it won't come up again?" Tyden asked. "You know we can't play unless we have a fourth man. If you're not going to be there, we could ask someone else. . . ."

Milen sighed, then held up a hand, sharply gesturing to the side. The motion caught Vin's attention—she had only been half listening to the conversation. She looked to the side, and nearly jumped in shock as she saw an obligator approaching the group.

So far she'd managed to avoid obligators at the balls. After her first run-in with a high prelan, some months ago—and the subsequent alerting of an Inquisitor—she'd been apprehensive to even go near one.

The obligator approached, smiling in a creepy sort of way. Perhaps it was the arms clasped before him, hands hidden inside the gray sleeves. Perhaps it was the tattoos around the eyes, wrinkled with the aging skin. Perhaps it was the way his eyes regarded her; it seemed like they could see through her guise. This wasn't just a nobleman, this was an *obligator*—eyes of the Lord Ruler, enforcer of His law.

The obligator stopped at the group. His tattoos marked him as a member of the Canton of Orthodoxy, the primary bureaucratic arm of the Ministry. He eyed the group, speaking in a smooth voice. "Yes?"

Milen pulled out a few coins. "I promise to meet these two for shelldry tomorrow," he said, handing the coins to the aging obligator.

It seemed like such a silly reason to call over an obligator—or, at least, so Vin thought. The obligator, however, didn't laugh or point out the frivolity of the demand. He simply smiled, palming the coins as deftly as any thief. "I witness this, Lord Milen," he said.

"Satisfied?" Milen asked of the other two.

They nodded.

The obligator turned, not giving Vin a second glance, and strolled away. She released a quiet breath, watching his shuffling form.

They must know everything that happens in court, she realized. *If nobility call them over to witness things this simple . . .* The more she knew about the Ministry, the more she realized how clever the Lord Ruler had been in organizing them. They witnessed every mercantile contract; Dockson and Renoux had to deal with obligators nearly every day. Only they could authorize weddings, divorces, land purchases, or ratify inheritance of titles. If an obligator hadn't witnessed an event, it hadn't happened, and if one hadn't sealed a document, then it might as well not have been written.

Vin shook her head as the conversation turned to other topics. It had been a long night, and her mind was full of information to scribble down on her way back to Fellise.

"Excuse me, Lord Milen," she said, laying a hand on his arm—though touching him made her shiver slightly. "I think perhaps it is time for me to retire."

"I'll walk you to your carriage," he said.

"That won't be necessary," she said sweetly. "I want to refresh myself, and then I have to wait for my Terrisman anyway. I'll just go sit down at our table."

"Very well," he said, nodding respectfully.

"Go if you must, Valette," Kliss said. "But you'll never know the news I have about the Ministry. . . ."

Vin paused. "What news?"

Kliss's eyes twinkled, and she glanced at the disappearing obligator. "The Inquisitors are buzzing like insects. They've hit *twice* as many skaa thieving bands these last few months as usual. They don't even take prisoners for executions—they just leave them all dead."

"How do you know this?" Milen asked skeptically. He seemed so straight-backed and noble. You would never know what he really was.

"I have my sources," Kliss said with a smile. "Why, the Inquisitors found another band just this afternoon. One headquartered not far from here."

Vin felt a chill. They weren't *that* far from Clubs's shop. . . . *No, it couldn't be them. Dockson and the rest are too clever. Even without Kelsier in town, they'll be safe.*

"Cursed thieves," Tyden spat. "Damn skaa don't know their place. Isn't the food and clothing we give enough of a theft from our pockets?"

"It's amazing the creatures can even survive as thieves," said Carlee, Tyden's young wife, in her normal purring voice. "I can't imagine what kind of incompetent would let himself get robbed by skaa."

Tyden flushed, and Vin eyed him with curiosity. Carlee rarely spoke except to make some jab against her husband. *He must have been robbed himself. A scam, perhaps?*

Filing away the information for later investigation, Vin turned to go—a motion that put her face-to-face with a newcomer to the group: Shan Elariel.

Elend's former betrothed was immaculate, as always. Her long auburn hair had an almost luminous sheen, and her beautiful figure only reminded Vin how scrawny she herself was. Self-important in a way that could make even a confident person uncertain, Shan was—as Vin was beginning to realize—exactly what most of the aristocracy thought was the perfect woman.

The men in Vin's group nodded their heads in respect, and the women curtsied, honored to have their conversation joined by one so important. Vin glanced to the side, trying to escape, but Shan was standing right before her.

Shan smiled. "Ah, Lord Milen," she said to Vin's companion, "it's a pity that your original date this evening took sick. It appears you were left with few other options."

Milen flushed, Shan's comment expertly placing him in a difficult position. Did he defend Vin, possibly earning the ire of a very powerful woman? Or, did he instead agree with Shan, thereby insulting his date?

He took the coward's way out: He ignored the comment. "Lady Shan, it is a pleasure to have you join us."

"Indeed," Shan said smoothly, eyes glittering with pleasure as she regarded Vin's discomfort.

Cursed woman! Vin thought. It seemed that whenever Shan grew bored, she would seek out Vin and embarrass her for sport.

"However," Shan said, "I am afraid I didn't come to chat. Unpleasant though it may be, I have business with the Renoux child. Will you excuse us?"

"Of course, my lady," Milen said, backing away. "Lady Valette, thank you for your company this evening."

Vin nodded to him and the others, feeling a little like a wounded animal being abandoned by the herd. She *really* didn't want to deal with Shan this evening.

"Lady Shan," Vin said once they were alone. "I think your interest in me is unfounded. I haven't really been spending much time with Elend lately."

"I know," Shan said. "It appears I overestimated your competence, child. One would think that once you'd gained favor with a man so much more important than yourself, you wouldn't have let him slip away so easily."

Shouldn't she be jealous? Vin thought, suppressing a cringe as she felt the inevitable touch of Shan's Allomancy on her emotions. *Shouldn't she hate me for taking her place?*

But, that wasn't the noble way. Vin was nothing—a momentary diversion. Shan wasn't interested in recapturing Elend's affection; she just wanted a way to strike back at the man who had slighted her.

"A wise girl would put herself in a position where she could make use of the only advantage she has," Shan said. "If you think any other important nobleman will ever pay any attention to you, then you are mistaken. Elend likes to shock the court—and so, naturally, he chose to do so with the most homely and lumpish woman he could find. Take this opportunity; you shall not soon find another."

Vin gritted her teeth against the insults and the Allomancy; Shan had obviously made an art out of forcing people to take whatever abuse she sought fit to deliver.

"Now," Shan said, "I require information regarding certain texts Elend has in his possession. You *can* read, can't you?"

Vin nodded curtly.

"Good," Shan said. "All you need to do is memorize the titles of his books—don't look on the outside covers, they can be misleading. Read the first few pages, then report back to me."

"And if I should instead tell Elend what you're planning?"

Shan laughed. "My dear, you don't *know* what I'm planning. Besides, you seem to be making some headway in court. Surely you realize that betraying *me* is not something you want to even contemplate."

With that, Shan walked off, immediately gathering a collection of hangers-on from the surrounding nobility. Shan's Soothing weakened, and Vin felt her frustration and anger rise. There had been a time when she would have simply scampered away, ego already too beaten down to be bothered by Shan's insults. This night, however, she found herself wishing for a way to strike back.

Calm yourself. This is a good thing. You've become a pawn in Great House plans—most lesser nobility probably dream of such an opportunity.

She sighed, retreating toward the now empty table she had shared with Milen. The ball this evening was being held at the marvelous Keep Hasting. Its tall, round central keep was attended by six auxiliary towers, each set off from the main building a short distance and connected to it by walltop walkways. All seven towers were set with winding, curving patterns of stained glass.

The ballroom was at the top of the wide central tower. Fortunately, a system of skaa-powered pulley platforms kept noble guests from having to walk all the way to the top. The ballroom itself wasn't as spectacular as some Vin had visited—just a squarish chamber with vaulted ceilings and colored glass running around the perimeter.

Funny, how easily one can become jaded, Vin thought. *Perhaps that's how the noblemen can do such terrible things. They've been killing for so long that it doesn't unsettle them anymore.*

She asked a servant to go fetch Sazed, then sat down to rest her feet. *I wish Kelsier would hurry up and get back,* she thought. The crew, Vin included, seemed less motivated without him around. It wasn't that she didn't want to work; Kelsier's snappy wit and optimism just helped keep her moving.

Vin looked up idly, and her eyes caught sight of Elend Venture standing just a short distance away, chatting with a small group of young noblemen. She froze. Part of her—the Vin part—wanted to scurry away and hide. She'd fit beneath a table, dress and all.

Oddly, however, she found her Valette side stronger. *I have to talk to him,* she thought. *Not because of Shan, but because I have to find out the truth. Dockson was exaggerating. He* had *to be.*

When had she grown so confrontational? Even as she stood, Vin was amazed at her firm resolve. She crossed the ballroom—checking her black dress briefly as she walked. One of Elend's companions tapped him on the shoulder, nodding toward Vin. Elend turned, and the other two men withdrew.

"Why, Valette," he said as she paused in front of him. "I arrived late. I didn't even know you were here."

Liar. Of course you knew. Valette wouldn't miss the Hasting Ball. How to broach it? How to ask? "You've been avoiding me," she said.

"Now, I wouldn't say that. I've just been busy. House issues, you know. Besides, I warned you that I was rude, and . . ." he trailed off. "Valette? Is everything all right?"

Vin realized she was sniffling slightly, and she felt a tear on her cheek. *Idiot!* she thought, dabbing her eyes with Lestibournes's handkerchief. *You'll ruin your makeup!*

"Valette, you're shaking!" Elend said with concern. "Here, let's go to the balcony and get you some fresh air."

She let him lead her away from the sounds of music and chattering people, and they stepped into the quiet, dark air. The balcony—one of many jutting from the top of the central Hasting tower—was empty. A single stone lantern stood as part of the railing, and some tastefully placed plants lined the corners.

Mist floated in the air, prevalent as ever, though the balcony was close enough to the keep's warmth that the mist was weak. Elend didn't pay any attention to it. He, like most noblemen, considered fear of the mist to be a foolish skaa superstition—which, Vin supposed, was right.

"Now, what is this about?" Elend asked. "I'll admit, I have been ignoring you. I'm sorry. You didn't deserve it, I just . . . well, it seemed like you were fitting in so well that you didn't need a troublemaker like me being—"

"Have you ever slept with a skaa woman?" Vin asked.

Elend paused, taken aback. "Is *that* what this is all about? Who told you this?"

"Have you?" Vin demanded.

Elend paused.

Lord Ruler. It's true.

"Sit down," Elend said, fetching her a chair.

"It's true, isn't it?" Vin said, sitting. "You've done it. He was right, you're *all* monsters."

"I . . ." He laid a hand on Vin's arm, but she pulled it away, only to feel a teardrop drip down her face and stain her dress. She reached up, wiping her eyes, the handkerchief coming back colored with makeup.

"It happened when I was thirteen," Elend said quietly. "My father thought it was time that I became 'a man.' I didn't even know they were going to kill the girl afterward, Valette. Honestly, I didn't."

"And after that?" she demanded, growing angry. "How many girls have you murdered, Elend Venture?"

"None! Never again, Valette. Not after I found out what had happened that first time."

"You expect me to believe you?"

"I don't know," Elend said. "Look, I know that it's fashionable for the women of court to label all men brutes, but you have to believe me. We're not all like that."

"I was told that you are," Vin said.

"By whom? Country nobility? Valette, they don't know us. They're jealous because we control most of the canal systems—and they might just have a right to be. Their envy doesn't make us terrible people, however."

"What percentage?" Vin asked. "How many noblemen do these things?"

"Maybe a third," Elend said. "I'm not sure. They aren't the types I spend my time with."

She wanted to believe him, and that desire should have made her more skeptical. But, looking into those eyes—eyes she had always found so honest—she found herself swayed. For the first time she could remember, she completely pushed aside Reen's whispers, and simply believed.

"A third," she whispered. *So many. But, that's better than all of them.* She reached up to dab her eyes, and Elend eyed her handkerchief.

"Who gave you that?" he asked curiously.

"A suitor," Vin said.

"Is he the one who's been telling you these things about me?"

"No, that was another," Vin said. "He . . . said that all noblemen—or, rather, all Luthadel noblemen—were terrible people. He said that court women don't even consider it cheating when their men sleep with skaa whores."

Elend snorted. "Your informant doesn't know women very well, then. I dare you to find me one lady who isn't bothered when her husband dallies with another—skaa or noble."

Vin nodded, taking a deep breath, calming herself. She felt ridiculous . . . but she also felt at peace. Elend knelt beside her chair, still obviously concerned.

"So," she said, "your father is one of the third?"

Elend flushed in the wan light, looking down. "He likes all kinds of mistresses—skaa, noble, it doesn't matter to him. I still think about that night, Valette. I wish . . . I don't know."

"It wasn't your fault, Elend," she said. "You were just a thirteen-year-old boy who was doing what his father told him."

Elend looked away, but she had already seen the anger and guilt in his eyes. "Someone needs to stop these kinds of things from happening," he said quietly, and Vin was struck by the intensity in his voice.

This is a man who cares, she thought. *A man like Kelsier, or like Dockson. A good man. Why can't they see that?*

Finally, Elend sighed, standing and pulling over a chair for himself. He sat down, elbow resting against the railing, running his hand through his messy hair. "Well," he noted, "you probably aren't the first lady I've made cry at a ball, but you *are* the first one I've made cry that I sincerely care about. My gentlemanly prowess has reached new depths."

Vin smiled. "It's not you," she said, leaning back. "It's just been . . . a very draining few months. When I found out about these things, I just couldn't handle it all."

"The corruption in Luthadel needs to be dealt with," Elend said. "The Lord Ruler doesn't even see it—he doesn't want to."

Vin nodded, then she eyed Elend. "Why exactly *have* you been avoiding me lately, anyway?"

Elend flushed again. "I just figured you had enough new friends to keep you occupied."

"What is that supposed to mean?"

"I don't like a lot of the people you've been spending your time with, Valette," Elend said. "You've managed to fit very well into Luthadel society, and I generally find that playing politics changes people."

"That's easy to say," Vin snapped. "Especially when you're at the very *top* of the political structure. You can afford to ignore politics—some of us aren't so fortunate."

"I suppose."

"Besides," Vin said, "you play politics just as well as the rest. Or, are you going to try and tell me that your initial interest in me wasn't sparked by a desire to spite your father?"

Elend held up his hands. "All right, consider me suitably chastised. I was a fool and a twit. It runs in the family."

Vin sighed, sitting back and feeling the cool whisper of the mists on her tear-wetted cheeks. Elend wasn't a monster; she believed him on that count. Perhaps she was a fool, but Kelsier was having an effect on her. She was beginning to trust those around her, and there was no one she wanted to let herself trust more than Elend Venture.

And, when it wasn't connected directly to Elend, she found the horrors of the noble-skaa relationship easier to deal with. Even if a third of the noblemen were murdering skaa women, something was probably salvageable of the society. The nobility wouldn't have to be purged—that was *their* tactic. Vin would have to make certain that sort of thing didn't happen, no matter what bloodline one had.

Lord Ruler, Vin thought. *I'm starting to think like the others—it's almost like I think that we can change things.*

She glanced across at Elend, who sat with his back to the curling mists beyond. He looked morose.

I brought out bad memories, Vin thought guiltily. *No wonder he hates his father so much.* She longed to do something to make him feel better.

"Elend," she said, drawing his attention. "They're just like us."

He paused. "What?"

"The plantation skaa," Vin said. "You asked me about them once. I was afraid, so I acted like a proper noblewoman—but you seemed disappointed when I didn't have more to say."

He leaned forward. "So, you *did* spend time with the skaa?"

Vin nodded. "A lot of time. Too much, if you ask my family. That might be why they sent me out here. I knew some of the skaa very well—one older man, in particular. He lost someone, a woman he loved, to a nobleman who wanted a pretty thing for the evening's entertainment."

"At your plantation?"

Vin shook her head quickly. "He ran away and came to my father's lands."

"And you hid him?" Elend asked with surprise. "Runaway skaa are supposed to be executed!"

"I kept his secret," Vin said. "I didn't know him for very long, but . . . well, I can promise you this, Elend: His love was as strong as that of any nobleman. Stronger than most of them here in Luthadel, certainly."

"And intelligence?" Elend asked eagerly. "Did they seem . . . slow?"

"Of course not," Vin snapped. "I should think, Elend Venture, that I knew several skaa more clever than yourself. They may not have education, but they're still intelligent. And they're angry."

"Angry?" he asked.

"Some of them," Vin said. "About the way they're treated."

"They know, then? About the disparities between us and them?"

"How could they not?" Vin said, reaching up to wipe her nose with the handkerchief. She paused, however, noting just how much makeup she had rubbed across it.

"Here," Elend said, handing her his own handkerchief. "Tell me more. How do you know these things?"

"They told me," Vin said. "They trusted me. I know that they're angry because they would complain about their lives. I know they're intelligent because of the things they keep hidden from the nobility."

"Like what?"

"Like, the underground movement network," Vin said. "Skaa help runaways travel the canals from plantation to plantation. The noblemen don't notice because they never pay attention to skaa faces."

"Interesting."

"Plus," Vin said, "there are the thieving crews. I figure that those skaa must be fairly clever if they're able to hide from the obligators and the nobility, stealing from the Great Houses right beneath the Lord Ruler's nose."

"Yes, I know," Elend said. "I wish I could meet one of them, to ask them how they hide so well. They must be fascinating people."

Vin almost spoke further, but she held her tongue. *I've probably said too much already.*

Elend looked over at her. "You're fascinating too, Valette. I should have known better than to assume you'd been corrupted by the rest of them. Perhaps you'll be able to corrupt them instead."

Vin smiled.

"But," Elend said, rising. "I need to be leaving. I actually came to the party tonight for a specific purpose—some friends of mine are meeting together."

That's right! Vin thought. *One of the men Elend met with before—the ones that Kelsier and Sazed thought it was strange that he would associate with—was a Hasting.*

Vin stood as well, handing Elend back his handkerchief.

He didn't take it. "You might want to keep that. It wasn't intended to be simply functional."

Vin looked down at the handkerchief. *When a nobleman wants to court a lady seriously, he gives her a handkerchief.*

"Oh!" she said, pulling the handkerchief back. "Thank you."

Elend smiled, stepping close to her. "That other man, whoever he is, might have a lead on me because of my foolishness. However, I am not so foolish that I would pass up the chance to give him a little competition." He winked, bowed slightly, and walked back toward the central ballroom.

Vin waited a moment, then walked forward and slipped through the balcony doorway. Elend met up with the same two as before—a Lekal and a Hasting, political enemies of the Venture. They paused for a moment, then all three walked toward a stairwell at the side of the room.

Those stairwells only lead one place, Vin thought, slipping back into the room. *The auxiliary towers.*

"Mistress Valette?"

Vin jumped, turning to find Sazed approaching. "Are we ready to go?" he asked.

Vin moved over to him quickly. "Lord Elend Venture just disappeared down that stairwell with his Hasting and Lekal friends."

"Interesting," Sazed said. "And why would . . . Mistress, what happened to your makeup!"

"Never mind," Vin said. "I think I should follow them."

"Is that *another* handkerchief, Mistress?" Sazed asked. "You have been busy."

"Sazed, are you listening to me?"

"Yes, Mistress. I suppose you could follow them if you wish, but you would be fairly obvious. I don't know that it would be the best method of gaining information."

"I wouldn't follow them overtly," Vin said quietly. "I'd use Allomancy. But, I need your permission for that."

Sazed paused. "I see. How is your side?"

"It's been healed for ages," Vin said. "I don't even notice it anymore."

Sazed sighed. "Very well. Master Kelsier intended to begin your training in earnest again when he returned, anyway. Just . . . be careful. This is a ridiculous thing to say to a Mistborn, I think, but I ask anyway."

"I will," Vin said. "I'll meet you on that balcony over there in an hour."

"Good luck, Mistress," Sazed said.

Vin was already rushing back toward the balcony. She stepped around the corner, then stood before the stone railing and the mists beyond. The beautiful, swirling void. *It's been far too long,* she thought, reaching into her sleeve and pulling out a vial of metals. She downed it eagerly and got out a small handful of coins.

Then, blissfully, she hopped up onto the railing and threw herself out into the dark mists.

Tin gave her sight as the wind flapped at her dress. Pewter gave her strength as she turned her eyes toward the buttresslike wall running between the tower and the main keep. Steel gave her power as she threw a coin downward, sending it into the darkness.

She lurched in the air. The air resistance fluttered her dress, and she felt like she was trying to pull a bale of cloth behind her, but her Allomancy was strong enough to deal with that. Elend's tower was the next one over; she needed to get onto the walltop walkway that ran between it and the central tower. Vin flared steel, Pushing herself up a bit higher, then flung another coin into the mists behind her. When it hit the wall, she used it to shoot herself forward.

She slammed into her target wall just a bit too low—folds of cloth cushioning the blow—but she managed to grab the lip of the walkway above. An unenhanced Vin would have had trouble pulling herself up onto the wall, but Vin the Allomancer easily scrambled over the side.

She crouched in her black dress, moving quietly across the walltop pathway. There were no guards, but the tower ahead of her had a lit sentrypost at its base.

Can't go that way, she thought, glancing upward instead. The tower appeared to have several rooms, and a couple of them were lit. Vin dropped a coin and catapulted herself upward, then Pulled against a window mounting and yanked herself over to land lightly on the stone window ledge. The shutters were closed against the night, and she had to lean close, flaring tin, to hear what was going on inside.

". . . balls always last well into the night. We'll probably have to pull double duty."

Guards, Vin thought, jumping and Pushing against the top of the window. It rattled as she shot up the side of the tower. She caught the base of the next window ledge and pulled herself up.

". . . don't regret my tardiness," a familiar voice said from inside. Elend. "She happens to be far more attractive than you are, Telden."

A masculine voice laughed. "The mighty Elend Venture, finally captured by a pretty face."

"She's more than that, Jastes," Elend said. "She's kindhearted—she helped skaa runaways on her plantation. I think we should bring her in to talk with us."

"Not a chance," said a deep-voiced man. "Look, Elend, I don't mind if you want to talk philosophy. Hell, I'll even share a few drinks with you when you do. But I'm not going to let random people come join us."

"I agree with Telden," Jastes said. "Five people is enough."

"See, now," Elend's voice said. "I don't think you're being fair."

"Elend . . ." another voice said sufferingly.

"All right," Elend said. "Telden, did you read the book I gave you?"

"I tried," Telden said. "It's a bit thick."

"But it's good, right?" Elend said.

"Good enough," Telden said. "I can see why the Lord Ruler hates it so much."

"Redalevin's works are better," Jastes said. "More concise."

"I don't mean to be contrary," said a fifth voice. "But, is this all we're going to do? Read?"

"What's wrong with reading?" Elend asked.

"It's a bit boring," the fifth voice said.

Good man, Vin thought.

"Boring?" Elend asked. "Gentlemen, these ideas—these words—they're *everything*. These men knew that they'd be executed for their words. Can you not sense their passion?"

"Passion, yes," the fifth voice said. "Usefulness, no."

"We can change the world," Jastes said. "Two of us are house heirs, the other three are second heirs."

"Someday, we'll be the ones in charge," Elend said. "If we put these ideas into effect—fairness, diplomacy, moderation—we can exert pressure even on the Lord Ruler!"

The fifth voice snorted. "You might be heir to a powerful house, Elend, but the rest of us aren't as important. Telden and Jastes will probably never inherit, and Kevoux—no offense—is hardly that influential. We can't change the world."

"We can change the way our houses work," Elend said. "If the houses would stop squabbling, we might be able to gain some real power in the government— rather than just bow to the whims of the Lord Ruler."

"Every year, the nobility grows weaker," Jastes said in agreement. "Our skaa belong to the Lord Ruler, as does our land. His obligators determine who we can marry and what we can believe. Our canals, even, are officially 'his' property. Ministry assassins kill men who speak out too openly, or who are too successful. This is no way to live."

"I agree with you there," Telden said. "Elend's prattling about class imbalance seems like silliness to me, but I can see the importance of presenting a unified front before the Lord Ruler."

"Exactly," Elend said. "This is what we have to—"

"Vin!" a voice whispered.

Vin jumped, nearly falling off the window ledge in shock. She glanced around in alarm.

"Above you," the voice whispered.

She glanced up. Kelsier hung from another window ledge just above. He smiled, winked, then nodded down toward the wall-walkway below.

Vin glanced back at Elend's room as Kelsier dropped through the mists beside her. Finally, she pushed herself off and followed Kelsier down, using her same coin to slow her descent.

"You're back!" she said eagerly as she landed.

"Got back this afternoon."

"What are you doing here?"

"Checking up on our friend in there," Kelsier said. "Doesn't seem like much has changed since the last time."

"Last time?"

Kelsier nodded. "I've spied on that little group a couple of times since you told me about them. I shouldn't have bothered—they're not a threat. Just a bunch of noblelings getting together to drink and debate."

"But, they want to overthrow the Lord Ruler!"

"Hardly," Kelsier said with a snort. "They're just doing what noblemen do— planning alliances. It's not that unusual for the next generation to start organizing their house coalitions before they come to power."

"This is different," Vin said.

"Oh?" Kelsier asked with amusement. "You've been a noble so long that you can tell that already?"

She flushed, and he laughed, putting a friendly arm around her shoulders. "Oh, don't get like that. They seem like nice enough lads, for noblemen. I promise not to kill any of them, all right?"

Vin nodded.

"Perhaps we can find a way to use them—they do seem more open-minded than most. I just don't want you to be disappointed, Vin. They're still noblemen. Perhaps they can't help what they are, but that doesn't change their nature."

Just like Dockson, Vin thought. *Kelsier assumes the worst about Elend.* But, did she really have any reason to expect otherwise? To fight a battle like Kelsier and Dockson were, it was probably more effective—and better for the psyche—to assume that all of their enemies were evil.

"What happened to your makeup, by the way?" Kelsier asked.

"I don't want to talk about it," Vin said, thinking back to her conversation with Elend. *Why did I have to cry? I'm such an idiot! And, the way I blurted out that question about him sleeping with skaa.*

Kelsier shrugged. "Okay, then. We should get going—I doubt young Venture and his comrades will discuss anything relevant."

Vin paused.

"I've listened to them on three separate occasions, Vin," Kelsier said. "I'll summarize for you, if you want."

"All right," she said with a sigh. "But I told Sazed I'd meet him back up at the party."

"Off you go, then," Kelsier said. "I promise not to tell him you were sneaking around and using Allomancy."

"He told me I could," Vin said defensively.

"He did?"

Vin nodded.

"My mistake," Kelsier said. "You should probably have Saze fetch you a cloak before you leave the party—you've got ash all over the front of your dress. I'll meet you back at Clubs's shop—have the carriage drop you and Sazed off there, then continue on out of the city. That'll keep up appearances."

Vin nodded again, and Kelsier winked and jumped off the wall into the mists.

In the end, I must trust in myself. I have seen men who have beaten from themselves the ability to recognize truth and goodness, and I do not think I am one of them. I can still see the tears in a young child's eyes and feel pain at his suffering.

If I ever lose this, then I will know that I've passed beyond hope of redemption.

24

KELSIER WAS ALREADY AT THE SHOP when Vin and Sazed arrived. He sat with Ham, Clubs, and Spook in the kitchen, enjoying a late-night drink.

"Ham!" Vin said eagerly as she came in the back door. "You're back!"

"Yup," he said happily, raising his cup.

"It seems like you've been gone forever!"

"You're telling me," Ham said, his voice earnest.

Kelsier chuckled, rising to refill his drink. "Ham's a bit tired of playing general."

"I had to wear a uniform," Ham complained, stretching. He now wore his customary vest and trousers. "Even plantation skaa don't have to deal with that kind of torture."

"Try wearing a formal gown sometime," Vin said, seating herself. She'd brushed off the front of her dress, and it didn't look half as bad as she'd feared. The blackish gray ash still showed up a bit against the dark fabric, and the fibers were rough where she'd rubbed against stone, but both were barely noticeable.

Ham laughed. "It seems that you've turned into a proper young lady while I was gone."

"Hardly," Vin said as Kelsier handed her a cup of wine. She paused briefly, then took a sip.

"Mistress Vin is being modest, Master Hammond," Sazed said, taking a seat.

"She's growing quite proficient at courtly arts—better than many actual nobles that I have known."

Vin flushed, and Ham laughed again. "Humility, Vin? Where'd you ever learn a bad habit like that?"

"Not from me, certainly," Kelsier said, offering Sazed a cup of wine. The Terrisman raised his hand in a respectful refusal.

"Of course she didn't get it from *you*, Kell," Ham said. "Maybe Spook taught her. He seems to be the only one in this crew who knows how to keep his mouth shut, eh, kid?"

Spook flushed, obviously trying to avoid looking at Vin.

I'll have to deal with him sometime, she thought. *But . . . not tonight. Kelsier's back and Elend's not a murderer—this is a night to relax.*

Footsteps sounded on the stairs, and a moment later Dockson strolled into the room. "A party? And no one sent for me?"

"You seemed busy," Kelsier said.

"Besides," Ham added, "we know you're too responsible to sit around and get drunk with a bunch of miscreants like us."

"*Someone* has to keep this crew running," Dockson said lightheartedly, pouring himself a drink. He paused, frowning at Ham. "That vest looks familiar. . . ."

Ham smiled. "I ripped the arms off of my uniform coat."

"You didn't!" Vin said with a smile.

Ham nodded, looking self-satisfied.

Dockson sighed, continuing to fill his cup. "Ham, those things cost money."

"Everything costs money," Ham said. "But, what *is* money? A physical representation of the abstract concept of effort. Well, wearing that uniform for so long was a pretty mean effort. I'd say that this vest and I are even now."

Dockson just rolled his eyes. In the main room, the shop's front door opened and closed, and Vin heard Breeze bid hello to the apprentice on watch.

"By the way, Dox," Kelsier said, leaning with his back against a cupboard. "I'm going to need a few 'physical representations of the concept of effort' myself. I'd like to rent a small warehouse to conduct some of my informant meetings."

"That can probably be arranged," Dockson said. "Assuming we keep Vin's wardrobe budget under control, I—" He broke off, glancing at Vin. "What did you do to that gown, young lady!"

Vin flushed, scrunching down in her chair. *Perhaps it's a bit more noticeable than I thought. . . .*

Kelsier chuckled. "You may have to get used to dirtied clothing, Dox. Vin's back on Mistborn duty as of this evening."

"Interesting," Breeze said, entering the kitchen. "Might I suggest that she avoid fighting three Steel Inquisitors at once this time?"

"I'll do my best," Vin said.

Breeze strolled over to the table and chose a seat with his characteristic decorum. The portly man raised his dueling cane, pointing it at Ham. "I see that my period of intellectual respite has come to an end."

Ham smiled. "I thought up a couple beastly questions while I was gone, and I've been saving them just for you, Breeze."

"I'm dying of anticipation," Breeze said. He turned his cane toward Lestibournes. "Spook, drink."

Spook rushed over and fetched Breeze a cup of wine.

"He's such a fine lad," Breeze noted, accepting the drink. "I barely even have to nudge him Allomantically. If only the rest of you ruffians were so accommodating."

Spook frowned. "Niceing the not on the playing without."

"I have no idea what you just said, child," Breeze said. "So I'm simply going to pretend it was coherent, then move on."

Kelsier rolled his eyes. "Losing the stress on the nip," he said. "Notting without the needing of care."

"Riding the rile of the rids to the right," Spook said with a nod.

"What are you two babbling about?" Breeze said testily.

"Wasing the was of brightness," Spook said. "Nip the having of wishing of this."

"Ever wasing the doing of this," Kelsier agreed.

"Ever wasing the wish of having the have," Ham added with a smile. "Brighting the wish of wasing the not."

Breeze turned to Dockson with exasperation. "I believe our companions have finally lost their minds, dear friend."

Dockson shrugged. Then, with a perfectly straight face, he said, "Wasing not of wasing is."

Breeze sat, dumbfounded, and the room burst into laughter. Breeze rolled his eyes indignantly, shaking his head and muttering about the crew's gross childishness.

Vin nearly choked on her wine as she laughed. "What did you even say?" she asked of Dockson as he sat down beside her.

"I'm not sure," he confessed. "It just sounded right."

"I don't think you said anything, Dox," Kelsier said.

"Oh, he said something," Spook said. "It just didn't *mean* anything."

Kelsier laughed. "That's true pretty much all the time. I've found you can ignore half of what Dox tells you and not miss much—except for maybe the occasional complaint that you're spending too much."

"Hey!" Dockson said. "Once again, must I point out that *someone* has to be responsible? Honestly, the way you people go through boxings . . ."

Vin smiled. Even Dockson's complaints seemed good-natured. Clubs sat quietly by the side wall, looking as curmudgeonly as ever, but Vin caught sight of a slight smile on his lips. Kelsier rose and opened another bottle of wine, refilling cups as he told the crew about the skaa army's preparations.

Vin felt . . . contented. As she sipped at her wine, she caught sight of the open doorway leading into the darkened workshop. She imagined, just for a moment, that she could see a figure out in the shadows—a frightened wisp of a girl, untrusting, suspicious. The girl's hair was ragged and short, and she wore a simple, untucked dirty shirt and a pair of brown trousers.

Vin remembered that second night in Clubs's shop, when she had stood out in the dark workroom, watching the others share late-night conversation. Had she really been that girl—one who would hide in the cold darkness, watching the laughter and friendship with a hidden envy, but never daring to join it?

Kelsier made some particularly witty comment, drawing laughter from the entire room.

You're right, Kelsier, Vin thought with a smile. *This* is *better.*

She wasn't like them yet—not completely. Six months couldn't silence Reen's whispers, and she couldn't see herself ever being as trusting as Kelsier was. But . . . she could finally understand, at least a little bit, why he worked the way he did.

"All right," Kelsier said, pulling over a chair and sitting on it the wrong way. "It looks like the army will be ready on schedule, and Marsh is in place. We need to get this plan moving. Vin, news from the ball?"

"House Tekiel is vulnerable," she said. "Its allies are scattering, and the vultures are moving in. Some whisper that debts and lost business will force the Tekiel to sell off their keep by the end of the month. There's no way they can afford to continue paying the Lord Ruler's keep tax."

"Which effectively eliminates one entire Great House from the city," Dockson said. "Most of the Tekiel nobility—including Mistings and Mistborn—will have to move to outer plantations to try and recoup losses."

"Nice," Ham noted. Any noble houses they could frighten out of the city would make seizing it that much easier.

"That still leaves nine Great Houses in the city," Breeze noted.

"But they've started killing each other at night," Kelsier said. "That's only one step away from open war. I suspect we'll see an exodus start here pretty soon—anyone who isn't willing to risk assassination to maintain dominance in Luthadel will leave town for a couple of years."

"The strong houses don't seem very afraid, though," Vin said. "They're still throwing balls, anyway."

"Oh, they'll keep doing that right up until the end," Kelsier said. "Balls make great excuses to meet with allies and keep an eye on enemies. House wars are primarily political, and so they demand political battlefields."

Vin nodded.

"Ham," Kelsier said, "we need to keep an eye on the Luthadel Garrison. You're still planning to visit your soldier contacts tomorrow?"

Ham nodded. "I can't promise anything, but I should be able to reestablish some connections. Give me a bit of time, and I'll find out what the military is up to."

"Good," Kelsier said.

"I'd like to go with him," Vin said.

Kelsier paused. "With Ham?"

Vin nodded. "I haven't trained with a Thug yet. Ham could probably show me a few things."

"You already know how to burn pewter," Kelsier said. "We've practiced that."

"I know," Vin said. How could she explain? Ham had practiced with pewter exclusively—he was bound to be better at it than Kelsier.

"Oh, stop pestering the child," Breeze said. "She's probably just tired of balls and parties. Let her go be a normal street urchin again for a bit."

"Fine," Kelsier said, rolling his eyes. He poured himself another drink. "Breeze, how well could your Soothers manage if you were gone for a little while?"

Breeze shrugged. "I am, of course, the most effective member of the team. But, I *did* train the others—they'll recruit effectively without me, especially now that stories about the Survivor are getting so popular."

"We need to talk about that by the way, Kell," Dockson said, frowning. "I'm not sure if I like all this mysticism about you and the Eleventh Metal."

"We can discuss it later," Kelsier said.

"Why ask about my men?" Breeze said. "Have you finally grown so jealous of my impeccable fashion sense that you've decided to have me disposed of?"

"You might say that," Kelsier said. "I was thinking of sending you to replace Yeden in a few months."

"Replace Yeden?" Breeze asked with surprise. "You mean for *me* to lead the army?"

"Why not?" Kelsier asked. "You're great at giving orders."

"From the background, my dear man," Breeze said. "I don't stand out in front. Why, I'd be a *general*. Do you have any idea how ludicrous that sounds?"

"Just consider it," Kelsier said. "Our recruitment should be mostly done by then, so you might be most effective if you were to go to the caves and let Yeden come back to prepare his contacts here."

Breeze frowned. "I suppose."

"Regardless," Kelsier said, rising. "I don't think I've had *nearly* enough wine. Spook, be a good lad and run down to the cellar for another bottle, eh?"

The boy nodded, and the conversation turned back to lighter topics. Vin settled back in her chair, feeling the warmth of the coal stove at the side of the room, content for the moment to simply enjoy the peace of not having to worry, fight, or plan.

If only Reen could have known something like this, she thought, idly fingering her earring. *Perhaps then, things would have been different for him. For us.*

Ham and Vin left the next day to visit the Luthadel Garrison.

After so many months of playing a noblewoman, Vin had thought that it would feel strange to wear street clothing again. Yet, it really didn't. True, it was a bit *different*—she didn't have to worry about sitting properly or walking so that her dress didn't brush against dirty walls or floors. Yet, the mundane clothing still felt natural to her.

She wore a simple pair of brown trousers and a loose white shirt, tucked in at the waist, then overlaid by a leather vest. Her still lengthening hair was pulled up under a cap. Casual passers might think her a boy, though Ham didn't seem to think it mattered.

And it really didn't. Vin had grown accustomed to having people study and evaluate her, but no one on the street even bothered to give her a glance. Shuffling skaa workers, unconcerned low noblemen, even high-placed skaa like Clubs—they all ignored her.

I'd almost forgotten what it was like to be invisible, Vin thought. Fortunately, the old attitudes—looking down when she walked, stepping out of people's way, slouching to make herself inconspicuous—returned to her easily. Becoming Vin the street skaa felt as simple as remembering an old, familiar melody she used to hum.

This really is just another disguise, Vin thought as she walked beside Ham. *My makeup is a light coat of ash, carefully rubbed on my cheeks. My gown is a pair of trousers, rubbed to make them seem old and well used.*

Who, then, was she really? Vin the urchin? Valette the lady? Neither? Did any of her friends really know her? Did she even really know herself?

"Ah, I've missed this place," Ham said, walking happily beside her. Ham always seemed happy; she couldn't imagine him dissatisfied, despite what he'd said about his time leading the army.

"It's kind of strange," he said, turning to Vin. He didn't walk with the same careful air of despondence that Vin had cultivated; he didn't even seem to care that he stood out from other skaa. "I probably shouldn't miss this place—I mean, Luthadel is the dirtiest, most crowded city in the Final Empire. But, there's also something about it. . . ."

"Is this where your family lives?" Vin asked.

Ham shook his head. "They live in a smaller city outside of town. My wife is a seamstress there; she tells people I'm in the Luthadel Garrison."

"Don't you miss them?"

"Of course I do," Ham said. "It's hard—I only get to spend a few months at a time with them—but it's better this way. If I were to get killed on a job, the Inquisitors would have a tough time tracking my family. I haven't even told Kell which city they live in."

"You think the Ministry would go to that much trouble?" Vin asked. "I mean, you'd already be dead."

"I'm a Misting, Vin—that means that all of my descendants will have some noble blood. My children might turn out to be Allomancers, as might their children. No, when the Inquisitors kill a Misting, they make certain to wipe out his children too. The only way to keep my family safe is to stay away from them."

"You could just not use your Allomancy," Vin said.

Ham shook his head. "I don't know if I could do that."

"Because of the power?"

"No, because of the money," Ham said frankly. "Thugs—or, Pewterarms, as the nobility prefer to call them—are the most sought-after Mistings. A competent Thug can stand against a half-dozen regular men, and he can lift more, endure more, and move faster than any other hired muscle. Those things mean a lot when you have to keep your crews small. Mix a couple of Coinshots with five or so Thugs, and you've got yourself a small, mobile army. Men will pay a lot for protection like that."

Vin nodded. "I can see how the money would be tempting."

"It's more than tempting, Vin. My family doesn't have to live in packed skaa tenements, nor do they have to worry about starving. My wife only works to keep up appearances—they have a good life, for skaa. Once I have enough, we'll move away from the Central Dominance. There are places in the Final Empire that a lot of people don't know about—places where a man with enough money can live the life of a nobleman. Places where you can stop worrying and just live."

"That sounds . . . appealing."

Ham nodded, turning and leading them down a larger thoroughfare toward the main city gates. "I got the dream from Kell, actually. That's what he always said he wanted to do. I just hope I have more luck than he did. . . ."

Vin frowned. "Everyone says he was rich. Why didn't he leave?"

"I don't know," Ham said. "There was always another job—each one bigger than the last. I guess when you're a crewleader like him, the game can get addicting. Soon, money didn't even seem to matter to him. Eventually, he heard that the Lord Ruler was storing some incalculable secret in that hidden sanctum of his. If he and Mare had walked away before that job . . . But, well, they didn't. I don't know—maybe they wouldn't have been happy living lives where they *didn't* have to worry."

The concept seemed to intrigue him, and Vin could see another of his "questions" working within his mind.

I guess when you're a crewleader like him, the game can get addicting. . . .

Her earlier apprehensions returned. What would happen if Kelsier seized the imperial throne for himself? He couldn't possibly be as bad as the Lord

Ruler, but . . . she was reading more and more of the logbook. The Lord Ruler hadn't always been a tyrant. He'd been a good man, once. A good man whose life had gone wrong.

Kelsier's different, Vin told herself forcefully. *He'll do the right thing.*

Still, she wondered. Ham might not understand, but Vin could see the enticement. Despite noble depravity, there was something intoxicating about high society. Vin was captivated by the beauty, the music, and the dancing. Her fascination wasn't the same as Kelsier's—she wasn't as interested in political games or even scams—but she could understand why he would have been reluctant to leave Luthadel behind.

That reluctance had destroyed the old Kelsier. But, it had produced something better—a more determined, less self-serving Kelsier. Hopefully.

Of course, his plans before also cost him the woman he loved. Is that why he hates the nobility so much?

"Ham?" she asked. "Has Kelsier always hated the nobility?"

Ham nodded. "It's worse now, though."

"He frightens me sometimes. It seems like he wants to kill *all* of them, no matter who they are."

"I'm concerned about him too," Ham said. "This Eleventh Metal business . . . it's almost like he's making himself out to be some kind of holy man." He paused, then he looked toward her. "Don't worry too much. Breeze, Dox, and I have already talked about this. We're going to confront Kell, see if we can rein him in a bit. He means well, but he has a tendency to go a little overboard sometimes."

Vin nodded. Ahead, the customary crowded lines of people waited for permission to pass through the city gates. She and Ham walked quietly past the solemn group—workers being sent out to the docks, men off to work one of the outer mills alongside the river or lake, lesser noblemen wishing to travel. All had to have a good reason to leave the city; the Lord Ruler strictly controlled travel inside his realm.

Poor things, Vin thought as she passed a ragged band of children carrying pails and brushes—probably on duty to climb the wall and scrub mist-grown lichen off the parapets. Ahead, up near the gates, an official cursed and shoved a man out of the line. The skaa worker fell hard, but eventually picked himself back up and shuffled to the end of the line. It was likely that if he wasn't let out of the city, he wouldn't be able to do his day's work—and no work meant no food tokens for his family.

Vin followed Ham past the gates, heading down a street parallel to the city wall, at the end of which Vin could see a large building complex. Vin had never studied the Garrison headquarters before; most crewmembers tended to stay a good distance away from it. However, as they approached, she was impressed by its defensive appearance. Large spikes were mounted on the wall that ran around the entire complex. The buildings within were bulky and fortified. Soldiers stood at the gates, eyeing passersby with hostility.

Vin paused. "Ham, how are we going to get in *there?*"

"Don't worry," he said, stopping beside her. "I'm known to the Garrison. Besides, it's not as bad as it looks—the Garrison members just put on an intimidating face. As you can imagine, they aren't very well liked. Most of the soldiers in there are skaa—men who have, in exchange for a better life, sold out to the Lord Ruler. Whenever there are skaa riots in a city, the local garrison is usually hit pretty hard by malcontents. Hence the fortifications."

"So . . . you know these men?"

Ham nodded. "I'm not like Breeze or Kell, Vin—I can't put on faces and pretend. I'm just who I am. Those soldiers don't know I'm a Misting, but they know I work in the underground. I've known many of these guys for years; they've consistently tried to recruit me. They generally have better luck getting people like me, who are already outside mainstream society, to join their ranks."

"But, you're going to betray them," Vin said quietly, pulling Ham to the side of the road.

"Betray?" he asked. "No, it won't be a betrayal. Those men are mercenaries, Vin. They've been hired to fight, and they'll attack friends—even relatives—in a riot or rebellion. Soldiers learn to understand these kinds of things. We may be friends, but when it comes to fighting, none of us would hesitate to kill the others."

Vin nodded slowly. It seemed . . . harsh. *But, that's what life is. Harsh. That part of Reen's teaching wasn't a lie.*

"Poor lads," Ham said, looking at the Garrison. "We could have used men like them. Before I left for the caves, I managed to recruit the few that I thought would be receptive. The rest . . . well, they picked their path. Like me, they're just trying to give their kids a better life—the difference is, they're willing to work for *him* in order to do it."

Ham turned back to her. "All right, you wanted some tips on burning pewter?"

Vin nodded eagerly.

"The soldiers usually let me spar with them," Ham said. "You can watch me fight—burn bronze to see when I'm using Allomancy. The first, most important thing you'll learn about Pewterarming is when to use your metal. I've noticed that young Allomancers tend to always flare their pewter, thinking that the stronger they are, the better. However, you don't always want to hit as hard as you can with each blow.

"Strength is a big part of fighting, but it's not the only part. If you always hit your hardest, you'll tire faster and you'll give your opponent information about your limitations. A smart man hits his hardest at the *end* of a battle, when his opponent is weakest. And, in an extended battle—like a war—the smart soldier is the one who survives the longest. He'll be the man who paces himself."

Vin nodded. "But, don't you tire slower when you're using Allomancy?"

"Yes," Ham said. "In fact, a man with enough pewter can keep fighting at near-peak efficiency for hours. But pewter dragging like that takes practice, and you'll run out of metals eventually. When you do, the fatigue could kill you.

"Anyway, what I'm trying to explain is that it's usually best to vary your pewter burning. If you use more strength than you need, you could knock yourself off balance. Also, I've seen Thugs who rely on their pewter so much that they disregard training and practice. Pewter enhances your physical abilities, but not your innate skill. If you don't know how to use a weapon—or if you aren't practiced at thinking quickly in a fight—you'll lose no matter how strong you are.

"I'll have to be extra careful with the Garrison, since I don't want them to know I'm an Allomancer. You'll be surprised at how often that's important. Watch how I use pewter. I won't just flare it for strength—if I stumble, I'll burn it to give me an instant sense of balance. When I dodge, I might burn it to help me duck out of the way a little faster. There are dozens of little tricks you can do if you know when to give yourself a boost."

Vin nodded.

"Okay," Ham said. "Let's go, then. I'll tell the garrisoners that you're the daughter of a relative. You look young enough for your age that they won't even think twice. Watch me fight, and we'll talk afterward."

Vin nodded again, and the two of them approached the Garrison. Ham waved to one of the guards. "Hey, Bevidon. I've got the day off. Is Sertes around?"

"He's here, Ham," Bevidon said. "But I don't know that this is the best day for sparring. . . ."

Ham raised an eyebrow. "Oh?"

Bevidon shared a glance with one of the other soldiers. "Go fetch the captain," he said to the man.

A few moments later, a busy-looking soldier approached from a side building, waving as soon as he saw Ham. His uniform bore a few extra stripes of color and a few gold-colored bits of metal on the shoulder.

"Ham," the newcomer said, stepping through the gate.

"Sertes," Ham said with a smile, clasping hands with the man. "Captain now, eh?"

"Happened last month," Sertes said with a nod. He paused, then eyed Vin.

"She's my niece," Ham said. "Good lass."

Sertes nodded. "Could we speak alone for a moment, Ham?"

Ham shrugged and let himself get pulled to a more secluded place beside the complex gates. Vin's Allomancy let her make out what they were saying. *What did I ever do without tin?*

"Look, Ham," Sertes said. "You won't be able to come spar for a while. The Garrison is going to be . . . occupied."

"Occupied?" Ham asked. "How?"

"I can't say," Sertes said. "But . . . well, we could really use a soldier like you right now."

"Fighting?"

"Yeah."

"Must be something serious if it's taking the attention of the entire Garrison."

Sertes grew quiet for a moment, and then he spoke again in a hushed tone— so quiet that Vin had to strain to hear. "A rebellion," Sertes whispered, "right here in the Central Dominance. We just got word. An army of skaa rebels appeared and attacked the Holstep Garrison to the north."

Vin felt a sudden chill.

"*What?*" Ham said.

"They must have come from the caves up there," the soldier said. "Last word was that the Holstep fortifications are holding—but Ham, they're only a thousand men strong. They need reinforcements desperately, and the koloss will never get there in time. The Valtroux Garrison sent five thousand soldiers, but we're not going to leave it to them. This is apparently a very big force of rebels, and the Lord Ruler gave us permission to go help."

Ham nodded.

"So, what about it?" Sertes asked. "Real fighting, Ham. Real battle pay. We could really use a man of your skill—I'll make you an officer right off, give you your own squad."

"I . . . I'll have to think about it," Ham said. He wasn't good at hiding his emotions, and his surprise sounded suspicious to Vin. Sertes, however, didn't appear to notice.

"Don't take too long," Sertes said. "We plan to march out in two hours."

"I'll do it," Ham said, sounding stunned. "Let me go drop off my niece and get some things. I'll be back before you leave."

"Good man," Sertes said, and Vin could see him clap Ham on the shoulder.

Our army is exposed, Vin thought in horror. *They're not ready! They were supposed to take Luthadel quietly, quickly—not face the Garrison straight out.*

Those men are going to get massacred! What happened?

No man dies by my hand or command except that I wish there had been another way. Still, I kill them. Sometimes, I wish that I weren't such a cursed realist.

25

KELSIER TOSSED ANOTHER WATER JUG into his pack. "Breeze, make a list of all the hideouts where you and I recruited. Go warn them that the Ministry might soon have prisoners who could give them away."

Breeze nodded, for once refraining from making any witty remarks. Behind him, apprentices scrambled through Clubs's shop, gathering and preparing the supplies that Kelsier had ordered.

"Dox, this shop should be secure unless they capture Yeden. Keep all three of Clubs's Tineyes on watch. If there's trouble, head for the bolt-lair."

Dockson nodded in acknowledgment as he hurriedly gave orders to the apprentices. One had already left, bearing a warning to Renoux. Kelsier thought that the mansion would be safe—only that one group of barges had left from Fellise, and its men had thought that Renoux wasn't in on the plan. Renoux wouldn't pull out unless absolutely necessary; his disappearance would require removing both himself and Valette from their carefully prepared positions.

Kelsier stuffed a handful of rations into his pack, then swung it onto his back.

"What about me, Kell?" Ham asked.

"You're going back to the Garrison, like you promised. That was clever thinking—we need an informant in there."

Ham frowned apprehensively.

"I don't have time to deal with your nerves right now, Ham," Kelsier said. "You don't have to scam, just be yourself and listen."

"I won't turn against the Garrison if I go with them," he said. "I'll listen, but I'm not going to attack men who think I'm their ally."

"Fine," Kelsier said curtly. "But I sincerely hope you can find a way not to kill any of our soldiers, either. Sazed!"

"Yes, Master Kelsier?"

"How much speed do you have stored up?"

Sazed flushed slightly, glancing at the numerous people scurrying around. "Perhaps two, three hours. It is a very difficult attribute to collect."

"Not long enough," Kelsier said. "I'll go alone. Dox is in charge until I get back."

Kelsier spun, then paused. Vin stood behind him in the same trousers, cap, and shirt she had worn to the Garrison. She had a pack like his slung over her shoulder, and she looked up at him defiantly.

"This is going to be a difficult trip, Vin," he said. "You've never done anything like this before."

"That's fine."

Kelsier nodded. He pulled his trunk out from beneath the table, then opened it and poured Vin a small pouch of pewter beads. She accepted it without comment.

"Swallow five of those beads."

"*Five?*"

"For now," Kelsier said. "If you need to take some more, call to me so we can stop running."

"Running?" the girl asked. "We're not taking a canal boat?"

Kelsier frowned. "Why would *we* need a boat?"

Vin glanced down at the pouch, then grabbed a cup of water and began to swallow beads.

"Make sure you have enough water in that pack," Kelsier said. "Take as much as you can carry." He left her, walking over to lay a hand on Dockson's shoulder. "It's about three hours before sunset. If we push hard, we can be there by noon tomorrow."

Dockson nodded. "That might be early enough."

Maybe, Kelsier thought. *The Valtroux Garrison is only three days' march from Holstep. Even riding all night, a messenger couldn't have gotten to Luthadel in under two days. By the time I get to the army . . .*

Dockson could obviously read the worry in Kelsier's eyes. "Either way, the army is useless to us now," he said.

"I know," Kelsier said. "This is just about saving those men's lives. I'll get word to you as soon as I can."

Dockson nodded.

Kelsier turned, flaring his pewter. His pack suddenly became as light as if it had been empty. "Burn your pewter, Vin. We're leaving."

She nodded, and Kelsier felt a pulsing come from her. "Flare it," he ordered, pulling two mistcloaks from his trunk and tossing one to her. He put on the other, then walked forward, throwing open the back door to the kitchen. The red sun was bright overhead. Frantic crewmembers paused for a moment, turning to watch as Kelsier and Vin left the building.

The girl hurried forward to walk at Kelsier's side. "Ham told me that I should learn to use pewter only when I need it—he said it's better to be subtle."

Kelsier turned to face the girl. "This is not a time for subtlety. Stay close to me, try to keep up, and make absolutely certain you don't run out of pewter."

Vin nodded, suddenly looking a bit apprehensive.

"All right," Kelsier said, taking a deep breath. "Let's go."

Kelsier took off down the alleyway in a superhuman dash. Vin jumped into motion, following him out of the alley and onto the street. Pewter was a blazing fire within her. Flared as it was, she would probably go through all five beads in barely an hour.

The street was busy with skaa workers and noble carriages. Kelsier ignored the traffic, bolting out into the very center of the street, maintaining his ridiculous speed. Vin followed, growing increasingly worried about what she had gotten herself into.

I can't let him go alone, she thought. Of course, the last time she'd forced Kelsier to take her with him, she'd ended up half dead in a sickbed for a month.

Kelsier wove between carriages, brushing past pedestrians, charging down the street as if it were meant only for him. Vin followed as best as she could, the ground a blur beneath her feet, people passing too quickly to see their faces. Some of them called out after her, their voices annoyed. A couple of these, however, choked off immediately, falling silent.

The cloaks, Vin thought. *That's why we're wearing them—that's why we always wear them. Noblemen who see the mistcloaks will know to stay out of our way.*

Kelsier turned, running directly toward the northern city gates. Vin followed. Kelsier didn't slow as he approached the gates, and the lines of people began to point. Checkpoint guards turned with surprised faces.

Kelsier jumped.

One of the armored guards crumpled to the ground with a cry, smashed down by Kelsier's Allomantic weight as the crewleader passed overhead. Vin took a breath, dropped a coin to give herself a bit of lift, and jumped. She easily cleared a second guard, who looked up with surprise as his companion squirmed on the ground.

Vin Pushed against the soldier's armor, throwing herself higher into the air. The man staggered, but stayed on his feet—Vin was nowhere near as heavy as Kelsier.

She shot over the wall, hearing cries of surprise from the soldiers on top of it. She could only hope that nobody recognized her. It wasn't likely. Though her cap flew free as she soared through the air, those who were familiar with Valette the courtgoing lady would probably never connect her to a Mistborn in dirty trousers.

Vin's cloak whipped angrily in the passing air. Kelsier completed his arc before her and began to descend, and Vin soon followed. It felt very strange to use Allomancy in the sunlight. Unnatural, even. Vin made the mistake of looking down as she fell. Instead of comfortable swirling mists, she saw the ground far below.

So high! Vin thought with horror. Fortunately, she wasn't too disoriented to Push against the coin Kelsier had used to land. She slowed her descent to a manageable level before thumping against the ashen earth.

Kelsier immediately took off down the highway. Vin followed him, ignoring merchants and travelers. Now that they were out of the city, she had thought Kelsier might slow down. He didn't. He sped up.

And, suddenly, she understood. Kelsier didn't intend to walk, or even jog, to the caves.

He planned to dash all the way there.

It was a two-week trip by canal. How long would it take them? They were moving fast, horribly fast. Slower than a galloping horse, certainly, but surely a horse couldn't maintain such a gallop for very long.

Vin didn't feel fatigue as she ran. She relied on the pewter, only passing a little of the strain onto her body. She could barely feel her footsteps hitting the ground beneath her, and with such a large reserve of pewter, she felt that she could maintain the speed for a decent length of time.

She caught up to Kelsier, falling into place beside him. "This is easier than I thought it would be."

"Pewter enhances your balance," Kelsier said. "Otherwise you'd be tripping over yourself right now."

"What do you think we'll find? At the caves, I mean."

Kelsier shook his head. "No use talking. Save your strength."

"But, I'm not feeling weary at all!"

"We'll see what you say in sixteen hours," Kelsier said, speeding up even more as they turned off the highway, running onto the wide towpath beside the Luth-Davn Canal.

Sixteen hours!

Vin fell behind Kelsier slightly, giving herself plenty of space to run. Kelsier increased their speed until they were going at a maddening pace. He was right: In any other context, she would have quickly missed her step on the uneven road. Yet, with pewter and tin guiding her, she managed to stay on her feet—though doing so required increasing attention as the evening grew dark and the mists came out.

Occasionally, Kelsier threw down a coin and launched himself from one hilltop to another. However, he mostly kept them running at an even pace, sticking to the canal. Hours passed, and Vin began to feel the fatigue that he had implied would come. She maintained her speed, but she could feel something underneath it—a resistance within, a longing to stop and rest. Despite pewter's power, her body was running out of strength.

She made certain to never let her pewter run low. She feared that if it ever went out, the fatigue would come upon her so powerfully that she wouldn't be able to get started again. Kelsier also ordered her to drink a ridiculous amount of water, though she wasn't that thirsty.

The night grew dark and silent, no travelers daring to brave the mists. They passed canal boats and barges tied up for the night, as well as the occasional camp of canalmen, their tents huddled closely against the mists. Twice they saw mistwraiths on the road, the first one giving Vin a terrible start. Kelsier just passed it by—completely ignoring the terrible, translucent remnants of the people and animals who had been ingested, their bones now forming the mistwraith's own skeleton.

Still he kept running. Time became a blur, and the running came to dominate all that Vin was and did. Moving demanded so much attention that she could barely even focus on Kelsier ahead of her in the mists. She kept putting one foot ahead of the other, her body remaining strong—yet, at the same time, feeling terribly exhausted. Every step, quick though it was, became a chore. She began to yearn for rest.

Kelsier didn't give it to her. He kept running, forcing her on, maintaining the incredible speed. Vin's world became a timeless thing of forced pain and burgeoning enervation. They slowed occasionally to drink water or swallow more pewter beads—but she never stopped running. It was like . . . like she *couldn't* stop. Vin let the exhaustion overwhelm her mind. Flared pewter was everything. She was nothing else.

Light surprised her. The sun began to rise, the mists vanishing. But Kelsier didn't let the illumination stop them. How could he? They had to run. They had to just . . . had . . . to . . . keep . . . running. . . .

I'm going to die.

It wasn't the first time the thought had occurred to Vin during the run. In fact, the idea kept circling in her mind, picking at her brain like a carrion bird. She kept moving. Running.

I hate running, she thought. *That's why I've always lived in a city, not out on the countryside. So I wouldn't have to run.*

Something within her knew that the thought didn't make any kind of sense. However, lucidity was not currently one of her virtues.

I hate Kelsier too. He just keeps on going. How long has it been since the sun rose? Minutes? Hours? Weeks? Years? I swear, I don't think—

Kelsier slowed to a stop on the road ahead of her.

Vin was so stunned that she nearly collided with him. She stumbled, slowing herself maladroitly, as if she had forgotten how to do anything other than run. She stopped, then stared down at her feet, dumbfounded.

This is wrong, she thought. *I can't just stand here. I have to be moving.*

She felt herself begin to move again, but Kelsier grabbed her. She struggled in his grip, resisting weakly.

Rest, something within her said. *Relax. You've forgotten what that is, but it's so nice. . . .*

"Vin!" Kelsier said. "Don't extinguish your pewter. Keep burning it or you'll fall unconscious!"

Vin shook her head, disoriented, trying to make out his words.

"Tin!" he said. "Flare it. Now!"

She did so. Her head blazed with a sudden headache that she had almost forgotten, and she had to close her eyes against the blinding sunlight. Her legs ached, and her feet felt even worse. The sudden wash of senses restored her sanity, however, and she blinked, looking up at Kelsier.

"Better?" he asked.

She nodded.

"You've just done something incredibly unfair to your body," Kelsier said. "It should have shut down hours ago, but you have pewter to make it keep going. You'll recover—you'll even get better at pushing yourself like this—but right now you just have to keep burning the pewter and stay awake. We can sleep later."

Vin nodded again. "Why . . ." Her voice croaked as she spoke. "Why did we stop?"

"Listen."

She did. She heard . . . voices. Yelling.

She looked up at him. "A battle?"

Kelsier nodded. "The city of Holstep is about an hour more to the north, but I think we've found what we came for. Come on."

He released her, dropping a coin and jumping over the canal. Vin followed, following him as he rushed up a nearby hill. Kelsier crested it, peeking over the top. Then he stood up, staring at something to the east. Vin crested the hill, and easily saw the battle—such as it was—in the distance. A shift in the wind brought scents to her nose.

Blood. The valley beyond was speckled with corpses. Men still fought on the far side of the valley—a small, ragged group in unmatched clothing was surrounded by a much larger, uniformed army.

"We're too late," Kelsier said. "Our men must have finished off the Holstep Garrison, then tried to march back to the caves. But Valtroux City is only a few days away, and its garrison is five thousand strong. Those soldiers got here before we did."

Squinting, using tin despite the light, Vin could see that he was right. The larger army wore imperial uniforms, and if the line of corpses was any indication, it had ambushed the skaa soldiers as it passed. Their army didn't have a chance. As she watched, the skaa began to throw up their hands, but the soldiers just kept on killing them. Some of the remaining peasants fought desperately, but they were falling almost as quickly.

"It's a slaughter," Kelsier said angrily. "The Valtroux Garrison must have orders to wipe out the entire group." He stepped forward.

"Kelsier!" Vin said, grabbing his arm. "What are you doing?"

He turned back to her. "There are still men down there. My men."

"What are you going to do—attack an entire army by yourself? For what purpose? Your rebels don't have Allomancy—they won't be able to run away on swift feet and escape. You can't stop an entire army, Kelsier."

He shook himself free of her grip; she didn't have the strength to hold on. She stumbled, falling to the rough black dirt, throwing up a puff of ash. Kelsier began to stalk down the hill toward the battlefield.

Vin climbed to her knees. "Kelsier," she said, shaking quietly with fatigue. "We aren't invincible, remember?"

He paused.

"*You're* not invincible," she whispered. "You can't stop them all. You can't save those men."

Kelsier stood quietly, his fists clenched. Then, slowly, he bowed his head. In the distance, the massacre continued, though there weren't many rebels left.

"The caves," Vin whispered. "Our force would have left men behind, right? Maybe they can tell us why the army exposed itself. Maybe you can save the ones who stayed behind. The Lord Ruler's men will certainly search out the army's headquarters—if they aren't trying already."

Kelsier nodded. "All right. Let's go."

Kelsier dropped down into the cavern. He had to flare tin to see anything in the deep darkness, lit only by a bit of reflected sunlight from far above. Vin's scraping in the crack above sounded thunderous to his overenhanced ears. In the cavern itself . . . nothing. No sound, no light.

So she was wrong, Kelsier thought. *No one stayed behind.*

Kelsier breathed out slowly, trying to find an outlet for his frustration and anger. He'd abandoned the men on the battlefield. He shook his head, ignoring what logic told him at the moment. His anger was still too fresh.

Vin dropped to the ground beside him, her figure no more than a shadow to his straining eyes.

"Empty," he declared, his voice echoing hollowly in the cavern. "You were wrong."

"No," Vin whispered. "There."

Suddenly, she was off, scrambling across the floor with a catlike litheness. Kelsier called after her in the darkness, gritted his teeth, then followed her by sound down one of the corridors.

"Vin, get back here! There's nothing—"

Kelsier paused. He could just barely make out a flicker of light ahead of him in the corridor. *Bloody hell! How did she see it from so far away?*

He could still hear Vin ahead of him. Kelsier made his way more carefully, checking his metal reserves, worried about a trap left by Ministry agents. As he drew nearer to the light, a voice called out ahead. "Who's there? Say the password!"

Kelsier continued walking, the light growing bright enough for him to see a spear-holding figure backlit in the corridor ahead. Vin waited in the darkness, crouching. She looked up questioningly as Kelsier passed. She seemed to have gotten over the drain of the pewter drag, for the moment. When they finally stopped to rest, however, she'd feel it.

"I can hear you!" the guard said anxiously. His voice sounded slightly familiar. "Identify yourself."

Captain Demoux, Kelsier realized. *One of ours. It's not a trap.*

"Say the password!" Demoux commanded.

"I need no password," Kelsier said, stepping into the light.

Demoux lowered his spear. "Lord Kelsier? You've come . . . does that mean the army succeeded?"

Kelsier ignored the question. "Why aren't you guarding the entrance back there?"

"We . . . thought it would be more defensible to retreat to the inner complex, my lord. There aren't a lot of us left."

Kelsier glanced back toward the entrance corridor. *How long until the Lord Ruler's men find a captive willing to talk? Vin was right after all—we need to get these men to safety.*

Vin stood and approached, studying the young soldier with those quiet eyes of hers. "How many of you are there?"

"About two thousand," Demoux said. "We . . . were wrong, my lord. I'm sorry."

Kelsier looked back at him. "Wrong?"

"We thought that General Yeden was acting rashly," Demoux said, blushing in shame. "We stayed behind. We . . . thought we were being loyal to you, rather than him. But we should have gone with the rest of the army."

"The army is dead," Kelsier said curtly. "Gather your men, Demoux. We need to leave *now*."

That night, sitting on a tree stump with the mists gathering around him, Kelsier finally forced himself to confront the day's events.

He sat with his hands clasped before him, listening to the last, faint sounds of the army's men bedding down. Fortunately, someone had thought to prepare the group for quick departure. Each man had a bedroll, a weapon, and enough food for two weeks. As soon as Kelsier discovered who had been so foresighted, he intended to give the man a hefty promotion.

Not that there was much to command anymore. The remaining two thousand men included a depressingly large number of soldiers who were past or before their prime—men wise enough to see that Yeden's plan had been insane, or men young enough to be frightened.

Kelsier shook his head. *So many dead.* They'd gathered nearly seven thousand troops before this fiasco, but now most of them lay dead. Yeden had apparently decided to "test" the army by striking at night against the Holstep Garrison. What had led him to such a foolish decision?

Me, Kelsier thought. *This is my fault.* He'd promised them supernatural aid. He'd set himself up, had made Yeden a part of the crew, and had talked so casually about doing the impossible. Was it any wonder that Yeden had thought he could attack the Final Empire head on, considering the confidence Kelsier had given him? Was it any wonder the soldiers would go with the man, considering the promises Kelsier had made?

Now men were dead, and Kelsier was responsible. Death wasn't new to him. Neither was failure—not anymore. But, he couldn't get over the twisting in his gut. True, the men had died fighting the Final Empire, which was as good a death as any skaa could hope for—however, the fact that they'd likely died expecting some sort of divine protection from Kelsier . . . that was disturbing.

You knew this would be hard, he told himself. *You understood the burden you were taking upon yourself.*

But, what right had he? Even members of his own crew—Ham, Breeze, and the others—assumed that the Final Empire was invincible. They followed because of their faith in Kelsier, and because he had couched his plans in the form of a thieving job. Well, now that job's patron was dead; a scout sent to check the battlefield had, for better or worse, been able to confirm Yeden's death. The soldiers had put his head on a spear beside the road, along with several of Ham's officers.

The job was dead. They had failed. The army was gone. There would be no rebellion, no seizing of the city.

Footsteps approached. Kelsier looked up, wondering if he even had the strength to stand. Vin lay curled up beside his stump, asleep on the hard ground, only her mistcloak for a cushion. Their extended pewter drag had taken a lot out of the girl, and she had collapsed virtually the moment Kelsier had called a halt for the night. He wished he could do the same. However, he was far more experienced with pewter dragging than she was. His body would give out eventually, but he could keep going for a bit longer.

A figure appeared from the mists, hobbling in Kelsier's direction. The man was old, older than any that Kelsier had recruited. He must have been part of the rebellion from earlier—one of the skaa who had been living in the caves before Kelsier hijacked them.

The man chose a large stone beside Kelsier's stump, sitting with a sigh. It was amazing that one so old had even been able to keep up. Kelsier had moved the group at a fast pace, seeking to distance them as much as possible from the cave complex.

"The men will sleep fitfully," the old man said. "They aren't accustomed to being out in the mists."

"They don't have much choice," Kelsier said.

The old man shook his head. "I suppose they don't." He sat for a moment, aged eyes unreadable. "You don't recognize me, do you?"

Kelsier paused, then shook his head. "I'm sorry. Did I recruit you?"

"After a fashion. I was one of the skaa at Lord Tresting's plantation."

Kelsier opened his mouth slightly in surprise, finally recognizing a slight familiarity to the man's bald head and tired, yet somehow strong, posture. "The old man I sat with that night. Your name was . . ."

"Mennis. After you killed Tresting, we retreated up to the caves, where the rebels there took us in. A lot of the others left eventually, off to find other plantations to join. Some of us stayed."

Kelsier nodded. "You're behind this, aren't you?" he said, gesturing toward the camp. "The preparations?"

Mennis shrugged. "Some of us can't fight, so we do other things."

Kelsier leaned forward. "What happened, Mennis? Why did Yeden do this?"

Mennis just shook his head. "Though most expect young men to be fools, I've noticed that just a little bit of age can make a man far more foolish than he was as a child. Yeden . . . well, he was the type who was too easily impressed—both by you and by the reputation you left for him. Some of his generals thought it might be a good idea to give the men some practical battle experience, and they figured a night raid on the Holstep Garrison would be a clever move. Apparently, it was more difficult than they assumed."

Kelsier shook his head. "Even if they'd been successful, exposing the army would have made it useless to us."

"They believed in you," Mennis said quietly. "They thought that they couldn't fail."

Kelsier sighed, resting his head back, staring up into the shifting mists. He slowly let his breath exhale, its air mingling with the currents overhead.

"So, what becomes of us?" Mennis asked.

"We'll split you up," Kelsier said, "get you back into Luthadel in small groups, lose you among the skaa population."

Mennis nodded. He seemed tired—exhausted—yet he didn't retire. Kelsier could understand that feeling.

"Do you remember our conversation back on Tresting's plantation?" Mennis asked.

"A bit," Kelsier said. "You tried to dissuade me from making trouble."

"But it didn't stop you."

"Troublemaking is just about the only thing I'm good at, Mennis. Do you resent what I did there, what I forced you to become?"

Mennis paused, then nodded. "But, in a way, I'm thankful for that resentment. I believed that my life was over—I awoke each day expecting that I wouldn't have the strength to rise. But . . . well, I found purpose again in the caves. For that, I'm grateful."

"Even after what I did to the army?"

Mennis snorted. "Don't think quite so highly of yourself, young man. Those soldiers got *themselves* killed. You might have been their motivation, but you didn't make the choice for them.

"Regardless, this isn't the first skaa rebellion to get slaughtered. Not by far. In a way, you've accomplished a lot—you gathered an army of considerable size, and then you armed and trained it beyond what anyone had a right to expect. Things went a little more quickly than you anticipated, but you should be proud of yourself."

"Proud?" Kelsier asked, standing to work off some of his agitation. "This army was supposed to help overthrow the Final Empire, not get itself killed fighting a meaningless battle in a valley weeks outside of Luthadel."

"Overthrow the . . ." Mennis looked up, frowning. "You really expected to do something like that?"

"Of course," Kelsier said. "Why else would I gather an army like this?"

"To resist," Mennis said. "To fight. That's why those lads came to the caves. It wasn't a matter of winning or losing, it was a matter of doing something—anything—to struggle against the Lord Ruler."

Kelsier turned, frowning. "You expected the army to lose from the beginning?"

"What other end was there?" Mennis asked. He stood, shaking his head. "Some may have begun to dream otherwise, lad, but the Lord Ruler can't be defeated. Once, I gave you some advice—I told you to be careful which battles you chose to fight. Well, I've realized that this battle *was* worth fighting.

"Now, let me give you another piece of advice, Kelsier, Survivor of Hathsin. Know when to quit. You've done well, better than any would have expected. Those skaa of yours killed an entire garrison's worth of soldiers before they were caught and destroyed. This is the greatest victory the skaa have known in decades, perhaps centuries. Now it's time to walk away."

With that, the old man nodded his head in respect, then began to shuffle back toward the center of the camp.

Kelsier stood, dumbfounded. *The greatest victory the skaa have known in decades . . .*

That was what he fought against. Not just the Lord Ruler, not just the nobility. He fought against a thousand years of conditioning, a thousand years of life in a society that would label the deaths of five thousand men as a "great victory." Life was so hopeless for the skaa that they'd been reduced to finding comfort in expected defeats.

"That wasn't a victory, Mennis," Kelsier whispered. "I'll *show* you a victory."

He forced himself to smile—not out of pleasure, and not out of satisfaction. He smiled despite the grief he felt at the deaths of his men; he smiled because that was what he did. That was how he proved to the Lord Ruler—and to himself—that he wasn't beaten.

No, he wasn't going to walk away. He wasn't finished yet. Not by far.

THE END OF PART THREE

PART FOUR

DANCERS IN
A SEA OF MIST

I am growing so very tired.

26

VIN LAY IN HER BED at Clubs's shop, feeling her head throb.

Fortunately, the headache was growing weaker. She could still remember waking up on that first horrible morning; the pain had been so strong she'd barely been able to think, let alone move. She didn't know how Kelsier had kept going, leading the remnants of their army to a safe location.

That had been over two weeks ago. Fifteen full days, and her head *still* hurt. Kelsier said it was good for her. He claimed that she needed to practice "pewter dragging," training her body to function beyond what it thought possible. Despite what he said, however, she doubted something that hurt so much could possibly be "good" for her.

Of course, it might well be a useful skill to have. She could acknowledge this, now that her head wasn't pounding quite so much. She and Kelsier had been able to run to the battlefield in under a single day. The return trip had taken two weeks.

Vin rose, stretching tiredly. They'd been back for less than a day, in fact. Kelsier had probably stayed up half the night explaining events to the other crewmembers. Vin, however, had been happy to go straight to bed. The nights spent sleeping on the hard earth had reminded her that a comfortable bed was a luxury she'd started to take for granted.

She yawned, rubbed her temples again, then threw on a robe and made her way to the bathroom. She was pleased to see that Clubs's apprentices had remembered to draw her a bath. She locked the door, disrobed, and settled into the warm, lightly scented bathwater. Had she ever really found those scents obnoxious? The smell would make her less inconspicuous, true, but that seemed a slim price for ridding herself of the dirt and grime she'd picked up while traveling.

She still found longer hair an annoyance, however. She washed it, combing out the tangles and knots, wondering how the court women could stand hair that went all the way down their backs. How long must they spend combing and primping beneath a servant's care? Vin's hair hadn't even reached her shoulders yet, and she was already loath to let it get longer. It would fly about and whip her face when she jumped, not to mention provide her foes with something to grab on to.

Once finished bathing, she returned to her room, dressed in something practical, and made her way downstairs. Apprentices bustled in the workroom and housekeepers worked upstairs, but the kitchen was quiet. Clubs, Dockson, Ham, and Breeze sat at the morning meal. They looked up as Vin entered.

"What?" Vin asked grumpily, pausing in the doorway. The bath had soothed her headache somewhat, but it still pulsed slightly in the back of her head.

The four men exchanged glances. Ham spoke first. "We were just discussing the status of the plan, now that both our employer and our army are gone."

Breeze raised an eyebrow. "Status? That's an interesting way of putting it, Hammond. I would have said 'unfeasibility' instead."

Clubs grunted his assent, and the four turned to her, apparently waiting to see her reaction.

Why do they care so much what I think? she thought, walking into the room and taking a chair.

"You want something to eat?" Dockson said, rising. "Clubs's housekeepers fixed some baywraps for us to—"

"Ale," Vin said.

Dockson paused. "It's not even noon."

"Ale. Now. Please." She leaned forward, folding her arms on the table and resting her head on them.

Ham had the nerve to chuckle. "Pewter drag?"

Vin nodded.

"It'll pass," he said.

"If I don't die first," Vin grumbled.

Ham chuckled again, but the levity seemed forced. Dox handed her a mug, then sat, glancing at the others. "So, Vin. What *do* you think?"

"I don't know," she said with a sigh. "The army was pretty much the center of everything, right? Breeze, Ham, and Yeden spent all their time recruiting; Dockson and Renoux worked on supplies. Now that the soldiers are gone . . . well, that only leaves Marsh's work with the Ministry and Kell's attacks on the nobility—and neither are things he needs us for. The crew is redundant."

The room fell silent.

"She has a depressingly blunt way of putting it," Dockson said.

"Pewter drag will do that to you," Ham noted.

"When did *you* get back, anyway?" Vin asked.

"Last night, after you were asleep," Ham said. "The Garrison sent us part-time soldiers back early, so they wouldn't have to pay us."

"They're still out there, then?" Dockson asked.

Ham nodded. "Hunting down the rest of our army. The Luthadel Garrison relieved the Valtroux troops, who were actually pretty beat up from the fighting. The majority of the Luthadel troops should be out for a long while yet, searching for rebels—apparently, several very large groups broke off of our main army and fled before the battle started."

The conversation lulled into another period of silence. Vin sipped at her ale, drinking it more out of spite than any belief that it would make her feel better. A few minutes later, footsteps sounded on the stairs.

Kelsier swept into the kitchen. "Good morning, all," he said with customary cheerfulness. "Baywraps again, I see. Clubs, you really need to hire more imaginative housemaids." Despite the comment, he grabbed a cylindrical baywrap and took a large bite, then smiled pleasantly as he poured himself something to drink.

The crew remained quiet. The men exchanged glances. Kelsier remained standing, leaning back against the cupboard as he ate.

"Kell, we need to talk," Dockson finally said. "The army is gone."

"Yes," Kelsier said between bites. "I noticed."

"The job is dead, Kelsier," Breeze said. "It was a good try, but we failed."

Kelsier paused. He frowned, lowering his baywrap. "Failed? What makes you say that?"

"The army is gone, Kell," Ham said.

"The army was only one piece of our plans. We've had a setback, true—but we're hardly finished."

"Oh, for the Lord's sake, man!" Breeze said. "How can you stand there so cheerfully? Our men are *dead*. Don't you even care?"

"I care, Breeze," Kelsier said in a solemn voice. "But what is done is done. We need to move on."

"Exactly!" Breeze said. "Move on from this insane 'job' of yours. It's time to quit. I know you don't like that, but it's the simple truth!"

Kelsier set his plate on the counter. "Don't Soothe me, Breeze. *Never* Soothe me."

Breeze paused, mouth open slightly. "Fine," he finally said. "I won't use Allomancy; I'll just use truth. Do you know what I think? I think you never intended to grab that atium.

"You've been using us. You promised us wealth so we'd join you, but you never had any intention of making us rich. This is all about your ego—it's about becoming the most famous crewleader that ever lived. *That's* why you're spreading all these rumors, doing all this recruitment. You've known wealth—now you want to become a legend."

Breeze fell quiet, eyes hard. Kelsier stood with his arms folded, regarding the crew. Several glanced aside, shamed eyes proving that they had considered what Breeze was saying. Vin was one of those. The silence persisted, all of them waiting for a rebuttal.

Footsteps sounded on the stairs again, and Spook burst into the kitchen. "Willing the care and upping to see! A gathering, in the fountain square!"

Kelsier didn't look surprised by the boy's announcement.

"A gathering in the fountain square?" Ham said slowly. "That means . . ."

"Come on," Kelsier said, standing up straight. "We're going to watch."

"I'd rather not do this, Kell," Ham said. "I avoid these things for a reason."

Kelsier ignored him. He walked at the head of the crew, who all—even Breeze—wore mundane skaa clothing and cloaks. A light ashfall had begun, and careless flakes floated down from the sky, like leaves dropped from some unseen tree.

Large clusters of skaa clogged the street, most of them workers from factories or mills. Vin knew of only one reason why the workers would be released and sent to gather in the city's central square.

Executions.

She'd never gone to them before. Supposedly, all the men in the city—skaa or noble—were required to attend execution ceremonies, but thieving crews knew how to remain hidden. Bells rang in the distance, announcing the event, and obligators watched at the sides of the streets. They would go into mills, forges, and random houses searching for those who disobeyed the call, meting out death as a punishment. Gathering this many people was an enormous undertaking—but, in a way, doing things like this simply worked to prove how powerful the Lord Ruler was.

The streets grew even more crowded as Vin's crew approached the fountain square. Building roofs were packed, and people filled the streets, pressing forward. *There's no way they'll all fit.* Luthadel wasn't like most other cities; its population was enormous. Even with only the men in attendance, there was no way everyone would have a view of the executions.

Yet, they came anyway. Partially because they were required, partially because they wouldn't have to work while they watched, and partially—Vin suspected—because they had the same morbid curiosity that all men possessed.

As the crowds grew thicker, Kelsier, Dockson, and Ham began to shove the crew a path through the onlookers. Some of the skaa gave the crew looks of resentment, though many were just dull-eyed and compliant. Some appeared surprised, even excited, when they saw Kelsier, though his scars were not showing. These people moved aside eagerly.

Eventually, the crew reached the outer row of buildings surrounding the square. Kelsier picked one, nodding toward it, and Dockson moved forward. A man at the doorway tried to bar his entrance, but Dox pointed toward the roof, then hefted his coinpouch suggestively. A few minutes later, the crew had the entire rooftop to themselves.

"Smoke us please, Clubs," Kelsier said quietly.

The gnarled craftsman nodded, making the crew invisible to Allomantic bronze senses. Vin walked over and crouched beside the roof's lip, hands on the short stone railing as she scanned the square down below. "So many people . . ."

"You've lived in cities all your life, Vin," Ham said, standing next to her. "Surely you've seen crowds before."

"Yes, but . . ." How could she explain? The shifting, overpacked mass was unlike anything she'd seen. It was expansive, almost endless, its trails filling every street leading away from the central square. The skaa were packed so closely, she wondered how they even had room to breathe.

The noblemen were at the center of the square, separated from the skaa by soldiers. They were close to the central fountain patio, which stood about five feet above the rest of the square. Someone had constructed seating for the nobility, and they lounged, as if they were visiting some show or horse race. Many had servants holding up parasols against the ash, but it was falling lightly enough that some just ignored it.

Standing beside the noblemen were the obligators—regular ones in gray, Inquisitors in black. Vin shivered. There were eight Inquisitors, their lanky forms standing a head above the obligators. But, it wasn't just height that separated the dark creatures from their cousins. There was an air, a distinctive posture, about the Steel Inquisitors.

Vin turned, studying the regular obligators instead. Most of them held themselves proudly in their administrative robes—the higher their position, the finer the robes. Vin squinted, burning tin, and recognized a moderately familiar face.

"There," she said, pointing. "That one's my father."

Kelsier perked up. "Where?"

"At the front of the obligators," Vin said. "The shorter one with the golden robe-scarf."

Kelsier fell silent. "*That's* your father?" he finally asked.

"Who?" Dockson asked, squinting. "I can't make out their faces."

"Tevidian," Kelsier said.

"The *lord prelan?*" Dockson asked with shock.

"What?" Vin asked. "Who's that?"

Breeze chuckled. "The lord prelan is the leader of the Ministry, my dear. He's the most important of the Lord Ruler's obligators—technically, he's even higher ranked than the Inquisitors."

Vin sat, dumbfounded.

"The lord prelan," Dockson mumbled, shaking his head. "This just keeps getting better."

"Look!" Spook suddenly said, pointing.

The crowd of skaa began to shuffle. Vin had assumed that they were too packed to move, but apparently she was wrong. The people began to pull back, making a large corridor leading to the central platform.

What could make them—

Then she felt it. The oppressive numbness, like a massive blanket pressing down, choking away her air, stealing her will. She immediately burned copper. Yet, like before, she swore that she could feel the Lord Ruler's Soothing despite the metal. She sensed him coming closer, trying to make her lose all will, all desire, all strength of emotion.

"He's coming," Spook whispered, crouching down beside her.

A black carriage drawn by a pair of massive white stallions appeared down a side street. It rolled down the corridor of skaa, moving with a sense of . . . inevitability. Vin saw several people get clipped by its passing, and suspected that if a man were to fall into the carriage's path, the vehicle wouldn't even slow as it crushed him to death.

The skaa sagged a bit more as the Lord Ruler arrived, a visible ripple washing across the crowd, their postures drooping as they felt his powerful Soothing. The background roar of whispers and chatting dampened, an unreal silence falling over the enormous square.

"He's so *powerful*," Breeze said. "Even at my best, I can only Soothe a couple hundred men. There have to be tens of thousands of people here!"

Spook looked over the rim of the rooftop. "It makes me want to fall. To just let go . . ."

Then, he paused. He shook his head, as if waking up. Vin frowned. Something felt different. Tentatively, she extinguished her copper, and realized that she could no longer feel the Lord Ruler's Soothing. The feeling of awful depression—of soullessness and emptiness—had strangely disappeared. Spook looked up, and the rest of the crewmembers stood just a little straighter.

Vin glanced around. The skaa below looked unchanged. Yet, her friends—

Her eyes found Kelsier. The crewleader stood straight-backed, staring resolutely at the approaching carriage, a look of concentration on his face.

He's Rioting our emotions, Vin realized. *He's counteracting the Lord Ruler's power.* It was obviously a struggle for Kelsier to protect even their small group.

Breeze is right, Vin thought. *How can we fight something like this? The Lord Ruler is Soothing a hundred thousand people at once!*

But, Kelsier fought on. Just in case, Vin turned on her copper. Then she burned zinc and reached out to help Kelsier, Rioting the emotions of those around her. It felt like she was Pulling against some massive, immobile wall. Yet, it must have helped, for Kelsier relaxed slightly, shooting her a grateful look.

"Look," Dockson said, probably unaware of the unseen battle that occurred around him. "The prisoner carts." He pointed toward a set of ten large, bar-lined carts traveling down the corridor behind the Lord Ruler.

"Do you recognize anyone in them?" Ham said, leaning forward.

"I'm not of the seeing," Spook said, looking uncomfortable. "Uncle, you really the burn, right?"

"Yes, my copper is on," Clubs said testily. "You're safe. We're far enough away from the Lord Ruler that it wouldn't matter anyway—that plaza is enormous."

Spook nodded, then obviously began burning tin. A moment later, he shook his head. "Notting of the recognizing anyone."

"You weren't there for a lot of the recruiting, though, Spook," Ham said, squinting.

"True," Spook replied. Though his accent remained, he was obviously making an effort to speak normally.

Kelsier stepped up to the ledge, holding a hand up to shade his eyes. "I can see the prisoners. No, I don't recognize any of the faces. They aren't captive soldiers."

"Who, then?" Ham asked.

"Mostly women and children, it appears," Kelsier said.

"The families of the soldiers?" Ham asked, horrified.

Kelsier shook his head. "I doubt it. They wouldn't have taken the time to identify dead skaa."

Ham frowned, looking confused.

"Random people, Hammond," Breeze said with a quiet sigh. "Examples—casual executions made in order to punish the skaa for harboring rebels."

"No, not even that," Kelsier said. "I doubt the Lord Ruler even knows, or cares, that most of those men were recruited from Luthadel. He probably just assumes that it was another countryside rebellion. This . . . this is just a way of reminding everyone who is in control."

The Lord Ruler's carriage rolled up a platform onto the central patio. The ominous vehicle pulled to a stop in the exact center of the square, but the Lord Ruler himself remained inside.

The prisoner carts pulled to a stop, and a group of obligators and soldiers began to unload them. Black ash continued to fall as the first group of prisoners—most struggling only weakly—were dragged up onto the raised central platform. An Inquisitor directed the work, gesturing for prisoners to be gathered beside each of the platform's four bowl-like fountains.

Four prisoners were forced to their knees—one beside each running fountain—and four Inquisitors raised obsidian axes. Four axes fell, and four heads were sheared free. The bodies, still held by soldiers, were allowed to spurt their last lifeblood into the fountain basins.

The fountains began to glisten red as they sprayed into the air. The soldiers tossed the bodies aside, then brought four more people forward.

Spook looked away sickly. "Why . . . why doesn't Kelsier do something? To saving them, I mean?"

"Don't be foolish," Vin said. "There are *eight* Inquisitors down there—not to mention the Lord Ruler himself. Kelsier would be an idiot to try something."

Though I wouldn't be surprised if he considered it, she thought, remembering when Kelsier had been ready to rush down and take on an entire army by himself. She glanced to the side. Kelsier looked like he was forcibly holding himself back—white-knuckled hands gripping the chimney beside him—to keep himself from rushing down to stop the executions.

Spook stumbled over to another part of the rooftop where he could retch without spilling bile onto the people below. Ham groaned slightly, and even Clubs looked saddened. Dockson watched solemnly, as if witnessing the deaths were some sort of vigil. Breeze just shook his head.

Kelsier, however . . . Kelsier was angry. His face red, his muscles tense, his eyes ablaze.

Four more deaths, one of them a child.

"This," Kelsier said, angrily waving his hand toward the central square. "*This* is our enemy. There is no quarter here, no walking away. This is no simple job, to be thrown aside when we encounter a few unexpected twists."

Four more deaths.

"Look at them!" Kelsier demanded, pointing at the bleachers full of nobility. Most of them appeared bored—and a few even seemed to be enjoying themselves, turning and joking with one another as the beheadings continued.

"I know you question me," Kelsier said, turning to the crew. "You think that I've been too hard on the nobility, think that I relish killing them too much. But, can you honestly see those men laughing and tell me that they don't *deserve* to die by my blade? I only bring them justice."

Four more deaths.

Vin searched the bleachers with urgent, tin-enhanced eyes. She found Elend sitting amid a group of younger men. None of them were laughing, and they weren't the only ones. True, many of the nobility made light of the experience, but there were some small minority who looked horrified.

Kelsier continued. "Breeze, you asked about the atium. I'll be honest. It was never my main goal—I gathered this crew because I wanted to change things. We'll grab the atium—we'll need it to support a new government—but this job isn't about making me, or any of you, wealthy.

"Yeden is dead. He was our excuse—a way that we could do something good while still pretending to just be thieves. Now that he's gone, you can give up, if you want. Quit. But, that won't change anything. The struggle will go on. Men will still die. You'll just be ignoring it."

Four more deaths.

"It's time to stop the charade," Kelsier said, staring at them each in turn. "If we're going to do this now, we have to be up-front and honest with ourselves. We have to admit that it isn't about money. It's about stopping *that*." He pointed at the courtyard with its red fountains—a visible sign of death for the thousands of skaa too far away to even tell what was happening.

"I intend to continue my fight," Kelsier said quietly. "I realize that some of you question my leadership. You think I've been building myself up too much with the skaa. You whisper that I'm making myself into another Lord Ruler—you think that my ego is more important to me than overthrowing the empire."

He paused, and Vin saw guilt in the eyes of Dockson and the others. Spook rejoined the group, still looking a bit sick.

Four more deaths.

"You're wrong," Kelsier said quietly. "You have to trust me. You gave me your confidence when we began this plan, despite how dangerous things seemed. I still need that confidence! No matter how things appear, no matter how terrible the odds, we have to keep fighting!"

Four more deaths.

The crew slowly turned toward Kelsier. Resisting the Lord Ruler's Pushing on their emotions didn't seem like half as much a struggle for Kelsier anymore, though Vin had let her zinc lapse.

Maybe . . . maybe he can *do it,* Vin thought, despite herself. If there was ever a man who could defeat the Lord Ruler, it would be Kelsier.

"I didn't choose you men because of your competence," Kelsier said, "though you are certainly skilled. I chose each of you specifically because I knew you to be men of conscience. Ham, Breeze, Dox, Clubs . . . you are men with reputations for honesty, even charity. I knew that if I were going to succeed at this plan, I would need men who actually *cared*.

"No, Breeze, this isn't about boxings or about glory. This is about war—a war we have been fighting for a thousand years, a war I intend to end. You may go, if you wish. You know I'll let any of you out—no questions asked, no repercussions exacted—if you wish to go.

"However," he said, eyes growing hard, "if you stay, you have to promise to stop questioning my authority. You can voice concerns about the job itself, but there will be no more whispered conferences about my leadership. If you stay, you follow me. Understood?"

One by one, he locked eyes with the crewmembers. Each one gave him a nod.

"I don't think we ever really questioned you, Kell," Dockson said. "We just . . . we're worried, and I think rightly so. The army was a big part of our plans."

Kelsier nodded to the north, toward the main city gates. "What do you see up in the distance, Dox?"

"The city gates?"

"And what is different about them recently?"

Dockson shrugged. "Nothing unusual. They're a bit understaffed, but—"

"Why?" Kelsier interjected. "Why are they understaffed?"

Dockson paused. "Because the Garrison is gone?"

"Exactly," Kelsier said. "Ham says that the Garrison could be out chasing remnants of our army for months, and only about ten percent of its men stayed behind. That makes sense—stopping rebels is the sort of thing the Garrison was created to do. Luthadel might be exposed, but no one ever attacks Luthadel. No one ever has."

A quiet understanding passed between the members of the crew.

"Part one of our plan to take the city has been accomplished," Kelsier said. "We got the Garrison out of Luthadel. It cost us far more than we expected—far more than it should have. I wish to the Forgotten Gods that those boys hadn't died. Unfortunately, we can't change that now—we can only use the opening they gave us.

"The plan is still in motion—the main peacekeeping force in the city is gone. If a house war starts in earnest, the Lord Ruler will have a difficult time stopping it. Assuming he wants to. For some reason, he tends to step back and let the nobility fight each other every hundred years or so. Perhaps he finds that letting them at each other's throats keeps them away from his own."

"But, what if the Garrison comes back?" Ham asked.

"If I'm right," Kelsier said, "the Lord Ruler will let them chase stragglers from our army for several months, giving the nobility a chance to blow off a little steam. Except, he's going to get a lot more than he expected. When that house war starts, we're going to use the chaos to seize the palace."

"With what army, my dear man?" Breeze said.

"We still have some troops left," Kelsier said. "Plus, we have time to recruit more. We'll have to be careful—we can't use the caves, so we'll have to hide our troops in the city. That will probably mean smaller numbers. However, that won't be an issue—you see, that garrison is going to return eventually."

The members of the group shared a look as the executions proceeded below. Vin sat quietly, trying to decide what Kelsier meant by that statement.

"Exactly, Kell," Ham said slowly. "The Garrison will return, and we won't have a big enough army to fight them."

"But we *will* have the Lord Ruler's treasury," Kelsier said, smiling. "What is it you always say about those Garrisoners, Ham?"

The Thug paused, then smiled too. "That they're mercenaries."

"We seize the Lord Ruler's money," Kelsier said, "and it means we get his army too. This can still work, gentlemen. We can *make* it work."

The crew seemed to grow more confident. Vin, however, turned her eyes back toward the square. The fountains ran so red that they seemed completely filled with blood. Over it all, the Lord Ruler watched from within his jet-black carriage. The windows were open, and—with tin—Vin could just barely see a silhouetted figure sitting within.

That's our real foe, she thought. *Not the missing garrison, not the Inquisitors with their axes. That man. The one from the logbook.*

We'll have to find a way to defeat him, otherwise everything else we do will be pointless.

I think I've finally discovered why Rashek resents me so very much. He does not believe that an outsider such as myself—a foreigner—could possibly be the Hero of Ages. He believes that I have somehow tricked the philosophers, that I wear the piercings of the Hero unjustly.

According to Rashek, only a Terrisman of pure blood should have been chosen as the Hero. Oddly, I find myself even more determined because of his hatred. I must prove to him that I can perform this task

27

IT WAS A SUBDUED GROUP that returned to Clubs's shop that evening. The executions had stretched for hours. There had been no denunciations, no explanations by the Ministry or the Lord Ruler—just execution, after execution, after execution. Once the captives were gone, the Lord Ruler and his obligators had ridden away, leaving a pile of corpses on the platform and bloodied water running in the fountains.

As Kelsier's crew returned to the kitchen, Vin realized that her headache no longer bothered her. Her pain now seemed . . . insignificant. The baywraps remained on the table, thoughtfully covered by one of the house maids. No one reached for them.

"All right," Kelsier said, taking his customary place leaning against the cupboard. "Let's plan this out. How should we proceed?"

Dockson recovered a stack of papers from the side of the room as he walked over to seat himself. "With the Garrison gone, our main focus becomes the nobility."

"Indeed," Breeze said. "If we truly intend to seize the treasury with only a few thousand soldiers, then we're certainly going to need something to distract the palace guard and keep the nobility from taking the city away from us. The house war, therefore, becomes of paramount importance."

Kelsier nodded. "My thoughts exactly."

"But, what happens when the house war is over?" Vin said. "Some houses will come out on top, and then we'll have to deal with them."

Kelsier shook his head. "I don't intend for the house war to ever end, Vin— or, at least, not for a long while. The Lord Ruler makes dictates, and the Ministry polices his followers, but the nobility are the ones who actually force the skaa to work. So, if we bring down enough noble houses, the government may just collapse on its own. We can't fight the entire Final Empire as a whole—it's too big. But, we might be able to shatter it, then make the pieces fight each other."

"We need to put financial strain on the Great Houses," Dockson said, flipping through his papers. "The aristocracy is primarily a financial institution, and lack of funds will bring *any* house down."

"Breeze, we might need to use some of your aliases," Kelsier said. "So far, I've really been the only one in the crew working on the house war—but if we're going to make this city snap before the Garrison returns, we'll need to step up our efforts."

Breeze sighed. "Very well. We'll just have to be very careful to make certain no one accidentally recognizes me as someone I shouldn't be. I can't go to parties or functions—but I can probably do solitary house visits."

"Same for you, Dox," Kelsier said.

"I figured as much," Dockson said.

"It will be dangerous for both of you," Kelsier said. "But speed will be essential. Vin will remain our main spy—and we'll probably want her to start spreading some bad information. Anything to make the nobility uncertain."

Ham nodded. "We should probably focus our attentions on the top, then."

"Indeed," Breeze said. "If we can make the most powerful houses look vulnerable, then their enemies will be quick to strike. Only after the powerful houses are gone will people realize that *they* were the ones really supporting the economy."

The room fell quiet for a second, then several heads turned toward Vin.

"What?" she asked.

"They're talking about House Venture, Vin," Dockson said. "It's the most powerful of the Great Houses."

Breeze nodded. "If Venture falls, the entire Final Empire would feel the tremors."

Vin sat quietly for a moment. "They're not all bad people," she finally said.

"Perhaps," Kelsier said. "But Lord Straff Venture certainly is, and his family sits at the very head of the Final Empire. House Venture needs to go—and you already have an in with one of its most important members."

I thought you wanted me to stay away from Elend, she thought with annoyance.

"Just keep your ears open, child," Breeze said. "See if you can get the lad to talk about his house's finances. Find us a bit of leverage, and we'll do the rest."

Just like the games Elend hates so much. However, the executions were still fresh in her mind. That sort of thing had to be stopped. Besides—even Elend said he didn't like his father, or his house, very much. Maybe . . . maybe she could find something. "I'll see what I can do," she said.

A knock came at the front door, answered by one of the apprentices. A few moments later, Sazed—clad in a skaa cloak to hide his features—entered the kitchen.

Kelsier checked the clock. "You're early, Saze."

"I try to make it a habit, Master Kelsier," the Terrisman replied.

Dockson raised an eyebrow. "That's a habit someone else could afford to pick up."

Kelsier snorted. "If you're always on time, it implies that you never have anything better you should be doing. Saze, how are the men?"

"As good as can be expected, Master Kelsier," Sazed replied. "But they can't hide in the Renoux warehouses forever."

"I know," Kelsier said. "Dox, Ham, I'll need you to work on this problem. There are two thousand men left from our army; I want you to get them into Luthadel."

Dockson nodded thoughtfully. "We'll find a way."

"You want us to keep training them?" Ham asked.

Kelsier nodded.

"Then we'll have to hide them in squads," he said. "We don't have the resources to train men individually. Say . . . a couple hundred men per team? Hidden in slums near one another?"

"Make sure none of the teams know about the others," Dockson said. "Or even that we still intend to strike at the palace. With that many men in town, there's a chance some of them will eventually get taken by the obligators for one reason or another."

Kelsier nodded. "Tell each group that it's the only one that didn't get disbanded, and that it's being retained just in case it's needed at some point in the future."

"You also said that recruitment needed to be continued," Ham said.

Kelsier nodded. "I'd like at least twice as many troops before we try and pull this off."

"That's going to be tough," Ham said, "considering our army's failure."

"What failure?" Kelsier asked. "Tell them the truth—that our army successfully neutralized the Garrison."

"Though most of them died doing it," Ham said.

"We can gloss over that part," Breeze said. "The people will be angry at the executions—that should make them more willing to listen to us."

"Gathering more troops is going to be your main task over the next few months, Ham," Kelsier said.

"That's not much time," Ham said. "But, I'll see what I can do."

"Good," Kelsier said. "Saze, did the note come?"

"It did, Master Kelsier," Sazed said, pulling a letter from beneath his cloak and handing it to Kelsier.

"And what would that be?" Breeze asked curiously.

"A message from Marsh," Kelsier said, opening the letter and scanning its contents. "He's in the city, and he has news."

"What news?" Ham asked.

"He doesn't say," Kelsier said, grabbing a baywrap. "But he gave instructions on where to meet him tonight." He walked over, picking up a regular skaa cloak. "I'm going to go scout the location before it gets dark. Coming, Vin?"

She nodded, standing.

"The rest of you keep working on the plan," Kelsier said. "In two months' time, I want this city to be so tense that when it finally breaks, even the Lord Ruler won't be able to hold it together."

"There's something you're not telling us, isn't there?" Vin said, looking away from the window, turning toward Kelsier. "A part of the plan."

Kelsier glanced over at her in the darkness. Marsh's chosen meeting place was an abandoned building within the Twists, one of the most impoverished skaa slums. Kelsier had located a second abandoned building across from the one they would meet in, and he and Vin waited on the top floor, watching the street for signs of Marsh.

"Why do you ask me that?" Kelsier finally said.

"Because of the Lord Ruler," Vin said, picking at the rotting wood of her windowsill. "I felt his power today. I don't think the others could sense it, not like a Mistborn can. But I know you must have." She looked up again, meeting Kelsier's eyes. "You're still planning to get him out of the city before we try to take the palace, right?"

"Don't worry about the Lord Ruler," Kelsier said. "The Eleventh Metal will take care of him."

Vin frowned. Outside, the sun was setting in a fiery blaze of frustration. The mists would come soon, and supposedly Marsh would arrive a short time later.

The Eleventh Metal, she thought, remembering the skepticism with which the other crewmembers regarded it. "Is it real?" Vin asked.

"The Eleventh Metal? Of course it is—I showed it to you, remember?"

"That's not what I mean," she said. "Are the legends real? Are you lying?"

Kelsier turned toward her, frowning slightly. Then he smirked. "You're a very blunt girl, Vin."

"I know."

Kelsier's smile deepened. "The answer is no. I'm not lying. The legends are real, though it took some time for me to find them."

"And that bit of metal you showed us really is the Eleventh Metal?"

"I think so," Kelsier said.

"But you don't know how to use it."

Kelsier paused, then shook his head. "No. I don't."

"That's not very comforting."

Kelsier shrugged, turning to look out the window. "Even if I don't discover the secret in time, I doubt the Lord Ruler will be as big a problem as you think. He's a powerful Allomancer, but he doesn't know everything—if he did, we'd be dead right now. He's not omnipotent, either—if he were, he wouldn't have needed to execute all of those skaa to try and frighten the city into submission.

"I don't know what he is—but I think he's more like a man than he is a god. The words in that logbook . . . they're the words of a regular person. His real power comes from his armies and his wealth. If we remove them, he won't be able to do anything to stop his empire from collapsing."

Vin frowned. "He might not be a god, but . . . he's something, Kelsier. Something different. Today, when he was in the square, I could feel his touch on my emotions even when I was burning copper."

"That's not possible, Vin," Kelsier said with a shake of his head. "If it were, Inquisitors would be able to sense Allomancy even when there was a Smoker nearby. If that were the case, don't you think they'd hunt down all of the skaa Mistings and kill them?"

Vin shrugged.

"You know the Lord Ruler is strong," Kelsier said, "and you feel like you *should* still be able to sense him. So you do."

Maybe he's right, she thought, picking off another bit of the windowsill. *He's been an Allomancer for far longer than I have, after all.*

But . . . I felt something, didn't I? And the Inquisitor that nearly killed me—somehow, he found me in the darkness and rain. He must have sensed something.

She let the matter drop, however. "The Eleventh Metal. Couldn't we just try it and see what it does?"

"It's not that simple," Kelsier said. "You remember how I told you never to burn a metal that wasn't one of the ten?"

Vin nodded.

"Burning another metal can be deadly," Kelsier said. "Even getting the wrong mixture in an alloy metal can make you sick. If I'm wrong about the Eleventh Metal . . ."

"It will kill you," Vin said quietly.

Kelsier nodded.

So, you're not quite as certain as you pretend, she decided. *Otherwise, you'd have tried it by now.*

"That's what you want to find in the logbook," Vin said. "A clue about how to use the Eleventh Metal."

Kelsier nodded. "I'm afraid we weren't very lucky in that respect. So far, the logbook hasn't even mentioned Allomancy."

"Though it does talk about Feruchemy," Vin said.

Kelsier eyed her as he stood by his window, one shoulder leaning against the wall. "So Sazed told you about that?"

Vin glanced down. "I . . . kind of forced him to."

Kelsier chuckled. "I wonder what I've unleashed upon the world by teaching you Allomancy. Of course, my trainer said the same thing about me."

"He was right to worry."

"Of course he was."

Vin smiled. Outside, the sunlight was nearly gone, and diaphanous patches of mist were beginning to form in the air. They hung like ghosts, slowly growing larger, extending their influence as night approached.

"Sazed didn't have time to tell me much about Feruchemy," Vin said carefully. "What kind of things can it do?" She waited in trepidation, assuming that Kelsier would see through her lie.

"Feruchemy is completely internal," Kelsier said in an offhand voice. "It can provide some of the same things we get from pewter and tin—strength, endurance, eyesight—but each attribute has to be stored separately. It can enhance a lot of other things too—things that Allomancy can't do. Memory, physical speed, clarity of thought . . . even some strange things, like physical weight or physical age, can be altered by Feruchemy."

"So, it's more powerful than Allomancy?" Vin said.

Kelsier shrugged. "Feruchemy doesn't have any external powers—it can't Push and Pull emotions, nor can it Steelpush or Ironpull. And, the biggest limitation to Feruchemy is that you have to store up all of its abilities by drawing them from your own body.

"Want to be twice as strong for a time? Well, you have to spend several hours being weak to store up the strength. If you want to store up the ability to heal quickly, you have to spend a great deal of time feeling sick. In Allomancy, the metals themselves are our fuel—we can generally keep going as long as we have enough metal to burn. In Feruchemy, the metals are just storage devices—your own body is the real fuel."

"So, you just steal someone else's storage metals, right?" Vin said.

Kelsier shook his head. "Doesn't work—Feruchemists can only access metal stores they themselves created."

"Oh."

Kelsier nodded. "So, no. I wouldn't say that Feruchemy is more powerful than Allomancy. They both have advantages and limitations. For instance, an Allomancer can only flare a metal so high, and so his maximum strength is bounded. Feruchemists don't have that kind of limitation; if a Feruchemist had enough strength stored up to be twice as strong as normal for an hour, he could choose instead to be *three* times as strong for a shorter period of time—or even four, five, or six times as strong for even shorter periods."

Vin frowned. "That sounds like a pretty big advantage."

"True," Kelsier said, reaching inside of his cloak and pulling out a vial containing several beads of atium. "But we have *this*. It doesn't matter if a Feruchemist is as strong as five men or as strong as fifty men—if I know what he's going to do next, I'll beat him."

Vin nodded.

"Here," Kelsier said, unstoppering the vial and pulling out one of the beads. He took out another vial, this one filled with the normal alcohol solution, and dropped the bead in it. "Take one of these. You might need it."

"Tonight?" Vin asked, accepting the vial.

Kelsier nodded.

"But, it's just Marsh."

"It might be," he said. "Then again, maybe the obligators caught him and forced him to write that letter. Maybe they're following him, or maybe they've since captured him and have tortured him to find out about the meeting. Marsh is in a very dangerous place—think about trying to do the same thing you're doing at those balls, except exchange all the noblemen for obligators and Inquisitors."

Vin shivered. "I guess you have a point," she said, tucking away the bead of atium. "You know, something must be wrong with me—I barely even stop to think how much this stuff is worth anymore."

Kelsier didn't respond immediately. "I have trouble forgetting how much it's worth," he said quietly.

"I . . ." Vin trailed off, glancing down at his hands. He usually wore long-sleeved shirts and gloves now; his reputation was making it dangerous for his identifying scars to be visible in public. Vin knew they were there, however. Like thousands of tiny white scratches, layered one over the other.

"Anyway," Kelsier said, "you're right about the logbook—I had hoped that it would mention the Eleventh Metal. But, Allomancy isn't even mentioned in reference to Feruchemy. The two powers are similar in many respects; you'd think that he would compare them."

"Maybe he worried that someone would read the book, and didn't want to give away that he was an Allomancer."

Kelsier nodded. "Maybe. It's also possible that he hadn't Snapped yet. Whatever happened in those Terris Mountains changed him from hero to tyrant; maybe it also awakened his powers. We won't know, I guess, until Saze finishes his translation."

"Is he close?"

Kelsier nodded. "Just a bit left—the important bit, hopefully. I feel a little frustrated with the text so far. The Lord Ruler hasn't even told us what he is supposed to accomplish in those mountains! He claims that he's doing something to protect the entire world, but that might just be his ego coming through."

He didn't seem very egotistical in the text to me, Vin thought. *Kind of the opposite, actually.*

"Regardless," Kelsier said, "we'll know more once the last few sections are translated."

It was growing dark outside, and Vin had to turn up her tin to see properly. The street outside her window grew visible, adopting the strange mixture of shadow and luminance that was the result of tin-enhanced vision. She knew it was dark, logically. Yet, she could still see. Not as she did in regular light—everything was muted—but it was sight nonetheless.

Kelsier checked his pocket watch.

"How long?" Vin asked.

"Another half hour," Kelsier said. "Assuming he's on time—and I doubt he will be. He *is* my brother, after all."

Vin nodded, shifting so that she leaned with arms crossed across the broken windowsill. Though it was a very small thing, she felt a comfort in having the atium Kelsier had given her.

She paused. Thinking of atium reminded her of something important. Something she'd been bothered by on several occasions. "You never taught me the ninth metal!" she accused, turning.

Kelsier shrugged. "I told you that it wasn't very important."

"Still. What is it? Some alloy of atium, I assume?"

Kelsier shook his head. "No, the last two metals don't follow the same pattern as the basic eight. The ninth metal is gold."

"Gold?" Vin asked. "That's it? I could have tried it a long time ago on my own!"

Kelsier chuckled. "Assuming you wanted to. Burning gold is a somewhat. . . . uncomfortable experience."

Vin narrowed her eyes, then turned to look back out the window. *We'll see,* she thought.

"You're going to try it anyway, aren't you?" Kelsier said, smiling.

Vin didn't respond.

Kelsier sighed, reaching into his sash and pulling out a golden boxing and a file. "You should probably get one of these," he said, holding up the file. "However, if you collect a metal yourself, burn just a tiny bit first to make certain that it's pure or alloyed correctly."

"If it isn't?" Vin asked.

"You'll know," Kelsier promised, beginning to file away at the coin. "Remember that headache you had from pewter dragging?"

"Yes?"

"Bad metal is worse," Kelsier said. "Far worse. Buy your metals when you can—in every city, you'll find a small group of merchants who provide powdered metals to Allomancers. Those merchants have a vested interest in making certain that all of their metals are pure—a grumpy Mistborn with a headache isn't exactly the kind of slighted customer one wants to deal with." Kelsier finished filing, then collected a few flakes of gold on a small square of cloth. He stuck one on his finger, then swallowed it.

"This is good," he said, handing her the cloth. "Go ahead—just remember, burning the ninth metal is a strange experience."

Vin nodded, suddenly feeling a bit apprehensive. *You'll never know if you don't try it for yourself,* she thought, then dumped the dustlike flakes into her mouth. She washed them down with a bit of water from her flask.

A new metal reserve appeared within her—unfamiliar and different from the nine she knew. She looked up at Kelsier, took a breath, and burned gold.

She was in two places at once. She could see herself, and she could see herself.

One of her was a strange woman, changed and transformed from the girl she had always been. That girl had been careful and cautious—a girl who would never burn an unfamiliar metal based solely on the word of one man. This woman was foolish; she had forgotten many of the things that had let her survive so long. She drank from cups prepared by others. She fraternized with strangers. She didn't keep track of the people around her. She was still far more careful than most people, but she had lost so much.

The other her was something she had always secretly loathed. A child, really. Thin to the point of scrawniness, she was lonely, hateful, and untrusting. She loved no one, and no one loved her. She always told herself, quietly, that she didn't care. Was there something worth living for? There had to be. Life couldn't be as pathetic as it seemed. Yet, it had to be. There wasn't anything else.

Vin was both. She stood in two places, moving both bodies, being both girl and woman. She reached out with hesitant, uncertain hands—one each—and touched herself on the faces, one each.

Vin gasped, and it was gone. She felt a sudden rush of emotions, a sense of worthlessness and confusion. There were no chairs in the room, so she simply squatted to the ground, sitting with her back to the wall, knees pulled up, arms wrapped around them.

Kelsier walked over, squatting down to lay a hand on her shoulder. "It's all right."

"What was that?" she whispered.

"Gold and atium are complements, like the other metal pairs," Kelsier said. "Atium lets you see, marginally, into the future. Gold works in a similar way, but it lets you see into the past. Or, at least, it gives you a glimpse of another version of yourself, had things been different in the past."

Vin shivered. The experience of being both people at once, of seeing herself twice over, had been disturbingly eerie. Her body still shook, and her mind didn't feel . . . right anymore.

Fortunately, the sensation seemed to be fading. "Remind me to listen to you in the future," she said. "Or, at least, when you talk about Allomancy."

Kelsier chuckled. "I tried to put it out of your mind for as long as possible. But, you had to try it sometime. You'll get over it."

Vin nodded. "It's . . . almost gone already. But, it wasn't just a vision, Kelsier. It was *real*. I could touch her, the other me."

"It may feel that way," Kelsier said. "But she wasn't here—I couldn't see her, at least. It's a hallucination."

"Atium visions aren't just hallucinations," Vin said. "The shadows really do show what people will do."

"True," Kelsier said. "I don't know. Gold is strange, Vin. I don't think anybody understands it. My trainer, Gemmel, said that a gold shadow was a person who didn't exist—but could have. A person you might have become, had you not made certain choices. Of course, Gemmel was a bit screwy, so I'm not sure how much I'd believe of what he said."

Vin nodded. However, it was unlikely that she'd find out more about gold anytime soon. She didn't intend to ever burn it again, if she could help it. She continued to sit, letting her emotions recover for a while, and Kelsier moved back over by the window. Eventually, he perked up.

"He's here?" Vin asked, crawling to her feet.

Kelsier nodded. "You want to stay here and rest some more?"

Vin shook her head.

"All right, then," he said, placing his pocket watch, file, and other metals on the windowsill. "Let's go."

They didn't go out the window—Kelsier wanted to maintain a low profile, though this section of the Twists was so deserted that Vin wasn't sure why he bothered. They left the building via a set of untrustworthy stairs, then crossed the street in silence.

The building Marsh had chosen was even more run-down than the one Vin and Kelsier had been sitting in. The front door was gone, though Vin could see remnants of it in the splintered refuse on the floor. The room inside smelled of dust and soot, and she had to stifle a sneeze.

A figure standing on the far side of the room spun at the sound. "Kell?"

"It's me," Kelsier said. "And Vin."

As Vin drew closer, she could see Marsh squinting in the darkness. It was odd to watch him, feeling like she was in plain sight, yet knowing that to him she and Kelsier were nothing more than shadows. The far wall of the building had collapsed, and mist floated freely in the room, nearly as dense as it was outside.

"You have Ministry tattoos!" Vin said, staring at Marsh.

"Of course," Marsh said, his voice as stern as ever. "I had them put on before I met up with the caravan. I had to have them to play the part of an acolyte."

They weren't extensive—he was playing a low-ranked obligator—but the pattern was unmistakable. Dark lines, rimming the eyes, running outward like crawling cracks of lightning. There was one, single line—much thicker, and in bright red, running down the side of his face. Vin recognized the pattern: These were the lines of an obligator who belonged to the Canton of Inquisition. Marsh hadn't just infiltrated the Ministry, he'd chosen the most dangerous section of it to infiltrate.

"But, you'll always have them," Vin said. "They're so distinctive—everywhere you go, you'll be known as either an obligator or a fraud."

"That was part of the price he paid to infiltrate the Ministry, Vin," Kelsier said quietly.

"It doesn't matter," Marsh said. "I didn't have much of a life before this anyway. Look, can we hurry? I'm expected to be somewhere soon. Obligators lead busy lives, and I only have a few minutes' leeway."

"All right," Kelsier said. "I assume your infiltration went well, then?"

"It went fine," Marsh said tersely. "Too well, actually—I think I might have distinguished myself from the group. I assumed that I would be at a disadvantage, since I didn't have the same five years of training that the other acolytes did. I made certain to answer questions as thoroughly as possible, and to perform my duties with precision. However, I apparently know more about the Ministry than even some of its members do. I'm certainly more competent than this batch of newcomers, and the prelans have noticed that."

Kelsier chuckled. "You always were an overachiever."

Marsh snorted quietly. "Anyway, my knowledge—not to mention my skill as a Seeker—has already earned me an outstanding reputation. I'm not sure how closely I want the prelans paying attention to me; that background we devised begins to sound a bit flimsy when an Inquisitor is grilling you."

Vin frowned. "You told them that you're a Misting?"

"Of course I did," Marsh said. "The Ministry—particularly the Canton of Inquisition—recruits nobleman Seekers diligently. The fact that I'm one is enough to keep them from asking too many questions about my background. They're happy enough to have me, despite the fact that I'm a fair bit older than most acolytes."

"Besides," Kelsier said, "he needed to tell them he was a Misting so that he could get into the more secretive Ministry sects. Most of the higher-ranking obligators are Mistings of one sort or another. They tend to favor their own kind."

"With good reason," Marsh said, speaking quickly. "Kell, the Ministry is far more competent than we assumed."

"What do you mean?"

"They make use of their Mistings," Marsh said. "*Good* use of them. They have bases throughout the city—Soothing stations, as they call them. Each one contains a couple of Ministry Soothers whose only duty is to extend a dampening influence around them, calming and depressing the emotions of everyone in the area."

Kelsier hissed quietly. "How many?"

"Dozens," Marsh said. "Concentrated in skaa sections of the city. They know that the skaa are beaten, but they want to make sure things stay that way."

"Bloody hell!" Kelsier said. "I always thought that the skaa inside Luthadel seemed more beaten down than others. No wonder we had so much trouble recruiting. The people's emotions are under a constant Soothing!"

Marsh nodded. "The Ministry Soothers are good, Kell—*very* good. Even better than Breeze. All they do is Soothe all day, every day. And, since they're not trying to get you to do anything specific—instead just keeping you from extreme emotional ranges—they're very hard to notice.

"Each team has a Smoker to keep them hidden, as well as a Seeker to watch for passing Allomancers. I'll bet this is where the Inquisitors get a lot of their leads—most of our people are smart enough not to burn when they know that there's an obligator in the area, but they're more lax in the slums."

"Can you get us a list of the stations?" Kelsier asked. "We need to know where those Seekers are, Marsh."

Marsh nodded. "I'll try. I'm on my way to a station right now—they always do personnel changes at night, to maintain their secret. The upper ranks have taken an interest in me, and they're letting me visit some stations to become familiar with their work. I'll see if I can get a list for you."

Kelsier nodded in the darkness.

"Just . . . don't be stupid with the information, all right?" Marsh said. "We have to be careful, Kell. The Ministry has kept these stations secret for quite some time. Now that we know about them, we have a serious advantage. Don't waste it."

"I won't," Kelsier promised. "What about the Inquisitors? Did you find anything out about them?"

Marsh stood quietly for a moment. "They're . . . strange, Kell. I don't know. They seem to have all of the Allomantic powers, so I assume that they were once Mistborn. I can't find out much else about them—though I do know that they age."

"Really?" Kelsier said with interest. "So, they're not immortal?"

"No," Marsh said. "The obligators say that Inquisitors change occasionally. The creatures are very long-lived, but they do eventually die of old age. New ones must be recruited from noblemen ranks. They're people, Kell—they've just been . . . changed."

Kelsier nodded. "If they can die of old age, then there's probably other ways to kill them too."

"That's what I think," Marsh said. "I'll see what I can find, but don't get your hopes up. The Inquisitors don't have many dealings with normal obligators—there's political tension between the two groups. The lord prelan leads the church, but the Inquisitors think that they should be in charge."

"Interesting," Kelsier said slowly. Vin could practically hear his mind working on the new information.

"Anyway, I should go," Marsh said. "I had to jog all the way here, and I'm going to be late getting to my appointment anyway."

Kelsier nodded, and Marsh began to move away, picking his way over the rubble in his dark obligator's robe.

"Marsh," Kelsier said as Marsh reached the doorway.

Marsh turned.

"Thank you," Kelsier said. "I can only guess how dangerous this is."

"I'm not doing this for you, Kell," Marsh said. "But . . . I appreciate the sentiment. I'll try and send you another missive once I have more information."

"Be careful," Kelsier said.

Marsh vanished out into the misty night. Kelsier stood in the fallen room for a few minutes, staring after his brother.

He wasn't lying about that either, Vin thought. *He really does care for Marsh.*

"Let's go," Kelsier said. "We should get you back to Mansion Renoux—House Lekal is throwing another party in a few days, and you'll need to be there."

Sometimes, my companions claim that I worry and question too much. However, while I may wonder about my stature as the hero, there is one thing that I have never questioned: the ultimate good of our quest.

The Deepness must be destroyed. I have seen it, and I have felt it. This name we give it is too weak a word, I think. Yes, it is deep and unfathomable, but it is also terrible. Many do not realize that it is sentient, but I have sensed its mind, such that it is, the few times I have confronted it directly.

It is a thing of destruction, madness, and corruption. It would destroy this world not out of spite or out of animosity, but simply because that is what it does.

28

KEEP LEKAL'S BALLROOM WAS SHAPED like the inside of a pyramid. The dance floor was set on a waist-high platform at the very center of the room, and the dining tables sat on four similar platforms surrounding it. Servants scuttled through the trenches running between the platforms, delivering food to the dining aristocrats.

Four tiers of balconies ran along the inside perimeter of the pyramidal room, each one a little closer to the point at the top, each one extending just a little bit more over the dance floor. Though the main room was well lit, the balconies themselves were shadowed by their overhangs. The design was intended to allow proper viewing of the keep's most distinctive artistic feature—the small stained-glass windows that lined each balcony.

Lekal noblemen bragged that while other keeps had larger windows, Keep Lekal had the most detailed ones. Vin had to admit that they were impressive. She'd seen so many stained-glass windows over the last few months that she was beginning to take them for granted. Keep Lekal's windows, however, put most of them to shame. Each of these was an extravagant, detailed marvel of resplendent color. Exotic animals pranced, distant landscapes enticed, and portraits of famous noblemen sat proudly.

There were also, of course, the requisite pictures dedicated to the Ascension. Vin could recognize these more easily now, and she was surprised to see references to things she had read in the logbook. The hills of emerald green. The steep mountains, with faint wavelike lines coming from the tips. A deep, dark lake. And . . . blackness. The Deepness. A chaotic thing of destruction.

He defeated it, Vin thought. *But . . . what was it?* Perhaps the end of the logbook would reveal more.

Vin shook her head, leaving the alcove—and its black window—behind. She strolled along the second balcony, wearing a pure white gown—an outfit she would never have been able to even imagine during her life as a skaa. Ash and soot had been too much a part of her life, and she didn't think she'd even had a concept of what a pristine white looked like. That knowledge made the dress even more wondrous to her. She hoped she would never lose that—the sense within herself of how life had been before. It made her appreciate what she had so much more than the real nobility seemed to.

She continued along the balcony, seeking her prey. Glittering colors shone from backlit windows, sparkling light across the floor. Most of the windows glowed inside small viewing alcoves along the balcony, and so the balcony before her was interspersed with pockets of dark and color. Vin didn't stop to study any more of the windows; she'd done quite a bit of that during her first balls at Keep Lekal. This night she had business to attend to.

She found her quarry halfway down the east balcony walkway. Lady Kliss was speaking with a group of people, so Vin paused, pretending to study a window. Kliss's group soon broke up—one could generally only take so much of Kliss at a time. The short woman began to walk along the balcony toward Vin.

When she drew close, Vin turned, as if in surprise. "Why, Lady Kliss! I haven't seen you all evening."

Kliss turned eagerly, obviously excited by the prospect of another person with whom to gossip. "Lady Valette!" she said, waddling forward. "You missed Lord Cabe's ball last week! Not due to a relapse of your earlier malady, I hope?"

"No," Vin said. "I spent that evening dining with my uncle."

"Oh," Kliss said, disappointed. A relapse would have made a better story. "Well, that's good."

"I hear you have some interesting news about Lady Tren-Pedri Delouse," Vin said carefully. "I myself have heard some interesting things lately." She eyed Kliss, implying that she'd be willing to trade tidbits.

"Oh, that!" Kliss said eagerly. "Well, *I* heard that Tren-Pedri isn't at all interested in a union with House Aime, though her father is implying that there will be a wedding soon. You know how the Aime sons are, though. Why, Fedren is an *absolute* buffoon."

Inwardly, Vin rolled her eyes. Kliss just kept on talking, not even noticing that Vin had something she herself wanted to share. *Using subtlety on this woman is about as effective as trying to sell bathwater perfumes to a plantation skaa.*

"That *is* interesting," Vin said, interrupting Kliss. "Perhaps Tren-Pedri's hesitance comes because of House Aime's connection to House Hasting."

Kliss paused. "Why would that be?"

"Well, we all know what House Hasting is planning."

"We do?" Kliss asked.

Vin pretended to look embarrassed. "Oh. Perhaps that isn't known yet. Please, Lady Kliss, forget that I said anything."

"Forget?" Kliss said. "Why, it's already forgotten. But, come now, you can't just stop. What do you mean?"

"I shouldn't say," Vin said. "It's just something I overheard my uncle talking about."

"Your uncle?" Kliss asked, growing more eager. "What did he say? You know that you can trust me."

"Well . . ." Vin said. "He said that House Hasting was relocating a lot of resources back to its plantations in the Southern Dominance. My uncle was quite happy—Hasting has withdrawn from some of its contracts, and my uncle was hoping to get them instead."

"Relocating . . ." Kliss said. "Why, they wouldn't do that unless they were planning to withdraw from the city. . . ."

"Could you blame them?" Vin asked quietly. "I mean, who wants to risk what happened to House Tekiel?"

"Who indeed . . ." Kliss said. She was practically shaking with eagerness to go share the news.

"Anyway, please, this is obviously only hearsay," Vin said. "You probably shouldn't tell anyone about it."

"Of course," Kliss said. "Um . . . excuse me. I need to go refresh myself."

"Of course," Vin said, watching the woman zip away toward the balcony stairs.

Vin smiled. House Hasting was making no such preparations, of course; Hasting was one of the strongest families in the city, and wouldn't likely withdraw. However, Dockson was back at the shop forging documents which, when delivered to the right places, would imply that Hasting was planning to do what Vin had said.

If all went well, the entire city would soon expect a Hasting withdrawal. Their allies would plan for it, and might even begin to withdraw themselves. People seeking to buy weapons would instead look other places, fearing that Hasting wouldn't be able to make good on contracts once it left. When Hasting *didn't* withdraw, it would make them look indecisive. Their allies gone, their income weakened, they could very well be the next house to fall.

House Hasting, however, was one of the easy ones to work against. It had a reputation for extreme subterfuge, and people would believe that it was planning a secret retreat. In addition, Hasting was a strong mercantile house—meaning it depended a great deal upon its contracts to survive. A house with such an obvious, dominating source of income also had an obvious weakness. Lord Hasting had worked hard to increase his house's influence over the last few decades, and in doing so he had extended his house's resources to their limits.

Other houses were far more stable. Vin sighed, turning and strolling down the walkway, eyeing the massive clock set between the balconies on the other side of the chamber.

Venture would not fall easily. It remained powerful through the sheer force of fortune; though it participated in some contracts, it didn't rely on them like other houses. Venture was rich enough, and powerful enough, that even mercantile disaster would only jostle it.

In a way, Venture's stability was a good thing—for Vin, at least. The house had no obvious weaknesses, so maybe the crew wouldn't be too disappointed when she couldn't discover any way to bring it down. After all, they didn't *absolutely* need to destroy House Venture; doing so would simply make the plan go more smoothly.

Whatever happened, Vin had to make sure that Venture didn't suffer the same fate as House Tekiel. Their reputation destroyed, their finances unhinged, the Tekiel had tried to pull out of the city—and this final show of weakness had been too much. Some of Tekiel's nobility had been assassinated before they left; the rest had been found in the burned-out ruins of their canal boats, apparently hit by bandits. Vin, however, knew of no thieving band who would dare slaughter so many noblemen.

Kelsier still hadn't been able to discover which house was behind the murders, but the Luthadel nobility didn't seem to care who the culprit was. House Tekiel had allowed itself to grow weak, and nothing was more embarrassing to the aristocracy than a Great House that couldn't maintain itself. Kelsier had been right: Though polite groups met at balls, the nobility were more than willing to stab each other square in the chest if it benefited them.

Kind of like thieving crews, she thought. *The nobility really aren't that different from the people I grew up around.*

The atmosphere was only made more dangerous by its polite niceties. Underneath that front were plots, assassinations, and—perhaps most importantly—Mistborn. It was no accident that all of the balls she had attended recently had displayed great numbers of guards, both wearing armor and not. The parties now served the additional purpose of warning and showing strength.

Elend is safe, she told herself. *Despite what he thinks of his family, they've done a good job of maintaining their place in the Luthadel hierarchy. He's the heir—they'll protect him from assassins.*

She wished those assertions sounded just a bit more convincing. She knew that Shan Elariel was planning something. House Venture might be safe, but Elend himself was a little bit . . . oblivious sometimes. If Shan did something against him personally, it might or might not be a major blow against House Venture—but it would certainly be a major blow against Vin.

"Lady Valette Renoux," a voice said. "I do believe that you're late."

Vin turned to see Elend lounging in an alcove to her left. She smiled, glancing down at the clock, noticing that it was indeed a few minutes past the time when she had promised to meet him. "I must be picking up bad habits from some friends of mine," she said, stepping into the alcove.

"Now, see, I didn't say it was a *bad* thing," Elend said, smiling. "Why, I'd say that it is a lady's courtly duty to be a bit dilatory. It does gentlemen good to be forced to wait upon a woman's whims—or, so my mother was always fond of telling me."

"It sounds like she was a wise woman," Vin said. The alcove was just large enough for two people standing sideways. She stood across from him, the balcony overhang a short distance to her left, a marvelous lavender window to her right, their feet nearly touching.

"Oh, I don't know about that," Elend said. "She married my father, after all."

"Thereby joining the most powerful house in the Final Empire. You can't do much better than that—though, I suppose she could have tried to marry the Lord Ruler. Last I knew, though, he wasn't in the market for a wife."

"Pity," Elend said. "Maybe he'd look a little less depressed if there were a woman in his life."

"I guess that would depend on the woman." Vin glanced to the side as a small group of courtgoers strolled past. "You know, this isn't exactly the most private location. People are giving us odd looks."

"You're the one who stepped in here with me," Elend pointed out.

"Yes, well, I wasn't thinking about the gossip we might start."

"Let it start," Elend said standing up straight.

"Because it will make your father angry?"

Elend shook his head. "I don't care about that anymore, Valette." Elend took a step forward, bringing them even closer together. Vin could feel his breath. He stood there for a moment before speaking. "I think I'm going to kiss you."

Vin shivered slightly. "I don't think you want to do that, Elend."

"Why?"

"How much do you really know about me?"

"Not as much as I'd like to," he said.

"Not as much as you need to, either," Vin said, looking up into his eyes.

"So tell me," he said.

"I can't. Not right now."

Elend stood for a moment, then nodded slightly and pulled away. He walked out onto the balcony walkway. "So, shall we go for a stroll, then?"

"Yes," Vin said, relieved—yet just a bit disappointed as well.

"It's for the best," Elend said. "That alcove has absolutely *terrible* reading light."

"Don't you dare," Vin said, eyeing the book in his pocket as she joined him on the walkway. "Read when you're with someone else, not me."

"But that's how our relationship began!"

"And that's how it could end too," Vin said, taking his arm.

Elend smiled. They weren't the only couple walking the balcony, and down below, other pairs spun slowly to the faint music.

It seems so peaceful. Yet, just a few days ago, many of these people stood and watched idly as women and children were beheaded.

She felt Elend's arm, his warmth beside her. Kelsier said that he smiled so much because he felt he needed to take what joy he could in the world—to relish the moments of happiness that seemed so infrequent in the Final Empire. Strolling for a time beside Elend, Vin thought she was beginning to understand how Kelsier felt.

"Valette . . ." Elend said slowly.

"What?"

"I want you to leave Luthadel," he said.

"*What?*"

He paused, turning to look at her. "I've thought about this a lot. You may not realize it, but the city is becoming dangerous. Very dangerous."

"I know."

"Then you know that a small house without allies has no place in the Central Dominance right now," Elend said. "Your uncle was brave to come here and try to establish himself, but he chose the wrong time. I . . . I think things are going to get out of hand here very soon. When that happens, I can't guarantee your safety."

"My uncle knows what he's doing, Elend."

"This is *different*, Valette," Elend said. "Entire houses are falling. The Tekiel family wasn't slaughtered by bandits—that was the work of House Hasting. Those won't be the last deaths we see before this is through."

Vin paused, thinking of Shan again. "But . . . you're safe, right? House Venture—it's not like the others. It's stable."

Elend shook his head. "We're even more vulnerable than the rest, Valette."

"But, your fortune is large," Vin said. "You don't depend on contracts."

"They may not be visible," Elend said quietly, "but they're there, Valette. We put on a good show, and the others assume that we have more than we do. However, with the Lord Ruler's house taxings . . . well, the only way we maintain so much power in this city is through income. Secret income."

Vin frowned, and Elend leaned closer, speaking almost in a whisper. "My family mines the Lord Ruler's atium, Valette," he said. "That's where our wealth comes from. In a way, our stability depends almost completely on the Lord Ruler's whims. He doesn't like to bother collecting the atium himself, but he gets *very* perturbed if the delivery schedule is disrupted."

Find out more! instinct told her. *This is the secret; this is what Kelsier needs.* "Oh, Elend," Vin whispered. "You shouldn't be telling me this."

"Why not?" he said. "I trust you. Look, you need to understand how dangerous things are. The atium supply has been having some troubles lately. Ever since. . . . well, something happened a few years ago. Ever since then, things have been different. My father can't meet the Lord Ruler's quotas, and last time that happened . . ."

"What?"

"Well," Elend said, looking troubled. "Let's just say that things could soon grow very bad for the Ventures. The Lord Ruler depends on that atium, Valette—it's one of the prime ways he controls the nobility. A house without atium is a house that can't defend itself from Mistborn. By keeping a large reserve, the Lord Ruler controls the market, making himself extremely wealthy. He funds his armies by making atium scarce, then selling extra bits for lavish amounts. If you knew more about the economics of Allomancy, this would probably make a lot more sense to you."

Oh, trust me. I understand more than you think. And now I know far more than I should.

Elend paused, smiling pleasantly as an obligator strolled along the balcony walkway beside them. The obligator looked them over as he passed, eyes thoughtful within their web of tattoos.

Elend turned back to her as soon as the obligator had passed. "I want you to leave," he repeated. "People know that I've paid attention to you. Hopefully, they'll assume it was just to spite my father, but they could still try to use you. The Great Houses wouldn't have any qualms about crushing your entire family just to get at me and my father. You have to go."

"I'll . . . think about it," Vin said.

"There isn't much time left for thinking," Elend warned. "I want you to leave before you get too involved with what is going on in this city."

I'm already involved so much more than you think. "I said I'd think about it," she said. "Look, Elend, I think you should be more worried about yourself. I think Shan Elariel is going to try something to strike against you."

"Shan?" Elend said with amusement. "She's harmless."

"I don't think she is, Elend. You need to be more careful."

He laughed. "Look at us . . . each one trying to convince the other how dreadfully dire the situation is, each one bullheadedly refusing to listen to the other."

Vin paused, then smiled.

Elend sighed. "You're not going to listen to me, are you? Is there anything I can do to make you leave?"

"Not right now," she said quietly. "Look, Elend, can't we just enjoy the time we have together? If things continue as they are, we might not have many more opportunities like this for a while."

He paused, then finally nodded. She could see he was still troubled, but he did turn back to their walk, letting her gently take his arm again as they strolled. They walked together for a time, silent until something drew Vin's attention. She removed her hands from his arm, instead reaching down to take his hand in her own.

He glanced at her, frowning in confusion as she tapped the ring on his finger. "It really is metal," she said, a bit surprised, despite what she'd been told.

Elend nodded. "Pure gold."

"Don't you worry about . . ."

"Allomancers?" Elend asked. He shrugged. "I don't know—they're not the sort of thing that I've ever had to deal with. You don't wear metal, out on the plantations?"

Vin shook her head, tapping one of the barrettes in her hair. "Painted wood," she said.

Elend nodded. "Probably wise," he said. "But, well, the longer you stay in Luthadel, the more you'll realize that little we do here is done in the name of wisdom. The Lord Ruler wears metal rings—and so, therefore, does the nobility. Some philosophers think that's all part of His plan. The Lord Ruler wears metal because he knows that the nobility will mimic him, and therefore give his Inquisitors power over them."

"Do you agree?" Vin asked, taking his arm again as they walked. "With the philosophers, I mean?"

Elend shook his head. "No," he said in a quieter voice. "The Lord Ruler . . . he's just arrogant. I've read of warriors, long ago, who would run into battle without armor on, supposedly to prove how brave and strong they were. That's how this is, I think—though admittedly on a far more subtle level. He wears metal to flaunt his power, to show how unfrightened—how unthreatened—he is by anything we could do to him."

Well, Vin thought, *he's willing to call the Lord Ruler arrogant. Perhaps I can get him to admit a little more. . . .*

Elend paused, glancing over at the clock. "I'm afraid I don't have a whole lot of time tonight, Valette."

"That's right," Vin said. "You'll need to go off and meet with your friends." She glanced at him, trying to gauge his reaction.

He didn't seem very surprised. He simply raised an eyebrow in her direction. "Indeed, I will. You're very observant."

"It doesn't take much observing," Vin said. "Anytime we're at Keeps Hasting, Venture, Lekal, or Elariel, you run off with the same people."

"My drinking friends," Elend said with a smile. "An unlikely group in today's political climate, but one that helps annoy my father."

"What do you do at these meetings?" Vin asked.

"We talk philosophy, mostly," Elend said. "We're kind of a stuffy lot—which isn't too surprising, I guess, if you know any of us. We talk about the government, about politics . . . about the Lord Ruler."

"What about him?"

"Well, we don't like some of the things he's done with the Final Empire."

"So you *do* want to overthrow him!" Vin said.

Elend gave her a strange look. "Overthrow him? What gave you that idea, Valette? He's the Lord Ruler—he's God. We can't do anything about him being in charge." He looked away as they continued to walk. "No, my friends and I, we just . . . wish the Final Empire could be a little different. We can't change things now, but maybe someday—assuming we all survive the next year or so—we'll be in positions to influence the Lord Ruler."

"To do what?"

"Well, take those executions a few days ago," Elend said. "I don't see that they did any good. The skaa rebelled. In reprisal, the Ministry executed a few hundred random people. What is that going to do besides make the populace even *more* angry? So, next time the rebellion will be bigger. Does that mean that the Lord Ruler will order more people beheaded? How long can that continue before there just aren't any skaa left?"

Vin walked thoughtfully. "And what would you do, Elend Venture?" she finally said. "If you were in charge."

"I don't know," Elend confessed. "I've read a lot of books—some that I'm not supposed to—and I haven't found any easy answers. I'm pretty certain, however, that beheading people won't solve anything. The Lord Ruler has been around for a long time—you'd think that he'd have found a better way. But, anyway, we'll have to continue this later. . . ." He slowed, turning to look at her.

"Time already?" she asked.

Elend nodded. "I promised I'd meet them, and they kind of look to me. I suppose I could tell them I'll be late. . . ."

Vin shook her head. "Go drink with your friends. I'll be fine—I have a few more people I need to talk to anyway." She did need to get back to work; Breeze and Dockson had spent hours planning and preparing the lies that she was supposed to spread, and they would be waiting for her report back at Clubs's shop after the party.

Elend smiled. "Maybe I shouldn't worry about you so much. Who knows—considering all of your political maneuvering, maybe House Renoux will soon be the power in town, and I'll just be a lowly beggar."

Vin smiled, and he bowed—winking at her—then was off toward the stairs. Vin walked slowly over to the balcony railing, looking down at the people dancing and dining below.

So he's not a revolutionary, she thought. *Kelsier was right again. I wonder if he ever gets tired of that.*

But still, she couldn't feel too disappointed with Elend. Not everyone was so insane that they'd think to overthrow their god-emperor. The mere fact that Elend was willing to think for himself set him apart from the rest; he was a good man, one who deserved a woman who was worthy of his trust.

Unfortunately, he had Vin.

So House Venture secretly mines the Lord Ruler's atium, she thought. *They must be the ones who administer the Pits of Hathsin.*

It was a frighteningly precarious position for a house to be in—their finances depended directly on pleasing the Lord Ruler. Elend thought that he was being careful, but Vin was worried. He wasn't taking Shan Elariel seriously enough—of that, Vin was certain. She turned, walking intently from the balcony and down to the main floor.

She found Shan's table easily; the woman always sat with a large group of attendant noblewomen, presiding like a lord over his plantation. Vin paused. She'd never approached Shan directly. Someone, however, needed to protect Elend; he was obviously too foolish to do it himself.

Vin strode forward. Shan's Terrisman studied Vin as she approached. He was so different from Sazed—he didn't have the same . . . spirit. This man maintained a flat expression, like some creature carved of stone. A few of the ladies shot disapproving glances toward Vin, but most of them—Shan included—ignored her.

Vin stood awkwardly beside the table, waiting for a lull in the conversation. There was none. Finally, she just took a few steps closer to Shan.

"Lady Shan?" she asked.

Shan turned with an icy glare. "I didn't send for you, country girl."

"Yes, but I've found some books like you—"

"I no longer require your services," Shan said, turning away. "I can deal with Elend Venture on my own. Now, be a good little twit and stop bothering me."

Vin stood, stunned. "But, your plan—"

"I *said* that you are *no longer needed.* You think I was harsh on you before, girl? That was when you were on my good side. Try annoying me now."

Vin wilted reflexively before the woman's demeaning gaze. She seemed . . . disgusted. Angry, even. Jealous?

She must have figured it out, Vin thought. *She finally realized out that I'm not just playing with Elend. She knows that I care for him, and doesn't trust me to keep her secrets.*

Vin backed away from the table. Apparently, she would have to use other methods to discover Shan's plans.

Despite what he often said, Elend Venture did not consider himself to be a rude man. He was more of a . . . verbal philosopher. He liked to test and turn conversation to see how people would react. Like the great thinkers of old, he pushed boundaries and experimented with unconventional methods.

Of course, he thought, holding his cup of brandy up before his eyes, inspecting it musingly, *most of those old philosophers were eventually executed for treason.* Not exactly the most successful role models.

His evening political conversation with his group was finished, and he had retired with several friends to Keep Lekal's gentlemen's lounge, a small chamber adjacent to the ballroom. It was furnished in deep green colors, and the chairs were comfortable; it would have been a nice place to read, had he been in a slightly better mood. Jastes sat across from him, puffing contentedly on his pipe. It was good to see the young Lekal looking so calm. These last few weeks had been difficult for him.

House war, Elend thought. *What terrible timing. Why now? Things were going so well. . . .*

Telden returned with a refilled drink a few moments later.

"You know," Jastes said, gesturing with his pipe, "any one of the servants in here would have brought you a new drink."

"I felt like stretching my legs," Telden said, settling into the third chair.

"And you flirted with no less than three women on your way back," Jastes said. "I counted."

Telden smiled, sipping his drink. The large man never just "sat"—he lounged. Telden could look relaxed and comfortable no matter what the situation, his sharp suits and well-styled hair enviably handsome.

Maybe I should pay just a little more attention to things like that, Elend thought to himself. *Valette suffers my hair the way it is, but would she like it better if I had it styled?*

Elend often intended to make his way to a stylist or tailor, but other things tended to steal his attention. He'd get lost in his studies or spend too long reading, then find himself late for his appointments. Again.

"Elend is quiet this evening," Telden noticed. Though other groups of gentlemen sat in the dim lounge, the chairs were spread out enough to allow for private conversations.

"He's been like that a lot, lately," Jastes said.

"Ah, yes," Telden said, frowning slightly.

Elend knew them well enough to take the hint. "Now, see, why must people be like this? If you have something to say, why not simply say it?"

"Politics, my friend," Jastes said. "We are—if you haven't noticed—noblemen."

Elend rolled his eyes.

"All right, I'll say it," Jastes replied, running his hand through his hair—a nervous habit that Elend was sure contributed somewhat to the young man's growing baldness. "You've been spending a lot of time with that Renoux girl, Elend."

"There is a simple explanation for that," Elend said. "You see, I happen to like her."

"Not good, Elend," Telden said with a shake of his head. "Not good."

"Why?" Elend asked. "You seem pleased enough to ignore class variances yourself, Telden. I've seen you flirt with half the serving girls in the room."

"I'm not heir to my house," Telden said.

"And," Jastes said, "these girls are trustworthy. My family hired these women—we know their houses, their backgrounds, and their allegiances."

Elend frowned. "What are you implying?"

"Something's strange about that girl, Elend," Jastes said. He'd gone back to his normal nervous self, his pipe sitting unnoticed in its holder on the table.

Telden nodded. "She got too close to you too quickly, Elend. She wants something."

"Like what?" Elend asked, growing annoyed.

"Elend, Elend," Jastes said. "You can't just avoid the game by saying you don't want to play. It'll find you. Renoux moved into town just as house tensions began to rise, and he brought with him an unknown scion—a girl who immediately began to woo the most important and available young man in Luthadel. Doesn't that seem odd to you?"

"Actually," Elend noted, "I approached her first—if only because she had stolen my reading spot."

"But, you have to admit that it's suspicious how quickly she latched on to you," Telden said. "If you're going to dabble with romance, Elend, you need to learn one thing: You can play with women if you want, but don't let yourself get too close to them. That's where the trouble starts."

Elend shook his head. "Valette is different."

The other two shared a look, then Telden shrugged, turning back to his drink. Jastes, however, sighed, then stood and stretched. "Anyway, I should probably be going."

"One more drink," Telden said.

Jastes shook his head, running a hand through his hair. "You know how my parents are on ball nights—if I don't go out and bid farewell to at least *some* of the guests, I'll be nagged about it for weeks."

The younger man wished them good night, walking back toward the main ballroom. Telden sipped his drink, eyeing Elend.

"I'm not thinking about her," Elend said testily.

"What, then?"

"The meeting tonight," Elend said. "I'm not sure if I like how it went."

"Bah," the large man said with a wave of his hand. "You're getting as bad as Jastes. What happened to the man who attended these meetings just to relax and enjoy time with his friends?"

"He's worried," Elend said. "Some of his friends might end up in charge of their houses sooner than he expected, and he's worried that none of us are ready."

Telden snorted. "Don't be so melodramatic," he said, smiling and winking to the serving girl who came to clear away his empty cups. "I have a feeling that this is all just going to blow over. In a few months, we'll look back and wonder what all the fretting was about."

Kale Tekiel won't look back, Elend thought.

The conversation waned, however, and Telden eventually excused himself. Elend sat for a while longer, opening *The Dictates of Society* for another read, but he had trouble concentrating. He turned the cup of brandy in his fingers, but didn't drink much.

I wonder if Valette's out yet. . . . He'd tried to find her once his meeting was over, but apparently she'd been in a private gathering of her own.

That girl, he thought lazily, *is far too interested in politics for her own good.* Perhaps he was just jealous—only a few months in court, and she already seemed to be more competent than he was. She was so fearless, so bold, so . . . interesting. She didn't fit any of the courtly stereotypes he'd been taught to expect.

Could Jastes be right? he wondered. *She certainly is different from other women, and she did imply there were things about her I didn't know.*

Elend pushed the thought out of his mind. Valette was different, true—but she was also innocent, in a way. Eager, full of wonder and spunk.

He worried about her; she obviously didn't know how dangerous Luthadel could be. There was so much more to politics in the city than simple parties and petty intrigues. What would happen if someone decided to send a Mistborn to deal with her and her uncle? Renoux was poorly connected, and none of the court's members would blink twice at a few assassinations in Fellise. Did Valette's uncle know how to take the proper precautions? Did he even worry about Allomancers?

Elend sighed. He'd just have to make certain that Valette left the area. That was the only option.

By the time his carriage reached Keep Venture, Elend had decided that he'd drunk too much. He made his way up to his rooms, looking forward to his bed and pillows.

The hallway to his bedroom, however, passed by his father's study. The door was open, and light still spilled out despite the late hour. Elend tried to walk quietly on the carpeted floor, but he'd never really been all that stealthy.

"Elend?" his father's voice called from the study. "Come in here."

Elend sighed quietly. Lord Straff Venture didn't miss much. He was a Tineye—his senses were so keen that he'd probably heard Elend's carriage approaching outside. *If I don't deal with him now, he'll just send the servants to pester me until I come down to speak with him. . . .*

Elend turned and walked into the study. His father sat in his chair, speaking quietly with TenSoon—the Venture Kandra. Elend still wasn't used to the creature's most recent body, which had once belonged to a servant in the Hasting household. Elend shivered as it noticed him. It bowed, then quietly retreated from the room.

Elend leaned against the doorframe. Straff's chair sat in front of several shelves of books—not a single one of which, Elend was confident, his father had ever read. The room was lit by two lamps, their hoods mostly closed to allow out only a bit of light.

"You attended the ball tonight," Straff said. "What did you learn?"

Elend reached up, rubbing his forehead. "That I have a tendency to drink far too much brandy."

Straff was not amused by the comment. He was the perfect imperial nobleman—tall, firm-shouldered, always dressed in a tailored vest and suit. "You met with that . . . woman again?" he asked.

"Valette? Hum, yes. Not for as long as I would have liked, though."

"I forbade you from spending time with her."

"Yes," Elend said. "I remember."

Straff's expression darkened. He stood, walking over to the desk. "Oh, Elend," he said. "When are you going to get over this childish temperament you have? Do you think I don't realize that you act foolishly simply to spite me?"

"Actually, I got over my 'childish temperament' some time ago, Father—it just seems that my natural inclinations work even better to annoy you. I wish I had known that earlier; I could have saved a great deal of effort in my younger years."

His father snorted, then held up a letter. "I dictated this to Staxles a short time ago. It is an acceptance of a lunch appointment with Lord Tegas tomorrow afternoon. If a house war *does* come, I want to make certain we are in a position to destroy the Hastings as quickly as possible, and Tegas could be a strong ally. He has a daughter. I'd like you to dine with her at the luncheon."

"I'll consider it," Elend said, tapping his head. "I'm not sure what kind of state I'll be in tomorrow morning. Too much brandy, remember?"

"You'll be there, Elend. This is not a request."

Elend paused. A part of him wanted to snap back at his father, to make a stand—not because he cared about where he dined, but because of something far more important.

Hasting is the second-most-powerful house in the city. If we made an allegiance with them, together we could keep Luthadel from chaos. We could stop the house war, not enflame it.

That's what his books had done to him—they had changed him from rebellious fop into would-be philosopher. Unfortunately, he'd been a fool for so long. Was it any wonder that Straff hadn't noticed the change in his son? Elend himself was only starting to realize it.

Straff continued to glare at him, and Elend looked away. "I'll think about it," he said.

Straff waved his hand dismissively, turning.

Trying to salvage something of his pride, Elend continued. "You probably don't even have to worry about the Hastings—it seems that they're making preparations to bolt the city."

"*What?*" Straff asked. "Where did you hear that?"

"At the ball," Elend said lightly.

"I thought you said you didn't learn anything important."

"Now, see, I never said anything of the sort. I just didn't feel like sharing with you."

Lord Venture frowned. "I don't know why I even care—anything you learn is bound to be worthless. I tried to train you in politics, boy. I really did. But now . . . well, I hope I live to see you dead, because this house is in for dire times if you ever take control."

"I know more than you think, Father."

Straff laughed, walking back to sit in his chair. "I doubt that, boy. Why, you can't even bed a woman properly—the last, and only, time I know about you trying it, *I* had to take you to the brothel myself."

Elend flushed. *Careful,* he told himself. *He's bringing that up on purpose. He knows how much it bothers you.*

"Get to bed, boy," Straff said with a wave of his hand. "You look terrible."

Elend stood for a moment, then finally ducked out into the hallway, sighing quietly to himself.

That's the difference between you and them, Elend, he thought. *Those philosophers you read—they were revolutionaries. They were willing to risk execution. You can't even stand up to your father.*

He walked tiredly up to his rooms—where, oddly, he found a servant waiting for him.

Elend frowned. "Yes?"

"Lord Elend, you have a guest," the man said.

"At this hour?"

"It's Lord Jastes Lekal, my lord."

Elend cocked his head slightly. *What in the Lord Ruler's name . . . ?* "He's waiting in the sitting room, I assume?"

"Yes, my lord," the servant said.

Elend turned regretfully away from his chambers, walking back down the hallway. He found Jastes waiting impatiently.

"Jastes?" Elend said tiredly, walking into the sitting room. "I hope you have something *very* important to tell me."

Jastes shuffled uncomfortably for a moment, looking even more nervous than normal.

"What?" Elend demanded, his patience waning.

"It's about the girl."

"Valette?" Elend asked. "You came here to discuss Valette? *Now?*"

"You should trust your friends more," Jastes said.

Elend snorted. "Trust *your* knowledge of women? No offense, Jastes, but I think not."

"I had her followed, Elend," Jastes blurted out.

Elend paused. "What?"

"I had her carriage followed. Or, at least, I had someone watch for it at the city gates. She wasn't in it when it left the city."

"What do you mean?" Elend asked, his frown deepening.

"She wasn't *in the carriage,* Elend," Jastes repeated. "While her Terrisman was producing papers for the guards, my man snuck up and peeked through the carriage window, and there was nobody inside.

"The carriage must have dropped her off somewhere in town. She's a spy from one of the other houses—they're trying to get at your father through you. They created the perfect woman to attract you—dark-haired, a bit mysterious, and outside of the regular political structure. They made her lowborn enough that it would be a scandal for you to be interested in her, then set her on you."

"Jastes, this is ridicu—"

"Elend," Jastes interrupted. "Tell me one more time: How did you meet her the first time?"

Elend paused. "She was standing on the balcony."

"In your reading spot," Jastes said. "Everyone knows that's where you usually go. Coincidence?"

Elend closed his eyes. *Not Valette. She* can't *be part of all this.* But, immediately, another thought occurred to him. *I told her about the atium! How could I be so stupid?*

It couldn't be true. He wouldn't believe that he had been duped so easily. But . . . could he risk it? He was a bad son, true, but he was no traitor to the house. He didn't want to see Venture fall; he wanted to lead it someday, so that perhaps he'd be able to change things.

He bid Jastes farewell, then walked back to his rooms with a distracted step. He felt too tired to think about house politics. However, when he finally got into bed, he found that he couldn't sleep.

Eventually, he rose, sending for a servant.

"Tell my father I want to make a trade," Elend explained to the man. "I'll go to his luncheon tomorrow, just as he wants." Elend paused, standing in his evening robe by his bedroom door.

"In exchange," he finally said, "tell him I want to borrow a couple of spies so that they can follow someone for me."

The others all think I should have had Kwaan executed for betraying me. To tell the truth, I'd probably kill him this moment if I knew where he'd gone. At the time, however, I just couldn't do it.

The man had become like a father to me. To this day, I don't know why he suddenly decided that I wasn't the Hero. Why did he turn against me, denouncing me to the entire Conclave of Worldbringers?

Would he rather that the Deepness win? Surely, even if I'm not the right one—as Kwaan now claims—my presence at the Well of Ascension couldn't possibly be worse than what will happen if the Deepness continues to destroy the land.

29

IT'S ALMOST OVER, Vin read.

We can see the cavern from our camp. It will take a few more hours of hiking to reach it, but I know that it is the right place. I can feel it somehow, feel it up there . . . pulsing, in my mind.

It's so cold. I swear that the rocks themselves are made of ice, and the snow is deep enough in places that we have to dig our way through. The wind blows all the time. I fear for Fedik—he hasn't been quite the same since the creature made of mist attacked him, and I worry that he will wander off a cliffside or slip through one of the many icy rifts in the ground.

The Terrismen, however, are a wonder. It is fortunate that we brought them, for no regular packmen would have survived the trip. The Terrismen don't seem to mind the cold—something about their strange metabolisms gives them a supernatural ability to resist the elements. Perhaps they have "saved up" heat from their bodies for later use?

They won't talk about their powers, however—and I am sure that Rashek is to blame. The other packmen look to him for leadership, though I don't think he has complete control over them. Before he was stabbed, Fedik feared that the Terrismen would abandon us up here in the ice. I don't think that will happen, however. I am here by providence of Terris prophecies—these men will not disobey their own religion simply because one of their number has taken a dislike to me.

I did finally confront Rashek. He did not want to speak to me, of course, but I forced him. Unleashed, he spoke at great length regarding his hatred of Khlennium and my people. He thinks that we have turned his people into little more than slaves. He thinks that Terrismen deserve far more—he keeps saying that his people should be "dominant" because of their supernatural powers.

I fear his words, for I see some truth in them. Yesterday, one of the packmen lifted a boulder of enormous size, then tossed it out of our way with an almost casual throw. I have not seen such a feat of strength in all my days.

These Terrismen could be very dangerous, I think. Perhaps we have treated them unfairly. However, men like Rashek must be contained—he irrationally believes that all people outside of Terris have oppressed him. He is such a young man to be so angry.

It is so cold. When this is finished, I think I should like to live where it is warm all year. Braches has told of such places, islands to the south where great mountains create fire.

What will it be like, when this is all over? I will be just a regular man again. An unimportant man. It sounds nice—more desirable, even, than a warm sun and a windless sky. I am so tired of being the Hero of Ages, tired of entering cities to find either armed hostility or fanatic adoration. I am tired of being loved and hated for what a bunch of old men say I will eventually do.

I want to be forgotten. Obscurity. Yes, that would be nice.

If men read these words, let them know that power is a heavy burden. Seek not to be bound by its chains. The Terris prophecies say that I will have the power to save the world. They hint, however, that I will have the power to destroy it as well.

I will have the ability to fulfill any wish of my heart. "He will take upon himself authority that no mortal should hold." Yet, the philosophers warned me that if I am self-serving with the power, my selfishness will taint it.

Is this a burden that any man should bear? Is this a temptation any man could resist? I feel strong now, but what will happen when I touch that power? I will save the world, certainly—but will I try to take it as well?

Such are my fears as I scribble with an ice-crusted pen on the eve before the world is reborn. Rashek watches. Hating me. The cavern lies above. Pulsing. My fingers quiver. Not from the cold.

Tomorrow, it will end.

Vin eagerly turned the page. The back page of the booklet, however, was empty. She turned it over, rereading the last few lines. Where was the next entry?

Sazed must not have finished the last part yet. She stood, sighing as she stretched. She'd finished the entire newest portion of the logbook in one sitting, a feat that surprised even her. The gardens of Mansion Renoux extended before her, the cultured pathways, broad-limbed trees, and quiet stream creating her favorite reading spot. The sun was low in the sky, and it was beginning to get chilly.

She wound her way up the path toward the mansion. Despite the chill evening, she could barely imagine a place like the one the Lord Ruler described. She had seen snow on some distant peaks, but she had rarely seen it fall—and even then it was usually just an icy slush. To experience that much snow day after day, to be in danger of having it fall upon you in great crushing avalanches . . .

A part of her wished that she could visit such places, no matter how dangerous. Though the logbook didn't describe the Lord Ruler's entire journey, some of the marvels it did include—the ice fields to the north, the great black lake, and the Terris waterfalls—sounded amazing.

If only he'd put in more detail about what things look like! she thought with annoyance. The Lord Ruler spent far too much time worrying. Though, admittedly, she was beginning to feel an odd sort of . . . familiarity with him through his words. She found it hard to associate the person in her mind with the dark creature that had caused so much death. What had occurred at the Well of Ascension? What could have changed him so drastically? She had to know.

She reached the mansion and went searching for Sazed. She was back to wearing dresses—it felt odd to be seen in trousers by anyone but the crewmembers. She smiled at Lord Renoux's interior steward as she passed, eagerly climbing the main entryway stairs and seeking out the library.

Sazed wasn't inside. His small desk sat empty, the lamp extinguished, the inkwell empty. Vin frowned in annoyance.

Wherever he is, he'd better be working on the translation!

She went back down the stairs, asking after Sazed, and a maid directed her to the main kitchen. Vin frowned, making her way down the back hallway. *Getting himself a snack, perhaps?*

She found Sazed standing amongst a small group of servants, pointing toward a list on the table and speaking in a low voice. He didn't notice Vin as she entered.

"Sazed?" Vin asked, interrupting him.

He turned. "Yes, Mistress Valette?" he asked, bowing slightly.

"What are you doing?"

"I am seeing to Lord Renoux's food stores, Mistress. Though I have been assigned to assist you, I am still his steward, and have duties to attend to when I am not otherwise occupied."

"Are you going to get back to the translation soon?"

Sazed cocked his head. "Translation, Mistress? It is finished."

"Where's the last part, then?"

"I gave it to you," Sazed said.

"No, you didn't," she said. "This part ends the night before they go into the cavern."

"That is the end, Mistress. That is as far as the logbook went."

"*What?*" she said. "But . . ."

Sazed glanced at the other servants. "We should speak of these things in private, I think." He gave them a few more instructions, pointing at the list, then nodded for Vin to join him as he made his way out the back kitchen exit and into the side gardens.

Vin stood dumbfounded for a moment, then hurried out to join him. "It can't end like that, Saze. We don't know what happened!"

"We can surmise, I think," Sazed said, walking down the garden path. The eastern gardens weren't as lavish as the ones Vin frequented, and were instead made up of smooth brown grass and the occasional shrub.

"Surmise what?" Vin asked.

"Well, the Lord Ruler must have done what was necessary to save the world, for we are still here."

"I suppose," Vin said. "But then he took the power for himself. That must have been what happened—he couldn't resist the temptation to use the power selfishly. But, why isn't there another entry? Why wouldn't he speak further of his accomplishments?"

"Perhaps the power changed him too much," Sazed said. "Or, maybe he simply didn't feel a need to record any more. He had accomplished his goal, and had become immortal as a side benefit. Keeping a journal for one's posterity becomes somewhat redundant when one is going to live forever, I think."

"That's just . . ." Vin ground her teeth in frustration. "It's a very unsatisfying end to a story, Sazed."

He smiled in amusement. "Be careful, Mistress—become too fond of reading, and you may just turn into a scholar."

Vin shook her head. "Not if all the books I read are going to end like this one!"

"If it is of any comfort," Sazed said, "you are not the only one who is disappointed by the logbook's contents. It didn't contain much that Master Kelsier could use—certainly, there was nothing about the Eleventh Metal. I feel somewhat guilty, since I am the one who benefited most from the book."

"But, there wasn't very much about the Terris religion either."

"Not much," Sazed agreed. "But, truly and regretfully, 'not much' is far more than we knew previously. I am only worried that I will not have an opportunity to pass this information on. I have sent a translated copy of the logbook to a location where my brethren and sister Keepers will know to check—it would be a pity if this new knowledge were to die with me."

"It won't," Vin said.

"Oh? Has my lady suddenly become an optimist?"

"Has my Terrisman suddenly become a smart-mouth?" Vin retorted.

"He always has been, I think," Sazed said with a slight smile. "It is one of the things that made him a poor steward—at least, in the eyes of most of his masters."

"Then they must have been fools," Vin said honestly.

"So I was inclined to think, Mistress," Sazed replied. "We should return to the mansion—we should not be seen out in the gardens when the mists arrive, I think."

"I'm just going to go back out into them."

"There are many of the grounds staff that do not know you are Mistborn, Mistress," Sazed said. "It would be a good secret to keep, I think."

"I know," Vin said, turning. "Let's go back then."

"A wise plan."

They walked for a few moments, enjoying the eastern garden's subtle beauty. The grasses were kept carefully trimmed, and they had been arranged in pleasant tiers, the occasional shrubbery giving accent. The southern garden was far more spectacular, with its brook, trees, and exotic plants. But the eastern garden had its own peace—the serenity of simplicity.

"Sazed?" Vin said in a quiet voice.

"Yes, Mistress?"

"It's all going to change, isn't it?"

"What specifically do you mean?"

"Everything," Vin said. "Even if we aren't all dead in a year, the crewmembers will be off working on other projects. Ham will probably be back with his family, Dox and Kelsier will be planning some new escapade, Clubs will be renting his shop to another crew. . . . Even these gardens that we've spent so much money on—they'll belong to someone else."

Sazed nodded. "What you say is likely. Though, if things go well, perhaps the skaa rebellion will be ruling Luthadel by this time next year."

"Maybe," Vin said. "But even still . . . things will change."

"That is the nature of all life, Mistress," Sazed said. "The world must change."

"I know," Vin said with a sigh. "I just wish . . . Well, I actually *like* my life now, Sazed. I like spending time with the crew, and I like training with Kelsier. I love going to balls with Elend on the weekends, love walking in these gardens with you. I don't want these things to change. I don't want my life to go back to the way it was a year ago."

"It doesn't have to, Mistress," Sazed said. "It could change for the better."

"It won't," Vin said quietly. "It's starting already—Kelsier has hinted that my training is almost finished. When I practice in the future, I'll have to do it alone.

"As for Elend, he doesn't even know that I'm skaa—and it's my job to try and destroy his family. Even if House Venture doesn't fall by my hand, others will bring it down—I know Shan Elariel is planning something, and I haven't been able to discover anything about her schemes.

"That's only the beginning, though. We face the Final Empire. We'll probably fail—to be honest, I don't see how things could possibly turn out otherwise. We'll fight, we'll do some good, but we won't change much—and those of us who survive will spend the rest of our lives running from the Inquisitors. Everything's going to change, Sazed, and I can't stop it."

Sazed smiled fondly. "Then, Mistress," he said quietly, "simply enjoy what you have. The future will surprise you, I think."

"Maybe," Vin said, unconvinced.

"Ah, you just need to have hope, Mistress. Perhaps you've earned a little bit of good fortune. There were a group of people before the Ascension known as the Astalsi. They claimed that each person was born with a certain finite amount of ill luck. And so, when an unfortunate event happened, they thought themselves blessed—thereafter, their lives could only get better."

Vin raised an eyebrow. "Sounds a bit simpleminded to me."

"I do not believe so," Sazed said. "Why, the Astalsi were rather advanced— they mixed religion with science quite profoundly. They thought that different colors were indications of different kinds of fortune, and were quite detailed in their descriptions of light and color. Why, it's from them that we get some of our best ideas as to what things might have looked like before the Ascension. They had a scale of colors, and used it to describe the sky of the deepest blue and various plants in their shades of green.

"Regardless, I find their philosophies regarding luck and fortune enlightened. To them, a poor life was only a sign of fortune to come. It might be a good fit for you, Mistress; you could benefit from the knowledge that your luck cannot always be bad."

"I don't know," Vin said skeptically. "I mean, if your bad luck were limited, wouldn't your *good* luck be limited too? Every time something good happened, I'd be worried about using it all up."

"Hum," Sazed said. "I suppose that depends on your viewpoint, Mistress."

"How can you be so optimistic?" Vin asked. "You and Kelsier both."

"I don't know, Mistress," Sazed said. "Perhaps our lives have been easier than yours. Or, perhaps we are simply more foolish."

Vin fell silent. They walked for a short time longer, weaving their way back toward the building, but not rushing the walk. "Sazed," she finally said. "When you saved me, that night in the rain, you used Feruchemy, didn't you?"

Sazed nodded. "Indeed. The Inquisitor was very focused on you, and I was able to sneak up behind him, then hit him with a stone. I had grown many times stronger than a regular man, and my blow threw him into the wall, breaking several of his bones, I suspect."

"Is that it?" Vin asked.

"You sound disappointed, Mistress," Sazed noted, smiling. "You expected something more spectacular, I suppose?"

Vin nodded. "It's just . . . you've been so quiet about Feruchemy. That makes it seem more mystical, I guess."

Sazed sighed. "There is really little to hide from you, Mistress. The truly unique power of Feruchemy—the ability to store and recover memories—you must surely have already guessed. The rest of the powers are not different, really, from the powers granted to you by pewter and tin. A few of them are a little more odd—making a Feruchemist heavier, or changing his age—but they offer little martial application."

"Age?" Vin said, perking up. "You could make yourself younger?"

"Not really, Mistress," Sazed said. "Remember, a Feruchemist must draw his powers from his own body. He could, for instance, spend a few weeks with his body aged to the point that it felt and looked ten years older than he really was. Then, he could withdraw that age to make himself seem ten years younger for an equal amount of time. However, in Feruchemy, there must be a balance."

Vin thought about that for a moment. "Does the metal you use matter?" she asked. "Like in Allomancy?"

"Most certainly," Sazed said. "The metal determines what can be stored."

Vin nodded and continued to walk, thinking over what he'd said. "Sazed, can I have a bit of your metal?" she finally asked.

"My metal, Mistress?"

"Something you've used as a Feruchemical store," Vin said. "I want to try burning it—maybe that will let me use some of its power."

Sazed frowned curiously.

"Has anyone ever tried it before?"

"I'm sure someone must have," Sazed said. "But, I honestly can't think of a specific example. Perhaps if I were to go search my memory copperminds . . ."

"Why not just let me try it now?" Vin asked. "Do you have something made from one of the basic metals? Something you haven't stored anything too valuable in?"

Sazed paused, then reached up to one of his oversized earlobes and undid an earring much like the one Vin wore. He handed the earring's tiny backing, used to hold the earring in place, to Vin. "It is pure pewter, Mistress. I have stored a moderate amount of strength in it."

Vin nodded, swallowing the tiny stud. She felt at her Allomantic reserve, but the stud's metal didn't seem to do anything different. She tentatively burned pewter.

"Anything?" Sazed asked.

Vin shook her head. "No, I don't . . ." She trailed off. There *was* something there, something different.

"What is it, Mistress?" Sazed asked, uncharacteristic eagerness sounding in his voice.

"I . . . can feel the power, Saze. It's faint—far beyond my grasp—but I swear that there's another reserve within me, one that only appears when I'm burning your metal."

Sazed frowned. "It's faint, you say? Like . . . you can see a shadow of the reserve, but can't access the power itself?"

Vin nodded. "How do you know?"

"That's what it feels like when you try to use another Feruchemist's metals, Mistress," Sazed said, sighing. "I should have suspected this would be the result. You cannot access the power because it does not belong to you."

"Oh," Vin said.

"Do not be too disappointed, Mistress. If Allomancers could steal strength from my people, it would already be known. It was a clever thought, however." He turned, pointing toward the mansion. "The carriage has already arrived. We are late for the meeting, I think."

Vin nodded, and they hurried their pace toward the mansion.

Funny, Kelsier thought to himself as he slipped across the darkened courtyard before Mansion Renoux. *I have to sneak into my own house, as if I were attacking some nobleman's keep.*

There was no avoiding it, however—not with his reputation. Kelsier the thief had been distinctive enough; Kelsier the rebellion instigator and skaa spiritual leader was even more infamous. That didn't, of course, keep him from spreading his nightly chaos—he just had to be more careful. More and more families were pulling out of the city, and the powerful houses were growing increasingly paranoid. In a way, that made manipulating them easier—but sneaking around their keeps was getting very dangerous.

In comparison, Mansion Renoux was virtually unprotected. There were guards, of course, but no Mistings. Renoux had to keep a low profile; too many Allomancers would make him stand out. Kelsier kept to the shadows, carefully making his way around to the east side of the building. Then he Pushed off a coin and guided himself up onto Renoux's own balcony.

Kelsier landed lightly, then peeked through the glass balcony doors. The drapes were shut, but he could pick out Dockson, Vin, Sazed, Ham, and Breeze standing around Renoux's desk. Renoux himself sat in the far corner of the room, staying out of the proceedings. His contract included playing the part of Lord Renoux, but he didn't wish to be involved in the plan anymore than he had to.

Kelsier shook his head. *It would be far too easy for an assassin to get in here. I'll have to make sure that Vin continues to sleep at Clubs' shop.* He wasn't worried about Renoux; the kandra's nature was such that he didn't need to fear an assassin's blade.

Kelsier tapped lightly on the door, and Dockson strolled over, pulling it open.

"And he makes his stunning entry!" Kelsier announced, sweeping into the room, throwing back his mistcloak.

Dockson snorted, shutting the doors. "You're truly a wonder to behold, Kell. Particularly the soot stains on your knees."

"I had to do some crawling tonight," Kelsier said, waving an indifferent hand. "There's an unused drainage ditch that passes right under Keep Lekal's defensive wall. You'd think they'd get that patched up."

"I doubt they need worry," Breeze said from beside the desk. "Most of you Mistborn are probably too proud to crawl. I'm surprised you were willing to do so yourself."

"Too proud to crawl?" Kelsier said. "Nonsense! Why, I'd say that we Mistborn are too proud *not* to be humble enough to go crawling about—in a dignified manner, of course."

Dockson frowned, approaching the desk. "Kell, that didn't make any sense."

"We Mistborn need not make sense," Kelsier said haughtily. "What's this?"

"From your brother," Dockson said, pointing at a large map laid across the desk. "It arrived this afternoon in the hollow of a broken table leg that the Canton of Orthodoxy hired Clubs to repair."

"Interesting," Kelsier said, scanning the map. "It's a list of the Soothing stations, I assume?"

"Indeed," Breeze said. "It's quite the discovery—I've never seen such a detailed, carefully drawn map of the city. Why, it not only shows every one of the thirty-four Soothing stations, but also locations of Inquisitor activity, as well as places that the different Cantons are concerned about. I haven't had the opportunity to associate much with your brother, but I must say that the man is obviously a genius!"

"It's almost hard to believe he's related to Kell, eh?" Dockson said with a smile. He had a notepad before him, and was in the process of making a list of all the Soothing stations.

Kelsier snorted. "Marsh might be the genius, but I'm the handsome one. What are these numbers?"

"Inquisitor raids and dates," Ham said. "You'll notice that Vin's crewhouse is listed."

Kelsier nodded. "How in the world did Marsh manage to steal a map like this?"

"He didn't," Dockson said as he wrote. "There was a note with the map. Apparently, high prelans *gave* it to him—they've been very impressed with Marsh, and wanted him to look over the city and recommend locations for new Soothing stations. It seems that the Ministry is a bit worried about the house war, and they want to send out some extra Soothers to try and keep things under control."

"We're supposed to send the map back inside the repaired table leg," Sazed said. "Once we are done this evening, I shall endeavor to copy it in as short a time as possible."

And memorize it as well, thereby making it part of every Keeper's record, Kelsier thought. *The day when you'll stop memorizing and start teaching is coming soon, Saze. I hope your people are ready.*

Kelsier turned, studying the map. It was as impressive as Breeze had said. Indeed, Marsh must have taken an extremely great risk in sending it away. Perhaps a foolhardy risk, even—but the information it contained . . .

We'll have to get this back quickly, Kelsier thought. *Tomorrow morning, if possible.*

"What is this?" Vin asked quietly, leaning across the large map and pointing. She wore a noblewoman's dress—a pretty one-piece garment that was only slightly less ornate than a ball gown.

Kelsier smiled. He could remember a time when Vin had looked frighteningly awkward in a dress, but she seemed to have taken an increasing liking to them. She still didn't move *quite* like a noble-born lady. She was graceful—but it was the dexterous grace of a predator, not the deliberate grace of a courtly lady. Still, the gowns seemed to fit Vin now—in a way that had nothing at all to do with tailoring.

Ah, Mare, Kelsier thought. *You always wanted a daughter you could teach to walk the line between noblewoman and thief.* They would have liked each other; they both had a hidden streak of unconventionality. Perhaps if his wife were still alive, she could have taught Vin things about pretending to be a noblewoman that even Sazed didn't know.

Of course, if Mare were still alive, I wouldn't be doing any of this. I wouldn't dare.

"Look!" Vin said. "One of these Inquisitor dates is new—it's marked as yesterday!"

Dockson shot a glance at Kelsier.

We would have had to tell her eventually anyway. . . . "That was Theron's crew," Kelsier said. "An Inquisitor hit them yesterday evening."

Vin paled.

"Should I recognize that name?" Ham asked.

"Theron's crew was part of the team that was trying to dupe the Ministry with Camon," Vin said. "This means . . . they probably still have my trail."

The Inquisitor recognized her that night when we infiltrated the palace. He wanted to know who her father was. It's fortunate that those inhuman things make the nobility uncomfortable—otherwise, we'd have to worry about sending her to balls.

"Theron's crew," Vin said. "Was . . . it like last time?"

Dockson nodded. "No survivors."

There was an uncomfortable silence, and Vin looked visibly sick.

Poor kid, Kelsier thought. There was little they could do but move on, though. "All right. How are we going to use this map?"

"It has some Ministry notes on house defenses," Ham said. "Those will be useful."

"There doesn't appear to be any pattern in the Inquisitor hits, however," Breeze said. "They probably just go where the information leads them."

"We'll want to refrain from being too active near Soothing stations," Dox said, lowering his pen. "Fortunately, Clubs's shop isn't close to any specific station—most of them are in the slums."

"We need to do more than just avoid the stations," Kelsier said. "We need to be ready to take them out."

Breeze frowned. "If we do, we risk playing our hand recklessly."

"But think of the damage it would do," Kelsier said. "Marsh said there were at least three Soothers and a Seeker at *every* one of these stations. That's a hundred and thirty Ministry Mistings—they must have recruited across the entire Central Dominance to gather those kinds of numbers. If we were to take them all out at once . . ."

"We'd never be able to kill that many ourselves," Dockson said.

"We could if we used the rest of our army," Ham said. "We've got them stashed throughout the slums."

"I have a better idea," Kelsier said. "We can hire other thieving crews. If we had ten crews, each assigned to take out three stations, we could clear the city of Ministry Soothers and Seekers in barely a few hours."

"We'd have to discuss timing, though," Dockson said. "Breeze is right— killing that many obligators in one evening means making a major commitment. It won't take the Inquisitors long to retaliate."

Kelsier nodded. *You're right, Dox. Timing will be vital.* "Would you look into it? Find some appropriate crews, but wait until we decide on a time before giving them the locations of the Soothing stations."

Dockson nodded.

"Good," Kelsier said. "Speaking of our soldiers, Ham, how are things going with them?"

"Better than I expected, actually," Ham said. "They went through training in the caves, and so they're fairly competent. And, they consider themselves the more 'faithful' segment of the army, since they didn't follow Yeden to battle against your will."

Breeze snorted. "That's a convenient way of looking past the fact that they lost three-fourths of their army in a tactical blunder."

"They're good men, Breeze," Ham said firmly. "And so were those who died.

Don't speak ill of them. Regardless, I worry about hiding the army as we are—it won't be too long before one of the teams gets discovered."

"That's why none of them know where to find the others," Kelsier said.

"I do want to mention something about the men," Breeze said, seating himself in one of Renoux's desk chairs. "I see the importance of sending Hammond to train the soldiers—but honestly, what is the reason for forcing Dockson and myself to go and visit them?"

"The men need to know who their leaders are," Kelsier said. "If Ham were to become indisposed, someone else will need to take command."

"Why not you?" Breeze asked.

"Just bear with me," Kelsier said, smiling. "It's for the best."

Breeze rolled his eyes. "Bear with you. We seem to do an awful lot of that. . . ."

"Anyway," Kelsier said. "Vin, what news from the nobility? Have you discovered anything useful about House Venture?"

She paused. "No."

"But the ball next week will be at Keep Venture, right?" Dockson asked.

Vin nodded.

Kelsier eyed the girl. *Would she even tell us if she knew?* She met his eyes, and he couldn't read a thing in them. *Blasted girl's far too experienced a liar.*

"All right," he said to her. "Keep looking."

"I will," she said.

Despite his fatigue, Kelsier found sleep elusive that night. Unfortunately, he couldn't go out and roam the hallways—only certain servants knew he was at the mansion, and he needed to keep a low profile, now that his reputation was building.

His reputation. He sighed as he leaned against the balcony railing, watching the mists. In a way, the things he did worried even him. The others didn't question him out loud, as per his request, but he could tell that they were still bothered by his growing fame.

It's the best way. I may not need all of this . . . but, if I do, I'm going to be glad I went to the trouble.

A soft knock came at his door. He turned, curious, as Sazed peeked his head into the room.

"I apologize, Master Kelsier," Sazed said. "But a guard came to me and said he could see you up on your balcony. He was worried that you'd give yourself away."

Kelsier sighed, but backed away from the balcony, pulling the doors closed and shutting the drapes. "I'm not meant for anonymity, Saze. For a thief, I'm really not all that good at hiding."

Sazed smiled and began to withdraw.

"Sazed?" Kelsier asked, causing the Terrisman to pause. "I can't sleep—do you have a new proposal for me?"

Sazed smiled deeply, walking into the room. "Of course, Master Kelsier. Lately, I've been thinking that you should hear about the Truths of the Bennet. They fit you quite well, I think. The Bennet were a highly developed people who lived on the southern islands. They were brave seafarers and brilliant cartographers; some of the maps the Final Empire still uses were developed by Bennet explorers.

"Their religion was designed to be practiced aboard ships that were away at sea for months at a time. The captain was also their minister, and no man was allowed to command unless he had received theological training."

"Probably weren't very many mutinies."

Sazed smiled. "It was a good religion, Master Kelsier. It focused on discovery and knowledge—to these people, the making of maps was a reverent duty. They believed that once all of the world was known, understood, and catalogued, men would finally find peace and harmony. Many religions teach such ideals, but few actually managed to practice them as well as the Bennet."

Kelsier frowned, leaning back against the wall beside the balcony drapes. "Peace and harmony," he said slowly. "I'm not really looking for either right now, Saze."

"Ah," Sazed said.

Kelsier looked up, staring at the ceiling. "Could you . . . tell me about the Valla again?"

"Of course," Sazed said, pulling a chair over from beside Kelsier's desk and seating himself. "What specifically would you like to know?"

Kelsier shook his head. "I'm not sure," he said. "I'm sorry, Saze. I'm in a strange mood tonight."

"You are always in a strange mood, I think," Sazed said with a slight smile. "However, you choose an interesting sect to ask after. The Valla lasted longer into the Lord Ruler's dominion than any other religion."

"That's why I ask," Kelsier said. "I . . . need to understand what kept them going for so long, Saze. What made them keep fighting?"

"They were the most determined, I think."

"But they didn't have any leaders," Kelsier said. "The Lord Ruler had slaughtered the entire Vallan religious council as part of his first conquest."

"Oh, they had leaders, Master Kelsier," Sazed said. "Dead ones, true, but leaders nonetheless."

"Some men would say that their devotion didn't make sense," Kelsier said. "The loss of the Vallan leaders should have broken the people, not made them more determined to keep going."

Sazed shook his head. "Men are more resilient than that, I think. Our belief is often strongest when it should be weakest. That is the nature of hope."

Kelsier nodded.

"Did you want further instruction on the Valla?"

"No. Thanks, Saze. I just needed to be reminded that there were people who fought even when things looked hopeless."

Sazed nodded, rising. "I think I understand, Master Kelsier. Good evening, then."

Kelsier nodded distractedly, letting the Terrisman withdraw.

Most of the Terrismen are not as bad as Rashek. However, I can see that they believe him, to an extent. These are simple men, not philosophers or scholars, and they don't understand that their own prophecies say the Hero of Ages will be an outsider. They only see what Rashek points out—that they are an ostensibly superior people, and should be "dominant" rather than subservient.

Before such passion and hatred, even good men can be deceived.

30

IT TOOK RETURNING TO THE VENTURE ballroom to remind Vin what true majesty was.

She'd visited so many keeps that she had begun to grow desensitized to the splendor. There was something special about Keep Venture, however—something that the other keeps strived for, but never quite achieved. It was as if Venture were the parent, and the others were well-taught children. All of the keeps were beautiful, but there was no denying which one was the finest.

The enormous Venture hall, lined by a row of massive pillars on each side, seemed even more grand than usual. Vin couldn't quite decide why. She thought about it as she waited for a servant to take her shawl. The normal limelights shone outside the stained-glass windows, spraying the room with shards of light. The tables were immaculate beneath their pillared overhang. The lord's table, set on the small balcony at the very end of the hallway, looked as regal as ever.

It's almost . . . too perfect, Vin thought, frowning to herself. Everything seemed slightly exaggerated. The tablecloths were even whiter, and pressed even flatter, than usual. The servants' uniforms seemed particularly sharp. Instead of regular soldiers at the doors, hazekillers stood looking intentionally impressive, distinguished by their wooden shields and lack of armor. All together, the room made it seem as if even the regular Venture perfection had been heightened.

"Something's wrong, Sazed," she whispered as a servant moved off to prepare her table.

"What do you mean, Mistress?" the tall steward asked, standing behind her and to the side.

"There are too many people here," Vin said, realizing one of the things that was bothering her. Ball attendance had been tapering off during the last few months. Yet, it seemed like everyone had returned for the Venture event. And they all wore their finest.

"Something's going on," Vin said quietly. "Something we don't know about."

"Yes . . ." Sazed said quietly. "I sense it too. Perhaps I should go to the stewards' dinner early."

"Good idea," Vin said. "I think I might just skip the meal this evening. We're a bit late, and it looks like people have already started chatting."

Sazed smiled.

"What?"

"I remember a time when you would *never* skip a meal, Mistress."

Vin snorted. "Just be glad I never tried to stuff my pockets with food from one of these balls—trust me, I was tempted. Now, get going."

Sazed nodded and moved off toward the stewards' dinner. Vin scanned the chatting groups. *No sign of Shan, thankfully,* she thought. Unfortunately, Kliss was nowhere to be seen either, so Vin had to choose someone else to go to for gossip. She strolled forward, smiling at Lord Idren Seeris, a cousin to House Elariel and a man she had danced with on several occasions. He acknowledged her with a stiff nod, and she joined his group.

Vin smiled at the other members of the group—three women and one other lord. She knew them all at least passingly, and had danced with Lord Yestal. However, this evening all four of them gave her cold looks.

"I haven't been to Keep Venture in a while," Vin said, falling into her persona as a country girl. "I'd forgotten how majestic it is!"

"Indeed," said one of the ladies. "Excuse me—I'm going to go get something to drink."

"I'll go with you," one of the other ladies added, both of them leaving the group.

Vin watched them go, frowning.

"Ah," Yestal said. "Our meal has arrived. Coming, Triss?"

"Of course," the final lady said, joining Yestal as they walked away.

Idren adjusted his spectacles, shooting Vin a halfhearted look of apology, then withdrew. Vin stood, dumbfounded. She hadn't received such an obviously cold reception since her first few balls.

What's going on? she thought with increasing trepidation. *Is this Shan's work? Could she turn an entire room full of people against me?*

No, that didn't feel right. It would have required too much effort. In addition, the oddity wasn't just around her. All of the groups of noblemen were . . . different this evening.

Vin tried a second group, with an even worse result. As soon as she joined, the members pointedly ignored her. Vin felt so out of place that she withdrew, fleeing to get herself a cup of wine. As she walked, she noticed that the first group—the one with Yestal and Idren—had re-formed with exactly the same members.

Vin paused, standing just inside the shade of the eastern overhang and scanning the crowd. There were very few people dancing, and she recognized them all as established couples. There also seemed to be very little mingling between groups or tables. While the ballroom was filled, it seemed most of the attendees were distinctly trying to ignore everyone else.

I need to get a better view of this, she thought, walking to the stairwell. A short climb later, she came out on the long, corridorlike balcony set into the wall above the dance floor, its familiar blue lanterns giving the stonework a soft, melancholy hue.

Vin paused. Elend's cubbyhole sat between the rightmost column and the wall, well lit by a single lantern. He almost always spent Venture balls reading there; he didn't like the pomp and ceremony that came from hosting a party.

The cubbyhole was empty. She approached the railing, then craned out to look toward the far end of the grand hallway. The host's table sat on an overhang at the same level as the balconies, and she was shocked to see Elend sitting there dining with his father.

What? she thought incredulously. Never once, during the half-dozen balls she'd attended at Keep Venture, had she seen Elend sit with his family.

Down below, she caught sight of a familiar, colorful-robed figure moving through the crowd. She waved toward Sazed, but he had obviously already seen her. As she waited for him, Vin thought she faintly heard a familiar voice coming from the other end of the balcony. She turned and checked, noticing a short figure she'd missed before. Kliss was speaking with a small group of minor lords.

So that's where Kliss went, Vin thought. *Maybe she'll talk to me.* Vin stood, waiting for either Kliss to finish her conversation or Sazed to arrive.

Sazed came first, leaving the stairwell, breathing heavily. "Mistress," he said in a low voice, joining her by the railing.

"Tell me you discovered something, Sazed. This ball feels . . . creepy. Everyone's so solemn and cold. It's almost like we're at a funeral, not a party."

"It is an apt metaphor, my lady," Sazed said quietly. "We have missed an important announcement. House Hasting said it is not going to hold its regular ball this week."

Vin frowned. "So? Houses have canceled balls before."

"House Elariel canceled as well. Normally, Tekiel would come next—but that house is defunct. House Shunah has already announced that it won't be holding any more balls."

"What are you saying?"

"It appears, Mistress, that this will be the last ball for a time . . . perhaps a very long time."

Vin glanced down at the hall's magnificent windows, which stood above the independent—almost hostile—groups of people.

"*That's* what's going on," she said. "They're finalizing alliances. Everyone is standing with their strongest friends and supporters. They know this is the last ball, and so they all came to put in an appearance, but they know they've no time left for politicking."

"It seems that way, Mistress."

"They're all going on the defensive," Vin said. "Retreating behind their walls, so to speak. That's why no one wants to talk to me—we made Renoux too neutral a force. I don't have a faction, and it's a bad time to be gambling on random political elements."

"Master Kelsier needs to know this information, Mistress," Sazed said. "He planned on pretending to be an informant again tonight. If he's ignorant of this situation, it could seriously damage his credibility. We should leave."

"No," Vin said, turning toward Sazed. "I can't go—not when everyone else is staying. They all thought it was important to come and be seen at this last ball, and so I shouldn't leave until they start to."

Sazed nodded. "Very well."

"You go, Sazed. Hire a carriage and go tell Kell what we've learned. I'll stay for a little longer, then leave when it won't make House Renoux look weak."

Sazed paused. "I . . . don't know, Mistress."

Vin rolled her eyes. "I appreciate the help you've given me, but you don't need to keep holding my hand. Plenty of people come to these balls without their stewards to watch after them."

Sazed sighed. "Very well, Mistress. I shall return, however, after I have located Master Kelsier."

Vin nodded, bidding him farewell, and he retreated down the stone stairwell. Vin leaned against the balcony in Elend's spot, watching until Sazed appeared below and disappeared toward the front gates.

Now what? Even if I can find someone to talk to, there's really no point in spreading rumors now.

She felt a feeling of dread. Who would have thought that she would come to enjoy noble frivolity so much? The experience was tainted by her knowledge of what many noblemen were capable of, but even still, there had been a . . . dreamlike joy to the entire experience.

Would she ever attend balls like these again? What would happen to Valette the noblewoman? Would she have to put away her dresses and makeup, and return to simply being Vin the street thief? There probably wouldn't be room for things like grand balls in Kelsier's new kingdom, and that might not be a bad thing—what right did she have to dance while other skaa starved? Yet . . . it seemed like the world would be missing something beautiful without the keeps and dancers, the dresses and the festivities.

She sighed, leaning back from the railing, glancing down at her own dress. It was of a deep shimmering blue, with white circular designs sewn around the base of the skirt. It was sleeveless, but the blue silk gloves she wore ran all the way past her elbows.

Once she would have found the outfit frustratingly bulky. Now, however, she found it beautifying. She liked how it was designed to make her look full through the chest, yet accentuated her thin upper torso. She liked how it flared at the waist, slowly fanning out into a wide bell that rustled as she walked.

She'd miss it—she'd miss it all. But, Sazed was right. She couldn't stop the progression of time, she could only enjoy the moment.

I'm not going to let him sit up there at the high table all evening and ignore me, she decided.

Vin turned and walked along the balcony, nodding to Kliss as she passed. The balcony ended in a corridor that turned, and—as Vin had correctly guessed—led out onto the ledge that held the host's table.

She stood inside the corridor for a moment, looking out. Lords and ladies sat in regal outfits, basking in the privilege of being invited up to sit with Lord Straff Venture. Vin waited, trying to get Elend's attention, and finally one of the guests noticed her, then nudged Elend. He turned with surprise, saw Vin, then flushed slightly.

She waved briefly, and he stood, excusing himself. Vin ducked back into the stone corridor a bit so they could speak more privately.

"Elend!" she said as he walked into the corridor. "You're sitting with your father!"

He nodded. "This ball has turned into something of a special event, Valette, and my father was fairly insistent that I obey protocol."

"When are we going to have time to talk?"

Elend paused. "I'm not sure that we will."

Vin frowned. He seemed . . . reserved. His usual, slightly worn and wrinkled suit had been replaced by a sharp, well-fitted one. His hair was even combed.

"Elend?" she said, stepping forward.

He raised a hand, warding her back. "Things have changed, Valette."

No, she thought. *This can't change, not yet!* "Things? What 'things'? Elend, what are you talking about?"

"I am heir to House Venture," he said. "And dangerous times are coming. House Hasting lost an entire convoy this afternoon, and that's only the beginning. Within the month, the keeps will openly be at war. These aren't things I can ignore, Valette. It's time I stopped being a liability to my family."

"That's fine," Vin said. "That doesn't mean—"

"Valette," Elend interrupted. "You are a liability too. A very big one. I won't lie and claim that I never cared for you—I did, and I still do. However, I knew from the start—as you did—that this could never be anything more than a passing dalliance. The truth is, my house needs me—and it's more important than you are."

Vin paled. "But . . ."

He turned to go back to dinner.

"Elend," she said quietly, "please don't turn away from me."

He paused, then looked back at her. "I know the truth, Valette. I know how you've lied about who you are. I don't care, really—I'm not angry, or even disappointed. The truth is, I expected it. You're just . . . playing the game. Like we all are." He paused, then shook his head and turned away from her. "Like I am."

"Elend?" she said, reaching for him.

"Don't make me embarrass you in public, Valette."

Vin paused, feeling numb. And then, she was too angry to be numb—too angry, too frustrated . . . and too terrified.

"Don't leave," she whispered. "Don't you leave me too."

"I'm sorry," he said. "But I have to go meet with my friends. It was . . . fun."

And he left.

Vin stood in the darkened corridor. She felt herself shiver quietly, and she turned to stumble back out onto the main balcony. To the side, she could see Elend bid good evening to his family, then head through a back corridor toward the keep's living section.

He can't do this to me. Not Elend. Not now . . .

However, a voice from within—a voice she had nearly forgotten—began to speak. *Of course he left you,* Reen whispered. *Of course he abandoned you. Everyone will betray you, Vin. What did I teach you?*

No! she thought. *It's just the political tension. Once this is over, I'll be able to convince him to come back. . . .*

I never came back for you, Reen whispered. *He won't either.* The voice felt so real—it was almost like she could hear him beside her.

Vin leaned up against the balcony railing, using the iron grating for strength, holding herself up. She wouldn't let him destroy her. A life on the streets hadn't been able to break her; she wouldn't let a self-important nobleman do so. She just kept telling herself that.

But, why did this hurt so much more than starvation—so much more than one of Camon's beatings?

"Well, Valette Renoux," a voice said from behind.

"Kliss," Vin said. "I'm . . . not in the mood to talk right now."

"Ah," Kliss said. "So Elend Venture finally spurned you. Don't worry, child—he'll get what he deserves shortly."

Vin turned, frowning at the odd tone in Kliss's voice. The woman didn't seem like herself. She seemed too . . . controlled.

"Deliver a message to your uncle for me, will you dear?" Kliss asked lightly. "Tell him that a man such as himself—without house alliances—might have a difficult time gathering intelligence in the upcoming months. If he needs a good source of information, tell him to send for me. I know lots of interesting things."

"You're an informant!" Vin said, pushing aside her pain for the moment. "But, you're . . ."

"A foolish gossip?" the short woman asked. "Why, yes I am. It's fascinating, the kinds of things you can learn when you're known as the court gossip. People come to you to spread obvious lies—such as the things you told me about House Hasting last week. Why would you want me to spread such untruths? Could House Renoux be making a bid for the weapons market during the house war? Indeed—could Renoux be *behind* the recent attack on the Hasting barges?"

Kliss's eyes twinkled. "Tell your uncle that I can be made to keep quiet about what I know—for a small fee."

"You've been duping me all along. . . ." Vin said numbly.

"Of course, dear," Kliss said, patting Vin's arm. "That's what we do here at court. You'll learn eventually—if you survive. Now, be a good child and deliver my message, all right?"

Kliss turned, her squat, gaudy dress suddenly seeming a brilliant costume to Vin.

"Wait!" Vin said. "What was that you said about Elend earlier? He's going to get what he deserves?"

"Hum?" Kliss said, turning. "Why . . . that's right. You've been asking after Shan Elariel's plans, haven't you?"

Shan? Vin thought with rising concern. "What is she planning?"

"Now *that*, my dear, is an expensive secret indeed. I could tell you . . . but then, what would I have in return? A woman of an unimportant house like myself needs to find sustenance somewhere. . . ."

Vin pulled off her sapphire necklace, the only piece of jewelry she was wearing. "Here. Take it."

Kliss accepted the necklace with a thoughtful expression. "Hum, yes, very nice indeed."

"What do you know?" Vin snapped.

"Young Elend is going to be one of the first Venture casualties in the house war, I'm afraid," Kliss said, stuffing the necklace into a sleeve pocket. "It's unfortunate—he really does seem like a nice boy. Too nice, probably."

"When?" Vin demanded. "Where? How?"

"So many questions, but only one necklace," Kliss said idly.

"It's all I have right now!" Vin said truthfully. Her coin pouch contained only bronze clips for Steelpushing.

"But it's a *very* valuable secret, as I've said," Kliss continued. "By telling you, my own life would be—"

That's it! Vin thought furiously. *Stupid aristocratic games!*

Vin burned zinc and brass, hitting Kliss with a powerful blast of emotional Allomancy. She Soothed away all of the woman's feelings but fear, then took hold of that fear and yanked on it with a firm tug.

"Tell me!" Vin growled.

Kliss gasped, wobbling and nearly falling to the ground. "An Allomancer! No *wonder* Renoux brought such a distant cousin with him to Luthadel!"

"Speak!" Vin said, taking a step forward.

"You're too late to help him," Kliss said. "I'd never sell a secret like this if it had a chance of turning on me!"

"Tell me!"

"He'll be assassinated by Elariel Allomancers this evening," Kliss whispered. "He might be dead already—it was supposed to happen as soon as he withdrew from the lord's table. But if you want revenge, you'll have to look toward Lord Straff Venture too."

"Elend's father?" Vin asked with surprise.

"Of course, foolish child," Kliss said. "Lord Venture would love nothing more than an excuse to give the house title to his nephew instead. All Venture had to do was withdraw a few of his soldiers from the rooftop around young Elend's room to let in the Elariel assassins. And, since the assassination will occur during one of Elend's little philosophy meetings, Lord Venture will be able to rid himself of a Hasting and a Lekal too!"

Vin spun. *I have to do something!*

"Of course," Kliss said with a chuckle, standing up. "Lord Venture is in for a surprise himself. I've heard that your Elend has some very . . . choice books in his possession. Young Venture should be much more careful about the things he tells his women, I think."

Vin turned back to the smiling Kliss. The woman winked at her. "I'll keep your Allomancy a secret, child. Just make certain I get payment by tomorrow afternoon. A lady must buy food—and as you can see, I need a lot of it.

"As for House Venture . . . well, I'd distance myself from them, if I were you. Shan's assassins are going to make *quite* the disturbance tonight. I wouldn't be surprised if half the court ended up in the boy's room to see what the ruckus was about. When the court sees those books Elend has . . . well, let's just say that the obligators are going to become very interested in House Venture for a time. Too bad Elend will already be dead—we haven't had an open execution of a nobleman in quite some time!"

Elend's room, Vin thought desperately. *That's where they must be!* She turned, holding the sides of her dress and rustling frantically down the balcony walkway toward the corridor she had left moments before.

"Where are you going?" Kliss asked with surprise.

"I have to stop this!" Vin said.

Kliss laughed. "I already told you that you're too late. Venture is a very old keep, and the back passages leading to the lords' quarters are quite the maze. If you don't know your way, you'll end up lost for hours."

Vin glanced around, feeling helpless.

"Besides, child," Kliss added, turning to walk away. "Didn't the boy just spurn you? What do you owe him?"

Vin paused.

She's right. What do *I owe him?*

The answer came immediately. *I love him.*

With that thought came strength. Vin rushed forward despite Kliss's laughter. She had to try. She entered the corridor and moved into the back passageways. However, Kliss's words soon proved true: The dark stone passageways were narrow and unadorned. She'd never find her way in time.

The roof, she thought. *Elend's rooms will have an outside balcony. I need a window!*

She dashed down a passage, kicking off her shoes and pulling off her stockings, then running as best she could in the dress. She searched frantically for a window big enough to fit through. She burst out into a larger corridor, empty save for flickering torches.

A massive lavender rose window stood on the far side of the room.

Good enough, Vin thought. With a flare of steel, she threw herself into the air, Pushing against a massive iron door behind her. She flew forward for a moment, then Pushed powerfully against the rose window's iron bindings.

She lurched to a stop in the air, Pushing both backward and forward at the same time. She strained, hanging in the empty corridor, flaring her pewter to keep from being crushed. The rose window was enormous, but it was mostly glass. How strong could it be?

Very strong. Vin groaned beneath the strain. She heard a snap behind her, and the door began to twist in its mountings.

You . . . must . . . give! she thought angrily, flaring her steel. Chips of stone fell around the window.

Then, with a *crack* of sound, the rose window burst free from the stone wall. It fell backward into the dark night, and Vin shot out behind it.

Cool mist enveloped her. She Pulled slightly against the door inside the room, keeping herself from going out too far, then Pushed mightily against the falling window. The enormous dark-glassed window tumbled beneath her, churning the mists as Vin shot away from it. Straight up, toward the roof.

The window crashed to the ground just as Vin flew up over the edge of the rooftop, her dress fluttering madly in the wind. She landed on the bronze-plated roof with a thump, falling to a crouch. The metal was cool beneath her toes and fingers.

Tin flared, illuminating the night. She could see nothing out of the ordinary.

She burned bronze, using it as Marsh had taught her, searching for signs of Allomancy. There weren't any—the assassins had a Smoker with them.

I can't search the entire building! Vin thought, desperately, flaring her bronze. *Where are they?*

Then, oddly, she thought she sensed something. An Allomantic pulse in the night. Faint. Hidden. But enough.

Vin rose to dash across the rooftop, trusting her instincts. As she ran, she flared pewter and grabbed her dress near the neck, then ripped the garment down the front with a single yank. She pulled her coin pouch and metal vials from a hidden pocket, and then—still running—she ripped the dress, petti-coats, and attached leggings free, tossing it all aside. Her corset and gloves went next. Underneath, she wore a thin, sleeveless white shift and a pair of white shorts.

She dashed frantically. *I can't be too late,* she thought. *Please. I can't.*

Figures resolved in the mists ahead. They stood beside an angled rooftop skylight; Vin had passed several similar ones as she ran. One of the figures pointed toward the skylight, a weapon glittering in its hand.

Vin cried out, Pushing herself off the bronze roof in an arcing jump. She landed in the very center of the surprised group of people, then thrust her coin pouch upward, ripping it in two.

Coins sprayed into the air, reflecting light from the window below. As the glistening shower of metal fell around Vin, she *Pushed.*

Coins zipped away from her like a swarm of insects, each one leaving a trail in the mist. Figures cried out as coins hit flesh, and several of the dark forms dropped.

Several did not. Some of the coins snapped away, Pushed aside by invisible Allomantic hands. Four people remained standing: Two of them wore mist-cloaks; one of them was familiar.

Shan Elariel. Vin didn't need to see the cloak to understand; there was only one reason a woman as important as Shan would come on an assassination like this. She was a Mistborn.

"*You?*" Shan asked in shock. She wore a black outfit of trousers and shirt, her dark hair pulled back, her mistcloak worn almost stylishly.

Two Mistborn, Vin thought. *Not good.* She scrambled away, ducking as one of the assassins swung a dueling cane at her.

Vin slid across the rooftop, then Pulled herself to a brief halt, spinning with one hand resting against the cold bronze. She reached out and Pulled against the few coins that hadn't escaped out into the night, yanking them back into her hand.

"Kill her!" Shan snapped. The two men Vin had felled lay groaning on the rooftop. They weren't dead; in fact, one was climbing unsteadily to his feet.

Thugs, Vin thought. *The other two are probably Coinshots.*

As if to prove her right, one of the men tried to Push away Vin's vial of metals. Fortunately, there weren't enough metals in the vial to give him a very good anchor, and she kept hold of it easily.

Shan turned her attention back to the skylight.

No you don't! Vin thought, dashing forward again.

The Coinshot cried out as she approached. Vin flipped a coin and shot it at him. He, of course, Pushed back—but Vin anchored herself against the bronze roof and flared Steel, Pushing with a firm effort.

The man's own Steelpush—transmitted from the coin, to Vin, to the roof—launched him out into the air. He cried out, shooting off into the darkness. He was only a Misting, and couldn't Pull himself back to the rooftop.

The other Coinshot tried to spray Vin with coins, but she deflected them with ease. Unfortunately, he wasn't as foolish as his companion, and he released the coins soon after Pushing them. However, it was obvious that he couldn't hit her. Why did he keep—

The other Mistborn! Vin thought, ducking to a roll as a figure leaped from the dark mists, glass knives flashing in the air.

Vin just barely got out of the way, flaring pewter to give herself balance. She came to her feet beside the wounded Thug, who stood on obviously weak legs. With another flare of pewter, Vin slammed her shoulder into the man's chest, shoving him to the side.

The man stumbled maladroitly, still holding his bleeding side. Then he tripped and fell right into the skylight. The fine, tinted glass shattered as he fell, and Vin's tin-enhanced ears could hear cries of surprise from below, followed by a crash as the Thug hit the ground.

Vin looked up, smiling evilly at the stunned Shan. Behind her, the second Mistborn—a man—swore quietly.

"You . . . You . . ." Shan sputtered, her eyes flaring dangerously with anger in the night.

Take the warning, Elend, Vin thought, *and escape. It's time for me to go.*

She couldn't face two Mistborn at once—she couldn't even beat Kelsier most nights. Flaring Steel, Vin launched herself backward. Shan took a step forward and—looking determined—Pushed herself after Vin. The second Mistborn joined her.

Bloody hell! Vin thought, spinning in the air and Pulling herself to the rooftop's edge near where she had broken the rose window. Below, figures scrambled about, lanterns brightening the mists. Lord Venture probably thought that the fuss meant his son was dead. He was in for a surprise.

Vin launched herself into the air again, jumping out into the misty void. She could hear the two Mistborn land behind her, then push off as well.

This isn't good, Vin thought with trepidation as she hurled through the misty air currents. She didn't have any coins left, nor did she have daggers—and she faced two trained Mistborn.

She burned iron, searching frantically for an anchor in the night. A line of blue, moving slowly, appeared beneath her to the right.

Vin yanked on the line, changing her trajectory. She shot downward, the Venture grounds wall appearing as a dark shadow beneath her. Her anchor was the breastplate of an unfortunate guard, who lay atop the wall, holding frantically to a tooth in the battlements to keep himself from being pulled up toward Vin.

Vin slammed feet-first into the man, then spun in the misty air, flipping to land on the cool stone. The guard collapsed to the stone, then cried out, desperately grabbing his stone anchor as another Allomantic force Pulled against him.

Sorry, friend, Vin thought, kicking the man's hand free from the battlement tooth. He immediately snapped upward, yanked into the air as if pulled by a powerful tether.

The sound of bodies colliding sounded from the darkness above, and Vin saw a pair of forms drop limply to the Venture courtyard. Vin smiled, dashing along the wall. *I sure hope that was Shan.*

Vin jumped up, landing atop the gatehouse. Near the keep, people were scattering, climbing in carriages to flee.

And so the house war starts, Vin thought. *Didn't think I'd be the one to officially begin it.*

A figure plummeted toward her from the mists above. Vin cried out, flaring pewter and jumping to the side. Shan landed dexterously—mistcloak tassels billowing—atop the gatehouse. She had both daggers out, and her eyes burned with anger.

Vin jumped to the side, rolling off the gatehouse and landing on the walltop below. A pair of guards jumped back in alarm, surprised to see a half-naked girl fall into their midst. Shan dropped to the wall behind them, then Pushed, throwing one of the guards in Vin's direction.

The man cried out as Vin Pushed against his breastplate as well—but he was far heavier than she, and she was thrown backward. She Pulled on the guard to slow herself, and the man crashed down to the walltop. Vin landed lithely beside him, then grabbed his staff as it rolled free from his hand.

Shan attacked in a flash of spinning daggers, and Vin was forced to jump backward again. *She's so good!* Vin thought with anxiety. Vin herself had barely trained with daggers; now she wished she'd asked Kelsier for a little more practice. She swung the staff, but she'd never used one of the weapons before, and her attack was laughable.

Shan slashed, and Vin felt a flare of pain in her cheek as she dodged. She dropped the staff in shock, reaching up to her face and feeling blood. She stumbled back, seeing the smile on Shan's face.

And then Vin remembered the vial. The one she still carried—the one Kelsier had given her.

Atium.

She didn't bother to grab it from the place she had tucked it at her waist. She burned steel, Pushing it out into the air in front of her. Then, she immediately burned iron and yanked on the bead of atium. The vial shattered, the bead heading back toward Vin. She caught it in her mouth, swallowing the lump and forcing it down.

Shan paused. Then, before Vin could do anything, she downed a vial of her own.

Of course she has atium!

But, how much did she have? Kelsier hadn't given Vin much—only enough for about thirty seconds. Shan jumped forward, smiling, her long black hair flaring in the air. Vin gritted her teeth. She didn't have much choice.

She burned atium. Immediately, Shan's form shot forth dozens of phantom atium shadows. It was a Mistborn standoff: The first one who ran out of atium would be vulnerable. You couldn't escape an opponent who knew exactly what you were going to do.

Vin scrambled backward, keeping an eye on Shan. The noblewoman stalked forward, her phantoms forming an insane bubble of translucent motion around her. She seemed calm. Secure.

She has plenty of atium, Vin thought, feeling her own storage burn away. *I need to get away.*

A shadowy length of wood suddenly shot through Vin's chest. She ducked to the side just as the real arrow—apparently made with no arrowhead—passed through the air where she had been standing. She glanced toward the gatehouse, where several soldiers were raising bows.

She cursed, glancing to the side, into the mists. As she did so, she caught a smile from Shan.

She's just waiting for my atium to burn out. She wants me to run—she knows she can chase me down.

There was only one other option: attack.

Shan frowned in surprise as Vin dashed forward, phantom arrows snapping against the stones just before their real counterparts arrived. Vin dodged between two arrows—her atium-enhanced mind knowing exactly how to move—passing so close that she could feel the missiles in the air to either side of her.

Shan swung her daggers, and Vin twisted to the side, dodging one slice and blocking the other with her forearm, earning a deep gash. Her own blood flew in the air as she spun—each droplet tossing out a translucent atium image—and flared pewter, punching Shan square in the stomach.

Shan grunted in pain, bending slightly, but she didn't fall.

Atium's almost gone, Vin thought desperately. *Only a few seconds left.*

So, she extinguished her atium early, exposing herself.

Shan smiled wickedly, coming up from her crouch, right-hand dagger swinging confidently. She assumed that Vin had run out of atium—and therefore assumed that she was exposed. Vulnerable.

At that moment, Vin burned her last bit of atium. Shan paused just briefly in confusion, giving Vin an opening as a phantom arrow streaked through the mists overhead.

Vin caught the real arrow as it followed—the grainy wood burning her fingers—then rammed it down into Shan's chest. The shaft snapped in Vin's hand, leaving about an inch protruding from Shan's body. The woman stumbled backward, staying on her feet.

Damn pewter, Vin thought, ripping a sword from a sheath beside the unconscious soldier at her feet. She jumped forward, gritting her teeth in determination, and Shan—still dazed—raised a hand to Push against the sword.

Vin let the weapon go—it was just a distraction—as she slammed the second half of the broken arrow into Shan's chest just beside its counterpart.

This time, Shan dropped. She tried to rise, but one of the shafts must have done some serious damage to her heart, for her face paled. She struggled for a moment, then fell lifeless to the stones.

Vin stood, breathing deeply as she wiped the blood from her cheek—only to realize that her bloody arm was just making her face worse. Behind her, the soldiers called out, nocking more arrows.

Vin glanced back toward the keep, bidding farewell to Elend, then Pushed herself out into the night.

Other men worry whether or not they will be remembered. I have no such fears; even disregarding the Terris prophecies, I have brought such chaos, conflict, and hope to this world that there is little chance that I will be forgotten.

I worry about what they will say of me. Historians can make what they wish of the past. In a thousand years' time, will I be remembered as the man who protected mankind from a powerful evil? Or, will I be remembered as a tyrant who arrogantly tried to make himself a legend?

31

"I DON'T KNOW," KELSIER SAID, SMILING as he shrugged. "Breeze would make a pretty good Minister of Sanitation."

The group chuckled, though Breeze just rolled his eyes. "Honestly, I don't see why *I* consistently prove to be the target of you people's humor. Why must you choose the only dignified person in this crew as the butt of your mockery?"

"Because, my dear man," Ham said, imitating Breeze's accent, "you are, by far, the best butt we have."

"Oh, please," Breeze said as Spook nearly collapsed to the floor with laughter. "This is just getting juvenile. The teenage boy was the only one who found *that* comment amusing, Hammond."

"I'm a soldier," Ham said, raising his cup. "Your witty verbal attacks have no effect on me, for I'm far too dense to understand them."

Kelsier chuckled, leaning back against the cupboard. One problem with working at night was that he missed the evening gatherings in Clubs's kitchen. Breeze and Ham continued their general banter. Dox sat at the end of the table, going over ledgers and reports, while Spook sat by Ham eagerly, trying his best to take part in the conversation. Clubs sat in his corner, overseeing, occasionally smiling, and generally enjoying his ability to give the best scowls in the room.

"I should be leaving, Master Kelsier," Sazed said, checking the wall clock. "Mistress Vin should be about ready to leave."

Kelsier nodded. "I should get going myself. I still have to—"

The outside kitchen door slammed open. Vin stood silhouetted by the dark mist, wearing nothing but her dressing undergarments—a flimsy white shirt and shorts. Both were sprayed with blood.

"Vin!" Ham exclaimed, standing.

Her cheek bore a long, thin gash, and she had a bandage tied on one forearm. "I'm fine," she said wearily.

"What happened to your dress?" Dockson immediately demanded.

"You mean this?" Vin asked apologetically, holding up a ripped, soot-stained blue mass of cloth. "It . . . got in the way. Sorry, Dox."

"Lord Ruler, girl!" Breeze said. "Forget the dress—what happened to *you!*"

Vin shook her head, shutting the door. Spook blushed furiously at her outfit, and Sazed immediately moved over, checking the wound on her cheek.

"I think I did something bad," Vin said. "I . . . kind of killed Shan Elariel."

"You did *what?*" Kelsier asked as Sazed tisked quietly, leaving the small cheek cut alone as he undid the bandage on her arm.

Vin flinched slightly at Sazed's ministrations. "She was Mistborn. We fought. I won."

You killed a fully-trained Mistborn? Kelsier thought with shock. *You've practiced for barely eight months!*

"Master Hammond," Sazed requested, "would you fetch my healer's bag?"

Ham nodded, rising.

"You might want to grab her something to wear too," Kelsier suggested. "I think poor Spook's about to have a heart attack."

"What's wrong with this?" Vin asked, nodding toward her clothing. "It's not that much more revealing than some of the thief's clothing I've worn."

"Those are undergarments, Vin," Dockson said.

"So?"

"It's the principle of the matter," Dockson said. "Young ladies do not run around in their undergarments, no matter how much those undergarments may resemble regular clothing."

Vin shrugged, sitting as Sazed held a bandage to her arm. She seemed . . . exhausted. And not just from the fighting. *What else happened at that party?*

"Where did you fight the Elariel woman?" Kelsier asked.

"Outside Keep Venture," Vin said, looking down. "I . . . think some of the guards spotted me. Some of the nobles might have too, I'm not certain."

"That's going to be trouble," Dockson said, sighing. "Of course, that cheek wound is going to be pretty obvious, even with makeup. Honestly, you Allomancers . . . Don't you ever worry about what you're going to look like the day *after* you get into one of these fights?"

"I was kind of focused on staying alive, Dox," Vin said.

"He's just complaining because he's worried about you," Kelsier said as Ham returned with the bag. "That's what he does."

"Both wounds will require immediate stitching, Mistress," Sazed said. "The one on your arm hit the bone, I think."

Vin nodded, and Sazed rubbed her arm with a numbing agent, then began to work. She bore it without much visible discomfort—though she obviously had her pewter flared.

She looks so exhausted, Kelsier thought. She was such a frail-looking thing, mostly just arms and legs. Hammond put a cloak around her shoulders, but she appeared too tired to care.

And I brought her into this.

Of course, she should know better than to get herself into this kind of trouble. Eventually, Sazed finished his efficient sewing, then tied a new bandage around the arm wound. He moved onto the cheek.

"Why would you fight a Mistborn?" Kelsier asked sternly. "You should have run. Didn't you learn anything from your battle with the Inquisitors?"

"I couldn't get away without turning my back on her," Vin said. "Besides, she had more atium than me. If I hadn't attacked, she would have chased me down. I had to strike while we were equally matched."

"But how did you get into this in the first place?" Kelsier demanded. "Did she attack you?"

Vin glanced down at her feet. "I attacked first."

"Why?" Kelsier asked.

Vin sat for a moment, Sazed working on her cheek. "She was going to kill Elend," she finally said.

Kelsier exhaled in exasperation. "Elend Venture? You risked your life— risked the plan, and our lives—for that fool of a boy?"

Vin looked up, glaring at him. "Yes."

"What is wrong with you, girl?" Kelsier asked. "Elend Venture isn't worth this."

She stood angrily, Sazed backing away, the cloak falling the floor. "He's a good man!"

"He's a nobleman!"

"*So are you!*" Vin snapped. She waved a frustrated arm toward the kitchen and the crew. "What do you think *this* is, Kelsier? The life of a skaa? What do any of you know about skaa? Aristocratic suits, stalking your enemies in the night, full meals and nightcaps around the table with your friends? That's not the life of a skaa!"

She took a step forward, glaring at Kelsier. He blinked in surprise at the outburst.

"What do you know about them, Kelsier?" she asked. "When's the last time you slept in an alley, shivering in the cold rain, listening to the beggar next to you cough with a sickness you knew would kill him? When's the last time you had to lay awake at night, terrified that one of the men in your crew would try to rape you? Have you ever knelt, starving, wishing you had the courage to knife the crewmember beside you just so you could take his crust of bread? Have you ever cowered before your brother as he beat you, all the time feeling thankful because at least you *had someone who paid attention to you?*"

She fell silent, puffing slightly, the crewmembers staring at her.

"Don't talk to me about noblemen," Vin said. "And don't say things about people you don't know. You're no skaa—you're just noblemen without titles."

She turned, stalking from the room. Kelsier watched her go, shocked, hearing her footsteps on the stairs. He stood, dumbfounded, feeling a surprising flush of ashamed guilt.

And, for once, found himself without anything to say.

Vin didn't go to her room. She climbed to the roof, where the mists curled in the quiet, unlit night. She sat down in the corner, the rough stone lip of the flat rooftop against her nearly bare back, wood beneath her.

She was cold, but she didn't care. Her arm hurt a bit, but it was mostly numb. She didn't feel nearly numb enough herself.

She crossed her arms, huddling down, watching the mists. She didn't know what to think, let alone what to feel. She shouldn't have exploded at Kelsier, but everything that had happened . . . the fight, Elend's betrayal . . . it just left her feeling frustrated. She needed to be angry at *someone*.

You should just be angry at yourself, Reen's voice whispered. *You're the one who let them get close. Now they're all just going to leave you.*

She couldn't make it stop hurting. She could only sit and shiver as the tears fell, wondering how everything had collapsed so quickly.

The trap door to the rooftop opened with a quiet creak, and Kelsier's head appeared.

Oh, Lord Ruler! I don't want to face him now. She tried to wipe away her tears, but she only succeeded in aggravating the freshly stitched wound on her cheek.

Kelsier closed the trap door behind him, then stood, so tall and proud, staring up at the mists. *He didn't deserve the things I said. None of them did.*

"Watching the mists is comforting, isn't it?" Kelsier asked.

Vin nodded.

"What is it I once told you? The mists protect you, they give you power . . . they hide you. . . ."

He looked down, then he walked over and crouched before her, holding out a cloak. "There are some things you can't hide from, Vin. I know—I've tried."

She accepted the cloak, then wrapped it around her shoulders.

"What happened tonight?" he asked. "What *really* happened?"

"Elend told me that he didn't want to be with me anymore."

"Ah," Kelsier said, moving over to sit beside her. "Was this before or after you killed his former fiancée?"

"Before," Vin said.

"And you still protected him?"

Vin nodded, sniffling quietly. "I know. I'm an idiot."

"No more than the rest of us," Kelsier said with a sigh. He looked up into the mists. "I loved Mare too, even after she betrayed me. Nothing could change how I felt."

"And that's why it hurts so much," Vin said, remembering what Kelsier had said before. *I think I finally understand.*

"You don't stop loving someone just because they hurt you," he said. "It would certainly make things easier if you did."

She started to sniffle again, and he put a fatherly arm around her. She pulled close, trying to use his warmth to push away the pain.

"I loved him, Kelsier," she whispered.

"Elend? I know."

"No, not Elend," Vin said. "Reen. He beat me over, and over, and over. He swore at me, he yelled at me, he told me he'd betray me. Every day, I thought about how much I hated him.

"And I loved him. I still do. It hurts so much to think that he's gone, even though he always told me he would leave."

"Oh, child," Kelsier said, pulling her close. "I'm sorry."

"Everyone leaves me," she whispered. "I can barely remember my mother. She tried to kill me, you know. She heard voices, in her head, and they made her kill my baby sister. She was probably going to kill me next, but Reen stopped her.

"Either way, she left me. After that, I clung to Reen. He left too. I love Elend, but he doesn't want me anymore." She looked up at Kelsier. "When are you going to go? When will you leave me?"

Kelsier looked sorrowful. "I . . . Vin, I don't know. This job, the plan . . ."

She searched his eyes, looking for the secrets therein. *What are you hiding from me, Kelsier? Something that dangerous?* She wiped her eyes again, pulling away from him, feeling foolish.

He looked down, shaking his head. "Look, now you got blood all over my nice, dirty, pretend informant's clothing."

Vin smiled. "At least some of it is noble blood. I got Shan pretty good."

Kelsier chuckled. "You're probably right about me, you know. I don't give the nobility much of a chance, do I?"

Vin flushed. "Kelsier, I shouldn't have said those things. You're good people, and this plan of yours . . . well, I realize what you're trying to do for the skaa."

"No, Vin," Kelsier said, shaking his head. "What you said was true. We're not really skaa."

"But, that's good," Vin said. "If you were regular skaa, you wouldn't have the experience or courage to plan something like this."

"They might lack experience," Kelsier said. "But not courage. Our army lost, true, but they were willing—with minimal training—to charge a superior force. No, the skaa don't lack courage. Just opportunity."

"Then it's your position as half skaa, half nobleman that has given *you* opportunity, Kelsier. And you've chosen to use that opportunity to help your skaa half. That makes you worthy of being a skaa if anything does."

Kelsier smiled. "Worthy to be a skaa. I like the sound of that. Regardless, perhaps I need to spend a little less time worrying about which noblemen to kill, and a little more time worrying about which peasants to help."

Vin nodded, pulling the cloak close as she stared up into the mists. *They protect us. . . . give us power . . . hide us. . . .*

She hadn't felt like she needed to hide in a long time. But now, after the things she'd said below, she almost wished that she could just blow away like a wisp of mist.

I need to tell him. It could mean the plan's success or failure. She took a deep breath. "House Venture has a weakness, Kelsier."

He perked up. "It does?"

Vin nodded. "Atium. They make certain the metal is harvested and delivered—it's the source of their wealth."

Kelsier paused for a moment. "Of course! That's how they can pay the taxes, that's why they're so powerful. . . . He *would* need someone to handle things for him. . . ."

"Kelsier?" Vin asked.

He looked back at her.

"Don't . . . do anything unless you have to, all right?"

Kelsier frowned. "I . . . don't know that I can promise anything, Vin. I'll try and think of another way, but as things stand now, Venture has to fall."

"I understand."

"I'm glad you told me, though."

She nodded. *And now I've betrayed him too.* There was a peace in knowing, however, that she hadn't done it out of spite. Kelsier was right: House Venture was a power that needed to be toppled. Oddly, her mention of the house seemed to bother Kelsier more than it did her. He sat, staring into the mists, strangely melancholy. He reached down, absently scratching his arm.

The scars, Vin thought. *It isn't House Venture he's thinking about—it's the Pits. Her.* "Kelsier?" she said.

"Yes?" His eyes still looking a bit . . . absent as he watched the mists.

"I don't think that Mare betrayed you."

He smiled. "I'm glad you think that way."

"No, I really mean it," Vin said. "The Inquisitors were waiting for you when you got to the center of the palace, right?"

Kelsier nodded.

"They were waiting for us too."

Kelsier shook his head. "You and I fought some guards, made some noise. When Mare and I went in, we were quiet. We'd planned for a year—we were stealthy, secretive, and very careful. Someone set a trap for us."

"Mare was an Allomancer, right?" Vin asked. "They could have just sensed you coming."

Kelsier shook his head. "We had a Smoker with us. Redd was his name—the Inquisitors killed him straight off. I've wondered if he was the traitor, but that just doesn't work. Redd didn't even know about the infiltration until that night, when we went and got him. Only Mare knew enough—dates, times, objectives—to have betrayed us. Besides, there's the Lord Ruler's comment. You didn't see him, Vin. Smiling as he thanked Mare. There was . . . honesty in his eyes. They say the Lord Ruler doesn't lie. Why would he need to?"

Vin sat quietly for a moment, considering what he'd said. "Kelsier," she said slowly, "I think that Inquisitors can sense our Allomancy even when we're burning copper."

"Impossible."

"I did it tonight. I punctured Shan's coppercloud to locate her and the other assassins. That's how I got to Elend in time."

Kelsier frowned. "You've got to be mistaken."

"It happened before too," Vin said. "I can feel the Lord Ruler's touch on my emotions, even when I'm burning copper. And I swear that when I was hiding from that Inquisitor who was hunting me, he found me when he shouldn't have been able to. Kelsier, what if it's possible? What if hiding yourself by Smoking isn't just a simple matter of whether or not your copper is on? What if it just depends on how strong you are?"

Kelsier sat thoughtfully. "It could be possible, I suppose."

"Then Mare wouldn't have had to betray you!" Vin said eagerly. "Inquisitors are extremely powerful. The ones who were waiting for you, maybe they just felt you burning metals! They knew that an Allomancer was trying to sneak into the palace. Then, the Lord Ruler thanked her because she was the one who gave you away! She was the Allomancer, burning tin, that led them to you."

Kelsier's face took on a troubled expression. He turned, sitting himself so he was directly in front of her. "Do it now, then. Tell me what metal I'm burning."

Vin closed her eyes, flaring bronze, listening . . . feeling, as Marsh had taught her. She remembered her solitary trainings, time spent focusing on the waves Breeze, Ham, or Spook gave off for her. She tried to pick out the fuzzing rhythm of Allomancy. Tried to . . .

For a moment, she thought she felt something. Something very strange—a slow pulsing, like a distant drum, unlike any Allomantic rhythm she'd felt before. But it wasn't coming from Kelsier. It was distant . . . far away. She focused harder, trying to pick out the direction it was coming from.

But suddenly, as she focused harder, something else drew her attention. A more familiar rhythm, coming from Kelsier. It was faint, difficult to feel over the pulsing of her own heartbeat. It was a bold beat, and quick.

She opened her eyes. "Pewter! You're burning pewter."

Kelsier blinked in surprise. "Impossible," he whispered. "Again!"

She closed her eyes. "Tin," she said after a moment. "Now steel—you changed as soon as I spoke."

"Bloody hell!"

"I was right," Vin said eagerly. "You *can* feel Allomantic pulses through copper! They're quiet, but I guess you just have to focus hard enough to—"

"Vin," Kelsier interrupted. "Don't you think Allomancers have tried this before? You don't think that after a thousand years' time, someone would have noticed that you could pierce a coppercloud? *I've* even tried it. I focused for hours on my Master, trying to sense something through his coppercloud."

"But . . ." Vin said. "But why . . . ?"

"It must have to do with strength, like you said. Inquisitors can Push and Pull harder than any regular Mistborn—perhaps they're so strong that they can overwhelm someone else's metal."

"But, Kelsier," Vin said quietly. "I'm not an Inquisitor."

"But you're strong," he said. "Stronger than you have any right to be. You killed a full Mistborn tonight!"

"By luck," Vin said, face flushing. "I just tricked her."

"Allomancy is nothing *but* tricks, Vin. No, there's something special about you. I noticed it on that first day, when you shrugged off my attempts to Push and Pull your emotions."

She flushed. "It can't be that, Kelsier. Maybe I've just practiced with bronze more than you. . . . I don't know, I just . . ."

"Vin," Kelsier said, "you're still too self-effacing. You're good at this—that much is obvious. If that's why you can see through copperclouds . . . well, I don't know. But learn to take a little pride in yourself, kid! If there's anything I can teach you, it's how to be self-confident."

Vin smiled.

"Come on," he said, standing and holding out a hand to help her up. "Sazed is going to fret all night if you don't let him finish stitching that cheek wound, and Ham's dying to hear about your battle. Good job leaving Shan's body back at Keep Venture, by the way—when House Elariel hears that she was found dead on Venture property . . ."

Vin allowed him to pull her up, but she glanced toward the trapdoor apprehensively. "I . . . don't know if I want to go down yet, Kelsier. How can I face them?"

Kelsier laughed. "Oh, don't worry. If you didn't say some stupid things every once in a while, you certainly wouldn't fit in with *this* group. Come on."

Vin hesitated, then let him lead her back down to the warmth of the kitchen.

"Elend, how can you read at times like this?" Jastes asked.

Elend looked up from his book. "It calms me."

Jastes raised an eyebrow. The young Lekal sat impatiently in the coach, tapping his fingers on the armrest. The window shades were drawn, partially to hide the light of Elend's reading lantern, partially to keep out the mists. Though Elend would never admit it, the swirling fog made him just a bit nervous. Noblemen weren't supposed to be afraid of such things, but that didn't change the fact that the deep, caliginous mist was just plain creepy.

"Your father is going to be livid when you get back," Jastes noted, still tapping the armrest.

Elend shrugged, though this comment did make him a little bit nervous. Not because of his father, but because of what had happened this night. Some Allomancers had, apparently, been spying on Elend's meeting with his friends. What information had they gathered? Did they know about the books he'd read?

Fortunately, one of them had tripped, falling through Elend's skylight. After that, it had been confusion and chaos—soldiers and ballgoers running about in a semi-panic. Elend's first thought had been for the books—the dangerous ones, the ones that if the obligators found he possessed, could get him into serious trouble.

So, in the confusion, he'd dumped them all in a bag and followed Jastes down to the palace side exit. Grabbing a carriage and sneaking out of the palace grounds had been an extreme move, perhaps, but it had been ridiculously easy. With the number of carriages fleeing the Venture grounds, not a single person had paused to notice that Elend himself was in the carriage with Jastes.

It's probably all died down by now, Elend told himself. *People will realize that House Venture wasn't trying to attack them, and that there wasn't really any danger. Just some spies who got careless.*

He should have returned by now. However, his convenient absence from the palace gave him a perfect excuse to check on another group of spies. And this time, Elend himself had sent them.

A sudden knock on the door made Jastes jump, and Elend closed his book, then opened the carriage door. Felt, one of the House Venture chief spies, climbed into the carriage, nodding his hawkish, mustached face respectfully to Elend, then Jastes.

"Well?" Jastes asked.

Felt sat down with the keen litheness of his kind. "The building is ostensibly a woodcrafter's shop, m'lord. One of my men has heard of the place—it's run by one Master Cladent, a skaa carpenter of no small skill."

Elend frowned. "Why did Valette's steward come here?"

"We think that the shop is a front, m'lord," Felt said. "We've been observing it ever since the steward led us here, as you ordered. However, we've had to be very careful—there are several watchnests hidden on its roof and top floors."

Elend frowned. "An odd precaution for a simple craftsman's shop, I should think."

Felt nodded. "That's not the half of it, m'lord. We managed to sneak one of our best men up to the building itself—we don't think he was spotted—but he had a remarkably difficult time hearing what's going on inside. The windows are sealed and stuffed to keep in sound."

Another odd precaution, Elend thought. "What do you think it means?" he asked Felt.

"It's got to be an underground hideout, m'lord," Felt said. "And a good one. If we hadn't been watching carefully, and been certain what to look for, we would never have noticed the signs. My guess is that the men inside—even the Terrisman—are members of a skaa thieving crew. A very well-funded and skilled one."

"A skaa thieving crew?" Jastes asked. "And Lady Valette too?"

"Likely, m'lord," Felt said.

Elend paused. "A . . . skaa thieving crew . . ." he said, stunned. *Why would they send one of their members to balls? To perform a scam of some sort, perhaps?*

"M'lord?" Felt asked. "Do you want us to break in? I've got enough men to take their entire crew."

"No," Elend said. "Call your men back, and tell no one of what you've seen this night."

"Yes, m'lord," Felt said, climbing out of the coach.

"Lord Ruler!" Jastes said as the carriage door closed. "No wonder she didn't seem like a regular noblewoman. It wasn't her rural upbringing—she's just a thief!"

Elend nodded, thoughtful, not certain what to think.

"You owe me an apology," Jastes said. "I was right about her, eh?"

"Perhaps," Elend said. "But . . . in a way, you were wrong about her too. She wasn't trying to spy on me—she was just trying to rob me."

"So?"

"I . . . need to think about this," Elend said, reaching out and knocking for the carriage to start moving. He sat back as the coach began to roll back toward Keep Venture.

Valette wasn't the person that she'd said she was. However, he'd already prepared himself for that news. Not only had Jastes's words about her made him suspicious, Valette herself hadn't denied Elend's accusations earlier in the night. It was obvious; she had been lying to him. Playing a part.

He should have been furious. He realized this, logically, and a piece of him did ache of betrayal. But, oddly, the primary emotion he felt was one of . . . relief.

"What?" Jastes asked, studying Elend with a frown.

Elend shook his head. "You've had me worrying over this for days, Jastes. I felt so sick that I could barely function—all because I thought that Valette was a traitor."

"But she *is*. Elend, she's probably trying to scam you!"

"Yes," Elend said, "but at least she probably isn't a spy for another house. In the face of all the intrigue, politics, and backbiting that has been going on lately, something as simple as a robbery feels slightly refreshing."

"But . . ."

"It's only money, Jastes."

"Money is kind of important to some of us, Elend."

"Not as important as Valette. That poor girl . . . all this time, she must have been worrying about the scam she would have to pull on me!"

Jastes sat for a moment, then he finally shook his head. "Elend, only *you* would be relieved to find out that someone was trying to steal from you. Need I remind you that the girl has been lying this entire time? You might have grown attached to her, but I doubt her own feelings are genuine."

"You may be right," Elend admitted. "But . . . I don't know, Jastes. I feel like I *know* this girl. Her emotions . . . they just seem too real, too honest, to be false."

"Doubtful," Jastes said.

Elend shook his head. "We don't have enough information to judge her yet. Felt thinks she's a thief, but there have to be other reasons a group like that would send someone to balls. Maybe she's just an informant. Or, maybe she is a thief—but not one who ever intended to rob me. She spent an awful lot of time mixing with the other nobility—why would she do that if I was her target? In fact, she spent relatively *little* time with me, and she never plied me for gifts."

He paused—imagining his meeting Valette as a pleasant accident, an event that had thrown a terrible twist into both of their lives. He smiled, then shook his head. "No, Jastes. There's more here than we're seeing. Something about her still doesn't make sense."

"I . . . suppose, El," Jastes said, frowning.

Elend sat upright, a sudden thought occurring to him—a thought that made his speculations about Valette's motivation seem far less important. "Jastes," he said. "She's skaa!"

"And?"

"And she fooled me—fooled us both. She acted the part of an aristocrat almost perfectly."

"An inexperienced aristocrat, perhaps."

"I had a real skaa thief with me!" Elend said. "Think of the questions I could have asked her."

"Questions? What kind of questions?"

"Questions about being skaa," Elend said. "That's not the point. Jastes, she *fooled* us. If we can't tell the difference between a skaa and a noblewoman, that means that the skaa can't be very different from us. And, if they're not that different from us, what right do we have treating them as we do?"

Jastes shrugged. "Elend, I don't think you're looking at this in perspective. We're in the middle of a house war."

Elend nodded distractedly. *I was so hard on her this evening. Too hard?*

He had wanted her to believe, totally and completely, that he didn't want anything more to do with her. Part of that had been genuine, for his own worries had convinced him that she couldn't be trusted. And she couldn't be, not at the moment. Either way, he'd wanted her to leave the city. He'd thought that the best thing to do was break off the relationship until the house war was through.

But, assuming she's really not a noblewoman, then there's no reason for her to leave.

"Elend?" Jastes asked. "Are you even paying attention to me?"

Elend looked up. "I think I did something wrong tonight. I wanted to get Valette out of Luthadel. But, now I think I hurt her for no reason."

"Bloody hell, Elend!" Jastes said. "Allomancers were listening to our conference this night. Do you realize what could have happened? What if they'd decided to kill us, rather than just spy on us?"

"Ah, yes, you're right," Elend said with a distracted nod. "It's best if Valette leaves anyway. Anyone close to me will be in danger during the days to come."

Jastes paused, his annoyance deepening, then he finally laughed. "You're hopeless."

"I try my best," Elend said. "But, seriously, there's no use worrying. The spies gave themselves away, and likely got chased off—or even captured—in the chaos. We now know some of the secrets that Valette is hiding, so we're ahead there too. It's been a very productive night!"

"That's an optimistic way of looking at it, I guess. . . ."

"Once again, I try my best." Even still, he would feel more comfortable when they got back to Keep Venture. Perhaps it had been foolhardy to sneak away from the palace before hearing the details of what had happened, but Elend hadn't exactly been thinking carefully at the time. Besides, he'd had the previously arranged meeting with Felt to attend, and the chaos had made a perfect opportunity to slip away.

The carriage slowly pulled up to the Venture gates. "You should go," Elend said, slipping out of the carriage door. "Take the books."

Jastes nodded, grabbing the sack, then bidding Elend farewell as he shut the carriage door. Elend waited as the carriage rolled back away from the gates, then he turned and walked the rest of the way to the keep, the surprised gate guards letting him pass with ease.

The grounds were still ablaze with light. Guards were already waiting for him at the front of the keep, and a group of them rushed out into the mists to meet him. And surround him.

"My lord, your father—"

"Yes," Elend interrupted, sighing. "I assume I'm to be taken to him immediately?"

"Yes, my lord."

"Lead on, then, Captain."

They entered through the lord's entrance on the side of the building. Lord Straff Venture stood in his study, speaking with a group of guard officers. Elend could tell from the pale faces that they had received a firm scolding, perhaps even threats of beatings. They were noblemen, so Venture couldn't execute them, but he was very fond of the more brutal disciplinary forms.

Lord Venture dismissed the soldiers with a sharp gesture, then turned to Elend with hostile eyes. Elend frowned, watching the soldiers go. Everything all seemed a little too . . . tense.

"Well?" Lord Venture demanded.

"Well what?"

"Where have you been?"

"Oh, I left," Elend said offhandedly.

Lord Venture sighed. "Fine. Endanger yourself if you wish, boy. In a way, it's too bad that Mistborn *didn't* catch you—they could have saved me a great deal of frustration."

"Mistborn?" Elend asked, frowning. "What Mistborn?"

"The one that was planning to assassinate you," Lord Venture snapped.

Elend blinked in startlement. "So . . . it wasn't just a spying team?"

"Oh, no," Venture said, smiling somewhat wickedly. "An entire assassination team, sent here after you and your friends."

Lord Ruler! Elend thought, realizing how foolish he had been to go out alone. *I didn't expect the house war to get so dangerous so quickly! At least, not for me . . .*

"How do we know it was a Mistborn?" Elend asked, gathering his wits.

"Our guards managed to kill her," Straff said. "As she was fleeing."

Elend frowned. "A full Mistborn? Killed by common soldiers?"

"Archers," Lord Venture said. "Apparently, they took her by surprise."

"And the man who fell through my skylight?" Elend asked.

"Dead," Lord Venture said. "Broken neck."

Elend frowned. *That man was still alive when we fled. What are you hiding, Father?* "The Mistborn. Anyone I know?"

"I'd say so," Lord Venture said, settling into his desk chair, not looking up. "It was Shan Elariel."

Elend froze in shock. *Shan?* he thought, dumbfounded. They'd been engaged, and she'd never even mentioned that she was an Allomancer. That probably meant . . .

She'd been a plant all along. Perhaps House Elariel had planned to have Elend killed once an Elariel grandson was born to the house title.

You're right, Jastes. I can't avoid politics by ignoring it. I've been a part of it all for much longer than I assumed.

His father was obviously pleased with himself. A high-profile member of House Elariel was dead on Venture grounds after trying to assassinate Elend. . . . With such a triumph, Lord Venture would be insufferable for days.

Elend sighed. "Did we capture any of the assassins alive, then?"

Straff shook his head. "One fell to the courtyard as he was trying to flee. He got away—he might have been Mistborn too. We found one man dead on the roof, but we aren't sure if there were others in the team or not." He paused.

"What?" Elend asked, reading the slight confusion in his father's eyes.

"Nothing," Straff said, waving a dismissive hand. "Some of the guards claim there was a third Mistborn, fighting the other two, but I doubt the reports—it wasn't one of ours."

Elend paused. *A third Mistborn, fighting the other two* . . . "Maybe someone found out about the assassination and tried to stop it."

Lord Venture snorted. "Why would someone else's Mistborn try to protect *you?*"

"Maybe they just wanted to stop an innocent man from being murdered."

Lord Venture shook his head, laughing. "You are an idiot, boy. You understand that, right?"

Elend flushed, then turned away. It didn't appear that Lord Venture wanted anything more, so Elend left. He couldn't go back to his rooms, not with the broken window and the guards, so he made his way to a guest bedroom, calling for a set of hazekillers to watch outside his door and balcony—just in case.

He prepared for bed, thinking about the conversation. His father was probably right about the third Mistborn. That just wasn't the way things worked.

But . . . that's the way it should be. The way it could be, maybe.

There were so many things Elend wished he could do. But, his father was healthy, and young for a lord of his power. It would be decades before Elend assumed the house title, assuming he even survived that long. He wished he could go to Valette, talk to her, explain his frustrations. She'd understand what he was thinking; for some reason, she always seemed to understand him better than others.

And, she's skaa! He couldn't get over the thought. He had so many questions, so many things he wanted to find out from her.

Later, he thought as he climbed into bed. *For now, focus on keeping the house together.* His words to Valette in that area hadn't been false—he needed to make certain his family survived the house war.

After that . . . well, perhaps they could find a way to work around the lies and the scams.

Though many Terrismen express a resentment of Khlennium, there is also envy. I have heard the packmen speak in wonder of the Khlenni cathedrals, with their amazing stained-glass windows and broad halls. They also seem very fond of our fashion—back in the cities, I saw that many young Terrismen had traded in their furs and skins for well-tailored gentlemen's suits.

32

TWO STREETS OVER FROM CLUBS'S SHOP, there was a building of unusual height compared with those surrounding it. It was some kind of tenement, Vin thought—a place to pack skaa families. She'd never been inside of it, however.

She dropped a coin, then shot herself up along the side of the six-story building. She landed lightly on the rooftop, causing a figure crouching in the darkness to jump in surprise.

"It's just me," Vin whispered, sneaking quietly across the sloped roof.

Spook smiled at her in the night. As the crew's best Tineye, he usually got the most important watches. Recently, those were the ones during the early evening. That was the time when conflict among the Great Houses was most likely to turn to outright fighting.

"Are they still going at it?" Vin asked quietly, flaring her tin, scanning the city. A bright haze shone in the distance, giving the mists a strange luminescence.

Spook nodded, pointing toward the light. "Keep Hasting. Elariel soldiers with the attacking tonight."

Vin nodded. Keep Hasting's destruction had been expected for some time— it had suffered a half-dozen raids from different houses during the last week. Allies withdrawing, finances wrecked, it was only a matter of time before it fell.

Oddly, none of the houses attacked during the daytime. There was a feigned air of secrecy about the war, as if the aristocracy acknowledged the Lord Ruler's dominance, and didn't want to upset him by resorting to daylight warfare. It was all handled at night, beneath a cloak of mists.

"Wasing the *want* of this," Spook said.

Vin paused. "Uh, Spook. Could you try to speak . . . normal?"

Spook nodded toward a distant, dark structure in the distance. "The Lord Ruler. Liking he wants the fighting."

Vin nodded. *Kelsier was right. There hasn't been much of an outcry from the Ministry or the palace regarding the house war, and the Garrison is taking its time getting back to Luthadel. The Lord Ruler expected the house war—and intends to let it run its course. Like a wildfire, left to blaze and renew a field.*

Except this time, as one fire died, another would start—Kelsier's attack on the city.

Assuming Marsh can find out how to stop the Steel Inquisitors. Assuming we can take the palace. And, of course, assuming Kelsier can find a way to deal with the Lord Ruler . . .

Vin shook her head. She didn't want to think poorly of Kelsier, but she just didn't see how it was all going to happen. The Garrison wasn't back yet, but reports said it was close, perhaps only a week or two out. Some noble houses were falling, but there didn't seem to be the air of general chaos that Kelsier had wanted. The Final Empire was strained, but she doubted that it would crack.

However, maybe that wasn't the point. The crew had done an amazing job of instigating a house war; three entire Great Houses were no more, and the rest were seriously weakened. It would take decades for the aristocracy to recover from their own squabbling.

We've done an amazing job, Vin decided. *Even if we don't attack the palace— or if that attack fails—we'll have accomplished something wonderful.*

With Marsh's intelligence about the Ministry and Sazed's translation of the logbook, the rebellion would have new and useful information for future resistance. It wasn't what Kelsier had hoped for; it wasn't a complete toppling of the Final Empire. However, it was a major victory—one that the skaa could look to for years as a source of courage.

And, with a start of surprise, Vin realized that she felt proud to have been part of it. Perhaps, in the future, she could help start a real rebellion—one in a place where the skaa weren't quite so beaten down.

If such a place exists . . . Vin was beginning to understand that it wasn't just Luthadel and its Soothing stations that made skaa subservient. It was *every-thing*—the obligators, the constant work in field and mill, the mind-set encouraged by a thousand years of oppression. There was a reason why skaa rebellions were always so small. The people knew—or thought they knew—that there was no fighting against the Final Empire.

Even Vin—who'd assumed herself a "liberated" thief—had believed the same. It had taken Kelsier's insane, over-the-top plan to convince her otherwise. Perhaps that was why he'd set such lofty goals for the crew—he'd known that only something this challenging would make them realize, in a strange way, that they *could* resist.

Spook glanced at her. Her presence still made him uncomfortable.

"Spook," Vin said, "you know that Elend broke off his relationship with me."

Spook nodded, perking up slightly.

"But," Vin said regretfully, "I still love him. I'm sorry, Spook. But it's true."

He looked down, deflating.

"It's not you," Vin said. "Really, it isn't. It's just that . . . well, you can't help who you love. Trust me, there are some people I really would rather *not* have loved. They didn't deserve it."

Spook nodded. "I understand."

"Can I still keep the handkerchief?"

He shrugged.

"Thank you," she said. "It does mean a lot to me."

He looked up, staring out into the mists. "I'm notting a fool. I . . . knew it wasing not to happen. I see things, Vin. I see lots of things."

She laid a comforting hand on his shoulder. *I see things.* . . . An appropriate statement, for a Tineye like him.

"You've been an Allomancer for a long time?" she asked.

Spook nodded. "Wasing the Snap when I was five. Barely even remember it."

"And since then you've been practicing with tin?"

"Mostly," he said. "Wasing a good thing for me. Letting me see, letting me hear, letting me feel."

"Any tips you can pass on?" Vin asked hopefully.

He paused thoughtfully, sitting by the edge of the slanted rooftop, one foot dangling over the side. "Tin burning . . . Notting about the seeing. Wasing about the *not seeing*."

Vin frowned. "What do you mean?"

"When burning," he said, "everything comes. Lots of everything. Distractions here, there. Iffing the power of wants, *ignoring* the distractions of both."

If you want to be good at burning tin, she thought, translating as best she could, *learn to deal with distraction. It isn't about what you see—it's about what you can ignore.*

"Interesting," Vin said thoughtfully.

Spook nodded. "When looking, seeing the mist and seeing the houses and feeling the wood and hearing the rats below. Choose one, and don't get distracted."

"Good advice," Vin said.

Spook nodded as a sound thumped behind them. They both jumped and ducked down, and Kelsier chuckled as he walked across the rooftop. "We really have to find a better way of warning people that we're coming up. Every time I visit a spynest, I worry that I'm going to startle someone off the rooftop."

Vin stood, dusting off her clothing. She wore mistcloak, shirt, and trousers; it had been days since she'd worn a dress. She only put in token appearances at Mansion Renoux. Kelsier was too worried about assassins to let her stay there for long.

At least we bought Kliss's silence, Vin thought, annoyed at the expense. "It's time?" she asked.

Kelsier nodded. "Nearly so, at least. I want to stop somewhere on the way."

Vin nodded. For their second meeting, Marsh had chosen a location that he was supposedly scouting for the Ministry. It was a perfect opportunity to meet, since Marsh had an excuse to be in the building all night, ostensibly Seeking for any Allomantic activity nearby. He would have a Soother with him for a good deal of the time, but there would be an opening near the middle of the night when Marsh figured he would have a good hour alone. Not much time if he had to sneak out and back, but plenty of time for a pair of stealthy Mistborn to pay him a quick visit.

They bid farewell to Spook and Pushed off into the night. However, they didn't travel the rooftops for long before Kelsier led them down onto the street, landing and walking to conserve strength and metals.

It's kind of odd, Vin thought, remembering her first night practicing Allomancy with Kelsier. *I don't even think of the empty streets as creepy anymore.*

The cobblestones were slick from mistwater, and the deserted street eventually disappeared into the distant haze. It was dark, silent, and lonely; even the war hadn't changed very much. Soldier groups, when they attacked, went in clumps, striking quickly and trying to overrun the defenses of an enemy house.

Yet, despite the emptiness of the nighttime city, Vin felt comfortable in it. The mists were with her.

"Vin," Kelsier said as they walked. "I want to thank you."

She turned to him, a tall, proud figure in a majestic mistcloak. "Thank me? Why?"

"For the things you said about Mare. I've been thinking a lot about that day . . . about her. I don't know if your ability to see through copperclouds explains everything, but . . . well, given the choice, I'd rather believe that Mare *didn't* betray me."

Vin nodded, smiling.

He shook his head ruefully. "It sounds foolish, doesn't it? As if . . . all these years, I've just been waiting for a reason to give in to self-delusion."

"I don't know," Vin said. "Once, maybe I would have thought you a fool, but . . . well, that's kind of what trust is, isn't it? A willful self-delusion? You have to shut out that voice that whispers about betrayal, and just hope that your friends aren't going to hurt you."

Kelsier chuckled. "I don't think you're helping the argument any, Vin."

She shrugged. "Makes sense to me. Distrust is really the same thing—only on the other side. I can see how a person, given the choice between two assumptions, would choose to trust."

"But not you?" Kelsier asked.

Vin shrugged again. "I don't know anymore."

Kelsier hesitated. "This . . . Elend of yours. There's a chance that he was just trying to scare you into leaving the city, right? Perhaps he said those things for your own good."

"Maybe," Vin said. "But, there was something different about him . . . about the way he looked at me. He knew I was lying to him, but I don't think he realized that I was skaa. He probably thought I was a spy from one of the other houses. Either way, he seemed honest in his desire to be rid of me."

"Maybe you thought that because you were already convinced that he was going to leave you."

"I . . ." Vin trailed off, glancing down at the slick, ashen street as they walked. "I don't know—and it's your fault, you know. I used to understand everything. Now it's all confused."

"Yes, we've messed you up right properly," Kelsier said with a smile.

"You don't seem bothered by the fact."

"Nope," Kelsier said. "Not a bit. Ah, here we are."

He stopped beside a large, wide building—probably another skaa tenement. It was dark inside; skaa couldn't afford lamp oil, and they would have put out the building's central hearth after preparing the evening meal.

"This?" Vin asked uncertainly.

Kelsier nodded, walking up to tap lightly on the door. To Vin's surprise, it opened hesitantly, a wiry skaa face peeking out into the mists.

"Lord Kelsier!" the man said quietly.

"I told you I'd visit," Kelsier said, smiling. "Tonight seemed like a good time."

"Come in, come in," the man said, pulling the door open. He stepped back, careful not to let any of the mist touch him as Kelsier and Vin entered.

Vin had been in skaa tenements before, but never before had they seemed so . . . depressing. The smell of smoke and unwashed bodies was almost overpowering, and she had to extinguish her tin to keep from gagging. The wan light of a small coal stove showed a crowd of people packed together, sleeping on the floor. They kept the room swept of ash, but there was only so much they could do—black stains still covered clothing, walls, and faces. There were few furnishings, not to mention far too few blankets to go around.

I used to live like this, Vin thought with horror. *The crew lairs were just as packed—sometimes more so. This . . . was my life.*

People roused as they saw that they had a visitor. Kelsier had his sleeves rolled up, Vin noticed, and the scars on his arms were visible even by emberlight. They stood out starkly, running lengthwise up from his wrist past his elbows, crisscrossing and overlapping.

The whispers began immediately.

"The Survivor . . ."

"He's here!"

"Kelsier, the Lord of the Mists . . ."

That's a new one, Vin thought with a raised eyebrow. She stayed back as Kelsier smiled, stepping forward to meet the skaa. The people gathered around him with quiet excitement, reaching out to touch his arms and cloak. Others just stood and stared, watching him with reverence.

"I come to spread hope," Kelsier said to them quietly. "House Hasting fell tonight."

There were murmurs of surprise and awe.

"I know many of you worked in the Hasting smithies and steel mills," Kelsier said. "And, honestly, I cannot say what this means for you. But it is a victory for all of us. For a time, at least, your men won't die before the forges or beneath the whips of Hasting taskmasters."

There were murmurs through the small crowd, and one voice finally spoke the concern loud enough for Vin to hear. "House Hasting is gone? Who will feed us?"

So frightened, Vin thought. *I was never like that . . . was I?*

"I'll send you another shipment of food," Kelsier promised. "Enough to last you for a while, at least."

"You've done so much for us," another man said.

"Nonsense," Kelsier said. "If you wish to repay me, then stand up just a little straighter. Be a little less afraid. They *can* be beaten."

"By men like you, Lord Kelsier," a woman whispered. "But not by us."

"You'd be surprised," Kelsier said as the crowd began to make way for parents bringing their children forward. It seemed like everyone in the room wanted their sons to meet Kelsier personally. Vin watched with mixed feelings. The crew still had reservations regarding Kelsier's rising fame with the skaa, though they kept their word and remained silent.

He really does seem to care for them, Vin thought, watching Kelsier pick up a small child. *I don't think it's just a show. This is how he is—he loves people, loves the skaa. But . . . it's more like the love of a parent for a child than it is like the love of a man for his equals.*

Was that so wrong? He was, after all, a kind of father to the skaa. He was the noble lord they always *should* have had. Still, Vin couldn't help feeling uncomfortable as she watched the faintly illuminated, dirty faces of those skaa families, their eyes worshipful and reverent.

Kelsier eventually bid the group farewell, telling them he had an appointment. Vin and he left the cramped room, stepping out into blessedly fresh air. Kelsier remained quiet as they traveled toward Marsh's new Soothing station, though he did walk with a bit more of a spring in his step.

Eventually, Vin had to say something. "You visit them often?"

Kelsier nodded. "At least a couple of houses a night. It breaks up the monotony of my other work."

Killing noblemen and spreading false rumors, Vin thought. *Yes, visiting the skaa would be a nice break.*

The meeting place was only a few streets away. Kelsier paused in a doorway as they approached, squinting in the dark night. Finally, he pointed at a window, just faintly lit. "Marsh said he'd leave a light burning if the other obligators were gone."

"Window or stairs?" Vin asked.

"Stairs," Kelsier said. "The door should be unlocked, and the Ministry owns the entire building. It will be empty."

Kelsier was right on both counts. The building didn't smell musty enough to be abandoned, but the bottom few floors were obviously unused. Vin and he quickly climbed up the stairwell.

"Marsh should be able to tell us the Ministry reaction to the House War," Kelsier said as they reached the top floor. Lanternlight flickered through the door at the top, and he pushed it open, still speaking. "Hopefully, that Garrison won't get back too quickly. The damage is mostly done, but I'd like the war to go on for—"

He froze in the doorway, blocking Vin's view.

She flared pewter and tin immediately, falling to a crouch, listening for attackers. There was nothing. Just silence.

"No . . ." Kelsier whispered.

Then Vin saw the trickle of dark red liquid seeping around the side of Kelsier's foot. It pooled slightly, then began to drip down the first step.

Oh, Lord Ruler . . .

Kelsier stumbled into the room. Vin followed, but she knew what she'd see. The corpse lay near the center of the chamber, flayed and dismembered, the head completely crushed. It was barely recognizable as human. The walls were sprayed red.

Could one body really produce this much blood? It was just like before, in the basement of Camon's lair—only with a single victim.

"Inquisitor," Vin whispered.

Kelsier, heedless of the gore, stumbled to his knees beside Marsh's corpse. He raised a hand as if to touch the skinless body, but remained frozen there, stunned.

"Kelsier," Vin said urgently. "This was recent—the Inquisitor could still be near."

He didn't move.

"Kelsier!" Vin snapped.

Kelsier shook, looking around. His eyes met hers, and lucidity returned. He stumbled to his feet.

"Window," Vin said, rushing across the room. She paused, however, when she saw something sitting on a small desk beside the wall. A wooden table leg, tucked half-hidden beneath a blank sheet of paper. Vin snatched it as Kelsier reached the window.

He turned back, looking over the room one last time, then jumped out into the night.

Farewell, Marsh, Vin thought regretfully, following.

"'I think that the Inquisitors suspect me,'" Dockson read. The paper—a single sheet recovered from inside the table leg—was clean and white, free from the blood that stained Kelsier's knees and the bottom of Vin's cloak.

Dockson continued, reading as he sat at Clubs's kitchen table. "'I've been asking too many questions, and I know they sent at least one message to the corrupt obligator who supposedly trained me as an acolyte. I thought to seek out the secrets that the rebellion has always needed to know. How does the Ministry recruit Mistborn to be Inquisitors? Why are Inquisitors more powerful than regular Allomancers? What, if any, are their weaknesses?

"'Unfortunately, I've learned next to nothing about the Inquisitors—though the politicking within the regular Ministry ranks continues to amaze me. It's like the regular obligators don't even care about the world outside, except for the prestige they earn by being the most clever or successful in applying the Lord Ruler's dictates.

"'The Inquisitors, however, are different. They are far more loyal to the Lord Ruler than the regular obligators—and this is, perhaps, part of the dissension between the two groups.

"'Regardless, I feel that I am close. They *do* have a secret, Kelsier. A weakness. I'm sure of it. The other obligators whisper of it, though none of them know it.

"'I fear that I've prodded too much. The Inquisitors tail me, watch me, ask after me. So, I prepare this note. Perhaps my caution is unnecessary.

"'Perhaps not.'"

Dockson looked up. "That's . . . all it says."

Kelsier stood at the far side of the kitchen, back to the cupboard, reclining in his usual position. But . . . there was no levity in his posture this time. He stood with arms folded, head slightly bowed. His disbelieving grief appeared to have vanished, replaced with another emotion—one Vin had sometimes seen smoldering darkly behind his eyes. Usually when he spoke of the nobility.

She shivered despite herself. Standing as he was, she was suddenly aware of his clothing—dark gray mistcloak, long-sleeved black shirt, charcoal trousers. In the night, the clothing was simply camouflage. In the lit room, however, the black colors made him look menacing.

He stood up straight, and the room grew tense.

"Tell Renoux to pull out," Kelsier said softly, his voice like iron. "He can use the planned exit story—that of a 'retreat' back to his family lands because of the house war—but I want him gone by tomorrow. Send a Thug and a Tineye with him as protection, but tell him to abandon his canal boats one day out of the city, then return to us."

Dockson paused, then glanced at Vin and the others. "Okay . . ."

"Marsh knew everything, Dox," Kelsier said. "They broke him before they killed him—that's how Inquisitors work."

He let the words hang. Vin felt a chill. The lair was compromised.

"To the backup lair, then?" Dockson asked. "Only you and I knew its location."

Kelsier nodded firmly. "I want everyone out of this shop, apprentices included, in fifteen minutes. I'll meet you at the backup lair in two days."

Dockson looked up at Kelsier, frowning. "Two days? Kell, what are you planning?"

Kelsier strode over to the door. He threw it open, letting in the mist, then glanced back at the crew with eyes as hard as any Inquisitor's spikes.

"They hit me where it couldn't have hurt worse. I'm going to do likewise."

Walin pushed himself in the darkness, feeling his way through the cramped caverns, forcing his body through cracks nearly too small. He continued downward, searching with his fingers, ignoring his numerous scrapes and cuts.

Must keep going, must keep going . . . His remaining sanity told him that this was his last day. It had been six days since his last success. If he failed a seventh time, he would die.

Must keep going.

He couldn't see; he was too far beneath the surface to catch even a reflected glimpse of sunlight. But, even without light, he could find his way. There were only two directions: up and down. Movements to the side were unimportant, easily disregarded. He couldn't get lost as long as he kept moving down.

All the while, he quested with his fingers, seeking the telltale roughness of budding crystal. He couldn't return this time, not until he'd been successful, not until . . .

Must keep going.

His hands brushed something soft and cold as he moved. A corpse, stuck rotting between two rocks. Walin moved on. Bodies weren't uncommon in the tight caverns; some of the corpses were fresh, most were simply bones. Often, Walin wondered if the dead ones weren't really the lucky ones.

Must keep going.

There wasn't really "time" in the caverns. Usually, he returned above to sleep—though the surface held taskmasters with whips, they also had food. It was meager, barely enough to keep him alive, but it was better than the starvation that would come from staying below too long.

Must keep—

He froze. He lay with his torso pinched in a tight rift in the rock, and had been in the process of wiggling his way through. However, his fingers—always searching, even when he was barely conscious—had been feeling the walls. And they'd found something.

His hand quivered with anticipation as he felt the crystal buds. Yes, yes, that was them. They grew in a wide, circular pattern on the wall; they were small at the edges, but got gradually bigger near the center. At the direct middle of the circular pattern, the crystals curved inward, following a pocketlike hollow in the wall. Here, the crystals grew long, each one having a jagged, sharp edge. Like teeth lining the maw of a stone beast.

Taking a breath, praying to the Lord Ruler, Walin rammed his hand into the fist-sized, circular opening. The crystals ripped his arm, tearing long, shallow gashes in his skin. He ignored the pain, forcing his arm in further, up to his elbow, searching with his fingers for . . .

There! His fingers found a small rock at the center of the pocket—a rock formed by the mysterious drippings of the crystals. A Hathsin geode.

He grasped it eagerly, pulling it out, ripping his arm again as he withdrew it from the crystal-lined hole. He cradled the small rock sphere, breathing heavily with joy.

Another seven days. He would live another seven days.

Before hunger and fatigue could weaken him further, Walin began the laborious climb back upward. He squeezed through crevasses, climbed up juttings in walls. Sometimes he had to move to the right or left until the ceiling opened up, but it always did. There were really only two directions: up and down.

He kept a wary ear out for others. He had seen climbers killed before, slain by younger, stronger men who hoped to steal a geode. Fortunately, he met nobody. It was good. He was an older man—old enough to know that he never should have tried to steal food from his plantation lord.

Perhaps he had earned his punishment. Perhaps he deserved to die in the Pits of Hathsin.

But I won't die today, he thought, finally smelling sweet, fresh air. It was night above. He didn't care. The mists didn't bother him anymore—even beatings didn't bother him much anymore. He was just too tired to care.

Walin began to climb out of the crack—one of dozens in the small, flat valley known as the Pits of Hathsin. Then he froze.

A man stood above him in the night. He was dressed in a large cloak that appeared to have been shredded to strips. The man looked at Walin, quiet and powerful in his black clothing. Then he reached down.

Walin cringed. The man, however, grabbed Walin's hand and pulled him out of the crack.

"Go!" the man said quietly in the swirling mists. "Most of the guards are dead. Gather as many prisoners as you can, and escape this place. You have a geode?"

Walin cringed again, pulling his hand toward his chest.

"Good," the stranger said. "Break it open. You'll find a nugget of metal inside—it is very valuable. Sell it to the underground in whatever city you eventually find yourself; you should earn enough to live on for years. Go quickly! I don't know how long you have until an alarm is raised."

Walin stumbled back, confused. "Who . . . who are you?"

"I am what *you* will soon be," the stranger said, stepping up to the rift. The ribbons of his enveloping black cloak billowed around him, mixing with the mists as he turned toward Walin. "I am a survivor."

Kelsier looked down, studying the dark scar in the rock, listening as the prisoner scrambled away in the distance.

"And so I return," Kelsier whispered. His scars burned, and memories returned. Memories of months spent squeezing through cracks, of ripping his arms on crystalline knives, of seeking each day to find a geode . . . just one, so that he could live on.

Could he really go back down into those cramped, quiet depths? Could he enter the darkness again? Kelsier held up his arms, looking at the scars, still white and stark on his arms.

Yes. For her dreams, he could.

He stepped over to the rift and forced himself to climb down inside of it. Then he burned tin. Immediately, he heard a cracking sound from below.

Tin illuminated the rift beneath him. Though the crack widened, it also branched, sending out twisting rifts in all directions. Part cavern, part crack, part tunnel. He could already see his first crystalline atium-hole—or what was left of it. The long, silvery crystals were fractured and broken.

Using Allomancy near atium crystals caused them to shatter. That was why the Lord Ruler had to use slaves, and not Allomancers, to collect his atium for him.

Now the real test, Kelsier thought, squeezing down further into the crack. He burned iron, and immediately he saw several blue lines pointing downward, toward atium-holes. Though the holes themselves probably didn't have an atium geode in them, the crystals themselves gave off faint blue lines. They contained residual amounts of atium.

Kelsier focused on one of the blue lines and Pulled lightly. His tin enhanced ears heard something shatter in the crack beneath him.

Kelsier smiled.

Nearly three years before, standing over the bloody corpses of the taskmasters who had beaten Mare to death, he had first noticed that he could use iron to sense where crystal pockets were. He'd barely understood his Allomantic powers at the time, but even then, a plan had begun to form in his mind. A plan for vengeance.

That plan had evolved, growing to encompass so much more than he'd originally intended. However, one of its key parts had remained sequestered away in a corner of his mind. He could find the crystal pockets. He could shatter them, using Allomancy.

And they were the only means of producing atium in the entire Final Empire.

You tried to destroy me, Pits of Hathsin, he thought, climbing down further into the rift. *It's time to return the favor.*

We are close now. Oddly, this high in the mountains, we seem to finally be free from the oppressive touch of the Deepness. It has been quite a while since I knew what that was like.

The lake that Fedik discovered is below us now—I can see it from the ledge. It looks even more eerie from up here, with its glassy—almost metallic—sheen. I almost wish I had let him take a sample of its waters.

Perhaps his interest was what angered the mist creature that follows us. Perhaps . . . that was why it decided to attack him, stabbing him with its invisible knife.

Strangely, the attack comforted me. At least I know that since another has seen it. That means I'm not mad.

33

"SO . . . THAT'S IT?" Vin asked. "For the plan, I mean."

Ham shrugged. "If the Inquisitors broke Marsh, that means they know everything. Or, at least, they know enough. They'll know that we plan to strike the palace, and that we're going to use the house war as a cover. We'll never get the Lord Ruler out of the city now, and we'll certainly never get him to send the palace guard into the city. It doesn't look good, Vin."

Vin sat quietly, digesting the information. Ham sat cross-legged on the dirty floor, leaning against the bricks of the far wall. The backup lair was a dank cellar with only three rooms, and the air smelled of dirt and ash. Clubs's apprentices took up one room to themselves, though Dockson had sent away all of the other servants before coming to the safe house.

Breeze stood by the far wall. He occasionally shot uncomfortable looks at the dirty floor and dusty stools, but then decided to remain standing. Vin didn't see why he bothered—it was going to be impossible to keep his suits clean while living in what was, essentially, a pit in the ground.

Breeze wasn't the only one taking their self-imposed captivity resentfully; Vin had heard several of the apprentices grumble that they'd almost rather have been taken by the Ministry. Yet, during their two days in the cellar, everyone had stayed in the safe house except when absolutely necessary. They understood the danger: Marsh could have given the Inquisitors descriptions and aliases for each crewmember.

Breeze shook his head. "Perhaps, gentlemen, it is time to pack up this operation. We tried hard, and considering the fact that our original plan—gathering the army—ended up so dreadfully, I'd say that we've done quite a marvelous job."

Dockson sighed. "Well, we certainly can't live off of saved funds for much longer—especially if Kell keeps giving our money away to the skaa." He sat beside the table that was the room's only piece of furniture, his most important ledgers, notes, and contracts organized into neat piles before him. He had been remarkably efficient at gathering every bit of paper that could have incriminated the crew or given further information about their plan.

Breeze nodded. "I, for one, am looking forward to a change. This has all been fun, delightful, and all of those other fulfilling emotions, but working with Kelsier can be a bit draining."

Vin frowned. "You're not going to stay on his crew?"

"It depends on his next job," Breeze said. "We aren't like other crews you've known—we work as we please, not because we are told to. It pays for us to be very discerning in the jobs we take. The rewards are great, but so are the risks."

Ham smiled, resting with his arms behind his head, completely unconcerned about the dirt. "It kind of makes you wonder how we ended up on this particular job, eh? Very high risk, very little reward."

"None, actually," Breeze noted. "We'll never get that atium now. Kelsier's words about altruism and working to help the skaa were all well and good, but I was always hoping that we'd still get to take a swipe at that treasury."

"True," Dockson said, looking up from his notes. "But, was it worth it anyway? The work we did—the things we accomplished?"

Breeze and Ham paused, then they both nodded.

"And that's why we stayed," Dockson said. "Kell said it himself—he picked us because he knew we would try something a little different to accomplish a worthwhile goal. You're good men—even you, Breeze. Stop scowling at me."

Vin smiled at the familiar banter. There was a sense of mourning regarding Marsh, but these were men who knew how to move on despite their losses. In that way, they really were like skaa, after all.

"A house war," Ham said idly, smiling to himself. "How many noblemen dead, do you think?"

"Hundreds, at least," Dockson said without looking up. "All killed by their own greedy noble hands."

"I'll admit that I had my doubts about this entire fiasco," Breeze said. "But the interruption in trade this will cause, not to mention the disorder in the government . . . well, you're right, Dockson. It was worth it."

"Indeed!" Ham said, mimicking Breeze's stuffy voice.

I'm going to miss them, Vin thought regretfully. *Maybe Kelsier will take me with him on his next job.*

The stairs rattled, and Vin moved reflexively back into the shadows. The splintery door opened, and a familiar, black-clothed form strode in. He carried his mistcloak over his arm, and his face looked incredibly wearied.

"Kelsier!" Vin said, stepping forward.

"Hello, all," he said in a tired voice.

I know that tiredness, Vin thought. *Pewter drag. Where has he been?*

"You're late, Kell," Dockson said, still not looking up from his ledgers.

"I strive for nothing if not consistency," Kelsier said, dropping his mistcloak on the floor, stretching, then sitting down. "Where are Clubs and Spook?"

"Clubs is sleeping in the back room," Dockson said. "Spook went with Renoux. We figured you'd want him to have our best Tineye to keep a watch."

"Good idea," Kelsier said, letting out a deep sigh and closing his eyes as he leaned against the wall.

"My dear man," Breeze said, "you look terrible."

"It's not as bad as it looks—I took it easy coming back, even stopped to sleep for a few hours on the way."

"Yes, but where *were* you?" Ham asked pointedly. "We've been worried sick that you were out doing something . . . well, stupid."

"Actually," Breeze noted, "we took it for granted that you were doing something stupid. We've just been wondering *how* stupid this particular event would turn out to be. So, what is it? Did you assassinate the lord prelan? Slaughter dozens of noblemen? Steal the cloak off the Lord Ruler's own back?"

"I destroyed the Pits of Hathsin," Kelsier said quietly.

The room fell into a stunned silence.

"You know," Breeze finally said, "you'd think that by now we'd have learned not to underestimate him."

"Destroyed them?" Ham asked. "How do you destroy the Pits of Hathsin? They're just a bunch of cracks in the ground!"

"Well, I didn't actually destroy the pits themselves," Kelsier explained. "I just shattered the crystals that produce atium geodes."

"All of them?" Dockson asked, dumbstruck.

"All of them that I could find," Kelsier said. "And that was several hundred pockets' worth. It was actually a lot easier to get around down there, now that I have Allomancy."

"Crystals?" Vin asked, confused.

"Atium crystals, Vin," Dockson said. "They produce the geodes—I don't think anyone actually knows how—that have atium beads at the center."

Kelsier nodded. "The crystals are why the Lord Ruler can't just send down Allomancers to Pull out the atium geodes. Using Allomancy near the crystals makes them shatter—and it takes centuries for them to grow back."

"Centuries during which they won't produce atium," Dockson added.

"And so you . . ." Vin trailed off.

"I pretty much ended atium production in the Final Empire for the next three hundred years or so."

Elend. House Venture. They're in charge of the Pits. How will the Lord Ruler react when he finds out about this?

"You madman," Breeze said quietly, eyes open wide. "Atium is the foundation of the imperial economy—controlling it is one of the main ways that the Lord Ruler maintains his hold over the nobility. We may not get to his reserves, but this will eventually have the same effect. You blessed lunatic . . . you blessed *genius!*"

Kelsier smiled wryly. "I appreciate both compliments. Have the Inquisitors moved against Clubs's shop yet?"

"Not that our watchmen have seen," Dockson said.

"Good," Kelsier said. "Maybe they didn't get Marsh to break. At the very least, maybe they don't realize that their Soothing stations were compromised. Now, if you don't mind, I'm going to sleep. We have a lot of planning to do tomorrow."

The group paused.

"Planning?" Dox finally asked. "Kell . . . we were kind of thinking that we should pull out. We caused a house war, and you just took out the imperial economy. With our cover—and our plan—compromised . . . Well, you can't honestly expect us to do anything more, right?"

Kelsier smiled, staggering to his feet and moving into the back room. "We'll talk tomorrow."

"What do you think he's planning, Sazed?" Vin asked, sitting on a stool beside the cellar's hearth as the Terrisman prepared the afternoon meal. Kelsier had slept through the night, and had yet to rise this afternoon.

"I really have no idea, Mistress," Sazed replied, sipping the stew. "Though, this moment—with the city so unbalanced—does seem like the perfect opportunity to move against the Final Empire."

Vin sat thoughtfully. "I suppose we could still seize the palace—that's what Kell always wanted to do. But, if the Lord Ruler has been warned, the others don't see that happening. Plus, it doesn't seem like we have enough soldiers to do much in the city. Ham and Breeze never finished their recruiting."

Sazed shrugged.

"Maybe Kelsier plans to do something about the Lord Ruler," Vin mused.

"Perhaps."

"Sazed?" Vin said slowly. "You collect legends, right?"

"As a Keeper I collect many things," Sazed said. "Stories, legends, religions. When I was young, another Keeper recited all of his knowledge to me so that I could store it, and then add to it."

"Have you ever heard about this 'Eleventh Metal' legend that Kelsier talks about?"

Sazed paused. "No, Mistress. That legend was new to me when I heard of it from Master Kelsier."

"But he swears that it's true," Vin said. "And I . . . believe him, for some reason."

"It is very possible that there are legends I haven't heard of," Sazed said. "If the Keepers knew everything, then why would we need to keep searching?"

Vin nodded, still a bit uncertain.

Sazed continued to stir the soup. He seemed so . . . dignified, even while performing such a menial task. He stood in his steward's robes, unconcerned with how simple a service he was performing, easily taking over for the servants the crew had dismissed.

Quick footsteps sounded on the stairs, and Vin perked up, sliding off her stool.

"Mistress?" Sazed asked.

"Someone on the stairs," Vin said, moving to the doorway.

One of the apprentices—Vin thought his name was Tase—burst into the main room. Now that Lestibournes was gone, Tase had become the crew's main lookout.

"People are gathering in the square," Tase said, gesturing toward the stairs.

"What's this?" Dockson said, entering from the other room.

"People in the fountain square, Master Dockson," the boy said. "Word on the street is that the obligators are planning more executions."

Retribution for the Pits, Vin thought. *That didn't take long.*

Dockson's expression darkened. "Go wake Kell."

"I intend to watch them," Kelsier said, walking through the room, dressed in simple skaa clothing and cloak.

Vin's stomach twisted. *Again?*

"You all may do as you wish," Kelsier said. He looked much better after his extended rest—his exhaustion was gone, replaced with the characteristic strength Vin had come to expect from him.

"The executions are probably a reaction to what I did at the Pits," Kelsier continued. "I'm going to watch those people's deaths—because indirectly, I caused them."

"It's not your fault, Kell," Dockson said.

"It's all of our faults," Kelsier said bluntly. "That doesn't make what we do wrong—however, if it weren't for us, these people wouldn't have to die. I, for one, think that the least we can do for these people is bear witness to their passing."

He pulled open the door, climbing the steps. Slowly, the rest of the crew followed him—though Clubs, Sazed, and the apprentices remained with the safe house.

Vin climbed the musty-aired steps, eventually joining the others on a grimy street in the middle of a skaa slum. Ash fell from the sky, floating in lazily flakes. Kelsier was already walking down the street, and the rest of them—Breeze, Ham, Dockson, and Vin—quickly moved to catch up with him.

The safe house wasn't far from the fountain square. Kelsier, however, paused a few streets away from their destination. Dull-eyed skaa continued walking around them, jostling the crew. Bells rang in the distance.

"Kell?" Dockson asked.

Kelsier cocked his head. "Vin, you hear that?"

She closed her eyes, then flared her tin. *Focus,* she thought. *Like Spook said. Cut through the shuffling feet and murmuring voices. Hear over the doors shutting and the people breathing. Listen. . . .*

"Horses," she said, dampening her tin and opening her eyes. "And carriages."

"Carts," Kelsier said, turning toward the side of the street. "The prisoner carts. They're coming this way."

He looked up at the buildings around him, then grabbed hold of a raingutter and began to shimmy up a wall. Breeze rolled his eyes, nudging Dockson and nodding toward the front of the building, but Vin and Ham—with pewter—easily followed Kelsier up to the roof.

"There," Kell said, pointing at a street a short ways away. Vin could just barely make out a row of barred prison carts rolling toward the square.

Dockson and Breeze entered the slanted rooftop through a window. Kelsier remained where he was, standing by the roof's lip, staring out at the prison carts.

"Kell," Ham said warily. "What are you thinking?"

"We're still a short distance from the square," he said slowly. "And the Inquisitors aren't riding with the prisoners—they'll come down from the palace, like last time. There can't be more than a hundred soldiers guarding those people."

"A hundred men are plenty, Kell," Ham said.

Kelsier didn't seem to hear the words. He took another step forward, approaching up onto the roof's edge. "I can stop this. . . . I can save them."

Vin stepped up beside him. "Kell, there might not be many guards with the prisoners, but the fountain square is only a few blocks away. It's packed with soldiers, not to mention the Inquisitors!"

Ham, unexpectedly, didn't back her up. He turned, glancing at Dockson and Breeze. Dox paused, then shrugged.

"Are you all crazy?" Vin demanded.

"Wait a moment," Breeze said, squinting. "I'm no Tineye, but don't some of those prisoners look a bit too well dressed?"

Kelsier froze, then he cursed. Without warning, he jumped off the rooftop, dropping to the street below.

"Kell!" Vin said. "What—" Then she paused, looking up in the red sunlight, watching the slowly approaching procession of carts. Through tin-enhanced eyes, she thought that she recognized someone sitting near the front of one of the carts.

Spook.

"Kelsier, what's going on!" Vin demanded, dashing down the street behind him.

He slowed just a bit. "I saw Renoux and Spook in that first cart. The Ministry must have hit Renoux's canal procession—the people in those cages are the servants, staff, and guards we hired to work at the mansion."

The canal procession . . . Vin thought. *The Ministry must know that Renoux was a fake. Marsh broke after all.*

Behind them, Ham appeared out of the building and onto the street. Breeze and Dockson were slower in coming.

"We have to work quickly!" Kelsier said, picking up his pace again.

"Kell!" Vin said, grabbing his arm. "Kelsier, you can't save them. They're too well guarded, and it's daylight in the middle of the city. You'll just get yourself killed!"

He paused, halting in the street, turning in Vin's grasp. He looked into her eyes, disappointed. "You don't understand what this is all about, do you, Vin? You never did. I let you stop me once before, on the hillside by the battlefield. Not this time. This time I can do something."

"But . . ."

He shook his arm free. "You still have some things to learn about friendship, Vin. I hope someday you realize what they are."

Then he took off, charging in the direction of the carts. Ham barreled past Vin, heading in a different direction, pushing his way through skaa on their way to the square.

Vin stood stupidly for a few moments, standing in the falling ash as Dockson caught up to her.

"It's insanity," she mumbled. "We can't do this, Dox. We're not invincible."

Dockson snorted. "We're not helpless either."

Breeze puffed up behind them, pointing toward a side street. "There. We need to get me to a place where I can see the soldiers."

Vin let them tow her along, suddenly feeling shame mix with her worry.

Kelsier . . .

Kelsier tossed away a pair of empty vials, their contents ingested. The vials sparkled in the air beside him, falling to shatter against the cobblestones. He ducked through one final alleyway, bursting out onto an eerily empty thoroughfare.

The prisoner carts rolled toward him, entering a small courtyard square formed by the intersection of two streets. Each rectangular vehicle was lined with bars; each one was packed with people who were now distinctly familiar. Servants, soldiers, housekeepers—some were rebels, many were just regular people. None of them deserved death.

Too many skaa have died already, he thought, flaring his metals. *Hundreds. Thousands. Hundreds of thousands.*

Not today. No more.

He dropped a coin and jumped, Pushing himself through the air in a wide arc. Soldiers looked up, pointing. Kelsier landed directly in their center.

There was a quiet moment as the soldiers turned in surprise. Kelsier crouched amid them, bits of ash falling from the sky.

Then he Pushed.

He flared steel with a yell, standing and Pushing outward. The burst of Allomantic power hurled soldiers away by their breastplates, tossing a dozen men into the air, sending them crashing into companions and walls.

Men screamed. Kelsier spun, Pushing against a group of soldiers and sending himself flying toward a prison cart. He smashed into it, flaring his steel and grabbing the metal door with his hands.

Prisoners huddled back in surprise. Kelsier ripped the door free with a burst of pewter-enhanced power, then tossed it toward a group of approaching soldiers.

"Go!" he told the prisoners, jumping down and landing lightly in the street. He spun.

And came face-to-face with a tall figure wearing a brown robe. Kelsier paused, stepping back as the tall form reached up, lowering his hood, revealing a pair of eyes impaled by spikes.

The Inquisitor smiled, and Kelsier heard footsteps approaching down side alleyways. Dozens. Hundreds.

"Damnation!" Breeze swore as soldiers flooded the square.

Dockson pulled Breeze into an alley. Vin followed them in, crouching in the shadows, listening to soldiers yelling in the crossroads outside.

"What?" she demanded.

"Inquisitor!" Breeze said, pointing toward a robed figure standing before Kelsier.

"*What?*" Dockson said, standing.

It's a trap, Vin realized with horror. Soldiers began to pile into the square, appearing from hidden side streets. *Kelsier, get out of there!*

Kelsier Pushed off a fallen guard, throwing himself backward in a flip over one of the prison carts. He landed in a crouch, eyeing the new squads of soldiers. Many of them carried staves and wore no armor. Hazekillers.

The Inquisitor Pushed himself through the ash-filled air, landing with a thump in front of Kelsier. The creature smiled.

It's the same man. The Inquisitor from before.

"Where's the girl?" the creature said quietly.

Kelsier ignored the question. "Why only one of you?" he demanded.

The creature's smile deepened. "I won the draw."

Kelsier flared pewter, dashing to the side as the Inquisitor pulled out a pair of obsidian axes. The square was quickly becoming clogged with soldiers. From inside the carts he could hear people crying out.

"Kelsier! Lord Kelsier! Please!"

Kelsier cursed quietly as the Inquisitor bore down on him. He reached out, Pulling against one of the still full carts and yanking himself into the air over a group of soldiers. He landed, then dashed to the cart, intending to free its occupants. As he arrived, however, the cart shook. Kelsier glanced up just in time to see a steel-eyed monster grinning down at him from atop the vehicle.

Kelsier Pushed himself backward, feeling the wind of an axehead swing beside his head. He landed smoothly, but immediately had to jump to the side as a group of soldiers attacked. As he landed, he reached out—Pulling against one of the carts to anchor himself—and Pulled against the fallen iron door he had thrown before. The barred door lurched into the air and crashed through the squad of soldiers.

The Inquisitor attacked from behind, but Kelsier jumped away. The still tumbling door careened across the cobblestones in front of him, and as he passed over it, Kelsier Pushed, sending himself streaking into the air.

Vin was right, Kelsier thought with frustration. Below, the Inquisitor watched him, trailing him with unnatural eyes. *I shouldn't have done this.* Below, a group of soldiers rounded up the skaa that he had freed.

I should run—try to lose the Inquisitor. I've done it before.

But . . . he couldn't. He wouldn't, not this time. He had compromised too many times before. Even if it cost him everything else, he *had* to free those prisoners.

And then, as he began to fall, he saw a group of men charging the crossroads. They bore weapons, but no uniforms. At their head ran a familiar form.

Ham! So that's where you went.

"What is it?" Vin asked anxiously, craning to see into the square. Above, Kelsier's form plunged back toward the fight, dark cloak trailing behind him.

"It's one of our soldier units!" Dockson said. "Ham must have fetched them."

"How many?"

"We kept them in patches of a couple hundred."

"So they'll be outnumbered."

Dockson nodded.

Vin stood. "I'm going out."

"No, you're not," Dockson said firmly, grabbing her cloak and pulling her back. "I don't want a repeat of what happened to you last time you faced one of those monsters."

"But . . ."

"Kell will be just fine," Dockson said. "He'll just try to stall long enough for Ham to free the prisoners, then he'll run. Watch."

Vin stepped back.

To her side, Breeze was mumbling to himself. "Yes, you're afraid. Let's focus on that. Soothe everything else away. Leave you terrified. That's an Inquisitor and a Mistborn fighting—you don't want to interfere with *that*. . . ."

Vin glanced back toward the square, where she saw a soldier drop his staff and flee. *There are other ways to fight,* she realized, kneeling beside Breeze. "How can I help?"

Kelsier ducked back from the Inquisitor again as Ham's unit crashed into the imperial soldiers and began cutting its way toward the prisoner carts. The attack diverted the attention of the regular soldiers, who appeared all too happy to leave Kelsier and the Inquisitor to their solitary battle.

To the side, Kelsier could see skaa beginning to clog the streets around the small courtyard, the fighting drawing the attention of those waiting up above at the fountain square. Kelsier could see other squads of imperial soldiers trying to push their way toward the fight, but the thousands of skaa crowding the streets seriously slowed their progress.

The Inquisitor swung, and Kelsier dodged. The creature was obviously growing frustrated. To the side, a small group of Ham's men reached one of the prisoner carts and broke open its lock, freeing the prisoners. The rest of Ham's men kept the imperial soldiers busy as the prisoners fled.

Kelsier smiled, eyeing the annoyed Inquisitor. The creature growled quietly.

"Valette!" a voice screamed.

Kelsier turned in shock. A well-dressed nobleman was pushing his way through the soldiers toward the center of the fighting. He carried a dueling cane and was protected by two beleaguered bodyguards, but he mostly avoided harm by virtue of neither side being certain of wanting to strike down a man of obvious noble blood.

"Valette!" Elend Venture yelled again. He turned to one of the soldiers. "Who told you to raid House Renoux's convoy! Who authorized this!"

Great, Kelsier thought, keeping a wary eye on the Inquisitor. The creature regarded Kelsier with a twisted, hateful expression.

You just go right on hating me, Kelsier thought. *I only have to hang on long enough for Ham to free the prisoners. Then, I can lead you away.*

The Inquisitor reached out and casually beheaded a fleeing servant as she ran by.

"No!" Kelsier yelled as the corpse fell at the Inquisitor's feet. The creature grabbed another victim and raised its axe.

"All right!" Kelsier said, striding forward, pulling a pair of vials from his sash. "All right. You want to fight me? Come on!"

The creature smiled, pushing the captured woman aside and striding toward Kelsier.

Kelsier flicked the corks off and downed both vials at once, then tossed them aside. Metals flared in his chest, burning alongside his rage. His brother, dead. His wife, dead. Family, friends, and heroes. All dead.

You push me to seek revenge? he thought. *Well, you shall have it!*

Kelsier paused a few feet in front of the Inquisitor. Fists clinched, he flared his steel in a massive Push. Around him, people were thrown back by their metal as they were hit by the awesome, invisible wave of power. The square—packed with imperial soldiers, prisoners, and rebels—opened up in a small pocket around Kelsier and the Inquisitor.

"Let's do it, then," Kelsier said.

I never wanted to be feared.

If I regret one thing, it is the fear I have caused. Fear is the tool of tyrants. Unfortunately, when the fate of the world is in question, you use whatever tools are available.

34

DEAD AND DYING MEN COLLAPSED TO the cobblestones. Skaa crowded the roads. Prisoners cried out, calling his name. Heat from a smoky sun burned the streets.

And ash fell from the sky.

Kelsier dashed forward, flaring pewter and whipping out his daggers. He burned atium, as did the Inquisitor—and they both probably had enough to last for an extended fight.

Kelsier slashed twice in the hot air, striking at the Inquisitor, his arms a blur. The creature dodged amid an insane vortex of atium-shadows, then swung an axe.

Kelsier jumped, pewter lending his leap inhuman height, and passed just over the swinging weapon. He reached out and Pushed against a group of fighting soldiers behind him, throwing himself forward. He planted both feet in the Inquisitor's face and kicked off, flipping backward in the air.

The Inquisitor stumbled. As Kelsier fell, he Pulled on a soldier, yanking himself backward. The soldier was pulled off his feet by the force of the Iron-pull, and he began to streak toward Kelsier. Both men flew in the air.

Kelsier flared iron, Pulling against a patch of soldiers to his right while still Pulling against the single soldier. The result was a pivot. Kelsier flew to the side, and the soldier—held as if by tether to Kelsier's body—swung in a wide arc like a ball on a chain.

The unfortunate soldier crashed into the stumbling Inquisitor, smashing them both into the bars of an empty prison cart.

The soldier toppled, unconscious, to the ground. The Inquisitor bounced off the iron cage, falling to its hands and knees. A line of blood ran down the creature's face, across its eye tattoos, but it looked up, smiling. It didn't seem the least bit dizzy as it stood.

Kelsier landed, cursing quietly to himself.

With an incredible burst of speed, the Inquisitor grabbed the empty, boxlike prison cell by a pair of bars, then ripped the entire thing free of the cart wheels.

Bloody hell!

The creature spun and hurled the massive iron cage at Kelsier, who stood only a few feet away. There was no time to dodge. A building stood right behind him; if he Pushed himself back, he'd be crushed.

The cage crashed toward him, and he jumped, using a Steelpush to guide his body through the open doorway of the spinning cage. He twisted within the cell, Pushing outward in all directions, holding himself in the metal cage's exact center as it smashed into the wall, then bounced free.

The cage rolled, then began to skid across the ground. Kelsier let himself drop, landing on the underside of the roof as the cage slowly slid to a halt. Through the bars, he could see the Inquisitor watching him amid a sea of fighting soldiers, its body surrounded by a twisting, dashing, moving cloud of atium-images. The Inquisitor nodded its head to Kelsier in a slight sign of respect.

Kelsier Pushed out with a yell, flaring pewter to keep from crushing himself. The cage exploded, the metal top flipping into the air, the bars ripping free and bursting outward. Kelsier Pulled the bars behind him and Pushed the ones in front of him, sending a stream of metal shooting toward the Inquisitor.

The creature raised a hand, expertly dividing the large missiles. Kelsier, however, followed the bars with his own body—shooting himself toward the Inquisitor with a Steelpush. The Inquisitor Pulled himself to the side, using an unfortunate soldier as an anchor. The man cried out as he was wrenched away from his duel—but he choked off as the Inquisitor jumped, Pushing against the soldier and crushing the man to the ground.

The Inquisitor shot into the air. Kelsier slowed himself with a Push against a group of soldiers, tracking the Inquisitor. Behind him, the top of the cage crashed back to the ground, throwing up chips of stone. Kelsier blasted against it and hurled himself upward, after the Inquisitor.

Flakes of ash streaked past him. Ahead, the Inquisitor turned, Pulling against something below. The creature switched directions immediately, instead hurling toward Kelsier.

Head-on collision. Bad idea for the guy without spikes in his head. Kelsier frantically Pulled against a soldier, lurching downward as the Inquisitor passed diagonally overhead.

Kelsier flared pewter, then crashed into the soldier he had Pulled up toward him. The two of them spun in midair. Fortunately, the soldier wasn't one of Ham's.

"Sorry, friend," Kelsier said conversationally, Pushing himself to the side.

The soldier shot away, eventually smashing into the side of a building as Kelsier used him to soar over the battlefield. Below, Ham's main squad had finally reached the last prison cart. Unfortunately, several more groups of imperial soldiers had pushed their way through the gawking skaa crowds. One of them was a large team of archers—armed with obsidian-tipped arrows.

Kelsier cursed, letting himself fall. The archers set up, obviously preparing to fire straight into the fighting crowd. They would kill some of their own soldiers, but the brunt of their attack would be borne by the fleeing prisoners.

Kelsier dropped to the cobblestones. He reached to the side, Pulling against some discarded bars from the cage he had destroyed. They flew toward him.

The archers drew. But he could see their atium-shadows.

Kelsier released the bars and Pushed himself to the side just slightly, allowing the bars to fly between the archers and the fleeing prisoners.

The archers fired.

Kelsier grabbed the bars, flaring both steel and iron, Pushing against one tip of each bar and Pulling against the opposite tip. The bars lurched in the air, immediately beginning to spin like furious, lunatic windmills. Most of the flying arrows were sprayed to the side by the spinning rods of iron.

The bars clanged to the ground amid the scattered, discarded arrows. The archers stood, stupefied, as Kelsier jumped to the side again, then Pulled lightly on the bars, flipping them up into the air in front of him. He Pushed, sending the bars crashing toward the archers. He turned away as men screamed and died, his eyes seeking his true foe.

Where is that creature hiding?

He looked into a scene of chaos. Men fought, ran, fled, and died—each one bearing a prophetic atium-shadow to Kelsier's eyes. In this case, however, the shadows effectively doubled the number of people moving on the battlefield, and only served to increase the sense of confusion.

More and more soldiers were arriving. Many of Ham's men were down, most of the rest were retreating—fortunately, they could simply discard their armor and blend into the skaa crowds. Kelsier was more worried about that last prisoner cart—the one with Renoux and Spook in it. The trajectory at which Ham's group had entered the battle had required them to move up the line of carts, back to front. Trying to get to Renoux first would have required passing by the five other carts, leaving their people still trapped.

Ham obviously didn't intend to leave until Spook and Renoux were free. And, where Ham fought, the rebel soldiers held. There was a reason Pewterarms were also called Thugs: there was no subtlety to their fighting, no clever Ironpulls or Steelpushes. Ham simply attacked with raw strength and speed, throwing enemy soldiers out of his way, laying waste to their ranks, leading his squad of fifty men toward the final prison cart. As they reached it, Ham stepped back to fight off a group of enemy soldiers as one of his men broke the cart's lock.

Kelsier smiled with pride, eyes still searching for the Inquisitor. His men were few, but the enemy soldiers seemed visibly unsettled by the skaa rebels' determination. Kelsier's men fought with passion—despite their other, numerous hindrances, they still had this one advantage.

This is what happens when you finally convince them to fight. This is what hides within them all. It's just so hard to release. . . .

Renoux exited the cart, then stepped to the side, watching as his servants rushed free from their cage. Suddenly, a well-dressed figure burst from the melee, grabbing Renoux by the front of his suit.

"Where's Valette?" Elend Venture demanded, his desperate voice carrying to Kelsier's tin-enhanced ears. "Which cage was she in?"

Kid, you're really starting to annoy me, Kelsier thought, Pushing himself a path through the soldiers as he ran toward the cart.

The Inquisitor appeared, leaping out from behind a pile of soldiers. It landed on top of the cage, shaking the entire structure, an obsidian axe grasped in each clawlike hand. The creature met Kelsier's eyes and smiled, then dropped from the top of the cage and buried an axe in Renoux's back.

The kandra jerked, eyes opening wide. The Inquisitor turned toward Elend next. Kelsier wasn't certain if the creature recognized the boy. Perhaps the Inquisitor thought Elend to be a member of Renoux's family. Perhaps it didn't care.

Kelsier paused for just a moment.

The Inquisitor raised his axe to strike.

She loves him.

Kelsier flared steel within, stoking it, raging it until his chest burned like the Ashmounts themselves. He blasted against the soldiers behind him—throwing dozens of them backward—and streaked toward the Inquisitor. He crashed into the creature as it began to swing.

The discarded axe clicked against the stones a few feet away. Kelsier gripped the Inquisitor by its neck as the two hit the ground; then he began to squeeze with pewter-enhanced muscles. The Inquisitor reached up, grabbing Kelsier's hands, desperately trying to force them apart.

Marsh was right, Kelsier thought through the chaos. *It fears for its life. It can be killed.*

The Inquisitor gasped raggedly, the metal spikeheads protruding from its eyes just inches from Kelsier's face. To his side Kelsier saw Elend Venture stumble back.

"The girl is fine!" Kelsier said through gritted teeth. "She wasn't on the Renoux barges. Go!"

Elend paused uncertainly; then one of his bodyguards finally appeared. The boy let himself get dragged away.

Can't believe I just saved a nobleman, Kelsier thought, struggling to choke the Inquisitor. *You'd better appreciate this, girl.*

Slowly, with straining muscles, the Inquisitor forced Kelsier's hands apart. The creature began to smile again.

They're so strong!

The Inquisitor pushed Kelsier back, then Pulled against a soldier, yanking itself in a skidding motion across the cobblestones. The Inquisitor hit a corpse and flipped backward, up to its feet. Its neck was red from Kelsier's grip, bits of flesh torn by his fingernails, but it smiled still.

Kelsier Pushed against a soldier, flipping himself up as well. To his side, he saw Renoux leaning against the cart. Kelsier caught the kandra's eyes and nodded slightly.

Renoux dropped to the ground with a sigh, axe in his back.

"Kelsier!" Ham yelled over the crowd.

"Go!" Kelsier told him. "Renoux is dead."

Ham glanced at Renoux's body, then nodded. He turned to his men, calling orders.

"Survivor," a rasping voice said.

Kelsier spun. The Inquisitor strode forward, stepping with pewter's lithe power, surrounded by a haze of atium-shadows.

"Survivor of Hathsin," it said. "You promised me a fight. Must I kill more skaa?"

Kelsier flared his metals. "I never said we were done." Then, he smiled. He was worried, he was pained, but he was also exhilarated. All of his life, there had been a piece of him that had wished to stand and fight.

He'd always wanted to see if he could take an Inquisitor.

Vin stood, trying desperately to see over the crowd.

"What?" Dockson asked.

"I thought I saw Elend!"

"Here? That sounds a bit ridiculous, don't you think?"

Vin flushed. *Probably.* "Regardless, I'm going to try and get a better view." She grabbed the side of the alleyway.

"Be careful," Dox said. "If that Inquisitor sees you . . ."

Vin nodded, scrambling up the bricks. Once she got high enough, she scanned the intersection for familiar figures. Dockson was right: Elend was nowhere to be seen. One of the carts—the one off of which the Inquisitor had ripped the cage—lay on its side. Horses stomped about, hedged in by the fighting and the skaa crowds.

"What do you see?" Dox called up.

"Renoux is down!" Vin said, squinting and burning tin. "Looks like an axe in his back."

"That may or may not be fatal for him," Dockson said cryptically. "I don't know a lot about kandra."

Kandra?

"What about the prisoners?" Dox called.

"They're all free," Vin said. "The cages are empty. Dox, there are a *lot* of skaa out there!" It looked like the entire population from the fountain square had crowded down to the small intersection. The area was in a small depression, and Vin could see thousands of skaa packing the streets sloping upward in all directions.

"Ham's free!" Vin said. "I don't see him—alive or dead—anywhere! Spook's gone too."

"And Kell?" Dockson asked urgently.

Vin paused. "He's still fighting the Inquisitor."

Kelsier flared his pewter, punching the Inquisitor, careful to avoid the flat disks of metal sticking out the front of its eyes. The creature stumbled, and Kelsier buried his fist in its stomach. The Inquisitor growled and slapped Kelsier across the face, throwing him down with one blow.

Kelsier shook his head. *What does it take to kill this thing?* he thought, Pushing himself up to his feet, backing away.

The Inquisitor strode forward. Some of the soldiers were trying to search the crowd for Ham and his men, but many just stood still. A fight between two powerful Allomancers was something whispered about, but never seen. Soldier and peasant stood dumbfounded, watching the battle with awe.

He's stronger than I am, Kelsier acknowledged, watching the Inquisitor warily. *But strength isn't everything.*

Kelsier reached out, grabbing smaller metal sources and Pulling them away from their owners—metal caps, fine steel swords, coin pouches, daggers. He threw them at the Inquisitor—carefully manipulating Steelpushes and Ironpulls—and kept his atium burning so that each item he controlled would have a fanning multitude of atium-images in the Inquisitor's eyes.

The Inquisitor cursed quietly as it deflected the swarming bits of metal. Kelsier, however, just used the Inquisitor's own Pushes against it, Pulling each item back, whipping them around at the creature. The Inquisitor blasted outward, Pushing against all the items at once, and Kelsier let them go. As soon as the Inquisitor stopped Pushing, however, Kelsier Pulled his weapons back.

The imperial soldiers formed a ring, watching warily. Kelsier used them, Pushing against breastplates, lurching himself back and forth in the air. The quick changes in position let him move constantly, disorienting the Inquisitor, allowing him to Push his different flying pieces of metal where he wanted them.

"Keep an eye on my belt buckle," Dockson asked, wobbling slightly as he clung to the bricks beside Vin. "If I fall off, give me a Pull to slow the fall, eh?"

Vin nodded, but she wasn't paying much attention to Dox. She was watching Kelsier. "He's incredible!"

Kelsier lurched back and forth in the air, his feet never touching the ground. Bits of metal buzzed around him, responding to his Pushes and Pulls. He controlled them with such skill, one would have thought they were living things. The Inquisitor slapped them away with a fury, but was obviously having trouble keeping track of them all.

I underestimated Kelsier, Vin thought. *I assumed that he was less skilled than the Mistings because he'd spread himself too thin. But that wasn't it at all. This. This is his specialty—Pushing and Pulling with expert control.*

And iron and steel are the metals he personally trained me in. Maybe he understood all along.

Kelsier spun and flew amid a maelstrom of metal. Every time something hit the ground, he flicked it back up. The items always flew in straight lines, but he kept moving, Pushing himself around, keeping them in the air, periodically shooting them at the Inquisitor.

The creature spun, confused. It tried to Push itself upward, but Kelsier shot several larger pieces of metal over the creature's head, and it had to Push against them, throwing off its jump.

An iron bar hit the Inquisitor in the face.

The creature stumbled, blood marring the tattoos on the side of its face. A steel helmet struck it in the side, tossing it backward.

Kelsier began to shoot pieces of metal quickly, feeling his rage and anger mount. "Were you the one who killed Marsh?" he yelled, not bothering to listen for an answer. "Were you there when I was condemned, years ago?"

The Inquisitor raised a warding hand, Pushing away the next swarm of metals. It limped backward, putting its back against the overturned wooden cart.

Kelsier heard the creature growl, and a sudden Push of strength washed through the crowd, toppling soldiers, causing Kelsier's metal weapons to shoot away.

Kelsier let them go. He dashed forward, rushing the disoriented Inquisitor, scooping up a loose cobblestone.

The creature turned toward him, and Kelsier yelled, swinging the cobblestone, his strength fueled almost more by rage than by pewter.

He hit the Inquisitor square in the eyes. The creature's head snapped back, smacking against the bottom of the overturned cart. Kelsier struck again, yelling, repeatedly smashing his cobblestone into the creature's face.

The Inquisitor howled in pain, reaching clawlike hands for Kelsier, moving as if to jump forward. Then it suddenly jerked to a stop, its head stuck against the cart's wood. The spike tips that jutted from the back of its skull had been pounded into the wood by Kelsier's attack.

Kelsier smiled as the creature screamed in rage, struggling to pull its head free from the wood. Kelsier turned to the side, seeking an item he had seen on the ground a few moments before. He kicked over a corpse, snatching the obsidian axe off the ground, its rough-chipped blade glittering in the red sunlight.

"I'm glad you talked me into this," he said quietly. Then he swung with a two-handed blow, slamming the axehead through the Inquisitor's neck and into the wood behind.

The Inquisitor's body slumped to the cobblestones. The head remained where it was, staring out with its eerie, tattooed, unnatural gaze—pinned to the wood by its own spikes.

Kelsier turned to face the crowd, suddenly feeling incredibly wearied. His body ached from dozens of bruises and cuts, and he didn't even know when his cloak had ripped free. He faced the soldiers defiantly, however, his scarred arms plainly visible.

"The Survivor of Hathsin!" one whispered.

"He killed an Inquisitor. . . ." said another.

And then the chanting began. The skaa in the surrounding streets began to scream his name. The soldiers looked around, realizing with horror that they were surrounded. The peasants began to press in, and Kelsier could feel their anger and hope.

Maybe this doesn't have to go the way I assumed, Kelsier thought triumphantly. *Maybe I don't have—*

Then it hit. Like a cloud moving before the sun, like a sudden storm on a quiet night, like a pair of fingers snuffing a candle. An oppressive hand stifled the budding skaa emotions. The people cringed, and their cries died out. The fire Kelsier had built within them was too new.

So close . . . he thought.

Up ahead, a single, black carriage crested the hill and began to move down from the fountain square.

The Lord Ruler had arrived.

Vin nearly lost her grip as the wave of depression hit her. She flared her copper, but—as always—she could still slightly feel the Lord Ruler's oppressive hand.

"Lord Ruler!" Dockson said, though Vin couldn't tell if it was a curse or an observation. Skaa that had been packed in to view the fight somehow managed to make room for the dark carriage. It rolled down a corridor of people toward the corpse-littered square.

Soldiers pulled back, and Kelsier stepped away from the fallen cart, moving out to face the oncoming carriage.

"What is he doing?" Vin asked, turning toward Dockson, who had propped himself up on a small outcropping. "Why doesn't he run? This is no Inquisitor—this isn't something to fight!"

"This is it, Vin," Dockson said, awed. "This is what he's been waiting for. A chance to face the Lord Ruler—a chance to prove those legends of his."

Vin turned back toward the square. The carriage rolled to a stop.

"But . . ." she said quietly. "The Eleventh Metal. Did he bring it?"

"He must have."

Kelsier always said that the Lord Ruler was his task, Vin thought. *He let the rest of us work on the nobility, the Garrison, and the Ministry. But this . . . Kelsier always planned to do this himself.*

The Lord Ruler stepped from his carriage, and Vin leaned forward, burning tin. He looked like . . .

A man.

He was dressed in a black and white uniform somewhat like a nobleman's suit, but far more exaggerated. The coat reached all the way to his feet, and trailed behind him as he walked. His vest wasn't colored, but a pure black, though it was accented with brilliant white markings. As Vin had heard, his fingers glittered with rings, the symbol of his power.

I'm so much stronger than you, the rings proclaimed, *that it doesn't matter if I wear metal.*

Handsome, with jet black hair and pale skin, the Lord Ruler was tall, thin, and confident. And he was young—younger than Vin would have expected, even younger than Kelsier. He strode across the square, avoiding corpses, his soldiers pulling back and forcing the skaa away.

Suddenly, a small group of figures burst through the line of soldiers. They wore the mismatched armor of rebels, and the man leading them looked just a bit familiar. He was one of Ham's Thugs.

"For my wife!" the Thug said, holding up a spear and charging.

"For Lord Kelsier!" yelled the other four.

Oh no . . . Vin thought.

The Lord Ruler, however, ignored the men. The lead rebel bellowed in defiance, then rammed his spear through the Lord Ruler's chest.

The Lord Ruler just continued to walk, passing the solider, spear sticking all the way through his body.

The rebel paused, then grabbed a spear from one of his friends and drove this one through the Lord Ruler's back. Again, the Lord Ruler ignored the men—as if they, and their weapons, were completely beneath his contempt.

The lead rebel stumbled back, then spun as his friends began to scream under an Inquisitor's axe. He joined them shortly, and the Inquisitor stood above the corpses for a moment, hacking gleefully.

The Lord Ruler continued forward, two spears sticking—as if unnoticed—from his body. Kelsier stood waiting. He looked ragged in his ripped skaa clothing. Yet, he was proud. He didn't bend or bow beneath the weight of the Lord Ruler's Soothing.

The Lord Ruler stopped a few feet away, one of the spears nearly touching Kelsier's chest. Black ash fell lightly around the two men, bits of it curling and blowing in the faint wind. The square fell horribly silent—even the Inquisitor stopped his gruesome work. Vin leaned forward, clinging precariously to the rough brickwork.

Do something, Kelsier! Use the metal!

The Lord Ruler glanced at the Inquisitor that Kelsier had killed. "Those are very hard to replace." His accented voice carried easily to Vin's tin-enhanced ears.

Even from a distance, she could see Kelsier smile.

"I killed you, once," the Lord Ruler said, turning back to Kelsier.

"You tried," Kelsier replied, his voice loud and firm, carrying across the square. "But you can't kill me, Lord Tyrant. I represent that thing you've *never* been able to kill, no matter how hard you try. I am hope."

The Lord Ruler snorted in disdain. He raised a casual arm, then backhanded Kelsier with a blow so powerful that Vin could hear the crack resound through the square.

Kelsier lurched and spun, spraying blood as he fell.

"*NO!*" Vin screamed.

The Lord Ruler ripped one of the spears from his own body, then slammed it down through Kelsier's chest. "Let the executions begin," he said, turning toward his carriage and ripping out the second spear, then tossing it aside.

Chaos followed. Prompted by the Inquisitor, the soldiers turned and attacked the crowd. Other Inquisitors appeared from the square above, riding black horses, ebony axes glistening in the afternoon light.

Vin ignored it all. "Kelsier!" she screamed. His body lay where it had fallen, spear jutting from his chest, scarlet blood pooling around him.

No. No. NO! She jumped from the building, Pushing against some people and throwing herself over the massacre. She landed in the center of the oddly empty square—Lord Ruler gone, Inquisitors busy killing skaa. She scrambled to Kelsier's side.

There was almost nothing remaining of the left side of his face. The right side, however . . . it still smiled faintly, single dead eye staring up into the red-black sky. Bits of ash fell lightly on his face.

"Kelsier, no . . ." Vin said, tears streaming down her face. She prodded his body, feeling for a pulse. There was none.

"You said you couldn't be killed!" she cried. "What of your plans? What of the Eleventh Metal? What of *me*?"

He didn't move. Vin had trouble seeing through the tears. *It's impossible. He always said we aren't invincible . . . but that meant me. Not him. Not Kelsier. He was* invincible.

He should have been.

Someone grabbed her, and she squirmed, crying out.

"Time to go, kid," Ham said. He paused, looking at Kelsier, assuring for himself that the crewleader was dead.

Then he towed her away. Vin continued to struggle weakly, but she was growing numb. In the back of her mind, she heard Reen's voice.

See. I told you he would leave you. I warned you.

I promised you. . . .

THE END OF PART FOUR

PART FIVE

BELIEVERS IN A
FORGOTTEN WORLD

I know what will happen if I make the wrong choice. I must be strong; I must not take the power for myself.

For I have seen what will happen if I do.

35

TO WORK WITH ME, **KELSIER HAD** said, *I only ask that you promise one thing—to trust me.*

Vin hung in the mist, immobile. It flowed around her like a quiet stream. Above, ahead, to the sides, and beneath. Mist all around her.

Trust me, Vin, he'd said. *You trusted me enough to jump off the wall, and I caught you. You're going to have to trust me this time too.*

I'll catch you.

I'll catch you. . . .

It was as if she were nowhere. Among, and *of*, the mist. How she envied it. It didn't think. Didn't worry.

Didn't hurt.

I trusted you, Kelsier, she thought. *I actually did—but you let me fall. You promised that your crews had no betrayals. What of this? What of your betrayal?*

She hung, her tin extinguished to let her better see the mists. They were slightly wet, cool upon her skin. Like the tears of a dead man.

Why does it matter, anymore? she thought, staring upward. *Why does anything matter? What was it you said to me, Kelsier? That I never really understood? That I still needed to learn about friendship? What about you? You didn't even fight him.*

He stood there again, in her mind. The Lord Ruler struck him down with a disdainful blow. The Survivor had died like any other man.

Is this why you were so hesitant to promise that you wouldn't abandon me?

She wished she could just . . . go. Float away. Become mist. She'd once wished for freedom—and then had assumed she'd found it. She'd been wrong. This wasn't freedom, this grief, this hole within her.

It was the same as before, when Reen had abandoned her. What was the difference? At least Reen had been honest. He'd always promised that he would leave. Kelsier had led her along, telling her to trust and to love, but Reen had always been the truthful one.

"I don't want to do this anymore," she whispered to the mists. "Can't you just take me?"

The mists gave no answer. They continued to spin playfully, uncaring. Always changing—yet somehow, always the same.

"Mistress?" called an uncertain voice from below. "Mistress, is that you up there?"

Vin sighed, burning tin, then extinguishing steel and letting herself drop. Her mistcloak fluttered as she fell through the mists; she landed quietly on the rooftop above their safe house. Sazed stood a short distance away, beside the steel ladder that the lookouts had been using to get atop the building.

"Yes, Saze?" she asked tiredly, reaching out to Pull up the three coins she'd been using as anchors to stabilize her like the legs of a tripod. One of them was twisted and bent—the same coin she and Kelsier had gotten into a Pushing match over so many months ago.

"I'm sorry, Mistress," Sazed said. "I simply wondered where you had gone."

She shrugged.

"It is a strangely quiet night, I think," Sazed said.

"A mournful night." Hundreds of skaa had been massacred following Kelsier's death, and hundreds more had been trampled during the rush to escape.

"I wonder if his death even meant anything," she said quietly. "We probably saved a lot fewer than were killed."

"Slain by evil men, Mistress."

"Ham often asks if there even *is* such a thing as 'evil.'"

"Master Hammond likes to ask questions," Sazed said, "but even he doesn't question the answers. There are evil men . . . just as there are good men."

Vin shook her head. "I was wrong about Kelsier. He wasn't a good man—he was just a liar. He never had a plan for defeating the Lord Ruler."

"Perhaps," Sazed said. "Or, perhaps he never had an opportunity to fulfill that plan. Perhaps we just don't understand the plan."

"You sound like you still believe in him." Vin turned and walked to the edge of the flat-topped roof, staring out over the quiet, shadowy city.

"I do, Mistress," Sazed said.

"How? How can you?"

Sazed shook his head, walking over to stand beside her. "Belief isn't simply a thing for fair times and bright days, I think. What is belief—what is faith—if you don't continue in it after failure?"

Vin frowned.

"Anyone can believe in someone, or something, that always succeeds, Mistress. But failure . . . ah, now, that is hard to believe in, certainly and truly. Difficult enough to have value, I think."

Vin shook her head. "Kelsier doesn't deserve it."

"You don't mean that, Mistress," Sazed said calmly. "You're angry because of what happened. You hurt."

"Oh, I mean it," Vin said, feeling a tear on her cheek. "He doesn't deserve our belief. He never did."

"The skaa think differently—their legends about him are growing quickly. I shall have to return here soon and collect them."

Vin frowned. "You would gather stories about Kelsier?"

"Of course," Sazed said. "I collect all religions."

Vin snorted. "This is no religion we're talking about, Sazed. This is Kelsier."

"I disagree. He is certainly a religious figure to the skaa."

"But, we *knew* him," Vin said. "He was no prophet or god. He was just a man."

"So many of them are, I think," Sazed said quietly.

Vin just shook her head. They stood there for a moment, watching the night. "What of the others?" she finally asked.

"They are discussing what to do next," Sazed said. "I believe it has been decided that they will leave Luthadel separately and seek refuge in other towns."

"And . . . you?"

"I must travel north—to my homeland, to the place of the Keepers—so that I can share the knowledge that I possess. I must tell my brethren and sisters of the logbook—especially the words regarding our ancestor, the man named Rashek. There is much to learn in this story, I think."

He paused, then glanced at her. "This is not a journey I can take with another, Mistress. The places of the Keepers must remain secret, even from you."

Of course, Vin thought. *Of course he'd go too.*

"I will return," he promised.

Sure you will. Just like all of the others have.

The crew had made her feel needed for a time, but she'd always known it would end. It was time to go back to the streets. Time to be alone again.

"Mistress . . ." Sazed said slowly. "Do you hear that?"

She shrugged. But . . . there was something. Voices. Vin frowned, walking to the other side of the building. They grew louder, becoming easily distinct even without tin. She peered over the side of the rooftop.

A group of skaa men, perhaps ten in number, stood in the street below. *A thieving crew?* Vin wondered as Sazed joined her. The group's numbers were swelling as more skaa timidly left their dwellings.

"Come," said a skaa man who stood at the front of the group. "Fear not the mist! Didn't the Survivor name himself Lord of the Mists? Did he not say that we have nothing to fear from them? Indeed, they will protect us, give us safety. Give us power, even!"

As more and more skaa left their homes without obvious repercussion, the group began to swell even further.

"Go get the others," Vin said.

"Good idea," Sazed said, moving quickly to the ladder.

"Your friends, your children, your fathers, your mothers, wives, and lovers," the skaa man said, lighting a lantern and holding it up. "They lie dead in the street not a half hour from here. The Lord Ruler doesn't even have the decency to clean up his slaughter!"

The crowd began to mutter in agreement.

"Even when the cleaning occurs," the man said, "will it be the Lord Ruler's hands that dig the graves? No! It will be our hands. Lord Kelsier spoke of this."

"Lord Kelsier!" several men agreed. The group was getting large now, being joined by women and youths.

Clanking on the ladder announced Ham's arrival. He was joined shortly by Sazed, then Breeze, Dockson, Spook, and even Clubs.

"Lord Kelsier!" proclaimed the man below. Others lit torches, brightening the mists. "Lord Kelsier fought for us today! He slew an immortal Inquisitor!"

The crowd grumbled in assent.

"But then he died!" someone yelled.

Silence.

"And what did we do to help him?" the leader asked. "Many of us were there—thousands of us. Did we help? No! We waited and watched, even as he fought for us. We stood dumbly and let him fall. We watched him die!

"Or did we? What did the Survivor say—that the Lord Ruler could never really kill him? Kelsier is the Lord of the Mists! Is he not with us now?"

Vin turned to the others. Ham was watching carefully, but Breeze just shrugged. "The man's obviously insane. A religious nut."

"I tell you, friends!" screamed the man below. The crowd was still growing, more and more torches being lit. "I tell you the truth! *Lord Kelsier appeared to me this very night!* He said that he would always be with us. Will we let him down again?"

"No!" came the reply.

Breeze shook his head. "I didn't think they had it in them. Too bad it's such a small—"

"What's that?" Dox asked.

Vin turned, frowning. There was a pocket of light in the distance. Like . . . torches, lit in the mists. Another one appeared to the east, near a skaa slum. A third appeared. Then a fourth. In a matter of moments, it seemed like the entire city was glowing.

"You insane genius . . ." Dockson whispered.

"What?" Clubs asked, frowning.

"We missed it," Dox said. "The atium, the army, the nobility . . . that wasn't the job Kelsier was planning. *This* was his job! Our crew was never supposed to topple the Final Empire—we were too small. An entire city's population, however . . ."

"You're saying he did this on purpose?" Breeze asked.

"He always asked me the same question," Sazed said from behind. "He always asked what gave religions so much power. Each time, I answered him the same. . . ." Sazed looked at them, cocking his head. "I told him that it was because their believers had something they felt passionate about. Something . . . or someone."

"But, why not tell us?" Breeze asked.

"Because he knew," Dox said quietly. "He knew something we would never agree to. He knew that he would have to die."

Breeze shook his head. "I don't buy it. Why even bother with us, then? He could have done this on his own."

Why even bother . . . "Dox," Vin said, turning. "Where's that warehouse Kelsier rented, the one where he held his informant meetings?"

Dockson paused. "Not far away, actually. Two streets down. He said he wanted it to be near the bolt-lair. . . ."

"Show me!" Vin said, scrambling over the side of the building. The gathered skaa continued to yell, each cry louder than the one before. The entire street blazed with light, flickering torches turning the mist into a brilliant haze.

Dockson led her down the street, the rest of the crew trailing behind. The warehouse was a large, run-down structure squatting disconsolately in the slum's industrial section. Vin walked up to it, then flared pewter and smashed off the lock.

The door slowly swung open. Dockson held up a lantern, and its light revealed sparkling piles of metal. Weapons. Swords, axes, staves, and helmets glittered in the light—an incredible silvery hoard.

The crew stared at the room in wonder.

"*This* is the reason," Vin said quietly. "He needed the Renoux front to buy weapons in such numbers. He knew his rebellion would need these if they were going to succeed in taking the city."

"Why gather an army, then?" Ham said. "Was it just a front too?"

"I guess," Vin said.

"Wrong," a voice said, echoing through the cavernous warehouse. "There was so much more to it than that."

The crew jumped, and Vin flared her metals . . . until she recognized the voice. "Renoux?"

Dockson held his lantern higher. "Show yourself, creature."

A figure moved in the far back of the warehouse, staying to shadow. However, when it spoke, its voice was unmistakable. "He needed the army to provide a core of trained men for the rebellion. That part of his plan was . . . hampered by events. That was only one bit of why he needed you, however. The noble houses needed to fall to leave a void in the political structure. The Garrison needed to leave the town so that the skaa wouldn't be slaughtered."

"He planned this all from the start," Ham said with wonder. "Kelsier knew that the skaa wouldn't rise up. They'd been beaten down for so long, trained to think that the Lord Ruler owned both their bodies and their souls. He understood that they would never rebel . . . not unless he gave them a *new* god."

"Yes," Renoux said, stepping forward. The light glittered off his face, and Vin gasped in surprise.

"Kelsier!" she screamed.

Ham grabbed her shoulder. "Careful, child. It's not him."

The creature looked at her. It wore Kelsier's face, but the eyes . . . they were different. The face didn't bear Kelsier's characteristic smile. It seemed hollow. Dead.

"I apologize," it said. "This was to be my part in the plan, and is the reason Kelsier originally contracted with me. I was to take his bones once he was dead, then appear to his followers to give them faith and strength."

"What are you?" Vin asked with horror.

Renoux-Kelsier looked at her, and then his face shimmered, becoming transparent. She could see his bones through the gelatinous skin. It reminded her of . . .

"A *mistwraith*."

"A kandra," the creature said, its skin losing its transparency. "A mistwraith that has . . . grown up, you might say."

Vin turned away in revulsion, remembering the creatures she had seen in the mist. Scavengers, Kelsier had said . . . creatures that digested the bodies of the dead, stealing their skeletons and images. *The legends are even more true than I thought.*

"You were part of this plan too," the kandra said. "All of you. You ask why he needed a crew? He needed men of virtue, men who could learn to worry more for the people than for coin. He put you before armies and crowds, letting you practice leadership. He was using you . . . but he was also training you."

The creature looked to Dockson, Breeze, then Ham. "Bureaucrat, politician, general. For a new nation to be born, it will need men of your individual talents." The kandra nodded to a large sheet of paper affixed to a table a short distance away. "That is for you to follow. I have other business to be about."

It turned as if to leave, then paused beside Vin, turning toward her with its disturbingly Kelsier-like face. Yet, the creature itself wasn't like Renoux or Kelsier. It seemed passionless.

The kandra held up a small pouch. "He asked me to give you this." It dropped the pouch into her hand, then continued on, the crew giving it a wide berth as it left the warehouse.

Breeze started toward the table first, but Ham and Dockson beat him to it. Vin looked down at the bag. She was . . . afraid to see what it contained. She hurried forward, joining the crew.

The sheet was a map of the city, apparently copied from the one Marsh had sent. Written at the top were some words.

My friends, you have a lot of work to do, and you must do it quickly. You must organize and distribute the weapons in this warehouse, then you must do the same in two others like it located in the other slums. There are horses in a side room for ease of travel.

Once you distribute the weapons, you must secure the city gates and subdue the remaining members of the Garrison. Breeze, your team will do this—march on the Garrison first, so that you can take the gates in peace.

There are four Great Houses that retain a strong military presence in the city. I have marked them on the map. Ham, your team will deal with these. We don't want an armed force other than our own inside the city.

Dockson, remain behind while the initial strikes happen. More and more skaa will come to the warehouses once word gets out. Breeze and Ham's armies will include the troops we have trained, as well as augmentations—I hope—from the skaa gathering in the streets. You will need to make certain that the regular skaa get their weapons, so that Clubs can lead the assault on the palace itself.

The Soothing stations should already be gone—Renoux delivered the proper order to our assassin teams before he came to get you to bring you here. If you have time, send some of Ham's Thugs to check out those stations. Breeze, your own Soothers will be needed amongst the skaa to encourage them to bravery.

I think that's everything. It was a fun job, wasn't it? When you remember me, please remember that. Remember to smile. Now, move quickly.

May you rule in wisdom.

The map had the city divided, with the various divisions labeled with various crewmembers' names. Vin noticed that she, along with Sazed, were left out.

"I'll go back to that group we left by our house," Clubs said in a grumbling voice. "Bring them here to get weapons." He began to hobble away.

"Clubs?" Ham said, turning. "No offense, but . . . why did he include you as an army leader? What do you know of warfare?"

Clubs snorted, then lifted up his trouser leg, showing the long, twisting scar that ran up the side of his calf and thigh—obviously the source of his limp. "Where do you think I got this?" he said, then began to move away.

Ham turned back with wonder. "I don't believe this is happening."

Breeze shook his head. "And I assumed that *I* knew something about manipulating people. This . . . this is amazing. The economy is on the verge of collapsing, and the nobility that survive will soon be at open warfare on the countryside. Kell showed us how to kill Inquisitors—we'll just need to pull down the others and behead them. As for the Lord Ruler . . ."

Eyes turned on Vin. She looked down at the pouch in her hand, and pulled it open. A smaller sack, obviously filled with atium beads, fell into her hand. It was followed by a small bar of metal wrapped in a sheet of paper. The Eleventh Metal.

Vin unwrapped the paper.

Vin, it read. *Your original duty tonight was going to be to assassinate the high noblemen remaining in the city. But, well, you convinced me that maybe they should live.*

I could never figure out how this blasted metal was supposed to work. It's safe to burn—it won't kill you—but it doesn't appear to do anything useful. If you're reading this, then I failed to figure out how to use it when I faced the Lord Ruler. I don't think it matters. The people needed something to believe in, and this was the only way to give it to them.

Please don't be angry at me for abandoning you. I was given an extension on life. I should have died in Mare's place years ago. I was ready for this.

The others will need you. You're their Mistborn now—you'll have to protect them in the months to come. The nobility will send assassins against our fledgling kingdom's rulers.

Farewell. I'll tell Mare about you. She always wanted a daughter.

"What does it say, Vin?" Ham asked.

"It . . . says that he doesn't know how the Eleventh Metal works. He's sorry—he wasn't certain how to defeat the Lord Ruler."

"We've got an entire city full of people to fight him," Dox said. "I seriously doubt he can kill us all—if we can't destroy him, we'll just tie him up and toss him in a dungeon."

The others nodded.

"All right!" Dockson said. "Breeze and Ham, you need to get to those other warehouses and begin giving out weapons. Spook, go fetch the apprentices—we'll need them to run messages. Let's go!"

Everyone scattered. Soon, the skaa they had seen earlier burst into the warehouse, holding their torches high, looking in awe at the wealth of weaponry. Dockson worked efficiently, ordering some of the newcomers to be distributors, sending others to go gather their friends and family. Men began to gear up, gathering weapons. Everyone was busy except for Vin.

She looked up at Sazed, who smiled at her. "Sometimes we just have to wait long enough, Mistress," he said. "Then we find out why exactly it was that we kept believing. There is a saying that Master Kelsier was fond of."

"There's always another secret," Vin whispered. "But Saze, everyone has something to do except me. I was originally supposed to go assassinate noblemen, but Kell doesn't want me to do that anymore."

"They have to be neutralized," Sazed said, "but not necessarily murdered. Perhaps your place was simply to show Kelsier that fact?"

Vin shook her head. "No. I have to do more, Saze." She gripped the empty pouch, frustrated. Something crinkled inside of it.

She looked down, opening the pouch and noticing a piece of paper that she hadn't seen before. She pulled it out and unfolded it delicately. It was the drawing that Kelsier had shown her—the picture of a flower. Mare had always kept it with her, dreaming of a future where the sun wasn't red, where plants were green. . . .

Vin looked up.

Bureaucrat, politician, soldier . . . there's something else that every kingdom needs.

A good assassin.

She turned, pulling out a vial of metal and drinking its contents, using the liquid to wash down a couple beads of atium. She walked over to the pile of weapons, picking up a small bundle of arrows. They had stone heads. She began breaking the heads off, leaving about a half inch of wood attached to them, discarding the fletched shafts.

"Mistress?" Sazed asked with concern.

Vin walked past him, searching through the armaments. She found what she wanted in a shirtlike piece of armor, constructed from large rings of interlocking metal. She pried a handful of these free with a dagger and pewter-enhanced fingers.

"Mistress, what are you doing?"

Vin walked over to a trunk beside the table, within which she had seen a large collection of powdered metals. She filled her pouch with several handfuls of pewter dust.

"I'm worried about the Lord Ruler," she said, taking a file from the box and scraping off a few flakes of the Eleventh Metal. She paused—eyeing the unfamiliar, silvery metal—then swallowed the flakes with a gulp from her flask. She put a couple more flakes in one of her backup metal vials.

"Surely the rebellion can deal with him," Sazed said. "He is not so strong without all of his servants, I think."

"You're wrong," Vin said, rising and walking toward the door. "He's strong, Saze. Kelsier couldn't feel him, not like I can. He didn't know."

"Where are you going?" Sazed asked behind her.

Vin paused in the doorway, turning, mist curling around her. "Inside the palace complex, there is a chamber protected by soldiers and Inquisitors. Kelsier tried to get into it twice." She turned back toward the dark mists. "Tonight, I'm going to find out what's inside of it."

I have decided that I am thankful for Rashek's hatred. It does me well to remember that there are those who abhor me. My place is not to seek popularity or love; my place is to ensure mankind's survival.

36

VIN WALKED QUIETLY TOWARD KREDIK SHAW. The sky behind her burned, the mists reflecting and diffusing the light of a thousand torches. It was like a radiant dome over the city.

The light was yellow, the color Kelsier had always said the sun should be.

Four nervous guards waited at the same palace doorway that she and Kelsier had attacked before. They watched her approach. Vin stepped slowly, quietly, on the mist-wetted stones, her mistcloak rustling solemnly.

One of the guards lowered a spear at her, and Vin stopped right in front of him.

"I know you," she said quietly. "You endured the mills, the mines, and the forges. You knew that someday they would kill you, and leave your families to starve. So, you went to the Lord Ruler—guilty but determined—and joined his guards."

The four men glanced at each other, confused.

"The light behind me comes from a massive skaa rebellion," she said. "The entire city is rising up against the Lord Ruler. I don't blame you men for your choices, but a time of change is coming. Those rebels could use your training and your knowledge. Go to them—they gather in the Square of the Survivor."

"The . . . Square of the Survivor?" a soldier asked.

"The place where the Survivor of Hathsin was killed earlier today."

The four men exchanged looks, uncertain.

Vin Rioted their emotions slightly. "You don't have to live with the guilt anymore."

Finally, one of the men stepped forward and ripped the symbol off his uniform, then strode determinedly into the night. The other three paused, then followed—leaving Vin with an open entrance to the palace.

Vin walked down the corridor, eventually passing the same guard chamber as before. She strode inside—stepping past a group of chatting guards without hurting any of them—and entered the hallway beyond. Behind her, the guards shook off their surprise and called out in alarm. They burst into the corridor, but Vin jumped and Pushed against the lantern brackets, hurling herself down the hallway.

The men's voices grew distant; even running, they wouldn't be able to keep up with her. She reached the end of the corridor, then let herself drop lightly to the ground, enveloping cloak falling around her body. She continued her resolute, unhurried pace. There was no reason to run. They'd be waiting for her anyway.

She passed through the archway, stepping into the dome-roofed central chamber. Silver murals lined the walls, braziers burned in the corners, the floor was an ebony marble.

And two Inquisitors stood blocking her path.

Vin strode quietly through the room, approaching the building-within-a-building that was her goal.

"We search all this time," said an Inquisitor in his grinding voice. "And you come to us. A second time."

Vin stopped, standing about twenty feet in front of the pair. They loomed, each of them nearly two feet taller than she, smiling and confident.

Vin burned atium, then whipped her hands from beneath her cloak, tossing a double handful of arrowheads into the air. She flared steel, Pushing powerfully against the rings of metal wrapped loosely around the arrowheads' broken hafts. The missiles shot forward, ripping across the room. The lead Inquisitor chuckled, raising a hand and Pushing disdainfully against the missiles.

His Push ripped the unattached rings free from the hafts, shooting the bits of metal backward. The arrowheads themselves, however, continued forward—no longer Pushed from behind, but still carried by a deadly momentum.

The Inquisitor opened his mouth in surprise as two dozen arrowheads struck him. Several punched completely through his flesh, continuing on to snap against the stone wall behind him. Several others struck his companion in the legs.

The lead Inquisitor jerked, spasming as he collapsed. The other growled, staying on his feet, but wobbling a bit on the weakened leg. Vin dashed forward, flaring her pewter. The remaining Inquisitor moved to block her, but she reached inside her cloak and threw out a large handful of pewter dust.

The Inquisitor stopped, confused. To his "eyes" he would see nothing but a mess of blue lines—each one leading to a speck of metal. With so many sources of metal concentrated in one place, the lines would be virtually blinding.

The Inquisitor spun, angry, as Vin dashed past him. He Pushed against the dust, blowing it away, but as he did so, Vin whipped out a glass dagger and flipped it toward him. In the confusing mess of blue lines and atium shadows, he missed noticing the dagger, and it took him square in the thigh. He fell, cursing in a crackly voice.

Good thing that worked, Vin thought, leaping over the groaning body of the first Inquisitor. *Wasn't sure about those eyes of theirs.*

She threw her weight against the door, flaring pewter and tossing up another handful of dust to keep the remaining Inquisitor from targeting any metals on her body. She didn't turn back to fight the two further—not with the trouble one of the creatures had given Kelsier. Her goal this infiltration wasn't to kill, but to gather information, then run.

Vin burst into the building-within-a-building, nearly tripping on a rug made from some exotic fur. She frowned, scanning the chamber urgently, searching for whatever the Lord Ruler hid inside of it.

It has to be here, she thought desperately. *The clue to defeating him—the way to win this battle.* She was counting on the Inquisitors being distracted by their wounds long enough for her to search out the Lord Ruler's secret and escape.

The room had only one exit—the entrance she'd come through—and a hearth burned in the center of the chamber. The walls were decorated with odd trappings; furs hung from most places, the pelts dyed in strange patterns. There were a few old paintings, their colors faded, their canvases yellowed.

Vin searched quickly, urgently, looking for anything that could prove to be a weapon against the Lord Ruler. Unfortunately, she saw nothing useful; the room felt foreign, but unremarkable. In fact, it had a comfortable hominess, like a study or den. It was packed full of strange objects and decorations—like the horns of some foreign beast and a strange pair of shoes with very wide, flat bottoms. It was the room of a pack rat, a place to keep memories of the past.

She jumped as something moved near the center of the room. A pivoting chair stood by the hearth, and it spun slowly, revealing the wizened old man who sat in it. Bald, with liver-spotted skin, he appeared to be in his seventies. He wore rich, dark clothing, and he frowned angrily at Vin.

That's it, Vin thought. *I've failed—there's nothing here. Time to get out.*

Just as she was spinning to dash away, however, rough hands grabbed her from behind. She cursed, struggling as she glanced down at the Inquisitor's bloodied leg. Even with pewter, he shouldn't have been able to walk on it. She tried to twist away, but the Inquisitor had her in a powerful grasp.

"What is this?" the old man demanded, standing.

"I'm sorry, Lord Ruler," the Inquisitor said deferentially.

Lord Ruler! But . . . I saw him. He was a young man.

"Kill her," the old man said, waving his hand.

"My lord," the Inquisitor said. "This child is . . . of special interest. Might I keep her for a time?"

"What special interest?" the Lord Ruler said, sighing as he sat again.

"We wish to petition you, Lord Ruler," said the Inquisitor. "Regarding the Canton of Orthodoxy."

"This again?" the Lord Ruler said wearily.

"Please, my lord," said the Inquisitor. Vin continued to struggle, flaring her pewter. The Inquisitor pinned her arms to her sides, however, and her backward kicking did very little good. *He's so strong!* she thought with frustration.

And then, she remembered it. The Eleventh Metal, its power sitting within her, forming an unfamiliar reserve. She looked up, glaring at the old man. *This had better work.* She burned the Eleventh Metal.

Nothing happened.

Vin struggled in frustration, her heart sinking. And then she saw him. Another man, standing right beside the Lord Ruler. Where had he come from? She hadn't seen him enter.

He had a full beard and wore a thick, woolen outfit with a fur-lined cloak. It wasn't rich clothing, but it was well constructed. He stood quietly, seeming . . . content. He smiled happily.

Vin cocked her head. There was something familiar about the man. His features looked very similar to those of the man who had killed Kelsier. However, this man was older and . . . more alive.

Vin turned to the side. There was another unfamiliar man beside her, a young nobleman. He was a merchant, from the looks of his suit—and a very wealthy one at that.

What is going on?

The Eleventh Metal burned out. Both newcomers vanished like ghosts.

"Very well," said the elderly Lord Ruler, sighing. "I agree to your request. We will meet in several hours' time—Tevidian has already requested a gathering to discuss matters outside the palace."

"Ah," said the second Inquisitor. "Yes . . . it will be good for him to be there. Good indeed."

Vin continued to squirm as the Inquisitor pushed her to the ground, then lifted his hand, gripping something she couldn't see. He swung, and pain flashed through her head.

Despite her pewter, all went black.

Elend found his father in the north entryway—a smaller, less daunting entrance to Keep Venture, though only when compared with the majestic grand hall.

"What's going on?" Elend demanded, pulling on his suit coat, his hair disheveled from sleep. Lord Venture stood with his guard captains and canalmasters. Soldiers and servants scattered through the white-and-brown hallway, rushing about with an air of apprehensive fright.

Lord Venture ignored Elend's question, calling for a messenger to ride for the east river docks.

"Father, what's happening?" Elend repeated.

"Skaa rebellion," Lord Venture snapped.

What? Elend thought as Lord Venture waved for another group of soldiers to approach. *Impossible.* A skaa rebellion in Luthadel itself . . . it was unthinkable. They didn't have the disposition to try such a bold move, they were just . . .

Valette is skaa, he thought. *You have to stop thinking like other noblemen, Elend. You have to open your eyes.*

The Garrison was gone, off to slaughter a different group of rebels. The skaa had been forced to watch those gruesome executions weeks ago, not to mention the slaughter that had come this day. They had been stressed to the point of breaking.

Temadre predicted this, Elend realized. *So did half a dozen other political theorists. They said that the Final Empire couldn't last forever. God at its head or not, the people would someday rise up. . . . It's finally happening. I'm living through it!*

And . . . I'm on the wrong side.

"Why the canalmasters?" Elend asked.

"We're leaving the city," Lord Venture said tersely.

"Abandon the keep?" Elend asked. "Where's the honor in that?"

Lord Venture snorted. "This isn't about bravery, boy. It's about survival. Those skaa are attacking the main gates, slaughtering the remnants of the Garrison. I have no intention of waiting until they come for noble heads."

"But . . ."

Lord Venture shook his head. "We were leaving anyway. Something . . . happened at the Pits a few days ago. The Lord Ruler isn't going to be happy when he discovers it." He stepped back, waving over his lead narrowboat captain.

Skaa rebellion, Elend thought, still a little numb. *What was it that Temadre warned in his writings? That, when a real rebellion finally came, the skaa would slaughter wantonly . . . that every nobleman's life would be forfeit.*

He predicted that the rebellion would die out quickly, but that it would leave piles of corpses in its wake. Thousands of deaths. Tens of thousands.

"Well, boy?" Lord Venture demanded. "Go and organize your things."

"I'm not going," Elend surprised himself by saying.

Lord Venture frowned. "What?"

Elend looked up. "I'm not going, Father."

"Oh, you're going," Lord Venture said, eyeing Elend with one of his glares.

Elend looked into those eyes—eyes that were angry not because they cared for Elend's safety, but because Elend dared defy them. And, strangely, Elend didn't feel the least bit cowed. *Someone has to stop this. The rebellion could do some good, but only if the skaa don't insist on slaughtering their allies.*

And, that's what the nobility should be—their allies against the Lord Ruler. He's our enemy too.

"Father, I'm serious," Elend said. "I'm going to stay."

"Bloody hell, boy! Must you insist on mocking me?"

"This isn't about balls or luncheons, father. It's about something more important."

Lord Venture paused. "No flippant comments? No buffoonery?"

Elend shook his head.

Suddenly, Lord Venture smiled. "Stay, then, boy. That's a good idea. Someone should maintain our presence here while I go rally our forces. Yes . . . a very good idea."

Elend paused, frowning slightly at the smile in his father's eyes. *The atium—Father is setting me up to fall in his place! And . . . even if the Lord Ruler doesn't kill me, Father assumes I'll die in the rebellion. Either way, he's rid of me.*

I'm really not very good at this, am I?

Lord Venture laughed to himself, turning.

"At least leave me some soldiers," Elend said.

"You can have most of them," Lord Venture said. "It will be hard enough to get one boat out in this mess. Good luck, boy. Say hello to the Lord Ruler in my absence." He laughed again, moving toward his stallion, which was saddled and readied outside.

Elend stood in the hall, and suddenly he was the focus of attention. Nervous guards and servants, realizing that they'd been abandoned, turned to Elend with desperate eyes.

I'm . . . in charge, Elend thought with shock. *Now what?* Outside, he could see the mists flaring with the light of burning fires. Several of the guards were yelling about an approaching mob of skaa.

Elend walked to the open doorway, staring out into the chaos. The hall grew quiet behind him, terrified people realizing the extent of their danger.

Elend stood for a long moment. Then he spun. "Captain!" he said. "Gather your forces and the remaining servants—don't leave anyone behind—then march to Keep Lekal."

"Keep . . . Lekal, my lord?"

"It's more defensible," Elend said. "Plus, both of us have too few soldiers—separated, we'll be destroyed. Together, we might be able to stand. We'll offer our men to the Lekal in exchange for protecting our people."

"But . . . my lord," the soldier said. "The Lekal are your enemies."

Elend nodded. "Yes, but someone needs to make the first overture. Now, get moving!"

The man saluted, then rushed into motion.

"Oh, and Captain?" Elend said.

The soldier paused.

"Pick out five of your best soldiers to be my honor guard. I'll be leaving you in charge—those five and I have another mission."

"My lord?" the captain asked with confusion. "What mission?"

Elend turned back toward the mists. "We're going to go turn ourselves in."

Vin awoke to wetness. She coughed, then groaned, feeling a sharp pain in the back of her skull. She opened dizzy eyes—blinking away the water that had been thrown on her—and immediately burned pewter and tin, bringing herself completely awake.

A pair of rough hands hoisted her into the air. She coughed as the Inquisitor shoved something into her mouth.

"Swallow," he ordered, twisting her arm.

Vin cried out, trying without success to resist the pain. Eventually, she gave in and swallowed the bit of metal.

"Now burn it," the Inquisitor ordered, twisting harder.

Vin resisted nonetheless, sensing the unfamiliar metal reserve within her. The Inquisitor could be trying to get her to burn a useless metal, one that would make her sick—or, worse, kill her.

But, there are easier ways to kill a captive, she thought in agony. Her arm hurt so much that it felt like it would twist free. Finally, Vin relented, burning the metal.

Immediately, all of her other metal reserves vanished.

"Good," the Inquisitor said, dropping her to the ground. The stones were wet, pooled with a bucketful of water. The Inquisitor turned, leaving the cell and slamming its barred door; then he disappeared through a doorway on the other side of the room.

Vin crawled to her knees, massaging her arm, trying to sort out what was going on. *My metals!* She searched desperately inside, but she found nothing. She couldn't feel any metals, not even the one she had ingested moments before.

What was it? A twelfth metal? Perhaps Allomancy wasn't as limited as Kelsier and the others had always assured her.

She took a few deep breaths, climbing to her knees, calming herself. There was something . . . Pushing against her. The Lord Ruler's presence. She could feel it, though it wasn't as powerful as it had been earlier, when he had killed Kelsier. Still, she didn't have copper to burn—she had no way to hide from the Lord Ruler's powerful, almost omnipotent, hand. She felt depression twisting her, telling her to just lie down, to give up. . . .

No! she thought. *I have to get out. I have to stay strong!*

She forced herself to stand and inspect her surroundings. Her prison was more like a cage than a cell. It had bars running along three of the four sides, and it contained no furniture—not even a sleeping mat. There were two other cell-cages in the room, one to either side of her.

She had been stripped, they had only left her with her undergarments. The move was probably to make certain that she didn't have any hidden metals. She glanced around the room. It was long and thin, and had stark stone walls. A stool sat in one corner, but the room was otherwise empty.

If I could find just a bit of metal . . .

She began to search. Instinctively, she tried to burn iron, expecting the blue lines to appear—but, of course, she had no iron to burn. She shook her head at the foolish move, but it was simply a sign of how much she'd come to rely on her Allomancy. She felt . . . blinded. She couldn't burn tin to listen for voices. She couldn't burn pewter to strengthen her against the pain of her hurting arm and head. She couldn't burn bronze to search for nearby Allomancers.

Nothing. She had nothing.

You functioned without Allomancy before, she told herself sternly. *You can do it now.*

Even so, she searched the bare floor of her cell, hoping for the chance existence of a discarded pin or nail. She found nothing, so she turned her attention to the bars. However, she couldn't think of a way to get off even a flake of the iron.

So much metal here, she thought with frustration. *And I can't use any of it!*

She sat back on the ground, huddling up against the stone wall, shivering quietly in her damp clothing. It was still dark outside; the room's window casually allowed in a few trails of mist. What had happened with the rebellion? What about her friends? She thought that the mists outside looked a bit brighter than usual. Torchlight in the night? Without tin, her senses were too weak to tell.

What was I thinking? she thought with despair. *Did I presume to succeed where Kelsier had failed? He knew that the Eleventh Metal was useless.*

It had done something, true—but it certainly hadn't killed the Lord Ruler. She sat, thinking, trying to figure out what had happened. There had been an odd familiarity about the things the Eleventh Metal had shown her. Not because of the way the visions had appeared, but because of the way Vin had felt when burning the metal.

Gold. The moment when I burned the Eleventh Metal felt like that time when Kelsier had me burn gold.

Could it be that the Eleventh Metal wasn't really "eleventh" at all? Gold and atium had always seemed oddly paired to Vin. All of the other metals came in pairs that were similar—a base metal, then its alloy, each doing opposite things. Iron Pulled, steel Pushed. Zinc Pulled, brass Pushed. It made sense. All except for atium and gold.

What if the Eleventh Metal was really an alloy of atium or of gold? *It would mean . . . that gold and atium aren't paired. They do two different things. Similar, but different. They're like . . .*

Like the other metals, which were grouped into larger bases of four. There were the physical metals: iron, steel, tin, and pewter. The mental metals: bronze, copper, zinc, and brass. And . . . there were the time-affecting metals: gold and its alloy, and atium and its alloy.

That means there's another metal. One that hasn't been discovered—probably because atium and gold are too valuable to forge into different alloys.

But, what good was the knowledge? Her "Eleventh Metal" was probably just a paired opposite of gold—the metal Kelsier had told her was the most useless of them all. Gold had shown Vin herself—or, at least, a different version of her that had felt real enough to touch. But, it had simply been a vision of what she could have become, had the past been different.

The Eleventh Metal had done something similar: Instead of showing Vin's own past, it had shown her similar images from other people. And that told her . . . nothing. What difference did it make what the Lord Ruler *could* have been? It was the current man, the tyrant that ruled the Final Empire, that she had to defeat.

A figure appeared in the doorway—an Inquisitor dressed in a black robe, the hood up. His face was shadowed, but his spike-heads jutted from the front of the cowl.

"It is time," he said. Another Inquisitor waited in the doorway as the first creature pulled out a set of keys and moved to open Vin's door.

Vin tensed. The door clicked, and she sprang to her feet, scrambling forward.

Have I always been this slow without pewter? she thought with horror. The Inquisitor snatched her arm as she passed, his motions unconcerned, almost casual—and she could see why. His hands moved supernaturally quickly, making her seem even more sluggish by comparison.

The Inquisitor pulled her up, twisting her and easily holding her. He smiled with an evil grin, his face pocked with scars. Scars that looked like . . .

Arrowhead wounds, she thought with shock. *But . . . healed already? How can it be?*

She struggled, but her weak, pewterless body was no match for the Inquisitor's strength. The creature carried her toward the doorway, and the second Inquisitor stepped back, regarding her with spikes that peeked out from beneath its cowl. Though the Inquisitor who carried her was smiling, this second one had a flat line of a mouth.

Vin spat at the second Inquisitor as she passed, her spittle smacking it right on one of its spike-heads. Her captor carried her out of the chamber and through a narrow hallway. She cried out for help, knowing that her screams—in the middle of Kredik Shaw itself—would be useless. At least she succeeded in annoying the Inquisitor, for he twisted her arm.

"Quiet," he said as she grunted in pain.

Vin fell silent, instead focusing on their location. They were probably in one of the lower sections of the palace; the hallways were too long to be in a tower or spire. The decorations were lavish, but the rooms looked . . . unused. The carpets were pristine, the furniture unmarked by scuff or scratch. She had the feeling that the murals were rarely seen, even by those who often passed through the chambers.

Eventually, the Inquisitors entered a stairwell and began to climb. *One of the spires,* she thought.

With each climbing step, Vin could feel the Lord Ruler getting closer. His mere presence dampened her emotions, stealing her willpower, making her numb to everything but lonely depression. She sagged in the Inquisitor's grip, no longer struggling. It took all of her energy to simply resist the Lord Ruler's pressure on her soul.

After a short time in the tunnel-like stairwell, the Inquisitors carried her out into a large, circular room. And, despite the power of the Lord Ruler's Soothing, despite her visits to noble keeps, Vin took just a brief moment to stare at her surroundings. They were majestic like none she'd ever seen.

The room was shaped like a massive, stocky cylinder. The wall—there was only one, running in a wide circle—was made entirely of glass. Lit by fires from behind, the room glowed with spectral light. The glass was colored, though it didn't depict any specific scene. Instead, it seemed crafted from a single sheet, the colors blown and melded together in long, thin trails. Like . . .

Like mist, she thought with wonder. *Colorful streams of mist, running in a circle around the entire room.*

The Lord Ruler sat in an elevated throne in the very center of the room. He wasn't the old Lord Ruler—this was the younger version, the handsome man who had killed Kelsier.

Some kind of impostor? No, I can feel him—just as I could feel the one before. They're the same man. Can he change how he looks, then? Appearing young when he wishes to put forth a pretty face?

A small group of gray-robed, eye-tattooed obligators stood conversing on the far side of the room. Seven Inquisitors stood waiting, like a row of shadows with iron eyes. That made nine of them in all, counting the two that had escorted Vin. Her scar-faced captor delivered her to one of the others, who held her with a similarly inescapable grip.

"Let us be on with this," said the Lord Ruler.

A regular obligator stepped forward, bowing. With a chill, she realized that she recognized him.

Lord Prelan Tevidian, she thought, eyeing the thin balding man. *My . . . father.*

"My lord," Tevidian said, "forgive me, but I do not understand. We have already discussed this matter!"

"The Inquisitors say they have more to add," the Lord Ruler said in a tired voice.

Tevidian eyed Vin, frowning in confusion. *He doesn't know who I am,* she thought. *He never knew he was a father.*

"My lord," Tevidian said, turning away from her. "Look outside your window! Do we not have better things to discuss? The entire *city* is in rebellion! Skaa torches light up the night, and they dare go out into the mists. They blaspheme in riots, attacking the keeps of the nobility!"

"Let them," the Lord Ruler said in an uncaring voice. He seemed so . . . worn. He sat strongly on his throne, but there was still a weariness to his posture and his voice.

"But my lord!" Tevidian said. "The Great Houses are falling!"

The Lord Ruler waved a dismissive hand. "It is good for them to get purged every century or so. It fosters instability, keeps the aristocracy from growing too confident. Usually, I let them kill each other in one of their foolish wars, but these riots will work."

"And . . . if the skaa come to the palace?"

"Then I will deal with them," the Lord Ruler said softly. "You will not question this further."

"Yes, my lord," Tevidian said, bowing and backing away.

"Now," the Lord Ruler said, turning to the Inquisitors. "What is it you wished to present?"

The scarred Inquisitor stepped forward. "Lord Ruler, we wish to petition that leadership of your Ministry be taken from these . . . men and granted to the Inquisitors instead."

"We have discussed this," the Lord Ruler said. "You and your brothers are needed for more important tasks. You are too valuable to waste on simple administration."

"But," the Inquisitor said, "by allowing common men to rule your Ministry, you have unwittingly allowed corruption and vice to enter the very heart of your holy palace!"

"Idle claims!" Tevidian spat. "You say such things often, Kar, but you never offer any proof."

Kar turned slowly, his eerie smile lit by the twisting, colored windowlight. Vin shivered. That smile was nearly as unsettling as the Lord Ruler's Soothing.

"Proof?" Kar asked. "Why, tell me, *Lord Prelan.* Do you recognize that girl?"

"Bah, of course not!" Tevidian said with a wave of his hand. "What does a skaa girl have to do with the government of the Ministry?"

"Everything," Kar said, turning to Vin. "Oh, yes . . . everything. Tell the Lord Ruler who your father is, child."

Vin tried to squirm, but the Lord Ruler's Allomancy was so oppressive, the Inquisitor's hands were so strong. "I don't know," she managed to say through gritted teeth.

The Lord Ruler perked up slightly, turning toward her, leaning forward.

"You cannot lie to the Lord Ruler, child," Kar said in a quiet, rasping voice. "He has lived for centuries, and has learned to use Allomancy like no mortal man. He can see things in the way your heart beats, and can read your emotions in your eyes. He can sense the moment when you lie. He knows . . . oh, yes. He knows."

"I never knew my father," Vin said stubbornly. If the Inquisitor wanted to know something, then keeping it a secret seemed like a good idea. "I'm just a street urchin."

"A Mistborn street urchin?" Kar asked. "Why, that's interesting. Isn't it, Tevidian?"

The lord prelan paused, his frown deepening. The Lord Ruler stood slowly, walking down the steps of his dais toward Vin.

"Yes, my lord," Kar said. "You felt her Allomancy earlier. You know that she is a full Mistborn—an amazingly powerful one. Yet, she claims to have grown up on the street. What noble house would have abandoned such a child? Why, for her to have such strength, she must be of an extremely pure line. At least . . . *one* of her parents must have been from a very pure line."

"What are you implying?" Tevidian demanded, paling.

The Lord Ruler ignored them both. He strode through the streaming colors of the reflective floor, then stopped right in front of Vin.

So close, she thought. His Soothing was so strong that she couldn't even feel terror—all she felt was the deep, overpowering, *horrible* sorrow.

The Lord Ruler reached out with delicate hands, taking her by the cheeks, tilting her face up to look into his eyes. "Who is your father, girl?" he asked quietly.

"I . . ." Despair twisted inside of her. Grief, pain, a desire to die.

The Lord Ruler held her face close to his own, looking into her eyes. In that moment, she knew the truth. She could see a piece of him; she could sense his power. His . . . godlike power.

He wasn't worried about the skaa rebellion. Why would he have to worry? If he wished, he could slaughter every person in the city by himself. Vin knew it to be the truth. It might take him time, but he could kill forever, tirelessly. He need fear no rebellion.

He'd never needed to. Kelsier had made a terrible, terrible mistake.

"Your father, child," the Lord Ruler prompted, his demand like a physical weight upon her soul.

Vin spoke despite herself. "My . . . brother told me that my father was that man over there. The lord prelan." Tears rolled down her cheeks, though when the Lord Ruler turned from her, she couldn't quite remember why she had been crying.

"It's a lie, my lord!" Tevidian said, backing away. "What does she know? She's just a silly child."

"Tell me truthfully, Tevidian," the Lord Ruler said, walking slowly toward the obligator. "Have you ever bedded a skaa woman?"

The obligator paused. "I followed the law! Each time, I had them slain afterward."

"You . . . lie," the Lord Ruler said, as if surprised. "You're uncertain."

Tevidian was visibly shaking. "I . . . I think I got them all, my lord. There . . . there was one I may have been too lax with. I didn't know she was skaa at first. The soldier I sent to kill her was too lenient, and he let her go. But I found her, eventually."

"Tell me," the Lord Ruler said. "Did this woman bear any children?"

The room fell silent.

"Yes, my lord," the high prelan said.

The Lord Ruler closed his eyes, sighing. He turned back toward his throne. "He is yours," he said to the Inquisitors.

Immediately, six Inquisitors dashed across the room, howling in joy, pulling obsidian knives from sheaths beneath their robes. Tevidian raised his arms, crying out as the Inquisitors fell on him, exulting in their brutality. Blood flew as they plunged their daggers over and over again into the dying man. The other obligators backed away, looking on in horror.

Kar remained behind, smiling as he watched the massacre, as did the Inquisitor who was Vin's captor. One other Inquisitor remained back as well, though Vin didn't know why.

"Your point is proven, Kar," the Lord Ruler said, sitting wearily on his throne. "It seems that I have trusted too much in the . . . obedience of mankind. I did not make a mistake. I have never made a mistake. However, it is time for a change. Gather the high prelans and bring them here—rouse them from their beds, if need be. They will witness as I grant the Canton of Inquisition command and authority over the Ministry."

Kar's smile deepened.

"The half-breed child will be destroyed."

"Of course, my lord," Kar said. "Though . . . there are some questions I wish to ask her first. She was part of a team of skaa Mistings. If she can help us locate the others . . ."

"Very well," the Lord Ruler said. "That is your duty, after all."

Is there anything more beautiful than the sun? I often watch it rise, for my restless sleep usually awakens me before dawn.

Each time I see its calm yellow light peeking above the horizon, I grow a little more determined, a little more hopeful. In a way, it is the thing that has kept me going all this time.

37

KELSIER, YOU CURSED LUNATIC, DOCKSON THOUGHT, scribbling notes on the table map, *why do you always just saunter away, leaving me to handle your messes?* However, he knew his frustration wasn't real—it was simply a way of keeping himself from focusing on Kell's death. It worked.

Kelsier's part in the plan—the vision, the charismatic leadership—was finished. Now it was Dockson's turn. He took Kelsier's original strategy and modified it. He was careful to keep the chaos at a manageable level, rationing the best equipment to the men who seemed the most stable. He sent contingents to capture points of interest—food and water deposits—before general rioting could steal them.

In short, he did what he always did: He made Kelsier's dreams become reality.

A disturbance came from the front of the room, and Dockson looked up as a messenger rushed in. The man immediately sought out Dockson at the center of the warehouse.

"What news?" Dockson asked as the man approached.

The messenger shook his head. He was a young man, in an imperial uniform, though he had removed the jacket to make himself look less obtrusive. "I'm sorry, sir," the man said quietly. "None of the guards have seen her come out, and . . . well, one claimed he saw her being carried toward the palace dungeons."

"Can you get her out?" Dockson asked.

The soldier—Goradel—paled. Until just a short time before, Goradel had been one of the Lord Ruler's own men. In truth, Dockson wasn't even certain how much he trusted the man. Yet, the soldier—as a former palace guardsman—could get into places that other skaa could not. His former allies didn't know he'd switched sides.

Assuming he really has switched sides, Dockson thought. But . . . well, things were moving too quickly now for self-doubt. Dockson had decided to use this man. He'd have to trust his initial instincts.

"Well?" Dockson repeated.

Goradel shook his head. "There was an *Inquisitor* holding her captive, sir. I couldn't free her—I wouldn't have the authority. I don't . . . I . . ."

Dockson sighed. *Damn fool girl!* he thought. *She should have had better sense than this. Kelsier must have rubbed off on her.*

He waved the soldier away, then looked up as Hammond walked in, a large sword with a broken hilt resting on his shoulder.

"It's done," Ham said. "Keep Elariel just fell. Looks like Lekal is still holding, however."

Dockson nodded. "We'll need your men at the palace soon." *The sooner we break in there, the better chance we have of saving Vin.* However, his instincts told him that they'd be too late to help her. The main forces would take hours to gather and organize; he wanted to attack the palace with all of their armies in tandem. The truth was he just couldn't afford to spare men on a rescue operation at the moment. Kelsier would probably have gone after her, but Dockson wouldn't let himself do something that brash.

As he always said—*someone* on the crew needed to be realistic. The palace was not a place to attack without substantial preparation; Vin's failure proved that much. She'd just have to look after herself for the moment.

"I'll get my men ready," Ham said, nodding as he tossed his sword aside. "I'm going to need a new sword, though."

Dockson sighed. "You Thugs. Always breaking things. Go see what you can find, then."

Ham moved off.

"If you see Sazed," Dockson called, "tell him that . . ."

Dockson paused, his attention drawn by a group of skaa rebels who marched into the room, pulling a bound prisoner with a cloth sack on his head.

"What is this?" Dockson demanded.

One of the rebels elbowed his captive. "I think he's someone important, m'lord. Came to us unarmed, asked to be brought to you. Promised us gold if we did it."

Dockson raised an eyebrow. The grunt pulled off the hood, revealing Elend Venture.

Dockson blinked in surprise. "You?"

Elend looked around. He was apprehensive, obviously, but held himself well, all things considered. "Have we met?"

"Not exactly," Dockson said. *Blast. I don't have time for captives right now.* Still, the son of the Ventures . . . Dockson was going to need leverage with the powerful nobility when the fighting was over.

"I've come to offer you a truce," Elend Venture said.

". . . excuse me?" Dockson asked.

"House Venture will not resist you," Elend said. "And I can probably talk the rest of the nobility into listening as well. They're frightened—there's no need to slaughter them."

Dockson snorted. "I can't exactly leave hostile armed forces in the city."

"If you destroy the nobility, you won't be able to hold on for very long," Elend said. "We control the economy—the empire will collapse without us."

"That is kind of the point of this all," Dockson said. "Look, I don't have time—"

"You *must* hear me out," Elend Venture said desperately. "If you start your rebellion with chaos and bloodshed, you'll lose it. I've studied these things; I know what I'm talking about! When the momentum of your initial conflict runs out, the people will start looking for other things to destroy. They'll turn on themselves. *You must keep control of your armies.*"

Dockson paused. Elend Venture was supposed to be a fool and a fop, but now he just seemed . . . earnest.

"I'll help you," Elend said. "Leave the noblemen's keeps alone and focus your efforts on the Ministry and the Lord Ruler—they're your real enemies."

"Look," Dockson said, "I'll pull our armies away from Keep Venture. There's probably no need to fight them now that—"

"I sent my soldiers to Keep Lekal," Elend said. "Pull your men away from *all* the nobility. They're not going to attack your flanks—they'll just hole up in their mansions and worry."

He's probably right about that. "We'll consider . . ." Dockson trailed off, noticing that Elend wasn't paying attention to him anymore. *Blasted hard man to have a conversation with.*

Elend was staring at Hammond, who had returned with a new sword. Elend frowned, then his eyes opened wide. "I know you! You were the one who rescued Lord Renoux's servants from the executions!"

Elend turned back to Dockson, suddenly eager. "Do you know Valette, then? She'll tell you to listen to me."

Dockson shared a look with Ham.

"What?" Elend asked.

"Vin . . ." Dockson said. "Valette . . . she went into the palace a few hours back. I'm sorry, lad. She's probably in the Lord Ruler's dungeons right now—assuming she's even still alive."

Kar tossed Vin back into her cell. She hit the ground hard and rolled, her loose undershirt twisting around her, her head knocking against the cell's back wall.

The Inquisitor smiled, slamming the door. "Thank you very much," he said through the bars. "You just helped us achieve something that has been a long time in coming."

Vin glared up at him, the effects of the Lord Ruler's Soothing weaker now.

"It is unfortunate that Bendal isn't here," Kar said. "He chased your brother for years, swearing that Tevidian had fathered a skaa half-breed. Poor Bendal . . . If only the Lord Ruler had left the Survivor to us, so that we could have had revenge."

He looked over at her, shaking his spike-eyed head. "Ah, well. He was vindicated in the end. The rest of us believed your brother, but Bendal . . . even then he wasn't convinced—and he found you in the end."

"My brother?" Vin said, scrambling to her feet. "He sold me out?"

"Sold you out?" Kar said. "He died promising us that you had starved to death years ago! He screamed it night and day beneath the hands of Ministry torturers. It is very hard to hold out against the pains of an Inquisitor's torture . . . something you shall soon discover." He smiled. "But, first, let me show you something."

A group of guards dragged a naked, bound figure into the room. Bruised and bleeding, the man stumbled to the stone floor as they pushed him into the cell beside Vin's.

"*Sazed?*" Vin cried, rushing to the bars.

The Terrisman lay groggily as the soldiers tied his hands and feet to a small metal ring set into the stone floor. He had been beaten so severely that he barely seemed conscious, and he was completely naked. Vin turned away from his nudity, but not before she saw the place between his legs—a simple, empty scar where his manhood should have been.

All Terrisman stewards are eunuchs, he had told her. That wound wasn't new—but the bruises, cuts, and scrapes were fresh.

"We found him sneaking into the palace after you," Kar said. "Apparently, he feared for your safety."

"What have you done to him?" she asked quietly.

"Oh, very little . . . so far," Kar said. "Now, you may wonder why I spoke to you of your brother. Perhaps you think me a fool for admitting that your brother's mind snapped before we drew out his secret. But, you see, I am not so much a fool that I will not admit a mistake. We should have drawn out your brother's torture . . . made him suffer longer. That was an error indeed."

He smiled wickedly, nodding to Sazed. "We won't make that mistake again, child. No—this time, we're going to try a different tactic. We're going to let you watch us torture the Terrisman. We're going to be very careful, making certain his pain is lasting, and quite vibrant. When you tell us what we want to know, we'll stop."

Vin shivered in horror. "No . . . please . . ."

"Oh, yes," Kar said. "Why don't you take some time to think about what we're going to do to him? The Lord Ruler has commanded my presence—I need to go and receive formal leadership of the Ministry. We'll begin when I return."

He turned, black robe sweeping the ground. The guards followed, likely taking positions in the guard chamber just outside the room.

"Oh, Sazed," Vin said, sinking to her knees beside the bars of her cage.

"Now, Mistress," Sazed said in a surprisingly lucid voice. "What did we tell you about running around in your undergarments? Why, if Master Dockson were here, he would scold you for certain."

Vin looked up, shocked. Sazed was smiling at her.

"Sazed!" she said quietly, glancing in the direction the guards had gone. "You're awake?"

"Very awake," he said. His calm, strong voice was a stark contrast to his bruised body.

"I'm sorry, Sazed," she said. "Why did you follow me? You should have stayed back and let me be stupid on my own!"

He turned a bruised head toward her, one eye swollen, but the other looking into her eyes. "Mistress," he said solemnly, "I vowed to Master Kelsier that I would see to your safety. The oath of a Terrisman is not something given lightly."

"But . . . you should have known you'd be captured," she said, looking down in shame.

"Of course I knew, Mistress," he said. "Why, how else was I going to get them to bring me to you?"

Vin looked up. "Bring you . . . to me?"

"Yes, Mistress. There is one thing that the Ministry and my own people have in common, I think. They both underestimate the things that we can accomplish."

He closed his eyes. And then, his body changed. It seemed to . . . deflate, the muscles growing weak and scrawny, the flesh hanging loosely on his bones.

"Sazed!" Vin cried out, pushing herself against the bars, trying to reach him.

"It is all right, Mistress," he said in a faint, frighteningly weak voice. "I just need a moment to . . . gather my strength."

Gather my strength. Vin paused, lowering her hand, watching Sazed for a few minutes. *Could it be . . .*

He looked so weak—as if his strength, his very muscles, were being drawn away. And perhaps . . . stored somewhere?

Sazed's eyes snapped open. His body returned to normal; then his muscles continued to grow, becoming large and powerful, growing bigger, even, than Ham's.

Sazed smiled at her from a head sitting atop a beefy, muscular neck; then he easily snapped his bindings. He stood, a massive, inhumanly muscular man—so different from the lanky, quiet scholar she had known.

The Lord Ruler spoke of their strength in his logbook, she thought with wonder. *He said the man Rashek lifted a boulder by himself and threw it out of their way.*

"But, they took all of your jewelry!" Vin said. "Where did you hide the metal?"

Sazed smiled, grabbing the bars separating their cages. "I took a hint from you, Mistress. I swallowed it." With that, he ripped the bars free.

She ran into the cage, embracing him. "Thank you."

"Of course," he said, gently pushing her aside, then slamming a massive palm against the door to his cell, breaking the lock, sending the door crashing open.

"Quickly now, Mistress," Sazed said. "We must get you to safety."

The two guards who had thrown Sazed into the chamber appeared in the doorway a second later. They froze, staring up at the massive beast who stood in place of the weak man they had beaten.

Sazed jumped forward, holding one of the bars from Vin's cage. His Feruchemy, however, had obviously given him strength only, no speed. He stepped with a lumbering gait, and the guards dashed away, crying for help.

"Come now, Mistress," Sazed said, tossing aside the bar. "My strength will not last long—the metal I swallowed wasn't large enough to hold much of a Feruchemical charge."

Even as he spoke, he began to shrink. Vin moved past him, scrambling out of the room. The guard chamber beyond was quite small, set with only a pair of chairs. Beneath one, however, she found a cloak rolled around one of the guards' evening meals. Vin shook the cloak free, tossing it to Sazed.

"Thank you, Mistress," he said.

She nodded, moving to the doorway and peeking out. The larger room outside was empty, and had two hallways leading off of it—one going right, one extending into the distance across from her. The wall to her left was lined with wooden trunks, and the center of the room held a large table. Vin shivered as she saw the dried blood and the set of sharp instruments lying in a row on the table's side.

This is where we'll both end up if we don't move quickly, she thought, waving Sazed forward.

She froze mid-step as a group of soldiers appeared in the far hallway, led by one of the guards from before. Vin cursed quietly—she would have heard them earlier if she'd had tin.

Vin glanced backward. Sazed was hobbling through the guard chamber. His

Feruchemical strength was gone, and the soldiers had obviously beaten him soundly before tossing him into the cell. He could barely walk.

"Go, Mistress!" he said, waving her forward. "Run!"

You still have some things to learn about friendship, Vin, Kelsier's voice whispered in her mind. *I hope someday you realize what they are. . . .*

I can't leave him. I won't.

Vin dashed toward the soldiers. She swiped a pair of torturing knives from the table, their bright, polished steel glistening between her fingers. She jumped atop the table, then leapt off of it toward the oncoming soldiers.

She had no Allomancy, but she flew true anyway, her months of practice helping despite her lack of metals. She slammed a knife into a surprised soldier's neck as she fell. She hit the ground harder than she had expected, but managed to scramble away from a second soldier, who cursed and swung at her.

The sword clanged against the stone behind her. Vin spun, slashing another soldier across the thighs. He stumbled back in pain.

Too many, she thought. There were at least two dozen of them. She tried to jump for a third soldier, but another man swung his quarterstaff, slamming the weapon into Vin's side.

She grunted in pain, dropping her knife as she was thrown to the side. No pewter strengthened her against the fall, and she hit the hard stones with a crack, rolling to a dazed stop beside the wall.

She struggled, unsuccessfully, to rise. To her side, she could barely make out Sazed collapsing as his body grew suddenly weak. He was trying to store up strength again. He wouldn't have enough time. The soldiers would be on him soon.

At least I tried, she thought as she heard another group of soldiers charging down the rightmost hallway. *At least I didn't abandon him. I think . . . think that's what Kelsier meant.*

"Valette!" a familiar voice cried.

Vin looked up with shock as Elend and six soldiers burst into the room. Elend wore a nobleman's suit, a little ill-fitting, and carried a dueling cane.

"Elend?" Vin asked, dumbfounded.

"Are you all right?" he said with concern, stepping toward her. Then he noticed the Ministry soldiers. They seemed a bit confused to be confronted by a nobleman, but they still had superior numbers.

"I'm taking the girl with me!" Elend said. His words were brave, but he was obviously no soldier. He carried only a nobleman's dueling cane as a weapon, and he wore no armor. Five of the men with him wore Venture red—men from Elend's keep. One, however—the one who had been leading them as they charged into the room—wore a palace guard's uniform. Vin realized that she recognized him just vaguely. His uniform jacket was missing the symbol on its shoulder. *The man from before,* she thought, stupefied. *The one I convinced to change sides . . .*

The lead Ministry soldier apparently made his decision. He waved curtly, ignoring Elend's command, and the soldiers began to edge around the room, moving to surround Elend's band.

"Valette, you have to go!" Elend said urgently, raising his dueling cane.

"Come, Mistress," Sazed said, reaching her side, moving to lift her to her feet.

"We can't abandon them!" Vin said.

"We have to."

"But you came for me. We have to do the same for Elend!"

Sazed shook his head. "That was different, child. I knew I had a chance to save you. You cannot help here—there is beauty in compassion, but one must learn wisdom too."

She allowed herself to be pulled to her feet, Elend's soldiers obediently moving to block off the Ministry soldiers. Elend stood at their front, obviously determined to fight.

There has to be another way! Vin thought with despair. *There has to . . .*

And then she saw it sitting discarded in one of the trunks along the wall. A familiar strip of gray cloth, one single tassel, hanging over the trunk's side.

She pulled free of Sazed as the Ministry soldiers attacked. Elend cried out behind her, and weapons rang.

Vin threw the top pieces of cloth—her trousers and shirt—out of the trunk. And there, at the bottom, lay her mistcloak. She closed her eyes and reached into the side cloak pocket.

Her fingers found a single glass vial, cork still in place.

She pulled the vial out, spinning toward the battle. The Ministry soldiers had retreated slightly. Two of their members lay wounded on the floor—but three of Elend's men were down. The small size of the room had, fortunately, kept Elend's men from being surrounded at first.

Elend stood sweating, a cut in his arm, his dueling cane cracked and splintered. He grabbed the sword from the man he had felled, holding the weapon in unpracticed hands, staring down a much larger force.

"I was wrong about that one, Mistress," Sazed said softly. "I . . . apologize."

Vin smiled. Then she flipped the cork free from her vial and downed the metals in one gulp.

Wells of power exploded within her. Fires blazed, metals raging, and strength returned to her weakened, tired body like a dawning sun. Pains became trivial, dizziness disappeared, the room became brighter, the stones more *real* beneath her toes.

The soldiers attacked again, and Elend raised his sword in a determined, but unhopeful, posture. He seemed utterly shocked when Vin flew through the air over his head.

She landed amid the soldiers, blasting outward with a Steelpush. The soldiers on either side of her smashed into the walls. One man swung a quarter-staff at her, and she slapped it away with a disdainful hand, then smashed a fist into his face, spinning his head back with a crack.

She caught the quarterstaff as it fell, spinning, slamming it into the head of the soldier attacking Elend. The staff exploded, and she let it drop with the corpse. The soldiers at the back began to yell, turning and dashing away as she Pushed two more groups of men into the walls. The final soldier left in the room turned, surprised, as Vin Pulled his metal cap to her hands. She Pushed it back at him, smashing it into his chest and anchoring herself from behind. The soldier flew down the hallway toward his fleeing companions, crashing into them.

Vin breathed out in excitement, standing with tense muscles amidst the groaning men. *I can . . . see how Kelsier would get addicted to this.*

"Valette?" Elend asked, stupefied.

Vin jumped up, grabbing him in a joyful embrace, hanging onto him tightly and burying her face into his shoulder. "You came back," she whispered. "You came back, you came back, you came back. . . ."

"Um, yes. And . . . I see that you're a Mistborn. That's rather interesting. You know, it's generally common courtesy to tell one's friends about things like that."

"Sorry," she mumbled, still holding on to him.

"Well, yes," he said, sounding very distracted. "Um, Valette? What happened to your clothes?"

"They're on the floor over there," she said, looking up at him. "Elend, how did you find me?"

"Your friend, one Master Dockson, told me that you'd been captured in the palace. And well, this fine gentleman here—Captain Goradel, I believe his name is—happens to be a palace soldier, and he knew the way here. With his help—and as a nobleman of some rank—I was able to get into the building without much problem, and then we heard screaming down this hallway. . . . And, um, yes. Valette? Do you think you could go put your clothes on? This is . . . kind of distracting."

She smiled up at him. "You found me."

"For all the good it did," he said wryly. "It doesn't look like you needed our help very much. . . ."

"That doesn't matter," she said. "You came back. No one's ever come back before."

Elend looked down at her, frowning slightly.

Sazed approached, carrying Vin's clothing and cloak. "Mistress, we need to leave."

Elend nodded. "It's not safe anywhere in the city. The skaa are rebelling!" He paused, looking at her. "But, uh, you probably already know that."

Vin nodded, finally letting go of him. "I helped start it. But, you're right about the danger. Go with Sazed—he's known by many of the rebel leaders. They won't hurt you as long as he vouches for you."

Elend and Sazed both frowned as Vin pulled on her trousers. In the pocket, she found her mother's earring. She put it back on.

"Go with Sazed?" Elend asked. "But, what about you?"

Vin pulled on her loose overshirt. Then she glanced upward . . . sensing through the stone, feeling *him* up above. He was there. Too powerful. Now, having faced him directly, she was certain of his strength. The skaa rebellion was doomed as long as he lived.

"I have another task, Elend," she said, taking the mistcloak from Sazed.

"You think you can defeat him, Mistress?" Sazed said.

"I have to try," she said. "The Eleventh Metal worked, Saze. I saw . . . something. Kelsier was convinced it would provide the secret."

"But . . . the Lord Ruler, Mistress . . ."

"Kelsier died to start this rebellion," Vin said firmly. "I have to see that it succeeds. This is *my* part, Sazed. Kelsier didn't know what it was, but I do. I have to stop the Lord Ruler."

"The Lord Ruler?" Elend asked with shock. "No, Valette. He's immortal!"

Vin reached over, grabbing Elend's head and pulling him down to kiss her. "Elend, your family delivered the atium to the Lord Ruler. Do you know where he keeps it?"

"Yes," he said with confusion. "He keeps the beads in a treasury building just east of here. But—"

"You *have* to get that atium, Elend. The new government is going to need that wealth—and power—if it's going to keep from getting conquered by the first nobleman who can raise an army."

"No, Valette," Elend said shaking his head. "I have to get you to safety."

She smiled at him, then turned to Sazed. The Terrisman nodded to her.

"Not going to tell me not to go?" she asked.

"No," he said quietly. "I fear that you are right, Mistress. If the Lord Ruler is not defeated . . . well, I will not stop you. I will bid you, however, good luck. I will come to help you once I see young Venture to safety."

Vin nodded, smiled at the apprehensive Elend, then looked up. Toward the dark force waiting above, pulsing with a tired depression.

She burned copper, pushing aside the Lord Ruler's Soothing.

"Valette . . ." Elend said quietly.

She turned back to him. "Don't worry," she said. "I think I know how to kill him."

Such are my fears as I scribble with an ice-crusted pen on the eve before the world is reborn. Rashek watches. Hating me. The cavern lies above. Pulsing. My fingers quiver. Not from the cold.

Tomorrow, it will end.

38

VIN PUSHED HERSELF THROUGH THE AIR above Kredik Shaw. Spires and towers rose around her like the shadowed tines of some phantom monster lurking below. Dark, straight, and ominous, for some reason they made her think of Kelsier, lying dead in the street, an obsidian-tipped spear jutting from his chest.

The mists spun and swirled as she blew through them. They were still thick, but tin let her see a faint glistening on the horizon. Morning was near.

Below her, a greater light was building. Vin caught hold of a thin spire, letting her momentum spin her around the slick metal, giving her a sweeping view of the area. Thousands of torches burned in the night, mixing and merging like luminescent insects. They were organized in great waves, converging on the palace.

The palace guard doesn't have a chance against such a force, she thought. *But, by fighting its way into the palace, the skaa army will seal its own doom.*

She turned to the side, the mist-wetted spire cold beneath her fingers. The last time she had jumped through the spires of Kredik Shaw, she had been bleeding and semiconscious. Sazed had arrived to save her, but he wouldn't be able to help this time.

A short distance away, she could see the throne tower. It wasn't difficult to spot; a ring of blazing bonfires illuminated its outside, lighting its single stained-glass window to those inside. She could feel Him inside. She waited for a few moments, hoping, perhaps, that she might be able to attack after the Inquisitors had left the room.

Kelsier believed that the Eleventh Metal was the key, she thought.

She had one idea. It would work. It had to.

"As of this moment," the Lord Ruler proclaimed in a loud voice, "the Canton of Inquisition is granted organizational dominance of the Ministry. Inquiries once addressed to Tevidian should now go to Kar."

The throne room fell silent, the collection of high-ranking obligators dumbfounded by the night's events. The Lord Ruler waved a hand, indicating that the meeting was finished.

Finally! Kar thought. He raised his head, his eye-spikes throbbing as always, bringing him pain—but, this evening it was the pain of joy. The Inquisitors had been waiting for two centuries, carefully politicking, subtly encouraging corruption and dissension among the regular obligators. And finally it had worked. The Inquisitors would no longer bow before the dictates of inferior men.

He turned and smiled toward the group of Ministry priests, knowing full well the discomfort the gaze of an Inquisitor could cause. He couldn't see anymore, not as he once had, but he had been given something better. A command of Allomancy so subtle, so detailed, that he could make out the world around him with startling accuracy.

Almost everything had metal in it—water, stone, glass . . . even human bodies. These metals were too diffuse to be affected by Allomancy—indeed, most Allomancers couldn't even sense them.

With his Inquisitor's eyes, however, Kar could see the ironlines of these things—the blue threads were fine, nearly invisible, but they outlined the world for him. The obligators before him were a shuffling mass of blues, their emotions—discomfort, anger, and fear—showing in their postures. Discomfort, anger, and fear . . . so sweet, all three. Kar's smile widened, despite his fatigue.

He had been awake for too long. Living as an Inquisitor drained the body, and he had to rest often. His brethren were already shuffling from the room, heading toward their rest chambers, which lay intentionally close to the throne room. They would sleep immediately; with the executions earlier in the day and the excitement of the night, they would be extremely fatigued.

Kar, however, stayed behind as both Inquisitors and obligators left. Soon, only he and the Lord Ruler remained, standing in a room lit by five massive braziers. The external bonfires slowly went out, extinguished by servants, leaving the glass panorama dark and black.

"You finally have what you want," the Lord Ruler said quietly. "Perhaps now I can have peace in this matter."

"Yes, Lord Ruler," Kar said, bowing. "I think that . . ."

A strange sound snapped in the air—a soft click. Kar looked up, frowning as a small disk of metal bounced across the floor, eventually rolling to a stop against his foot. He picked up the coin, then looked up at the massive window, noting the small hole broken through it.

What?

Dozens more coins zipped through the window, scattering it with holes. Metallic clinks and tinkling glass rang in the air. Kar stepped back in surprise.

The entire southern section of the window shattered, blasting inward, the glass weakened by coins to the point that a soaring body could break through.

Shards of colorful glass spun in the air, spraying before a small figure clad in a fluttering Mistcloak and carrying a pair of glittering black daggers. The girl landed in a crouch, skidding a short distance on the bits of glass, mist billowing through the opening behind her. It curled forward, drawn by her Allomancy, swirling around her body. She crouched for just a moment in the mists, as if she were some herald of the night itself.

Then she sprang forward, dashing directly toward the Lord Ruler.

Vin burned the Eleventh Metal. The Lord Ruler's past-self appeared as it had before, forming as if out of mist to stand on the dais beside the throne.

Vin ignored the Inquisitor. The creature, fortunately, reacted slowly—she was halfway up the dais steps before it thought to chase her. The Lord Ruler, however, sat quietly, watching her with a barely interested expression.

Two spears through the chest didn't even bother him, Vin thought as she leapt the last bit of distance up to the top of the dais. *He has nothing to fear from my daggers.*

Which was why she didn't intend to attack him with them. Instead, she raised her weapons and plunged directly toward the past-self's heart.

Her daggers hit—and passed right through the man, as if he weren't there. Vin stumbled forward, skidding directly through the image, nearly slipping off the dais.

She spun, slicing at the image again. Again, her daggers passed through it harmlessly. It didn't even waver or distort.

My gold image, she thought in frustration, *I was able to touch that. Why can't I touch this?*

It obviously didn't work the same way. The shadow stood still, completely oblivious of her attacks. She'd thought that maybe, if she killed the past version of the Lord Ruler, his current form would die as well. Unfortunately, the past-self appeared to be just as insubstantial as an atium shadow.

She had failed.

Kar crashed into her, his powerful Inquisitor's grip grabbing her at the shoulders, his momentum carrying her off the dais. They tumbled down the back steps.

Vin grunted, flaring pewter. *I'm not the same powerless girl you held prisoner just a short time ago, Kar,* she thought with determination, kicking him upward as they hit the ground behind the throne.

The Inquisitor grunted, her kick tossing him into the air and ripping his grip free of her shoulders. Her Mistcloak came off in his hands, but she flipped to her feet and scrambled away.

"Inquisitors!" the Lord Ruler bellowed, standing. *"Come to me!"*

Vin cried out, the powerful voice striking pain in her tin-enhanced ears.

I have to get out of here, she thought, stumbling. *I'll need to come up with a different way to kill him. . . .*

Kar tackled her again from behind. This time he got his arms wrapped completely around her, and he squeezed. Vin cried out in pain, flaring her pewter, pushing back, but Kar forced her to her feet. He dexterously wrapped one arm around her throat while pinning her own arms behind her back with his other. She fought angrily, squirming and struggling, but his grip was tight. She tried throwing them both back with a sudden Steelpush against a doorlatch, but the anchor was too weak, and Kar barely stumbled. His grip held.

The Lord Ruler chuckled as he sat back down on his throne. "You'll have little success against Kar, child. He was a soldier, many years ago. He knows how to hold a person so that they can't break his grip, no matter how strong they may be."

Vin continued to struggle, gasping for breath. The Lord Ruler's words proved true, however. She tried ramming her head back against Kar's, but he was ready for this. She could hear him in her ear, his quick breathing almost . . . passionate as he choked her. In the reflection on the window, she could see the door behind them open. Another Inquisitor strode into the room, his spikes gleaming in the distorted reflection, his dark robe ruffling.

That's it, she thought in a surreal moment, watching the mists on the ground before her, creeping through the shattered window wall, flowing across the floor. Oddly, they didn't curl around her as they usually did—as if something were pushing them away. To Vin, it seemed a final testament to her defeat.

I'm sorry, Kelsier. I've failed you.

The second Inquisitor stepped up beside his companion. Then, he reached out and grabbed something at Kar's back. There was a ripping sound.

Vin dropped immediately to the ground, gasping for breath. She rolled, pewter allowing her to recover quickly.

Kar stood above her, teetering. Then, he toppled limply to the side, sprawling to the ground. The second Inquisitor stood behind him, holding what appeared to be a large metal spike—just like the ones in the Inquisitor eyes.

Vin glanced toward Kar's immobile body. The back of his robe had been ripped, exposing a bloody hole right between the shoulder blades. A hole big enough for a metal spike. Kar's scarred face was pale. Lifeless.

Another spike! Vin thought with wonder. *The other Inquisitor pulled it out of Kar's back, and he died. That's the secret!*

"What?" the Lord Ruler bellowed, standing, the sudden motion tossing his throne backwards. The stone chair toppled down the steps, chipping and cracking the marble. "Betrayal! From one of my own!"

The new Inquisitor dashed toward the Lord Ruler. As he ran, his robe cowl fell back, giving Vin a view of his bald head. There was something familiar about the newcomer's face despite the spike-heads coming out the front—and the gruesome spike-tips jutting from the back—of his skull. Despite the bald head and the unfamiliar clothing, the man looked a little like Kelsier.

No, she realized. *Not Kelsier.*

Marsh!

Marsh took the dais steps in twos, moving with an Inquisitor's supernatural speed. Vin struggled to her feet, shrugging off the effects of her near-choking. Her surprise, however, was more difficult to dismiss. Marsh was alive.

Marsh was an Inquisitor.

The Inquisitors weren't investigating him because they suspected him. They intended to recruit him! And now he looked like he intended to fight the Lord Ruler. *I've got to help! Perhaps . . . perhaps he knows the secret to killing the Lord Ruler. He figured out how to kill Inquisitors, after all!*

Marsh reached the top of the dais.

"Inquisitors!" the Lord Ruler yelled. "Come to—"

The Lord Ruler froze, noticing something sitting just outside the door. A small group of steel spikes, just like the one Marsh had pulled from Kar's back, lay piled on the floor. There looked to be about seven of them.

Marsh smiled, the expression looking eerily like one of Kelsier's smirks. Vin reached the bottom of the dais and Pushed herself off a coin, throwing herself up toward the top of the platform.

The awesome, full power of the Lord Ruler's fury hit her halfway up. The depression, the anger-fueled asphyxiation of her soul, pushed through her copper, hitting her like a physical force. She flared copper, gasping slightly, but wasn't completely able to push the Lord Ruler off of her emotions.

Marsh stumbled slightly, and the Lord Ruler swung a backhand much like the one that had killed Kelsier. Fortunately, Marsh recovered in time to duck. He spun around the Lord Ruler, reaching up to grab the back of the emperor's black, robelike suit. Marsh yanked, ripping the cloth open along the back seam.

Marsh froze, his spike-eyed expression unreadable. The Lord Ruler spun, slamming his elbow into Marsh's stomach, throwing the Inquisitor across the room. As the Lord Ruler turned, Vin could see what Marsh had seen.

Nothing. A normal, if muscular, back. Unlike the Inquisitors, the Lord Ruler didn't have a spike driven through his spine.

Oh, Marsh . . . Vin thought with a sinking depression. It had been a clever idea, far more clever than Vin's foolish attempt with the Eleventh Metal—however, it had proven equally faulty.

Marsh finally hit the ground, his head cracking, then slid across the floor un-

til he ran into the far wall. He lay slumped against the massive window, immobile.

"Marsh!" she cried, jumping and Pushing herself toward him. However, as she flew, the Lord raised his hand absently.

Vin felt a powerful . . . *something* crash into her. It felt like a Steelpush, slamming against the metals inside her stomach—but of course it couldn't have been that. Kelsier had promised that no Allomancer could affect metals that were inside of someone's body.

But he had also said that no Allomancer could affect the emotions of a person who was burning copper.

Discarded coins shot away from the Lord Ruler, streaking across the floor. The doors wrenched free from their mountings, shattering and breaking away from the room. Incredibly, bits of colored glass even quivered and slid away from the dais.

And Vin was tossed to the side, the metals in her stomach threatening to rip free from her body. She slammed to the ground, the blow knocking her nearly unconscious. She lay in a daze, addled, confused, able to think of only one thing.

Such power . . .

Clicks sounded as the Lord Ruler walked down his dais. He moved quietly, ripping off his torn suit coat and shirt, leaving himself bare from the waist up save for the jewelry sparkling on his fingers and wrists. Several thin bracelets, she noticed, pierced the skin of his upper arms.

Clever, she thought, struggling to her feet. *Keeps them from being Pushed or Pulled.*

The Lord Ruler shook his head regretfully, his steps kicking up trails in the cool mist that poured across the floor from the broken window. He looked so strong, his torso erupting with muscles, his face handsome. She could feel the power of his Allomancy snapping at her emotions, barely held back by her copper.

"What did you think, child?" the Lord Ruler asked quietly. "To defeat me? Am I some common Inquisitor, my powers endowed fabrications?"

Vin flared pewter. She then turned and dashed away—intending to grab Marsh's body and break through the glass at the other side of the room.

But then, *he* was there, moving with a speed as if to make the fury of a tornado's winds seem sluggish. Even within a full pewter flare, Vin couldn't outrun him. He almost seemed casual as he reached out, grabbing her shoulder and yanking her backward.

He flung her like a doll, tossing her toward one of the room's massive support pillars. Vin quested desperately for an anchor, but he had blown all of the metal out of the room. Except . . .

She Pulled on one of the Lord Ruler's own bracelets, ones that didn't pierce his skin. He immediately whipped his arm upward, throwing off her Pull, making her spin maladroitly in the air. He slammed her with another of his power-ful Pushes, blasting her backward. Metals in her stomach wrenched, glass quivered, and her mother's earring ripped free of her ear.

She tried to spin and hit feet-first, but she crashed into a stone pillar at a terrible speed, and pewter failed her. She heard a sickening snap, and a spear of pain shot up her right leg.

She collapsed to the ground. She didn't have the will to look, but the agony from her torso told her that her leg jutted from beneath her body, broken at an awkward angle.

The Lord Ruler shook his head. No, Vin realized, he didn't worry about wearing jewelry. Considering his abilities and strength, a man would have to be foolish—as Vin had been—to try and use the Lord Ruler's jewelry as an anchor. It had only let him control her jumps.

He stepped forward, feet clicking against broken glass. "You think this is the first time someone has tried to kill me, child? I've survived burnings and be-headings. I've been stabbed and sliced, crushed and dismembered. I was even flayed once, near the beginning."

He turned toward Marsh, shaking his head. Strangely, Vin's earlier impression of the Lord Ruler returned. He looked . . . tired. Exhausted, even. Not his body—it was still muscular. It was just his . . . air. She tried to climb to her feet, using the stone pillar for stability.

"I am God," he said.

So different from the humble man in the logbook.

"*God* cannot be killed," he said. "*God* cannot be overthrown. Your rebellion—you think I haven't seen its like before? You think I haven't destroyed entire armies on my own? What will it take before you people stop questioning? How many centuries must I prove myself before you *idiot* skaa see the truth? How many of you must I kill!"

Vin cried out as she twisted her leg the wrong way. She flared pewter, but tears came to her eyes anyway. She was running out of metals. Her pewter would be gone soon, and there was no way she would be able to remain conscious without it. She slumped against the pillar, the Lord Ruler's Allomancy pressing against her. The pain in her leg throbbed.

He's just too strong, she thought with despair. *He's right. He is God. What were we thinking?*

"How dare you?" the Lord Ruler asked, picking up Marsh's limp body with a bejeweled hand. Marsh groaned slightly, trying to lift his head.

"How dare you?" the Lord Ruler demanded again. "After what I gave you? I made you superior to regular men! I made you dominant!"

Vin's head snapped up. Through the haze of pain and hopelessness, something triggered a memory inside of her.

He keeps saying . . . he keeps saying that his people should be dominant. . . .

She reached within, feeling her last little bit of Eleventh Metal reserve. She burned it, looking through tearstained eyes as the Lord Ruler held Marsh in a one-handed grip.

The Lord Ruler's past self appeared next to him. A man in a fur cloak and heavy boots, a man with a full beard and strong muscles. Not an aristocrat or a tyrant. Not a hero, or even a warrior. A man dressed for life in the cold mountains. A herdsman.

Or, perhaps, a packman.

"Rashek," Vin whispered.

The Lord Ruler spun toward her in startlement.

"Rashek," Vin said again. "That's your name, isn't it? You aren't the man who wrote the logbook. You're not the hero that was sent to protect the people . . . you're his servant. The packman who hated him."

She paused for a moment. "You . . . you killed him," she whispered. "That's what happened that night! That's why the logbook stopped so suddenly! You killed the hero and took his place. You went into the cavern in his stead, and you claimed the power for yourself. But . . . instead of saving the world, you took control of it."

"You know nothing!" he bellowed, still holding Marsh's limp body in one hand. "You know nothing of that!"

"You hated him," Vin said. "You thought that a Terrisman should have been the hero. You couldn't stand the fact that he—a man from the country that had oppressed yours—was fulfilling your own legends."

The Lord Ruler lifted a hand, and Vin suddenly felt an impossible weight press against her. Allomancy, Pushing the metals in her stomach and in her body, threatening to crush her back against the pillar. She cried out, flaring her last bit of pewter, struggling to remain conscious. Mists curled around her, creeping through the broken window and across the floor.

Outside, through the broken window, she could hear something ringing faintly in the air. It sounded like . . . like cheering. Yells of joy, thousands in chorus. It sounded almost like they were cheering her on.

What does it matter? she thought. *I know the Lord Ruler's secret, but what does it tell me? That he was a packman? A servant? A Terrisman?*

A Feruchemist.

She looked through dazed eyes, and again saw the pair of bracelets glittering on the Lord Ruler's upper arms. Bracelets made of metal, bracelets that pierced his skin in places. So . . . so that they couldn't be affected by Allomancy. Why do that? He supposedly wore metal as a sign of bravado. He wasn't worried about people Pulling or Pushing against his metals.

Or, that was what he claimed. But, what if all the other metals he wore—the rings, the bracelets, the fashion that had made its way to the nobility—were simply a distraction?

A distraction to keep people from focusing on this one pair of bracers, twisting around the upper arms. *Could it really be that easy?* she thought as the Lord Ruler's weight threatened to crush her.

Her pewter was nearly gone. She could barely think. Yet, she burned iron. The Lord Ruler could pierce copperclouds. She could too. They were the same, somehow. If he could affect metals inside of a person's body, then she could as well.

She flared the iron. Blue lines appeared pointing to the Lord Ruler's rings and bracelets—all of them but the ones on his upper arms, piercing his skin.

Vin stoked her iron, concentrating, Pushing it as hard as she could. She kept her pewter flared, struggling to keep from being crushed, and she knew somehow that she was no longer breathing. The force pushing against her was too strong. She couldn't get her chest to go up and down.

Mist spun around her, dancing because of her Allomancy. She was dying. She knew it. She could barely even feel the pain anymore. She was being crushed. Suffocated.

She drew upon the mists.

Two new lines appeared. She screamed, *Pulling* with a strength she had never known before. She flared her iron higher and higher, the Lord Ruler's own Push giving her the leverage she needed to Pull against his bracelets. Anger, desperation, and agony mixed within her, and the Pull became her only focus.

Her pewter ran out.

He killed Kelsier!

The bracelets ripped free. The Lord Ruler cried out in pain, a faint, distant sound to Vin's ears. The weight suddenly released her, and she dropped to the floor, gasping, her vision swimming. The bloody bracelets hit the ground, released from her grip, skidding across the marble to land before her. She looked up, using tin to clear her vision.

The Lord Ruler stood where he had been before, his eyes widening with terror, his arms bloodied. He dropped Marsh to the ground, rushing toward her and the mangled bracelets. However, with her last bit of strength—pewter gone—Vin Pushed on the bracelets, shooting them past the Lord Ruler. He spun in horror, watching the bracelets fly out the broken wall-window.

In the distance, the sun broke the horizon. The bracelets dropped in front of its red light, sparkling for a moment before plunging down into the city.

"*No!*" the Lord Ruler screamed, stepping toward the window.

His muscles grew limp, deflating as Sazed's had. He turned back toward Vin, angry, but his face was no longer that of a young man. He was middle-aged, his youthful features matured.

He stepped toward the window. His hair grayed, and wrinkles formed around his eyes like tiny webs.

His next step was feeble. He began to shake with the burden of old age, his back stooping, his skin sagging, his hair growing limp.

Then, he collapsed to the floor.

Vin leaned back, her mind fuzzing from the pain. She lay there for . . . a time. She couldn't think.

"Mistress!" a voice said. And then, Sazed was at her side, his brow wet with sweat. He reached over and poured something down her throat, and she swallowed.

Her body knew what to do. She reflexively flared pewter, strengthening her body. She flared tin, and the sudden increase of sensitivity shocked her awake. She gasped, looking up at Sazed's concerned face.

"Careful, Mistress," he said, inspecting her leg. "The bone is fractured, though it appears only in one place."

"Marsh," she said, exhausted. "See to Marsh."

"Marsh?" Sazed asked. Then he saw the Inquisitor stirring slightly on the floor a distance away.

"By the Forgotten Gods!" Sazed said, moving to Marsh's side.

Marsh groaned, sitting up. He cradled his stomach with one arm. "What . . . is that . . . ?"

Vin glanced at the withered form on the ground a short distance away. "It's him. The Lord Ruler. He's dead."

Sazed frowned curiously, standing. He wore a brown robe, and had brought a simple wooden spear with him. Vin shook her head at the thought of such a pitiful weapon facing the creature that had nearly killed her and Marsh.

Of course. In a way, we were all just as useless. We should be dead, not the Lord Ruler.

I pulled his bracelets off. Why? Why can I do things like he can?

Why am I different?

"Mistress . . ." Sazed said slowly. "He is not dead, I think. He's . . . still alive."

"What?" Vin asked, frowning. She could barely think at the moment. There would be time to sort out her questions later. Sazed was right—the aged figure wasn't dead. Actually, it was moving pitifully on the floor, crawling toward the broken window. Toward where his bracelets had gone.

Marsh stumbled to his feet, waving away Sazed's ministrations. "I will heal quickly. See to the girl."

"Help me up," Vin said.

"Mistress . . ." Sazed said disapprovingly.

"Please, Sazed."

He sighed, handing her the wooden spear. "Here, lean on this." She took it, and he helped her to her feet.

Vin leaned on the shaft, hobbling with Marsh and Sazed toward the Lord Ruler. The crawling figure reached the edge of the room, overlooking the city through the shattered window.

Vin's footsteps crackled on broken glass. People cheered again below, though she couldn't see them, nor see what they were cheering about.

"Listen," Sazed said. "Listen, he who would have been our god. Do you hear them cheering? Those cheers aren't for you—this people never cheered for you. They have found a new leader this evening, a new pride."

"My . . . obligators . . ." the Lord Ruler whispered.

"Your obligators will forget you," Marsh said. "I will see to that. The other Inquisitors are dead, slain by my own hand. Yet, the gathered prelans saw you transfer power to the Canton of Inquisition. I am the only Inquisitor left in Luthadel. *I* rule your church now."

"No . . ." the Lord Ruler whispered.

Marsh, Vin, and Sazed stopped in a ragged group, looking down at the old man. In the morning light below, Vin could see a massive collection of people standing before a large podium, holding up their weapons in a sign of respect.

The Lord Ruler cast his eyes down at the crowd, and the final realization of his failure seemed to hit him. He looked back up at the ring of people who had defeated him.

"You don't understand," he wheezed. "You don't know what I do for mankind. I *was* your god, even if you couldn't see it. By killing me, you have doomed yourselves. . . ."

Vin glanced at Marsh and Sazed. Slowly, each of them nodded. The Lord Ruler had begun coughing, and he seemed to be aging even further.

Vin leaned on Sazed, her teeth gritted against the pain of her broken leg. "I bring you a message from a friend of ours," she said quietly. "He wanted you to know that he's not dead. He can't be killed.

"He is hope."

Then she raised the spear and rammed it directly into the Lord Ruler's heart.

Oddly, on occasion, I sense a peacefulness within. You would think that after all I have seen—after all I have suffered—my soul would be a twisted jumble of stress, confusion, and melancholy. Often, it's just that.

But then, there is the peace.

I feel it sometimes, as I do now, staring out over the frozen cliffs and glass mountains in the still of morning, watching a sunrise that is so majestic that I know that none shall ever be its match.

If there are prophecies, if there is a Hero of Ages, then my mind whispers that there must be something directing my path. Something is watching; something cares. These peaceful whispers tell me a truth I wish very much to believe.

If I fail, another shall come to finish my work.

EPILOGUE

"THE ONLY THING I CAN CONCLUDE, Master Marsh," Sazed said, "is that the Lord Ruler was both a Feruchemist *and* an Allomancer."

Vin frowned, sitting atop an empty building near the edge of a skaa slum. Her broken leg—carefully splinted by Sazed—hung over the edge of the rooftop, dangling in the air.

She'd slept most of the day—as, apparently, had Marsh, who stood beside her. Sazed had carried a message to the rest of the crew, telling them of Vin's survival. Apparently, there had been no major casualties among the others—for which Vin was glad. She hadn't gone to them yet, however. Sazed had told them that she needed to rest, and they were busy setting up Elend's new government.

"A Feruchemist and an Allomancer," Marsh said speculatively. He had recovered quickly indeed—though Vin still bore bruises, fractures, and cuts from the fight, he seemed to have already healed his broken ribs. He leaned down, resting one arm on his knee, staring out over the city with spikes instead of eyes.

How does he even see? Vin wondered.

"Yes, Master Marsh," Sazed explained. "You see, youth is one of the things that a Feruchemist can store. It's a fairly useless process—in order to store up the ability to feel and look a year younger, you would have to spend part of your life feeling and looking one year older. Often, Keepers use the ability as a disguise, changing ages to fool others and hide. Beyond this, however, no one has ever seen much use for the ability.

"However, if the Feruchemist were *also* an Allomancer, he might be able to burn his own metal storages, releasing the energy within them tenfold. Mistress Vin tried to burn some of my metals earlier, but couldn't access the power. However, if you were able to make up the Feruchemical storages yourself, then burn them for the extra power . . ."

Marsh frowned. "I don't follow you, Sazed."

"I apologize," Sazed said. "This is, perhaps, a thing that is difficult to understand without a background in both Allomantic and Feruchemical theory. Let me see if I can explain it better. What is the main difference between Allomancy and Feruchemy?"

"Allomancy draws its power from metals," Marsh said. "Feruchemy draws its powers from the person's own body."

"Exactly," Sazed said. "So, what the Lord Ruler did—I presume—was *combine* these two abilities. He used one of the attributes only available to Feruchemy—that of changing his age—but fueled it with *Allomancy* instead. By burning a Feruchemical storage that he himself had made, he effectively made a new Allomantic metal for himself—one that made him younger when he burned it. If my guess is correct, he would have gained a limitless supply of youth, since he was drawing most of his power from the metal itself, rather than his own body. All he would have to do was spend the occasional bit of time aged to give himself Feruchemical storages to burn and stay young."

"So," Marsh said, "just burning those storages would make him even younger than when he started?"

"He would have had to place that excess youth inside of another Feruchemical storage, I think," Sazed explained. "You see, Allomancy is quite spectacular—its powers generally come in bursts and flares. The Lord Ruler wouldn't have wanted all of that youth at once, so he'd have stored it inside of a piece of metal which he could slowly drain, keeping himself young."

"The bracelets?"

"Yes, Master Marsh. However, Feruchemy gives decreasing returns—it takes more than the proportionate amount of strength, for instance, to make yourself four times as strong as a regular man, as opposed to simply twice as strong. In the Lord Ruler's case, this meant that he had to spend more and more youth to keep from aging. When Mistress Vin stole the bracelets, he aged incredibly quickly because his body was trying to stretch back to where it should have been."

Vin sat in the cool evening wind, staring out toward Keep Venture. It was bright with light; not even a single day had passed, and Elend was already meeting with skaa and noblemen leaders, drafting a code of laws for his new nation.

Vin sat quietly, fingering her earring. She'd found it in the throne room, had put it back in her torn ear as it began to heal. She wasn't certain why she kept it. Perhaps because it was a link to Reen, and the mother who had tried to kill her. Or, perhaps, simply because it was a reminder of things she shouldn't have been able to do.

There was much to learn, still, about Allomancy. For a thousand years, the nobility had simply trusted what the Inquisitors and Lord Ruler told them. What secrets had they shadowed, what metals had they hidden?

"The Lord Ruler," she finally said. "He . . . just used a trick to be immortal, then. That means he wasn't ever really a god, right? He was just lucky. Anyone who was both a Feruchemist and an Allomancer could have done what he did."

"It appears that way, Mistress," Sazed said. "Perhaps that was why he feared Keepers so much. He hunted and killed Feruchemists, for he knew that the skill was hereditary—just as Allomancy is. If the Terris lines ever mixed with those of the imperial nobility, the result could very well have been a child who could challenge him."

"Hence the breeding programs," Marsh said.

Sazed nodded. "He needed to make absolutely sure that the Terrismen weren't allowed to mix with the regular populace, lest they pass on latent Feruchemical abilities."

Marsh shook his head. "His own people. He did such horrible things to them just to keep hold of his power."

"But," Vin said, frowning, "if the Lord Ruler's powers came from a mixture of Feruchemy and Allomancy, what happened at the Well of Ascension? What was the power that the man who wrote the logbook—whoever he was—was supposed to find?"

"I don't know, Mistress," Sazed said quietly.

"Your explanation doesn't answer everything," Vin said, shaking her head. She hadn't spoken of her own strange abilities, but she had spoken of what the Lord Ruler had done in the throne room. "He was so *powerful*, Sazed. I could feel his Allomancy. He was able to Push on metals inside my body! Perhaps he could enhance his Feruchemy by burning the storages, but how did he get so strong at Allomancy?"

Sazed sighed. "I fear that the only person who could have answered these questions died this morning."

Vin paused. The Lord Ruler had held secrets about the Terris religion that Sazed's people had been searching for centuries to find. "I'm sorry. Maybe I shouldn't have killed him."

Sazed shook his head. "His own aging would have killed him soon anyway, Mistress. What you did was right. This way, I can record that the Lord Ruler was struck down by one of the skaa he had oppressed."

Vin flushed. "Record?"

"Of course. I am still a Keeper, Mistress. I must pass these things on—history, events, and truths."

"You won't . . . say too much about me, will you?" For some reason the idea of other people telling stories about her made her uncomfortable.

"I wouldn't worry too much, Mistress," Sazed said with a smile. "My brethren and I will be very busy, I think. We have so much to restore, so much to tell the world. . . . I doubt details about you need to be passed on with any urgent timing. I will record what happened, but I will keep it to myself for a while, if you wish."

"Thank you," Vin said, nodding.

"That power that the Lord Ruler found in the cave," Marsh said speculatively, "perhaps it was just Allomancy. You said that there is no record of any Allomancers before the Ascension."

"It is indeed a possibility, Master Marsh," Sazed said. "There are very few legends about the origins of Allomancy, and nearly all of them agree that Allomancers first 'appeared with the mists.'"

Vin frowned. She'd always assumed that the title "Mistborn" had come about because Allomancers tended to do their work at night. She'd never considered that there might be a stronger connection.

Mist reacts to Allomancy. It swirls when an Allomancer uses his abilities nearby. And . . . what did I feel at the end? It was like I drew something from the mists.

Whatever she'd done, she hadn't been able to replicate it.

Marsh sighed and stood. He had been awake only a few hours, but he already seemed tired. His head hung slightly, as if the weight of the spikes were pulling it down.

"Does that . . . hurt, Marsh?" she asked. "The spikes, I mean?"

He paused. "Yes. All eleven of them . . . throb. The pain reacts to my emotions somehow."

"Eleven?" Vin asked with shock.

Marsh nodded. "Two in the head, eight in the chest, one in the back to seal them together. That's the only way to kill an Inquisitor—you have to separate the top spikes from the bottom ones. Kell did it through a beheading, but it's easier to just pull out the middle spike."

"We thought you were dead," Vin said. "When we found the body and the blood at the Soothing station . . ."

Marsh nodded. "I was going to send word of my survival, but they watched me fairly closely that first day. I didn't expect Kell to make his move so quickly."

"None of us did, Master Marsh," Sazed said. "None of us expected it at all."

"He actually did it, didn't he?" Marsh said, shaking his head in wonder. "That bastard. There are two things I'll never forgive him for. The first is for stealing my dream of overthrowing the Final Empire, then actually succeeding at it."

Vin paused. "And the second?"

Marsh turned spike-heads toward her. "Getting himself killed to do it."

"If I may ask, Master Marsh," Sazed said. "Who *was* that corpse that Mistress Vin and Master Kelsier discovered at the Soothing station?"

Marsh looked back over the city. "There were several corpses, actually. The process to create a new Inquisitor is . . . messy. I'd rather not speak about it."

"Of course," Sazed said, bowing his head.

"*You*, however," Marsh said, "could tell me about this creature that Kelsier used to imitate Lord Renoux."

"The kandra?" Sazed said. "I fear even the Keepers know little of them. They are related to mistwraiths—perhaps even the same creatures, just older. Because of their reputation, they generally prefer to remain unseen—though some of the noble houses hire them on occasion."

Vin frowned. "So . . . why didn't Kell just have this kandra impersonate him and die in his stead?"

"Ah," Sazed said. "You see, Mistress, for a kandra to impersonate someone, they first must devour that person's flesh and absorb their bones. Kandra are like mistwraiths—they have no skeletons of their own."

Vin shivered. "Oh."

"He is back, you know," Marsh said. "The creature is no longer using my brother's body—he has another one—but he came looking for you, Vin."

"Me?" Vin asked.

Marsh nodded. "He said something about Kelsier transferring his contract to you before he died. I believe the beast sees you as its master, now."

Vin shivered. *That . . . thing ate Kelsier's body.* "I don't want it around," she said. "I'll send it away."

"Do not be quite so hasty, Mistress," Sazed said. "Kandra are expensive servants—you must pay them in atium. If Kelsier bought an extended contract for one, it would be foolish to waste its services. A kandra might prove a very useful ally in the months to come."

Vin shook her head. "I don't care. I don't want that thing around. Not after what it did."

The trio fell silent. Finally, Marsh stood, sighing. "Anyway, if you will excuse me, I should go make an appearance at the keep—the new king wants me to represent the Ministry in his negotiations."

Vin frowned. "I don't see why the Ministry deserves any say in things."

"The obligators are still quite powerful, Mistress," Sazed said. "And, they are the most efficient and well-trained bureaucratic force in the Final Empire. His majesty would be wise to try and bring them to his side, and recognizing Master Marsh may help achieve this."

Marsh shrugged. "Of course, assuming I can establish control over the Canton of Orthodoxy, the Ministry should . . . change during the next few years. I'll move slowly and carefully, but by the time I'm done, the obligators won't even realize what they've lost. Those other Inquisitors could present a problem, though."

Vin nodded. "How many are there outside of Luthadel?"

"I don't know," Marsh said. "I wasn't a member of the order for very long before I destroyed it. However, the Final Empire was a big place. Many speak of there being around twenty Inquisitors in the empire, but I never was able to pin anyone down on a hard number."

Vin nodded as Marsh left. However, the Inquisitors—while dangerous—worried her far less now that she knew their secret. She was more concerned about something else.

You don't know what I do for mankind. I was your god, even if you couldn't see it. By killing me, you have doomed yourselves. . . .

The Lord Ruler's final words. At the time, she thought he'd been referring to the Final Empire as the thing he did "for mankind." However, she wasn't so certain anymore. There had been . . . fear in his eyes when he'd spoken those words, not pride.

"Saze?" she said. "What was the Deepness? The thing that the Hero from the logbook was supposed to defeat?"

"I wish that we knew, Mistress," Sazed said.

"But, it didn't come, right?"

"Apparently not," Sazed said. "The legends agree that had the Deepness not been stopped, the very world would have been destroyed. Of course, perhaps these stories have been exaggerated. Maybe the danger of the 'Deepness' was really just the Lord Ruler himself—perhaps the Hero's fight was simply one of conscience. He had to choose to dominate the world or to let it be free."

That didn't sound right to Vin. There was more. She remembered that fear in the Lord Ruler's eyes. Terror.

He said "do," not "did." "What I do for mankind." That implies that he was still doing it, whatever it was.

You have doomed yourselves. . . .

She shivered in the evening air. The sun was setting, making it even easier to see the illuminated Keep Venture—Elend's choice of headquarters for the moment, though he might still move to Kredik Shaw. He hadn't decided yet.

"You should go to him, Mistress," Sazed said. "He needs to see that you are well."

Vin didn't reply immediately. She stared out over the city, watching the bright keep in the darkening sky. "Were you there, Sazed?" she asked. "Did you hear his speech?"

"Yes, Mistress," he said. "Once we discovered that there was no atium in that treasury, Lord Venture insisted that we go seek help for you. I was inclined to agree with him—neither of us were warriors, and I was still without my Feruchemical storages."

No atium, Vin thought. *After all of this, we haven't found a speck of it. What did the Lord Ruler do with it all? Or . . . did someone else get to it first?*

"When Master Elend and I found the army," Sazed continued, "its rebels were slaughtering the palace solders. Some of them tried to surrender, but our soldiers weren't letting them. It was a . . . disturbing scene, Mistress. Your Elend . . . he didn't like what he saw. When he stood up there before the skaa, I thought that they would simply kill him too."

Sazed paused, cocking his head slightly. "But . . . the things he said, Mistress . . . his dreams of a new government, his condemnation of bloodshed and chaos . . . Well, Mistress, I fear that I cannot repeat it. I wish I'd had my metalminds, so that I could have memorized his exact words."

He sighed, shaking his head. "Regardless, I believe that Master Breeze was very influential in helping calm that riot. Once one group started listening to Master Elend, the others did too, and from there . . . well, it is a good thing that a nobleman ended up as king, I think. Master Elend brings some legitimacy to our bid for control, and I think that we will see more support from the nobility and the merchants with him at our head."

Vin smiled. "Kell would be angry with us, you know. He did all this work, and we just turned around and put a nobleman on the throne."

Sazed shook his head. "Ah, but there is something more important to consider, I think. We didn't just put a nobleman on the throne—we put a *good man* on the throne."

"A good man . . ." Vin said. "Yes. I've known a few of those, now."

Vin knelt in the mists atop Keep Venture. Her splinted leg made it harder to move around at night, but most of the effort she used was Allomantic. She just had to make certain that her landings were particularly soft.

Night had come, and the mists surrounded her. Protecting her, hiding her, giving her power . . .

Elend Venture sat at a desk below, beneath a skylight that still hadn't been patched from the time Vin had thrown a body through it. He didn't notice her crouching above. Who would? Who saw a Mistborn in her element? She was, in a way, like one of the shadow images created by the Eleventh Metal. Incorporeal. Really just something that *could* have been.

Could have been . . .

The events of the last day were difficult enough to sort through; Vin hadn't even tried to make sense of her emotions, which were a far bigger mess. She hadn't gone to Elend yet. She hadn't been able to.

She looked down at him, sitting in the lanternlight, reading at his desk and making scribbled notes in his little book. His meetings earlier had apparently gone well—everyone seemed willing to accept him as king. Marsh whispered that there were politics behind the support, however. The nobility saw Elend as a puppet they could control, and factions were already appearing amongst the skaa leadership.

Still, Elend finally had an opportunity to draft the law code he'd been dreaming of. He could try to create the perfect nation, try to apply the philosophies he had studied for so long. There would be bumps, and Vin suspected that he would ultimately have to settle for something far more realistic than his idealistic dream. That didn't really matter. He would make a good king.

Of course, compared with the Lord Ruler, a pile of soot would make a good king. . . .

She wanted to go to Elend, to drop down into the warm room, but . . . something kept her back. She'd been through too many recent twists in her fortune, too many emotional strains—both Allomantic and non-Allomantic. She wasn't certain what she wanted anymore; she wasn't certain if she were Vin or Valette, or even which of them she wished that she were.

She felt cold in the mists, in the quiet darkness. The mist empowered, protected, and hid . . . even when she didn't really want it to do any of the three.

I can't do this. That person who would be with him, that's not me. That was an illusion, a dream. I am that child who grew up in the shadows, the girl who should be alone. I don't deserve this.

I don't deserve him.

It was over. As she had anticipated, everything was changing. In truth, she'd never really made a very good noblewoman. It was time for her to go back to being what she was good at. A thing of shadows, not of parties and balls.

It was time to go.

She turned to leave, ignoring her tears, frustrated with herself. She left him, her shoulders slumped as she hobbled across the metallic roof and disappeared into the mist.

But then . . .

He died promising us that you had starved to death years ago.

With all the chaos, she'd nearly forgotten the Inquisitor's words about Reen. Now, however, the memory made her pause. Mists passed her, curling, coaxing.

Reen hadn't abandoned her. He'd been captured by the Inquisitors who had been looking for Vin, the unlawful child of their enemy. They'd tortured him.

And he had died protecting her.

Reen didn't betray me. He always promised that he would, but in the end, he didn't. He had been far from a perfect brother, but he had loved her nonetheless.

A whispered voice came from the back of her mind, speaking in Reen's voice. *Go back.*

Before she could convince herself otherwise, she dashed limpingly back to the broken skylight and dropped a coin to the floor below.

Elend turned curiously, looking at the coin, cocking his head. Vin dropped down a second later, Pushing herself up to slow the fall, landing only on her good leg.

"Elend Venture," she said, standing up. "There is something I've been meaning to tell you for some time." She paused, blinking away her tears. "You read too much. Especially in the presence of ladies."

He smiled, throwing back his chair and grabbing her in a firm embrace. Vin closed her eyes, simply feeling the warmth of being held.

And realized that was all she had ever really wanted.

ARS ARCANUM

Find extensive author's annotations of every chapter of this book, along with deleted scenes and expanded world information, at www.brandonsanderson.com.

ALLOMANCY QUICK-REFERENCE CHART

METAL	EFFECT	MISTING TITLE
Iron	Pulls on Nearby Metals	Lurcher
Steel	**Pushes on Nearby Metals**	**Coinshot**
Tin	Enhances Senses	Tineye
Pewter	**Enhances Physical Abilities**	**Pewterarm, Thug**
Zinc	Soothes Emotions	Soother
Brass	**Riots Emotions**	**Rioter**
Copper	Hides Allomancy	Smoker
Bronze	**Reveals Allomancy**	**Seeker**

(Note: External metals have been italicized. Pushing metals have been bolded.)

BRASS (EXTERNAL MENTAL PUSHING METAL)   A person burning brass can Riot another person's emotions, enflaming them and making particular emotions more powerful. It does not let one read minds or even emotions. A Misting who burns brass is known as a Rioter.

BRONZE (INTERNAL MENTAL PUSHING METAL)   A person burning bronze can sense when people nearby are using Allomancy. Allomancers burning metals nearby will give off "Allomantic pulses"—something like drumbeats that are audible only to a person burning bronze. A Misting who can burn bronze is known as a Seeker.

COINSHOT   A Misting who can burn steel.

COPPER (INTERNAL MENTAL PULLING METAL)   A person burning copper gives off an invisible cloud that protects anyone inside of it from the senses of a Seeker. While within one of these "copperclouds," an Allomancer can burn any metal they wish, and not worry that someone will sense their Allomantic pulses by burning bronze. As a side effect, the person burning copper is themselves immune to any form of emotional Allomancy (Soothing or Rioting). A Misting who can burn copper is known as a Smoker.

LURCHER   A Misting who can burn iron.

PEWTER (INTERNAL PHYSICAL PUSHING METAL)   A person burning pewter enhances the physical attributes of their body. They become stronger, more durable, and more dexterous. Pewter also enhances the body's sense of balance and ability to recover from wounds. Mistings who can burn pewter are known as both Pewterarms and Thugs.

PEWTERARM   A Misting who can burn pewter.

IRON (EXTERNAL PHYSICAL PULLING METAL)   A person burning iron can see translucent blue lines pointing to nearby sources of metal. The size and brightness of the line depends on the size and proximity of the metal source. All types of metal are shown, not just sources of iron. The Allomancer can then mentally yank on one of these lines to Pull that source of metal toward them. A Misting who can burn iron is known as a Lurcher.

RIOTER   A Misting who can burn brass.

SEEKER   A Misting who can burn bronze.

SMOKER   A Misting who can burn copper.

SOOTHER   A Misting who can burn zinc.

STEEL (EXTERNAL PHYSICAL PUSHING METAL)   A person burning iron can see translucent blue lines pointing to nearby sources of metal. The size and brightness of the line depends on the size and proximity of the metal source. All types of metal are shown, not just sources of steel. The Allomancer can then mentally Push on one of these lines to send that source of metal away from them. A Misting who can burn steel is known as a Coinshot.

TIN (INTERNAL PHYSICAL PULLING METAL)   A person burning tin gains enhanced senses. They can see farther and smell better, and their sense of touch becomes far more acute. This has the side effect of letting them pierce the mists, allowing them to see much farther at night than even their enhanced senses should have let them. A Misting who can burn tin is known as a Tineye.

TINEYE   A Misting who can burn tin.

THUG   A Misting who can burn pewter.

ZINC (EXTERNAL MENTAL PULLING METAL)   A person burning brass can Soothe another person's emotions, dampening them and making particular emotions less powerful. A careful Allomancer can Soothe away all emotions but a single one, essentially making a person feel exactly as they wish. Zinc, however, does not let that Allomancer read minds or even emotions. A Misting who burns zinc is known as a Soother.